UNIVERSAL PRAISE FOR AARON COOLEY'S

"A remarkable thriller ... would make a good series along the lines of *True Detective* or *The Killing*."

- MenReadingBooks.com

"Copious surprises ... delightfully puzzling ... a scorching pace makes this savvy thriller a quick read."

- Kirkus Reviews

"The action is explosive, the plot decently paced, and the tension steadily ratchets up with each new revelation ... literally, a television show in book form."

- IndieReader.com

"Cooley delivers again. A riveting political thriller that is somehow educational and page-turning at the same time."

- Dave Callaham, screenwriter, *Godzilla* and *The Expendables*

"Cooley writes with knowledge and skill about a shadowy world few truly understand… at times richly emotional, hilarious, and challenging."

- Eric Lodal, Creator & Exec Producer, TNT's *Murder in the First*

"*Four Seats* will be your must read this summer ... I seriously can't stop raving about it!"

- Jessica DeLuna, LiteraryEtc.com

"If you have time to read one book before you die, you should probably read the Bible. But if you have time for two, read *Four Seats* by Aaron Cooley."

- Jeremy Garelick, Director, *The Wedding Ringer*

A Thriller of the Supreme Court

Aaron Cooley

MELNORE PRESS

First published for public sale as an E-book Serial in six parts
by Melnore Press, June 2015
First Paperback Edition, November 2015

ISBN 978-0-9962967-8-6

Series & Paperback Covers Designed by June Cooley & Anna Mack
Title Design by Kathleen Chee
Cover Photo by Whitney Cooley
Back Cover Photo by John Easton

Melnore Press logo by Rick Thompson

For everyone who encouraged me everyday in this endeavor,
especially June, Craig, Joel S, Joe O,
and my best friend,
Whitney.

The Docket

FOUR SEATS

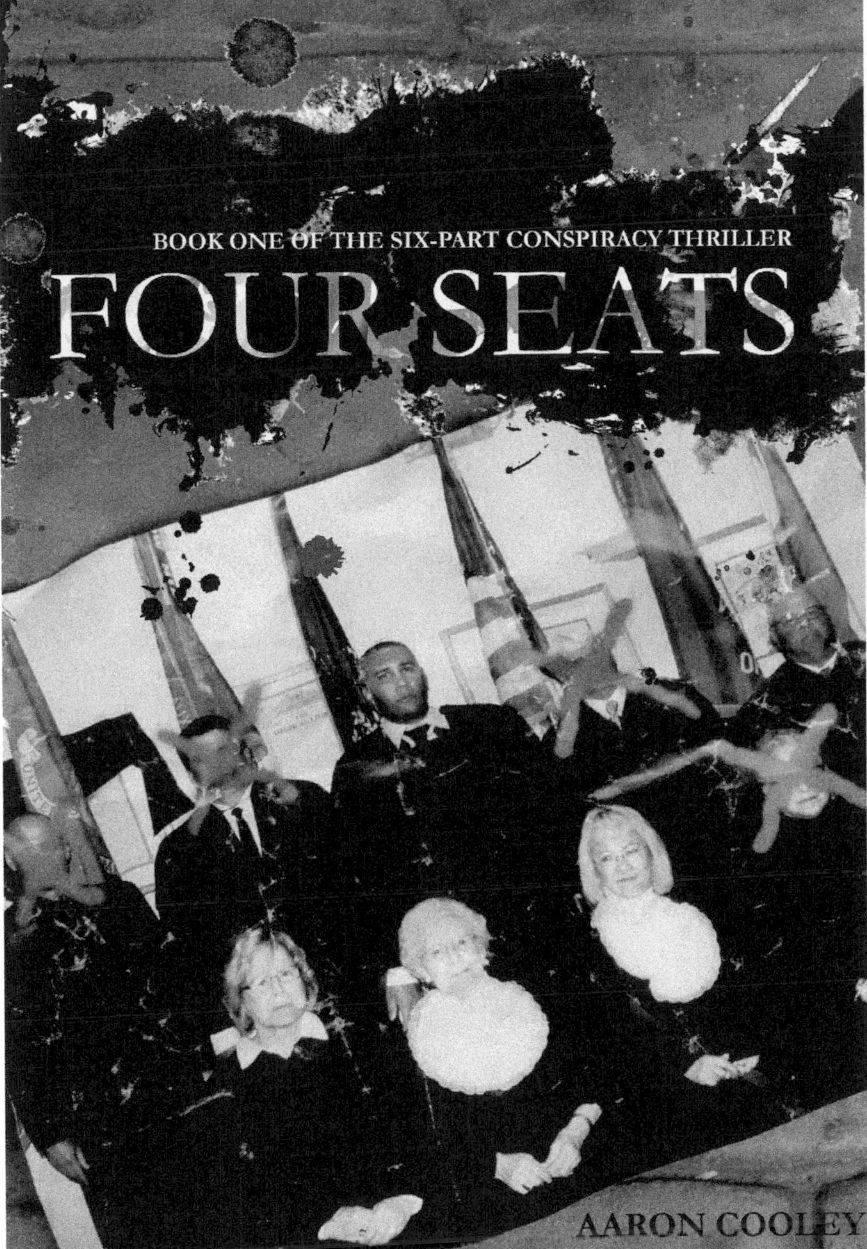
BOOK ONE OF THE SIX-PART CONSPIRACY THRILLER
FOUR SEATS
AARON COOLEY

THE FIRST MONDAY OF OCTOBER

Jason Lancaster couldn't remember how last night ended. He remembered meeting Miranda at Bullfeathers, just as she had asked in her cryptic email. He remembered his confusion when he saw the golden brown liquid sitting in the double shot glass she bounced around her fingers, two dry empties already discarded nearby.

He remembered her turning from the bar when he touched her shoulder. He remembered her eyes swollen with tears.

He remembered their sex, or fleeting visions of it at least. He remembered a thought crossing his mind right before he came with her, a thought that this might be their best sex in weeks, the first time they had *made love* in months. But maybe that was just his drunk talking.

His drunk? That's impossible. Jason hadn't had a drink in four years.

These quick little snaps were all he remembered through an otherwise blacked-out nothingness as he forced open his eyes the next morning. He grimaced, the flare of the early morning sun burning his pupils, the TV blaring from the next room taking sledgehammer swings at his hangover. "Rand?" he called out, but it wasn't Miranda that answered, just some car insurance singers from the living room TV.

Jason forced himself to his feet, stumbling on his own toes into the bathroom, catching himself on the sink. He ran the water, whether to splash on his face or wash his impending vomit down the drain, he wasn't yet sure. His back clenched at the very thought. A deep, guttural heave cannonballed out of his throat – and nothing came out. Of course nothing came out; they didn't eat at all last night, just drank and then fucked.

Drank? He didn't remember drinking. Why would he have drank? Why after four years of torturing himself, of planning his whole life around not being tempted to take even a sip or a smell or a glance at booze, would he have cracked last night?

He cupped some water in his palms, splashed it on his cheeks. It didn't help.

The sink was still running when he woke up who-the-hell-knows-how-much later, crumpled up in a little ball underneath the exposed pipes. He didn't even have the energy to climb up and turn it off, just to focus his eyes across the bedroom, to his bedside table, to his alarm clock – **8:11 AM**.

Shit, 8:11! *Shit shit shit.* He shot to his feet – still drunk, but with new energy to move and tear off his shirt and stammer into the closet. The first day of a new Court term, and he was going to be at least 15 minutes late – and that's if everything, every crosswalk, every train, every fucking Union Station commuter cooperated perfectly.

Goddammit, where the hell's Rand and why didn't she wake me? She would never let him be late like this. She would have woken him an hour ago; they should just be arriving at work *together* at 8:11.

The CNN morning host was introducing her guest, Vice Admiral Kennesaw MacTavish, when Jason crossed from his bedroom through the living room, reaching under his shirt to cake some deodorant onto his pits, then dropping the bar onto the couch before opening the front door and charging down to the sidewalk.

He was back seconds later, rushing to the kitchen counter – *Thank Christ.* As fucked up as he was last night, he still remembered to drop his lanyard, his Supreme Court Police badge, off in its trusty bowl. He had made it a rule to drop everything from his pockets into this same bowl every single time he walked in the door, ever since that day he was three minutes late because he couldn't remember setting his badge on a window sill then later lowering the blinds, hiding it behind them. *You like baseball, right, Lancaster?* Miranda had chastised him that morning. *In baseball, you get three strikes. In my Court, you only get two. You're four seconds late one more time, and you're out.*

That was over a year ago now, one of his first days at the Court. There had to be a statute of limitations on that first strike, right? And besides, how could she fire him the morning after their best sex in a year?

"*CNN This Morning* is back," the host recited off the teleprompter, "sitting down with our next guest, for the last nine years the commanding officer of the US Joint Special Operations Command, Vice Admiral Kennesaw MacTavish."

The buzz of the hot studio lights seemed to change in pitch as Mac's periphery caught the red light jumping from the host's close-up camera to the master two-shot which included him. He felt his neck moistening under his dress uniform collar, and shifted in his seat before replying smoothly, "Thanks for having me." His dulcet baritone soothed both the host and his own fluttering butterflies the same way he might a team of SEALs about to deploy.

"You have a new book out today, *A Theory of Special Ops.* It's a great book..."

"Thank you."

"—but you don't mention the Sheikh Alabar mission in the book once," she observed, reminding her audience that this was the man who had planned and commanded the apprehension of the most important terrorist since bin Laden. "That's no way to sell books, Admiral."

"I wasn't out to sell books," he said with a smile that could talk you into battle, "just get my theories on Joint Special Operations down on paper. When I retire, I'll write something that will sell more books."

"But you designed the missions that not only took out the Sheikh, but more recently rescued the Americans in Yemen. You do realize you're a hero, don't you?"

He chuckled with real modesty. "What's it say on my Wikipedia page?"

Though the host continued seamlessly, she was starting to become aware of the commotion building on the other side of the lights and cameras, PAs rushing in to whisper things to the floor director, a couple of cameramen sprinting out to take posts in adjacent studios. This wasn't normal; something was going down, but it was her job to pretend just the opposite until new instructions came through the tiny speaker pressed deep into her right ear. "Can you take us back to the Alabar mission, how you even begin to plan something like that?"

"Of course. As head of JSOC, I have about 60,000 men and women across all branches of the military at my disposal. So the first thing I do is assess--"

"I'm sorry, Admiral," the Host butted in, her fingers pressing her ear into which the explanations were finally starting to flow, "but we— I'm being told we need to go to our newsroom right away for some breaking news."

"And we're out," the floor director announced before Mac (a nickname that had stuck since Annapolis) could even respond. He didn't even get in a word, in fact, before the host was on her feet and charging for the passageway into the next studio. "How bad is it?" he heard her ask the PA at her side. "I need numbers--"

Starting to feel like perhaps a television studio wasn't the most responsible place for one of the most important military men in America to be right at this moment, Mac stood, removing the radio mic from his lapel and pulling it out through the bottom of his jacket. That's when the floor director approached him, he assumed for some sort of practiced apology written for guests who had been bumped.

Instead, he saw real fear in the director's eyes. "Admiral. You're gonna want to see this."

Admiral MacTavish's interview was just beginning when Janaki Singh poked her head into the courtroom of the Honorable Isaac Goldman on the 21st floor of Philly's James A. Byrne Courthouse. She would recall this for the rest of her life, never forget that the courtroom was absolutely empty when she stepped in, the only sound coming from behind the bench, CNN emanating (and rather loudly, too) from the TV in the federal judge's chambers.

"Judge Goldman?" Janaki called out tentatively, but no one answered, save the CNN host explaining, *"...for the last nine years the commanding officer of the US Joint Special Operations Command ..."* Janaki stepped in further to take in the giant seal of the United States Court of Appeals for the Third Circuit staring back at her from the front of Goldman's legal throne. It didn't fill her with the fear, intimidation, goose bumps or urge to piss herself which would have gripped any number of her former law school classmates at such a moment; the truth was, deep down, Janaki didn't really care about this interview. It was her parents who believed becoming either a doctor or lawyer were her only options, the only possible ways she wouldn't end up cleaning Days Inn toilets or slinging Chicken Tikka Masala. Of these two paths, Janaki had chosen to pursue the law for two reasons: (1) the D she had gotten in Orgo freshman year; and (2) the fact that all she really wanted to do was write. At least as a lawyer she would get to do a lot of stuff that she could *pretend* was writing: briefs, arguments, comments, and eventually, decisions. And maybe someday she could parlay a decade of law firm misery into becoming the female Grisham or Turow. (There are quite a few authors making their fortunes off legal thrillers; there's only one Robin Cook.)

Is what I'm doing verboten? she wondered as she made her way behind the bench, entering the Judge's personal office. *Am I violating his personal sanctum, spelling my certain doom? Or am I showing the kind of initiative that will make me stand apart from the rest of the applicants?*

"Morning," a voice sang out from behind her. She jumped back ten feet, 360ing in mid-air, ass pounding back into the desk, quaking every frame and tchotchke loitering its surface, even knocking a few over.

Though she had never met him before, Janaki recognized him instantly. For law school graduates, Circuit Court Judges are the equivalent of minor reality TV celebrities (actual Supreme Court Justices being the Kardashians), but Isaac Goldman had found renown even beyond legal circles with his quirky briefs, propensity to make bad jokes from behind the bench, and the national fascination with his habit of wearing shorts and Birkenstocks beneath his robes. This was exactly what he was wearing when Janaki met him, his tanned chicken legs descending from beneath his bottom hem. “If you know what’s good for you, you won’t go in there,” he chuckled with a nod back to the bathroom, then continued behind his desk, returning some of the clutter to its proper choreography as he went.

“Judge Goldman, I’m Janaki Singh. I’m interviewing to be your new clerk? You emailed me to be here at--”

“There’s just one problem, Ms. Singh. I don’t really need any more clerks.”

“What? But your email--”

The hard landing of a rather sizable document in the center of Goldman’s desk cut her off. “I lied.”

“What’s that?” she asked, finger quivering with dread as she pointed to the projectile.

“My contract with Farrar Straus. You’ll find my advance on page three. I’ll give you forty percent. I’ll even credit you.”

She leaned forward, getting her fingers around the thick document, raising it to her eyes. “You want me to help you write your biography?”

“I’m going to be up front with you. Empirical evidence indicates you’ll probably be writing the whole thing yourself. I signed that two years ago--”

“And you haven’t written a word.”

“Well, ‘Introduction’ is a word technically.”

Janaki looked down at the behemoth document again, hoping to get more information on this ridiculous task by perusing its first few pages. She didn’t get past the first one, and the proposed title of the book: “*The Circuit Breaker*?” she accidentally sneered aloud. “No.”

“It does say, ‘tentatively titled,’ doesn’t it?” He leaned forward to double-check, but Janaki was already returning it to his desk and trying to back her way out.

“With all due respect, Your Honor, if I had known this is what I’d be doing—”

"You're the best writer to come out of the last five classes of my alma mater. But, shit, if you'd really rather research precedent and proofread opinions for the next two years, I can make a couple phone calls."

Janaki snickered. She had no doubt it was probably true, but, "How could you possible know how good a writer I--"

"'The Artichoke and the Ship," he smiled. "'Burning Your Feet'? 'The 45th Annual Prom Punch Bowl'?" They spouted from his tongue like '80s sit com titles, but for Janaki, it was like hearing the names of her children announced magna cum laude at graduation. "You are the J. Singh who had three short stories published in *The Frontier,* aren't you?"

"You read those?" Janaki didn't think anyone beyond the magazine's editor had read all three of her stories (and she had to date him for a few months to make even that happen). "And if I were to help you … have you even started? Made any notes?"

Four minutes later, they were in the court's parking garage, staring in through the windows of a fourteen-year-old Hyundai Elantra. Boxes had been shoved into every inch, every nook and cranny from pleather to roof, forming a bubble around the open driver's seat. "I've made some notes," Judge Goldman said with a chuckle. "Here."

Janaki snatched the car keys from midair a second before they connected with her eyes. "What's this?"

"I understand you moved here from Millbourne without a car. Now you have one."

"But … what about you?"

"Girlfriend, please," he scoffed, then fired his own little key nob behind him, lighting up the beams of a Benz with a short burst of horn. "The Hyundai's my kid's car. He just left to become an Orangeman. Syracuse," he clarified off her look of confusion. "Spoiled little--"

He didn't finish that sentence, for it was right at this moment that the elevator beeped and the first load of people fleeing the court stampeded out. Bailiffs darted for their cars, paralegals charged out of the stairwell, public defenders shoved their briefcases into their trunks or onto their passenger seats and screeched out of their reserved spots.

"Fire drill?" Goldman asked an evacuee who looked the right age and demographic for a clerk.

"*Drill?*" she answered, not recognizing His Honor in a Hawaiian shirt and cargo shorts. "You better turn on the news!"

At law schools all across the country, few had any inkling yet that this would be the most tumultuous day in the history of American law. In South Bend, Indiana, Professor Cecilia Koh of Notre Dame's law school was unaware of what had just occurred 600 miles to the East as she convened her "Faith, Morality and Constitutional Law" seminar by calling on third year student Jane Norfleet to stand and subject herself to a Socratic interrogation. "The case you read last night, Ms. Norfleet. Explain for us why the Supreme Court ruled the way they did."

The student's chest welled with excitement, just as Professor Koh knew that it would. It was quite clear in the course catalog, let alone by reading the Professor's biography on the school website, what stance Koh would take on issues of morality in this class – not to mention the fact this was frigging Notre Dame – but every year, she would still without fail get two or three students who made it obvious from the first or second class meeting that they had enrolled to play contrarian, to try to put the stuffy conservative professor in her place and announce their own oh-so-enlightened political views to the world. This semester, Jane Norfleet was that student. And if Professor Koh were being honest, she would have to admit she called on Jane after very specific reading assignments because she wanted to turn the tables on the little snotnose. She knew after Jane's first diatribe a month ago (on the constitutionality of forcing religious hospitals to offer contraception) that she would be just the student she would call on after they read *Roe v. Wade*. And Norfleet began just as the Professor knew she would: "The Court ruled that the state of Texas violated Ms. McCorvey's right to privacy--"

"The right to privacy found where?"

"In the Constitution." Norfleet's defenses snapped up, as she intuited she was already walking into some sort of trap.

"Of course," the Professor smiled, using false encouragement to mask her glee at the ease of this. "Please cite the article or amendment guaranteeing privacy in the Constitution."

"It's the 14th Amendment--"

"Very good. Just read us the sentence in the 14th Amendment with the word 'privacy' in it."

Norfleet's fingers dug for her Government Printing Office pocket-sized edition of the Constitution, searching through its pages as she stalled. "It's here, it--"

"No, actually, the word 'privacy' isn't in there. Not in the original seven articles, not in the 27 amendments."

"But-- *but,* there are 'pemunbras and emanations' of protections, Justice Douglas wrote that, of protections not specifically--"

"Ms. Norfleet." Norfleet lowered into her seat, having already learned enough of the Professor's verbal cues to know when she was done with her, and ready to turn this q-&-a into a lecture. The class tittered amongst themselves at her limp attempt to recover. "The Court violated your Constitution in 1973, Ms. Norfleet. Interpreted it out of whole cloth."

Norfleet's humiliation only lasted for a few moments – before the giggles started to turn into frantic whispers, her classmates attempting to pull their iPhones out of their bags and switch them to life without the Professor noticing. This sort of thing never happened among the collection of perfect children and ne'er-do-wrongs that made up the law school. Something was going on, Norfleet realized. She reached down for her own purse.

"This class is about the Text," Koh continued, still oblivious that one of her most-important class tenants was being violated on a large scale. "The Text as it was originally meant to be interpreted. There is no such thing as a 'living' document. There is a document, written at one moment in time--"

"Professor!" Norfleet shot to her feet, not even bothering to stuff her Galaxy back into its hiding spot.

"What are the only two rules in my classroom, Ms. Norfleet?"

"No passing, and no connecting to the internet during class time."

"Then can you explain to me why everyone here is so fixated on their—"

"I think you better turn on the TV, Professor!"

Koh knew from her tone, from the tears already welling under her eyes, that whatever had driven Jane Norfleet so hysterical was real, very real, and very, very serious. She picked the projector's remote up off her podium, and as she rotated to face the screen with her class, started punching the series of buttons that would switch the image's feed to Fox News.

It had been five First October Mondays since William Quint had presided over the Supreme Court as its Chief. He had continued to follow the Court's docket like a hawk through the first year or two of his retirement, making frequent visits to One First Street to check in with his colleagues, spend the day in his small office there, give a short talk to the new batch of clerks, attend the occasional Court social function. But with 80 now well in his rearview mirror, he thought it was time to let his connection to the great temple of American justice fade, and on this glorious Virginia morning, he wasn't even aware it was October 7th, the first morning of a new Term, the first morning the Court would hear new oral arguments since the Spring.

He was aware that he had given his driver Eddie the day off, and more pressing, that he was out of Half-&-Half. He wasn't about to drink his Early Grey (as he had called it since the 1960s) with two percent, or whatever that swill made from nuts was that Darline loved so much. No, Chief Quint was going to back his 14-year-old Beemer out of the driveway *himself* for the first time in two years and drive *himself* to the store.

He could have sworn he had grunted the shift stick back to the "R." Eddie hadn't mentioned to him that there was something amiss in the connection between stick and dash, that you had to confirm the indicator on the dash also read "R," that they sometimes didn't match up; that was the only explanation for what happened next. Quint knew with every fiber of his being that he had pulled the stick back into Reverse, so after he lowered the E-brake and laid his right foot on the gas, the car should have moved *backwards.*

"Fuck a duck!" the elderly judge exclaimed as the car shot *forward* instead. He slammed the brake pedal, and with a brief little squeak of a screech the car wrenched to a stop – only after the front bumper had tapped the garage door.

Quint just sat there, counting to himself. His guess was that it would take her 45 seconds, but his count had only reached about 12 when he heard Darline call out, "William!" from the front door and charge down to his driver's side window. He lowered it without even looking up at her, after 51 years of marriage well familiar with the lecture that was about to ensue. "Just what do you think you're doing?"

"Eddie's daughter has her first soccer game this afternoon, so I gave him the day off."

"And so you're planning to drive *yourself,* without a license, all the way into Washington?"

"Washington?" he asked, confused. Had he forgotten some engagement he had committed to? Sadly, it wouldn't be the first time.

"Haven't you been listening to the radio?"

Chief Quint took the gear shift – moving it from, yes, D back to P – let his foot off the brake, and tapped the car stereo to life. Of course it was set to NPR, perhaps the only station this particular car stereo had ever played.

"*Getting reports of explosions, at least two separate explosions ...*"

The Reginald J. Irving Presidential Library and Museum was nothing more than a hollow shell, a skeleton of beams and girders and laid-out blue tape. The former President had been waiting for this day for weeks, the day when he could get back to Portland and see those plans he had approved over six months ago starting to come to life. Kevin Morrison, the hometown architect that Irving had taken pride in finding and awarding the job even after his Chief of Staff presented him with a list of 50 brand name candidates, was just walking him through what would be the main entrance of the library: where guests would check in and receive a map, which wall would be covered with a collage of images from his inaugurations, which video screen would be showing highlights from his annual appearance on CBS's SuperBowl pregame show.

"And the public transportation initiative?" Irving interrupted.

"Um, I'm sorry, Sir?"

"In our last meeting, a month ago in New York, we talked about covering this wall with images from cities that participated in the public transpo initiative. And over here, this was going to be images of my foreign policy accomplishments. Maybe Sheikh Alabar with the cuffs on?"

"Sir, I'm sorry, I thought--"

"I told him to change it," Rosemarie Irving spoke up from 30 yards behind the men, back by the work table covered with blueprints.

Irving turned to his wife; he had gotten in such a zone he had for a moment forgotten she was there. "*You* did?"

"Everyone who would plan a vacation around visiting your library is already going to know everything you achieved when you were in office. You need to remind them of your warmth. Your humanity. All those things everyone, even your own constituents, were saying you lacked when we left Washington."

“Have you seen these new ads the RNC’s running, honey? Or Brad Benedict’s first ad in New Hampshire? They’re still running against *me*, still saying I didn’t do anything, didn’t accomplish--”

“Reg. You’re retired. This building is a celebration. Not a stump speech.”

Her last words echoed up through the empty frame as silence descended on their discussion and Irving debated whether she was right. Rosemarie knew that within four to seven seconds he would realize she was; that’s about how long it always took him. Over 26 years of marriage and a couple more before that, he had conceded almost every debate to her but for a few you could count on one hand. And even those he later admitted he should have seen her way.

And indeed, just over five-and-a-half seconds later, he turned to his architect and grinned, “Kevin, I ever tell you marrying this woman was the smartest thing I ever did?”

“You didn’t have to, Mr.--”

“MR. PRESIDENT!” a loud voice boomed into the structure, overpowering their soft-spoken draftsman. “MR. PRESIDENT, MR. PRESIDENT, SIR!” the linebacker silhouette yelled as it ran full speed for them. The Irvings tensed up, not because they didn’t know who the intruder was – Mitchell Aldridge had been their lead Secret Service agent for almost ten years now – but because this was a tone they never heard injected into his voice. Seeing he had their attention, he pulled up to a stop, explaining, “There’s something you need to see!”

Irving looked to his wife, gave her those eyes he gave her whenever something terrible was in the process of going down. *Those eyes that always used to scream to me, “What the hell do I do now?”* she thought to herself in that one beat.

Then as soon as Irving moved – she had trained herself to always let him move first, he *was* the President – she was right on his heels, following Mitch back out of the building to their waiting Escalade.

The current POTUS was in a casino sports book when he heard the news. The one promise Antonio Salas had made to himself when he entered politics was that he wouldn’t miss a single match his beloved Lions of Athletic Bilbao played in their Spanish La Liga season. The higher the heights he reached, of course, the more difficult this became, but advances in DVR technology had allowed him to bend his rule without missing a single throw-in or yellow card. It was something he needed, he rationalized to himself (and his Chief of Staff) in order to clear and rest his brain every once in a while. And it reminded him of his roots: Bilbao had been his Grandfather Antonio's team, and when the family brought the younger Antonio to their namesake parish in northern Spain for the first time in 1982, his abuelo made a point of renting his own car and driving his only grandson (against 14 granddaughters!) the three and a half hours east to see the team that had always been near and dear to his heart, even after fleeing to Mexico during World War II.

There was no one else in the sports book on the morning of October 7th to hear President Salas's Spanish declarations of Bilbao's incompetency as they struggled at home against the goliath FC Barcelona, already in a two-nil hole as the second batch of forty-five minutes got underway, no one of course except his lead Secret Service guard Hifrael Fernandez. It was Hifrael who first got word over his earpiece that something was happening, that the President's Chief of Staff needed to see him immediately. "Tell her to check La Liga schedule and she'll know where to find me," POTUS snapped back in Español while waiting for a corner kick. (He had promoted Hifrael to his lead agent not only because he loved his calm demeanor, but also so he could speak to him in Spanish and fewer listeners might pick up on it, fewer TV viewers might read what he was saying as it came off his lips.)

Salas didn't understand the import of this emergency, and Hifrael wasn't about to try to impress it upon the Commandant-en-Jefe himself, especially during a Bilbao match. So, after what seemed like no more than 12, maybe 13 seconds, Rebecca Whitford was marching off the elevator, stepping into the one spot you never wanted to be – between the man and his La Liga. Not yet 40, Becks (call her "Becky" at your own risk) was the first female Chief of Staff in the White House's history, and she didn't get there by worrying about things like soccer. "We've been looking all over the building for you."

"All the matches are on the schedule, Becks. And I even double-checked with Delores this morning that nothing had been added--"

"It's the Supreme Court. It's bad."

A Barca defender was now rolling on the pitch, gripping his shin in faux agony; Salas knew this gave him a minute or two to spar with Becks. "I'm not the one who nominated Lapadula," he grinned--

– but when his eyes met hers, his lips flattened; there was serious shit behind Rebecca's eyes, the most serious he thought he had ever seen there. "We need to move you to the Bunker, Mr. President."

Salas rose without a word of protest, whipping his jacket off his chair and throwing his arms into it as he followed her to the elevators, Hifrael in step right behind. “Aguila on the move,” the guard said into his wrist, using the codename for the President, Spanish for ‘eagle.’

They passed all the empty slot machines and roulette wheels and craps tables and slid into the elevator where two other agents were already waiting for them. For a moment Salas wondered if any other Presidents had been made aware of crises in this room when it housed a bowling alley or a basketball court; but when the elevator doors brought together the image of the bald eagle and the Presidential seal in front of his eyes and Becks started giving him the gruesome basics of the catastrophe, all thoughts of football and Spain and casinos disappeared.

Jason Lancaster woke again each time the Metro car’s ungreased wheels screeched into another of the 11 stations between Maryland and the heart of DC. He was still too grogged to process the announcer’s voice coming over the PA, so he made a point of leaning against a bar as close to the door as he could find. From there, he could make sure to read each station’s name on the opposite wall every time they came to a stop.

But when they reached his intended stop, he was never able to read the black bar glued onto the wall reading, “UNION STATION.” There were too many people charging onto the car, too much pushing and shoving and scared-as-shit people for him to see through.

Though Jason couldn’t be certain this was Union Station, he knew he *had* to get off in this chaos. He was sure that whatever had happened to him the night before, whatever had made Miranda cry, whatever had made her disappear that morning, whoever had drugged him with something that was still very much controlling his system – it couldn’t be a coincidence, there were no coincidences in Washington, it all had to be connected to whatever shit storm he had just stumbled into. So just before the doors could close, Jason found a well of energy in his breast and launched forward, shoving through the wave of traffic surging the other direction, pounding past the Metro Cop yelling, “Station’s closed! Ladies and gentlemen, do not get off the train!”

Massachusetts Ave was a complete nightmare – people screaming, cars screaming, police sirens screaming – and Jason realized it had to be because of that giant black plume of smoke rising up from the trees above First Street NE, right about where he had been due for work 13 minutes ago. Jason sped up into a jog, navigating around the bumper-to-bumper strangling the web of streets spiraling out from the front of the station. And as he entered the mouth of First, everything he saw – the emergency vehicles jumping up onto the sidewalk to go around traffic; the girl he could swear he recognized sobbing as she looked for a paramedic, her left hand holding up the bloody stump where she used to have a right forearm; the warping of his vision as he drew closer and closer to the source of raging heat – *everything* pushed his feet faster.

He shot past Rusty, the pro-life hobo always stationed on the corner of First and Maryland, rattling his cup and shaking his 'Kill No More Babies' sign in front of the Methodist Building, hollering, "Save the children! Save the children!" as if this were any other day and there wasn't bedlam around him.

Jason suddenly pulled up to a stop right in the middle of the street. He turned to face the carnage on his left. His eyes stung not just from the smoke, but the sorrow and anger washing through him as he confirmed the source of the immense heat.

Someone had blown up the Supreme Court.

BOOK ONE

FOUR SEATS

TUESDAY

Less than 24 hours after the first explosion tore through the front of the Supreme Court building, President Salas was already taking it in the shorts. There was of course a grace period for leaders after great national tragedies, but in the era of the three second news and Facebook and tweet cycle, that grace period ended before 5 AM EST Tuesday morning when the executive producer of the *Fox & Friends* morning show told his staff he wanted to lead with the Justice Department's apparent lack of *any* leads in the bombing investigation, or at least any leads they were willing to share with the American people. It was a valid question to be asking even at this juncture, he argued; America after all has a fine tradition of quick, swift response to these sorts of wounds. Oswald was in custody in less than a day, the Boston Bombers in less than four.

The frightening truth was that the Justice Department *didn't* know anything, and no one had any idea this attack was coming. As *Fox & Friends* went to air, as CNN and MSNBC's own morning shows rushed to also weigh in on this budding controversy, Salas was in the Situation Room, chairing the tenth assemblage of America's brass since the attack. (The first eight had been in his Bunker under Pennsylvania Avenue, where he had stayed for over six hours until Secret Service had cleared him to the Oval Office for an address to the nation, then later to the Residence for about five hours of sleep.) The Joint Chiefs were all there on Tuesday morning, as were the Secretaries of Defense and Homeland Security, and the Directors of every Bureau and Agency that had been marshaled in this investigation.

Not one of them could tell POTUS jack shit.

Pulling two more clumps out of his hair, the President instead switched to playing defense. The bombs had gone off just early enough that not all nine of the Supreme Court Justices had arrived in the building for the day; the Administration didn't want to announce who or even how many had perished until they had confirmed remains, but they did at least know which Justices had survived. Was the attack a targeted strike against the Court and the Justices, or just an opportunity to hit any random American icon? No one knew yet, but Salas wasn't going to take any chances that it was the former, turning to the Director of the Secret Service to order, “I want teams on all the surviving Justices, Joe. I don’t want them leaving their homes. I want them to be the safest human beings on the planet until we’ve caught whoever’s responsible for this. Liaise with the Court police force, work with them on this.”

“Actually, Mr. President,” his Homeland Security Secretary piped up, “we think it might be best to keep the Supreme Court Police at an arm’s length at first, just for the time being.”

“You don’t think one of them had something to do with this?”

“Four of the seven explosives were planted in areas the general public doesn’t have access to. And we’re finding huge gaps in the Court’s surveillance recordings from over the weekend.”

“Jesus,” POTUS swallowed hard. “Has anyone put Alabar under some hot lights, or any of the terrorists we’ve got in custody? Sussed out if one of them knew this was coming?”

“Mr. President,” the Secretary of Defense chimed in, “this attack was much more advanced than a frat of Sunni cave dwellers could pull off. Much more *professional*.”

“Two of the explosives were set in the main climate control center,” FBI confirmed. “Flames poured through the ventilation system, engulfing rooms throughout the rest of the building.”

The DIA Director: “And radical Islamists would typically have claimed responbility sometime in the first 24, if not 12 hours.”

“We have had some luck, Sir. Only six of the seven explosives detonated successfully. We’re tearing apart the seventh now.” The DHS Secretary read off a sheet: “It’s a second-generation Kai-shek plastic explosive, but modified for extra punch--”

“Chinese?”

“Kai-sheks are also black market available, Sir,” the CIA Director explained. “Meaning this could have been anyone.”

“The majority of threats to judicial officials,” the FBI Director joined in, “are made by individuals directly affected by that court and its decisions. We’ve got a team carefully analyzing the decision history of each of the Justices, as well as the cases granted Cert this term. We’re talking everything from campaign finance to abortion to the detainment of terror suspects. This will give us a list of groups with motive.”

"Thousands of them," Salas sighed, "both domestic and international."

"Very few groups have the resources or the training to pull this off, Sir. The modifications on the explosive devices, the remote detonator we found on the unexploded ordnance--"

"Remote? They set them and ran. They weren't suiciders."

"No sir."

"They're still out there."

"We're collecting the weekend recordings of every camera in a five-mile radius," the director of the NSA contributed, "including every parking garage and Metro stop. It's going to take some time. But we're going to find some pictures of these guys, Mr. President. You can bet on it."

Chief of Staff Rebecca Whitford hadn't looked up from her left knee in more than ten minutes. That's where she held her BlackBerry, over which she was the only one in the room following the morning press coverage, the only one who knew they would be treading water until they had solid, concrete *answers* to share – and it sounded like they'd be waiting until Shavuot for that. She believed their top priority should be doing everything they could to make the American people feel safer *right now*, even if doing so was just a show. "When can we go off lockdown?" she spoke up from her chair off the main table, pushed up against one of the walls. "Open the White House to non-essentials?"

"There's been no chatter or any other indication of imminent threats to any other targets since the incident," NSA answered. "This appears to be a lone strike. At least for now."

Becks stood, nodding over to Secret Service. "Can we get the White House open by 11 then, Joe? The sooner we can get back to business as usual, the sooner the American people--"

She was cut off by Salas's open palms slamming down hard on the conference table. "Business as usual, Becks?" he spit in her direction as she lowered back into her chair. "Are any of you listening to yourselves? There was no *chatter* this weekend. Was there, Keith? John, I never saw an imminent threat like this even hinted at in one of my daily briefs. Did I? We had no fucking clue this was coming. They hit us blind. They're *laughing* at us right now. And planning their next one."

It took Salas just 45 minutes to apologize to Becks. She didn't even think an apology was necessary; he was the President of the United States, less than a day after the third deadliest day on her soil since the Civil War. But he insisted, just another example of how he was the best boss ever. They were in POTUS's private study off the Oval, going over the day's agenda – one which had opened up, everything cleared to make room for updates about the bombing and the casualties and the damage to the building and of course, the investigation. Salas wasn't listening as Becks recited the day's current plan, instead bouncing his favorite miniature rubber soccer ball off the five TVs, all showing variations of the same story, that this bombing had baffled everyone in the Antonio Salas Administration.

Reading how heavily these accusations weighed on his brow, Becks paused to look up from her tablet. "You can't listen to them. Every American knows you're doing everything you possibly can right now, no matter what those assholes might say."

"Not good enough. I should be out in front of this. Surveying the damage at the Court--"

"Which Secret Service promises me they'll have ready by 2 for the press event."

He glared at her. "A press event. I take back my apology."

She sighed, standing to collect her pile of things. "I think you need to blow off a little steam. 20 minutes in your casino, doctor's orders."

"*Now?*" Salas stood, still throwing his ball off any flat surface as he paced. "Can you imagine twenty years from now when it comes out that 24 hours after the bombing, I was playing pai gow?"

"Mr. President. There's someone down there to see you."

As soon as the Irvings had seen the first images of the smoldering Supreme Court from their Escalade, they had ordered their driver to get them back to their private plane at Hillsboro Municipal Airport just outside Portland. All traffic over American airspace was grounded for over eight hours after the bombing, but the Irvings were able to procure special permission to take off after just two. They spent the evening in their Spring Valley townhouse, but barely slept. Even after they had crawled into bed, put down their reading (his a Phil Jackson coaching chronicle, hers the latest Doris Kearns Goodwin), and switched off the light, they both could sense that the other's eyes never closed. There was too much excitement, too much opportunity in the air. They both had an uncanny talent to taste opportunity; that was one of the first qualities that drew them to one another. They lay awake for hours, just like the old days in rundown Shilo Inns at campaign stops across Oregon, making plans for their future.

The first step was getting in to see the current POTUS as soon as possible. Reg had predicted it would be Wednesday; Salas wouldn't be able to leave the Sit Room for the first 48 hours, no matter how much he owed Irving for his DNC showstopper three years ago, for his tireless campaigning for his chosen successor.

But Rosemarie Irving knew that there was much more behind Salas's loyalty to her husband than gratitude; like most men, *fear* drove him. She knew Salas spent most days submerging his fear that he didn't know what the hell he was doing. But after the events of Monday, she knew that fear must have bubbled to the surface, drowning him, choking him; today, he'd be shitting his figurative pants. He would be only too happy to take advice from any two-term former chief exec who offered. She wasn't half as surprised as her husband when Rebecca Whitford told them she could fit them in Tuesday morning, and even less surprised when the elevator opened and President Salas stepped out onto the carpeted casino floor an hour earlier than expected.

Their meeting was at first formal and stilted: Irving assured Salas that no one knew they were there, they had used the Tunnel to come straight to the casino so they could offer their services or counsel or whatever else he might need without undermining his authority. Salas thanked him like he was performing from a script, assuring his predecessor he didn't know anything more than what he had explained in his address to the nation on Monday night, but that he would include Irving the next time he did.

It was Rosemarie who dragged the elephant out of the corner and into the center of the room. "How many Justices, Mr. President?"

Salas didn't answer, a little taken aback by her boldness. Irving chuckled off his own slight embarrassment at her lack of tact (he had always been the perfect counterbalance to his wife, that's what made them such an unbeatable team), and explained, "Mr. President. This is going to be complicated. That's why we're here. We think we're in a unique position to help you with this."

"Help – with what exactly?"

"You've got a kick-off rally in three months, a convention in less than ten. Your next year has to be perfect. Including – *especially* – your nominations."

"Nominations?" Salas turned to his Chief of Staff. "Becks, did you know this is why they wanted to see us?"

She shrugged; of course she knew why the Irvings had asked for an audience now. She knew, she loved the idea, and she had encouraged them to come. "You said you wanted to take some action," she tried to explain.

"You want me to get into Supreme Court nominations *now?*"

"Not you," Irving continued. "You're going to be caught up in the attack, the investigation – and soon, the retaliation. That's the rest of your term. If you're going to rebuild this Court before the election – and you've earned the right to rebuild this Court – you're going to need help."

The President shook his head, nearly laughing at the audacity of the proposal. "I'm sorry. I appreciate you coming. But I can't *touch* this until we've got some suspects, a theory at least--"

"Respectfully, Mr. President," Rosemarie stepped forward, taking over for her husband, "we're talking about the heart of our democracy." Salas had heard the legends about Rosemarie being Irving's Mariano Rivera, his closer, and in just her eyes, he could now see how she got that rep. "This is the Court that invented judicial review. Ended segregation. The Court that made the New Deal a reality. The Court that chose the winner in a goddamn Presidential election."

"The Court of *Dred Scott,*" Salas retorted, citing the Court's 1857 decision that a slave could not sue for his freedom, as he was technically not a person but property; the ruling served to keep slavery alive for its final eight years.

"The Court that made 'separate-but-equal' segregation legal in *Plessy v. Ferguson,*" Rosemarie agreed. "The Court that said the government could end a labor strike if it was harming interstate commerce; the Court that has on numerous occasions declared corporations to be persons with the full protections of the Fourteenth Amendment. These are all perfect examples of why it's imperative we make sure the right person rebuilds this Court, and puts it in the right hands for decades to come. You don't want decisions like all of these hung on *your* legacy."

Irving stepped up beside his wife. "Without control of the Senate, you have to time the nominations perfectly. Time them just right, and the Republicans will have no choice but to confirm your nominees, or they'll risk being branded un-

American, accused of holding up the most important part of the rebuilding and healing process this nation must go through."

"But wait too long," Rosemarie continued, "let the calendar get too close to the election next year, and they'll be able to stall those confirmations until *after* the election, arguing that it's irresponsible to let a potential lame duck make these vital picks. It's exactly what they did to LBJ when he tried to promote Abe Fortas to Chief Justice. It was already June of an election year and the Republicans knew LBJ was out. They threatened to filibuster Fortas until Nixon was elected; Fortas resigned and the pick became Nixon's."

"You don't make nominations soon, and the Court will be frozen for, what, the next year and a half? Whoever did this will have succeeded, they'll have killed the Court. And when it finally re-opens? Who knows what kind of activists will be on the bench."

"Have you been watching the news?" Salas counterpunched. "They're already killing me for not having the bombers in chains after less than 24 hours. How do you think they're going to respond if I'm spending my days picking Supreme Court nominees while these killers are running the streets?"

"*You're* not going to do anything," Irving smiled. "Not until you're absolutely certain the time is right. Maybe it's the day you announce the arrest of the bombers. But you have to be ready for that moment. You have to have nominees ready to go."

"If we put a search committee on this," Becks joined the fray, "it will leak. If anyone from White House Counsel or the AG's office starts putting together a questionnaire or interview questions or so much as wikis the roster of appellate court judges, it will leak."

"But if in the coming weeks, Reg and I were to invite some old friends to dinner," Rosemarie closed, "if we were to vet those friends for positions in our foundation, if we were to bring some of them to Washington to check out our office space – who would even notice?"

For several seconds, Salas didn't speak. The room would have been silent, if not for the bells and whistles and bangs and bings of the slot machines gifted by casinos from all over the world. Salas knew that handling this, the nominations, more so than even the investigation, would pose the greatest challenge of his presidency.

It was Becks who broke the impasse: "Four. We're announcing it at the Court at 2 today. Four Justices had arrived at the building and swiped in by the time the bombs went off. We already have identified remains for Justice Salovey. But we believe Justices Biggs, Robinson--"

"And Lapadula," Salas added, still ashamed of the joke he had made in this room at the very moment the Chief Justice was most likely disintegrating in flames or crumbling under falling debris.

The Irvings didn't respond for several seconds. After all the figures and video footage and arguments over strategy that had filled the last 23 hours, putting names to the dead sobered everything.

"Two from each side," Reginald Irving finally observed. "Two liberals, two conservatives."

"That's why I find it hard to believe this was motivated by ideology," the President said.

"Unless it was someone who wanted you to turn the tide," Reg countered, "turn a 5-4 hole into a dominant 6-3."

"None of it matters until we get the first one," Rosemarie whispered, her gaze locked on the carpet patterns. "The quorum for any decisions is six Justices. The Court will be paralyzed until you can add at least one more." No one doubted she was to be trusted when it came to Supreme Court rules; she was the only one in the room, after all, who had spent a year at One First Street as a clerk.

Rosemarie looked up into the President's eyes. She didn't know this man well, but she had known enough in her life to know they weren't going to get an answer out of him right at this instant. It would take marination, rumination.

She moved past Salas, heading straight back for the elevators, stunning her husband. "Sweetheart, where--"

"We've made our recommendation," she explained as the elevator doors slid open behind her. "Our job now is to support our President, whatever he decides."

Reg smiled; as always, he knew his wife was right. "Thank you for your time, Mr. President," he said as he joined her on the elevator.

The back doors of their Escalade had been closed, Mitch had returned to his usual perch up in shotgun, and the wheels under them had started to roll back in the direction of Spring Valley before Irving turned to his wife with concern. "Are you all--"

"He's not going to give us enough time."

"What?"

"When he calls to give us the green light. He won't give us much time. We need to be ready."

Irving smiled and sat back with a laugh. 26 years of marriage, and he was still underestimating his wife.

"Nothing's wrong," Miranda said. That was the last thing Jason could remember her saying before the rest of his Sunday night blacked out.

Bullshit, he had thought, *something's very fucking wrong*. Miranda had been sober even longer than he had. He learned that the first time he was at Bullfeathers with her, when they realized they had both ordered ginger ales. That's all they had ordered, every visit to their favorite bar since. So why the hell was she drinking Sunday night? There was no doubt about it, that wasn't prune juice in her glass, not the way she bounced it between her fingers. Not the way her last two empties were still sitting there, as if she had asked the bartender not to clear them so their carcasses could stare up at her from the bar and gloat. What could drive the strongest, smartest, toughest, most grounded person he knew to break a now-nine-year-old pledge? Was it whatever had made her cry? What was it? She had been staring up at the TV over the bar when she cried – what had been on that TV? Was that what made her cry, was that what made her--

Jason would have to find his answers in the present. Sunday was in the past now, in his dreams. He wanted to keep poring over them, replaying them for answers, but the present was now shining its light on his face, waking him from a day-long stupor nap. A giant metal door was sliding open, light from behind it tearing apart the darkness that had been so comforting for God-knows-how-many hours now.

Where the hell was he? He was sprawled out, stomach down, on a cold concrete floor – he really had been drunk if he had found this comfortable enough to sleep. But the drunk was in the past now too. His head was clear, razor sharp for the first time since he saw Miranda's empties. Sober enough to see – metal bars. He was in some sort of cell, some sort of cage.

Jason rose to his feet and crossed to these bars, his eyes adjusting to make out the one figure on the other side of them, a strange little man pushing 60, in a suit, round glasses and blue bowtie, sitting cross-legged in a simple folding chair, several stacks of papers organized on his lap. "Where am I?" Jason asked him. "What the hell is this?"

"Mr. Lancaster. George Aug, Homeland Security," the older man answered, strangely genial for the situation. George was that kind of dying breed of man every family or company had, the droll intellectual who doesn't own any straight ties, who always finds a smile no matter how bad things are going. Right now, things couldn't have been going worse for anyone on the planet than Jason. "You collapsed at the Supreme Court. You were babbling incoherently."

It all rushed back to Jason – or parts of it at least, like he was a frat boy sucking in the cold, cleansing air of a dawn walk of shame. He had pulled out all stops to get into the burning building – one cop let him past the barricades when he flashed his Court Police ID, but a couple others he had to push aside and outrun up the marble steps. They had pulled up short, not wanting to enter the conflagration without a flame retardant suit or oxygen mask. Everyone Lancaster saw in the hellscape, in the Great Hall, was wearing one, including the man who accosted him and told him he should leave. He brandished his badge again, tried to explain that he was the head of Threat Assessment for the Supreme Court Police, but Haz Mat just chuckled, "You picked the wrong day to call in sick," and continued escorting him back towards the gaping hole where the interior heat had blown off the iconic bronze doors. Jason demanded he take him to the Marshal of the Court Police, to Miranda Whitney, that she was his CO and he needed to report to her, but Haz Mat wasn't listening.

Had Jason gotten rough with him? Violent? Is that what had landed him in the basement of Homeland Security's National Ops Center? (At least, that's where he prayed he was, still in Washington, still on American soil, not renditioned to some new hush-hush Guantanamo.) He squinted his eyes, gripped his aching temple, tapped his frontal lobe against the bars, but couldn't remember anything more.

"… claimed you were drugged," Aug was continuing as Jason's head came back to the present, "that someone didn't want you there--"

"How long have I been in here?"

"We're very grateful for your patience. There are a lot of people we need to chat with. You understand."

"Chat? This where you usually put people to *chat*?"

"We both know these are extenuating circumstances. You're late for work for the first time in your career--"

"Second."

Aug flipped through his papers, thrown for a loop. "It was never reported." Jason smiled, realizing Miranda had never written up his one day of tardiness. "Regardless, you're never late, you're late yesterday, and that happens to be the morning your workplace blows up."

"Yesterday? It's already Tuesday?"

"Like I said. You were in rough shape, Mr. Lancaster. They had to drag you down the floor of the Great Hall."

That came back too – he remembered how hot the floor had been, that marble floor that's usually cold to the touch even in summer. "Did you check my blood? For Rohypnol or--"

"There were no foreign chemicals of any kind in your blood sample, Mr. Lancaster. Just alcohol. Almost point two-two."

Jason shook his head. He knew he had been something *like* drunk – but until he remembered the smell and taste and warmth of the drink going down his throat, he refused to admit it was booze that had done him in. "I didn't drink Sunday night. You can ask my sponsor. I was with her. Miranda Whitney. Call her."

"We'll get to that. I want to start further back than Sunday."

"Don't I get a call? I want to call Miranda--"

"Could you tell me what this is?"

Aug was holding up a color photograph. Jason knew what it was – tight packages of some sort of variation of plastic explosive, C4 or Semtex wrapped in neat little black paper packages. If he saw it closer, he could nail its make, model, its country of origin, the organization that had trained its maker; but he wasn't going to do that right now. He knew where Aug was leading this interrogation, and he wasn't going to fall into that trap. "I want. My call."

"I will get you your call. I just can't do that until I can tell my bosses I've asked you a few more questions. Like about your Special Forces team." He pulled out a couple sheets of goldenrod, laid them on top of his pile, and smiled as he read; this was the moment Aug had been building up to. "'3rd SFG … sub-Saharan Africa … Afghanistan …' You've seen some serious shinola. And then … look at that. Arrested and court-martialed for beating the stuffing out of your Captain."

"What?"

"You didn't assault a Captain Lance Tyrol?"

"That was expunged from my record."

Aug held up the goldenrod sheets with a shit-eating grin. "Little talent I've always had. Gotten me where I am. I've always been able to find the *unabridged* versions of things." He returned the goldenrods to the pile and read on. "Hmm, let's see, you were a 12B, Combat Engineer. Sounds harmless enough. What's that mean exactly, you build bridges and things?"

"You know exactly what it means. It's why you put me in here."

Aug shifted his ream into one hand and stood, stepping right up to the bars. "You blew stuff up. And you enjoyed it too. You were pretty gosh darn good at it." He held up the photo of the explosive again, but still Jason wouldn't look at it. "So you recognize a grade-A Kai-Shek model Chinese firecracker when you see one, don't you? You'd know how to modify it, give it a little more yuck for its Yuan."

Jason raised his eyes, being careful to avoid even passing over the photo, lest some innate curiosity keep him locked on it for a second too long, get the wheels turning behind his eyes, and confirm for Aug that he was indeed the bomb savant all those papers said he was. He blinked off the photo, and instead just pierced his gaze right into Aug's. "Miranda. Whitney. She's the Marshal of the Supreme Court Police. She's my CO. I need to talk to her."

"I know who she is, Jason. Problem is, unlike you, Ms. Whitney was very punctual yesterday."

Jason's legs stopped working. He didn't feel his knees crash down onto the concrete, didn't feel the tears pouring suddenly down his cheeks, or his mouth opening wide in a silent scream. You've heard the expression about your life flashing before your eyes? At this moment, Jason's entire life *with Miranda* replayed over and over again for him, on an endless, uncontrollable loop: his first interview with her at the Court, afternoons spent hanging out at Bullfeathers, passionate midnight kisses under the darkened arches of a closed bank …

Aug nodded down the hall to unseen associates, and the heavy metal door started wheeling to a close over the bars, again closing Jason in complete and utter darkness.

It didn't matter. All he was seeing was that last beautiful time they made love. And then he was back at the Court again for his first interview, meeting Miranda all over again.

WEDNESDAY

The nation needed a funeral.

It was Becks who realized it, sitting next to the President in the back of his "Tanque" (his armored stretch Cadillac sedan) on the way to the ruins of the Court for Tuesday's afternoon press event. The plan had always been for POTUS to use this event to announce which Justices had been lost – but why not milk it even further? Why not have him take several minutes to go over detailed memorial arrangements for each? It would create an atmosphere in which the assembled reporters would surely feel it too tasteless to even *think* about asking him why there were no arrests or theories in the investigation as of yet.

A block from First Street NE and the waiting presser, Becks yelled up to Hifrael to do another lap, adding ten minutes to their journey; a minute later, POTUS had Chief Justice Lapadula's widow on the line agreeing that it would be quite all right if a memorial of some type were held for her husband the very next day. It couldn't be a "funeral" per se – they hadn't yet identified any of his remains among the other 124 victims; they couldn't yet do anything involving a coffin or urn. But why not get a group of his family and friends and colleagues gathered around his future gravesite at Arlington, why not bring in the Army Salute Guns Battery for a 19-gunner (an advantage of starting with the Chief, as the Associate Justices would warrant only 17 guns), why not *force* the press to spend at least part of their hump day celebrating this Justice's considerable legacy?

Twenty-four hours later, 'A Remembrance for Warren Lapadula' was a resounding success. Every network devoted much of their morning show to him, every network – cable and the big boys and even ESPN (the Chief had won the Heisman Trophy the year after OJ) – cut into their midday programming to cover the event, and the President's eulogy had the assembled celebrants in tears.

The only thing Becks hadn't foreseen was the role the *surviving* Justices would play in the early afternoon. Salas had bent his earlier edict restricting them to their homes of course (the more VIPs he could get sobbing in front of cameras, the more *moments* the media would have to replay and re-post and recycle throughout the day). So on this third day of their short careers as Secret Service protectees, each of the five survivors arrived at the nation's most famous cemetery surrounded by their own personal offensive lines. Predictably, some Fox News commentators asked if the President had only served to set up an easy one-stop-shop for the killers who had hit only four of their nine intended targets the first time. But Becks made sure Secret Service prepared for this; though to the television cameras it looked like a beautiful open-air Autumn event, in reality, the entire group was sitting within an oval of transparent bulletproof glass – and everyone save the President and the Justices underwent the equivalent of a TSA opt-out feel-up before being granted admittance.

No, it wasn't the logistics of having the Justices present that Becks fumbled – it was giving them access to POTUS. After Salas's speech and the 19-gun salute, he moved down the line of widows, widowers and finally the five survivors to offer his condolences. But Becks had never had a personal encounter with the second-to-last Justice in the President's path before. If she had, she would have known better than to give her personal, unfettered, unplanned access to her boss, even if just for a few seconds.

Claudine Egan would have been remembered as an historic figure even if she had never been nominated to the Supreme Court. She was the first female professor tenured at Harvard Law School and by the end of the 1970s had argued more cases in front of the Court than any other woman in history. It was Ronald Reagan who had nominated her to the 10th Circuit, and his former VP who later moved her up to the Supremes. There were three occasions during her 30-year tenure that she could have been named the first ever female Chief Justice, and all three times she was the most qualified candidate, but all three times had been passed over for a male colleague. This may well have been because as brilliant and historic a figure as she was, she was also ruthlessly cutthroat, never shying away from breaking convention or stepping on a contemporary's throat to boost herself up the next rung of the achievement ladder.

Being Chief means not only a lot more administrative duties, but taking on the uncomfortable role of keeping order in Conference, the private meeting between the Justices in which they each declare which way they intend to vote on a particular case, and try to convince their colleagues to change their minds. A traditionally civilized powwow, under Chief Justice Lapadula the Conferences had reportedly become louder, more passionate, and, rumor had it, even close to *physical* on more than one occasion. These are but a couple of the reasons that new Chief Justices often come from outside the Court – most Associate Justices are more than happy in their current positions, and don't ever dream of future promotion to the center chair.

Claudine Egan was not one of these Associate Justices. Being Chief had been her father's failed dream, a dream he later transferred to his only child, and for many years now the only unfulfilled dream she still harbored for herself—which she made clear to POTUS when he leaned over her at Chief Lapadula's Remembrance, took her hands in his own, and whispered, "Madame Justice, I know you two were particularly--"

"You need to show the American people the Court lives on," she barked in his face. Salas didn't move at first, not quite sure what he had heard. So Egan took the hands located around her own, and used them to yank him in even closer. "Appoint one of us the new Chief."

"Madame Justice, I have to say it's highly unusual for a member of the Court to engage in political--"

"Then you don't know this Court very well."

"Mr. President, we have to keep moving." Becks was already pushing on Salas's back, trying to encourage him onto the final Justice and then back to his vehicle.

"This is your last chance, you know," Egan continued in Salas's face without even flinching.

"I'm sorry?"

"Your last chance to prove to everyone who thinks you're just a pretty face that you actually *can* do something."

Salas slammed his door of the Tanque. Becks wanted to apologize as she crawled in next to him, but he had already ordered her to get the Irvings on the line. He'd barked it out before they had even exited the bulletproof bubble, so she knew when she got into her side of the car, he wouldn't want to hear anything except: "I've got the Irvings on the line."

Salas nodded; she thumbed the speaker phone button, holding the phone equidistant between them as the Tanque started its 2.5-mile trek back to 1600 Pennsylvania Avenue. "Mr. President?" former President Irving's voice came out of the phone's tinny speaker.

"I've always prided myself on not being one of those politicians who can't admit when he's wrong," Salas said as he hovered over Becks's phone. "I should've gotten this started when you told me to, 18 hours ago. But better late than never. Becks will brief you on our List. We've had a running one going since Super Tuesday, when we first thought I might get the nomination."

"I need to get it from the safe in my office," Becks chimed in, "but I know right at the top is--"

"Your List is useless," Rosemarie's voice interrupted from the handset.

"I'm sorry?" Salas asked.

"We can tell you without seeing it, it's going to be too partisan," Irving agreed with his wife.

"There's never been a scenario like this," the First Lady continued. "If you're going to get a Republican-controlled Senate to go for this, if you're going to get the American people to back you up, you're going to have to re-think every rule."

"So how do you suggest we start?"

"We have a List," Rosemarie explained.

"—crafted with a situation a lot like this in mind," Irving added.

"What? How the hell did you--"

"You remember when Chief Quint had just announced his retirement, and Egan went into the hospital?"

Becks nodded. "The routine gall stone. We had just won Iowa."

"There was nothing routine about it. Egan had liver cancer. We thought we were going to have to replace two at once."

Salas chuckled to himself at the notion that Egan would push herself for Chief Justice with that kind of medical history.

Rosemarie continued: "We came up with a list that can satisfy both sides of the aisle. Veras did all the vetting," she said of Irving's White House Counsel; she knew Salas trusted Farrah, as he had asked her to stay on as his own top in-house legal advisor.

"All right, let's go get one," Salas ordered. "Let's get the first one. I don't want him to even know what we're doing. Let's just get him to Washington."

You mean her, Rosemarie thought as her husband thumbed his phone dead. He giggled, giving her that smile he always flashed when her brilliance had borne fruit. It was her idea to get to Chicago. It was her idea to spend a couple nights at one of their favorite hotels, the Palmer House Hilton.

It was her idea that, when POTUS's call came in, they would be only 90 minutes from South Bend, Indiana.

This time, Jason was expecting the giant metal wall to slide open. He still had to squint as the first slivers of light burned his irises, his face cross-hatched by the shadows of the bars like a film noir heavy, but this time he was ready to receive George Aug. He was ready to take control of this little game.

"You asked to see me?" Aug asked.

"Yes," Jason answered with his first little smile since sometime during the 4th quarter of the Skins' win on Sunday.

"You're ready to share something that can help me?"

"There's something I think you should see," Jason grunted as he pushed himself to his feet. "In my house."

No one at Notre Dame Law School knew quite how to react to the bombing. For how many days should classes be cancelled? (The Dean settled on the remainder of the week.) Was this attack but the first of many on the American legal system? Were students who had always dreamed of arguing cases before the Supreme Court, or maybe someday even deciding them, supposed to now be fearful of entering the Law? Or should this be a call to arms, more reason than ever that the Law needed America's best and brightest to serve in her hour of greatest need?

Professor Cecilia Koh decided to take her frustrations out on some exams. She had never been one for grand, sweeping historical narratives or base paranoia – she was interested in the here and now. That's what had drawn her to Textualism: she believed in the *words,* the meaning of those words as intended by the framer at the moment he had won an argument against his peers and won the right to put pen to everlasting paper. She wasn't interested in how people thought and reasoned and *felt* a law should be interpreted today, under a myriad of new and more complicated circumstances. That all could change tomorrow, for God's sake, if not in an hour.

So with no class to teach for five more days, she decided to get the grading of the midterms (with the final, one of only two exams that would determine each student's entire grade for the semester) out of the way. Life would return to normal soon, she knew; her class would continue, and students would with almost shocking impatience demand to know their midterm grades. She was getting that out of the way now, with the added bonus of unleashing any anger or sorrow she may have retained over Monday's tragedy through the red of her pen. (And yes, she might have enjoyed the lousiest exams more than ever before, finding some sort of morose pleasure in bloodying their pages with such deep red it soaked through to the ones beneath them.)

She was in the middle of one of the better exams when the two flimsy Xeroxed pages landed on top of it. She didn't immediately look at them, instead turning to see who had disturbed her small office, her quiet reverie: that semester's nemesis. "My name is Jane Norfleet. Row J. You called on me on Monday--"

"And during our contraception discussion last month," Professor Koh sat back, pulling off her reading glasses and setting them on Norfleet's Xeroxes. "I remember you, Ms. Norfleet. What can I do for--"

"Mifa didn't give a last name."

Koh lunged back for her desk, knocking her reading glasses to the opposite edge of its surface as she grabbed those photocopies Norfleet had brought with her. The name was uncommon enough in this country, and one she had never heard before within the hallowed walls of Notre Dame. It was a beautiful name Cecilia thought would be a great honor to her Korean heritage. Her husband – though not Korean himself – knew how important it was to Cecilia to reconnect with her past, how she had been struggling to do it her whole adult life, and graciously said he loved the name too.

"I know Mifa's your daughter, Professor," Norfleet continued to crow. Koh had only been in Women's Health & Wellness – the clinic whose name was displayed at the top of the first photocopy – once, but she knew the exact day, the exact hour, the exact occasion for that visit. "My cousin works there," Norfleet explained. "She saw you pay cash. For your daughter's abortion."

For a moment, Professor Koh considered trying to explain everything – how her daughter had struggled with clinical depression, how Mifa was barely hanging on in school even before getting pregnant, how one day when Norfleet had a child of her own she would understand that when your son or daughter comes to you for help, there's only one course of action that makes any fucking sense at all – but came to her senses, remembering that this had nothing to do with her daughter. "I suppose you expect an A for this?"

"The *Journal of Law & Ethics.* I'm the editor this year. You're going to come clean for our next cover story."

"Come clean?" The words clicked off Koh's teeth like machine gun shells clattering to the floor.

"Welcome to Catholicism, Professor. This is where you confess. You've made a career out of dressing up your stone age morality in the *lie* of strict Constitutional interpretation. It's time you confessed your hypocrisy."

At this precise moment in Norfleet's practiced diatribe, Professor Koh stopped listening. Not out of spite for the student or what she was doing (although she had plenty for both), but because of the caravan of black SUVs pulling up in the parking lot right over Norfleet's shoulder, just beyond the office's only window, with two smaller tinted vehicles trailing just behind it. "Now the truth has finally come out," Norfleet was still going. "When life got real, you were just like everyone else."

A large African-American gentleman with a white cord coiling out of the back of his ear lobe got out of the Escalade, walked to the rear door, and opened it – and just *stood there*, as if he was guarding the secret entrance to some meat-packing district nightclub. "Professor?" Norfleet whined, but Cecilia Koh was already on her feet, already stepping out the door, already on her way to the large vehicle.

Stunned and offended at the Professor's gall, Jane Norfleet responded the only way kids these days know to respond to most things: she took a picture with her iPhone.

Koh had a feeling the SUV was there for her. There was no one else in the building that day (in fact, she had to get special permission from the Dean to convince security to open the doors for her in the first place), no other cars but her Acura in the parking lot. So when she approached Mitchell Aldridge and put a hand to her chest with eyes that asked, "Me?" she wasn't surprised when he nodded with a smile, then gave her a hand up into the vehicle, shutting the door after her heels.

She *was* surprised to find the last President and First Lady of the United States sitting in the back of the car waiting for her. But perhaps not as surprised as your average Joe might be, as she had met them on two previous occasions. "Mr. President. It's too late to change the C I gave your son."

"We're here out of gratitude, Professor. He's been at Williams & Connolly since June."

"You were just the kick in the ass he always needed," Rosemarie Irving chimed in with her husband.

"You came all this way to thank me? Today?"

Irving leaned forward, tapping her knee. "Your President needs you, Professor."

"And by that he means the current one," Rosemarie added.

Professor Koh didn't move, didn't say a word for several minutes. This reaction didn't shock the Irvings at all; they seemed to revel in it, their eyes gleaming as Reg signaled his driver it was okay to move.

They had just merged onto Interstate-70 when the Professor burst out into utter, hysterical laughter. "You can't possibly mean--"

"Professor," Irving soothed. "We've got a long drive ahead of us. You're going to want to get some rest."

Koh gasped. They weren't going in the direction of any airport she knew. They were driving her *to Washington.* This whole thing was so hush-hush, they didn't even want flight records in some rinky-dink municipal airport that could prove she had travelled with them. "I need to go home," she panicked. "I need to pack, I need to talk to my family--"

Rosemarie smiled, a smile that somehow calmed Koh even more than the President's had. "We've got someone there. It's all being handled. Just sit back. And relax."

Professor Koh tried to do just that. It was no easy task with the tears raining down her cheeks.

Jason heard the bootfalls and shouted orders even through the metal wall. *My ride is here*, he thought as he stood, just seconds before it slid open and light again penetrated his little cage. He knew the tease would work, knew Aug wouldn't be able to resist the notion that there was something in Jason's Maryland home that could open this investigation wide.

"But you won't find it without me," Jason had gloated – because he knew Aug would have no choice but to agree. It had already been over 60 hours, maybe even more, since the attack; if Homeland Security considered Jason some sort of suspect, any sort of suspect, they had already torn his house apart, dumped it upside down and shook out every last piece of lint. If Jason could convince Aug that the only way he was finding this new piece of evidence was with Jason's help, he would have his ticket out of this hole, into daylight, for a couple hours at least.

So he was expecting the DHS agents when they came to drag him from his cell to the Ops Center's motor pool. They threw him in the back of a surveillance van. Though the back of the van had no windows, the last rays of the day lit up the windshield in front. Jason wouldn't get to *feel* any daylight (Aug's one condition for this little boondoggle was that Jason wouldn't leave the van) but he'd get to see it at least. Jason didn't remember his mother well, but he did remember her always telling him how important the Vitamin D of the sun's rays was, remembered her always reading her romance novels outside in the New Mexico sun for at least an hour each day. On those couple days a year when it was too hot for even her to go outside, it almost drove her mad.

Soon after they had come to a stop in the middle of Jason's street, he could see the SWAT team charging up the steps of his brownstone and kicking open his front door. As Aug climbed into the back next to him, Jason grumbled under his breath, "I could've given you the key."

Aug chuckled, putting on headphones and sitting before the wall of monitors displaying every helmet cam feed. "Key? These boys don't know what a key is." Jason grimaced as he watched over Aug's shoulder; he expected the place to have already been ransacked, but when it's your home that's been desecrated, defiled and deflowered by search warrant, the aftermath is always much more gruesome than you even came close to imagining. "Okay, we're here," Aug turned to him, "where are they going?"

"There's a crawl space in the bedroom."

On Aug's subsequent command, the SWATs moved for the back of the apartment, pushing aside the bed like movers with three houses on the day's schedule. Two of them went to the wall, crouching to get their fingers in between the drywall and carpet fibers, wrenching back the rug until a floor hatch was visible.

"And what are they gonna find down there?"

"Miranda's a cop too. I had to go to special lengths to hide it from her."

The SWATs had already pulled the hatch open and were piercing the darkness with a first check of their flashlights. Not liking Jason's tone, Aug stood. "Listen up, I want EOD down there first. Anyone down there needs to be locked, loaded and heavily caffeinated."

It took nearly forty minutes to get the Explosive Ordnance Disposal specialist into her *Hurt Locker* space suit and lower her down into the crawl space. It didn't take even four for her to realize the anomaly down there, the item you wouldn't expect to find in a crawl space: a plastic retail shopping bag. Though her helmet wasn't outfitted with a video camera, Jason could picture the whole scene when he heard her curse over the radio, "Oh, Jesus Christ."

The bag of robin's egg blue was very carefully brought out to Aug in the DHS surveillance van. The sight of it brought a thicker lump to Jason's throat than he had expected. What the hell was he supposed to do with it now? The thought of returning it just made him sick to his stomach, but he was also sure he wasn't ever going to meet anyone else he wanted to give it to. He tried to just put the whole thing out of his mind, but that proved impossible when Aug pulled out the bag's only contents: a tiny jewelry box, also robin's egg, some pearl-white ribbon wrapped around it. He tore it open to reveal the diamond ring Jason had intended to use to ask for Miranda's hand in marriage.

"Now you know," Jason explained to the gobsmacked Aug, "I could never have done it. Not with her inside."

The frustrated Aug spiked the box back into the bag, then glared at Jason. "Someone who's planning to blow up one of our greatest institutions? That's a guy who would go to great lengths to mask his motive."

Jason leaned forward, digging into Aug's eyes with his own. "Look in my eyes. Look in them, and if you still think I could do this, then go ahead and lock me up and throw away the key." Aug did look back. Jason could sense something churning in there, concern and confusion clouding his pupils. Was he getting through to him?

What he was seeing behind those eyes was Aug's realization that his time with Jason had run out over ten hours ago, and he still had nothing to show for it.

THURSDAY

The greatest controversy since the bombing came courtesy of the AG's office. Attorney General Patrick Naftalis was pretty much asking for it when at 6:13 PM EST on Monday night – less than an hour after the President's own first address had ended – he declared for any microphones within shouting distance that this was *not* 2001 and the Justice Department would be handling this investigation and eventual prosecution much differently than 9/11 had been handled. What had occurred on Monday morning in Washington was a heinous crime – and it would be handled as such. (Needless to say, there were several Republican members of Congress – who as a group had already declared war in the media on four different nations and three different terror groups – who had some issues with this mannered approach.) There would be no bending of civil liberties or illegal wiretapping this time, Antonio Salas's Attorney General promised, no Patriot Act, no Guantanamo.

In other words, George Aug and Homeland Security could only hold a suspect like Jason Lancaster for 48 hours of questioning without charging him with a crime. And as Thursday dawned on the nation's capital, he had already spent over 70 in the hole. Empty handed, Aug's superiors wished they had given another interrogator a shot at Jason, but Aug had never before failed like this to get somewhere, *anywhere* with a suspect.

Which was what made George Aug so confident that Jason really was innocent, really wasn't hiding anything. He had indeed looked in those eyes, and he believed he had seen the honest soul of a loyal American. More than that: he had heard in his voice when he spoke of Miranda Whitney – when he spoke of that ring – the warm warble of a deep love story, one that reminded George of the one he had recently lost in his own life.

All of this was why he argued so hard – and convinced – the CO of his division, the Under Secretary of Intelligence & Analysis, that they didn't need to keep a 24/7 surveillance team on Lancaster, that it was a waste of resources that could be better spent elsewhere.

Well, that was one reason. The other reason stemmed from the conversation he had with Jason when George came down to the Ops Center basement to bid him farewell as he collected his personal effects. "Probably a good idea to stay in town," Aug smiled, "for when we have additional questions."

At first, Jason didn't answer, just put his wallet in his back pocket, then looked down at his Supreme Court Police badge on its lanyard, and realizing he might not need it for a good while, stuffed it in a front pocket. He turned to mount the ramp up to daylight and freedom – but looked back once more, with one tantalizing final thought: "That bomb you recovered. If you let me see it, I could tell you where it came from." No, Jason didn't feel like this agency *deserved* his help after how they had treated him, but he was still a law enforcement officer. More than anything, he was a grieving lover who would do anything, work with *anyone* to bring about justice.

"Aw, why would I need you to do that?" Aug replied with a grin. "I've got a 61 billion dollar federal agency to do that for me."

"You're right," Jason nodded. "They already know where it came from." That was a test, a measuring stick of how much information DHS did have. Aug's eyes gave Jason all the answer he needed – they still hadn't cracked the origin of those bombs; or if they had, they hadn't shared this information with George Aug.

"No, they don't. If they did, I would know it," George couldn't help but retort.

Jason started backpedalling up the exit ramp, keeping his eyes locked on Aug's for one more reply: "Whoever told you they don't has got a good reason for lying to you."

He turned and was gone, disappearing into the sun like an apparition returning to the hereafter, leaving George Aug to question, well, *everything* upon which he had built his life.

It was the just-walking-around that Reginald Irving missed most, the unplanned strolls through the halls of the Eisenhower Exec Office Building or the Treasury on the opposite side of the White House, the drinking in of all the gasps, failed attempts at composure, running for cover and swooning as the President of the United States just sauntered by unannounced. It was the part he had always dreamed about as a late bloomer growing up in Oregon, a revenge of sorts on all his peers who had ignored him, especially those of the fairer sex. As he rose in politics, he swore he could feel the humidity rise whenever he entered a room, the panties all around him instantly dampening. He still got that reaction, would continue to get it for the rest of his life, but it's not the same when you're just going to your foundation offices every day, or presiding over the smallest staff you've had in a decade. There were still a few events a year – world summits, political conventions – during which he got to play the rock star again, but they were maybe monthly, rather than daily, occurrences now.

Farrah Veras had never swooned for Irving, or if she did, was damn good at concealing it beneath multiple layers of professionalism. That was one big reason he liked her so much, he acknowledged to himself, because she was a challenge for him, someone he had to *convince* to like him, much like he'd had to do his absolute God damnedest to convince Rosemarie 28 years ago. Farrah was one of the rare people who could make a POTUS feel like she was interviewing him, like it wasn't up to him whether or not she would be his next White House Counsel, it was a question of whether or not she even wanted the job. Irving knew she was perfect; if there was one person at the White House who can't be scared of the President, shouldn't it be his lawyer? She took the job of course – and turned out to be good at it too, which is what had kept her in it for an unprecedented nine years. And eventually, he *had* convinced her to like him, and very, very much so.

After a nostalgic walk of points and whispers and moist undergarments, Irving found Veras doing what he always found her doing in her EEOB office. "I ever tell you how sexy you are when you're reading?" he stirred her, putting on the smile he knew to be his most seductive as he leaned against the open door frame of her office.

She didn't even need to look up to confirm the origin of that voice, that silky tone she knew so well. "Only about twelve hundred times," she replied.

"Well, that's not as bad as I would have guessed--"

"In your first term." She leaned forward, tightening the sandwich of her breasts with her forearms. "To what do I owe the pleasure today, Mr. President?"

"You've always had an amazing nose for new talent, Farrah. I want to meet the best, hungriest, most trustworthy young guy you've got."

"DENNIS!" she screamed, aiming her voice around Irving's shoulder and down the long corridor of offices housing her associates and deputies. "GET IN HERE!"

And seconds later, wet-behind-the-ears Dennis Coutts, in only his fourth month on the job, ran into the same room as a former President of the United States.

"Did you call me, Ms. Ver— *Oh my God!"*

"No, just a President," Veras chuckled.

A product of an Arizonan Navajo reservation, Dennis might have been the least likely person working in Washington, second only to President Salas himself. Even on the day he graduated top of his class from Sandra Day O'Connor School of Law (his parents had guilted him into staying close to home at Arizona State), he would have considered the notion of working in the White House Counsel's office crazy. Yet, a month later he received a job offer from the Bureau of Indian Affairs and packed up his car for a cross-country drive to Washington; a year later, he moved a block east to the White House.

The third job offer he would receive in his short career would sound the most insane, like the stuff of a fevered peyote trip.

"Dennis, Farrah here tells me you're the most promising Deputy Associate she's got these days. What are you working on right now?"

Dennis's shoulders clenched up. "Um, Sir … all due respect, Sir … unless you're *currently* serving in the Administration … I'm not authorized to discuss--"

Irving put his hand on Dennis's shoulder. The young man gasped, recoiling like a trapped animal. "Right answer, Dennis."

Dennis's tension released with a hard exhale and a relieved smile. "Thank you Sir!"

"I'm afraid you've been fired."

"*What?!*" Dennis and Farrah exclaimed in unison, the latter leaping to her feet.

"Good news is, you've already got a new job. Follow me."

Not one to defy a President, the confused Dennis did just that, out of Farrah's office and down the hall. "But, but, you said--"

"Which one's yours?" Irving cut him off with a nod to the open doors, many of which had faces peeking out.

Dennis swallowed, then traipsed into his own small, windowless office. The President and his rather large African-American guard stood just outside the door as Dennis cleared the top of his desk into a banker's box. "Um, what will I be doing … ?" he inquired, to which Irving just chuckled. Dennis went back to packing up his life, pulling out his center drawer of supplies and assorted other knickknacks and dumping that into the box too.

Then it was down an elevator to the basement level of the building, a humid brick corridor lined with pipes and tubes housing the cables that made the building hum. Irving's guard (who had by now been introduced as Mitch Aldridge) led them a few yards to another door which he opened with a key card, revealing yet another stairwell down into the earth. The President took the steep stairs like this was a practiced route and at Mitch's urging, Dennis followed. Their descent ended in yet another locked door, again opened with a key card. Dennis tingled with excitement, picturing some dingy, 18th Century Presidential bunker on the other side, long ago hidden under Washington when the city was first built.

But instead, he now stepped out into a long, sleek tunnel, a Disneyfied or Spielbergian vision of the future, Dennis thought: bright lights recessed in a white ceiling, walls lined with tanned leather, floors carved from polished marble. Dennis looked both directions in wonder, one way going on to infinity, the other forking into a few different passageways. *Holy shit*, he thought, *am I actually in the secret White House tunnel system?* "Is this—?"

Irving returned his hand to Dennis's shoulder with that famous smile that could end wars. "Let's go." They turned what Dennis believed was East, down the infinity tunnel, in what he reasoned had to be the direction of the White House. But after a football field or so, Irving stopped, turning left to face the smooth wall. He opened his right palm, winked back at Dennis, and placed his mitt flat on the wall.

And nothing happened. Irving moved his hand around the wall, as if he was searching for something. "I guess Tony moved the thing," he said back to Dennis with a sheepish grin.

As if on cue, a square of green lit up the leather underneath his hand. Dennis jumped a little as two panels in the wall slid open, revealing a hidden elevator. He followed Irving and Mitch inside, then felt his skin crawl with goose bumps when the doors slid shut, forming the eagle of the Presidential seal. He stayed silent between them, fighting the urge to hum along with the Muzak version of "Hail to the Chief" as the elevator descended what felt like a *long way,* Dennis's throat flying up into his skull on the first initial drop. *We're going to China. The White House has a frigging elevator to China.*

But before he knew it, the elevator was binging and they were coming to a smooth stop. In that instant before the doors slid open again, Dennis's overactive young imagination again swam with visions of what he was about to walk into – *Some sort of secret bunker? A nuclear launch command center? NORAD? USCYBERCOM? SHIELD?!? Maybe SHIELD is real, and it's behind these doors!* The eagle parted, and Dennis stepped out into--

A casino. There were slot machines chirping, there were tables for blackjack and roulette and craps, there were TVs lining the back wall showing seven different sports channel feeds. And sitting in two chairs right in the middle of it all was President Irving's First Lady and a tiny Asian woman with a sharp gaze.

Rosemarie Irving stood. "Hello Dennis."

She knows my name. Holy shit, Rosemarie Irving knows my name!

"I'd like to introduce you to Cecilia Koh, the next Associate Justice of the Supreme Court. You're going to vet her."

The next sound Dennis heard was his banker's box crashing to the floor, his pencils and staple gun and three-hole punch rattling out onto the floor.

"I came here to speak to you tonight, because that's what the families who suffered tragedy on Monday would want me doing," President Salas said to the assembled analysts and field agents and janitors and every Homeland Security employee they could fit into the Ops Center's largest conference room. "What all the Justices, what Chief Justice Lapadula, would want us doing. Every minute, their killers get further and further away. We've already given them a head start of over forty-eight hundred minutes. I know you're all doing everything you possibly can in this effort. But we don't sleep, none of us, myself included, until we make that time up."

George Aug wasn't so sure they were doing everything they could. Jason had filled his mind with doubt, had inspired in him a sinking, sick feeling that they should indeed know much more about the bombs, much more about who planted them and how they got into the building, by this stage of the game. He knew these thoughts could well be ridiculous; he was taking Jason's words at face value, the words of a vindictive man whom they'd just held in a windowless hole for three days, for God's sake. Letting Jason's words get to him like this, haunt him like this, this was rookie baloney, George chided himself. Aug needed to get Jason's words out of his brain – and the best way to do that was to expose their flaws, find out exactly what his agency knew about the bombs, snuff out the minor bureaucratic snafu that had kept this information from reaching his desk, assure himself that nothing was being swept under the rug despite Jason's insinuation.

George's current superior was Kingman Summers, the Under Secretary of Intelligence & Analysis – okay, actually, the *Assistant* Under Secretary, but holding the higher post until the President's nominee could be confirmed by the Senate, which they'd already delayed for over nine months. George tried his darnedest to give this kid (Kingman was 41, but that was almost 20 years younger than George, definitely qualifying for 'kid' status) the benefit of the doubt, to put out of his mind that *Assistant* part of his title. Unfortunately, Kingman Summers made that nearly impossible. He was everything George couldn't stand about government. George was a law enforcement lifer, now working under an unqualified appointee who'd been named after a former president of Yale and had everything in his life handed to him on a silver tray, probably procuring this position by playing soccer with President Salas every Saturday.

He waited until the Under Secretary had been through the Salas receiving line and was alone in the hall, walking back to his office. "Kingman," George called out as he caught up to him from behind. "Great speech, wasn't it? I've always thought he was--"

"I don't want to rush you, Georgie," the Under Secretary cut him off, not slowing his pace, "but it turns out they don't cancel school plays at Sidwell for national tragedies."

Georgie? He had never called George that before. No one had, at least not since he was a boy growing up in Long Island City, Queens. He didn't like the sound of it any more as an adult than he had as a child. "I was hoping you could tell me where EXD has gotten with the unexploded device."

Kingman stopped, turning to bore into George with a sinister, almost melting gaze. "What are you worried about the bomb for?"

"It's … something that Lancaster said, actually--"

"Wait a minute. You told me that guy was clean."

"He is. But he does know a thing or two about bombs. He made some interesting points. We should know something about it by now."

Kingman laughed. "Oh should we? Don't tell me you fell for his Special Forces psy-ops bullshit."

"I've been doing this for a few years, Sir."

The Under Secretary took a menacing step forward, raising a sharp forefinger in George's face. "You listen to me, Georgie." *There it is again.* "The bomb's a dead end."

"I'm one of the lead analysts on this case. I probably should play a role in declaring when things are dead ends."

Summers looked away with a chuckle and an eyeroll. "By my scorecard, you either spent the first three days of this investigation on your own dead end, or you failed to keep a bad guy off the streets. So don't you think you best stop worrying about the bomb, Dr. Strangelove, and get your nose back on Lancaster, or some other suspect, or some piece of actionable intelligence that might actually help us break this thing? You know, *do your job*."

"And you don't think knowing everything there is to know about the bomb might help me, might help all of us, do just that?"

The Under Secretary's laugh dripped with condescension. "I know you've been here a long time and go home and tell your wife and your kids and all your drinking buddies at the Caps game that you really run this place. But the President, that same President you just spent 20 minutes salivating over, he appointed me your boss. That means I'm the one who gets to decide what will or won't help you do your job. We clear?"

George nodded, turned and marched back to his desk. "And it's Mr. Under Secretary," Kingman called after him. But George didn't hear it. He was too busy going through a roll call of all his DHS colleagues in his head, trying to decide if he there was a single one of them he could trust.

It was on the return trip from his visit to the Ops Center that President Salas was informed that the Irvings were recommending Cecilia Koh as his first nominee to the Supreme Court. By the time he was perusing their file on her, Dennis had already been questioning her for about three hours. It had been over seven since Irving first led the young lawyer into the White House casino and introduced him to the Professor, but the first four were spent vomiting, telling Mitch Aldridge where he lived and how to get in and from what drawers to retrieve him more clothes, reading every document that had ever been created about Professor Koh, going upstairs for a shower and some fresh clothes and some godsend *mouthwash,* then finally, a laid back lunch with Rosemarie Irving for instructions on how she would like him to conduct the vetting. "We had her fully vetted five years ago," she explained. "The FBI did a background. The ABA rated her 'well qualified.' She passed everything with flying colors. So there's no pressure on you, Dennis. We don't need an exhaustive body cavity. Just walk her politely through the basics. Then eventually, get into anything from the last five years that you or she think may have adversely affected her stellar fitness for the Court."

Rosemarie was running the show now; they had decided that President Irving should keep up his public commitments, get in front of just enough cameras to throw the media off any potential scent of what they were really doing. So he was at a banquet dinner with ambassadors from five different African nations ("Don't you let them cancel," he had instructed his Chief of Staff), when the current President called in from the Tanque to the casino.

"It's Águila, ma'am." Mitch handed Rosemarie the house phone.

"Thank you, Mitch. Mr. President?"

"Pull the plug, Rosemarie," his voice barked through the phone.

"Excuse me?"

"Former counsel to the Heritage Foundation? Law journal articles defending the Patriot Act and enhanced interrogation? This woman can't be my first nominee to the Court."

"With all due respect, Sir, *this woman* must be your first nominee." Rosemarie cupped a hand around the phone as she stepped away from the Roulette table where Professor Koh and Dennis were faced off like *Super Password* teammates, every inch of the table's felt covered with the history of Cecilia Koh's life and legal career. "The Republicans aren't going to allow you to replace their two seats with liberals and you know it. But you start off by giving them this gift, they'll have no choice but to support your next three nominees or be crucified for playing politics with the rebuilding of the Court."

"But, Madame First Lady, an academic?" Becks piped up over the line. "Shouldn't we be looking at circuit judges--"

"She's better. She was nominated to the federal bench by Bush 43, but not confirmed by the end of his second term, and the offer was revoked when he left office. She has the gold star of already being worthy of a presidential appointment, minus the paper trail of batshit judicial opinions to hang herself with."

"She's not right, Rosemarie," POTUS laid down the law. "Pull it."

As the line went dead, the First Lady could already feel the hot stares branding the back of her neck from the Roulette table. "I'm going home, aren't I?" Cecilia Koh asked.

"Not at all," she smiled as she spun around to them. "Just back to the hotel for the night."

Jason had returned two pieces of furniture to their usual positions, had picked up the glass of just one felled picture frame, when he realized he couldn't spend another minute in his apartment. It was that one picture, face down in the living room carpet, that had done it. It had only been in the house for the last nine, ten months, since the day Miranda delivered it to his office. It was a photo of the two of them from his first weeks at the Court, long before they were even romantically involved. In a stroke of hazing, Miranda had told Jason he should show up to work everyday in a full morning suit with tails. After a couple of weeks of catching constant snickers behind his back, Jason found Miranda in his office one morning also dressed in the tails she usually only wore for oral arguments in the courtroom. They had gotten their photo taken by an admiring clerk, their arms around each other as if they had some inkling of their future together.

A month later, when she spent her first night in his brownstone, she noticed the photo propped up on his desk. "You liked me long before you let on, didn't you?" she teased him.

"You kidding?" he smirked back. "With how big a bitch you were to me at first?"

"Hey!" She raised a finger in his face. "Don't ever use that word with me."

He grabbed that hand, pulled the finger down, yanked her face right up into his. "Or what?"

"It's such an ugly word."

"I'm sorry." He apologized with a kiss, then roughly undid her pants, taking her right there in the living room (they would have their first official bedroom romp the very next morning). And the next time she visited, she brought with her a frame into which the photo fit perfectly.

A tear hit a shard of glass, then rolled onto the photo paper, discoloring the image of Jason's tie. He swiped his forearm across his eyes, tossed the wrecked keepsake back up on its perch, then turned for the front door and went out to drink himself into oblivion. And why the hell shouldn't he? If the complete destruction of his life wasn't enough excuse for him to leap off the wagon, the fact that someone had already pushed him off four days ago was all he needed. He still didn't know what drug had fucked him up so royally, but it was close enough to the feeling of a booze bender that Jason didn't see any reason to be precious about his sobriety any longer.

Though hoping for his second blackout of the week, Jason was only up to his second Dewar's and third tequila shot when a grating voice observed from over his shoulder, "I thought the wagon seemed lighter."

Jason didn't react as George Aug took the stool next to him and ordered himself a ginger ale. "No, I don't have someone watching you," George grinned. "No need, long as you're planning on using your credit card from time to time."

Jason grunted, taking another long pull of his scotch. "Not even 12 hours and you already have more questions to harass me with?"

"Just one, actually." George swiveled his stool towards Jason, so he could murmur right into his ear without being overheard. "What reasons could an Under Secretary at Homeland Security possibly have for lying to me?"

Eighty-four minutes later, George Aug's 2007 Volvo pulled up to the front guard gate of the National Ops Center. Security computers recorded his ID being swiped over the reader, just as the surveillance cameras caught the back of his white mane nodding hello to the guard, then his vehicle advancing under the rising entrance arm. The parking lot cams watched his vehicle bounce into the lot, then the feeds in each corridor followed his course on foot from his assigned parking spot to the building housing the Science & Tech Directorate, onto an elevator up to the 12th floor where Advanced Research Projects kept their slew of offices, to a plain, unmarked office door he accessed using his key card.

Sensing the movement of a visitor, the overheads popped to life, lighting up the main laboratory of EXD, Homeland Security's bomb division. Hundreds of tiny electronic parts covered their work table, puzzle pieces that once made up a modified Kai-shek plastic explosive meant for the Supreme Court building. The lab's cameras followed George as he moved around the table, using the magnifying arm to examine each piece, from one section of the table to another as if he was a wide-eyed young boy following an elaborate treasure map. Studying the video later, the Under Secretary of Intelligence & Analysis would remark that he didn't realize George knew his way around a bomb so well, and the truth is he didn't. But the surveillance cameras weren't close enough to see the seam between his hairline and scalp; and George made a point of never facing or looking up to a camera lens.

Hence, no one who reviewed the tapes, including his CO, would ever realize that this wasn't George at all, but Jason Lancaster blinking through a pair of George's prescription glasses, wearing a wig purchased in a dedicated Halloween shop that was only open one month each year.

George had coached Jason on the exact location of each camera, so when he found the piece that might hold answers for them, he had made sure he was far enough away from each lens that it was easy to make it appear as if he was returning the piece to the table, while actually keeping the part stuffed in his palm and transferring it to his pocket.

He also knew he only had about three or four minutes – about the time it would take for the guard on camera duty to notice "George" in the bomb lab and call the Under Secretary who had asked to be notified whenever anyone went in there. Kingman Summers would tell the guard to send a patrol there, but in the time it took to radio a night guard doing his or her rounds, then for that guard to walk the one or two buildings, the several floors, over to Jason, he had seen enough. It took Jason only three minutes and seventeen seconds to find something no one at DHS had allegedly been able to find in over three days: a clue.

And when the night guard did peek into the EXD lab, Jason had been gone for 15 seconds.

Jason and George planned their exchange for right about the time some newly released comic book sequel let out of the Regal Bethesda Cinema. The garage under the theatre was packed with departing vehicles and chatty pedestrians, no one noticing the two men just there to trade cars.

Jason pulled George's Volvo into the open spot next to his Jeep, then the two men crossed behind the sedan for the key exchange, George taking back his Volvo key-- but holding back Jason's keys. Jason stared at him, confused, until the older man whispered, "You find anything?"

Jason looked around, not comfortable discussing this out in the open, then grunted, "Maybe."

Jason reached for his keys again, but George pulled them back even further, at the same time showing surprising quickness and strength in grabbing Jason's right wrist. George knew he had to get some answers out of Jason now, or he might never see him again. "I didn't get you in there to shut me out like my boss is doing," he grit through clenched teeth.

Jason rolled his eyes, then pulled his left hand from his pocket, offering a closed fist to George. Aug cupped his open palm under Jason's hand, until Jason opened his fingers to drop something into it. George held his cupped palm up close to his tired old eyes, examining the tiny black chip sitting in the crevices of his life lines. "It's a cellular antenna," Jason explained, "with one hell of an RF amplifier."

"Jesus Christ. Cell phone detonators. A fucking high school kid could've done this."

"Your lab had already separated the antenna."

"Okay."

"Meaning your boss has already been told what number called that bomb to detonate it."

George rubbed his scrunched brow. "And for whatever reason, he chose to bury it."

"Maybe he checked it out, and it led nowhere."

"No. I would've heard about that. I would know all this already."

Jason opened his hand again. "Give me a couple days."

George nodded, returning the antenna and keys to that hand. He had no choice. Jason was now the only resource in his life he trusted.

House Speaker Robert Hatfield (R-OH) thought his work day was coming to an end. He was in the back of his Suburban with his Chief of Staff, going over the next day's agenda, making sure his Judiciary Committee meeting wasn't bumping up too close to the end of the all-important CPAC lunch – where a strong showing was imperative if he was going to make it onto Bradley Benedict's eventual short list of Vice Presidential candidates – when he noticed the black Escalade parked on the curb in front of his brownstone. No, this would not normally be a newsworthy item in Georgetown, except for the large linebacker of a Secret Service agent standing sentry next to it.

"Sir, you expecting someone tonight?" his Chief of Staff asked.

"Someone with an earpiece detail? I most definitely am not."

Speaker Hatfield had his driver pull up parallel to the Escalade, and as he got out, the Secret Service agent opened the rear door of the other SUV just as he thought he might. Inside, Hatfield found the wife of his greatest political nemesis. "Madame First Lady. To what do I owe this pleasure?"

"It's always bothered me, Bob," Rosemarie greeted him, "that my husband never properly rewarded you for ending the shutdown."

Hatfield held up a hand. "No, no, no, I just did my job. We had the votes to end it, even if they weren't the loudest votes. The blowhards had their day, then we got back to big boy politics."

"You and Reg," she opined with a wistful gleam to her eye, "that was when politics was done the right way."

Rosemarie and her husband had good reason for gratitude. Every pundit had declared Irving's Presidency dead when the Republicans won control of the House in the midterms of his second four years, and indeed, when the budget next expired, the House Republicans elected to shut the government down rather than approve a new one. That is, *half* the House Republicans did. The other half revolted, replacing their first Speaker of the session with Hatfield in a midnight coup. Hatfield ended the shutdown, vowing to work towards further compromises with the President; as promised, he went on to form a formidable bi-partisan team with Irving, passing more bills than in any session since Reagan & O'Neill. But sadly, this success soon backfired on the Speaker, with Irving riding such an approval ratings high, he was not only able to handpick Antonio Salas as his successor, but usher in another Democratic takeover of both houses, costing Hatfield his Speakership.

Luckily, as had many first term Presidents before him, Salas failed to capitalize on his own majorities, leading to a reversal of fortune in both houses in the previous year's midterms, and Bob Hatfield being handed the Speaker's gavel for the second time.

"Madame First Lady, is this really why you've dropped by tonight?"

"Please. Rosemarie. We've always been on the lookout for a way to thank you for your cooperation while my husband was in office. I think we might have found it." She leaned forward, taking the Speaker's hands in her own. "Have you heard these whisperings about who the President is considering nominating to the Court?"

"Can't say I have, no."

"Reg and I, we believe that nothing is more important to our democracy than balance on the Court. You're not really going to stand for Salas replacing Lapadula and Robinson with two liberals, are you?"

Hatfield scoffed. "What can I do about it? The House doesn't vote on nominations."

"So think of how historic it would be if you did."

FRIDAY

The desire to hold some sort of immediate remembrance for the victims of the attack was not exclusive to the White House. All across Washington, the families of Supreme Court employees or visitors who hadn't been heard from since the bombing held private gatherings and candlelit vigils well before any remains were identified or any loved ones given official death notifications. This included the family of the Supreme Court Marshal, the most important non-Justice of all Supreme Court employees, responsible for a myriad of duties from administrating renovations to paying the Justices' salaries to running the Supreme Court Police.

No one in the Whitney family had heard from Miranda since she called her father to wish him a happy birthday last Saturday; none of their initial Monday morning calls or emails asking her if she was all right had ever been answered. So on Wednesday morning, Ellen and Ken Whitney met with their parish priest Perry Gentry about holding some sort of prayer vigil for their daughter, and that afternoon composed the short and respectful email invitation they would send out to a select group of family and friends.

They included Jason Lancaster on their invite list, despite the fact they had never really connected with Jason. This was by Miranda's choice; by the time Jason was a part of her life, Ken and Ellen were only a perfunctory part of it themselves. Miranda had idolized her father growing up, eventually enlisting in the Marine Corps because of him. But as often happens between military generations, as Miranda became more disillusioned with the way things were run and – especially after she became a Marine MP – with what people got away with, she clashed more and more with her dad, in whose eyes the Corps could do no wrong.

As for her mother, tom boy Miranda had never been as close to her as most girls, and as she grew older and more independent, she also grew more and more disgusted by the old fashioned household Ken ran – one of those households from 'the perfect '50s' in which the man gets to do whatever he wants and the woman does all the shopping, cooking, cleaning and laundering. Miranda lost all respect for her mother for never complaining, never leaving, never breaking that pathetic smile through forty plus years of a life like that.

So Jason had met Ken and Ellen, but just twice. *Connections* had never been forged.

Miranda's parents had invited Jason to this event, but he had failed to respond to their email. It wasn't that he hadn't seen it –his BlackBerry hadn't left his person since his release from the Ops Center, in case someone, *anyone* had any sort of news or information or lead that could help him figure out how the hell to start looking for Miranda's killers. But he hadn't *replied* to any emails; he hadn't opened up the mail program to flip through old ones to remind himself of important missives that had come and gone; his in-box felt like one big omnibus of the trivial in the midst of the worst pain he had ever known.

It wasn't until his eyes popped open on Friday morning that he remembered the invitation to a prayer lunch celebrating Miranda, set for 11 AM Friday morning, that morning, at the Whitney home in Gaithersburg. Jason rolled off his couch (his bed was too covered with detritus to be usable), checked that he had just 80 minutes to get there, and dragged himself to the shower.

Jason quietly stepped in the Whitneys' front door at 11:24, foregoing the doorbell as he was sure the festivities had already begun. Indeed, Father Gentry was seated on the hearth with his eyes closed, all the guests in a circle around him, every hand held, his voice taking that pleading, heavenward tone of prayer as he recited what Jason recognized to be the end of the 23rd Psalm, personalized to include Miranda: "… surely your goodness and love will follow Miranda wherever her spirit may go, and she will dwell in your house forever, Lord. Amen."

Every hand was squeezed, every mouth responded with its own Amen, and the group let out that first after-prayer exhale. "Thank you, Father," Ellen took over, her throat quaking as if each word might break her. "And thank you everyone, who all meant so much to Miranda, for coming to this impromptu gathering. I know she's here with us, and is so grateful herself. We promise to have a more formal memorial when--"

That's when her eyes first noticed the new addition, standing in the back of the living room behind the prayer circle. "Oh, Jason," she cried, standing to open her arms. Jason realized he had no choice, and broke through the circle to make his way into her embrace, the first hug he had ever received from her. She sobbed into his shoulder, squeezing the back of his shirt into fists of anger and confusion as she moaned, "I am so, so sorry."

There were tears of joy mixed in with Ellen's wails of sorrow. When Ken and Ellen hadn't heard from Jason, they were sure he too had perished on Monday. Seeing him alive, standing here in his living room, even old Marine Ken Whitney was overwhelmed by a compulsion to get to his feet, offer his hand to this man he should know so much better. No words needed to be exchanged between these men, just a good, hearty grip.

Ellen pulled back from his chest, dark oil spills down her cheeks. "Jason, do you know where Gordon is?"

"Who?" Jason asked. He had never heard this name. Ellen didn't explain, just returned her face and her sobs to his chest, until Ken pulled her away.

That's when Jason noticed the man he was really here to see out in the backyard smoking a Pall Mall.

Jason Lancaster never liked Oliver Whitney. To him, Oliver equaled an upset Miranda, Miranda getting off a phone call with her parents to complain that all they had talked about was Oliver's latest attention-grabbing suicide threat, or Miranda driving home from another Thanksgiving or Christmas or Birthday at the Whitney home complaining that the Little Shit had ruined yet another holiday with his perfectly-timed return to rehab or jail. As tough as Miranda Whitney and her Marine father and her ER nurse of a mother were, Oliver Whitney could drive them all to their knees.

Like many tortured souls, Oliver was as much of a genius as he was a head case. Jason didn't know this when he got him his job at FirmWall, one of the hot new cybersecurity subcontractors springing up around Washington. He hadn't even met Ollie at that point; Miranda had come into his office a wreck and begged his help finding her troubled little bro a job in the tech or computer world, any job – making coffee, changing paper towel dispensers, any would do. As luck would have it, Jason had just had lunch with a buddy from his old unit who had told him all about FirmWall, and through him, Jason was able to hook Ollie up with an entry-level at this new company.

And Ollie had almost proceeded to fuck it up. Jason's buddy called him a month later to tell him how Oliver had shown up drunk to work one day and pissed down the corner of the break room during lunch. Jason's fist slammed down into his desk as he asked what jail he needed to bail the kid out of this time. "Oh, he's not going to jail, Jase," his buddy reported. "He's too fucking good." A savant-level hacker, Ollie was just the sort of little virtuoso FirmWall needed to go toe-to-toe with the sociopathic wizards wreaking havoc on our internet.

So no, Jason hadn't come to the prayer lunch to pray or cry or even offer his condolences to Ken and Ellen. He had come for Ollie. His buddy had moved on from FirmWall, moved home to Ohio to run the family hardware supply business – but Ollie was still there, still a star there.

As soon as he had broken their parental embrace, Jason made a beeline for the back door. He pulled out his flask as he stepped down two concrete steps and over the green garden hose, offering it up to Ollie, perched atop their above-ground hot tub.

"I thought you quit," the kid sneered.

"I thought you did too."

Ollie shrugged, took the flask and sucked a third of it down. Then offered up his red pack to Jason in exchange, one inviting stick extended for his taking. Jason put it in his mouth, where Oliver lit it.

For a few minutes, they just puffed and exhaled, occasionally tipping back the flask for a quick rush of warmth. It was the younger man who broke the silence. "Hadn't talked to her in a month. We had this stupid Facebook-fight about unions." Ollie didn't have any political beliefs beyond that he loved taking the opposite view of whoever he was arguing with. He loved his sister, but loved fucking with her even more.

"I know doing things for others has always been a foreign concept for you," Jason said, pulling a small Ziploc out of his pocket. Ollie saw it was that thin little variety of baggie that always looked to him like it was designed specifically to carry joints. Jason held it up in front of Ollie's face, shaking it a little so the tiny black chip he took from the DHS bomb lab bounced up and down inside. "This is for her, Ollie." Confused, Ollie took the bag in his fingers, not sure what he was looking at. "It's a cellular antenna. I need you to tell me any numbers that have ever called into it."

"What, I look like mother fucking Verizon to you?"

"You work with people a lot smarter than Verizon. Even if you can't figure this out, someone there can."

"Except I'm on bereavement, Homes. I ain't going back there for a while."

The conversation was progressing how Jason thought it would. He had practiced his response in the shower, then on the drive over. What he hadn't planned on doing was grabbing Ollie's shirt in both hands and pulling his nose into his own. "Even after all you put this family through over the years—whenever Rand talked about you, she'd get tears in her eyes. Not tears of anger, or tears of sadness. Tears of love. She was so proud of how you'd turned everything around. And so happy she never gave up on you."

At the very mention of tears, Ollie's own ran down his cheeks. He nodded acceptance of his mission. Jason released him, looked up towards the gasp from the window where Ellen and three other women were watching, then turned and walked back to his car.

House Concurrent Resolution 1790 (so named in honor of the first meeting of the Supreme Court on February 2, 1790), "Expressing the opposition of the Congress to any Supreme Court nominations or confirmations until justice has been found for those Justices and other Court personnel murdered while fulfilling their duties to this nation," passed in almost record time, with the swiftness of emergency responses or calls to military action.

The night before, Rosemarie Irving's Escalade hadn't even left his cul-de-sac before Speaker Hatfield had the Chairman of the Judiciary Committee on the phone. "You won't believe what I just heard," he teased salaciously. "President *Salsa* actually has the gall to be vetting nominees for the Court."

"No."

"I didn't believe it myself when I heard it. But he's already got his first nominee teed up, ready to be announced. Could even happen Sunday – you know, he's doing a full Ginsburg." The Speaker used the slang term that in Washington parlance meant appearing on at least five network morning shows on the same Sunday, named for Monica Lewinsky's lawyer, the first to pull off such a feat.

"Shit, he's going to do it, isn't he? He's going to announce one. I didn't think even he was capable of playing politics *this soon*."

"He's young. I think someone should probably educate him on the proper way to do these things." They shared a chuckle, then the Speaker unveiled his plan: the Chairman would introduce a Concurrent Resolution the next morning declaring the vociferous disapproval of the Congress of any nominations or appointments before there was clarity in the mystery of the bombing itself.

Usually reserved for such earth-jarring matters as the date Congress would gather for their next session or who the Congress would really love to see celebrated on the next round of postage stamps, Concurrent Resolutions don't require the Chief Executive's signature, don't create any actual *law*, and therefore, don't need to be dissected word for word in committee or debated in front of C-SPAN cameras before they go up for a vote. With the Republicans controlling 235 seats to the Dems' 200, there was no doubt HCON 1790 would garner the required 218. But the impressive number of Democratic votes it notched as well turned the debate over whether this President would *ever* get the opportunity to nominate replacement Justices into the biggest news story of the day.

Senate Majority Leader Clyde Dudley (R-KY) told Fox News's Bret Baier that the Senate would add their votes to the Resolution come Monday morning; no one doubted that all 59 Senate Republicans would vote for it, or that the Democrats wouldn't have the stones to filibuster it. A resolution wasn't law, and wouldn't bar POTUS from doing anything, but once the Senate passed it, they wouldn't be able to open their arms to any judiciary nominees for weeks, maybe even months, without appearing to be complete hypocrites.

President Salas was in his private study after the House vote, bouncing his soccer ball off the image of Hatfield's gloating face on all his TVs. The Speaker was giving a press conference just outside the House Chamber, the congressional equivalent of a lap around the ice with the Stanley Cup held aloft; for the first time in history, the House of Representatives was playing a role in the Supreme Court nomination process, and he wanted the world to know that he had orchestrated it.

Of course, the first question shouted out of every reporter's mouth was some sort of variation on, "Did Congress schedule this vote because the President *is* planning on making nominations soon?"

Speaker Hatfield danced around their questions like a seasoned vet of the Bolshoi. "The American people aren't ready for a confirmation process right now. They want answers, they want suspects. They want justice. That's why we had this vote, that's why we passed this Resolution, and we urge our brethren in the Senate to do the same on Monday morning in the name of national unity. They need to send a message to the President that they will not accept any nominations until there is justice for the Justices who have fallen."

"Shit!" Salas exclaimed as his ball disappeared behind a file cabinet.

"We can get you another one." Becks tried to find a positive spin as Salas bent down behind the cabinets to attempt to retrieve it. "They really think they can keep the Supreme Court closed for a year and a half until Benedict gets in?"

"Hey!" Salas rose to point in her face, the retrieved soccer ball scrunched into the fist beneath that extended finger. "That asshole will *never* beat me."

Becks laughed, slapping her open palms down on her desk. *That* was the Antonio Salas she went to work for, the scrappy brawler who never saw a fight, never saw a war he didn't want to win. They went to work, planning how they were going to turn this around, turn this Resolution into a win, how they were going to wrest control of the nomination process back from the Congress. The coming weekend would be their battlefield.

SATURDAY

Jason was back in Bullfeathers, back with Miranda, back with her emptied Scotches and her tear-drenched eyes.

"Rand," he asked, "what's wrong?" That's what you're supposed to ask when the person you love more than any other in the world, more than you've ever loved anyone before, falls off the wagon or cries in a bar.

"Nothing's wrong," the lady didst protest too much – then looked away.

I'm remembering more. Yes, the tape of his memory was going further. *That's right, she looked away, up at the TV above the bar –*

The TV was on C-SPAN. Only in fucking Washington is a TV in a bar set to C-SPAN. It's the deadest month of the year – the Nats are done, the Wizards and Hoyas haven't started, and if the Caps aren't playing, a mindless bartender might leave his TV on something like C-SPAN all night, replaying interviews with authors of Korean War books no one would read, or speeches Congresspeople had made that day to an empty chamber.

LAST THURSDAY, it read in the upper left-hand corner of the screen; then at the bottom, *CHIEF JUSTICE LAPADULA - GUEST LECTURE AT HARVARD LAW SCHOOL.* That's right; the TV had drawn his attention because he knew the guy on it: the big cheese of the Court, about 14 hours from becoming much more famous in death than he ever was in life.

And a cell was ringing. Was it Miranda's? No, hers was inert on the bar, and it wasn't her ring anyway. It was *his* ring, it was Jason's. He reached into his pocket-- No, he didn't reach into his pocket, that's not what he did next, his phone wasn't ringing then.

It was ringing on Saturday morning. Jason woke up in his bed for the first time in five mornings, and his BlackBerry was singing and vibrating across the bedside table Miranda had picked out when she put her decorating stamp on the place. Its crash to the floor was the final wake up he needed. He grabbed it as it shook across the hardwood, reading the caller's name on the display:

"Ollie?"

"The calls came from a blocked number," the voice of Miranda's brother came through the line. "But one of my boys was able to triangulate them."

Jason sat straight up – that's right, he had given Ollie a mission. The Little Shit had come through for him. "Calls into that antenna I gave you?"

"No one called it on Monday."

"The detonation call didn't get through – that's why that one didn't go off."

"But there was a call the night before – and two calls the week before that."

"Test calls."

"All three calls originated in Detroit."

Jason shoved himself to his feet. "Thanks. You did good." He threw the phone back on top of the duvet, grabbed yesterday's jeans up off the floor, started pulling them on—

And his shoulder erupted in white heat. He slammed back against the wall with a whimper. Something made him whimper like a little fucking baby. Pain, pain made him whimper: blood all over his white ribbed undershirt, expanding from his left shoulder. He had been shot. All his years in the military and law enforcement, he had never been shot – until right this very instant.

"Holy shit!" He dove down behind the bed – and the walls started raining bullets.

He was moving. Glass was breaking, plaster splintering, little craters of impact blowing open in the beautiful hardwood as bullets tore into it. Jason hung tight to the floor, not feeling any more shells finding paydirt in his flesh.

What the fuck was this? The timing of it, right after Ollie's call – someone had to be listening to them, there's no such thing as a coincidence in assassination, someone heard them and *We're on the right track,* so someone had to take him out. He was lucky only his shoulder had been hit. *Have to keep moving.* He crab-crawled into the hall – the exploding walls following him – onto his feet in the living room. The bullets were moving with him, glass and dry wall symphony now tearing through the living room –

The pantry. He had to get to the pantry, the only room with no north-facing windows. But the bullets were right on his heels, the hardwood impacts getting closer and closer to his pumping Achilles.

He dove into the pantry, scrunching his body behind the waist-high safe hidden there –

And after a few more cracks of punctured timber, the hailstorm ceased, just as he had hoped. The brick matter and wood chips settled, then silence descended.

Jason swiveled around the safe for the keypad, pressing 2 twice, then 1-7-9-0, the code Miranda had set when she moved in with him, and added her collection to his own. He pulled the door wide, grabbing his Kimber 1911, custom made for LAPD SWAT, the .45 he carried with him every day to work. He shoved it in the back of his belt, then reached for the two halves of the M4 rifle he had kept from the military. He aligned the upper and lower halves and snapped the takedown pins into place. He hadn't used the weapon in years, hadn't even needed to keep it stored in one piece, but it still felt natural in his palms. He wouldn't take the time to pull out the collapsible stock or look through the sight, wouldn't need them; all he needed was a distraction, four seconds or so to get to the back door. He grabbed a mag, shoved it up into the weapon, charged it –

And thrust up on top of the safe, eyes going to the holes high up on the wall near the ceiling – where the last bullets had come through, after the shooter had followed him from the hall. Jason aimed for those holes and lay on his trigger, blowing back through them, in the hope they would follow the reverse trajectory of his enemy's rounds. As he fired, there was no return fire coming through – it was working. The shooter must have ducked down when Jason's bullets started flying up at him. He wouldn't stay ducked for long – he would realize Jason wasn't coming close, that he must be firing blind.

Jason got to his feet, rushing back for the kitchen. He blew out the kitchen window glass with a few more rounds, just to be safe, then tossed the rifle onto the kitchen table, threw open the back door and hurdled down the back concrete steps. To the fence, up and over into his neighbor's yard. He heard the sniper get started again, heard a couple rounds penetrate brick, then lodge in the wood of the fence behind him. It wouldn't last long: the shooter wouldn't be very mobile, not with the size of gun Jason figured he had to be firing to do the damage he had done. Jason just had to keep moving – over another fence, and another, past some kids already spending maybe the last warm Saturday of the year in their plastic pool, over one more. He turned right, charging for the door in a fence, kicking it open, marching out to the sidewalk.

The fire was continuing. As long as the shooter could see him, he might be able to follow him for literally miles. He had to take some turns; the left up ahead could take him to a denser block.

It's stopped. The fire has stopped. I'm in the clear.

"There!" Jason's head whipped to the voice a block back: two guys in suits, both bigger than him, both with white coiled wires tucked into their ear holes.

They're bigger than me, but I bet they aren't faster. Jason started running – around a corner, then another. *Just keep turning,* he thought. *You know this neighborhood better than them. As they get farther and farther back, it'll get harder for them to figure out which way you went.*

He saw a break in the traffic, and darted to his right, crossing the street, then down another alley.

As he turned the next time, he threw a glance over his left shoulder – *Shit, they're still there, they're still coming.*

Jason headed for an area he knew would be busy, especially for a Saturday, even at this early hour – the shopping at Friendship Heights. He darted onto Wisconsin Ave, heading into the foot traffic around the Wisconsin Place shops and the nearby entrance to Bloomingdale's. *Goddammit, Rand, thank you for making me come here so many Sundays, I'm sorry I'm so sorry I ever bitched and moaned about it.*

But his true destination was the entrance to the Friendship Heights metro station, where maybe he could lose these guys on the busy Red Line. As he rounded the top of the escalator, he could see the southbound train into the District idling on the platform, people already trickling on. *No one's disembarking. It's been here for ten, fifteen seconds already. If I hurry –*

Jason shot down the escalator, giving one brief look over his shoulder – the two suits were still behind him, although they were moving so fast, one of them lost his balance, going down, pulling a woman shopper onto the metal stairs with him. But the other was still coming, just a few feet from Jason now.

Jason turned back to the train – *the doors are shutting don't shut don't shut* – "Hold the train!" he screamed, reaching a hand out, trying to get it between the doors before they could close on him –

But he was too late. The door sealed with a swish, the train's brakes exhaled, and the giant steel centipede started chugging away, leaving the platform empty, save for Jason and one of his assailants.

Jason turned back, as if accepting his fate. The Brooks Brothers thug grabbed his right biceps in a tight grip, smiling, "All right, Lancaster, we're gonna go for a little walk."

Jason took a step to walk with him – then drove his skull right into the guy's nose, smashing it in a burst of blood. He staggered back with a scream, gripping his gushing nostrils, giving Jason one free moment--

--to leap off the platform! He reached out his right hand – his left might shoot too much pain through his wounded shoulder, and make him let go -- his right hand had to be enough --

His right grabbed onto one of the handles on the rear of the train. He swung into the car, forearm twisting as his back slammed against metal. He hung there for three seconds, like a plastic bag caught on a fence on a blustery day.

Then he pulled himself up onto the tiny step beneath the train's rear door. He smiled back at his assailant, who was just stamping his feet with a "Fuck!" when the dark of the tunnel swallowed Jason's vision whole.

The Under Secretary himself didn't call, but the operator who reached George on his cell phone that afternoon made a point of mentioning that the head of Intelligence & Analysis had personally requested he join the team responding to the reports of a shooting at Jason Lancaster's address in Maryland.

Montgomery County PD had already been there for over an hour when George and his team showed up. (The neighbors had called the local Police, of course, and DHS had only picked up on it when the computer server they have monitoring emergency bands around the country pinged a match with Jason's red-flagged address.) The officer-in-charge gave Aug the quick dime tour of the place: the Army-issue M4 discarded on the kitchen table, the gun safe left open in the pantry, the windows broken in every room – climaxing with the blood smeared on the white wall next to the bed and pooled on the floor below it. "They got him good," the officer whistled, and George nodded, hoping they hadn't gotten him too good. He ordered his team to run the DNA off the blood, and start checking hospitals for Lancaster. Then he stepped to the window, wondering if he would ever see Jason again.

That's when he noticed the building looking down on them from across the street: a window on its top floor was broken, a row of bullet-sized holes swerving from the window up to the roofline.

Three minutes later, George and another agent stepped off the elevator on the top floor of that building, spinning around to figure out which door must lead to the broken glass. George picked one, knocked three different times, giving the occupant several seconds to respond each time, then nodded to his partner, who proceeded to kick the deadbolt off and the door open in three kicks. (Off George's impressed look, he smiled, "You know I played for DC United, right?" George responded, "Who?") No, they didn't have a warrant, but George had been through 9/11, and didn't figure DHS was going to get more than a wrist-slap for any civil liberties lapses that might occur in the first week after a terrorist attack on our soil.

The unit was empty, save for the corners of dust and the pile of glass below the window. Whoever was here, whoever had shot at Jason, had taken every trace of himself with him, even the discarded shells from his weapon. "Let's give this place the full sweep," George ordered out of habit, but he knew they wouldn't find anything. He knew the only one who might know anything about who had been here was Jason, and there was a 50-50 chance he would never see him again.

A lifelong conspiracy theorist, Blake Lancaster taught his children to always be prepared to have to go on the run. Jason had mixed feelings about his father – okay, he thought 'Sarge' was a misogynist nut bag with refried brains from two too many tours' worth of Vietnamization. But it's amazing how even the most deranged ramblings of a crazy parent can get mixed into your blood. So about the time Jason first realized he was going to be staying in Washington for a while, he found himself renting a storage unit under a false name and filling it with the barest essentials needed to survive a terrorist attack, zombie plague, or you know, the time he would inevitably be stalked by a sniper.

Three or four days, that's how many minimum he should spend in his unit, he figured. Give it enough time that whoever hired that sniper starts wondering if Jason died somewhere from his shoulder injury and exhales a little. *Relaxes* – that's when his nemesis, whoever the hell he is, will screw up.

The storage unit had everything Jason would need to survive for weeks – plus everything Miranda had forbidden him from keeping in their cramped apartment, like his approximately 1200 comic books from the years 1986-92 that he knew must be worth something (including every issue of Marvel's *GI Joe* and *The 'nam* from those years), if only he could figure out how to post something on eBay. More important to him right now was the dark green foot locker painted with the green bereted skull of the Special Forces seal, above a ribbon proclaiming their motto: *'De Oppresso Liber.'* 'Liberate the oppressed.' Jason looked around and sighed. *Who the fuck's gonna liberate me?*

He released the padlock and threw open the top of the locker. He was exhausted (it was amazing how tired your muscles could get just from tightening with fear), but he had work to do. He had already pried the SIM card out of the back of his BlackBerry and left it to burn up in a glass of lemon juice in a diner that afternoon – that was the most important thing he would do today, ensure that no one could track him.

Now the harder part: prying the bullet out of his shoulder. He knew it hadn't hit any vital organs, cut any vital connections, or he would be dead on the side of the road or in an ER right about now. Check that; if he had been taken to an ER, his name would have gone into a computer, those dudes in suits would have found him and again, in this scenario as well, he would be dead by now.

No, he was lucky that the shooter hadn't been very skilled. That was his assessment: failing to take Jason's head off with his first shot, then following his movement with wild, loose spray, that was rookie shit, not SEAL team. What the hell that meant, Jason couldn't answer, not yet. But it meant something. To call his assailant a sniper was an affront to the true artistes of the profession; whoever-it-was had come close to ending his life, but he wasn't a sniper, just a well-armed *shooter.*

He laid out his tools on a clean hand towel before him: exacto knife, tweezers, the side view mirror off a Jeep he had found in some roadside gravel one weekend, a needle and thread. Then he bit down on the cap of a bottle of Wild Turkey, twisted it off in his teeth, and started chugging down his anesthetic.

SUNDAY

If it's Sunday, it's *Meet the Press.*

The original thought behind booking President Salas for a Full Ginsburg (plus two, actually: he was appearing on seven network shows counting visits to Univision and Telemundo, leading staffers to joke he was doing a "Ginsburg Siete") had nothing to do with Supreme Court nominations, or playing defense against the House's petulant Concurrent Resolution. Salas himself had asked his press office to set it up; he wanted to speak to every corner of the population, he wanted to give them the chance to look into his chocolate eyes in close up, he wanted them to see his worried age lines in hard, cynical HD, and see that he was just as rattled and devastated and frightened by what had occurred six days ago as they were. He wanted them to hear that his administration was doing everything they could to bring the bombers to justice; he wanted them to see in the blue craters under his eyes that this quest had robbed him of sleep. He saw Sunday morning as his best opportunity to reconnect with the people who had elected him.

Friday's House vote meant he needed to go into these shows more on the offensive, ready to tell the American people exactly why the timings of nominations would be up to him and only him. Becks had provided him some talking points, and they had rehearsed them loosely throughout Saturday. They had assumed the Sunday hosts would offer him their shows as warm, safe places from which he could deliver his message to the voting public.

This was a devastating error. All six hosts – even the Spanish-language ones who were so elated to have the first Latino in the highest office, they had given him a free pass for the last three years – now saw him as a President under siege, a President in over his head. This was the national narrative now and thus, it was their duty as Important journalists (with yes a capitol I) to put the entire, brief Salas Presidency on the witness stand.

He was scheduled to hit *Meet the Press* last, making it the coup de grace, the grand finale. But perhaps because of the rapport they had built over the years since Salas's first visit to the show while Governor of California, Chuck Todd felt he could be the most brutally honest about POTUS's record, and asked the fiercest questions:

"Do you see these Court vacancies as an opportunity for a signature achievement in a Presidency that seems to have lacked one?"

"Do you now look back on last year's midterms and wish you'd done more to get more Democrats elected to Congress, so you'd have a better chance of getting judicial nominees confirmed?"

"Do you think this is even appropriate while the country's mourning? It's been said that even just *talking* about who you might nominate is premature, maybe even insensitive or classless. But you and your staff have been talking about it, haven't you, Mr. President?"

If the President wanted the American people to see how tired he was, *Meet the Press* accomplished that mission, as he stumbled and struggled to put coherent answers together, often falling back on his rote talking points that had nothing to do with the question that had just been asked.

Silence filled the Tanque on the drive back to 1600 Penn, not a word passing between President and Chief of Staff. Finally, when they rounded the circle before the private entrance to the White House, Becks opened her door before she realized she hadn't waited for POTUS to open his first. She looked over at him, still staring straight ahead with a fiery glare, then pulled her door closed to keep their privacy. She could feel a reaming coming her way and didn't need anyone else hearing it. "Mr. President?"

"You wanted to listen to them," he said through clenched teeth, without moving his eyes off the windshield. "You wanted to listen to the Irvings. You wanted to get into nominations. Now I'm being punished for vetting a woman I never even approved."

"We can find out how the Republicans found out we were vetting--"

"It's done," he spit. This was the trait she perhaps admired most in him, the ability to never be vindictive, but accept what had occurred and move on from there. "What you're going to do now is figure out how to fix it. You're going to figure out how we make sure we get at least nine Senate Republicans to vote in my favor tomorrow."

Becks's BlackBerry was already on her ear before the Tanque shook with the impact of the President's door slamming. "Please tell me you know how the fuck we fix this," she said into the phone when the other end of the line picked up.

"Time to send in the closer," Reginald Irving replied.

Sunday mornings were George's time.

It was four years ago, after his wife was gone and he'd had a particularly frustrating, violent day with Brenda, that his therapist had recommended he find sometime each week – most of her clients chose Sunday – to do something that would take his mind off work, off his epically imploding family, and put it squarely on peace and serenity, a time to just relax and be one with nature. A time for mindfulness. Maybe it would be a jog he loved to do, maybe a hike, maybe even just a quiet cup of coffee in his favorite park with the arts or sports sections of the Sunday *Post.* George had devoted his life to everyone else: to his mother, to his job, to his country, to his wife, to his daughter. It was about time that George carved out a weekly space for *himself,* some time to be selfish.

George already knew how he would spend this time. Whenever he had trouble sleeping throughout his adult life, or needed to relax through a turbulent flight, he had closed his eyes and transported himself back to his Boy Scout troop canoeing the Chesapeake and Ohio Canal, parallel to the Potomac. He could still remember the algal smells, or the sounds of splashing water against utter calm. He had taken Brenda out on the canal one summer Sunday when she was nine or ten, and it had been one of their best-ever days together. Then he tried again, a year or two after her break, and she was miserable – didn't speak, didn't smile, never looked up from her crossed arms.

George suspected that the canal was something only he understood, that only he could appreciate and had to appreciate all on his own; he finally put that theory to the test after the prodding from his therapist. He fell so in love with his weekly float, he eventually even crafted his own canoe by hand, devoting his entire garage to the endeavor for weeks. Once completed, he moved the vessel to the Boathouse at Fletcher's Cove, and tried to take it out for a stroll down the canal every Sunday between May and October.

He usually liked to get out on the water much earlier in the day (a necessity in the summer), but with the lack of sleep on which he had been operating since the bombing, he thought it more important on this particular Sunday that he sleep in. And, as hoped, with the weather getting chillier, the Skins back on the field and the kids back in school, the traffic on the water was still light when he tipped the two boathouse boys for carrying his craft out to the water, then stepped down into the vessel and picked up his paddle.

The canoe shook with the impact of another passenger plopping down on the other side of it, burning into George with his laser eyes. "Who tried to kill me?" Jason Lancaster demanded. He was armed with his own paddle pilfered from somewhere off the dock, and with one hand awkwardly used it to push them off into the middle of the water where they could have some privacy. That was when George noticed his other arm hung in a T-shirt tied around his shoulder in a makeshift sling.

"Kill you? What?" George stammered, not happy to have his only personal time interrupted. But he knew Lancaster wouldn't hear that excuse. He looked awful beyond just the sling: hair greased and wiry, eyes red, jowls unshaven since the attack, long patches of brown down the front of his pant legs. George wasn't sure, but he thought Jason might even smell a little rancid – he had been canoeing this water for years, and was now smelling something he hadn't ever smelled there before.

Jason replied by retrieving his Kimber .45 from the back of his jeans. He slammed the top of the weapon into his hip, using his belt as leverage to pull a round into the chamber.

"*Hey-hey-hey--*" George put up his hands.

"I pulled a .338 Lapua out of this shoulder last night."

"A sniper?"

"Don't give him so much credit. I'm here. But *someone* shot up my house looking for me. You know anything about this?"

"No, no I don't know what the heck you're talking about, I swear--"

"You can prove it by figuring out what's in Detroit."

"Detroit?"

"Whoever built those bombs tested them in Detroit. And as soon as I got that information, they start taking target practice at me. I'd like to know what the hell I'm getting into before I go up there."

The boat bumped into the mud embankment opposite the boathouse, startling George. He hadn't realized how they'd already floated all the way across to the opposite shore. Jason reached over for some grass, pulling them taut with the mud so he could stand up and start to get out. "Wait, how will I find you?" George asked. "You coming to my Tuesday morning squash game too?"

"Leave a message on my cell. I burn bagged the SIM, but I'll check the voice mail." And without a goodbye, he traipsed away.

George sighed. He pushed off the bank, and started paddling his canoe straight back to the boathouse.

"You haven't changed *anything*?"

Noting the pitch of surprise in her voice, President Salas turned from the bar – or "the Betty Ford Bar" as Reginald Irving loved calling it – a fixture Rosemarie Irving had herself added just to the left of the iconic window of the West Sitting Room of the White House Residence. (They had decided the East Sitting Room would host more formal occasions, and designed the West as more of the kick-your-feet-up, laid back party room where their son could have a beer with his college buddies, for example.) At the sight of his predecessor's wife, Salas started pouring her a small glass of the Gran Patrón Platinum he had been drinking for close to an hour. For the President, tequila wasn't just a drink, it was as much an expression of his heritage as a Bilbao match, and a nod to Guadalajara, to Jalisco, where the spirit was produced and his grandparents had first set up a new life after fleeing Spain.

Rosemarie took a step further into the room, pivoting on a heel to look up to the ceiling and then behind her. She hadn't been in the West Sitting Room since sometime in her last week in the Residence, but not a thing had changed. When her gaze returned to Salas, she caught and collected herself. "My apologies, Mr. President. I meant no offense, but usually when someone new takes over, they--"

"None taken," Salas smiled as he offered up the fresh liquor to her. "Not to be a pig, but there are some things you need a FLOTUS for." He sat on one of the couches, keeping his ass on the edge of the cushions and his back arched. Rosemarie smiled as she sat across from him; she remembered these couches were much more pleasing to the eye than they were to the lumbar. "I did meet with three decorators my staff recommended," he explained.

"Oh, you did?" she teased back.

"I did. I even hired one." He took a sip, then shrugged. "But that night, I couldn't sleep. I fired her the next morning. From time to time, we'll go over new resumes and portfolios. I've just never seen—'The One,' you know?"

"Please don't ever tell that story into a microphone."

Salas finished his drink and stood, crossing to look out at the Eisenhower across the lawn. The room was dark, and in contrast to her husband's lankier physique, Antonio's toned, compact body cast an impressive silhouette over the giant, basketball key-shaped Tiffany window, Rosemarie thought.

"How fast can you get the next name on your list here?" he asked without turning back to her.

"Look--"

"I need someone here by Friday." He whipped around, returning to the bar for more. "I need to show them their fucking Resolution isn't going to scare me. I will nominate someone when I want to nominate someone."

"Respectfully, Mr. President--"

"Jesus *Christ*!" He slammed his glass down on the wooden bar top with such force she was shocked it didn't shatter. "I'm so goddamn tired of everyone in this town acting like they care about being respectful."

"Fine. Since Monday, you've really done everything you can to screw the pooch."

He looked at her. Didn't move, didn't say a word. Rosemarie stood, moving in to hammer home her plan. "You announce Cecilia Koh at 9 AM *tomorrow*. You do that, and the Senate will never even vote on the Concurrent Resolution. The Republicans will realize they can't go on the record trying to block the first pro-life nominee in over a decade, and Dudley will have to pull the vote off the floor."

He nodded to himself, even chuckled a little. She was everything his administration lacked, everything he had hoped Becks would provide before he had realized she was really too young and inexperienced: an advisor, a sounding board, a cool head. Of course Rosemarie was right. He didn't believe in a single thing Cecilia Koh stood for, but she was the only thing that could save his Presidency now.

Rosemarie retreated back into her regal, controlled, camera-ready self, crossing past him to return her empty glass to the bar. "My apologies, Mr. President. I forget this isn't my house any--"

"Does everyone else in your life believe all your apologies?"

She looked up in his eyes, raising an eyebrow with the smirk of a child caught peeking at Christmas gifts through little gaps in the wrapping paper.

"Why are you doing this?" he asked quietly.

"I clerked on the Supreme Court. I understand how vital a role--"

"*Rosemarie.* Your President's asking you a question. Why are you doing this?"

She took a moment to answer, to choose the words she had never said aloud, at least not to anyone besides Reg. "For my husband. For his legacy. Presidents can't make their legacies in office anymore – they're under too much scrutiny, too much fire, too much attack. Look at Reagan, look at Carter. They cemented their legacies *after* office. Being the face of humanitarian aid, lending a hand in diplomacy. But filling four seats of the Supreme Court? This is Reg's chance to cement his."

As she started for the door, he called out, "Is your whole life for him?"

She stopped against the bright hall lights, a sleek counterpoint to his silhouette. "Someday you'll find someone who does the same for you." She spun on a heel. "There are some things you need a FLOTUS for."

Dennis had been sitting on the ottoman for literally three days. He didn't even understand why the hallway of the 12th floor of the Sheraton needed an ottoman, anyway – it wasn't paired with any easy chair, you couldn't lift the top and store things inside (he had checked more than once). It was just there to fill the empty space, to decorate, and for the last three days, to serve as the place that a Supreme Court vetter currently without a vettee could sit.

Dennis figured it had been seventy-six hours since Rosemarie Irving had asked him to accompany Professor Koh back to her hotel. Seventy-five since his ride from Washington to Alexandria with the Professor, thinking to himself it was sure going overboard to make a candidate for the Supreme Court stay at a Sheraton in Virginia, rather than the Mandarin Oriental or the Willard or the Hay-Adams, all in the name of keeping her selection under wraps. *Aw well,* he assured himself, *it's the last time she'll have to stay four star or less in her life, I hope she enjoys it.*

He had left each night for about seven hours to eat dinner and sleep, then maybe another hour or ninety minutes each day for other meals; he figured he had spent at least forty-six of the last seventy-five hours sitting on the ottoman, ready to jump back into the vetting when the signal was given. He also secretly pretended he was packing heat, there to protect her life, keep her safe from whomever was bent on killing Supreme Court justices. What else do you do when you realize you've read all the literature on the Professor three times over, not to mention everything on your Kindle?

Just as he entered his forty-seventh hour sitting sentry, his pocket vibrated. He pulled out his iPhone 7, and seeing the magic word "BLOCKED" across his display, yelped with delirious joy. Only one person with a blocked number would call him. "Hello!" he answered.

"We're back on," the First Lady's voice replied.

Dennis checked his watch: just after 9 PM, he figured they could get in a good two, two-and-a-half hours before calling it a night. "How long till the car's downstairs?"

"The car isn't coming."

"Huh?"

"You have less than 12 hours to finish vetting her, Dennis. I don't want you wasting any time sleeping, any time eating, or any time riding in the back of a town car. I want you to go into her room and finish vetting her there."

And the line went dead.

Dennis moved to knock on the door, but it yanked open before his knuckles met wood. "Hi. I heard your yelp," Professor Koh smiled meekly. "So I listened to your call a little. Hope you don't mind."

"I promise not to put that in my vetting report," Dennis joked, then followed her inside.

Rosemarie had spent the first five minutes of her ride home from the White House wracking her brain for the right taste maker, the right morning radio or Fox News host, or a retired elder statesman even, who could help ensure her plan didn't fail.

When the Escalade passed under the billboard for BabySoft paper towels, she remembered instantly that BabySoft was owned by Zellerman Paper, a division of Sacerdoti Industries. Perfect.

Rosemarie pulled out her BlackBerry and placed a call to Christian Sacerdoti's office. A man like Sacerdoti always had someone manning his phones, someone to make sure he received any important call, no matter the day or the hour.

Yes, Sacerdoti was perfect. This was Washington, after all. Money trumped all else.

MONDAY

Senate Majority Leader Clyde Dudley polished off his coffee at 9:21 AM, then got up from his desk to begin making his way down to the Senate Chamber for the vote. He wanted to get the Concurrent Resolution passed as soon as possible to add immediate insult to all the injuries the President had suffered across the nation's televisions on Sunday. He felt a little bad for the younger man, so unqualified for this job in the first place, now forced to navigate this nation through its greatest tragedy of almost two decades. But 'Salsa' signed up for politics, and this was how politics was waged, especially in a Presidential Election year for God's sake (and everyone knows that Presidential Election "years" start three Januarys before the actual election, or 34 months before the first mail-in votes were cast).

There were very few men on this Earth who could keep Dudley—once diagnosed as borderline OCD – from making everything on his schedule on time, be it a vote, a PTA meeting, or a University of Kentucky basketball game. Christian Sacerdoti was of course one of those men.

Sacerdoti made a fortune not just by figuring out how to program advertising before every video on YouTube, before every cute cat or local news blooper, but by designing qualitative analyses of those ad placements that helped ensure an advertiser's dollars were making it in front of more and more of its model customers, by designing software that could judge by a user's viewing habits if they would likely make it through a full thirty-second ad or would require the five-second 'Skip Ad' button to stay engaged. At age 23, he started his online agency with two friends, but after advertisers realized that in the age of the DVR more people were seeing commercials online than on their TVs, he was able to sell the company for nine figures.

That's when he went into politics, with the zeal you would expect from a Conservative who had spent his formative years being teased and ridiculed by California lefties. He threw a large portion of his new fortune behind his Super-PAC, FreedomLovers, in the form of 'dark money' (meaning his identity as the source of the cash was not publicly disclosed) going to support not only Republican and Libertarian candidates around the country, but even helping primary GOP incumbents that had gotten on Sacerdoti's bad side. Clyde Dudley would never have won a sixth term had FreedomLovers not so generously triaged his campaign in its final months. So when Senator Dudley found Sacerdoti sitting beside his receptionist's desk, he had no choice but to delay his march to the Capitol to lead the Resolution vote. "Chris. What brings you to Washington this fine morning?"

Sacerdoti stood, his patented billion-dollar grin sparkling back at the Senator. "You did."

Dudley looked to his secretary in a panic. "Me? I don't remember--"

"Well, to be fair, Bob Hatfield started this shit storm, didn't he? But you're about to step right in line and help him cock block Cecilia Koh's nomination."

"I'm sorry, who?"

"I can't let you hold this vote, Clyde."

The majority leader nearly spit up at the audacity. "With all due respect, Chris--"

"Sir!" Dudley's secretary pawed for the remote control lost in the clutter of her desk. She aimed it at the TV hanging in the upper-North corner of the ceiling, cranking the volume so they could hear what the President was saying.

"In the last week, there has been much debate about how this country should proceed from one of our greatest tragedies. Rest assured, this administration, this nation, her every citizen, shall not rest until those individuals behind this abomination are brought to justice. Whoever you are, hear my voice, and know that we will find you."

The feed snapped to a wide angle, revealing that he was standing behind a podium erected just in front of the crumbled marble and melted iron of the Supreme Court ruins. The chyron at the bottom of the screen read, *"PRESIDENT SALAS TO INTRODUCE SUPREME COURT NOMINEE."*

And Clyde Dudley took a seat. He knew there would be no vote on the Concurrent Resolution now.

President Antonio Ramón Salas's introduction of Cecilia Koh to the nation was one of the great speeches of his presidency. Nominees were traditionally introduced for a gathering of press at the White House, but POTUS and his Chief of

Staff had agreed that, as this was the most important nomination in the Court's history, it warranted several extra degrees of theater: in front of the ruins of the Court, all the surviving Justices and many members of the Cabinet in attendance, plus every enthusiastic aide and intern they could cram between the President's podium and the barricades holding back the press. Every network preempted their usual programming; having a suspect in custody would have been a wonderful third act to the tragic week that had just passed, but in lieu of that, POTUS had crafted the next best thing.

Salas recruited his three best speech writers to each draw up a draft for that morning, and as they rode over, Becks handed them to him in a stack, topped by her preferred choice. "We need to get our final to the prompter typist by--"

"Don't need it," he grinned. This made her nerves clench, as she had never known him to write his own speeches.

But an hour later, as his every word sent tendrils of new goose bumps down her arms, her fear had been proved unwarranted.

"To find an enemy, we must understand his goals, his twisted motivation. And our enemy's objective here was nothing short of denying our citizens their most inalienable right: 'Equal Justice Under Law.' Those were the words above this building just one week ago. You may knock those words off our buildings, but you cannot erase them from our souls. We will rebuild this building you see behind me. We will rebuild those sacred words. We will rebuild this Supreme Court. Starting with the exceptionally qualified nominee it is my honor to introduce to you today – the first Asian-American nominee in the Court's history, Cecilia Elizabeth Koh."

Everyone shot to their feet as the tiny Asian professor emerged from the wreckage and stepped up next to POTUS at his podium. Every young aide, every member of Congress who had wandered over applauded not just her, but the very catharsis of the moment; even members of the press tucked their notepads under an arm or shoved their iPhones into a pocket and clapped at this defiant American celebration. Though no records were kept of such things, it was surely the longest and most raucous standing ovation a nominee to the Supreme Court had ever received.

Cecilia Koh's acceptance speech was brief and gracious, barely touching on the political firestorm her nomination had avoided and would have sparked under any other circumstances. She never mentioned the buzz words that had come to define her career, not "textualism" nor "strict constructionism." She knew today was not appropriate for explaining and defending her views on these matters; her next month (if not longer) would be devoted to that battle.

As she soaked in the encore of applause following her speech, she wondered for a fleeting moment if perhaps she should have told Dennis Coutts about her daughter Mifa, and hoped that Jane Norfleet, wherever she might be watching, would have the decency to not force a 17-year-old girl into the coming fray.

Rebecca Whitford hadn't watched this much TV since college, since she and her two best girlfriends had watched their 50 favorite *Friends* episodes over one week in preparation for the series finale. But she wanted to soak this moment in, the moment that every network that had filleted the President, *her* President, was now basically fellating him for the tact and political skill he had exhibited in nominating Cecilia Koh just one week after the bombing. She cracked open a beer, then another, not moving from her office desk chair for nearly two hours as CNN declared that the President had heroically defied not just Congress but the terrorists; MSNBC trotted out guest after guest promising that Salas had nominated a Conservative as a gesture of good faith to Senate Republicans and would get more progressive with his subsequent nominees; and Fox News played one political conventiony slow motion documentary after another chronicling the life and achievements of the American hero that was Cecilia Koh.

"Today happened because of you," a voice said from her door.

"Mr. President!" IPA dribbled out of Becks's nose as she shot to her feet, hiding the bottle behind her thigh and snapping to attention for the Chief Executive leaning against the frame of her office door. But it wasn't *her* Chief Executive. It was the last one. "Is the First Lady--"

He took a step in, shutting the door behind him with a coy smile. "Prepping for our next nominee." He crossed the room, coming up around the side of her desk, taking the beer out of her hand and sucking down half of it. "I wanted to make sure someone properly acknowledged you for putting us in front of the President. For getting this whole process started."

He set the bottle down, and she just stared up into his eyes, now inches from her own. She just breathed him in. It had been over four years since she had been this close, close enough to just breathe him in.

He grabbed her, spinning her around, shoving her down across the desk, her ass served up for him like a platter for a king. He reached up into her skirt, pushing aside the sliver of cotton so he could run his fingers down her damp slit. Becks bit her lower lip, closed her eyes, trying to hold back from releasing just at his very touch.

Becks heard his belt buckle jangle loose, then felt his hand balling her panties up into a fist. "I don't have another pair," she protested, but he had already torn them clean off. She gasped, more fluid squirting down the back of her thigh.

"Oops," he chuckled, then shoved himself all the way up into her. She grunted with ecstasy, and he growled with pleasure. He loved that first initial penetration, that first cry of helpless pain.

Becks loved it too. She wrapped her fingers over the front end of her desk, and buried her face into the wood, hoping to dampen her screams as he thrust in and out of her.

"Who's next?" Dennis asked as he moved the headshot of Professor Koh they had printed off Notre Dame's website to the empty left side of the corkboard. He stepped under the populated side on the right, staring up with wonder at the 20 or so faces of American legal luminaries, some which he recognized instantly, some which he still couldn't believe were qualified to be up there. *I wonder if any of them are already thinking about it,* he thought to himself, *wondering if they're going to be called to serve? Or, who's going to be so completely surprised they break down in tears? Or pee all over themselves? That's what I'd probably do, just piss myself.*

"Next," Rosemarie Irving answered behind him, and Dennis whipped around. She stood on the other side of their new vacant office in the musty ground floor of the Capitol's North Wing, just down the hall from the Supreme Court's first dedicated courtroom, its home from 1810-1860. There wasn't anything in this empty, forgotten room yet, just the corkboard on an easel and Dennis's satchel on the floor, shoved up against one wall like he had come here for a yoga class. Yet, the First Lady filled the entire empty, dim space with her Renaissance regality. "Next, you get me every relevant piece of material you can find on *Aguire v. Detroit.*"

"Say that again?"

"It was a case the Court granted certiorari and heard last Term. But they never issued a ruling. It was relisted for early this Term."

It took Dennis a moment to process this odd request: *Isn't that a little weird, FLOTUS wanting to read up on a case at the exact same time she's helping pick nominees for the Court?*

He shook this off and started moving for the door. *What the hell are you doing, Coutts, trying to screw up the job of a lifetime? Your job isn't to question, just to kick ass doing exactly as you're told.* "On it," he assured Mrs. Irving.

"Dennis," she said, then waited a moment for him to turn back. "Everything. The Justices' confidential internal cert memos. *Everything*."

This time, Dennis didn't even stumble. "Of course, Ma'am."

He disappeared down the dark, empty hall. And Rosemarie Irving moved closer to the corkboard to take in all those faces herself. She couldn't help but snicker. Most of them were just filler. *Some of them will never have any idea they're being used as decoys.* She already knew which three of these faces she would be seeing in person very, very soon. She already knew that the military hero and the former Chief Justice would be getting calls from her in the coming months.

She pulled down the photo of the white-haired judge with the warm hazel eyes. She already knew she would be visiting this eccentric adjudicator of the Third Circuit in Philly next.

For the first time in a week, President Salas was sitting down for a meeting in his Situation Room with a smile on his face, buoyed by the confidence that comes with a win, maybe the greatest of his Presidency.

He didn't even notice that his Chief of Staff's hair was a little mussed, uncharacteristic for her, nor that she chose a chair even further away from the main table than usual, hiding herself in the dark shadows and keeping one knee locked tight on top of the other.

"Let's end a good day with some great news," POTUS smiled as he took the head of the table, turning to his Homeland Security secretary. "What do you say, Janette?"

"I'm sorry, Mr. President. We've identified every body in the building now. And we have found no traces of Chief Justice Lapadula."

"Excuse me?"

"One hundred twenty-three dead accounted for," the Secretary read off a list. "But not the Chief."

"We already had a goddamn funeral for him."

"A Remembrance," Becks corrected.

"I thought Lapadula had swiped in for the day--"

"That is correct, Sir."

"Then where the hell is he?"

ONE WEEK LATER

There was a DoubleTree less than three miles from Jason's new storage facility home. It was a big enough hotel that when he nodded to the front desk staff on his way to the elevators, they all just nodded back with delight, none of them aware they hadn't actually seen him before. To the desk staff of the DoubleTree Bethesda, Jason was just another brown haired six-foot white guy going in and out of their hotel on a Monday at lunchtime.

He picked the '7' button of the elevator. When the doors slid aside on that floor, he looked both ways, determining the hall was empty, every room door closed. So he moved for the stairs and took them two-at-a-time up to the 8th. *Bingo.* He could already hear the dueling vacuums before he opened the stairwell door onto this hall. There were two carts stationed on opposite ends, two doors propped open, the windows inside the rooms casting a glow onto the corridor carpet.

Jason entered the nearest open room, sitting down on one of the beds as he picked up the phone stationed between them and dialed.

"You want us to--?" one of the maids asked after shutting off her Hoover.

"No, no, keep doing your thing. Just forgot one phone call I have to make." She nodded and returned to her cart to grab a stack of new towels, giving him a break from the vacuum for his call. His own voice answered without a ring, and he punched in #, followed by his PIN (again, 2-2-1-7-9-0, the same code he had used for everything since Miranda moved into his life).

"First new message," the Voicemail Lady responded.

George Aug's voice came next. "I think I know what's there. See you soon." Those were his only words before the beep, but it was enough. It had taken him a week, but George had dug up something about Detroit, something that might offer a clue to that city's connection to the bombings. Jason stood, pulling the receiver off his ear to return it to its dock--

"Next new message," the Voicemail Lady continued. Jason returned the phone to his ear, surprised. Who else would leave him a message? Must have been George again, maybe cryptically leaving him a time or place for their rendezvous.

"Jason. It's me."

Jason's entire soul shot up into his throat.

It *was* her. There was no fabricating it, no duplicating it.

And this wasn't an old message. It was brand fucking new. He had re-listened to Miranda's three old messages a dozen different times over the last two weeks, even during one of his hotel visits since jettisoning the BlackBerry itself. He knew those three precious messages word-for-word by now. And none of them started with, "Jason. It's me."

"I'm not supposed-- I miss you bad," she continued. "I wanted you to know … I am okay. I did a bad thing, Jason …" He could hear her throat quivering, her nostrils clenching as she fought flowing tears. This was only the third time he had known her to cry. Four years he had known Rand, and two of the three times she had cried were in the days surrounding the attack. "Someone's coming-- I can't--"

Beep. "End of messages."

Jason Lancaster would listen to that message three more times before he would get up from that bed and leave that room.

He wouldn't remember his walk back to the storage facility, or the rest of his day. And it would be 24 hours before he would find the strength to go find George Aug and find out what the hell Detroit had done to all their lives.

MARTIAL LAW

BOOK TWO OF THE SIX-PART CONSPIRACY THRILLER

FOUR SEATS

DETROIT HOSPITAL

AARON COOLEY

FEBRUARY

It hadn't snowed in nearly three weeks, but the dirty black ice mounds still lined every Washington street like bowling lane bumpers. The rain refused to abate for more than ten minutes at a time, the sun couldn't penetrate its solitary confinement of dark clouds for more than five, and any skin bared for more than two would crack and redden with frost. But to hell with what he saw outside; for President Antonio Salas, winter was finally breaking.

Salas marched down the East Room's strip of red carpet with a pep he hadn't had in his step since his inauguration. But before he could reach his podium, every member of the press, Congress and the Court rose to their feet to fete him with applause. He stopped a few paces short of his mic, taken aback; he hadn't received this kind of reception before the swearings-in of any of the other judicial nominees. Looking around the gallery, taking in those smiling, appreciative faces – appreciative of *him* – he realized that they were all, every last one of them, just as *relieved* as he was that this was all over, that maybe after lunch, Washington would feel normal again.

POTUS stepped up to his podium where his prepared remarks sat waiting, raising his hands to signal the adoring guests to take their seats. None of them were here for him, after all.

"Thank you, ladies and gentlemen, members of the United States Congress, and Supreme Court Justices both senior and new. We are all here to celebrate and bear witness to the investiture of the nineteenth Chief Justice of the United States.

"When I set out to select my nominee for this vital position, I knew that whoever took the center chair would inherit a Court at the most tumultuous moment in its history: a Court under attack, not yet recovered from the destruction of its home or the loss of so many of her personnel from both behind the bench and behind the scenes. Truth be told, we as a nation, and our Court, must never fully recover, or ever fully forget, those wounds.

But there is no doubt in my mind that the person I selected to replace the late Chief Justice Lapadula is better qualified, prepared and willing to lead our Court into its future than any other human being on this planet. Ladies and gentlemen, I am truly humbled to introduce to you, the next Chief--"

The gunshot cut off the President mid-sentence.

Everyone exhaled that strange mix of gasp and scream that signaled the start of a horrific crisis, most ducking for cover as Secret Service agents yanked out sidearms and rushed in front of POTUS, his personal guard Hifrael Fernandez shoving him to the ground with one hand as he screamed into his opposite wrist for a report. On the floor behind the podium, Salas felt around his chest, then pulled his white shirt taut to check for red. Nothing. Wherever or from whomever that shot had originated, it hadn't hit him.

His mind swam with questions: was it even meant for him? If not him, then who was the target? Could the Court be under attack once again?

"The Green Room, the shot came from the Green Room!" he heard Hifrael yell to his men, several of them rushing down the red carpet back into the room from whence the President had emerged moments ago.

The Green Room.

Salas rose, puffing his chest to follow his men. But Hifrael grabbed him from behind, hard, holding the former Team USA goalkeeper in place. "No, Sir," he whispered in Español. "This is our job." Salas nodded, but grit his teeth in agony. If shots had been fired in the Green Room, he knew who they were intended for.

The target had been his new Chief Justice.

BOOK TWO

MARTIAL LAW

THREE MONTHS EARLIER
A MONDAY IN NOVEMBER

Janaki Singh was more nervous on Monday morning than she had been on any other morning working in the chambers of the Third Circuit's Judge Isaac Goldman. She was even more nervous than on that first morning she had come for an interview nearly one month before. She didn't get nervous proofreading opinions or drafting a memo in the Judge's voice. But on this morning, it was *her writing* that was going before the Judge.

Goldman had promised her some 'regular' clerking duties in return for her help with his book, and on this Monday she was presenting a chapter outline for *The Circuit Breaker* to His Honor for the first time. She had planned out the whole thing in her head: what time she would knock on his door from her outer office, how she would work her way into the meat of what she really needed to discuss with him, how she would broach the topic of what the book was missing, what she needed in order to make the book as juicy as possible (and interesting enough for her to spend the next year of her life – at least – writing it).

She hadn't foreseen pulling into the garage of the James A. Byrne Courthouse only seconds before him. So when she heard the honk of his Benz as he whipped around the corner, when his tires screeched right into the spot next to where she was unloading the trunk of his old/her new Hyundai, her grand plans for the day went right out the window.

"How we doin'?" the Judge grinned as he popped out of his car.

Fuck it, she thought, and pulled the outline from her leather messenger bag, offering it up to him without even a word of preface.

"Already?" Goldman exclaimed as he flipped through the stapled document, his green eyes dancing with elation. He didn't even care about its content yet; all that mattered was that this document represented the most progress he had made since signing his book contract over two years before. This girl was going to save his bacon! "You're incredible!"

She gave him the basics of the book's structure, all the while burying the lede, dancing around what she really needed to discuss with him. "It starts in law school, a chapter on clerking for Souter, your practice, your appointment--"

"It's the perfect legal memoir."

"It needs to get more personal." The words shot from her mouth almost of their own volition. She had fretted over how to broach this with him for the past three days – longer than that, three *weeks*, since she first started organizing his boxes of notes – so there was no way she could keep it pent inside any longer.

"I'm sorry?" the Judge responded.

"Why did your wife leave you?"

The Judge smiled it off. Then, realizing how serious she was, flattened his expression. "Don't take this the wrong way, Singh. But have you ever been checked out for Asperger's?"

Janaki opened her mouth to answer – when a caravan of black SUVs appeared over the Judge's shoulder, descending around the corner from the level above them. One big black Escalade wouldn't normally be noteworthy in a garage populated by the cars of high-powered super lawyers and famous judges. But three of them, all with windows tinted dark as slate?

They danced around each other in practiced choreographic unity, then slid backwards into three adjacent parking spots like champion synchronized swimmers. Someone important was parking on their level of the garage – and right across from the spots reserved for the Judge's staff.

A large African-American gentleman dropped out of the front passenger side of the central Escalade, and as he shut his door, Janaki noticed the white plastic cord wrapping around his right ear lobe. "Judge Isaac Goldman?" his baritone bounced across the concrete.

"If you're who the mob sends, tell them yes, I can be bought, no problem. I'm not even that expensive."

The black man smiled, then stepped back to open the rear door of the Escalade, gesturing with an inviting hand for the Judge to get in.

"Not without her."

"Excuse me?" Janaki's horrored eyes whipped over to her boss.

"Yep, that's right. I'm not going anywhere without my girl Friday here." The bruiser spun to look into that backdoor of the Escalade. After receiving some form of confirmation, he nodded to the Judge that it would be all right.

Goldman took a deep breath, then started shuffling to the back of the car. It took him three steps to notice Janaki hadn't moved. "Singh. What're you doing? You're coming with me--"

"No way."

"That's an order. And I have leverage. Your eating options will diminish considerably if I put a halt to that direct deposit thing we got going."

Janaki rolled her eyes, but followed. She was only a step or two behind him when he stuck his head into the car and exclaimed, "Holy Christ!" Janaki recoiled with a gasp of terror. "Singh, you gotta see how much these people …" But by this time, Janaki had rounded the side of the door herself, able to make out the handsome middle-aged couple seated in the back of the vehicle, smiling out at them. "... look like Reginald and Rosemarie Irving!" the Judge finished.

"We don't just look like them," Rosemarie replied.

"Got a minute, Your Honor?" Reg joined in.

Janaki felt Goldman's hand go around her wrist as he lowered himself into the car – whether he was using her to balance himself or was pulling her in after him, she couldn't quite be sure. But she wasn't going to miss maybe the only chance she would have in her life to meet a former President and First Lady. The door slammed behind her heels and she fell into the seat next to the Judge. The engine restarted, the wheels moving under their feet.

"And by a minute," Irving chuckled, "I was hoping you'd be free for a few days."

Janaki spun around in her leather seat, trying to get her bearings on where they were going – what garage exit they would come out of, which direction they would head down which street – when she noticed the cute young man with golden skin and oil-black hair one row behind them, working away on something on his laptop. "Say hello to Dennis," Rosemarie nodded. "He's assisting with this little project we're working on."

Dennis looked up for just a second – just long enough to get caught in Janaki's eyes. He had never seen anything quite like them. "Hi," his voice quavered, the laptop long forgotten.

Janaki wanted to stare back – she found him just as intriguing as he found her, maybe even more – but Janaki had always been a world-class prioritizer, and right now, the Irvings were the priority. *I'm sorry,* she chided herself, *former Presidents over cute guys.*

"Mrs. Irving," Goldman made chit-chat, "good to see you again. How long's it been exactly--?"

"Since you ruled against my client Michael Kestenbaum? Twenty-four years."

"And here I hoped you had put it behind you rather nicely."

"Then you don't know me very well."

Janaki remembered the Kestenbaum case from her perusal of Goldman's book notes – the visit of a future FLOTUS to his courtroom was worthy of inclusion, of course – but hadn't had the time to study the anecdote enough to understand this bitterness behind her tongue.

"Truthfully, Your Honor," Reginald Irving leaned forward to interrupt their sparring, "Rosemarie's admired you from afar ever since. That's why we're here."

"Your President needs you, Judge Goldman."

"And by that she means the current one," Reg smirked, remembering his wife's clever line from the recruitment of their first nominee.

The five of them sat in silence for a mile or two, Dennis's clattering away on his laptop behind them the only sound. Janaki looked down at her fingers – they were shaking. *Is this happening? Are they offering him ...?*

Judge Goldman burst out into raucous laughter; the Irvings joined in on the uproarious good time, which went on and on for another mile.

But Janaki couldn't move. Was she witnessing what she thought she was witnessing? Was this like being there when Thurgood Marshall received The Call from LBJ? Sandra Day O'Connor from Reagan, Ruth Bader Ginsburg from Clinton?

Goldman's laughter cut off like his power plug had been yanked from an outlet far behind them. "Jesus fucking Christ, you're serious."

The Irvings just smiled back.

Janaki looked down at the chapter outline in her lap – Goldman had handed it back to her when the caravan was parking across from them. Twenty-one chapter titles descended down the front page. No one noticed as she pulled out a pen and added one to the bottom of the list: "*22. Justice Goldman*?"

The Irvings had taken a break from the confirmation hearings of Antonio Salas's first nominee to the Supreme Court to travel to Philadelphia and recruit his second. And why not? The first two days of Cecilia Koh's hearings had been smooth sailing, a celebration of the Professor's early legal career and her more recent dedication to education. It seemed as if the last thing the members of the Senate Judiciary Committee wanted to do in this time of crisis was torture the American people with a long, drawn-out public flogging like confirmation hearings past.

And Professor Koh had been even more skilled at navigating her way through the hearing than they could have hoped; parrying with idealistic students, it turned out, prepared one for sparring with frothy Senators as much if not more than years spent soliciting juries or cross-examining witnesses. She brought charm and wit to her every answer, and at several different moments of Thursday and Friday elicited long rounds of good ol' belly laughter throughout the Kennedy Caucus Room of the Russell Office Building, that wonderful mutual laughter that came at no one's expense, just wink-winked at the silliness of the proceedings themselves.

So the Irvings felt more than comfortable leaving her to fend for herself on what should have been the last day of hearings before the Judiciary kicked the vote up to the Senate itself. POTUS wanted to capitalize on the smoothness of the last three weeks, he told Reg and Rosemarie Sunday night, and get his next nominee all teed up to be announced perhaps even at Koh's own swearing-in. The Irvings drove down to Philadelphia on Sunday night to pick up Nominee #2, figuring they would be back early enough on Monday to watch the Professor wrap up her hearings with handshakes, back slaps and a unanimous committee vote to recommend.

How were they to know the tide was about to turn?

Monday morning brought ranking Democrat Geoff Wyley's turn to question the nominee. Cecilia's team of preppers had warned her Wyley would undoubtedly shine close scrutiny upon the curriculum of her Notre Dame Law class, "Faith, Morality and Constitutional Law," which to this point had barely been mentioned. Professor Koh was prepared for Wyley's assault, and at first eased through it with effortless aplomb.

"Were you aware, Professor," the Senator began, "that Notre Dame is now offering videos of your course on their NotreDameOnline service?"

"I'm afraid I don't get any royalties from that, if that's what you're asking, Senator." The room filled with its first chortles of the new week.

"The camera does love you, Professor," Wyley laughed along, "and you are quite a riveting orator. I enjoyed watching some of your highlights this past weekend." He brought his reading glasses to his nose and a piece of paper closer to his eyes to read aloud: "'The word privacy isn't in the Constitution. Not in the original seven articles, not in the twenty-seven amendments.'" He looked up off the paper, beading down onto Koh over the top of his frames. He had practiced this all weekend, and knew the rest of it by heart. "'By invoking privacy in 1973, the Supreme Court violated your Constitution. Interpreted it out of whole cloth.' This is taken from the transcript of one of your videos, Professor. You're clearly referring to the Court's decision in *Roe v. Wade*, are you not?"

Prepared for this volley, Koh leaned into the mic. "That is correct, Senator."

"My question, Professor, is whether this *diatribe* on *Roe v. Wade* offers us a preview of how you will vote when cases involving a woman's right to a legal and safe abortion come before the Court."

"With all due respect, Senator, I think the word diatribe implies a passion that could only be fueled by my own personal beliefs--"

"Do you deny these are your beliefs?"

"I was hired by Notre Dame Law School to teach a class, to teach a curriculum and a history of the law that reflects the moral and legal philosophies of the school. That's what they asked me to do on the day they hired me, to replace a very learned and respected professor who was retiring after 30 years of teaching that same philosophy."

"And that philosophy is--"

"That philosophy is Originalism, sometimes called Textualism, a belief that the Constitution should be interpreted as the Framers intended it when they ratified it over two hundred years ago, or when each Amendment is put into law by the legislative and executive branches. Regardless of my personal beliefs, that is the philosophy that Notre Dame asked me to teach in my class, and that's what I have been doing to the best of my ability."

"Professor Koh, I think you know what I'm asking here. If an opportunity to overturn *Roe v. Wade* comes before the Supreme Court, how will you vote?"

"Senator Wyley, I think it would be inappropriate for me to comment on specific cases in this hearing, as that would leave the impression I have prejudged future cases. What I will say is that I have done my job as a Notre Dame Law professor to the best of my ability, and if I am blessed to be confirmed as an Associate Justice of the Supreme Court, I will do the same there. And that job, any judging job, is to weigh the myriad different factors involved in any case, not just things like the original intent of the Constitution, but *stare decisis* – the precedent of past cases like *Roe v. Wade* or *Planned Parenthood v. Casey* which have already dealt with many of the toughest issues in this debate."

The room hummed at the skill with which she had handled this line of attack, and every Republican sitting high behind the committee bench smiled and nodded. She had answered the queries of the most progressive member of their group without allowing him to paint her as a flawed, one-issue nominee. The conservatives were confident how she would vote on abortion, on any moral issue that mattered to their constituents, but no liberal was going to get her to admit it into the microphone.

Wyley wasn't finished. He put down the transcript from her class and picked up a second piece of paper, again reading aloud.

"'The Pope has said it's a waste of time for Catholics to fight for issues like abortion and gay marriage. Well, that doesn't sound like any Pope of mine. This organization will spend every last dime crusading for these causes that represent the degradation of our society, and we won't rest until they are eradicated from our society.'"

"I'm sorry, Senator, I don't understand--"

"You don't recognize those words, Professor?"

"No, Senator. I can tell you they're not mine."

"This was a speech your husband Lindsey Campbell gave to the organization Catholic Crusaders. Do you know this group, Professor?"

"Ah. Yes, of course. They're a very passionate, opinionated organization on the fringes of Catholicism. My husband is a member of the group, but I assure you I personally am not."

"To paraphrase that old commercial, he's not just a member, he's also the president. Isn't he, Professor?"

"With all due respect, Senator, I'm not sure what relevance my husband's affiliation with this group has on my--"

"I'm getting to that, Professor. Did you know the Catholic Crusaders own a publishing arm?"

"Like I said, Senator Wyley, I'm not familiar with every--"

"*Pink Alert: Homosexuality Warning Signs in Early Childhood. The Dirty Little Secret: The Covered-Up Link Between Birth Control and Cancer*. These are some of the titles offered by Crusader Press on Amazon-dot-com, Professor."

Cecilia took a sip of water, giving the assembled onlookers a moment to buzz at the first moment of real drama in her three days of hearings. The Senator had succeeded in venturing into territory not rehearsed with her prep team. Sure, she had seen those kitschy books for sale on a small side table whenever she attended a Catholic Crusaders event with Lindsey, but never in her wildest dreams had she imagined the Senate of the United States questioning her about them.

"And they also have a political action arm, did you know that? CFF. Catholics for Freedom. In this calendar year alone, CFF has raised over fifteen million dollars to be used in next year's elections. Now, Professor, my question is this: do you think it just might be a conflict of interest for a Supreme Court Justice to be married to a man who is out collecting millions of dollars from donors who support conservative political candidates, conservative causes, and of course, conservative rulings on cases that might come before her court?"

The hearing room erupted into a symphony of unrest. Someone had done it, someone had rattled Cecilia Koh. Her eyes glazed over for several seconds; she knew about Catholic Crusaders, of course, and had practiced a response several times over the weekend with her preppers. But her husband had never told her about the PAC arm of the group. She wanted to proclaim that he had no affiliation with that side of the organization, but knew she shouldn't open her mouth on that until she knew for certain.

When Senator Dudley called a short recess, everyone jumped to their feet, except the Professor herself. One of her preppers leaned into her to whisper encouragement, but she didn't hear a word he said, the C-SPAN and CNN and MSNBC and Fox News cameras leaning in on her doubt-plagued eyes.

"Smile," Rosemarie Irving cursed under her breath. "Smile-smile-smile." She, her husband, and an assortment of Salas staffers were stationed in one of the small antechambers down the hall from the committee hearing room. Rosemarie wasn't worried; she was the only one in the room who wasn't, the rest of them moaning through the last several minutes of Koh's testimony. She wanted a smile not because she was worried in the least, but just to make the optics better, to make it seem that the Professor wasn't worried either – and to deny that progressiver-than-thou twit Wyley the satisfaction of having made her squirm.

The President's Chief of Staff Rebecca Whitford had accosted the Irvings the second they entered Russell upon their return from Philadelphia. "She's blowing it," Becks exclaimed. "Wyley's pinned her in a corner and she's fucking blowing it."

Rosemarie brushed this off, charging right past her and heading for their temporary office. There was no way the Professor could blow anything. The Republicans controlled the Senate, they controlled the Committee, and they were going to confirm her no matter what one liberal quack made her say on the stand.

That's why Rosemarie was the only one on the Salas team not sweating as the latest session went into recess. It would be nice if the Professor could smile; the Irvings had never liked Wyley, they knew he had been one of those backstabbers always bitching off-record to *Mother Jones* or *The Nation* that they weren't liberal enough when they were in office, and she despised the idea of him getting any moment in the sun. If the Professor could just smile, it would drain him of all his power, his little fifteen second victory.

But that was a minor quibble. Whether she smiled or not, by the end of this week, Cecilia Koh was going to be the next Associate Justice of the Supreme Court. Senate Democrats were furious about it. But what the hell could they do?

Detroit has always been bloody.

Fought over in the French and Indian War, burnt to the ground in 1805, surrendered to the British without a fight in 1812, ravaged by race riots in the 20th Century, abandoned as a ghost town in the 21st, Detroit's history was perhaps more turbulent than any other American city's.

And that was even before the last two years.

Six years had passed since the Governor of Michigan had handed control of the city over to an Emergency Manager via a controversial law that stripped the local government – the mayor, the city council – of all its power and placed it in the hands of one man tasked with curing the city's financial ills. It was meant to be a temporary means to an end, a band-aid. But six years and three Emergency Managers later, nothing had changed. The city was still in the throes of Bankruptcy, and Allied Armament still ruled her streets.

Jason Lancaster had seen the trademark matte-black vehicles adorned with the red intertwined A, A, S, and C (for Allied Armament Security Consultants), couldn't miss their legions of ex-grunts and jarheads with wrap-around Oakleys and tatted biceps patrolling the avenues, hanging their assault rifles out the windows of their SUVs like Mexican federales. Jason was familiar with the company – several Army buddies had gone to work for the security contractors after leaving the military – but this was his first real personal encounter with them.

The company was founded by F. Walsh Howard III, scion of a lumber empire who had himself grown close to military culture – seen its needs and deficiencies – in a tour in Afghanistan. In its short history, Allied Armament's press had been no less than glowing, especially after its Domestic Operations Division performed valiantly when called upon to aid FEMA after two recent hurricanes and a devastating South American earthquake. When Detroit Emergency Manager Gibson called Howard to float the idea of Allied Armament replacing Detroit's entire police and fire departments, AASC had landed the most profitable account in its history. The citizenry of Detroit, however, was not so keen about 4000 of its workforce being laid off and replaced with an army of mercenaries, and they had responded to the change with almost immediate violence. Though AASC had quelled those first uprisings, the rioting had continued throughout the last 27 months; Allied Armament men had exchanged fire on numerous occasions with youths described in their reports as 'gangbangers;' and more businesses had packed up and left town in the time AASC was in charge than in the five previous years combined. By replacing his cops with soldiers of fortune, the Emergency Manager had somehow succeeded in making Detroit an even bloodier place.

Jason had only been in Detroit for about 48 hours; he hadn't come immediately after Oliver Whitney gave him the address at which one of the Supreme Court bombs had been tested, nor after he heard Miranda's voice mail message that she had survived the bombing (and even implied she might have had something to do with it). First, Jason had some groundwork to lay: getting a clean, unregistered car in which he could make the eight hour drive from Washington; getting as much of his checking and savings accounts converted to cash in one quick, perfectly-timed, in-and-out bank visit; figuring out the highest ranked person at AASC he could get to; letting his shoulder heal, his left shoulder that had taken a .338 Lapua round when someone shot up his Bethesda brownstone.

But 48 hours was enough to get the lay of Detroit; to walk her deserted neighborhoods overgrown with chest-high grass; long enough to see all the buildings burnt and sidewalks blood-stained in the new rash of riots; long enough to see the pimps and streetwalkers, malnourished dogs and starving addicts; to witness firsthand the dregs of society that came out to play and terrorize when the sun went down. Enough time to see Allied Armament in action, keeping these dregs out of the downtown waterfront area, away from the affluent and predominantly white suburbanites driving in for the opera or the Lions or the Red Wings.

And enough time to walk the perimeter of the address Ollie had given him, the abandoned five story '70s modern building at Michigan Ave and 20th. Unfortunately, he couldn't get any closer than the perimeter; AASC had barbed wired the entire property line and wouldn't let Jason in the one gated entrance. He knew it was time to flex what little muscle he had.

Mooner, an old buddy of Jason's from his time in the 'Stan, had e-troduced him two weeks before to Dean Rikeman, Allied Armament City Commander for all Detroit forces. (Mooner was the highest-ranking spook Jason knew, running a CIA Special Activities team overseas, a team that Jason's Special Forces group had worked with on more than one mission. Mooner loved Jason, and tried to get him to apply to the Company when he left the Army. But Jason's father was gravely ill, and Jason thought he should get a job that would bring him home where he could take care of the old man he not-so-affectionately referred to as 'Sarge.' (His sister was so over the man, she refused to commit to coming up from Charlottesville more than once a month.) Little did he know his dear ol' dad would be dead before he would even start his new job at the Supreme Court, but once he met Miranda, he never harbored a regret about the choice.)

"That's United Community Hospital," Rikeman said as he flipped Jason's tablet through the roll of photos he had taken outside the barbed wire on Sunday night. "Or Southwest Detroit. That's what it was originally called, so a lot of locals will still refer to it with that name, or SDH."

Jason was in Rikeman's spacious office in the former Detroit Public Safety HQ at 1301 Third Street, the building itself a quasi-border between the glistening downtown and the desolation further west on the Detroit River. The office had once belonged to the Detroit Chief of Police; Rikeman struck Jason more as a West Point-grad Lieutenant who had probably never seen real combat himself.

"You mind if I ask what you guys are doing with it?"

"Nothing. Just keeping it locked up. United Community's been closed up since we got here. It was still fully stocked with drugs when they closed down, so the EM doesn't want us to let anyone in."

"But there are people in there," Jason leaned forward to flip to one particular photo, in which the flames of a small fire could be seen in an upper floor window.

Rikeman sat back with a sigh. "When we took over, DPD had left the place open and it was a fucking free-for-all. We try to go in there and pull everyone out, we'd be asking for a total YouTube shit show. So we cut our losses. Don't let anyone new in, and don't let anyone out."

"And eventually, they take enough drugs and little enough food that they all die in there."

Rikeman shrugged and lifted his eyebrows with a smile. "Rumor has it there's enough rats and stray cats in there to keep 'em going for years."

"I need to get in there."

"Sorry, man. Moon says you're a good guy, but this one's above me. We're not even allowed in ourselves without some sort of probable cause."

"It has to do with the Supreme Court."

Rikeman sat forward, his attention piqued. "The bombing?"

Jason nodded. "The cell phone detonator for one of the bombs was tested in that building before it went to Washington. Those bombs came from the United Community Hospital."

Rikeman picked up his phone. "That's all you had to say. Trust me, corporate would love to be able to say we're assisting in that investi--"

Jason's fingers slammed down into the phone's cradle, killing the dial tone in Rikeman's ear. "Please," Jason pleaded. "Just me for now." He let his fingers off the phone and Rikeman returned the handset, a tacit agreement to not report this intel just yet. But Jason could read he would need more before he would actually acquiesce to his request. "It's personal."

Jason had to get to the bottom of all this himself. If Miranda was waiting at the bottom of all this, maybe he could help her, maybe she didn't have to get arrested or go to the electric chair. Maybe there was some huge misunderstanding he could help her fix. But bring in the big guns on this, and he would never get his chance.

"Look, I know you can't sit on this for long," Jason said as he stood. "Just do me a favor. If you're going to report this, give me a day or two at least. To try to figure out if there's any way I can do this on my own."

Rikeman nodded. They shook hands and Jason turned to go.

"Oh, one more thing," Jason remembered, and pulled a stack of small photo cards from his pocket. He took several off the top, and set them down on Rikeman's desk, situated so Miranda's eyes stared back at the City Commander. "I'd love to know if any of your men have seen her," Jason explained.

"She also has to do with the bombing?"

"I'm hoping not."

Rikeman took the top one off the stack and looked at her closely. "Pretty." It actually wasn't even her prettiest photo on Jason's old Blackberry, but it was the one he thought looked most like she looked on a day-to-day basis. "Doesn't look familiar to me, but I'll distribute them and tell everyone to keep an eye out."

"I'd appreciate it." Jason made his way to the door and out.

And Rikeman made that call he aborted earlier. He didn't break his promise and mention what Jason had told him, about the bombs coming from inside that hospital. All he said into the receiver was, "He's here."

"Filibuster?" Reginald Irving pushed off from the conference table and sat back with a laugh.

It was Washington's worst kept secret that the Irvings were running Salas's Supreme Court process, so when the Dems on the Judiciary Committee needed someone to bitch to, they set a meeting with Reg and Rosemarie. Professor Koh had cleared the Judiciary hurdle earlier that day in a surprisingly close 11-8 vote, and her confirmation by the end of the week seemed assured. The Senate Democrats were running out of time to block the most Conservative nominee to the Court in almost a decade and a half. There was only one course of action left open to them.

"You can't filibuster her, Geoff," the former POTUS shook his head.

"We absolutely can," Senator Wyley replied with confidence, doing everything he could to avoid calling Irving *Mr. President* – an oversight the Irvings had no trouble noticing. Wyley had succeeded in getting all 40 of his fellow Senate Democrats on the phone or gathered in his office that afternoon, and all 40 had promised without reservation to join him in his filibuster of the Cecilia Koh vote. It would take 60 GOP votes to break the filibuster, but with only 59 seats in Republican hands, the math was in Geoff Wyley's favor. ('The Nuclear Option,' which eliminated the possibility of filibuster from judicial appointments, did not apply to the Supreme Court process.)

"Right now?" Irving mocked. "You realize there's never been a filibuster of a Supreme Court nominee? And you're going to do it *right now* – when this nation's still healing, and overwhelmingly approves the President's drive to rebuild the Court?"

"My constituents don't approve of this activist nominee. They elected a Democratic President to put Democratic values on the Court, and then he goes and does this."

"It's all part of a process," the smooth voice rang out from the door, taking the words right out of Rosemarie's own mouth. Everyone recognized the sonorous voice that had once made Antonio Ramón Salas a Spanish soap star, and shot to their feet. "Please," he encouraged them to sit, crossing to the open chair in the midst of the angry Dems, directly across from his predecessor and First Lady. Becks followed him in, but stayed leaned against the wall just behind him. "You have to trust it's all part of our process," the President continued. "We've got four open seats. And at the end of our process, I promise you're going to be very happy with the new makeup of the Court. But the Right controls the Senate. They understand as well as you do that we have a chance here to weigh down the Court with six liberals. We have to give them some sort of balance, even one tipped in our favor. We give them one, we still end up with a 5-4 head count."

"All we're doing with Koh is lubing them up for what we're gonna do to them later," Reg chuckled.

"Respectfully, Mr. President," Wyley replied – and Salas had to fight to not roll his eyes at his least favorite of all Washington words. "You were never in the Senate. I've been in this body almost my entire adult life, for almost four decades now. This is not the way you deal with them, Mr. President, by acting from weakness, by capitulating right from go. You need a strong, progressive nominee, someone who shows them, goddammit, I'm the President and I mean business and I'm not going to compromise in this process."

"Respectfully, Senator, you've never been the President," Rosemarie shot back. "I think you can trust these two gentlemen that they know how to do that job."

Wyley kept his eyes trained on Salas, never acknowledging the First Lady. "Sir, I would be betraying my constituents if I allowed this nominee to be confirmed."

"What do you want me to do, Geoff? Pull my first nominee? How is that going to look? Is that going to look like I'm acting from strength?"

"What will look worse: that, or a President's own party filibustering his first nominee?"

"They're not going to move on to other business," Reg Irving said. "This is the Supreme Court we're talking about, Geoff. You say you're filibustering, they're going to make you do it for real." Usually, the Senate was free to move on to new business while a bill was being filibustered. But should the Majority Leader – who in this case would be a Republican – refuse to refer further business to the Senate, the filibustering party would have to actually keep speaking for the duration of the filibuster.

"I have to tell you, Sir, my caucus wants to go all out on this. We are prepared to fight for this, for days if we have to. This is going to be the biggest news of the year after the bombing, Sir. But it doesn't have to be like this." He rose from his chair, and his sycophants followed. "Thank you for your time, Mr. President."

The two POTUSes and Rosemarie waited for their surprising nemeses to clear the room before they spoke. Reg was first, rising to his own feet. "This is no problem. We only need to get one of them to break and we've got our vote. Some of these assholes still owe me favors." He followed the Senate procession into the hall, closing the door behind him.

"You're not supposed to come down here," Rosemarie barked at Salas. In just a month of this process, she had discovered she could talk to him like no other person on the planet; he knew that's exactly what he needed and never fought it. "You let me run this and I call you when the champagne's chilled."

"We need to get some blue votes."

"Their filibuster won't last more than a day. They're going to get killed in the media, then they'll make a big to-do about how they said their piece and now the democratic process can continue."

"Show her the numbers, Becks."

Becks pulled a sheet of paper from her leather folder and set it before Rosemarie. It was just large enough for four polls – NBC News, PPP, Quinnipiac, *New York Times* – all pitting Salas against the presumptive GOP nominee in the next year's presidential election.

"Brad Benedict? They're hasn't even been one primary yet, we have no idea who their nominee--"

"Some evangelical might win Iowa, or get some publicity off some fire and brimstone debate blabber, but everyone knows Benedict's the only one their party's going to let through the process. He's the only one who has a chance in a general. And he's only two points behind me."

"And those are in polls usually very favorable to us," Becks chimed in. "Fox News has him up--"

"A year out."

"I need the base, Rosemarie. I won three years ago by getting out the base in church busloads, by getting more young Latinos, more young Latino *women* to vote than ever before. Geoff Wyley has made a career off the black vote in Florida, and he delivered that vote to me. If he paints me as a traitor to the party on my very first Supreme Court nomination, a traitor to everyone whose church takes their souls to the polls on the Sunday before Election Day for early voting--" here he stood, pointing a finger to the door "--if I don't have Geoff Wyley and every one of those goddamn Senators barnstorming for me in their home states, we're going to lose the White House."

Becks opened the door for him, and Salas buttoned his jacket as he moved for it, pausing to turn back for just one last beat. "I want you to get me ten blue votes for Cecilia Koh. Or I can't let that vote happen."

TUESDAY

***F**ucking Jason,* Oliver Whitney thought as he dragged his Galaxy through the detritus of his bedside table and over to his eyes. *For a brilliant girl, Randi always picked dickheads.* If not for Jason, Ollie wouldn't have gone back to the office so soon, and he would still be on Bereavement Leave. If not for Jason, Ollie could chase Falcor to his heart's content and not have to confine his favorite activity to hours away from FirmWall. If not for Jason, his Morphine ringtone wouldn't be waking his ass up before 5 AM on a Tuesday morning.

Ollie thumbed the green answer square, then held the phone up to his ear. But he wasn't even able to muster enough strength to say hello, drifting back into slumber for a few seconds before he heard, "—llie? Ollie? OLLIE!"

"What? Goddamn. You know what time I went to bed last night, bitch?"

"Try to imagine how little I give a shit," Jason spit into the cold Detroit air. A flashlight beam cut through the blackness as an Allied Armament guard started traipsing along the barbed wire in his direction, moving closer to investigate who the hell was having such a loud phone conversation at three o'clock in the morning. Jason had done another sweep of the hospital perimeter, another search for a way in through the fence or into the building. But the one thing he didn't need to do was draw the suspicions of the company now ruling this town. So he moved on, lowering his voice as he disappeared into the shadows under the Michigan Avenue overpass, continuing onto the uninhabited urban green belt north of the hospital. "United Community Hospital, in Detroit."

"What the hell you saying?"

"I need you to find out everything you can about it."

"Hold on, I'm hooked up to the wi-fi, I can get you the address while we're connected--"

"I don't need a Google search, Ollie, I need you to go to work and pull out every little stop to get me every little piece of information you can dig up on this place. Government records, everything. Who owns it. I mean *really* owns it. Maybe even plans of the building, anything you can get me."

"And this couldn'ta waited till 9 or 10 or normal-mother-fucking-o'clock?"

"We need to figure out who could've been in there five weeks ago practicing how to blow up the Supreme Court."

Ollie sat up in bed, Jason's last words a bucket of ice water to his face. "Got it."

"Good." Jason hung up, then opened up the back of the burner, tearing out its battery, tossing the pieces around the grass. Whoever it was that had tried to kill him in Washington would have no way of knowing about this phone, or the five others he had bought with cash in five different stores between Maryland and Michigan – no way of knowing, that is, until he used it to call Ollie. They were surely listening in on Ollie. They had heard their call a month ago, the initial one about the bomb test calls occurring in Detroit, so they'd be listening in on him and waiting for Jason to call so they could track that new number and find him.

As he dismantled the phone, he thought about how Ollie's tone had changed; he had done the right thing, entrusting the kid with all the facts, making him feel included, letting him know how important this effort was. He still hadn't told him about Miranda's message, not in the three conversations they'd had since he first heard it. He was saving that nugget for when he really needed to light a fire under the kid's ass.

Ollie, meanwhile, was already out of the shower, waiting for his hair to dry and coffee to percolate, staring at the red digits of his cable box. Despite his sudden surge of motivation, it was going to be another two and a half hours before he could get into work. With the clients they had, the sensitive shit they were trading in, the FirmWall bosses didn't want anyone in there when there wasn't a full security department watching every camera and internet connection, when there weren't enough co-workers around to dissuade anyone from doing anything devious. Two hours and twenty-seven more minutes until the doors opened at 8 AM and Ollie was the first one to arrive (a first in his FirmWall career).

Two twenty-seven: more than enough time. *Yeah, that's perfect*, he thought as he tore off a clean square of aluminum foil. *This'll wake my ass all the way up, then wear off right about the time I need my head clear and my eyes pearly white. Perfect.*

The steel-cut oats of the Hay-Adams kitchen weren't half as good as Lindsey's; they left some sort of paste in Cecilia's mouth and crunchy grit between her teeth. Professor Koh's husband had made her steel cut oatmeal every morning of the past 21 years, or every morning they were in the same city at least; she didn't know what he put in them, how much water he included per quarter-cup of oats, how long he kept those oats simmering, but she had never found a hotel in the world that could match them in flavor or smoothness. Cecilia grinned as she chewed through that first bite; she missed her husband, even after hearing such sharp criticisms of him for 24 straight hours now.

As she ate the hotel oats, she perused the first few paragraphs of each of the three papers she had picked up between her room and this corner table in the hotel's ground floor restaurant. The *Post, USA Today,* even the *New York Times* all portrayed her Monday performance as not nearly the disaster she thought it had been. (Maureen Dowd had even written an op-ed criticizing Geoff Wyley's attacks as sexist and applauding her poise in the face of them.) Sure, they were all going easy on her because that's what polls said Americans wanted, to just get this whole process over and done with, but Cecilia liked to think she had done her part in making that possible, handling the Senator's attacks with calm, coolness and collection. These reviews confirmed it.

"*USA Today*? Really, Professor?" Jane Norfleet appeared from over Cecilia's shoulder and sat down in the chair across from her. "Is someone sitting here? Your husband? No, he's probably the last person you'd want anywhere near this town and all its cameras, isn't he?" She leaned forward, smiling as if she had practiced this speech throughout her entire journey from South Bend. "Well, maybe not the last person. That'd be me."

"How'd you find me?" Cecilia clenched, her voice shaking with more timidity than at any point of the Senate proceedings.

"Um, you're checked in under your own name, Professor. You're not Oprah now or something." She reached into her messenger bag, pulling out a magazine, tossing it on top of Koh's reading pile. "I'm disappointed to see you reading those fish rags. How 'bout something a little more befitting your intellectual reputation?" It was *The Notre Dame Journal of Law & Ethics,* the law review Norfleet edited. "Although, I must admit I was a little disappointed in this month's issue. You were supposed to write the cover story, remember?"

"You made a grave mistake coming here--"

"All articles for the December issue were due last Friday. I hadn't received a draft from you, so I thought I'd better come check on you. I know you don't want to miss another issue. I might have to write your piece myself. You wouldn't want that."

"You can't be serious." Cecilia leaned forward, hissing out the words in whispered exasperation; it wasn't just the ears of the walls that scared her in Washington, it was the microphones under all the tables, the dictaphones behind every curtain. "Don't you think the situation has changed just slightly? Are you really threatening to drag my daughter into the spotlight right now, drag her into a Congressional hearing--?"

"I don't know how many times I have to say it. This isn't about your daughter. This is about you, Professor. I believe in your daughter's right to a safe and legal abortion. Apparently, so do you. I just want you to admit that in my law journal, that's all." She leaned in, eyes gleaming with delight. "But I'll make you a deal. I know how slammed you must be right now, practicing all the different ways to disown your husband or rationalize your class curriculum. So here's what I'm gonna do for you: you come clean, you tell your little story into a microphone anytime between now and the confirmation vote, and you're off the hook. You don't have to write the article."

She stood, looking down at Cecilia shrinking in her chair like a cowering animal. "Your choice."

"It's a former daycare slash pre-K facility," Salas's Homeland Security Secretary explained as the Situation Room's center flat screen filled with satellite surveillance footage of a rainy urban street. "Kingman?"

The Secretary turned to Kingman Summers, her acting Under Secretary for Intelligence & Analysis. Kingman stood, hiding the grimace that accompanied any strain put on that knee he had ravaged in too many pick up games, and carried his tall frame over to the screen. He worked the remote to zoom in on a large circular building, an extended playground area extending behind it. "It was called Pencil Pals. Open from the late 1990s until about three years ago. It seems they were running their budget pretty hand-to-mouth, and couldn't keep up when the Old Town neighborhood of Portland got hot again and their rent picked up. The management company that owns the building, Waugh Properties, has had it listed for sale ever since, but until they find takers, they wanted to keep it occupied—

and as you can imagine, the available renters for an abandoned pre-school are limited, Sir."

Salas leaned forward. "So who'd they rent it to?"

Kingman thumbed the remote, cutting to another moment in the recording, the picture brightening with a sunny day. He held down a button, zooming in closer on the playground – until POTUS could make out several men on their knees, on some sort of yoga mats laid out on the back lawn, dipping their heads in unison supplication. "They're praying to Mecca, Sir."

"It's some kind of mosque?"

"That, and much more," the Secretary joined back in. "For anyone who flees Iran and ends up in Oregon, the renters of the Pencil Pals building have offered a warm, safe place to crash while they get their new lives kickstarted. It's a half-way house for Iranians."

"At least, that's what we're supposed to believe it is," Kingman added, flipping the feed again – now the men in the playground were on their feet, paired up, throwing punches at each other, grabbing each other in fighting holds, flipping each other onto the ground, practicing hand-to-hand combat techniques.

"How many of them are there?"

"We have no way of knowing, Sir," Kingman answered. "As far as we can tell, they keep only paper records. And we've only been watching them closely for the past two weeks."

The Secretary read from a prepared stat sheet. "The building is about three thousand square feet: a ring of classrooms surrounding a center circular play or gathering area, with small cafeteria in back."

"There could be as many as a couple hundred of them in there. We're using recognition software now to try to get a count of how many unique faces come in and out."

"Assuming they all do come out." The Secretary pursed her lips. "There's no way to be sure."

Salas sat back, crossing his arms over his chest. He wasn't sure yet what to think of this notion his DHS team had brought to him, so he tried to change the subject to something that he knew caused him unmitigated indigestion. "What about the Chief Justice? Lapadula? Any new ideas on how the hell he got out of the building, or where he is now?"

The DHS Secretary shook her head. "Not yet, Sir, I'm sorry."

"This," Salas stammered, holding his hand up to the flat screen, "this is a community service, not a crime. Holding personal defense classes for Muslims is not a crime. I don't see what--"

Kingman aimed the remote at the screen once again, replacing the surveillance video with a driver's license photo: an Iranian young man, late 20s, his eyes holding back the type of history with which no one in the Sit Room could identify. "This is Mohammed Mullin. 'Mo' to his friends. Born Ronald Eric Mullin in Good Samaritan Hospital in the Beaverton suburb of Portland in 1989. His parents fled Iran right before the Shah did and changed their last names in the early '80s to try to hide their heritage. Rebelling against his secular upbringing, Mullin changed his first name and went out and joined a mosque on his own at age 17. He's been active in Muslim causes ever since. He's now a partner at the local law firm of Pagon & Fitzgerald, and with no wife or kids of his own, donates a considerable portion of his salary to the halfway house inside Pencil Pals."

"More importantly," the Secretary added, "he's a graduate of Stanford Law School who, in his third year, applied for a clerkship with one Supreme Court Associate Justice Frederick Biggs. God rest his soul."

"When Mullin didn't get the job, he launched into a tirade on a Muslim discussion board, all over the map, but mostly about how the Court's whole hiring process is anti-Muslim. Several news aggregator websites picked up his most choice little morsels. Facebook and Twitter did their thing. Gave him a little taste of the fame that comes with Muslim activism."

"Wait a second," Salas held up a hand, "let's think through this theory. How the hell could this kid get into the building, get into all the restricted areas, knock out the surveillance system--?"

"This *kid's* in the legal community, Sir," the Director of the CIA retorted. "Who knows who he's friends with, who he went to law school with, who he's fucked."

"Mr. President," the DHS Secretary tried to restore order. "We're not saying we've got this all mapped out yet. We're just saying this is the best lead we've got right now."

Salas found Rebecca's eyes, looking for some guidance. In moments like these, he often wished he had a more senior, trusted advisor, someone his equal, someone he hadn't met in just the last three years who brought to his or her job an elaborate agenda. That's what he had enjoyed so much about the Court nomination process, having that sort of advisor in Rosemarie Irving. But she wouldn't be permitted in the Sit Room; he had to trust his own gut when it came to the investigation.

"Keep following that lead," Salas ordered as he pushed back from the table. "Get me more."

"There's no nice way to put this," Rosemarie began after the room had cleared of Cecilia's entire prep team save her and Reg. "You need to distance yourself from your husband."

Professor Koh nodded. She knew this was coming.

"You don't have to go overboard. You can unquestionably say he's been a faithful husband and exemplary father. You've just always disagreed on many issues. Debating over issues of the day was your favorite shared activity when you were dating--"

"It sure was ours," Reginald Irving smiled.

"--and today, it's what your family does over the dinner table every night. We've had someone from the White House Communications staff put a rough framework of talking points like this together for you. All we need is for you to add in some personal examples, and we can get the interview done first thing tomorrow--"

"I should withdraw," Cecilia blurted out.

Rosemarie took a breath. She expected trepidation from the Professor, not outright surrender. "No. Cecilia, that's not what anyone wants."

"Wyley was just doing what he thought he needed to do to keep his base frothy," Irving agreed, "bring their favorite issues front and center."

"The public is overwhelmingly behind you and your confirmation. The President just wants to make sure he gets a bipartisan vote on this, after everything the country's been through. The best way to do that is to make sure everyone understands you're a legal *scholar*, not an activist like your--"

"I took my daughter to get an abortion."

The entire room seemed to grind to a halt. Rosemarie could swear she even heard the heating system choose that very moment to shut down.

"My daughter Mifa was pregnant, she didn't want the child – *God knows* she couldn't even begin to handle a child, and I didn't want to handle it for her. So I took her for an abortion. I paid cash for it. My husband-- he nearly divorced me over this last year." She looked up, trying to focus her eyes with thoughts of practicality. “He told me I shouldn’t come to Washington, I shouldn’t do this. He was right. When the Republicans find out what I did, I’m going to go from fifty-five votes to five. It will screw up your whole strategy for the other nominees. I don’t want to do that. I should withdraw.”

Rosemarie looked at her husband, and he got the hint. They both stood, and as he made his way out of their conference room-turned-prep space, she crossed around to the seat next to Cecilia, taking her small hands in her own. “Look, I can’t even begin to imagine what that whole experience was like. Our son barely talked to women before he turned 20. You obviously have some very conflicted, very complicated feelings wrapped up into this whole thing. But those feelings are yours and yours alone. This is no one’s business, except you and your daughter’s. And I promise you, it’s going to stay that way. No one’s going to find out. The hearings are over. The Dems might make some noise for a day or two, but the vote’s going to be--”

“A student knows.”

“*What?*”

“A Notre Dame student found out – her cousin or something works in the clinic we went to – and she’s extorting me.”

“Extorting how?”

“She’s giving me until the vote to admit what I did, or she’s going to print it in the law review she edits.” Cecilia looked down to the floor, but Rosemarie could see the first drips falling off her cheeks.

Rosemarie felt the heat building behind her eyes, and took a lap of the room to ice it down. She harbored a typical Polish woman’s temper, but had learned long ago how to control it, how to harness it. Reaching the door, she opened it to invite her lead Secret Service agent Mitchell Aldridge in with a nod. Returning to Cecilia as MMA stepped in and closed the door, she asked, “When did this student last contact you? And how?”

“This morning. She’s here, she’s in Washington.”

“What’s her name?”

Cecilia thought for a moment about where this line of questioning must be leading, and shook her head. “Oh no, I don’t know if she’d even be in a hotel--”

Rosemarie nodded back to Mitch with a smile. “I hang out with Secret Service agents all day long. What’s her name?”

“Jane Norfleet.”

"Listen to me. What she's threatening to do, not to you, but to your daughter, is absolutely disgusting. I'm just going to let her know that. She's going to keep your secret safe." Rosemarie took Cecilia's chin between her forefinger and thumb, raising her damp eyes back up again. "This information doesn't change anything. I promised you when you first told me, and I promise you now: *no one* will learn your secret. Just you, Reg and I, and this Jane Norfleet and her cousin, we're the only people who know about it now, and we're the only people who are going to know about it when this is all done. I give you my word."

Cecilia nodded the green light. Rosemarie stood, and as she made her way out, had to use every fiber of strength to avoid saying, *Don't worry. When I'm through with that little cunt, she won't know what hit her.*

"Fuck," Jason cursed as he pulled his left foot from the puddle. If he had stayed in his motel room, he never would have had to brave this driving, torrential, monsoon rain. But he needed a few fingers of whiskey. Six hours spent wracking his memory banks and making calls, searching for anyone who might be able to get him into a locked-down, abandoned hospital in a city under martial law – he *deserved* a few fingers of whiskey.

Of course, as long as he was in a bar, why not have all his fingers and toes worth of whiskey. It still wasn't enough to make him forget that without a way into United Community, his investigation had ground to a standstill. Not nearly enough to drown out the frustration simmering in his sternum as more and more people failed to recognize the girl in the photo cards he was liberally handing out.

Not even a little sparring had made Jason feel better; you could now add guilt into his cocktail of emotions. He felt bad for the two local dumbshits who thought he'd be fun to talk shit to. The way he looked, the way he was drinking, the wear on his hairline, they obviously thought they were picking on some middle-aged drunk, not a green beret who had learned from his pappy to hold his liquor with the best of them. They each left the bar with a souvenir for their mistake, one a broken jaw, the other a right arm. If he had been just a tad more sober, Jason might have escaped unscathed, but one of his punches had missed, smashing into the Pabst's mirror on the wall, shattering it and slicing up his knuckles. Jason left two hundred in cash for the bartender for the damage he had caused, and walked out with his right sock wrapped around his fist, soaked through with red like it had come off Curt Schilling's foot.

So when he slammed his foot into that puddle, Jason cursed Murphy, whoever the fuck he was, and his damn law. Jason was walking back to his motel with one sock on one foot, and of course that was the foot that landed in the puddle, instantly soaking it all the way through. When he rounded the corner to the avenue where he'd find his motel (a former Motel 8 or Super-6 or some combination of those words), he had already grown tired of the alternating patter of his dry foot with the squish-squish-squish of his saturated sock. He was tempted to remove both shoes and his sock, and just finish the journey barefoot – but with a sudden flash of Stephen King's Misery Chastain axing off Paul Sheldon's frost-blackened foot, he decided against it. Only a couple more blocks to go, besides.

As he approached his fleabag-away-from-home, he noticed one of Allied Armament's matte-black Hummers sitting on the curb, engine idling. The passenger door flew open and City Commander Rikeman lowered himself onto the sidewalk. "Mr. Lancaster. Thought you might like to know one of my patrols picked up a streetwalker with a purse full of valium and other prescription bottles, all with United Community pharmacy labels."

Jason was a little slower to get Rikeman's drift in his current state of mind, but soon smiled. "Probable cause."

"Bingo. I thought if we were opening 'er up, what the hell, no reason you couldn't join us for a quick spin through the place."

Jason turned for the motel. "Let me get some socks."

WEDNESDAY

The padlock clanged against the chain links as it fell open from Rikeman's hand. He dragged the gate wide and the four men waiting behind him giggled, lighting up the flashlights hanging from the barrels of their M4 assault rifles. They charged past him and onto the hospital grounds like a pack of rabid dobermans let off their leashes.

Allied Armament spoiled its men – when they left the company, they would be able to buy suburban McMansions three times bigger than most of them had grown up in, be able to afford three sports cars and the kinds of ritzy private schools for their kids that they used to mock. But beyond the pay and the benefits, patrolling Detroit's derelict streets was a thankless, unfulfilling job. These men were trained for combat, for missions with targets and objectives, for wars with end dates and victory parades, not for occupation, not for keeping watch over tenement avenues devoid of life or populated with homeless junkies. So any chance to *do* something – even just a couple laps of a hospital to round up some of the brain dead zombie squatters inside – was met with elation, with whooping and relished HOO-RAHs. Rikeman's small unit slipped and slid across the black ice between fence gate and Union Community's old ER entrance like school boys on a snow day, hollering with joy as they disappeared around the smashed remains of the automatic glass doors.

Only Rikeman and Jason remained outside the gate. The AASC officer nodded toward the towering building with a grin, as if to say, *After you.* Jason retrieved his own flashlight from his pocket, lit it up, and started to follow the grunts. "Hey, Bailiff," Rikeman's voice stopped him, "I can't let you in there with just that." Jason looked back with a smirk and removed his Kimber 1911 .45 from the back of his belt. "Holy shit, is that-- LAPD SWAT custom?" Rikeman noticed.

Jason just smirked back, pulled a round into the chamber, and continued on the same path as the men before him.

He stopped as he crossed over into this eerie wasteland of a building, surveying the waiting room lobby under his flashlight's circle of white light. The room was a disaster: chairs toppled, piled up or repurposed as barricades, every inch of the wraparound reception desk's surface covered with felled ceiling tiles and rifled-through patient files.

But one feature of this room had somehow been spared from the decay: a mural painted upon two walls, wrapping around one sharp corner. It was immaculate, as if one of the residents had each day spent his only hour of sobriety sponging it down. Jason drew closer to this work of art, undamaged by time or the elements. Several beautiful black bodies interwove in a sea of purple, old faces full of character, limbs and chests ripped tight with musculature, one man even sporting angel wings. But it was the hands that were so comforting, so inviting: the hands of the central figure, with massive kind face and white curly locks crossing over both halves of the painting, his giant hands reaching for Jason, some sort of brilliant, life-sustaining energy crackling between his palms. Jason had never been one for art, but this piece – where it was located amidst the ruination and crumbled drywall and unmistakable fetid piss stench – struck some sort of nerve inside him. The mural's central figure was supposed to keep a city and its people warm and safe and healthy, but his shamed eyes made Jason think he knew he had failed on all accounts.

Jason remembered his own mission, and shook off his trance. Clock was ticking. He moved on, finding the nearest stairwell.

He didn't know what he was looking for, hadn't even had the time to design the best way of doing the looking; all he knew was that Rikeman was giving him an hour to get through as much of the hospital as he could. He tried to cover each floor in some sort of efficient pattern so he didn't miss a square inch or a single room, didn't miss whatever evidence there might be that someone had built bombs in here.

No, he didn't know what the hell he was looking for; he just knew he wasn't finding it. Not in the Pharmacy where the Allied Armament guys had three gaunt, anemic addicts on the ground, flex-cuffing their wrists behind their backs, their ankles together, so they could drag them out. Not amongst the stacks of engorged red plastic bags on every floor, every one so full it was easy for Jason to read the words printed on their sides: "REGULATED MEDICAL WASTE – BIOHAZARD." And not in the exam room where a naked junkie was passed out over a table, another resident drilling away at the dryness between her legs with brutal pelvic thrusts, his eyes closed in some sort of fantasy world, any sort of fantasy world better than this place.

No, Jason didn't notice anything out of the extraordinary ordinary of this horrific place, nothing to give him pause or warrant closer examination, until the very moment his watch beeped the end of the hour. He was just opening the door into the nearest stairwell to return to the ground floor– when a piercing red light caught his eye.

There was no electricity in here; this was the first light besides his own flashlight he had seen in his sixty minutes. What was powering that red light, indicating the black surveillance camera hanging in the corner of this hallway's ceiling was recording? And how could this camera look so shiny black? Jason brought his flashlight beam right onto the lens: it was clean, no dust, none of the mold or grime that covered every other square inch of this place.

How and more importantly *why* was this camera, much newer than this hospital or anything else in it, getting power? And what was it supposed to be filming?

And who the hell was on the other side, who was monitoring its feed?

"Time's up, Bailiff," Rikeman's voice piped through the walkie on Jason's belt. *"We're out."*

Jason spun 180, debating going back – no, he had searched this fifth and final floor thoroughly. If that camera was there because this was the floor where the shit had gone down, where perhaps the bombs were built and stored and tested before delivery to Washington, all evidence of that was long gone. Jason could violate Rikeman's time limit and keep looking, but he was almost certain he wasn't going to find anything more a second time through. And all Rikeman would do is send those four rabid, starved drones up after him, to collect him before he was even a third of the way back down the hall.

Jason stared up into the eye of the camera one last time. He wanted to say something to whoever was on the other side, something like, *I'll find you*, something that masked how fucking lost he really was.

But he wasn't in an '80s Chuck Norris film. He was in awful reality. He turned and started his descent.

Rosemarie had committed the cardinal Washington sin. She had broken ranks. She called Clyde Dudley on Tuesday night following her last meeting with Cecilia and told the Senate Majority Leader she needed to see him and as much of the Republican Leadership as he could round up the next morning. After seeing how that student had broken the Professor, after hearing the tremble in her voice, she knew she wasn't going to be able to get an impassioned speech or press availability out of her. Rosemarie was going to have to take steps to fix this mess herself.

It went without saying that this meeting would have to be secret. The notion that the Irvings might have assisted with the selection of the current President's first Supreme Court nominee was already starting to make ripples through the media; if it was known Rosemarie was meeting with Republicans in the midst of his first confirmation battle, the American people – especially the Democratic Base, that nebulous group that was so important to Salas – would start to wonder whose side she, let alone the President, was really on. Was Salas's unity with the Irvings breaking down? Was Rosemarie Irving going behind the President's back? Who was in charge of this dog and pony show anyway? Confidence, party loyalty, Salas's coalition that had lifted him up to victory three years ago – all would start to fray.

More than anything, Rosemarie couldn't have the Democratic Leadership knowing about this meeting, not if she was going to pull off the maneuver she had in mind.

Dudley sat back to wipe his lips with the linen napkin from his lap. He had insisted Rosemarie come for breakfast, then emailed his Secretary an order she was to call into Pete's Diner first thing upon her arrival on Wednesday morning, before sending out a couple pages to retrieve it. Dudley's Whip was there, as was the Junior Senator from his state, plus four other Senators loyal to the cause. Dudley's Chief of Staff was the only non-elected official let into the room, eating his own order out of a styrofoam container while scribbling notes just off the main circle of power.

"Now I don't want you to worry for one little second, Madame First Lady," Dudley crooned in his quaint Kentucky drawl. "All of us in this room, we expect a filibuster. Oh, they just need to stamp their feet a little, make a good show of it, we understand that. We invented that. We just refuse to refer any further business, and they'll have to put their mouths where their money is. They'll get their camera time, then we'll move right along."

"We're not too worried about them breaking Senator Thurmond's record," the Republican Whip smiled. Majority Leader and future President Lyndon Johnson had refused to bring new business to the floor when it came time to vote on the 1957 Civil Rights Act, forcing Strom Thurmond to *actually* speak for the duration of his filibuster. He would last 24 hours, 18 minutes, a Senate record that still stood.

"I promise you gentlemen," Rosemarie said as she set down her fork, "they are not planning to go quietly into the night. They're ready to go to war over this one. They're ready to put on a spectacle."

"Standard operating procedure around here. We would have been disappointed with anything less."

"Nothing about this is standard operating procedure," Rosemarie replied, her eyes enough to wipe the smile off Dudley's face. "The President didn't want unrest on this one. He had hoped everyone would stow the usual partisan bullshit and do their part to help this process go as smoothly and painlessly as possible. He is very uncomfortable with how this is going down right now."

"Well of course he is," Dudley purred. "He was never in Congress. Ah, governors." His cohorts chortled their approval at this little dig. Reginald Irving had been in the House himself when he had moved over to the White House, so Dudley figured Rosemarie would appreciate, if not outright agree with, his sentiment.

"He's going to pull her." Rosemarie took that tone that had a way of sucking laughter right out of the throats of men.

"Bullshit."

Rosemarie nodded. "He'd rather the headlines say he was indecisive about his first pick – headlines that would disappear the second he announced a replacement – than that he's warring with his own party or that he doesn't share their values. He can't have that going into an election year. If the Democrats insist on embarrassing him, he's going to pull her."

Dudley sat forward, that calculated Southern affect disappearing for the first time (his true accent was forged in the Northeast prep schools he had attended from age five onward), his eyes blazing with concern. "You realize how difficult, how *ugly* this process is going to become if he teases us with this wonderful woman, then rips her right out from under us?"

"I've tried to tell him. Now I'm telling you."

"Us?" the Whip leaned forward. "All due respect, Ma'am, but what the hell can we do about it? *They're* the ones who're gonna filibuster."

"You're resourceful, powerful men," she smiled. "You need to find a way to convince them they *can't* filibuster."

After not returning to his motel from the hospital search until after 4 AM, Jason slept away most of the day. As crappy as the fleabag was, he was thankful his room at least had some semblance of black-out curtains. When he whipped them open near 4 PM, the sun had already descended behind the buildings of downtown, casting a dark shroud over the dregs of the city.

He took a hot, cleansing shower – the showerhead, more of an exposed pipe, shot out only one single, thin beam, but its hot stream was still enough to loosen his skin, its steam his pores – then unwrapped one of his other burner phones from its retail plastic and went for a long walk during which he would call Ollie. Whoever had tried to kill him in Washington would already know he was in Detroit from monitoring his last call with Miranda's brother. But he sure as hell didn't need to lead them right to his motel. So, under the assumption they would triangulate his calls with Ollie, he always made sure he was several miles away from the fleabag before placing one.

"Glad you called, dawg," Ollie's voice crackled into Jason's ear. "I didn't know how the hell I'm supposed to get in touch with you."

Jason winced; when he hadn't talked to Ollie in a while, it would always take him a moment to adjust to his forced ebonics. He may be a genius on a computer, but he was still just another suburban young white kid wishing his life would emulate his favorite hip hop albums. "You found something for me?" Jason continued.

"Public records had blueprints for the hospital – full floor plans, the whole nine. They 40 years old, so I don't know if they can help, but I'll leave 'em for you." Ollie had set up a Dropbox that Jason could access from any computer with an internet connection, and would dump things in there whenever Jason needed. Jason would just have to make sure, again, that whatever IP address he used to check the Dropbox was far, far away from his motel.

"Anything else?"

"It's owned by the April Group – April Group Property Development? You ever heard of them? They bought it about nine years ago."

"No, I haven't."

"Fifteen-year-old company. Based in Seattle. Private company."

Jason stopped walking, pointing a finger into the pavement for emphasis. "Did you see *anything* that could link them to the Supreme Court? Or politics or Washington at all? Any sort of lawsuit they're wrapped up in, or legislation they're trying to get passed? Anything at all that might give them some kind of motive?"

"Look, you're the Columbo, but it sure don't seem like it to me. Their most profitable subsidiary is called Waterford Villas. It's a bunch of care centers scattered throughout the country. For old folks and retards-- 'scuse me, the *handicapped*, mental and physical. These places are top of the line, raking in bank. They bought your hospital at auction in 2010 and filed paperwork to turn it into a Waterford."

"But?"

"You know how it works. Not as many white people moved in around it as they was hoping. The area never made a comeback. They haven't done anything with it since."

"Okay. Good work." Jason was grateful, and felt like the kid deserved a little reward, a little encouragement that his efforts were in pursuit of a worthy cause. "She's alive, Ollie."

"What?"

Jason took a deep breath. "Miranda."

The line went silent. Jason pushed a finger into his opposite ear to make sure he didn't miss any of Ollie's reaction.

"You know what, that isn't funny." Jason noticed Ollie's usage of a proper contraction and knew he really had his attention.

"I'm serious. She called me. She left me a message."

"That doesn't make any sense. Why would she just disappear like this—?"

"I'm going to find out. She's still out there. And this hospital is the only clue we've got that might lead to her."

He paused, but Ollie didn't say anything, trying to process this bombshell. Then, finally, he said, "And is Gordon with her?"

"What?" Jason said. "Who's Gordon?"

"Ah, no, nobody--"

"Ollie, your parents mentioned him too. Who the hell is Gordon?"

"He's my sponsor. Miranda hooked me up with him. I'm sorry, man, since she, she died or whatever, I've been doing things I shouldn't be doing. I just-- That's my guilt coming out, y'know, Gordon on my mind."

Jason considered how to respond. He knew this was a lie. "Ollie, if this Gordon could have something to do with where Miranda is now, with what she's done, I need to know …"

"Nah, man. You know I want you to find her as much as you do. I'm doing everything I can. I'm here when you need more help. Whatever you need."

The line went dead. Ollie had hung up. Jason wanted to push harder, but he also knew he couldn't stay on this phone, a homing beacon for whomever was looking for him, all through the night. He thumbed the power button dead, then dropped the phone into a wastebasket.

He stopped at the next corner to look around, scouring the streets for some sort of internet café or copy center, anything that might have computers with internet connections. But everything he could see was either boarded up or didn't offer much beyond liquor.

He was going to have to head downtown.

Jane Norfleet's throat burned like she had swallowed a handful of sewing needles. She could count on one hand the number of times she had smoked weed since graduating from Brown, leaving her well out-of-practice for the clearing of a two-foot bong. She tried to hold in the mouthful of smoke, but it wouldn't be contained, punching out of her lips and nostrils, her throat erupting into a violent cough that made her former college roommate Patty Jacobi laugh uncontrollably for the next several minutes.

Jane was in the bathroom, leaned over the sink, sucking in tap water to try to cool the burn, when she heard the doorbell ring. She was looking in the mirror examining her eyes – now reddened, watered down orbs that looked like Mars appearing through a rainstorm – when she heard Patty exclaim, "Holy fuck!"

"Patty? You all right?"

"She's here for *you*," Patty exclaimed, appearing in the doorway of the john. Jane noticed she was shaking.

"Who's here for me?"

"I think you better go out there," Patty implored her. "I'm really fucking high."

That makes two of us, Jane thought as she pushed past her old friend and stepped out into the living room of Patty's modest one-bedroom. The first person she noticed was the Secret Service agent posted in the corner. And then the woman examining the book case spun around. "Holy fuck," Jane echoed.

"You must be Jane," Rosemarie Irving smiled, stepping closer, making a point of not looking down at the grease-stained pizza boxes or smoldering bong.

"I, I, I'm sorry about my eyes. I've been sick."

"You don't have to worry. I'm here as a fan of yours. And a representative of Alterman & Richbourg. You know the firm?"

"Of course."

"Oh good. Then you may know I've had a long relationship with them. I worked at A&R after clerking for Chief Justice William Quint. I had just made partner when I met my husband and decided to join him in Oregon. But the partners and I have remained very close. They've asked me to extend an offer to you."

"An offer?"

"When you graduate from Notre Dame next year, they'd like you to join their firm as an Associate. Any of their fifteen offices, it's your choice. You would start September 1st." Rosemarie held out a large white envelope, the firm's fancy logo filling the upper right-hand corner. Typed in the center of the white were just two words: Jane's name.

Jane accepted the envelope, opening it and pulling out the cover letter inside. Her bloodshot eyes grew wide as she read the details of the offer.

Rosemarie smiled. "I think you'll agree the compensation package is quite generous."

Jane dropped the envelope to her waist, her shoulders sagging with annoyance. Every law student in America dreamt of this, the moment they received their first offer from a firm. Now Jane would always remember her moment as tainted. "You've got to be fucking kidding me."

"Excuse me?"

"You think I don't know what this is about?"

Rosemarie nodded. "You will have to sign a confidentiality agreement covering anything and everything you know about Cecilia Koh in order to make the offer official."

Jane shoved the cover sheet back into the envelope, then held the package out to the former FLOTUS. "Forget it."

"Ms. Norfleet--"

"With all due respect, Mrs. Irving, it's a lot of money. But my principles mean more to me than money."

"I think that's very admirable. That's why I spoke with Justice Winks about you, and he said he would love to hire you as a clerk for next term. And the A&R

offer will still be good a year later, when you complete your clerkship at the Supreme Court."

Jane shook the envelope, not relenting.

Rosemarie took a step forward, eyes burning with ferocity. "Young lady. I think you need to understand how much power I wield in the firm you'll be joining. They've agreed to guarantee you a partnership within two years of going to work there."

But Jane didn't move.

"Let me be absolutely clear about the word 'guarantee.' You don't even have to show up for work for two years, and you'll still be promoted to partner. That's how serious I am."

"Oh I understand, Mrs. Irving. I know exactly how serious you are. I know this is how everyone in Washington gets ahead, by trading favors and access. But the rest of us have to earn our place the old-fashioned way, through things like hard work and determination."

Rosemarie remembered being this young, this idealistic, this stupid. She was furious the impertinent little shit was making her perform such a dance, but she also knew better than almost anyone on the planet that no matter what she did, Jane wasn't going to budge, at least not yet.

So Rosemarie smiled, took the envelope back, and made her way out.

Jane heard Patty applauding from the hallway behind her right before she leaned over and covered the carpet with vomit.

Day Two and, like Professor Koh before him, Judge Goldman was sailing through the vetting process. Like the Professor, Goldman had been vetted and background checked five years before; the Irvings had considered him as a nominee when faced with the possibility of concurrent Court vacancies during Reginald's presidency. Goldman had never even been informed he had been considered then – Justice Claudine Egan returned to work less than two weeks after being secretly diagnosed with liver cancer, and therefore never had to be replaced – but he had passed the background and financial records checks with flying colors, was approved by the bar association, and remained on the list they dug out whenever rumors or innuendo of an impending open seat sprouted up.

Dennis was the first person to interview the Judge in person for a nomination, and he had a blast doing it. On Tuesday, Goldman filled out the 500-question "pop quiz" in under three hours. In the face-to-faces, he was insightful, brilliant, and often even hilarious. He also had insisted that his newest clerk Janaki Singh be allowed to listen in and take notes on the interviews, and Dennis enjoyed the sport of trying to sneak glances over to her without it being too obvious. He kicked himself after she caught him once. *Hey! What are you doing? What, bored already? Being the lone vetter for new Supreme Court justices isn't exciting enough for you? Eyes on the prize, buddy, eyes on what you're here to do. If Goldman gets nailed in his hearing for something you didn't warn the Irvings about, that's what's gonna go on your tombstone. So you better not screw this up. When this is all over, there will be plenty of girls just as pretty as— What the hell, there you go, staring at her again! Eyes back on the Judge!*

"So," Dennis recovered with a smile directed at Goldman, "your wife leaves you last year after … 26 years of marriage?"

Janaki looked at her watch. *Day Two, Hour Seven.* She had been waiting on pins and needles for this moment, wondering when Dennis was going to either stumble, or dive headfirst, into this most delicate area of Goldman's past. She had seen it in the Judge's eyes just two mornings ago when she herself had broached the topic. There was much more to the Goldmans' separation than boredom or a midlife crisis or two. She didn't know if there was infidelity involved – or on whose part – but when Janaki had surprised him with this topic during that initial discussion of her outline down in the Courthouse garage, the Judge had clenched up with more tension than she had seen in her entire first month in his employ.

But once he was being vetted, the Judge knew this question would be coming, and had prepared himself for it. He sat forward with calm eyes and answered, "Yeah. She thought we had grown apart. Sometimes that happens."

"So, you don't think it's relevant at all to this confirmation process?"

Goldman stuck out his lower lip. "I don't see how." As Dennis took a simple note on the subject and turned the page of his notebook to move on, Goldman smiled and added, "If the Court grants Cert to a case on the constitutionality of divorce, I promise to recuse myself."

Janaki was jotting down her own notes on the Judge's response – *Well thought out. Well-rehearsed. Totally unalarming. Complete and utter bullshit.* — when she noticed one of the guys from Secret Service crossing the floor of the White House's secret casino with phone in hand, offering it up to Dennis.

"Mr. Coutts. First Lady Irving for you."

Dennis smiled at Janaki, then caught himself again, turning all-business as he accepted the phone and stepped away from the vetting table for a moment. "This is Dennis."

"I need you to do something for me," Rosemarie said into her phone as she rode back to the White House in the Irvings' armored Escalade.

"Yes, Ma'am?"

"There's a current law student at Notre Dame named Jane Norfleet. She's enrolled in Professor Koh's course. I want you to spend tomorrow finding everything you can on her."

"Okay. I'm not a private investigator. You want me to vet her as it pertains to legal issues, or--"

"No, you're not a private investigator. You're one of the lawyers for the President of the United States. You have much better resources than a private investigator. Trust me when I say I'm asking you to use those resources in the service of this nation."

"Of course. I would never doubt--"

"Get me everything on this girl. *Everything.*"

Dennis nodded. "Yes, Ma'am." But the buzz in his ear from the connected line was already gone.

Jason felt like he had just got off a plane at JFK from some third world Central American country. He felt like that college girl returning to the States from a semester off to discover herself, smelling of patchouli oil, her hair pulled back off her crown in violent, defiant braids, her skin painted with the darkest shade of tan it would ever know. Jason had returned to civilization, to the clean and pristine, after spending what felt like weeks in another world. Everyone he passed as he walked Detroit's Cultural Center Historic District looked educated, pretentious, spoiled – just *stinking* of ignorance of what lay a few blocks away. But for those few who chose to notice, the signs were there: the giant Allied Armament vehicles parked every couple blocks, the boys inside stationed like safari guides ordered to put down any stray beasts who might show up to devour Detroit's most cherished citizens.

Jason wasn't here to pen a social commentary. He was just here for an internet connection. He mounted the short steps up to the main branch of the Detroit Public Library, a Renaissance-style masterpiece of marble. This block of Windward, the Library facing off against the Institute of Arts, was like a random block of central Vienna air dropped down into the middle of the ruthless city.

Jason felt a certain warmth wash over him as he entered the building, a comfort level that usually only came in places he had been before; perhaps he somehow intuited that the Library was designed by one Cass Gilbert, who would fourteen years later design the Supreme Court building. After a perusal of the floor map, he made his way to International Languages, a collection he thought might be on the less busy side and hence, offer more available computer terminals.

Ollie was right about April Group Property Development and its Waterford subsidiary. Jason spent two hours poring through Google, through every news item he could find on the company – but found nothing that might link it to the Supreme Court bombings. They weren't connected to any cases that had come before the Court, or were scheduled to do so soon. They hadn't even had any conflicts with the communities in which they opened their properties, always welcomed with open arms, their arrivals consistently lauded by local press.

Jason sat back, attempting to rub the ache of frustration from his temples; he was already tired of this search, this enigma, and was growing impatient waiting for answers, any answer, to fall in his lap. He remembered why he had never had an interest in going into law enforcement; yeah, he had worked for the Supreme Court *Police*, but his job had always been one of protection, of prevention. This was the first time he had been presented with a real mystery, and that mixed with his renewed diet of whiskey was killing him.

Jason sat forward with one last idea. He found the homepage for Gmail, and banged through the steps to open a new account. Then he cut-and-pasted the Wikipedia link about April Group into an email, and wrote below it: *This company might be involved, but I can't find it. Do you see something I don't? – JL.* He punched in what he thought he remembered as George Aug's email address at Homeland Security and sent it on its way.

Finally, it was time to access Ollie's Dropbox and move the hospital blueprints onto the thumb drive he had brought in his pocket. As soon as he did that, *someone* out there, whoever was looking for him, would know he was at this IP address – if they didn't already from the email to Aug, but he figured it would take some time, and some analysis, to realize that was from him – and track him to the Library. He had to make the transfer quickly and get out of there.

He shoved his mini-drive into a USB port, and started transferring the files over. But as he moved them, he couldn't help opening each PDF and giving them short glances. The first floor, second floor, third … as he zipped through them, he remembered walking down each corridor, re-cataloging what he had seen in every room. First floor, second floor, third … soon only the Basement file remained in the Dropbox.

Basement file? He hadn't seen the fucking basement.

Something had just fallen in his lap – and it was a whole hospital floor.

"Today happened because of you," Reginald Irving's voice echoed from off-screen. Rebecca Whitford shot to her feet, waiting for him to come around to her, and right into the webcam's gaze.

Becks wasn't sure how many times she had watched this video in the three weeks since the former POTUS had said those words to her. She hadn't *heard* those words almost any of the times she had watched it – most times, she had reviewed it with the sound off, fast forwarding in silence to the moment when he shoved her down across her desk and force fed his manhood to her backside. Her monitor was faced away from her office door, so even if it was open, no one could see what was on her computer screen, and she would have plenty of warning if anyone was approaching, more than enough time to kill the video, adjust her seated posture and pray her panties hadn't gotten too damp.

But today, she needed more. President Salas was wracked with stress over the ugly turns the Koh nomination had taken, and every time he spoke about it, Becks could hear behind his words a little bit of *blame* – blame of her, of course. It was her, after all, that had set up his initial meeting with the Irvings about spearheading the nomination process, it was Becks who had encouraged him to give them the green light. So who else's fault could it be when the process wasn't one hundred percent smooth? With the vote scheduled to go before the Senate and the Dems' fili-bluff called in less than 24 hours, Becks had more than a little tension to release. She knew she wasn't going to be going home anytime soon, so goddammit, she was going to release it here.

She wished Irving was willing to give her that release. She had hungered for him since that surprise visit three weeks ago, but whenever they had been in the same room, he hadn't returned her eye contact for even a second. Oh, he would brush his eyes over hers when it couldn't be avoided, but they never locked in; he was a consummate pro at conveying with just his eyes that there wasn't going to be a return visit, a second brief encounter, at least not for a very long while. Becks was prepared for this; it had been the same when he was in office, when she was just a press aide, then his Deputy Press Secretary; each time he threw her a fuck, he was sure to not return to the well for several more weeks after that, killing any chance of unrealistic expectations, of unwelcome clinginess. He knew she wouldn't complain publicly – he knew how ambitious she was, and that meant she had just as much to lose, if not more, than he did. Heard from Monica Lewinsky lately? If Becks had ever screwed-and-told, she would be ten times as famous today, but ten times as much of a joke, ten times less hirable. She wouldn't be in the West Wing, but back in Western Mass.

For over four years, she thought she'd had her final tryst with Irving. It was in the Oval, his Oval – that was one she would never forget. She had snuck in there between meetings to notify him that she had taken a job as Deputy Campaign Manager on the Committee to Elect Antonio Salas President. Irving held back a slight chuckle at the news – this was before anyone thought Salas had a Hostess Sno Ball's chance in hell (including Becks herself, if she had to be honest, but she needed a campaign on her resume). The President stood, coming over to shake her hand and congratulate her and wish her good luck and broken legs and all that.

The second their hands touched, he pulled her in hard to gnaw on her lips like a starved wolverine. Then he threw her down and fucked her brains out right on top of the Resolute Desk.

Becks had pleasured herself numerous times to those memories. She had always wished she had some sort of recording of that afternoon – not because she would ever need evidence of fucking the President, but because it was the hottest fuck of her life and she wished she had it recorded for posterity. She had always been turned on by videotaped sex, much more than any other woman she knew. (She still laughed at the memory of her freshman year roommate Jin Hee Kim walking in on her fingering herself to hardcore internet porn.) And so, when Irving appeared in the threshold of her office three weeks ago, her first thought had been to covertly move her mouse to activate her webcam and burn everything that came next onto her hard drive. She didn't move, waiting for him to come to her – and right into the webcam's gaze.

A month later, on this stress-filled Wednesday afternoon, she closed her office door and locked it before coming around to her desk. Sure, this wasn't a hundred percent secure: the Secret Service and White House Security had the means to open it, but that added to the thrill and excitement of what she was doing. She could use that.

She pulled her skirt up as she sat, bunching it up around the tops of her thighs so she could get at herself, then found the video hidden within three different pass-locked files with boring titles having to do with appropriations and the environment and the deficit. She cranked the volume dial on her left speaker – the office was soundproof, just in case she ever had to review something sensitive with Salas.

"I wanted to make sure someone properly acknowledged you for putting us in front of the President. For getting this whole process started." Becks was already touching herself over her panties when, onscreen, Irving moved her beer bottle to the desk and stared into her eyes. She could almost smell him again as she caressed cotton into her mound.

He grabbed her, spun her around, shoving her down across the desk, reaching up into her skirt.

Becks pushed her hand down the front of her panties, touching her wetness in unison with Irving, matching the movement of her hand to what she remembered of his caress. She closed her eyes as she heard his belt fall loose, then the ripping of her panties coming off. Her gasps fell into perfect harmony with her recorded panting as the President pushed up into her; and in the present, she slid a finger inside. She kept her eyes closed, just listening to his grunts and her moans.

There was a click at the door – *someone was opening it.* A Secret Service man was coming in, the President's lead guard, Hifrael. He had to have an urgent message about Salas if he was going to undo her locks to deliver it. But when he saw Becks with her hand between her legs, that was all forgotten. He kicked the door shut behind him, dropped his trousers, stroking himself as he marched over to fill himself with that last needed bit of blood, shoved her chair back up against the wall, pulled her underwear down onto one ankle, and drilled her into the wall, one hand gripping the back of her chair for leverage as he rutted away, deep and hard and primal.

Becks fell back against her chair after she came. Her computer speakers had gone silent, the video long complete. She was glad that the fantasy of Hifrael had popped into her head just in time to carry her across the finish line.

She pulled her panties off her left foot as she stood, wiped herself with some Kleenex, then replaced her underwear with a fresh pair from her desk. She was ready to face whatever the rest of the evening might bring.

It took the Allied Armament guard patrolling the United Community fence less than ten seconds to process the sounds of violence coming from just over the grassy ridge. "Hey!" he yelled, using his fist-sized Maglite to find the mass of bodies: two large black men beating on a third, a smaller white guy, beating and kicking on him and showing no signs of relenting until his body did. "Break it up!" the guard screamed – already quite sure they had no intention of obeying. He charged at them, holstering the mag, raising his rifle, the beam of its own barrel flashlight casting a jail yard spotlight on the tussle. "Freeze! I said freeze, goddammit!"

As soon as he was within ten feet, the three men broke apart, the flashlight's corona lighting up the small Caucasian's pale white face, somehow devoid of any damage from the beating he was just taking. It also lit up his shaking albino hand—the one brandishing a Glock back at the Allied Armament grunt. "Whoa-whoa-whoa, take it easy!" the mercenary recoiled. "We don't need to do this!"

"You don't tell me what I need or don't need, mu-mu-muther fucker," the white junkie spit, his whole body shaking with hunger for his next fix.

It's amazing what three hundred bucks can buy you, Jason thought as he watched this stand-off from under a tree located about a football field off the action.

"Let's just put it down," the Allied Armament soldier pleaded, "and everything's going to be okay."

"We've got a four-seventeen in process," another AASC grunt was reciting into his shoulder-mounted walkie as he approached his colleague, rifle also brandished at the armed junkie.

Jason knew he had only seconds to move, mere seconds before the area was crawling with back up. He marched out of the shadows of his tree, into the full moonlight, rushing for the gate, trying to stay calm and *quiet* and not draw the guards' attention off the diversion he had choreographed.

Reaching the gate, he pulled one side as wide as it would go from its mate. He crouched down, sticking his head under the taut padlock chain and through to the other side. *Shit.* The rest of his body wasn't getting through; it was too tight. He was stuck out here in the middle of a full moon night, a sitting duck. He sucked in – grit his teeth – pulled and wrestled with the shaking chain links –

One of the guards thought he heard this, and started to turn … The junkie with the gun, who had always prided himself on doing things to the fullest, on always completing goals (he once ran a marathon; now, his goals were more along the lines of doing as much smack as he could get his hands on in a 12-hour period), saw Jason's tussle with the fence, saw the guard turning, and knew he had only a millisecond to act, to get the guard's attention back. Fail, and he would have to live with the guilt that he had cheated that dude out of his hundred bucks. He already had way too much guilt in his life.

He moved the barrel of his gun to his own temple. The AASC guys tensed up again. "No, no, no, don't do that!" they seemed to cry in unison. But neither turned back to the hospital, both locked on the gun man, giving Jason just enough time--

--to pop through!

He looked back once more. *Thank God for junkies with good work ethic.* Seeing Jason was through and their deal thus complete, the junkie threw his gun at the grunts' feet, then went down on his stomach, hands clutched behind his head. The men who two minutes ago looked like they were beating the shit out of him followed suit. The guards moved in to flex cuff them, one of them looking back at the hospital fence for the first time in several minutes: the gate was still secure, the padlock locked tight, with no sign of anyone on either side of it.

Jason was already inside the building, bypassing the waiting room mural this time, jumping right into his quest to find a way into this basement he had somehow missed the first time. First the North stairwell: no, it was just as he remembered; it went no lower than this first floor. Same with the South. If there was a basement under his feet, how the hell did he get down there?

He reached into his inner jacket pocket, pulling out his tablet (the smallest he could find in any store between DC and Michigan), and punched open the PDF of the basement blueprint, dancing it around his screen with his finger. There was one stairwell in the drawing, on the West side of the building.

Wait – the *West* side of the building. He hadn't seen a stairwell there.

Jason consulted the first floor blueprint, while darting for where it looked like this phantom stairwell would be located: an employee break room, with small kitchen, a couple tables, and several vending machines lined up against the walls, all smashed open, the treasures inside long since emptied out. On the wall above a machine that once housed potato chip bags and candy boxes, Jason could see the top of a door frame. He navigated his hands around the shards of the machine's face and dragged it off the wall – until he could see the entire door hidden behind it, the words 'EMPLOYEES ONLY' stenciled upon it.

Five more minutes of grunting, and Jason had the machine far enough off the wall to open that door, and stare down the steep steps into the pitch black basement below. He powered his flashlight to life (he hadn't needed it yet with the moon full and plenty of first floor windows), lighting up the paisley '70s floor pattern spreading out from beneath the final step. He made his way down, off that last step –

"Shit!" he cursed as his boot dunked into freezing water for the second time in 24 hours. That wasn't a paisley floor pattern his flashlight had illuminated, it was a thick layer of debris floating atop a half-foot or so of standing water. Jason shook his head, then submerged both his feet in the murk, the water rising up to about mid-calf.

The basement level was just like the five floors he had explored before it, one room packed with old banker boxes full of patient files, another stacked with old computers and microfilm machines. The one big difference was the stench; judging by the line of brown about a foot higher than the water line on every white wall – everything below the line stained a deep, fungal green – Jason realized that the basement must flood with every rain, and what he was breathing in was long-gestating mold.

He stepped into the final room – and tensed up. For the first time in all his hours spent in this hospital, he had found something that didn't add up. It at first seemed like nothing more than a windowless closet, the shelves lining its walls filled with medical machine parts probably abandoned before Jason was born. But someone had also taken the time to set this room up like some kind of replica of an examination or operating room: a bed covered with ratty blankets and yellowed paper had been rolled into the middle of the room and locked off, an instrument table nearby, a bowl filled with the most gruesome and rusted of medical tools on top of it.

But what interested Jason most were the coils of wires and tubes taped and stapled around the ceiling in haphazard mania, many descending down onto shelves below or out the door.

"Help," a tiny voice whimpered from a dark corner of the room.

"Hello?" Jason stepped forward, his flashlight finding a small animal cage shoved into the back recesses of a high shelf behind discarded machines. As he got closer, a face grimed with dirt, a girl's face, appeared among the slats of the cage.

"Please." She was young, maybe no more than 13 or 14, barely dressed, shivering with a chill – and no doubt fright. "Please help me."

Jason examined the lock keeping the cage sealed. "Stand back," he told the girl. He spun his .45 in his hand, aimed the handle like a hammer – and brought it down hard on the lock. *Once-twice-thrice*—the girl gasped and shrieked as Jason pistol whipped the lock until it broke clean off. He returned his gun to the back of his belt, then pulled the cage open and reached a hand in. "It's okay. You don't have to be scared."

She took his hand and he lifted her down into his arms. She buried her face in his chest, the sobs pouring out now. "Thank you thank you thank you."

"Shhh," he assured her. "You don't have to--"

"DON'T FUCKING MOVE!" Jason's head whipped up – a frayed and ratty, skinny-as-a-bone middle-aged man blocked the doorway. He had dragged another girl in with him, his elbow cocked around her throat in a head lock. "I got this whole room wired! Ask the girls, they'll tell you! You're gonna put her down, and get the fuck out of here, or BOOM-- I blow the four of us straight up to the kingdom, the power and the glory, just like that!"

In the man's other hand was a small little box, wires pouring from the top of it and winding up to the array on the ceiling. "I'm fucking serious! I'll do it, man!" His thumb bounced on the box's red button, itching to depress it.

THURSDAY

Jason set the girl from the cage down, raising his arms to shoulder level.

"Good," the self-proclaimed bomb maker grinned. "Now you're just gonna slowly, calmly walk out of here. No one's gonna get hurt. You're gonna go back upstairs. And leave us be."

Jason yanked his Kimber .45 out of his belt again – everyone yelped, girls and bomber alike, as Jason took aim right at the bomber's head.

"What the fuck you think you doing?" the bomber screeched. "I said I'll do it, man, I'll blow these little girls up. I'll blow myself up! I don't fucking care, I got a lot less to live for than you do!"

"No shit. But you're not going to blow anyone up."

"Oh, you're so sure, are you?" the crazed sicko tightened his grip on the girl in his arms, making her suck in sharp gasps of fear. "You're so fucking sure?"

"I spent over a decade as a Combat Engineer with the Green Berets. You know what that means, smart guy?" The bomber was silent now, trying to just get his frantic breaths under control. "It means I spent over ten years building bombs, detecting bombs, taking bombs apart. Eating, drinking and sleeping with bombs. So, yes, I'm sure. You may have made these poor girls believe you'd turned this room into a bomb – you may even in the deep recesses of your sick little diseased brain believe it yourself – but I knew the second I looked around this place. Those wires coming out of that little box in your hand? They don't do jack shit."

The bomber's fingers quivered, until the box just fell from them, clattering onto the floor.

But he wasn't ready to give up just yet. He grabbed the top of his captive's matted hair with his now-free hand, pulling a handful into his fist to make her scream, tightening the grip of his headlock around her throat. She pawed at his forearm, choking out deep, breathless coughs. "I don't need a bomb to kill this bitch," he grit through clenched teeth. "I've killed before."

"I don't doubt it."

"I have. So you're still gonna leave. Yeah, you are. Or I take her head clean off."

Jason sighed. He hoped it wouldn't come to this.

He hoped he wouldn't have to put a slug right between the guy's eyes.

The girls both screamed as the bomber fell straight backwards without a peep, his convulsing body pulling his captive down onto the concrete floor on top of him.

Jason pried her free, pulling her loose from the bomber's death grasp. She moved right into a hug, pulling herself tight into Jason's chest.

"Shhh, it's all right," he tried to quiet her tears. "Everything's going to be all right now."

The spectacle began at 10:08 AM. That was when the President pro tempore of the Senate announced that debate would commence on the motion to Consent to the President's Nomination of Cecilia Elizabeth Koh as Associate Justice of the Supreme Court of the United States.

It was clear just 19 minutes into Wisconsin Democrat Theodore Werder's opening speech that the party in the minority intended this debate to go on for quite a while: the 19 minute mark was when he began a meticulous, dripping-with-dramaturgy reading of the Prologue to *Romeo & Juliet,* followed by a half-hour of wondering aloud how many "star-cross'd young lovers out there" would have the rest of their lives dictated by the mistakes of their youth if Cecilia Koh were confirmed to the bench.

It was in the second hour of Senator Werder's speech, when workmen started carrying cots through a corridor that wound right by a gathering of news cameras, that the whole thing graduated to spectacle. Every network cut into their regular programming to announce over shots of the cots that the first filibuster of a Supreme Court nominee in history had begun. The intended message of the temporary beds was clear: the Democrats planned to stay in the Capitol as many hours and days and nights as it took to force the withdrawal of Cecilia Koh. (The timing did inspire John Oliver to explain that the Dems had decided to institute a policy of midday naps into their legislative day.)

Minority Leader Geoff Wyley began his press availability at Noon sharp, beaming over to the 9 AM West Coast, his Whip and several of his most loyal followers arrayed behind him as he explained to the media that his forces were rested and ready to wage the great battle that lay before them. He had figured the more Senatorial faces behind him as he explained this, the better it would look on everyone's televisions back home in Tampa.

All that tableau of faces really did, however, was accentuate the confusion and horror when the first reporter brought up the joint press conference Clyde Dudley was giving with Bryce Lafayette at that very same moment. "I'm sorry?" Senator Wyley's beady eyes squinted out at whoever had asked that question. "I'm not aware of--"

"Senator Dudley is giving a press conference right now, as we speak, with the President of the NRA."

"I really know nothing about that, so I couldn't comment on--"

"They're both announcing their endorsement of the background check bill from last year."

For a few seconds, none of them, no one in Wyley's cute little tableau of solidarity, even moved. Then the whispers started spreading like wildfire; a couple of the Senators even broke from their assigned spots to go grab the nearest aide, anyone's aide, and ask what the hell was going on.

Much earlier in the Session, twenty-one months earlier to be precise, three Democratic Senators had sponsored a bill that would require all gun sellers – even private dealers at gun shows – to perform some sort of background check of potential buyers before completing any firearm sale. Though these checks had the support of over 90 percent of respondents polled in both parties, the NRA once again put enough pressure on the Republicans on the Judiciary Committee to make sure the bill died there and never made it before the full Senate body. Why would the NRA change their tune and endorse the bill *now*? Wyley – and every single Senator arrayed behind him – had a sinking feeling they knew why.

Wyley drew the press conference to a quick close, charging for the Democratic cloakroom – he was sure the TV there would be turned not to his, but Dudley's, spectacle. Indeed, Wyley entered right as NRA President Bryce Lafayette was completing an answer: *"... this country is ready for responsible background checks, and so is the NRA."*

"Senator Dudley, assuming the bill should have no problems getting through the Judiciary, when will you bring it before the Senate for a vote?"

"I'm standing here with Mr. Lafayette because I respect his organization so deeply," Dudley explained, his each and every word dripping with dramatic flourish. *"If they're ready to support background checks, then so am I, so is my*

caucus, and so, I'm sure, will our colleagues in the House. But the unfortunate truth is that we're running out of time in the legislative calendar. Thanksgiving is in two weeks, then we come back in December, and we've got to jump right into a tough budget discussion. The hard, cold facts are that we're not going to have time to consider the background check bill unless we get Cecilia Koh confirmed this week and can move on to other business."

"Senator Dudley! Can't you just table the Koh confirmation in order to vote on background checks?"

Dudley took his time with this answer, milking this moment he had so brilliantly crafted. *"Young man. Think about how irresponsible that would be. One of our three branches of government is just frozen right now. Unable to move, unable to do anything, unable to complete its part of the Constitutional bargain. Well, it is my duty to the Constitution to get that judicial branch back up and running. I can't with a clear conscience distract this body with anything else until we've done just that. But if the Democrats want to hold up the business of government over nitpicking a very qualified nominee, then that is their right of course, and when things like background checks fail to move forward as a result, they'll just have to answer to the American people."*

Wyley slammed his hand down on the nearest hard surface while the half-dozen other blue Senators in the room cursed or moaned. He didn't know Clyde Dudley was close enough to Bryce Lafayette to pull off a stunt like this – but of course, one wouldn't have to be very close to get Bryce Lafayette all hot and frothy about Cecilia Koh. Bryce Lafayette wasn't just the president of the NRA, he was also on the advisory board of the NRLC, the National Right to Life Committee.

The filibuster was finished. The Republicans only needed one Democratic vote to end it in cloture, and now that universal background checks waited on the other side of Koh's confirmation, they would probably get twenty- or even thirty-one.

"That goddamn bitch," Wyley growled deep in his throat. He knew who had orchestrated this, who had warned the Republicans they were going to filibuster, who had given them time to prepare this cunning counter-offensive.

The filibuster was finished. But Geoff Wyley wasn't.

Professor Koh's best friends had always been books. When her parents would move her from military base to military base, the only friends she could take with her with her books. Books were why she had chosen to give up a skyrocketing legal career (her firm had offered her partnership after just four years) and move into academia. She never loved the brief writing, the confrontation, the rainmaking. Cecilia loved libraries. She loved the smell of browned books and rotting spines wafting through her nostrils as she strolled through the dusty old stacks, then found herself a corner table where she could literally disappear from the world for days. Yes, in academia she had to devote several hours a week to *people,* to teaching and student interaction, but she would also have full access to the library, and time to read, full spring breaks and summers and two-week winter holidays to read.

On Thursday, with thousands of people all over the country discussing her life and her future, Cecilia decided to forget it all and devote her day to her two favorite things: disappearing and reading. She had been warned these days would be the worst of the whole process, maybe the worst of her whole life, worse even than the confirmation hearings, these days of sitting, *waiting* for a vote, unable to do anything except pray that no surprises popped up before the Senate got through their hours of preening and posing and just got the goddamn vote over with. She went to the most beautiful library on the planet, into the Law Library Reading Room at the Library of Congress, and got lost for hours.

Her hotel room was already shrouded by dusk when she returned in the late afternoon, and the blinking red light on her bedside phone was bouncing off the white wallpaper around it. Cecilia thought that was strange – wouldn't Lindsey, wouldn't her kids, wouldn't Dennis, wouldn't the First Lady have called her cell phone?

"You really shouldn't have fucked with me," Jane Norfleet's message played into her ear moments later. Cecilia didn't move, just sat on the bed, listening to the whole thing. Jane had found her room number, Jane had somehow figured out her alias. Okay, in hindsight, maybe she could've gone more obscure than Herbert Choy, first Asian-American to serve on the federal bench. "Sending *Rosemarie Irving,* a fucking First Lady, to try to intimidate me? To try to blackmail me? I thought I could make you an important symbol in the war on women. Now I just want to *ruin* you.

"Check your email." Cecilia picked up her phone, and thumbed the envelope icon. She hadn't opened her email in days, and sure enough, it quickly updated with over 100 new messages congratulating her, requesting an interview, or closer to the top, trying to console her after her toughest day of hearings. And at the very top, there was the message from jnorfleet@ndlaw.edu, the paperclip icon of an attachment next to her address. "I've sent you a press release about your daughter's abortion. Don't worry, I haven't circulated it yet. You're going to withdraw your name before I get a chance. You're going to go back to being just an unknown, faceless teacher of an outdated, dogmatic form of law that should be dead in a generation. And then I'll delete that from my hard drive.

"But you should read it. If the Senate gets to a vote and you haven't withdrawn your name yet, I will email blast that to every newspaper, aggregator and blog in the country – and you will not just go down in flames, you will go down as the biggest failure in Supreme Court history."

There was a click, followed by the robotic voice alerting her, "*End of message. To delete this message ...*" Cecilia didn't delete the message, didn't even hang up the phone. She just let the receiver drop to her shoulder and, for the first time since the Irvings offered her the nomination, let the tears roll down her cheeks.

Rikeman got in the back seat of his company Hummer. He preferred sitting behind the front passenger seat, but Jason was already there. "You were right," Rikeman said. "The wires weren't connected to anything. They were all pulled out of various pieces of old equipment the hospital had stored in the basement."

Jason's eyes stayed locked on the rain patterns of the windshield. "But you're going to tell me I need to make something up about how I thought he had a weapon."

"You're in Detroit, remember?" Rikeman smiled. When Jason didn't laugh back, his own countenance got serious again. "Bethany, the girl you saved, she says he was going to choke her out. You did what was necessary to save her. I see no reason to say anything different in my report." Still, Jason didn't respond. No word of thanks, not even eye contact. "They'd love to see you again," Rikeman fished. "Those girls. They want to thank you."

"I was glad to help. But I wasn't there to help them."

"We pulled that camera out of the wall on Five. As far as my guy can tell, it was just left on and was still sending its pictures back to the central hospital security office. But I told him to tear it open and look closer. I'll let you know if he finds anything."

Jason rubbed his chin with a sigh. That didn't fit. The camera was too new, too clean.

"There's nothing in that basement, Bailiff. If the bombers were in there, if they did use the hospital as their staging grounds, they're long gone and knew how to clean up after themselves. I'm sorry." Rikeman leaned forward, tapping his driver on the shoulder. The engine thundered to life and they started to roll over the weeds that had sprouted through the parking lot asphalt. "Give you a ride back to your motel?"

Even after a month working for the First Lady, Dennis still got a rush when he thought about the Access-with-a-capital-A he had unexpectedly acquired overnight. His flight into South Bend was just descending when he day dreamed about how he was going to use it against this Jane Norfleet, whoever she was. *"Dennis Coutts,"* he imagined announcing in his deepest Chris Meloni voice as he entered the Notre Dame registrar's office. *"I'm an investigator with the offices of Rosemarie Irving."* If only he had some sort of badge. He would have to work on that.

But he quickly shook this fantasy off – about the stupidest thing he'd ever day dreamt, in a life of doozies.

It was about two weeks into his new job that he had first realized this new power he wielded, starting when Rosemarie had given him the assignment of collecting everything he could find on a case that the Supreme Court was scheduled to hear in the current term, *Agguire v. Detroit.* An obscure claim barely covered in the media, Dennis figured the task to be a test, one he was determined to pass with flying colors. Unfortunately, most of the paper records of this term – every scrap from every Justice's office to every clerk's cubby hole – had been lost in the bombing, explained Acting Marshal Gregor Meyers, a tightly-wound baritone-voiced career government employee with an overgrown goatee of red.

"Of course," Meyers added just as Dennis was rising to his feet, "that whole case should've been copied and taken down to the Vault, too."

"The Vault?"

"Permanent Records. It's a vault two floors under ground, below the garage and mailroom level, basically a giant underground box encased on all sides in seven feet of concrete. Not a wisp of smoke from the fires got down there."

"And all paper records go down there?"

"Eventually. When a case is going to be heard in a current term, its paper trail is spread out amongst all the Justices who are in the process of reading about it and arguing it, plus their clerks who are sending memos back and forth about it. Then there's all the green briefs that come in from outside parties who feel like they should be heard ..."

"Uh huh?" Dennis pushed for the punch line.

"But as soon as a decision is announced, everything gets collected, organized and sent downstairs. We're required by law to have a complete paper record of every term in its entirety down in the Vault."

"And *Agguire v. Detroit* was originally heard last term," Dennis reminded himself, "before they postponed it."

Meyers nodded. "I can't guarantee it, but if regulations were strictly followed to the letter of the law here, then everything on that case should've been copied and sent down to the Vault."

And when Meyers heard that Dennis was working for Rosemarie Irving, he was more than happy to let him in down there to find out for sure. (Meyers had not only voted twice for Rosemarie's husband for President, but had just started in the Court Police the year she clerked for Justice Quint; though he had little to no direct interaction with her in that year, he still took pride in her future achievements, always referring to her with colleagues or family as "Court trained" or "one of the Court's own.")

It took over a week for approval to come in from Homeland Security and the Secret Service, but eventually, the Acting Marshal was granted entry onto the bombed-out ruins. Dennis had already been on these tragic grounds once before, on the day the President announced Cecilia Koh as his first nominee. But on this second trip, at dusk, the purple sun slowly disappeared through the melted columns and beheaded support beams, and Dennis felt like he was a first responder at Pompeii. They were escorted by two DC fire department personnel who cleared away debris to get them down into the basement garage. They thumbed their flashlights to life, and Dennis followed them through the maze of abandoned cars covered in soot and ash, some even with their roofs completely caved in by the toppled ceiling.

"Here you go," one of the firemen said as they sifted through enough rubble to uncover a stairwell door. At the bottom of the steps was a red metal door, with a keycard access pad mounted next to it. But when the Marshal's keycard failed to open the electronic locks, they had to wait yet another hour for this section of the grid to be turned back on.

At the stroke of 9 PM, they were finally stepping through the airtight seal, walking past the abandoned security desk, and entering this giant warehouse of a library, boxes upon boxes of old papers and files stacked upon shelves going a quarter-mile in every direction. "So this is where they took the Ark," Dennis smiled. Then, noticing Meyer's complete lack of recognition, tried to explain, "You know, the end of *Raiders*? Indiana Jones?"

The Acting Marshal may not have been gifted with the wit of his predecessor, but he was invaluably resourceful in leading Dennis to exactly the boxes he needed. He even helped stack them onto a dolly, then wheeled the heavy, awkward beast around every corner until they were pointed in the direction of the exits.

Dennis was just starting to push the cart up a ramp when he heard the Marshal's voice call out behind him one more time: "You can't forget this!" Meyers ran up the ramp to catch up with Dennis, handing him a small jewel case of clear plastic, its lid just transparent enough to see the compact disc inside.

"Ah, digital copies of everything," Dennis assumed.

"All the audio files. Oral arguments, the decision--"

"Or, in this case, the day they announced they were rescheduling the case for this term, I bet."

"Plus any inter-office phone calls pertaining to the case, a recording of the Justices' conference after orals, any personal audio recordings the Justices may have made while writing their opinions or dissents--"

"You keep all that?" Dennis was so flabbergasted, he let go of the dolly just long enough for the cart to start careening back down the ramp.

Meyers chuckled, reaching out and grabbing its handle before it plummeted to its doom. "This is the United States government. We keep everything."

Wyley and the Democratic Leadership met with Dudley and his Republicans about one hour after the background checks announcement. Though he held all the chips, Dudley accepted Wyley's first offer: the Democrats would end their filibuster without requiring the rigmarole of an official cloture vote, if Dudley would still honor the rule that kept debate open for another thirty hours following the end of a filibuster. The thirty hour requirement was noteworthy as, barring a late-night or weekend session, it would mean the vote wouldn't occur until first thing Monday morning. Dudley could live with that, especially considering that, barring any unforeseen surprises, this agreement virtually guaranteed Cecilia Koh's confirmation.

Wyley walked out of the conference room with the satisfaction of a small victory of his own, as he explained to the Irvings when he met with them privately that evening: "I have until Monday morning to convince the President to pull the Koh nomination. I won't need nearly all that time."

Rosemarie sat back with a laugh. She had won, and wasn't sure why they were even taking this meeting. But like it or not, Geoff Wyley was still one of the most powerful Democrats in Washington, and they still had three nominees to go. They still had to kiss the ring. "Senator," Rosemarie smiled, "I can't tell you how much I respect your conviction. But this round is over. It's time we all moved on – together."

Wyley opened a hand to his Chief of Staff on his right. She pulled a single piece of paper out of a leather binder and handed it to him. He slapped it down hard on the table, then pushed it across to the Irvings.

Reg picked it up, and over his shoulder Rosemarie could see it was a short letter addressed to President Salas, a dozen or so messy John Hancocks scribbled below it. "It's only thirteen signatures," Wyley explained. "But it will be more than enough to convince the President to see the error of his ways."

"Thirteen--?" Reg asked.

"Thirteen Senators who have pledged to vote down every Supreme Court nominee we see the rest of the President's term, should the Cecilia Koh nomination go through."

"You're in the minority," Reg smiled, laying the letter down flat on the surface of the table. "After Cecilia goes through, the Republicans are going to owe us big."

"How big, Mr. President? You have to ask yourself, will they owe us enough? Without our 13 votes, you'll only have 28 other blue votes guaranteed on each nomination. You'll need to recruit 22 more Republican votes on each one, to get to a tie that the Vice President can break." Wyley sat forward. "Are you really willing to give them that much power, just for Koh? Is she really that important to you? You know the kind of people you're going to need to nominate to get 22 Republicans? We're talking *four* Cecilia Kohs."

"Geoff," Reg implored, "you've just got to trust us on where this is going. We're *giving* them Koh, so that we can get nine of their votes on the progressive, liberal nominees I promise you we've got planned next."

Without another word, Wyley leaned forward, getting his fingers on the letter, pulling it back, then folding it up and returning it to the inside of his jacket. His Chief of Staff was already on her feet as Wyley stood.

Rosemarie couldn't control herself any longer. "I can't believe you're this myopic."

"Rosemarie," Reg implored with a raised hand.

"Worrying about the optics, the politics of this one vote, unable to see the big picture. Burning down our entire process, an entire presidency, all in the name of self-preservation. That's all this is about: you, and your political future. Well, we see right through it. It's the shallowest form of politics."

Wyley kept his back to them, hand on the door handle, for several seconds, before he uttered, "You know, Ivy League kids get hooked on meth too."

"What's that?" Irving asked.

"My daughter's freshman year at UPenn. Her first semester. We get a call she hasn't shown up for her first three finals. Four days later, we find her in a downtown Philly meth lab."

Reg stood. "We had no idea--"

"We promised her no one ever would. She had to take the rest of the year off. She wasn't just broken. She was pregnant. And if abortion had been illegal, her life from that moment forward would have been totally different. She might never have returned, never have graduated." A smile broke through his pursed lips. "I might still be going to her graduation from Stanford Law next May. Or maybe I wouldn't be. Who knows. But shouldn't a young person have every opportunity to correct their youthful wrongs? I sure did." He turned back to them, eyes ablaze. "There is a very thin line separating the two sides of this issue. That line protects young people just like my daughter. So don't you dare accuse me ever again of playing political games with that line. As far as I can tell, I'm the only person in this room who would never, *ever* do that."

Long after he left, the Irvings still couldn't look at each other.

FRIDAY

Rosemarie Irving would never admit to anyone, least of all herself, that as she looked over the corkboard of candidate headshots set up in her temporary office in the North Wing of the Capitol, she was considering who might make a good replacement for Cecilia Koh. Rosemarie Irving never acknowledged fear, never admitted defeat.

"Madame First Lady?" Cecilia's voice – it seemed to have gotten tinier and tinier as this process dragged on – squeaked from the door behind her.

"Professor," Rosemarie turned with a smile, "I thought you promised to call me Rosemarie."

Cecilia smiled. "It still feels a little strange. I knew who you were over-- Oh gosh, was it 30 years ago? When you won the national title for Moot Court?"

"Couldn't have been. We must both just be terrible at math."

"Yes, that must be it."

As the small talk continued, the Professor's eyes couldn't help but graze over to the board behind Rosemarie, one side blank save for an outdated photo of her (she wished she still looked that good) thumbtacked above a photo of a man with white hair and wide eyes; the other side of the board, populated with at least two dozen more photos. Processing what this display was, she darted back to the door, pushing it shut. "I'm so sorry! Am I even supposed to …? Dennis said I could find you in here."

"You've trusted us with your most precious secrets. We trust you with ours. Besides," Rosemarie turned to look up to the board with a grin, "you're the one who's going to have work with three of these people for the rest of your life."

"That's why I wanted to see you. My husband's coming in today."

Rosemarie whipped back around. "Reg and I would love to meet him. I hope you understand the things I said about him, that was purely strategic--"

"He's going to drive me back to South Bend." That's when Rosemarie noticed the envelope in Cecilia's hand. Tracking her gaze, the Professor held it up. "It's for the President. Thanking him. And withdrawing."

"I promised you I would handle Ms. Norfleet."

Cecilia turned away, walking to the other side of the room, looking around at the beautiful hand craftsmanship of the 200-year-old walls. "'The Face of the Movement.' That's what Pat Robertson called me today." She scoffed, shaking her head. "How can I be the face of the movement?" She turned back, holding up the envelope again. "This isn't because of the extortion. This is about my conscience."

"It's never coming out, Cecilia. I promised you. If you think what you did was a mistake – well, let that mistake fuel you. That mistake is what makes you the *perfect* face of the movement. And it's a mistake no one except your family will ever know."

"Maybe not in the next week. But I get on this Court, someone's always gonna be gunning for me, gunning for my husband, searching for dirt. You won't always be there to protect me."

Cecilia had to look away – Rosemarie's eyes were too powerful, too persuasive. "After my parents fled North Korea, they never talked to either of their families again. I never knew my family. And my husband's family never really embraced me. My children, they have their issues, but they're the only thing that's prevented me from being the loneliest person on the planet. I've spent my whole career being this perfect, by-the-book, unfeeling machine. My kids are the only thing that makes me human." She turned back, locking in on Rosemarie's eyes. "Nothing is more important than my kids. Nothing. Not even the Supreme Court."

Rosemarie nodded. Cecilia thought she might be getting through to her for the first time. "I understand, of course. If that's how you feel, I respect that." Rosemarie walked toward her, offering up her hand for a shake. "It's been wonderful getting to know you."

Cecilia smiled with unadulterated relief as she took that hand. "Thank you, you too."

But Rosemarie wouldn't let go. She put her other hand over Cecilia's, and brought it in close to her stomach. "Just do me this one favor. Stay the weekend with your husband. We've already paid for your hotel suite; the two of you should enjoy it. On Sunday, Mitch Aldridge, our Secret Service guard, he'll pick you up at 9:15 and take you to St. John Neumann, a lovely little church up in Maryland. Reg and I discovered it when he was in the House. No one will bother you there. I swear, no one even recognized him until the week after he officially received the nomination at the Convention. Don't even think about the National Cathedral, it's a scene. Go to our church on Sunday, pray on all of this, this insane last month of your life, and if you still feel withdrawing is the right call, we will of course honor that. We'll have your name pulled almost 24 hours before the vote, and Ms. Norfleet will never get the chance to follow through on her disgusting threat."

Cecilia chuckled; she knew Rosemarie wouldn't let go until she got the answer she was looking for. "Okay, it's a deal."

They shook again, and as Cecilia made her way to the exit, Rosemarie turned back to her corkboard. "And Judge Goldman is an excellent choice," the Professor added before opening the door and disappearing down the hall.

Annie Hall was on. The vetting process was going so well, Judge Goldman had been given the weekend off, even granted permission by Rosemarie Irving to return to Philadelphia, as long as he kept up the façade that he had just been on a writing retreat trying to make progress on his long-overdue book memoir.

But Goldman didn't have any reason to go home. So why the hell not stay? He had given Janaki permission to return to Philly as well, but evidently she also had no reason to return, and as Friday evening descended on Alexandria, she was sitting on the floor of his hotel room sharing gyoza and General Tso's chicken with him, laughing along with him to *Annie Hall.* He figured he would be introducing her to something new, sharing one of the great pleasures in life with the youth of America; then the movie began and she said, "Yeah, I know, and such small portions," right in unison with Woody Allen – and Goldman realized she knew the movie even better than he did.

"You know, Singh, you're acutally much cooler than I originally thought."

"Yeah, go fuck yourself. Your Honor."

Watching the movie was of course a huge mistake, as Goldman knew it would be. But they were into the red wine now and he had always been a glutton for punishment. He had taken Alice to this movie for their first date over forty years ago, and they had made a tradition of watching it on several Anniversaries over the years, so he should have known how painful an experience it might be for him. So painful, that by the time Alvy and Annie were in line to see a movie, Goldman was sneaking his cell phone into his pocket, then getting up and slinking into the bathroom.

"Alice, it's me," he whispered into her voice mail. It was the first time he'd had the courage to call her since she moved out, since she told him about Elia. "*Annie Hall* is on. USA, I think, if you want to catch the end of it. Anyway, it just made me think of the Brattle Theatre and smile."

He paused, wanting to hang up. Instead, he exhaled that first pant of an emotional torrent, failing to hold back the tears. "They're going to make me a Supreme Court justice, Alice. I'm in Washington, and they're vetting me right now. I thought you might be proud of me. I thought …" He put his forefinger under his running nose, sucking in hard. "I didn't think anything. I know you're happy. I'm happy for you. Have a good night."

This time, he did hang up. His forehead collapsed onto the phone in his hand. He shouldn't drink wine. He definitely should never watch *Annie Hall.*

"Was the stuff on Jane Norfleet helpful?" Dennis asked from his South Bend hotel. He had been trying to reach Rosemarie for the last twenty-four hours, ever since he had transmitted his collection of materials to her. He still remembered the elation that gushed from the First Lady when he had aced that first assignment and delivered everything on *Agguire v. Detroit*. Well, not *everything*.

Gregor Meyers had called him in a panic the day after his visit to the Vault, explaining he was just learning all the procedures of the Marshal's job, and that he wasn't supposed to have granted access to most of the audio recordings to anyone but the Chief Justice. Would Dennis mind destroying the disc, and keeping Gregor's mistake to himself? Dennis had secretly copied all the audio files onto his laptop in case Rosemarie was disappointed with his initial haul and the need arose to prove to her he could get even more, but out of respect for Meyers, he deleted them as soon as she approved of his first delivery.

Unfortunately, he had struggled to earn anything close to that first day's huge smile again, and hoped his Jane Norfleet report might do the trick.

But more importantly, he really just wanted to get back to Washington, and get through the Goldman vet. He knew the Irvings wanted to announce the Judge's nomination the second that Koh was confirmed, and he didn't want to be the one that held all that up.

In the back seat of her Escalade, Rosemarie rolled her eyes. There wasn't much she despised more than compliment fishing. But Dennis was young and had proved to be impressively resourceful, so she cut him some slack. "Very," she replied into her phone. "There was just one thing missing."

"Crap, really? What's that?"

"I need to know what cousins she has living in the South Bend area."

George Aug's time in the dog house was about to end.

"Meet Mohammed Mullin." Under Secretary Kingman Summers stood next to the same ID photo the President had seen in his Sit Room earlier that week, narrating for his senior analysts. "Well paid lawyer and generous benefactor to the Iranian sleepaway camp hidden away in an Oregonian preschool. Science & Tech's been remotely prostate-examining his home and office computers and Galaxy phone for the past three days." He picked up a list and read from it. "In the six months leading up to the bombing, he made regular visits to at least 14 different radical Islamic websites, once visited a webpage featuring a recipe for homemade C4, and on August 7th of this year watched a YouTube video on cell phone detonators all the way through to the end."

George adjusted the way his bowtie sat on his throat and started jotting notes. He had been frozen out of the bombing investigation since they had been forced to release Jason Lancaster – since George had failed to get him to spill anything they could use to keep holding him. George of course now believed that Jason had nothing to do with the bombing, and *that's* why he hadn't gotten anything out of him – there was nothing there to get. But that wasn't good enough for Kingman Summers. George had realized in watching him in this last month that Kingman could latch onto things, form an almost unhealthy attachment to certain concepts or theories. Jason Lancaster had become one of those fixations for Kingman, and he hadn't forgiven George for not humoring it. George had been on the outside looking in for the last three weeks, handling meaningless tasks on the periphery while the rest of the division threw all their resources into the bombing analysis.

And then, just two hours before this meeting, he got the email from Kingman's Chief of Staff inviting him to attend.

"Mullin also has exhibited what we can safely classify as an unhealthy obsession with one Sarah MacDonald," Kingman continued, posting a photo of an intellectual co-ed on the board behind him, "a Stanford Law classmate of his who got one of the Biggs clerkships when he didn't. Mullin checks MacDonald's Facebook page an average of three times daily, and did extensive Google searches of her seven different times after she sent an email to her entire contact list announcing the prestigious Washington firm she was joining when her clerkship ended this summer."

"Jilted lover?" one of the analysts scoffed a little too loudly. "That motive'll get torn apart."

"Look, it's just half a picture, we know that. But we believe this is further evidence of Mullin's maniacal fixation on one moment in his life, the moment he sees as his biggest failure, the moment he didn't get that clerkship. Lawyers from MacDonald's firm were supposed to make an argument before the Court two days after the bombing, Wednesday the 9th. Isn't it possible Mullin had the date confused, and believed her firm would be in the building on Monday the 7th?"

George sat back, tapping his pen against his front teeth. It had been a full month since he realized Kingman had buried the analysis of the bomb recovered from the Court. Was this whole line of investigation even legit, or also motivated by secrets of the Under Secretary?

"We've only had two people on this guy," Kingman explained. "The President agrees it's time to get more serious, really dig deep beneath the surface. That's why the Bureau, CIA, DHS – we're working together and sending a full Task Force out there." Kingman's eyes locked on George. "Georgie, you're going to head our presence. You'll leave tonight. The guys on the ground will brief you in the morning."

George almost couldn't believe it. He stayed in his state of shock as the meeting broke up, as his colleagues came around to pat his back and wish him good luck. Kingman was the last one there, cleaning up his presentation materials. George stood and walked to the front of the room – he knew the right political move was to thank him for his renewed confidence.

"I know Lancaster was just a minor blemish on what otherwise is the most sterling record in this building," Kingman assured him. "Tear this guy apart, Georgie. We need to start bringing the President, bringing the American people, results. I knew I couldn't do that without you."

"Yes, Sir," George said with a nod, then headed for his office to pack up. He still hated the nickname Summers had bestowed upon him, but had decided weeks ago to let that slide in the name of getting back in his boss's good graces. He knew his CO might be the enemy, but he was a man who believed in keeping one's enemies as close as possible. All the better to observe them, analyze them, understand them.

Once he had cleared his desk of everything he thought he would need and moved it to his leather satchel, he sat down at his desktop one last time and sent an email to Jason that he had been preparing in response to his query about April Group Property Development. It wasn't as complete an analysis as George would normally like to do, but he no longer had the time. And besides, the April Group couldn't have looked more squeaky-clean in his initial digging. He sent the email off, shut down the computer for the last time for who knows how long, and stood, throwing the strap of the satchel over a shoulder.

Then, with a thought, he sat once more, picking up his phone. He hadn't spoken to Jason in three weeks, and wanted him to know where he was headed and why. And, yeah, he could even admit he was a little worried about him. He had developed a soft spot for him in their week of Woodward-and-Deep Throat meetings.

After listening to the outgoing message on Jason's voice mail, George waited for the beep, then typed in a handful of random numbers (pulling his ear off the receiver as the beeps blared out) and hung up. They had set that as their code – Jason would hear the beeps, and know George needed to speak to him. And if George was ever questioned on why he had called Jason Lancaster's inert cell, he could point to the short duration of the call and claim he had dialed the wrong number when trying to call someone else. This clueless defense was one of the advantages of being one of the older guys still punching the clock for Uncle Sam.

From the door, George looked around his little cubby hole of an office one last time. He knew how long these excursions could last; he realized it might be years before they got enough on the Iranians to close that investigation and come home, return to this office. He said goodbye, killed the light and left.

Jason wouldn't be checking his messages any time soon, or logging into the new gmail address he had opened to contact George. Jason was getting fucking drunk.

He had known this night would come, had known for years, really. Not just the night that this investigation would grind to a halt, but something on a much grander scale. Starting with his very first night out with Miranda, to his first meal with her, from the first time she came to his brownstone to the day she moved in.

From *the very moment he first laid eyes on her*, he knew that she was too good for him, that everything that followed was all too good to be true. In their happiest days together, his overwhelming emotion wasn't joy, or at least, not for more than a couple of minutes at a time. That's all it would last before he would catch himself and remind himself that happiness couldn't last; it never lasted; it all had to come crashing down very soon. Every relationship ends, every life ends, every happiness ends. And unless you take a bullet or a blood clot to the brain, it's a very long, painful descent to that end. Jason was just more acutely aware of this from moment to moment than most human beings.

He was also aware that he didn't *deserve* happiness.

That had to be the explanation. He hadn't deserved to know his mother. He *deserved* to be shipped east when she died, to his raging alcoholic nutbag father who thought children should be disciplined like cadets at a Corps boot camp. Jason must have deserved living and working and breathing in the shit of Afghanistan and the hottest beds of Africa for almost a decade. He deserved, as soon as he was finding success and validation for and enjoyment out of the work he was doing over there, the ugly circumstances that led to his discharge.

He didn't know if he deserved all this as karma for a past life, or if he had just gotten the short stick in some cosmic lottery. He didn't know if he believed in God. He knew his Mom did, remembered going to church with her, one of maybe only six or seven memories he had of her – but a helluva lot of good church did her. All he knew was that this was the life he deserved. He had to believe that; he refused to drown in pity parties, his sister's specialty. He believed in acceptance. *This*, this misery and frustration and dirt and depression that gripped him throughout his stay in Detroit, this was what he deserved. He didn't deserve his life as it was six weeks ago. He didn't deserve the Supreme Court, didn't deserve Rand.

He *deserved* the whole thing blowing up – *literally* – in his face.

Those were his thoughts as he worked through his first whiskey. The second was all about how he hadn't killed anyone in almost three years as far as he could remember, since he left the 'Stan. Why had that goddamn pedophile made him kill again? Why, when he saw Jason's gun, hadn't he just let the girl go and run out of there?

The girl standing at the table by the door of the bar – she looked so much like the girl that crazed fuck had almost strangled to death. But it couldn't be her, could it? Dolled up like that, skinny young thighs wrapped in fish nets, talking to a table of guys with the crew cuts and bicep tats of off-duty Allied Armament, getting pulled down onto one of their laps with a laugh rather than a scream? Shouldn't she be in some sort of recovery facility? Shouldn't she be with her mother or sister or grandma or guardian?

Jason had to know for sure it wasn't her. After the first pull on whiskey number three, he stepped off his stool and sauntered over. *Well, I'll be damned.* Maybe he should've agreed to see the girls, should've let them thank him. Wouldn't it have been obvious to him that they were just going to head right back out onto the streets, out on the market? Could he have said something then, imparted some wisdom to talk them out of it? *I guess I better do it now.*

The entire table froze when Jason's hand locked around her elbow. "Hey you," she smiled as soon as she recognized him, and stood up off that lap. The AASC grunts weren't smiling.

"Bethany, right?"

"Yeah. I didn't get your name." She rolled her finger down his forearm. "We didn't get to thank you."

"Let's get out of here," he implored her. "That'll be thanks enough."

Jason heard the mercenaries giving shit to the guy who just seconds ago had Bethany in his lap. He knew the world of testosterone and machismo so well, he could have scripted what came next. The huge grunt rose up, his throat rising above the level of Jason's eyes. Jason pulled Bethany behind him. "We've already got plans," the steakhead growled.

"She was mistaken. Her calendar wasn't open after all."

"Why don't you mind your own goddamn business?"

Staying on the good side of Allied Armament had been Jason's most important objective when he arrived in Detroit. But he didn't deserve their good side, did he? He didn't deserve anyone's good side.

Especially after he fired his skull right into the grunt's Adam's apple. The merc went right down onto his knees, wheezing and choking. As his buddies rose to his defense, Bethany was pleading, "No, no, don't do this—"

But Jason deserved it. He was no slouch, able to break a nose here and finger there in the melee. But he was well outgunned, and deserved to get his ass worked. He deserved the bottle smashing across his back, putting him down on all fours. He deserved the kicks up into his stomach and ribs. He deserved to pass out to the sounds of Bethany's screams mixing with the brutal breaking of his own flesh.

SUNDAY

For the second time in a month, Jason woke up in a cage.

The Allied Armament thugs were the best-trained fighters in the world, artisans with tools of pain, be it guns or fists; they knew how to inflict the maximum amount of pain on Jason while doing the minimal amount of actual damage. So while he looked like absolute shit – one eye purpled shut, arms conveying the entire color spectrum from black to red – he didn't need a hospital. They charged him with five counts of Aggravated Assault of a Peace Officer and threw him in the drunk tank to cool off. The drunk tank was just an oversized chicken coop, a large pen in one corner of the abandoned Michigan Central Station that served as the holding cell for every arrestee waiting out the weekend for the Judges to come to work on Monday morning. Jason figured he still had another 24 hours at least, 24 more hours of sitting in a corner of the pen ignoring the crazed ramblings and manhood challenges of his cellmates. He wasn't expecting the two AASC guards who unlocked the cage and pulled him to his feet and escorted him out of there, leading him to the other side of the giant central concourse. The personnel who had seemed so loose the rest of Jason's stay stood at rapt attention, surrounding their surprise visitor, the City Commander.

"You look like absolute shit," Rikeman observed.

"Your guys are as good as advertised," Jason smiled through his split lip.

"And I'm sure you by no means did anything to deserve this." Rikeman pulled the phone off his belt, punched redial, listened for a beat, then said into it, "I found him."

He held the phone out for Jason. "Hello?" he asked into the handset.

"Where the heck have you been, Kid?" the voice of George Aug came through from the other end.

Jason took the phone in his own hand and stepped away from the collection of mercs. Rikeman raised a hand to his men, assuring them it was all right to give Jason some space. "You know where I am," Jason answered into the phone.

"I emailed you where I am now. The investigation is heating up out here. I think you're gonna want to get out here."

"What is it, who are you onto?"

"A cell of Iranian immigrants. Their bankroller has plenty of motive to hate the Supreme Court. We've got every agency converging on this place now."

Jason clenched with a slight, momentary panic, with images of the task force finding Miranda before he could, whisking her away to Guantanamo before he could see her and help her and ask her why the hell she had done whatever she had done.

He shook it off, asking, "What about this company I emailed you about?"

"April Properties? It's a total dead end. Totally clean, totally above board."

"The bombs were tested on their property, George, in their hospital."

"I've been doing this my whole life, Jason. They don't smell right. What I'm doing right now smells right. Oregon smells right."

Jason nodded. He had wasted a week; he didn't want to waste any more time. "I'll find you."

He thumbed the phone dead, walking over to return it to Rikeman. "How much longer till I can get out of there?" he nodded back toward the pen.

"Your lucky day, Bailiff. Your fairy Godfather on the phone there paid your bail. You're free to go."

One of the AASC mercs elbowed the guy next to him. "Bet I know where he's going first," he giggled, then mimed taking a girl from behind, slapping her imaginary backside in rhythm with each pelvic pump.

His buddy laughed back, offering him a fist bump. "Oh hells yeahs. She looked like she needed it bad, bro."

"What are you talking about?" Jason asked. "Who?"

"The chick who came to see you. Friday night, or early Saturday actually. Your ass was still passed out."

Jason stormed up to him, got right in his face. He couldn't help but think the impossible. "Describe her."

The grunt stumbled back a step. "I don't know, man, young as hell. I think she said her name was Beth or something?"

Jason wilted. He was so tired, so beat up, so wracked with every emotion, rational thought had for a second escaped him. Of course it wasn't Miranda. It wasn't going to be that easy to find Rand. He turned and headed for the exit.

Patty wasn't getting the damn door. The knocking woke Jane, and kept going for the five minutes she had been lying awake waiting for Patty to answer it. "PATTY?" she called out. "YOU GONNA GET THAT?"

She wasn't about to get up and answer Patty's door. But then her hook-up from the night before rolled over, his arm falling over her like he wanted to snuggle or something. *Eww,* Jane thought, crawling out from under him and off the fold-out. As she passed the front door, the knocking continued unabated. *Fuck it.*

"Brooke?" What the hell was Jane's cousin doing here in DC, standing out in the rain, knocking on Patty Jacobi's door? Why did she look so nervous, why were her hands shaking? "What the hell are you doing--?"

"They flew me out here," Brooke answered. "They called me yesterday and said the e-ticket was already in my in-box."

"Who? Who flew you out here?"

"They're putting me up at the Hay-Adams Hotel." Brooke's eyes were as wide as baseballs. "Have you ever seen this place? I can see the White House from my window!"

Jane's shoulders collapsed. Of course, it all made sense. They got to her.

Sensing this, Brooke swallowed hard, spitting out the line she had practiced the entire flight out here. "I'm not going to talk about what I know about Cecilia Koh. Not ever again. To anyone. I'm sorry, Janey."

"Goddammit, Brooke, come inside where it's dry and we can talk this out--"

"She's getting me a full ride to IU." She leaned in with an excited whisper. "And basketball season tickets."

Jane put her hands on her hips. She well knew who 'she' was. And Jane knew there was nothing she could do or say now that 'she' had acted.

"But, but she said if I tell anyone about the Kohs-- that would be a violation of my confidentiality agreement at work. They'd have to tell the school about it, and my scholarship will be pulled for lack of character."

Jane's front pocket started shaking. She pulled out her phone – the face read, 'BLOCKED,' but she knew who it was. She turned away from Brooke as she pushed the green answer button and spit into the tiny mic, "You are just an awful, awful person."

"Now, now, Jane," the voice of Rosemarie Irving hummed from the other side, "that's no way to treat the person who just helped your cousin get into college."

“Don’t think this changes anything. I still know what she did; I’ll still go public with it.”

“That’s your right as an American. But with no proof, and no one to corroborate your story, I think you’ll find the number of news outlets willing to run it has diminished. Oh, there’s of course a few out there who still love to peddle in conspiracy theories. They’ll be happy to run it, but I’m not sure you’ll get the type of attention you were hoping for.”

Jane squeezed her eyes tight, trying to swallow the tears. She rubbed her pounding forehead. Then finally said, “I was wrong. You were very generous to arrange the offer we spoke about earlier. I’d like to accept. I’d love to join Alterman & Richbourg.”

Rosemarie’s titter could be heard even through the phone connection. “Oh, Jane, you don’t want to do that. You want to earn your place the old-fashioned way, through things like hard work and determination. I wish you the best of luck.”

Cecilia was ashamed how often she spaced out during the reading of the Gospel, but in mass this morning, she hadn’t heard a word of it, her mind in other places, on other people. She was glad Father Gentry repeated some of it when he went into his homily: “‘Whoever loves father or mother more than me is not worthy of me,’ Jesus tells his new disciples. ‘Whoever loves son or daughter more than me is not worthy of me.’

“Now I don’t see any of you out there shaking your head at me or whispering to your spouse that you want to storm out. That’s probably because you’re not really listening to me.” The people in the St. John Neumann pews chuckled; Gentry smiled back and continued. “But the idea of loving anyone or anything more than our children is about the most foreign concept there ever could be. How could we love *anything* more than our kids? Even when they’re teenagers!”

Cecilia laughed. It felt so good to laugh. This priest was one of the more dynamic, charismatic, engaging she had ever heard give mass. She looked over – her husband was just as riveted to his every word. She was so grateful Rosemarie had suggested this church.

"So what could Jesus mean, how could He even think it was possible for us to place Him above the most cherished people in our lives? The truth is, in today's world we might be dedicating too much of our lives to our children, whether it be dedicating all our Facebook posts to their every menial action, or surrendering our careers, or taking out third and fourth mortgages in order to provide everything you think their happiness requires. When we're caught up in this whirlpool of dedicating our lives to our children's lives, we often forget to be *selfish.*

"'Wait a second, Father,' you're asking me, 'isn't selfishness a bad thing?' Sometimes. But sometimes, concentrating on ourselves is exactly what God wants. He didn't make you a talented writer or runner or actor or singer so you could give your talents up when you became a parent. God gave you those talents, and the opportunities that come with those talents, so you would *use* those talents – in service of Him.

"As you walk down this great long hallway called life, you're going to walk by many doors. Sometimes you'll get impatient and try to force open a door on your own." The crowd laughed as he got into it, grunting as he wrestled with an imaginary doorknob. "The key is to recognize the doors that God has opened for you, the opportunities He has created for you, and know when He wants us to walk right through those doors. How do we do that? We have to carefully examine *why* God is opening doors for us, and what he wants us to accomplish on the other side. Who is it, waiting on the other side of that door, that we will be carrying His messages to? And what messages will we be carrying exactly?

"Now sometimes the mission God has given us won't make any sense to us whatsoever. 'Father Gentry,' people ask me all the time, 'how can I teach my kids to not sin, when I myself have sinned so much?' That is the quintessence of *forgiveness.* God has forgiven us, and chosen us for a task specifically because we know the pain a sin brought to our lives, and can share that knowledge with others. It's time we realized, if God has forgiven us, then we can forgive ourselves, and put his mission above all else in our lives. Let us pray."

Cecilia was about to bring her hands together, when Lindsey grabbed her left hand hard and pulled it into his own. He squeezed her hand tight as he prayed. Then on "Amen," he looked over into her eyes, his irises damp with tears.

No words needed to be exchanged. Cecilia heard his message, and God's. It was God who had given her the opportunity to serve on the highest court in the greatest land ever known to man, and that alone made it worth risking her family's privacy. If their privacy was shattered, it would be in service of God. She knew everything that had come before – from Mifa's pregnancy, to her coming to her mother for help getting an abortion – all of that pain had been leading her to this moment, to this decision, to this door. She could not ignore God's wishes. She would walk through His open door, and if the truth about Mifa were to someday come out, she would know it was just part of God's plan that it come out, and they would be ready to deal with it as a family.

"The girl didn't give her last name," Brooke explained, "but when her mother opened up her wallet to get some cash, I saw the name on her driver's license, you know, displayed in that little plastic sleeve? It wouldn't have meant anything to me, except my cousin was in her class at Notre Dame, and all she talked about was how much of a ball-buster this Professor Koh was. So as soon as I got off work that night, I called Jane and asked her if her professor's first name happened to be Cecilia. Then of course, when I saw her on *Conan,* I recognized her again." Brooke stared out at the nine old men and four women examining her from the other side of the round table, salivating for more. "Um, that's it, I guess?"

"Just so I'm clear, Ms. Norfleet," the man in the center of the Senators, Geoff Wyley, leaned forward, "you would be willing to testify under oath that Cecilia Koh paid for her daughter Mifa's abortion?"

Brooke turned her panicked eyes to Rosemarie. "Um, you said I wouldn't have to--"

"You absolutely will not," Rosemarie answered with supreme confidence. "Senator Wyley means hypothetically. *Hypothetically* you are so confident in the truth of your story, you would be willing to recount it under oath. Everyone here understands our agreement that you will never tell this story again after today, they just want to be sure it is true."

"Yes." Brooke faced the Senators again. "It's true. Even under oath."

"Thank you, Brooke," Rosemarie smiled. "Why don't you wait out in the hall for me?"

Brooke got up with a smile of pure relief and exited. Rosemarie stood behind her empty chair, her eyes going immediately to Wyley's. His lips quivered, condensation welling in the lower lids. He looked away, coughed it off.

"Just because she gave her daughter an abortion doesn't guarantee she won't vote to repeal *Roe*," one of the women pointed at Rosemarie, trying to keep the heat on. "This town was built on votes of hypocrisy."

"No, it doesn't guarantee it. But let's say it did. Six months from today, after you've confirmed our next three nominees, this Court will be balanced six-to-three in favor of a woman's right to choose. The Court has walked the tightrope since the day *Roe* was written. This will be the best ratio you've ever had. You'll finally be able to breathe easy." Rosemarie threw up her arms, coming around to sit down in the seat Brooke left vacant. "If that's an opportunity the 13 of you want to throw away in the name of political grandstanding, well, I guess there really is nothing I can do to convince you."

Suddenly, Wyley stood. "We're done," he said. He didn't know how this woman would vote any more than anyone in the room did, but knowing she at least understood on some level what he had gone through with his own daughter eased his heart.

Nothing more needed to be said. One by one, the twelve other holdouts stood, each making his or her way to the door, several even placing a hand on Wyley's shoulder as they passed. They all knew what had happened to his daughter; all loved him as one of the few true, 'real,' good guys in the Senate; all would follow him off almost any cliff. They all felt they had made an important stand here, and had succeeded in getting an important pledge out of the Irvings as a result.

Soon, only the two recent adversaries remained. "Thank you," Wyley nodded to Rosemarie. "Thank you for listening to me."

He started to follow the others out the door, stopping only when she said, "Oh, don't worry, I'm sure you'll get a chance to make it up to me."

MONDAY

It had taken Jason over eight hours to find her.

He had spent all Sunday night driving around the streets, the corners he thought she might work. It was only when he was driving back to his motel just after dawn that he saw Bethany walking down a broken Detroit sidewalk, the *Detroit Free Press* over her head little shield against the driving rain.

He leaned across the cab of his truck, pushing open the door and barking, "Get in."

"I'm going home." She kept walking. "Been a long night."

Jason held up a wad of twenties, a couple hundreds; he was prepared for her to not come willingly. "C'mon. I'll make it worth your while." She stopped to consider the cash, then finally shrugged and got in. "This is how this is going to work. I'm going to pay you a thousand dollars--"

"You got a room, or are you expecting to come to my place?

"I want *you* to go up to your apartment, pack up all your stuff, then leave town with me."

"That's gonna cost you a lot more than a thousand dollars."

"I'll drop you anywhere you want. Anywhere in Michigan, or anywhere between here and Oregon. You just promise me you're done with Detroit."

"What's in Oregon?"

"Just promise me, Bethany."

She tried to respond, but she couldn't-- because of the tears suddenly pouring out of her eyes. She covered her face, but the compulsive sniffling was unmistakable. "I, I'm sorry, I don't know what's got over me--"

Jason put his truck in gear and started driving in the direction of her apartment.

A month since the bombing, Mac thought when NPR announced the final tally of the Koh confirmation vote, *and we got nothing*. A month since the bombing, and a new Supreme Court Justice had been nominated, vetted, cross-examined and confirmed in a resounding 69-29 vote. The Supreme Court was going to start hearing cases again. A month since the bombing, and the United States military had accomplished nothing. No intelligence-gathering, no message-sending, no retaliation – or at least, none that Vice Admiral Kennesaw MacTavish was aware.

The commanding officer of the Joint Special Operations Command had grown tired of fielding questions for which he had no answers. As an officer who interacted with, and drew his forces from, all branches of the military, MacTavish had four times as many people looking to him for updates, or at least, that's how it felt. Everywhere he went someone asked him the same thing in passing; every meeting he took ended with the same small talk: *"Have you heard anything new about/Why isn't there news on/When the hell are we gonna have some targets to strike in retaliation for the Supreme Court?"*

MacTavish thought if anyone could provide him with answers, or at least an understanding of why there weren't any, it would be Admiral Percy Holmes. Pers had been Mac's classmate at Annapolis, and their meteoric rises had almost paralleled one another: While MacTavish was now the commander of JSOC, Holmes had just in the last six months been installed as the Commander of Naval Operations, the Navy's representative on the Joint Chiefs of Staff. If anyone in the country knew anything about the Supreme Court investigation, it would be Percy, and he would know just the way to assuage Mac's impatience with little morsels of intel or an optimistic timetable for resolution.

The first hour of their lunch in one of the Pentagon's small private dining rooms was filled with their usual semiannual small talk: "Sir--" "Oh shut the hell up, Mac, it's always been Pers and as long as it's just the two of us at this table it will remain Pers." "How are Valerie and the kids, Pers?" And on and on it went. MacTavish had no answers to Pers's questions about his own dating life, but over the years, he had become a pro at deflecting them, at providing just enough detail on the one or two dates he had taken in the last month to mitigate any concern. Plus, no one was actually worried about a Navy man being married to his Navy, they were just repeating the questions their wives had told them to ask.

It was after their lunch plates had been whisked away and they waited on the obligatory dessert inquiry that Mac launched into his true mission. "We're just sitting by our phones at JSOC, Pers," he said, wobbling his coffee cup around its saucer. "Going a little stir crazy."

"Shit, Mac, you could've just asked--"

"I love our lunches. I'd be here even if I didn't have four branches of the armed forces up my ass begging for a chance to fry some bad guys."

"You know you're my first call when we get something actionable."

"So there really is nothing? Six weeks-- and nothing?"

"Oh, the spooks are out there doing what they do, scraping moss off rocks. The DCI was sitting here with us, he'd probably tell you they're drowning in 'promising leads.'" Percy shook his head. "Let's just say I haven't seen or heard of anything that got me excited enough to reach for my blood pressure meds."

Mac leaned in. It was just all beyond comprehension. "C'mon, what'd they find at the site? They think this is foreign, domestic …?"

"They found nothing, Mac. And no one knows what the hell to think. These were real pros. Hit us completely blind, then-- POOF. It's like they were never there."

Mac nodded. It was disconcerting, frightening, *infuriating* that someone could do this to America today.

But for Admiral MacTavish, it was also a bit of a relief. He'd had an ulterior motive for requesting lunch with Pers, for picking his brain about imminent JSOC action.

He waited until he had driven his vintage 911 several miles out of the Pentagon before he called his ulterior motive. "I need to see you," he said after he heard the speaker phone connect.

Jason drove Bethany the 68 miles northwest to the depressed suburb of Flint in which she grew up. It was 68 miles out of the way, off his path to Oregon, but as soon as she started debating aloud whether returning to her Mother or an old boyfriend in Ann Arbor was the best thing to do, Jason headed for I-75 N.

He asked her some questions along the way to confirm it wasn't a terrible choice: what kind of mother had she been, was she into drugs, did she play any part in Bethany's choice of careers? Her journey back through her childhood memories was a rocky one, and Bethany more than once demanded that Jason pull over or turn around for a new destination. Jason held firm that, from everything he had heard so far, she was making the right move. Their life didn't sound like a Norman Rockwell, but it was as decent a place as any for her to start over, get a job, pocket some cash to add to that thousand he had just given her, before eventually venturing out on her own again. No, he couldn't guarantee to himself that she wouldn't be right back on the streets of Detroit in two weeks, but he felt like he was giving her as much time as he – as Miranda – could afford right now.

Finally, he pulled up outside a drooping little bungalow, its roof wilting under the weight of the rain. She got out and jumped down from the cab, throwing her one bag over her shoulder. She looked back at him, not sure what she wanted to say. She wanted to say thanks, but also understood that the word wasn't sufficient. Why after all these hundreds of years of the English language had no one invented a word more powerful than thanks for people who did something like *this* for you?

But before she could find that word, her back pocket was singing a Miley Cyrus song. "Hello?" she answered into her phone.

"Is this Bethany Stern?" the male voice on the other side of the line asked.

"Um, yeah?"

"When was the last time you saw or spoke to Jason Lancaster?"

She locked eyes with Jason. She didn't like the way this character was asking questions. "Not since I visited him in the drunk tank, why?"

A loud sigh blew into her ear. "Tell him Dean Rikeman needs to speak with him. It's urgent."

Bethany thumbed the mute button, then held her palm over the mic just to be sure. "It's someone Rikeman?"

Jason reached out his hand for her phone. He unmuted it, then said, "It's me."

"We've been looking all over town for you."

"I'm not in town."

"Well, you better get yourself back here, or get yourself to a computer. There's something you need to see."

Admiral MacTavish didn't like how close the motel was to his house. He had told Shareef the last time he had rented a room at the Colony Inn that it was too close, that he wanted at least five miles distance between his home and their meeting place. (He had invited the kid to his actual house one night after an infuriating day, so Shareef knew where Mac lived, a momentary lapse in judgment the Admiral regretted intensely.) The Colony was barely a mile away, making it five times more likely that someone who knew Mac might see him there, see him parking ("I drive a canary yellow Porsch, for Chrissakes!") or walking to a room there.

Goddammit, why can't he remember these things? Mac slapped his steering wheel as he drove to the Colony. *Why do I always have to re-teach him these things?*

Mac pulled the 911 into the deepest open spot in the lot he could find, the furthest open spot from the road. He was glad it was raining, giving him the excuse to bury his face within the hood of his slicker. He took the nearest stairs, mounting them two-at-a-time to the second level. "*Jesus fucking Christ,*" he cursed under his breath when he realized the room the kid had checked out was way on the other side of the structure – as close to the road as could be. Mac stamped over there, copper-colored standing water splashing over the side of the railing under his heavy footfalls.

The door had been left ajar. Mac gave the wood four spread-out knocks – their code – then entered.

Shareef's muscular, sinewy back looked up at Mac from the floor. By the time Mac had dead bolted and chained them in, Shareef was finished with his prayers, rising back up onto his knees, revealing a beautiful hand-woven prayer mat lying across the carpet beneath him. He opened his eyes and looked up at the much-older Admiral.

Mac wanted to scold him, lecture him for everything he had done wrong, but started with the main reason he had called this meeting: "They're still completely in the dark," he reported of his meeting with Percy. "We're good."

Rosemarie popped the handsome black-&-white of Vice Admiral Kennesaw MacTavish off the populated side of the corkboard. She pulled the sheet of biographical bullet points off the back of the photo, handed that off to Dennis, then moved the Admiral under Cecilia and Judge Goldman on the emptier side of the board.

"Wow," Dennis whistled as he read Mac's bio. "Bold move."

"That's all we've got room for. He was squeaky clean five years ago. You'll find anything new?"

"Of course, ma'am," Dennis nodded, hiding the bio in the binder under his arm and heading out the door, bracing himself for another week of four-hour-night's-sleeps.

Rosemarie smiled as she took two more steps back from the board, staring at the three photos arrayed one on top of the other: from new Associate Justice, to next nominee, to next recruit. She then moved to her bag resting on the one table in this room, pulling out her Blackberry. "Suzie, it's me," she said when her husband's secretary picked up the line from the offices of their foundation. "Would you connect me to President Salas's office?"

"Of course, Mrs. Irving."

"Oh-- dammit. Suzie?"

"Yes, Mrs. Irving?"

"I keep forgetting. Will you send a $10,000 donation to St. John Neumann?"

"Of course, Mrs. Irving."

"Include a personalized note from both of us. 'Dear Father Gentry – Your spiritual guidance has once again saved another lost sheep. See you next Sunday. Love, R & R.'"

President Salas picked up the phone on the Resolute Desk. "I told you I would call when the champagne was chilled," a feminine voice teased from the other end of the line.

"Excuse me?" he chuckled.

"I think what we just accomplished is worthy of a celebration," Rosemarie continued. "And of course, I need to brief you on who's next. I'm in the room I decorated."

The President grinned at her dig that he still hadn't hired someone to re-decorate the West Sitting Room – or any room of the Residence, for that matter. "I'll be right there," he answered, then set the phone back in its handset.

He started to step around the desk, picking up his Blackberry with a last thought – just in time for it to vibrate in his hand with a new email. He glanced at the in-box, but when he saw the strange address of the latest sender, he stopped in his tracks. The latest sender didn't have an address; the line where the sender's name or even address was usually displayed was just blank. He could read the first line of the email, however: "Let a flunky see this video first, and you'll regret it."

Salas thought this through for a beat. His phone was supposed to be the most impenetrable on the planet; it wasn't supposed to be possible to hack it, or infect it with a virus. If the 'video' attached to this email was a scam, the phone would just refuse to open it or even shut down as a precautionary measure.

He tapped the video icon with his thumb, and it began to play.

"Today happened because of you," the unmistakable voice of former President Irving opened the video. But it was dark – and on this small screen, Salas couldn't make out what he was looking at. He squinted, trying to shield the screen from the bright lights of the Oval with his hand. There was movement in front of the lens, a male body appearing next to the female body already standing there. Both heads were above the top of the frame, but Salas could still hear Reg Irving: *"I wanted to make sure someone properly acknowledged you for putting us in front of the President. For getting this whole process started."*

And suddenly, the female in frame was being pushed down on top of the desk, her face coming right down into the eye of the camera's lens. It was Becks; it was Salas's Chief of Staff. And with the undoing of a belt buckle and the rip of panties, Salas's predecessor – and the husband of the First Lady he was about to meet in the West Sitting Room – was taking his Chief of Staff from behind.

"Okay, I'm here," Jason said into his phone.

He looked around this copy center, the closest he could find to Flint, examining the customers at the other computer terminals, the plump bearded guy feeding a stack of paper into a large color copier. No one paid him any mind, no one filled him with even the slightest hint of suspicion.

He opened up his Gmail, the address he had reluctantly given to Rikeman on his way over here. Indeed, there was an email from 'drikeman@aasc.com' waiting in his in-box. "And it looks like I've got it," Jason assured him. He opened it, and at the bottom of the blank message, a photo started to slowly appear, the top rolling down as it casually loaded.

"I sent you a photo."

"I've got it. I'll need a minute. Internet connection here sucks."

"It was taken by an undercover agent we have working the Minutemen."

"I'm sorry, who?"

"The Michigan Minutemen. They're a militia upstate--"

"Militia?"

"Real serious mother fuckers, Bailiff. Rumor has it, they've built some sort of compound in the Huron National Forest and are hiding away there waiting for the apocalypse. You're about to see an arms sale they came into Detroit to make just this last weekend."

Indeed, the first thing Jason could make out as the bottom edge of the photo got lower and lower was a tall truck in an alley, the back overloaded with wooden crates. One of the crates was on the ground, mountain men rocking green camo standing all around it, its top crowbarred open, the camoed militia men reaching in to pull out assault rifles and offer them to black youths smiling like they were pilfering Santa's bag. Rikeman continued: "We believe they have their own arms manufacturing capabilities on their compound. A party will venture back out into the real world about once a month to make some profit off those arms and turn it around into food and supplies. We believe the blonde guy at seven o'clock is the leader. You regonize him?"

Indeed, the bone-thin man holding an AR-15 in the lower left hand corner of the screen, the intensity of his eyes piercing through even the darkness of this night shot, did look familiar somehow.

"Benjamin Bratten," Rikeman explained.

"Wait-- the Solstice Bank shooter?"

"Missing for over two years. Until this photo. The whole thing loaded yet?"

"No."

"'cause you're gonna want to catch your breath and call me back when it does." Jason didn't have any idea what he was talking about--

--until the final person in the photo appeared. She only had one eye open, squinting her left closed to aim the Glock in her right hand straight into camera. Her hair had been chopped, and Jason had never seen her in anything as grungy as the dark-green surplus jacket she was wearing in this photo.

But Jason knew Miranda Whitney when he saw her.

GREEN BRIEF

BOOK THREE OF THE SIX-PART CONSPIRACY THRILLER

FOUR SEATS

AARON COOLEY

FEBRUARY

Jason Lancaster didn't care what everyone claimed, or what his father had always insisted. Mid-Atlantic winters weren't beautiful or glorious. Mid-Atlantic winters were shit.

It wasn't the snow Jason despised; the first morning flurry of the season still gave him a pinch of that elation of boyhood. He still got flashes of makeshift sleds, of catching ice-hard footballs between mittened fingers, of Sarge's favorite morning DJ including the name of his school in a long list of closures. No, Jason didn't mind the snow itself, even as the blizzards seemed to get worse and worse with each passing year. (He had no interest in even *thinking* about why they were getting worse; Jason avoided any argument tainted with politicization.)

No, what he hated was what the snow devolved into, those depressing masses of charred sludge lining the roads of February and March, as if someone (probably whoever was making the goddamn winters worse) had insisted on coating everyone's commute with a layer of whipped depression.

Winter is a microcosm of life itself, Jason thought as he jogged across the traffic of 15th St. NW and approached the Treasury-side entrance onto the White House grounds. *No matter how happy you are, no matter how well things seem to be going for you, in just a matter of weeks or days or hours everything's going to be dark and wet and dirty and sludgy again.* Every moment of happiness Jason had dared to cherish in his life, from his Mom to Miranda, had ended in sludge. *Everything,* he had gotten used to telling himself, *every moment and every life, ends in dirt and worms. Might as well stop getting your hopes up for any other outcome.*

As Jason watched the gate guard read his name off his Maryland license, then type it into his computer, he refused to tense up with nerves. He had disarmed IEDs in Afghanistan, for Chrissake; the fate he was tempting by venturing onto the White House grounds – time in a holding cell under Pennsylvania Avenue, followed by meals and health care and a roof over his head for the rest of his life

– was nothing compared to the fate he had tempted every time he removed wires from a homemade haji bomb. Still, as he watched the Asian-American guard stare at his screen, as he waited those excruciating thirty-seven seconds for his name to be processed, he could feel his pits start to dampen with concern.

"Oh, that's what's going on," the guard murmured to himself, just as Jason had planned. "Whoever put you on the guest list misspelled your first name. So I hope you don't mind the spelling on your badge." He smiled as the temporary White House ID for 'JAASON LANCASTER' popped out of the little box next to his hard drive, then handed it across to Jason. "There you go, Ja-ay-son," the guard laughed, and Jason smiled back. The plan had worked. Without an exact match for his real name in the system, no alarms had been set off; neither Secret Service nor Homeland Security nor anyone else had been alerted that a wanted fugitive had actually turned himself in at the Commander-in-Chief's residence. The only potential hiccup had been the possibility of the guard himself recognizing Jason's name from the news, remembering those reports from the Huron National Forest now several weeks old. Judging the sentry to be in his 20s, Jason figured he had filled his brain with so many Facebook posts and tweets and Instagrams and Snapchats in the weeks since Polis that the name of Jason Lancaster had long ago been pushed out of his memory cortices.

"You know where you're going, Mr. Lancaster?" Jason couldn't vocalize, just nodded, then started following the gaggle of press swarming for the east entrance of the President's home.

Jason was well aware he had embarked on a suicide mission, that today might very well be the day *he* ended in dirt and worms. But he had no choice, he had to stop this *now*. In thirty minutes, it would be too late. The person who had started all this, who had robbed him of Miranda, who had sent him on a 1700-mile round trip over the last four months in search of answers, the person who had branded him a criminal, the person who had brought down that temple of justice where Jason had last dared to be happy – *that person* was in the White House right at this moment. That person was doing something much more dangerous to this nation, much more deadly, than those bombs that went off four months ago. That person was about to wrest control of the judicial branch of the government. That person was about to be sworn in as Chief Justice of the United States.

As Jason approached the building, he saw the metal detector station awaiting him just inside the doors. "Everything in your pockets into a bowl," one of the rotund uniform guards commanded as Jason stepped inside, but he took care to remove only his cell phone, keys, and the simple little digital dictaphone he had cash purchased at a Best Buy two days earlier. The disparate pieces of plastic in his pockets shouldn't set off the machine, and they would look damn suspicious sitting in one of those plastic little bowls.

"Journalist?" a female guard smiled at him, nodding at the recorder.

"Something like that," he replied.

"You're a little late. They been up there setting up all morning. Hope you can get a seat."

Jason nodded, being sure to keep his hands on the plastic puzzle pieces in the deep pockets of his winter coat as he stepped through the detector arch--

And set it off with a piercing beep. His face clenched up. Was this going to be the way he went down? Was it possible the weapon did have some metal in it, even just a gram or two, after all?

"Your hands, Sir," the female guard barked at him. "Take your hands out."

Jason did slowly, quickly debating in his mind what he would do when she asked him to remove everything inside those pockets. Did he claim they were pieces of a toy he was going to give to his nephew or niece? Did he abort the whole thing?

"I ain't taking your belt off for you. You're gonna have to use those hands."

Jason let out a relieved smile, then pulled his belt off and returned to the other side of the detector to lay it on the conveyer belt. He stepped through the arch – this time, wth a silent result.

Once inside, he took a hard left to the first men's room, stowing himself in the last open stall. He quickly assembled the five pieces of plastic into the odd-looking pistol that had been guaranteed to pack a .357 punch. He wished for a moment he had his Kimber 1911 .45 pistol, the gun an LAPD SWAT officer had once given him as thanks for a good deed. All white with soft curved edges, this gun looked all wrong, like a prop from a Saturday morning sci fi show, much sillier than the guns he ran around his yard with as a kid. But it was the only thing he would ever have been able to get inside this building.

"Thank you, ladies and gentlemen, members of the United States Congress, and Supreme Court Justices both senior and new," Jason heard the President's voice echo from speakers lining the East Room as he topped the stairs on the State Floor. Jason couldn't help but wonder about the three new Justices confirmed so far; he had been so engrossed in his quest, he had only heard (and then forgotten) two of their names, and hadn't had the time to learn about any of them. (Nothing, that is, save for the dark facts he had compiled about the nominee for

Chief.) For a second, he missed the Justices he used to work with, each a quirky and engaging personality who almost without exception went out of their ways to acknowledge and even get to know Miranda and Jason and their colleagues. For a moment, he mourned the friends and mentors he had lost.

But he quickly snapped back into what he was here to do. He was nearly to the Green Room without being noticed at all: every aide, page and official had their head poked in an East Room door, savoring this historic moment. Only one Secret Service agent looked sideways at Jason as he passed, but when he held up his old Supreme Court Police badge, his thumb strategically placed to cover most of his name, the agent responded with a half-smile and turned back to the nearest door himself.

Jason laid his left fingers on the handle to the Green Room door, but before he opened it, he looked both ways down the corridor, then moved his right hand behind the small of his back and up under his jacket, to that area referred to in those yoga classes Miranda had talked him into attending as the 'sacrum.' Now sweating almost as much as he did in the one 'hot' class he had taken with her, he removed the plastic pistol from the back of his jeans and pushed open the door. For the hundredth-something time in the last week, he quickly ran through in his mind exactly how he saw this going down: *Don't just go in there blasting, but force a confession, acquire the evidence needed to close this case and clear Miranda's name, clear my name, once and for all.* (He knew Miranda could probably never be totally cleared, but when the full circumstances of her participation came out, there would be mercy and leniency. And whatever her penance might be, he would wait it out.)

"… I knew that whoever took the center chair," POTUS's voice rang through the open door on the opposite side of the room, "would inherit a Court at the most tumultuous moment in its history …" *You've got no idea,* Jason thought. Salas's nominee for Chief was the only other person in the Green Room, a silhouette filling that open door leading out onto the red carpet and the President's podium.

Jason raised his gun, aiming its mouth at the perfect spot to penetrate through to his target's spleen. The bullets were only plastic too, but when they hit just the right spot at a close enough range, they had been known to be lethal.

"I know you planned the bombings," he said in a low voice, just loud enough for the other occupant of the room to hear, but not enough to carry out into the East Room or for a microphone recording the press event to pick up.

The soon-to-be-Chief turned around with slow and calm, as if these words weren't surprising in the least. Jason swallowed, blinking the sweat out of his eyes. He was face to face with the person who had ruined his life.

"I know who you are," the nominee answered calmly. "I'm very sorry you got caught up in all of this."

"*You* blew up the Court," Jason continued, even quieter this time. "And I know why."

"... there is no doubt in my mind," the unaware President was continuing out at his podium, "that the person I selected to replace the late Chief Justice Lapadula is better qualified, prepared and willing to lead our Court into its future than any other human being on this planet. Ladies and gentlemen, I am truly humbled to introduce to you, the next Chief--"

The gunshot cut him off mid-sentence.

Secret Service agents yanked out sidearms and rushed in front of him, his personal guard Hifrael Fernandez shoving him to the ground with one hand as he screamed into his opposite wrist for a report.

"The Green Room, the shot came from the Green Room!" Salas heard Hifrael yell to his men, several of them rushing down the red carpet.

The Green Room. Salas felt his throat tighten.

The target had been his new Chief Justice.

BOOK THREE

GREEN BRIEF

TWO MONTHS EARLIER
A MONDAY IN DECEMBER

"And just where do you think you're going?" Reginald Irving rotated in front of his wife, stopping her path to the Republican cloakroom. Mitchell Aldridge, their trusted Secret Service agent for over a decade now, positioned his considerable chest at the perfect angle so no passersby or rubberneckers would come within twenty feet of the couple and pick up any word of their intimate interchange.

"Orals are starting in the old Court chambers downstairs," the former President continued, moving a step closer to his wife, taking her by the forearms, giving her those sideways eyes that had melted so many hearts and raised so many skirts over the years. "You've been down there everyday of the last three weeks. You're not going senile before me, are you?"

"You wish," Rosemarie shook her head. She had never let her husband forget that he was nine years her senior, but he reveled in finding opportunities to retort that their gap wasn't quite as pronounced as the numbers on their birth certificates might indicate. "I'm headed down there after I take a peek at how Goldman's goodwill tour is going."

"You pick 'em, I get 'em confirmed," Reg responded. "You changing the plan on me with only one down?"

"Honey, you know me too well to think I'd ever be comfortable with a total separation of powers."

Reg smiled, spinning on his heel to allow his First Lady to continue walking. "One thing both sides of the aisle always complimented me on was knowing when to cut my losses with a charming smile."

"You do everything with a charming smile," she said as she moved past him.

Rosemarie had underplayed the importance of the section of the confirmation process in which their second nominee, Judge Isaac Goldman, was engrossed. 'Courtesy calls'— visiting Senators, getting to know them personally, making them feel like their input was valued and even *needed*– was a vital part of getting confirmed to the Supreme Court. (Legend had it this tradition became popular following Richard Nixon's unsuccessful nomination of Judge Clement Haynsworth: several Senators later claimed to have voted against Haynsworth because they didn't appreciate the tone of his answers in his confirmation hearing, not realizing that much of this was due to a speech impediment which would have been quite obvious to them had they ever met him one-on-one.)

Rosemarie had heard that Judge Goldman's meetings had gone well so far – but that was with Democratic Senators. Today he would be meeting with Republicans for the first time, with the Majority Leader and a gaggle of his handpicked sycophants, with Kentucky Senator Clyde Dudley, a fool if Rosemarie had ever met one. And one thing she had learned about Judge Goldman in his three weeks of confirmation prep was that he did not suffer fools. He wouldn't hesitate to let anyone – not the green clerk he had brought with him from Philadelphia, not his prep team, not even the FLOTUS herself – know when he thought they were wrong or off-base. He would do it with charm and humor, of course, but do it he would. He had even gotten in a dig about President Salas's hometown Dodgers the first time he had been in the Oval Office; Rosemarie had exhaled hard when POTUS had just laughed it off and gave it right back to him about the travails of his own beloved Phillies.

Rosemarie rounded the corner to the cloakroom entrance and the Capitol Policeman stationed there stood from his stool with a nod. "Madam First Lady," he said as he opened the red velvet rope, then brought his keycard to the little box next to the door, a black plastic that almost blended in with the dark word of the wall paneling.

"Thank you Huston," she acknowledged back, showing off the talent for name recognition that had made her a favorite with all the worker bees to whom most politicians wouldn't even grant eye contact. Reginald followed right behind—

But as they stepped through the threshold into the moody cloakroom foyer, they ground to a halt. Someone was speaking in a raised voice, very raised, raised enough that you could almost go right ahead and call it a yell. And they both recognized that voice. "I'M A FEDERAL JUDGE. DON'T YOU UNDERSTAND WHAT THE HELL THAT MEANS?"

Reg grimaced. Rosemarie closed her eyes, her tactical mind switching to strategy: What had he done? What was *she* going to have to do to salvage yet another nominee from self-destruction, as she had done for Cecilia Koh a month ago?

"I CAN'T HAVE THIS SMUT ON MY COMPUTER! I MIGHT BE VETTED FOR THE SUPREME COURT ONE DAY!"

A chorus of raucous laughter sputtered off the end of Judge Goldman's last word. Rosemarie's head whipped up, face filling with a smile as she realized what was going on.

"But that approach wasn't working at all," Goldman continued. "They were all staring up at me like I was doing a staged reading of the Magna Carta. I realized I just had to level with them. So I said, 'Okay, guys, here's the truth: I thought that video was funny as hell.'"

As more laughs rang out, Rosemarie led her husband around the corner into the next room. There, they found Goldman, for lack of a better term, holding court. He stood in the dead center of the room, Dudley and his compatriots gathered around him like school kids at story time, several with handkerchiefs under their sobbing eyes as they laughed their hearts out. "Whoever admits to me, I told them, just admits that they used my computer in the middle of the night to watch this video is gonna get lunch on me today. In the private judicial dining room! Just like that--" --he clapped his hands together-- "every hand in the room shoots up!" This drove the Republicans to a new level of hysteria. "'Oh it was me, Your Honor, I used your computer last night, me, me!'"

Goldman looked up at Rosemarie, giving her a quick, almost imperceptible wink. Then he raised his hands. "I'm sorry, I'm sorry, I know we're supposed to be talking serious business here."

Dudley rose next to him, putting his hand on the Judge's shoulder. "No, Your Honor, we needed that. I don't think I've laughed that hard since I went into politics."

"Well, you guys were great practice. The truth is, the only reason I'm doing this is I bet Bernie Gamer, another circuit judge back in Philly, I bet him five thousand bucks I could make Justice Egan crack a smile."

This dig drove the laughter to its highest level. The Whip was slapping his knee so hard, Rosemarie thought he might pound it clean off. "That's *Chief* Justice Egan now!" Dudley screamed and pointed.

Having seen more than enough, Rosemarie turned back for the door. "Hey, we still doing Virginia today?" her husband whispered as she passed him.

"Let me see what cases are on the docket today," she nodded back, "and we'll be on the road by 11."

Alice Goldman cherished her walks to work. She loved the opportunity to breathe in a little fresh air and collect her thoughts before ensconcing herself away in her windowless medical offices for an eight hour workday. Even in the worst-weather months of last winter, even when she had to high-knee it through deep snow, she found that four and a half blocks wasn't too harrowing a distance to traverse.

When she emerged on Monday morning, Dr. Goldman was surprised there wasn't any snow yet. She could feel it coming in that biting cold in the air, that cold that stung your front teeth if you were out in it for too long, and she had an ominous feeling about what January and February might bring. (Winters only seemed to get worse and worse each year these days.) But there was no snow on the ground yet, not even frozen rain to slip upon. It was freezing, but it was bright and gorgeous as she pulled her building's front door closed behind her, squeezed her jacket tight around her neck, and turned in the direction of her office.

"Dr. Goldman!" She heard the pounding footfalls right after the voice. "Dr. Goldman, can I ask you a few questions?" She kept her head down and walked, cursing herself that she didn't heed Elia's advice and hire some security. *Security?* she had exclaimed. *Security for an oncologist?* Just until her husband's confirmation hearings were complete, Elia had replied. C'mon, it's just being safe, and we can afford it. But still, she hadn't been convinced. This was at least the fourth or fifth time the smarmy Fox News on-the-street reporter Jesse Watters and his cameraman had attempted to accost her – she found it pretty scary that she had lost count. "Just a couple of questions, Dr. Goldman," the reporter continued as he caught up with her, shoving his microphone up against her right shoulder.

She looked up and back, forcing a smile but not slowing her march. "I already told you that my husband is speaking for himself in Washington, and I don't need to do anything to intrude on that."

"Is he your *ex*-husband now, Dr. Goldman?"

"No, he's my husband." She was looking straight ahead now, the camera picking up only her profile, more than enough to see the smile had already evacuated her lips.

"Is there a reason he wouldn't want you in Washington? Wouldn't want you by his side? Is there something he doesn't want you testifying about, Dr. Goldman?"

She regretted giving him that first smile, that first answer – it only seemed to fuel him, encourage him, egg him on. Dr. Goldman kept marching, fighting to just outright ignore him.

"Why did you leave the Judge? Is there a reason that would be of interest to the American people when they're choosing a new Supreme Court Justice?"

Dr. Goldman had to laugh. "I don't know why you keep badgering me, when you know I'm not going to give you anything."

"Is there someone else you think we should be badgering?"

"You shouldn't be badgering anyone at all, you should be reading amicus briefs!"

Watters stopped in his tracks, his cameraman an instant later. He didn't know what the hell that meant, but he knew it was the first juicy thing he had gotten out of her. He could just hear it in her throat: the exasperation, the regret, the anger. He had broken through. He would be talking about an amicus brief, whatever the hell that was, on *O'Reilly* tonight.

As Dr. Goldman kept walking, dread seeped into her eyes. She was relieved she had found a way to get rid of the reporter, but hoped to God she hadn't sunk her husband's chances at a Supreme Court seat in the process.

Until four weeks ago, the old Supreme Court Chamber on the ground floor of the Capitol's North Wing was perhaps the most historic room in the country that no one knew anything about. It was in this room that Thomas Jefferson was inaugurated, that the first Morse code message was transmitted, that the decision in *Dred Scott v. Sanford* was handed down. It was in this room that Supreme Court Justices met before every presidential inauguration to don their robes. But it was just four weeks ago, when a special committee recommended to President Salas that the Supreme Court reconvene as soon as possible, that Capitol visitors and press and personnel started to notice the room undergoing a state-of-the-art security upgrade and the Chamber became the center of its first media firestorm in probably 160 years.

"Thank you, Counsel," Acting Chief Justice Egan cut off a lawyer as soon as the temporary red light installed on the petitioner's table started glowing. "The case is submitted."

The bearded solicitor shuffled his notes together into an unwieldy pile, turning and storming away from the odd-looking collection of six robed Justices, the Chief sitting off-center because of their current even numbers, Cecilia Koh three chairs to her left in the chair of the most junior Justice. Even from the rear of the chamber, Rosemarie could read the annoyance in the lawyer's eyes; was it frustration with himself for a bad performance, she wondered, or blame for the draconian system the acting Chief had instituted, a structure that put lawyers in the position of having no idea when they were going to be called to perform?

Concerned that the motive for the bombing may have been a specific case the Court was scheduled to hear, Chief Egan had decided that upon the return of the Court, their schedule would be much murkier than in years past: cases would be scheduled in two-week blocks, but which cases would be heard in each two-week cycle wouldn't be announced to the public or even the most veteran members of the press. Realizing that inevitably these lists of two-week case blocks might be leaked, Egan also decreed that even the lawyers in each case would be informed only that their case would be called in a certain two-week window, but would have no idea on which exact day of those two weeks, nor whether they might be called up first or second on a particular day of oral arguments. Acting Marshal Gregor Meyers, Homeland Security, even the President, loved this idea and gave the acting Chief their full support to run with it.

Rosemarie Irving did not love it. Every decision Egan had made so far as Chief had raised Rosemarie's hackles; this one made her blood boil. Not only did Egan's "pop orals" method lead to lawyers drowning in unpreparedness and lack of focus, mewling like wet-behind-the-ears 1Ls under the hot glare of the Socratic method, but Rosemarie believed every case heard while the Court had only six justices would be forever tainted with controversy, branded with asterisks that would make Roger Maris cringe. She predicted most of these cases would have to be reheard and many overturned.

But Rosemarie was biased. There was one case she thought especially inappropriate to hear with anything less than nine justices. This one case was the reason Rosemarie had been present for each day of oral arguments of the last three weeks; this case was the one she feared hearing whenever Egan read the docket number of the next claim to be brought before the Court.

"We will hear argument next this morning in Case 18-012," Egan read – and before she even got the title out, two distinct sectors of the room erupted into commotions, both sides of this case realizing that they had been summoned into action.

Rosemarie's sharp fingernails dug into her palms, leaving beet-red impressions that wouldn't fade for the rest of the day. She knew that docket number too. She hadn't noticed the lawyers in the gallery, but there they were, rising and collecting their notes and papers to bring up to their tables.

" ... *Agguire v. The City of Detroit, Michigan,*" Egan continued. She waited a moment for the lawyers to rush to their places behind the podium, one of them so discombobulated he stepped behind the wrong table before realizing his error and shuffling over to his left. "Mr. Pastor?" Egan asked this disheveled solicitor, without even a hint of amusement on her lips.

"Thank you, Madam Chief Justice," Pastor collected himself. He squeezed his eyes shut to summon all his concentration, then quickly snapped them back open to launch into his prepared monologue. "And may it please the Court: one of the tenants of American freedom, going back to the *Posse Comitatus Act* of 1878, is the right to home soil free from the control or oversight of the federal government, the right to streets policed by, and laws enforced by, local entities, rather than federal military forces. And yet today, the streets of one of America's proudest cities, Detroit, Michigan, are patrolled by one of this country's, one of the world's, most well-armed armies. Allied Armament is a military contractor, made up almost entirely of former military personnel. My client was a victim of unlawful arrest and harassment at the hands of this military contractor, an entity we contend the City of Detroit has illegally and unconstitutionally granted complete and unprecedented control over its police, its fire department – and through them, its people.

"Now counsel for the respondent is going to stand here and argue today that Allied Armament is not the military, but a private company. We have provided the Court with hundreds of pages of analysis comparing Allied Armament's personnel and materiel, its machinery and weapons of war, to that of our four main branches of armed forces, comparisons that will clearly show you that this company is equipped enough to qualify as a fifth branch. And in the 21st century, we as a nation have fully considered Allied Armament and other defense contractors a vital part of our military. In the decade following 9/11, the Defense Department paid out more than four hundred billion dollars to civilian contractors. We need look no further than the DoD's own Quadrennial Review of 2006, in which the

Pentagon defined the 'Department's Total Force' as, and I quote, 'its active and reserve military components, its civil servants, and its *contractors*.'"

Rosemarie couldn't concentrate, could barely take in let alone analyze what he was saying, so shocked and disgusted and *livid* was she that this case was being heard now. Didn't Egan understand its implications, that it would be the most important case the Court would hear this term, and maybe over the next several?

"Madams and Messrs. Justices," the lawyer continued, "Allied Armament is not some sort of small, homegrown mom-and-pop business helping little old ladies to cross dark Detroit streets. Allied Armament is a military force dependent on the federal government for over sixty percent of its annual revenue. Allied Armament might as well be a division of the US Army, holding Detroit in the grip of martial law."

"Wouldn't you say there have to be exceptions to *Posse Comitatus*," Egan leaned forward, interrupting him with that condescending tone already-decided Justices often took on when reciting a rebuttal they had thought up days in advance. "Natural disasters, local riots, even the enforcement of school desegregation – these are the type of crisis events that in the past have compelled Presidents to send troops into states. Would you claim these were illegal acts?"

"Of course not, Madam Chief Justice. But this is not a crisis event, this is a total, long term, with no end in sight, takeover."

"I think perhaps if you spent a week in the Michigan legislature, you might consider Detroit a crisis event," Egan replied, sending a wave of uncomfortable laughter echoing through the nine lobed vaults carved into the ceiling.

Of course she understands the case's importance, Rosemarie scowled to herself. *Why the hell do you think she called it while she's still in control?*

"The image is too grainy," George Aug said into his phone. "We couldn't get any hits on facial recognition. NCIC had nothing either."

George looked down at the photo Jason had emailed him four days earlier, a granular blow-up of a still-frame from a cheap, over-the-counter, black-&-white security camera, a shot of a white male standing in the lobby of a rundown motel. The quality of the pic was so poor, that's about all you could guarantee, that he was a white male; age, hair color, any facial features, all were impossible to discern. "Maybe if you gave me a little more on this guy? What do you know about him, anything?"

George paused as if an answer might be forthcoming, as if he wasn't conversing with Jason's voice mail. He shoved the photo back into his bag, then sat back with a sigh, pushing up his glasses to pinch the skin between his eyebrows with three fingers. His headache was a rager, but he was used to it by now – it had been unrelenting for weeks. He looked around as he dug into his bag for his little green Excedrin Migraine bottle, for a moment wishing Jason would appear, that they could spend just ten minutes catching up on everything, getting on the same damn page. He knew Jason wouldn't, couldn't answer his calls, in case George's phone was being tapped. They had been trading messages and emails like this for weeks now, Jason always switching to a new burner, or writing George from a new account. But George missed that connection, that rapport, he thought they had established before Jason left DC.

It had been so many weeks now, George wasn't sure if his memories of their interaction, their teaming were even accurate. He had gotten so little sleep in those weeks.

"I know you're still trying to find the Minutemen," George continued. He had his own personal worries and stresses he wanted to unload right now, but knew Jason didn't care. And it would only be ammo that whoever might be listening could use against him later. Instead, he stuck to verbalizing concern for the younger man. "Everything I've found on them tells me to tread carefully. They've got a whole subsection of their website about the Supreme Court, especially about those FISA appeals last year. The Court said the NSA could basically tap anyone they damn well please, and that drove libertarian nuts like this militia absolutely bonkers."

George chuckled. "What am I talking about? You know how the Court ruled. You were there. There's a whole hate page on Lapadula, on the judges he appointed to the FISA court while he was Chief Justice."

George raised a finger, as if he was lecturing his daughter, as if she could even hear or process what he was saying when he tried to teach her something. "You tread lightly around these guys. You find *anything* that seals up the link between this militia and what happened in October, you call me in *immediately*."

George sat back again, looking up at the flat screen hanging from a nearby post. "You were so smart to not come to Oregon. We've been *here* a month now"

– he was sure to remember in his wording that anyone, including his own Homeland Security superiors, might at some point hear this call – "and the Iranians haven't even played their music too loud. The Mossad wouldn't even find these guys suspicious anymore."

George noticed the cute redhead, the one he always gave a little oldman-flirt when he was here, stepping up to the podium and reaching for the PA handset. He knew he had only seconds to wrap up his call, or there would be evidence forever burned in behind his voice of where he was, what he was doing. It would be a simple matter to determine how many times he had done this over the last month. "I'm gonna close this snipe hunt as soon as I can, and get out to you. You be careful until then."

He thumbed the call dead just as the gate agent's voice blared throughout the terminal: "Ladies and gentlemen, we're gonna go ahead and start boarding Alaska flight 771 with service to Portland …"

George stood, throwing the strap of his leather computer case over his shoulder, with a quiet prayer that he could somehow fall asleep on this flight. He hadn't slept on any of his flights back and forth between Reagan National and PDX over these last four weeks, one of many reasons that sneaking back and forth like this had been so exhausting.

"Mr. President, I really want to thank you for sitting down with us today," George Stephanopoulos smiled across the Blue Room to Antonio Salas.

"The pleasure's been all mine."

"Before you go, I do have to ask if you've been watching the early Republican debates."

Salas chuckled, just as his Communications team had coached him. "You know, this job keeps me very busy. There will be plenty of time for me to get to know my opponent once the Republicans officially nominate someone next summer."

The political operative-turned-reporter expected this sort of response, and had planned ahead for it with his own staff. Long tired of the Right's accusations that he goes easy on liberal presidents, he was determined to challenge the current POTUS at least a little. "Then you probably missed this moment from Bradley Benedict last Thursday. I'd love to get your take on it--"

Before Salas could protest, the monitor stationed next to the camera switched from the ABC logo to video of the last GOP debate: the Republican candidates lined up on a stage, each behind his or her own mini-podium, the Fox News logo filling the cyc behind them. Greta Van Susteren squeezed down an audience aisle and handed her mic to a college-aged questioner. "Hi, my question is for Governor Benedict."

"What's your name, young man?" the charming Florida governor asked back.

"Beau, sir, I'm a sophomore at VMI. And I was wondering if you'd care to respond to the comments Governor Clark of California just made, about you using your influence to get your son out of the military early."

The audience buzzed. Governor Benedict had been the GOP frontrunner for weeks, but this recent revelation that he had asked one of the Joint Chiefs to get his son out of the Marines had been his first potential stumbling block, and had dropped him within five points of his competitors for the first time.

"Beau, I am so grateful you had the courage to ask me that question. I *did* take steps to get my son out of the Marines, and out of Afghanistan. As I'm sure you've read, I did go to college with General Fernie, Commandant of the Marines. And I did call him and ask his help in bringing Brad Jr. home."

A unison gasp sucked the air out of the room – everyone had expected some sort of rationalization, some sort of evasion, not actual *honesty* from a politician of all people.

"But let me tell you why I did that, Beau. My only nephew – my brother's son Charlie – he was killed last year in Afghanistan, in Kabul. And then, after what happened at the Supreme Court – I had seen enough. This President has failed to get us out of foreign wars we want no part of, and now this President opens us up to terrorist attacks? This President *fails* to bring any sort of justice to bear on the perpetrators of that attack, now over two months later? I'm sorry, but-" Benedict's voice cracked, and he paused for a moment, bringing his forefinger under his nose. "I'm sorry, but my family can't lose another member of the next generation, we can't *risk* another member of our next generation, until we have a Commander-in-Chief who knows what it feels like to have children, children who can die in wars or at the hands of terrorism. A Commander-in-Chief I can trust to keep my son safe."

The applause was already starting, but Benedict raised a finger, pointing down the stage at his fellow candidates. "And I have not one doubt that any of these fine people here are more equipped to do that than our current Commander-in-Chief. Elect one of us President, and I promise you we'll prove it!"

Whoever was running Stephanopoulos's monitor let it play a few seconds more. Salas had never seen anything like it (well, actually, he had seen it two nights ago when his Chief of Staff Rebecca Whitford had shown it to him the first time): candidates at a debate applauding one of their opponents. Now, four days later, Benedict's lead was bigger than it had ever been.

The monitor went dead, Stephanopoulos turning back to the President. "It's hard to deny that's powerful."

"I do feel for the Benedict family," Salas replied, "and I am so grateful to all families who have lost members in defense of this nation."

"And what do you think of his charges?"

Salas prayed his eyes weren't betraying his annoyance, his anger at what Benedict had said, but he had a sinking feeling they were all too easy to read. "Governor Benedict's a great man and a great governor, but obviously, there's a lot going on behind the scenes that a Governor who hasn't even won one Presidential primary yet just isn't privy to. I promise you, George, and I promise the American people, we have made great progress and are getting very, very close to bringing the Supreme Court bombers to justice."

Stephanopoulos leaned forward, offering his hand. "Thank you, Mr. President." Salas smiled and took it, as the temporary stage lights extinguished.

"And we're out," the field producer announced.

Stephanopoulos bounded up with a smile, removing his mic. "It'd be nice to get some bad guys behind bars before the election, huh?"

Jason had been in the bar so long, he had seen the entire second half of the Michigan State hoops game (live from the deck of some aircraft carrier), he had seen the President's national television interview, both silently displayed under the steady stream of John Cougar, Springsteen and whatever country pop the jukebox had decided to spit out on random. He'd had three Dewar's on the rocks and had just signaled the well-worn waitress for a fourth. And still, no one new had walked through the only door of the bar, the one he made sure he was facing when he selected his booth. No one entered who might be the man who had left the note at the front desk of his motel, the note telling Jason to be at the saloon about a mile and a half down Highway 33, across from a Rite Aid and adjacent a hardware store, at 5 PM.

Past 7 now, and it was still just him, the two men at the bar, the buxom waitress and the balding bartender.

Jason had heard George's message, that he had been unable to score a match on the image of the man from the motel's lobby security camera footage. (It was a minor miracle the Pinewood Motel even had a security camera installed, albeit a remedial, low-res one.) Jason had flashed his Supreme Court Police badge and said he was with the FBI in order to convince the girl on night duty she should hand over the security cam image of the man who had delivered that note for him. But alas, a day later in the Mio Saloon, Jason had no idea whom he was looking for, just that the note promised that the man would bring him the "information you seek."

Jason's fourth Dewar's came with an added bonus: the shiny-pated, gruff-voiced bartender sitting down on the other side of his booth across from him, his bulky shoulders blocking out the sun beading in from the open door. "He's not coming," the bartender hissed as he pushed Jason's Dewar's across the table to him.

"I'm sorry?"

"The man you thought you'd be meeting here. I can tell you he's not coming."

Jason was cautious not just in his verbal response, but in any physical cues he might give off. His first thought was to wonder if the bartender himself was the one who had delivered the note and this was his way of backing out after a change of heart – but that didn't make sense, unless he had worn a wig into the motel. The video image may have been grainy, but it was still clear enough to make out a full head of hair. Jason didn't say a word, just took a healthy pull off his Dewar's, by this point in the evening no longer tasting the burn of the alcohol, just the oak barrel sweetness.

"Everyone knows why you're in Mio," the bartender rattled on. "It's the only reason anyone who don't have family in town might stay in Mio for more than a night. Someone's here to camp, he stays one night, then heads right into the Huron at dawn the next morning. You're not here to camp. Not in this cold." He leaned in, his yellowed teeth stinking of old chaw shrapnel, "You're looking for the Minutemen."

It had taken Jason the better part of two weeks to determine that Mio was the jumping-off point for the Minutemen, the last bastion of civilization in which many of the militia's members were seen for the final time before disappearing into the 439,000 acres of the Huron National Forest. He had filled out the membership form on their website, requesting an invite to join the group, but had never heard anything back, so he knew he had to find them on his own. Ollie had struck out in his own exhaustive searches – the militia left no digital footprint beyond what one could find on their website, or the handful of conspiratorial articles written by local media that a Google search would turn up. Jason knew he had to go to the source, that he would only find them with his boots on the ground. He had been in Mio almost five days now, asking around at other bars, at hardware stores, at AA and Al-Anon meetings, even among the sparse crowd of last Friday night's Mio Au Sable High School basketball game. He had received almost universal tight lips and vicious scowls, until the anonymous note was delivered to his room late last night.

He finished his drink in a second pull. The cubes of ice jangled into new positions as he set the empty down on the table. "I don't know what you're talking about."

The bartender smiled and shrugged. "Having my business right here on the highway and all – I've always seen that as a responsibility. This is a stopping point for a lot of weary travelers, just passing through Mio, and I know it's up to me to welcome them to these parts. So why don't I give you a little tourist information? The Minutemen cherish their privacy. They don't tolerate anyone violating that privacy. Gentleman who told you to meet him here has come to his senses on that. People in the past who've poked their noses around where they're not supposed to end up leaving Mio with those noses bloodied."

Jason stood, pulling three twenties from his wallet and tossing them down before the older man. "Keep the change," he smiled and moved for the exit.

Vice Admiral Kennesaw MacTavish liked taking his frustrations out on paper targets, and his frustrations seemed to be mounting and mounting with each passing day, threatening to bury him under their weight. He might tell anyone who noticed his sour mood, his secretary or his mother perhaps, that he was disheartened with the lack of leads in the Supreme Court bombings, discouraged that he still didn't know where he would be deploying his best JSOC special forces teams for retribution.

But more than anything, he was frustrated with Shareef-- No, frustrated with *himself* for getting in so deep with Shareef, for letting the plans he had made with the young man, with the *boy*, cloud his judgment and threaten everything he had worked so hard over decades to achieve.

So as he fired his 9MM Beretta at a paper silhouette of a turbaned man 25 yards away, he wasn't picturing the mythical "enemy," he wasn't picturing a father who had beat him (his had never laid a hand on him), or a bully who had picked on him all through high school (he was the real bully back then, using machismo to mask his deepest fears). He was picturing his own face, his own stupid fucking face, doing all the stupid fucking things he had done over the past year. He was doing what he wished he had the courage do: he was killing himself.

Mac noticed the sticky film on his skin as he locked his weapon up in its metal case and stowed it in the nose of his canary yellow Porsche 911. It wasn't the shooting, the pumping of the trigger that had made him sweat, it was the anger, the fear and regret saturating his brain as he wasted over 200 rounds of ammunition over two hours. Neither his trigger finger nor forearms were sore even in the slightest, but his head ached a deep, dull burn, pains Mac thought he would drown in Jack as soon as he got home. (Jack on the rocks had been his drink of choice since hearing in junior high school that it was Sinatra's preferred beverage.)

It was after Mac slammed the nose closed that he first noticed the three large black SUVs with tinted windows sitting on the other side of the grass parking lot. It was the sort of sight he had never seen here; this outdoor range was preferred by the sort of local rednecks who considered Virginia part of the South and resented that so many Washington folk also called the state home. No P who was VI enough to travel in such a caravan would ever stoop to using this range, or Loebner would have bragged about it at some point (just as he was sure Loebner bragged about him to his other customers).

A large African-American tank of a man dropped out of the passenger side of the largest vehicle, then baritoned across to him, "Vice Admiral MacTavish?" And Mac understood: the occupant of this vehicle wasn't here to shoot, he was here for him.

Mac would soon learn there were *two* occupants of this vehicle. As furious as Rosemarie was with what she had witnessed back in the old Court chambers, she agreed with her husband that in order to keep everything moving forward, they needed to get down to Virginia and recruit their third nominee for the Court as soon as possible, especially considering how well Judge Goldman seemed to be doing in wooing votes. His confirmation seemed imminent by the end of the week, and that meant President Salas needed to have another candidate to announce by the beginning of next week. Rosemarie would have to find a way to deal with *Acting* Chief Justice Egan later.

Mitchell Aldridge opened the backdoor on her side, stepping aside to allow MacTavish entry – but after seeing who was sitting back there, the Admiral recoiled into a salute. "At ease, Admiral," Reg smiled, then opened his hand towards the seats across from them. "Please."

Mac obeyed and took a seat, Aldridge closing the door behind him "Sir. Ma'am. This is an unexpected pleasure."

"Not after all you did for us when we were in office," the former President smiled, and Mac smiled back. He had rarely agreed with Reginald Irving politically, and hadn't voted for him in either of his two campaigns, but it was undeniable that the greatest accomplishments of his professional career – from the apprehension of the terrorist Sheikh Alabar to the rescue of those journalism students from Yemen – had occurred while Irving was in office, green lighting even Mac's riskiest mission proposals without a hesitation.

The car started moving, and Mac looked around, confused about what was going on. This was an odd way for orders to be delivered. "If I may ask – is there news? On the Supreme Court?"

"There is. Time to brush off your old law books, Admiral."

"Excuse me?"

"You attended Duke Law School," Rosemarie reminded him as if he had forgotten. "Fifth in your class, in fact, weren't you?"

"Yes, but … I never practiced. Never even took a bar exam--"

"Because you were inspired into service after Mogadishu, right?" Reg chimed in, "Right after Black Hawk Down?"

"I don't think anyone would fault you for the service you've done for your country," Rosemarie smiled.

"We sure as hell wouldn't," her husband concurred.

"I'm sorry, I'm not following where this is--"

"Admiral," Rosemarie leaned forward, putting her hand on his knee. "There are no requirements in the Constitution that Supreme Court Justices have any legal background whatsoever. You've at least got a law degree."

"You don't seriously mean--"

"Your Commander-in-Chief needs you, Admiral," Reg smirked.

"You're an unconventional choice," his wife continued. "But in our view, you make more tough decisions in a month than most nominees do in their careers."

Mac couldn't help but chuckle. "Respectfully, Ma'am, Sir, the Bar Association will never endorse me, the Senate, they'll rip me apart--"

"Respectfully, Admiral," Rosemarie patted that knee, "you let us handle the politics."

"We're not worried about the Senate criticizing a military hero in this current climate," her husband added.

Mac sat back for a moment, transported to the Senate Judiciary Committee chambers, his mind swimming in all the questions they would ask him, the questions about the military choices he had made, the *personal* choices he had made …

"Stop the car!" he blurted out, turning to the front seat. "Please, can you stop the car?" He rotated back, noticing Reginald Irving nodding up to the front himself, a signal to the driver to do as Mac asked. The car rolled over to the side of the road and the Admiral reached for the door.

"Can't we take you back to your car?" Reg asked.

"That's all right, we haven't gone far, please, I just need to--"

But before he had even gotten it open, Rosemarie Irving's dulcet tones stopped him once again. "Admiral. Your trepidation is only natural. But the correlation between prior judicial experience and fitness for the functions of the Supreme Court is zero."

"Madam First Lady. You've always had a way with words. But--"

"They're not my words. They're Justice Felix Frankfurter's. And he should know. He served on the Court for 23 years."

"And we worked with the Court for eight. Rosemarie was a clerk there."

"We know better than almost anyone else on this planet when someone is going to make a marvelous Supreme Court Justice. And we know that when we look at you."

Mac shook his head with a laugh. This woman could talk a Superbowl ticket out of your fingers. "I'm honored. But I'm not the right person for this. I'm sure you'll find the right man or woman who is." He got out, shutting the door behind him.

Reg looked over to comment on how terribly that went, when he noticed Rosemarie was already on her phone. "Dennis. Have my office clear my schedule tomorrow morning. And tell Suzie to do the same for Reg's. We need to be back in Arlington in the morning."

The former President sat back, shaking his own head. He shouldn't have been surprised. He thought MacTavish's no was definitive. But he also knew Rosemarie Irving never accepted defeat.

Mac, meanwhile, hadn't moved since the Irvings' trio of Escalades had left him on the side of a Virginia road. Had he actually just turned down an opportunity to serve on the Supreme Court of the United States? *The goddamn Supreme Court. Are you really that stupid, Mac?*

And then he remembered the image that had made up his mind. He remembered that he had no idea how he would answer when a Senator asked if it was true he was in love with a male hustler twenty years his junior, a male hustler of Syrian descent.

It was in their first month together, back when Antonio Salas was a surprise nominee for President, that he had asked his lead Secret Service Agent Hifrael Fernandez to always, no matter what meeting Salas was in or where he was or what he was doing, to always let him know when he was going off-duty and leaving Salas in another agent's care. The future POTUS hadn't requested this for any particular reason beyond that he liked Hifrael, and wanted a personal bond with whomever his life was going to be entrusted on a daily basis. From that point forward, from that request, their relationship blossomed: he was often making cracks to Hifrael in Spanish about whatever meeting he was coming from, or whomever he was scheduled to meet with next, and kept a secret tally of how many smiles he was able to force out of the guard's ultra-serious visage. After growing up with six sisters, Hifrael was the closest thing to a little brother Salas had ever had.

And yet, in three weeks he still hadn't introduced the one topic he really wanted to broach with him. Maybe it was because they *were* so close that Salas hadn't brought it up, because he knew how inappropriate his request was and deep down, didn't want to put Hifrael in such a position.

But on this December night, when Hifrael stepped into the Oval Office to bid goodnight to his still-working President, Salas decided he couldn't wait any longer.

"Hey, do you know any of the guys on the Irvings' detail?" he asked Hifrael in Spanish before the agent could exit.

Hifrael didn't have to think about it for very long. "MMA. Mitchell Aldridge. We attended the Citadel together. That was many years ago, of course."

"C'mon, how many could it be? What are you guys, like 28?"

"Gracias, Sir," Hifrael smiled back with a wink.

Salas leaned forward, bringing the tips of his fingers together and resting the sides of his hands on the Resolute Desk. "If there was something we needed to ask him about the Irvings – something sensitive, but something I thought it imperative that I know – you could ask MMA about it?"

"I'm sorry, Sir … what kind of question do you mean?"

"Something that I wouldn't even think about asking if I didn't think it might be affecting the way this administration governs this country."

Hifrael tensed up for a moment. Was this a test of his loyalty? He had been the President's lead guy since his Democratic Convention three and a half years ago, since he won the nomination, why would he feel the need to test Hifrael *now?* Of course, this was politics, the most cutthroat, backstabbing business in America. Maybe the President didn't know whom to trust.

But how to answer? Was POTUS looking for undying loyalty to him and only him, loyalty that extended to even such an unethical request? Or was he testing to make sure the Secret Service agent remained ethical no matter who was giving the order?

Hifrael clenched up his body in obedient attention. "You know I serve at the pleasure of the President, Sir," he recited the Secret Service credo in English.

"Gracias, Hifrael," Salas replied. But he had seen the doubt tense up in the younger man's eyes. He knew that what he was considering asking was going to make Hifrael very uncomfortable. And did he *really* need an answer? Did he really need it right now? "Go home, Hifrael. Say hello to your wife and daughters for me. It's nothing that can't wait."

The President couldn't help but notice Hifrael's shoulders relaxing with relief before he turned for the door. "Thank you, Sir."

When Jason returned from the Mio Saloon, he found his door would barely open. The floor was crafted of old, warped wood, but it was the four-times-folded piece of paper shoved under it that stopped the door in its tracks just six inches from leaving its jamb.

After hearing such welcoming sentiments from the Saloon bartender, Jason made sure he was all the way into his room, the door locked and latched behind him, before he unfolded the paper. Two rows of numbers were hand scrawled on top of the creases, the first starting with 44, followed by three other numbers, with quotation marks and decimals mixed in. Below, a similar set of numbers, starting with 83.

44 degrees and change north, by 83 degrees and change west: it was coordinates.

Jason collapsed onto the creaky twin-sized bed with his boots still on. He would determine where those coordinates led in the morning. He would buy what he needed to get to them – out in the middle of the Huron National Forest, he would bet heavy money.

He was too drunk right now to do anything, and any store with the equipment he needed would be closed. He shut his eyes, letting his mind drift back to Miranda.

For the first few weeks after the bombing, he had avoided thinking of her, altering the course of his mind whenever he found himself starting to wander into memories of her. He couldn't control his dreams, of course, but found she was less and less frequently a part of them when he wasn't thinking of her during the course of a day.

But then he found out she was alive. Then he heard in the quaking tone of her voice mail *regret,* for whatever involvement she had in the bombings. Maybe, just maybe, he could even hear in her voice that it was something that had somehow been forced upon her (or so Jason hoped). He started thinking of her more and more, and such thoughts started to comfort him, fuel this long quest. Fantasies of what she might say when he someday saw her again kept him from giving up whenever there seemed to be no leads, no light at the end of the tunnel.

He had thought more and more about that last night he had spent with Miranda, about finding her off the wagon in Bullfeathers, her eyes red and tear-stained. What would have driven her to drink after more than a decade, what would have made her cry? Did she look up at the TV after he asked what was wrong – did she look up at Chief Justice Lapadula on the screen – just because she wanted to avoid answering Jason? Or did she turn that way because she *was* answering, because something on that screen, maybe the Chief himself, had something to do with her tears?

"What's wrong with my head?" Jason moaned from their bed, tearing at the hair nearest his temples. "Someone ... rufied me. Is this what it feels like to be rufied?"

"They're not rufies," Miranda answered from their bedroom window. "The next generation thing, still undetectable."

Jason's jaw dropped open as he looked up at her, her perfect naked form glowing in the moon. There was no surprise in her face, there was no denial.

"Rand ... are you saying ...?"

"I'm saving your life, Jason."

What memory was that? Jason sat up, tearing at the hair nearest his temple, just as he had that night. This was a new memory, a memory buried in the deepest, blackest realms of his skull, until tonight, when it seeped out again. Miranda had admitted to drugging his drink. Miranda was the reason he blacked out and didn't make it to the Court before the bombs went off.

More, more, he needed more.

There's earlier. They're making love – brief, rabid flashes of it – but no more of their words that night.

Nothing more about the Chief Justice, about Lapadula. *LAST THURSDAY,* the C-SPAN above the bar had read, *CHIEF JUSTICE LAPADULA - GUEST LECTURE AT HARVARD LAW SCHOOL.* Is that why, is *he* why, Miranda was crying?

Oh, what the hell did it matter anymore? The Chief was dead, killed in the bombing with three other Justices.

And trying to remember anything more just gave Jason a raging headache. He plopped that head back down on his pillow. And as he did every time he tried to remember that last night, Jason instead switched his brain over to happier thoughts, warmer thoughts, memories of Miranda from even further back, when everything seemed much simpler.

THIRTEEN MONTHS EARLIER

From that first second she rounded the corner into the office, Jason loved what he saw in the Supreme Court Marshal's eyes. "Oh," she rebounded with surprise. "Can I help you?"

He offered his hand as he stood from the couch. "Jason Lancaster. I'm interviewing for the Threat Assessment position. I thought your secretary said 8:30?"

The Marshal took his hand, gripping it with the most strength he had felt surging through female fingers since his days of playfully arm wrestling some of the tough chicks he knew back in the military. "She did, but I figured the blizzard out there might delay you at least a little." She nodded toward the window behind him, blurred with the unseasonably early November snow flurry.

"My father," Jason smiled down at the floor. "He drilled into my head to never be even a minute late. That minute you miss might be the most important minute of your life."

"Smart man," the Marshal smiled back.

"Not really," he replied as he followed her gesture to return to the couch.

"That's okay, mine isn't either." She spun a chair around from her desk to sit across from him. "Well, sorry to make you wait. Things are nuts here. We started a new term less than a month ago. My name is Miranda Whitney, I'm the Marshal of the Court. I basically do a little bit of everything to make this place go, including running the Supreme Court Police."

Jason realized it wasn't just that initial surprise, not just that small little victory of impressing her with his punctuality, that he loved in her eyes. He would never be able to put it into words, but there was a-- a *buzz,* a spark, an energy, an electricity in her eyes that drew him in, that made him want to know everything there was to know about this woman. There wasn't just one color in there, but three or four dancing around one another; he would come to learn that her mood or environment could make one color step out from the others and take center stage at any given moment: green on a hike, pale blue on a clear-sky drive to the beach.

Jason had locked into a few pairs of eyes like this in his life. He remembered when he first saw his best friend Paddy Brennan on the first day of seventh grade football practice, and he knew, *That guy's going to be my best friend.* Sometimes there's just an instantaneous connection between the eyes of two living beings. It was a feeling he even got when his Dad took him to an animal shelter when he was 8, and he first locked eyes with the beautiful German Shepherd they would take home that night. Thorn became Jason's dog in that very moment and remained his dog until his death the last month of Jason's senior year of high school, as if the dog somehow knew Jason would be leaving him soon, and understood that the loneliness and despair about to overtake him would be too much to bear.

Jason wasn't sure he believed in love-at-first-sight, but he did believe in connection-at-first-sight, and he had just that connection with this Miranda Whitney. He had never felt that connection with a woman before – sure, there were plenty of women who filled him with lust, whose bodies he wanted to devour the second he laid eyes upon them, but this was the first time he got that *buzz* from a woman's eyes.

Jason didn't even know if he was going to get this job yet, but he somehow knew that he was meant to be with Miranda Whitney.

"Mmm, you just took Gavin de Becker's course," Miranda read off his resume.

"That's right. Excellent course." De Becker was the foremost American expert in personal security, and held a course focusing on Threat Assessment in Lake Arrowhead, California. Jason's CIA buddy Mooner, who had recommended that he apply for this position with the Supreme Court Police, had also told him he wouldn't get any job ranked above hallway monitor if he didn't have de Becker's course on his CV.

Miranda tucked the resume away into the pile on her lap with a sigh, then sat back and drilled into Jason with those amazing eyes. "So why'd you decide to leave the military?"

"Almost a decade in the Middle East isn't reason enough?" he chuckled.

"Someone who puts that amount of time into the military can really turn it into anything he wants," she didn't smile back. "Any posting, any branch, any specialty. A lieutenant in Special Forces? You don't just throw that away."

Jason's smile was tightening under her hot glare. "I didn't throw anything away. It was a big part of my life. But I thought it was time I tried civilian life for a while."

“It didn’t have anything to do with Lance Tyrol?”

“I’m sorry?”

“Your CO over there, Captain Tyrol. Your discharge didn’t have anything to do with him?”

Jason just stared at her for several seconds, unsure how to proceed. She knew what she was digging at. Should he just come clean? He couldn’t tell her the truth, could he? Not if he wanted this job. But he also knew she could read the depth of his lies, and was probably judging him on his evasiveness.

Miranda dug into the pile, pulling out a photograph. She held it up for Jason to see. He had seen it before, but the surprise of seeing it here made him flinch. He had last seen it eight months ago, in a Military Police office. He moved his eyes to the floor, to the fibres of the Asian rug under the coffee table. It was a photo of Captain Tyrol, but with his face pounded in, his lips cracked and swollen, one eye purpled and distended, unable to open.

“You know … I was promised that had been buried, and was going to remain buried. Forever. No one was ever going to be able to find that.”

Miranda shrugged, tucking the photo away again. “It’s what I do. I can’t run this building properly unless I know everything there is to know about everyone in it. Especially the things they want to keep buried.”

Jason stood. He wasn’t sure if it was because he was disgusted to be ambushed like this, ashamed by what he had done, or just sure that there was no way in hell he was getting this job. “Thank you for your time,” he nodded to her, then stepped around the coffee table and made his way out.

He was proud of himself, for not losing his cool, for keeping his composure. Proud, but that was small consolation after losing a job that he knew would have been perfect for him.

On the elevator back down to the ground floor, as he passed the pro-life hobo wailing, “Save the children!” in front of the Methodist Building, on his walk to Union Station, on his entire train ride back up into Maryland, all he could think about was how wrong he had been about that woman’s eyes.

TUESDAY

Mac's eyes ached from being open for so many hours straight. They pulsed and throbbed, itched with dryness. He had never believed in all-nighters, and didn't think he had ever pulled one himself, not even back in Durham, at law school. He had gotten good at bagging Zs no matter where he was, no matter how loud or bright the environment around him was – a key skill honed when faced with the sleep deprivation of Naval OCS, and later, SEAL training.

No, if he failed to fall asleep tonight, it would be the first all-nighter of Kennesaw MacTavish's life. And there was no reason to believe he wasn't headed that way, still wide awake past 4 AM, now over five hours since he first crawled under the covers.

All the Admiral could think about was how he had sworn an oath to his country. Nothing had ever been more important than his country, not school, not God, *no* not his family, not even Shareef. And if his Country was now telling him, through her messengers the Irvings, that Mac could best serve her as a Justice of the Supreme Court, how *dare* he even consider turning that down?

He was a soldier. How dare he defy an order of his Commander-in-Chief, an order he had sent the Irvings to pass along?

But wasn't this debate moot? If he had no chance of being confirmed, what was the point of wasting his Country's time with the painful, ugly process that would ensue should he accept the nomination?

It was around 4:01 that Mac came to the realization that his mission had to be to do whatever it took to make sure he *was* confirmed.

At 4:02, he shot out of bed, storming right for the safe in his closet. There, he could procure everything he needed for this mission, items he had stashed away in case of national emergency. No, this wasn't the type of national emergency he had ever imagined, but it still qualified.

Nine minutes later, Mac's Porsch screeched onto the asphalt of the Colony Inn's parking lot. He marched up the stairs to the second level of the motel – he hadn't been sure that Shareef was here tonight, but the pounding Arab hip hop from the far corner window confirmed it.

Mac was surprised when he kicked open the door and found only four young men in that room; he had seen Shareef party with many more. Mac's Beretta was already raised – and at the sight of a barrel in their faces, the room's occupants recoiled into corners with frantic whimpers; even the guy on the bed shot up, the lines of coke that had been laid out on his perfect washboard abs poofing off his skin into clouds of white smoke.

"OUT!" Mac barked like he had stumbled onto a boot camp obstacle course, pushing them deeper up against the walls with quick lunges of his pistol. "EVERYONE THE FUCK OUT, RIGHT NOW!" The squealing boys grabbed their various clothing and paraphernalia, darting around the crazy old man with the gun. "MOVE! MOVE!"

Only the calmest, the handsomest among them, only Shareef, didn't move. He just rolled his eyes and moaned, "Really?"

Mac shut the door behind the last evacuee and turned back to the young Syrian. "It's over," Mac grunted as he dug deep into his pocket, pulling out an engorged white envelope, tossing it down onto the bed. "That's twenty thousand. Enough for you to take care of yourself for a long, long time. I can't do it anymore."

"But," Shareef protested, "but you said-- they don't know anything, you don't have a mission yet, you're not being deployed--"

"Something else has come up. I'm sorry. This has to be it. Goodbye."

And yet, Mac didn't move. He wanted to look away, but he couldn't pull himself out of the young man's beautiful brown eyes, couldn't help but notice the drops of wetness pooling under his pupils. *He's about to cry?* Mac swallowed a gasp. *For me.* Mac never realized Shareef cared that much. He didn't think this was a two-way street, he always figured he was just a silly old man with a fixation--

Shareef's lips landed hard on his, erasing all other thoughts save for the recognition of his precious taste. And Mac was doing nothing to stop him. Shareef's tongue was pushing in through Mac's lips, caressing his own. And Mac wasn't raising his gun, he was letting it drop from his limp fingers onto the bed.

Shareef was dropping to his knees, opening Mac's belt, then reaching one hand over the top of the elastic of Mac's boxer briefs and down onto that throb. Shareef was taking Mac in his mouth, and giving him more care, more affection, than he ever had before, more tenderness and selflessness and love than Mac had ever felt in his life.

And Mac wasn't going to do a thing to stop it.

The second Jason walked out of Glen's Market, white plastic bags full of canned foods and non-perishables hanging off his fingertips, he noticed the strange silhouette sitting in his car.

He took a hard left, then a long circle around the parking lot, coming up behind his own truck. Setting the bags down on the concrete just behind the truck bed, he pulled out his Kimber .45 and aimed it at the back of the head of the silhouette sitting in shotgun. One fellow shopper gasped and double-timed her cart away at the sight of his pistol, but Jason didn't move his eyes, didn't divert his focus from whomever was now sitting in his truck.

Keeping the gun trained with his right hand, he jerked the door wide with his left, startling the pasty, pudgy man inside. "Jesus!"

"You got in the wrong truck, pal," Jason said, pushing his barrel hard into the back of the guy's neck, forcing his face down in the direction of his knees.

"You're shopping for supplies, aren't you?" the stranger pleaded. "To hike out to those coordinates I left for you?"

Jason returned the pistol to his sacrum, deposited the groceries in the truck bed as he came back around the rear of the vehicle, then got in behind the steering wheel. "You coming with me?"

"No. I can't be seen there, I don't know what they'd do to me for deserting."

"Well, I give up. Why've you been helping me?"

"I just ..." He turned to Jason, stress-hardened eyes bloodshot and shaky. He reached into a pocket, pulling out a crumpled, tear-stained photo and handing it over. This man was center in the photo, his eyes happier, body healthier, arms around a beautiful woman and a young girl. "My wife, my daughter. Evelyn and Hope. They're still in there."

"With the Minutemen?"

The man broke, letting the tears gush out as he nodded. "In Polis."

"Polis?"

"That what the Ancient Greeks called their city-states. Totally independent, self-governed entities." He sucked in hard, wiping his dripping nose with the back of his hand. "It's my fault. It was my idea. I got us in. Then I realized how insane, how sadistic Benji was--"

"Benjamin Bratten?" Jason asked.

The man nodded. "You'll see. He's so charismatic. So-- *convincing.* Of anything he wants you to believe."

Jason wasn't sure how he would react if he came into contact with Benjamin Bratten. Three years ago, Bratten had walked into a Chicago branch of Solstice Bank with two assault rifles and mowed down seven people. His attack was precisely planned and lightning quick – Bratten avoided 'innocents,' taking out only bank personnel and security guards, and was out the door before an alarm even went off. He had boldly eschewed a mask for his attack, and an hour later, HD surveillance camera stills and other photos of his mug were plastered all over national networks and social media sites. And yet, Bratten was never seen again, except in a series of YouTubes espousing an anti-banking system manifesto that also called for open rebellion against all branches of government. An overnight cult hero, his disappearance became a national fascination to rival DB Cooper, Hoffa or Earhart. But eventually, another news cycle erased another 15-minute obsession, yet another push for gun rights was defeated, and it was as if the shooting had never happened.

Would that anger someone like Bratten? Jason had wondered, harkening back to the sorts of threat profiles he studied in Gavin de Becker's course. *Would he yearn to do something else to get back in the spotlight? Something like blowing up a government building?* These thoughts had been percolating in his mind since Allied Armament City Commander Dean Rikeman had emailed him the photo of both Bratten and Miranda making an arms deal in a Detroit alley.

Apprehending Benjamin Bratten wasn't Jason's quest, but he also knew he wouldn't hesitate to eliminate anyone who stood between him and getting Miranda back.

"By the time I wanted out," the man continued, "it was too late for my wife. She had fallen for Bratten, hook, line and sinker. A true believer."

"And you want me to get her out?"

"Please. Just tell her ... tell her I still love her." He couldn't hold back the sobs now, just pushing the words through them as best as he could manage. "And tell them I think about them every minute, every second of every day."

Jason offered the photo back to him, but the man shook his head. "No, you keep it – you'll need to recognize them--"

"I'll remember," Jason promised.

Mac was thankful he had made sure to not let Shareef pass out on top of him. He was easily able to sneak out of the motel room and back down to his Porsch. The younger man had turned him inside out – much more even than usual – but for Mac, not a thing had changed. He hoped when Shareef woke up and saw the envelope of two hundred Ben Franklins still resting on the bedside table, he would realize that Mac was standing by his words of the last night, realize that even the best things in life were finite. Mac promised himself to find some way to check on Shareef soon, before any sort of vetting got started, check and make sure he got the message.

But for now, he didn't have time. He didn't know how long it would take the Irvings to contact another potential nominee, but he expected they had a long list and would move down to their next name as soon as possible, probably even by the end of the day. Mac rushed home to shower and shave and put on his full service dress whites. He would start with the offices of the Irvings' foundation in Washington; he still remembered the President's secretary Suzie from his visits to the White House for various briefings and press conferences and medals and commendations, and if POTUS and FLOTUS weren't in their office this morning, he was confident he could sweet talk her into sharing their schedule for the rest of the day.

It wouldn't come to that. He was halfway down the driveway to his Porsche when he realized his view of the house across the street had been obstructed by the caravan of three black Escalades lined up along his curb.

As he turned and started marching for the center vehicle, Reginald Irving was lifting his rear off the backseat of the center SUV to retrieve his wallet. "Paying up already?" Rosemarie teased her husband with a cocky smile. "He may be coming over to tell us he's still out."

"In those whites?" Reg replied, pulling a c-note from his billfold and handing it across to her.

But Rosemarie wasn't just smiling about beating her husband, something that always filled her with joy. She was smiling that this was over, and she could return to the Capitol, return to dealing with the woman who had become the latest thorn in her side.

Judge Goldman silently congratulated himself on selecting the perfect tie, a dark blue with stripes of red outlined in white. Patriotic but not obvious. Classy but not staid. Conservative (it would be a Republican majority grilling him, after all) but not tight-assed.

"You were smart to not go with the green one," he heard Janaki say, then through the mirror saw her appear over his left shoulder.

Goldman turned with a smile; he had some news he had been waiting all morning to tell her. "Guess what? Farrar Strauss loved your outline. They changed their minds, I don't have to give my advance back." But for some reason, this news didn't even crack a smile into her tense features. "C'mon, what kind of a sour look is that? We're gonna have a book published!"

"If you get confirmed."

"Actually, I bet they'd love it just as much if I wasn't. Bork wrote some bestsellers--" He caught himself, shaking off this train of thought. "Wait a second, *if* I get confirmed? You're supposed to be my biggest fan. I made sure I put that in when I wrote the clerking contracts."

Janaki took a deep breath to organize the words she needed to say. She decided to keep it simple and to the point. "*Gonzalez v. Raich.*"

Goldman was already back to working on that knot in the mirror. "What about it?"

"It was the 2005 case in which the Supreme Court ruled Congress could criminalize marijuana use, even if certain states have legalized--"

"Yeah, I know what it is, what about it?"

"Fox News has your green brief."

Goldman paused, searching his brain, trying to remember how damaging it could be. He of course remembered writing and submitting an amicus brief – a legal opinion from someone who actually has nothing to do with a case – but couldn't remember any of his exact verbiage. "You're gonna have to give me more than that. Remember you're dealing with the elderly here."

Janaki raised the papers in her left hand to her eyes, reading some aloud. "'Cannabis poses less danger than alcohol, less danger than operating a motor vehicle, less danger than most drugs approved by our oh-so-above-reproach Food & Drug Administration. And I can promise you from personal experience that occasional use poses no impediment to any person reaching for such heights of success as say, a judgeship."

Goldman pursed his lips, confused. "Time out. You watch Fox News?"

"Some people watch reruns of *The Big Bang Theory* when they need to laugh. I watch *Hannity*."

"Okay, so I'll admit I smoke it from time to time. What's the big deal? Does anyone even care anymore?"

"No nominee has admitted to using it since Clarence Thomas. That was over 25 years ago. We have no idea what the reaction's going to be in there."

"Hey, he still got in," Goldman replied with a smile.

"Yeah, because everyone was too busy talking about something else he had done. Until he accused the Judiciary of racism and they *had* to confirm him."

Goldman was unfazed, already halfway out into the hall before Janaki brought up one more important aspect of Fox's scoop. "Your Honor. They got it from your wife." He turned back to her with perplexed eyes, as if it didn't make immediate sense to him. "The green brief. It was your wife that told Fox to look for it."

Goldman didn't move, frozen where he stood.

Three silent minutes later, Janaki would put her hand on his back and escort him down the hall to the Committee chamber. He shook it off and claimed he was fine, but she knew otherwise, knew that his wife's sudden involvement in this whole grand opera had rattled him. She regretted stabbing him like this, but better he hear it *before* the hearing began, and from her, than give every news network on the planet the opportunity to capture his reaction in real time. As bad as this wound hurt now, Janaki hoped this way it wouldn't be fatal.

Acting Chief Justice Egan considered it very important that the Supreme Court's 'robing room experience' was recreated in their new home as best as possible. The Robing Room had been the Supreme Court's equivalent of the locker room, a small chamber located just behind the Courtroom itself, where the Justices would congregate approximately five minutes before 10 AM to don their robes and shake one another's hands – thirty-six handshakes in all, a tradition that always helped ease any tensions left over from nasty conference squabbles or petty dissent language.

And so, even though the wooden lockers of the actual Robing Room had been charred to crisps in the bombing, a wall of replica lockers had been erected in the vacant office nearest to the old Court chamber on the Capitol's ground floor. Six of the lockers were emblazoned with golden plates carved with the

Justices' names, while two still remained blank. But the locker closest to the door read simply, 'THE CHIEF JUSTICE.' Egan had stared at that plate each morning as she opened her own locker; she was still resentful that the President had insisted on attaching the extra adjective to her title, that he had decided to name her only '*Acting* Chief Justice,' and wouldn't go ahead and officially nominate her for the middle chair. She should be celebrated as the first female Chief Justice, but without the official investiture, would instead someday soon become just another flotsam piece of Wiki-trivia. Everyone snickered throughout the corridors of power that President Salsa would never make her promotion permanent; she had asked her clerks to set up a Google News alert for any use of the term 'The Egan Court' by the media, but through three weeks it had only been used twice, both times by *The Daily Nebraskan*, the student newspaper of her alma mater. And many of the official duties of the Chief were being put on hold; neither the Judicial Conference nor the Smithsonian Board of Regents, both chaired by the Chief, would be meeting until a permanent replacement to Warren Lapadula had been named.

Yes, Antonio Salas would surely want his own nominee as Chief. She shuddered to think whom *this* President might nominate. In the meantime, she intended to take full advantage and do as much good as she could while control of this Court was in her hands.

"Um, Chief? You ready?" one of the other Justices broke her caustic reverie. She had insisted in their first meeting as an abridged Court that her colleagues honor the tradition of referring to her as Chief as long as she held the title, and in another gesture designed to make sure no one forgot to accord her the proper respect, added four gold stripes to the sleeves of her black robes, a sartorial choice originated by William Rehnquist (and not followed by any of the subsequent Chiefs).

Egan turned to her fellow Justices with a smile and took the hand nearest hers, starting the circle of handshakes. As she shook her fifth hand – the dainty, still-shaking fingers of the outmatched Cecilia Koh – Egan noticed this room had a seventh occupant: the last First Lady of the United States.

"No one but the Justices is allowed in the Robing Room before we enter the Courtroom," Egan hissed at Rosemarie.

"Two weeks ago this was the break room for Capitol janitorial. I just need five minutes."

Egan leered at Rosemarie. The First Lady's impertinence disgusted her. But not wanting to make a scene, she said over her shoulder, "Everyone line up outside the courtroom and I will join you before we go in."

Rosemarie smiled at the other Justices as they filed out, shut the door behind the last one, then turned back to Egan. "I really admire what you're doing, Claudine. Bringing the Court back to life, keeping it moving forward. Refusing to let the terrorists win."

"You're delaying the Supreme Court to pay me a compliment?"

"And offer a little advice, if I may. I think this country – and your legacy – would be best served by more carefully considering which cases you hear before the Court has a full complement of Justices. There are plenty of cases you can call now that will undoubtedly be decided by a 6-0 margin, something no one will ever be able to find fault with. But if you hand down a decision 4-2 or send it back down to the lower courts with a 3-3 tie ..."

Egan was already moving for the door. "With all due respect, Madame First Lady, you may not offer me any advice."

Rosemarie's hand grappled around the Chief's left bicep, holding her in place. "Take a case like *Agguire v. Detroit.* You rule on that, and next term it's going to have to be re-tried and overturned. You know it will. Your entire tenure will come off looking like a joke, like it didn't even count."

Egan didn't bother to pull her arm away, instead leaning in and bringing her eyes in close to Rosemarie's. "Who do you think you are? You haven't won anything since your sorority elections. You've never been grilled for five eight-hour days by a Senate committee. You were never appointed to anything more than the chairmanships of national weight loss programs, canned food drives and Easter egg hunts. You're a symbol of our most arcane, sexist, defunct traditions. You're more useless than a Vice President. Our current President didn't even need one of you to get elected. And now, because you spent twelve months as a clerk here twenty-some-odd years ago, you're suddenly the national expert on the Supreme Court? Well, I'm sorry, Madame First Lady, you may have the opportunity to inject your two cents with our gutless President, but in here, in *this* Court, everything is up to me. And I'm going to go ahead and trust the instincts I've honed over thirty-three years as an Associate Justice, observing four Chiefs, and hearing nearly *three thousand* cases." She yanked her arm free. "You're of course always more than welcome to listen in."

Egan exited, not realizing she had done something few other human beings to walk this Earth had ever accomplished: she had made Rosemarie Irving speechless.

Seated two rows behind Goldman at his nominee table, Janaki could already feel the sweat under her arms drying up, the airflow into her lungs coming in deeper, more relaxed breaths. It was the second Senator – and first Republican – to question him, Miriam Ekman of Utah, who brought up the judge's green brief. And though his clerk had warned him about this possible line of attack mere minutes before he walked into the committee hearing room, Judge Goldman handled this line of questioning with the skill and aplomb of someone who had practiced for it with his prep team for the last week.

"What you have to understand, Senator," he smiled into the thin mic snaking up from the table, making sure to lock eyes with his questioner, "is that *Gonzalez v. Raich* was heard three years before I was appointed to the federal bench. In 2005, I was serving as an Associate Justice of a state Supreme Court. I wrote that amicus brief as a representative of a state, of state judiciaries in general. Now that I am a representative of the *federal* government, the federal judicial system, and of course would continue to be such if I was lucky enough to be confirmed by the Senate, I would have to look at each issue, including this one, from a different perspective, that of the federal government.

"But I have to say, Senator," he had to add with a mischievous grin, "considering your own stances on health care, on gun control, on a national abortion policy … I would've thought you of all people would applaud my argument for states' rights."

The Kennedy Caucus Room filled with stifled chuckles, and deep in her lap so no one would notice, Janaki pumped her fist. The Boss had nailed the Senator with that one.

But Ekman wasn't backing down. She removed her reading glasses and tossed them down on the table before her, as if tossing off her kid gloves. "Are you trying to contend, Judge Goldman, that were a case to come before the Supreme Court that could result in the national legalization of marijuana, that we're supposed to believe you wouldn't vote on the side of legalization?"

"As you know, Senator, it's not really appropriate for me to comment on exact cases or situations in this hearing, and there are hundreds, thousands of variables that would go into any case, and any decision. But I will say that the most important variable to consider when deciding a case is stare decisis, all the precedents set previously by the Court, including the decision they reached in *Gonzalez v. Raich*, and those precedents of course are going to be much more important than any of my own personal considerations."

"Judge Goldman, I think you know the question most of America is asking as they watch this proceeding and consider your fitness for their Supreme Court." Ekman leaned in close to her mic, her voice reverberating with the bass of the voice of God. "Do you still smoke recreational marijuana as regularly as your amicus brief implied?"

The gallery stirred with the boldness of the question, but Goldman smirked. "I believe the word I used in the brief was *occasional* – and no, I don't smoke it recreationally."

This inspired an even larger reaction. Goldman milked it for a moment, even turning full around to wink at Janaki before he returned to the mic. "I have a prescription. You see, Senator, I wouldn't have been able to get into Harvard and start my path toward a legal career if I wasn't a halfway decent hockey player. But it turns out my technique left a lot to be desired: I led with my left shoulder a little too much in my fore-check. And *occasionally* I do ease my most debilitating pains with marijuana."

"Would you be able to define occasional for us?"

"I wouldn't be able to put an exact number on it, just that I think if you were to stay at my house for a year, I think you'd be surprised at how infrequent it really is."

Ekman's eyes filled with glee as she dug out a piece of paper; Goldman had walked right into her trap. "One of your former clerks has recently given an interview to the website *World Net Daily*. Have you read it?"

"Actually, I can't say I've ever even heard of that site."

"Your Honor," Clyde Dudley – himself surprised at just how fond he had become of the liberal judge – piped up, trying to come to the rescue, "with all due respect to the junior Senator from Utah, I wouldn't say it's the most reputable news source--"

But Ekman was in a rage, and not to be deterred. "This ex-clerk of yours claims your wife Dr. Alice Goldman left you because you smoke marijuana daily, if not twice daily, or even more. Is that not accurate, Judge Goldman?"

"Senator Ekman, you're in your last minute--"

"And in that remaining time, Mr. Chairman, I'd very much appreciate it if Judge Goldman could answer my question."

Janaki was glad she couldn't see Goldman's face. She shut her eyes, praying he was holding it together, hoping his eyes weren't full of terror, his forehead not shiny with sweat.

Finally, he leaned into the mic and, softer and weaker than he had spoken all day, said, "Senator. I wish I could just whip out a chart of how often I use cannabis. I really do. You'd see that whoever was interviewed by that website was greatly exaggerating. But unfortunately, I don't keep track. I guess you're just going to have to trust me."

Senator Ekman let out one grunt of a laugh and sat back in her chair, so very proud of herself. This one grunt of a laugh would be replayed throughout the day on political websites, social media feeds, and finally, evening news and gab shows. For an eventual accumulative audience in the millions, Ekman had successfully equated trusting Isaac Goldman with a joke. Dudley acknowledged the next Senator to speak, and another round of questions began. Nothing the rest of the day tripped Goldman up the way Ekman's interrogation had, but the damage had been done. He was never the same, the swagger drained out of him.

In the narrative of the day, he had been made more joke than Justice.

Ali had known for two weeks he was being surveilled, and now the others had to believe him.

He had seen that same black man too many times over the last couple of weeks for it to be a coincidence. He might not have ever noticed him in the first place if not for the man's slight lisp coming out when he ordered a mocha from the Stumptown Roasters at 3rd & Pine. Ali knew it was a waste of money, his tradition of having an espresso there every morning as he pored over online job listings with Yas blasting in his earbuds, but he also knew that couple hours a day was the only thing keeping him sane in his current situation: in a new country, with no friends or family, staying on a cot in a stuffy little room of a closed preschool with five other unwashed Iranian men.

"Thanks so much, have a great day." It was about ten days ago Ali realized how many times he had heard that black man say that, heard him shove his tongue too far between his teeth as he pronounced his S's. He had been here almost every day that Ali was. That didn't mean anything, of course – there were many people who went to this coffee shop every single day, including Ali himself. Wasn't that a tradition in this country, especially in his new city, Portland? *Dammit, Ali,* he chastised himself, *you're going to have to relax if you're ever going to learn to like this place.*

Ali prayed he would come to like it. He *had* to come to like it. His father had sacrificed so much to get Ali here, giving him his own Diversity Immigrant Visa when he won the previous year's 'Green Card Lottery.' Ali had to remember to respond whenever anyone called him by his father's name. He had almost blown it at the DMV: he was so hung over the day of his appointment (he had to be drunk every night to fall asleep in that hell hole halfway house), he had answered, "No, that's my father," when the government worker behind the desk read his father's name off his doctored passport. He quickly corrected himself, laughing off that line like it had been a joke, but by the time the worker handed the passport back with a smile, Ali had pissed himself a little in fear.

Every expat Iranian he had met loved it here – once they put in the time and effort to build their own lives and careers and families. Many of these families were so kind, opening their homes to newcomers for a home-cooked meal once or twice a week. *This truly is the land of opportunities,* the dinner hosts would assure their guests. *Give it time and patience and every effort you have inside of you and you will find the opportunity that is meant for you.*

Those dinners just angered Ali, made him stew with impatience, with a brutal rage that things were taking so long, that there were so many disadvantages here for foreigners. In his mind, Ali knew they were right, but in his heart fractious emotions burned white hot during each dinner at some rich asshole's suburban home: *It was so easy for you when you came over. You don't know what it's like now. Everyone hates us now. Their economy is shit. This place has been drained of every opportunity like a dirty old wet towel.*

A beautiful Iranian homemaker had reached across the table of a recent dinner to take his hand; she must have seen the pulsing behind his eyes. *You can't watch the news,* she said. *You must know that everyone here, everyone in this city, welcomes you and wants you to succeed.* Her words were the first to break through to Ali, much more so than those of Mo Mullin, the benefactor of the halfway house (and maybe the biggest hypocrite of them all, now getting rich through the Americans' corrupt legal system). No, the words of this beautiful woman were the first to relax Ali, to help him open his mind to the possibilities of the future. He could find a job. He could start a life. Maybe someday he could find the younger version of this wonderful woman.

And then Ali went for a bike ride. His friend Bahram had invited him to go for a ride on Saturday, four days ago, offering up his wife's bike for Ali's use. Even when they emerged from the Pencil Pals to find the skies gray and wet with drizzle, they had kept their plan. They had taken the Waterfront Park Trail all the way south along the Willamette, to the path's terminus under the Marquam Bridge.

That's when Ali saw the black man coming up behind them on his own bike.

They passed him going the opposite direction, and Ali looked back over his shoulder, confirming that the man was turning around as well, following after them, keeping at least 50 or so yards behind them. After they had passed under the Burnside Bridge and turned back onto Naito Parkway, about to enter back into their Old Town neighborhood, Ali stopped his bike, turning with his cell phone to snap several photos of the black man as he rode by, continuing up the waterfront. Bahram grabbed his arm, pulling the phone down, scolding him, "What are you doing? You can't take photos of someone without their permission." Ali said he would explain when they got back inside, that it wasn't safe out here. Bahram looked at him as if he was certifiable, then mounted his bike again and rode west towards the Pencil Pals building.

No one else believed Ali's claims that this man was following him, that this man was watching him. Okay, a couple of the residents considered to be the most unbalanced may have agreed, claiming they also had been under surveillance for months if not years. But none of the leadership figures bought into his theory. "I'm sure he lives in the neighborhood," Mo scoffed. "Where else is he going to get coffee and ride his bike on the weekend?"

"It was fucking pouring out there today," Ali railed. "There was no one else crazy enough to ride today – just us and this random black man! And you're telling me that's a coincidence?"

"Maybe you two should date," someone cat called from the back of the room, and the meeting ended in laughter.

Today, Ali was going to make them swallow those laughs. He had to wait until today because today was the first day a car was available to borrow from one of the other residents. Ali got in and just started driving. He didn't know where the hell he was going, he was just going to drive, down I-5 into the heart of suburbia, across 217 into Beaverton. After about an hour on the road, he entered 'Council Crest' into the maps app on his phone, and started following its directions.

Twenty minutes later, he was making his way up the windy roads to this park a thousand feet above sea level, which offered numerous views for hikers down onto the city. Best of all for Ali's purposes, there was only one road into – or out of – Council Crest. He rounded the one-way circle of pavement around the park's highest grassy knoll, then started descending back down into the adjacent neighborhood. But after going less than a block, he yanked the car over to the right and parked on the curb, getting out and darting into the nearest bushes, crouching there in the bark dust, behind the shrubs.

Three minutes later, the car went by: a charcoal Toyota Camry, maybe the most bland, forgettable car on the road today. Ali shot to his feet – he had seen the driver, he knew that his theory had been validated! He held up his phone, readying the camera function. He could hear the Camry rounding the circle, then coming out of the park again, coming his way, coming towards his car –

As the Camry drove by, Ali slapped his thumb against his phone screen, snapping off as many photos as he could. The car went by at not even ten miles per hour – the driver *peering into Ali's empty car as he passed.* Then it sped up again, disappearing down Council Crest Road.

Ali checked the photos. He didn't get the Camry driver's face in any of them, as he was turned towards Ali's car. But that didn't matter. He got the back of his head, the back of his hair, cropped close to his black skin.

The meeting had been going on for well over an hour, thirty-seven paragraphs dissected with fine tooth combs, when Salas's Deputy Communications Director said what was on everyone's mind. He was loathe to do it, but Becks had selected him before the President came in. He drew the proverbial short straw as the shortest-tenured of the senior staff (he had come on just after Labor Day); he was the one who was going to have to make the suggestion.

"If I may, Mr. President," he whimpered, "I think what it's really missing is national security." He looked around, expecting at least nods and grunts of assent, but no one moved. The echo of someone setting their pen down ricocheted through the silence. Everyone was waiting to gauge POTUS's reaction before they joined their fellow staffer on his creaky limb.

"What do you call Paragraph 22?" The President read from his own legal pad: "'With the fewest boots this country's had on the ground in Afghanistan in the last decade, our armed forces are safer than in a generation--" He grimaced, crossing out and scribbling an edit. "--the men and women of our armed forces are the safest they've been in a generation and ready to deploy at a moment's notice to any cry for help from any of the world's citizens.'"

"With all due respect," the staffer cleared his throat, looking around the table for help. He may be sinking, but he wasn't going to shirk the duty the President's Chief of Staff had assigned him; he doubted Antonio Salas knew his name yet, and only saw him once or twice a week, whereas he had to suffer at least two meetings with Rebecca Whitford a day. "All anyone really wants to know is what we're doing about the attack. What we've done."

Salas rubbed his forehead. "Okay, we've gone over this a lot with the press office, but I might as well make sure everyone here's heard it. The most capable men and women in all areas of law enforcement and homeland security have been working around the clock to find answers for the American people, and more importantly, make sure an incident like the Supreme Court doesn't happen again. But I'm not going to jeopardize any ongoing investigations for political purpose--"

"Sixty-one." Becks slammed a piece of paper down on the table, standing from her chair across from her boss. "Your approval rating two months ago, the highest of your Presidency, the day we announced Cecilia Koh as your first pick for the Court. Today you're at 37, your lowest, and the lowest of any President in over a decade." She lifted the paper to her eyes and read aloud: "'How confident are you in this President on matters of national security?' 25 percent. 'How confident are you this President will find the Supreme Court bombers?' *Nine* percent."

"And you think telling everyone what they don't want to hear is the way to raise those numbers?" Salas retorted. "Reminding them we don't have anyone in custody yet? That we may never find the answer?"

"Mr. President," Becks paused. She hated to ambush him like this, and wished she could've gone over these numbers with him in private, but she could tell he hadn't been listening to her in weeks. She didn't know why, she could just surmise from his mindless grunts when she spoke, from questions he would ask that she had answered a meeting or a day or even an hour before, that he wasn't hearing a word she said. She didn't know why things had changed, but they had.

She hoped that bringing something up in a large meeting like this, with a room full of eyes gazing upon him, on a topic he cared about like the State of the Union, would give him no excuse but to hear her this time. "In the weeks after the attack, the American people were all in our corner, rooting for us to repair the Court and find the bad guys. Unfortunately, we've only had the means to work on one of those missions they gave us. And their patience is wearing thin. This is your first State of the Union since the attack. And the final one you'll give before the election. This is your last chance to convince them again you're the right man to find justice for the attack."

Salas shook his head, flipping back through his legal pad of scribbles. "I don't know, Becks--"

"Everyone believes, everyone knows that you have done everything you can to bring the culprits to justice, Mr. President. Everyone hopes that so much has happened behind the scenes, and will continue to happen, that you just haven't been able to share with us yet. Maybe it's time we brought some of that in front of the scenes. Or this will be the last State of the Union we all work on together. And I think I speak for everyone in this room when I say we want to keep working for you, Mr. President."

The meeting would move on, not breaking up for another thirty minutes. Becks made sure she was at the President's side upon his departure, on his way back to the Oval for a sit-down with some Asian Ambassador. "I'm sorry to put you on the spot like that in front of the staff, Sir," she said, then held a piece of paper out over his chest with her left hand. He took it, never breaking his stride as he read. "The first poll not sponsored by Fox News that has Bradley Benedict beating you," she explained.

He shook his head, shoving the poll right back at her. "We don't even know if this guy can win Iowa and New Hampshire yet."

"You can keep saying that, but someone's going to win those states. And it really doesn't matter who it is, you're not beating their nominee without answers on--"

He stopped, turning to bore his eyes right into hers. On Hifrael's cue, his Secret Service escort stopped to form a tight perimeter around them. "Someone wants to take you down, Becks."

"Excuse me?"

He took another step toward her, lowering his voice into an intense whisper. "Sometimes, we spend so much time looking out for others, we fail to keep our own house in order."

“What are you talking about?”

He shook his head, already regretting even broaching the topic. “It’s not even worth getting into. I would just be on my best behavior if I were you. Someone out there is waiting to pounce on any wrong move you might make.”

“Sir-- You’re blindsiding me with this. Can’t you tell me anything? Tell me who it is?”

“How many people on this planet have the ability to get an email with a video attachment through to my Blackberry?”

Ali tossed away the clove cigarette and mounted the small mound of barkdust up to the fence. He felt its rough edges with his fingers in the dark – the hole he had cut through the wires with bolt cutters earlier that day was still there. As he ducked underneath and through, it was clear that no one had noticed his new backdoor behind the bushes: there were no other Pencil Pals residents anywhere near this section of the fence, no one keeping an eye on it to make sure it wasn’t used by intruders, no one patrolling the backyard at all. The fools. Didn’t they realize the targets they had become?

Ali couldn’t go in the front door tonight because of one of the rules Mohammed Mullin had imposed on all the residents. *Fucking arrogant asshole,* Ali thought in Persian as he entered the backdoor of the building, inconspicuously sliding in place at the end of the dinner line. *Thinks he’s so brilliant ‘cause he went into debt learning this country’s laws. He’s not so smart. I just outsmarted him.*

Ali had to come onto the property via his new backdoor because of an item Mo had expressly outlawed, now zippered in the deep inside pockets of his parka. It had been so easy to buy; sure, many of the camouflaged customers wandering the floor of the Portland Convention Center eyed his complexion with suspicion, sure they had a terrorist in their midst. But none of them *did* anything more than stare. Ali liked their stares, drew power from them. And when he found the nice older lady who was more than happy for his cash, when he had picked out the one he wanted, she was able to sell it to him right then and there with no delay, no background check, not even a recording of his name.

Whoever was surveilling the Pencil Pals would eventually take their surveillance to the next level. They would be coming. Ali would be the only one ready for them.

Clyde Dudley had a point. *World Net Daily,* or *WND,* was by no means a reputable news source. But by the time darkness fell on the nation's capital, that hardly mattered, as the banner headlines draped across every major network's video feed, even MSNBC's, were about Isaac Goldman's pot use, how it affected his relationship with his wife, and of course what it might mean for his performance as a Justice. He was compared not to Clarence Thomas, but Douglas Ginsburg, a Reagan Court nominee forced to withdraw his name after his own collegiate marijuana smoking came out. Every Republican, even those who thus far had come to his defense in the committee chamber, vowed to turn the rest of the week into not only a serious cross-examination of the judge, but a referendum on the loosening of morals in our drug-obsessed culture.

Goldman just flipped between each channel, enraptured with his own destruction, like a man granted the ability to watch his own car accident. Sequestered in his room at the Hay-Adams, he thought he better call the only person to whom he ever turned in times of crisis.

But Alice didn't answer. Of course she didn't, just like she hadn't answered the other five times he had called her over the past three weeks since the Irvings first contacted him about the Court.

Okay, he had called many more times than that; he wasn't even sure how many times total. But he had only left five messages. He hoped those were the only five calls she knew about, but it was so hard to tell, so many of his calls ringing just once very quickly, or just one and a half times, before transferring through to the voicemail. That had to mean she had her phone turned off, and hadn't seen those calls come in, didn't it?

Or did it ring once because she *had* seen who was calling, and had depressed the button on top of her phone to ignore the call? The judge tried to keep such horrific possibilities out of his mind.

"Alice," he breathed into his phone after the voicemail beeped. "I hope they're not bothering you with this circus. I know you might have gotten Fox started on it but ...I'm sure there's a misunderstanding there somewhere. Whatever happened, I don't care, I forgive you, I--"

He sighed, kneading his brow with his sweating fingers. "I know I'm the one who needs forgiveness. And I'm calling you for it now. I've changed. This last month, this is the biggest thing that ever happened to me, and all I can think about--" He sucked in hard, trying with all his might to avoid breaking. "--is how I wished I was experiencing it with you."

He stood, trying to pace out the emotion before it overtook him. "No, I know we're past that. But I thought you might want to know that I've changed. I've stopped smoking, I've given it up. Everything. I know it doesn't change a thing. But I hoped if you knew that, it might somehow make you happy. I love you."

He grimaced. He didn't mean to let that out. "I mean-- I always will. But I'm happy for your happiness now."

He killed the connection, throwing the phone across the desk of his hotel room with disgust at himself. Of all the calls he had made to her, all the messages he had left her, this was the weakest, the most simpering, the most deceitful.

He picked up his e-cigarette, depressed its tiny button until it lit up white, and sucked in the sweet THC vapor from its cartridge. If Alice had taught him one thing, it was that this, not her, was the only thing in the world he could count on in a time of crisis.

Dennis hadn't cried since freshman year at Window Rock High School. Okay, that wasn't true – he also cried when he didn't get tapped by Delta Tau Delta fraternity his freshman year at ASU (in hindsight: thank God). And at 3:06 AM the night before his first law school exam. And of course there was the twice during his first month as a Deputy Associate White House Counsel. Or was it three times? No, the third time was definitely in the second month.

This is not to say that the tears he shed after Rosemarie's lecture were routine, weren't from real pain, real fear.

He had expected some type of blowback after Goldman's grilling at the hands of Senator Ekman; this was the second straight vetting in which Dennis had missed something about the nominee. Cecilia Koh's complicity in her daughter's abortion had put her confirmation in doubt just last month, and now Fox News had Goldman's amicus brief, which Dennis also knew nothing about. If the green brief were to bring Goldman down, it would be Dennis's head on a stick.

He had met the attorney whom Farrah Veras had hired to replace him in Counsel's office – meaning, if the Irvings fired Dennis, he had no job to go back to. And unlike most of the Ivy Leaguers populating capital cafeterias and congressional staff offices, Dennis had no safety net, no security blanket. His dad was a walking stereotype, a (usually drunk) mechanic at a Ford dealership, his mom a (usually medicated) RN at Fort Defiance Indian Hospital who had to go back to working double-shifts to try to pay back the money they had taken out on their house. And all of this was occurring with a couple of their children still living at home. They couldn't keep themselves above water, let alone float Dennis a single cent if he himself became unemployed.

He had played out the whole thing in his mind: he needed to keep this job, or he would be forced to sling hashbrowns at Mickey D's just hours after losing it. With only government salaries on his resume so far that hadn't made a dent in either his law school debt or empty savings account, he had put himself in the frightening position of not being able to take even two weeks off. Get sacked, and he would have to go to work right away – but where? He couldn't just answer a 'Help Wanted' sign outside any Hardee's or Starbucks; pick one too close to Washington and he might end up serving someone he knows, or someone who might consider him for a job down the line. If they saw him there, his credibility as a hirable candidate would be destroyed; he wouldn't look like a brilliant young lawyer, but a fraud who had to mix chai tea lattes just to stay afloat. No, he would have to drive far, far away, deep into Virginia or up into Maryland, fifty miles minimum he figured, to assure himself of not being discovered.

All of this made his encounter with Rosemarie following the first day of Goldman hearings all the more horrific. Dennis was just starting his vet of their third nominee, Kennesaw MacTavish – asking him the basics, getting to know him, explaining the purposes of the 75-page questionnaire they were asking him to fill in by the next morning – when he noticed the Casino elevator opening over Mac's shoulder and the First Lady storming out, her face gripped with an intensity and anger he hadn't seen there before. No Secret Service agent had followed her off the elevator, almost as if she had eluded her escort on purpose. Something was really wrong. Seeing Dennis and Mac out of the corner of her eye, she kept her face down, darting behind the large display over the roulette wheel.

The exact middle of five children, number three, Dennis had always prided himself on having a talent for smoothing things over, for playing peacekeeper, for making people feel better when life appeared to have it out for them. He had kept his mother aloft, and had done the same for several of his siblings (his father was a hopeless cause). Sometimes he did it with his words, sometimes just by being there to listen to theirs. Seeing Rosemarie's frustrated expression as she marched off the elevator, he couldn't help but feel the urge to do the same for her. Sure, she was a First Lady of the United States, and he was just a lowly government attorney, but why the hell not, right? It was something he knew he was very good at, and she sure as hell looked like she needed it.

"Why don't we take a short break?" he whispered to Mac, then folded up his research on the Admiral, stood and crossed around behind the Roulette station. "Mrs. Irving?" he broached. But she didn't turn back to him, didn't respond. "You okay? Is there anything I can do? Whatever it is, you know I'm here for you."

Several seconds passed. Dennis was wondering if she had even heard him. Then, finally, just as he opened his mouth to say more, she raised her chin and replied with a perfect, calm tone, as if in seconds she had erased any muscle memory of whatever emotional ride she had just been on. "Do you take a lot of breaks like this, Dennis?"

"Um, no, Ma'am … I just saw you and thought--"

"I don't think now is the time for you to be slacking on this job, do you?"

"… Ma'am?"

"We are under attack, Dennis. We are a sinking ship. There are submarines firing torpedoes at us from all directions, and it sure seems like we have no defense. We're going down, primarily because we didn't see the submarines coming. No, actually, we knew they were coming. But we didn't realize what kind of torpedoes they had in their arsenals. We've been unprepared."

"I know, and I'm sorry. I take full responsibility--"

"Don't tell me you're sorry. Just tell me it will never happen again."

Dennis didn't know how he could promise that, not the way he had failed twice already, not with his confidence at an all-time low. But he couldn't let her down another time. He gulped. "It will never happen again."

That was good enough for FLOTUS, at least for now. She took leave of them, letting them return to their work. Dennis was proud he was able to hold in his emotions the rest of the evening, all the way through the ride back to the Alexandria Sheraton with the Vice Admiral, through handing off the questionnaire to Mac before he disappeared into the hotel elevator for the night. Dennis held it all in until he could get outside, dropping his weight down onto the built-in brick planter boxes extending from the main entrance. He could almost feel the tears crystalizing with ice on his cheeks as they dropped from his eyes down to his chin.

He was so overcome, lost in his own fear and misery, he didn't notice the black town car bouncing onto the driveway and rolling up to the entrance. He didn't even look at the girl getting out of the backseat – at least, not until he realized she was coming over and sitting down next to him.

"Can you believe they move my boss to the Hay-Adams and make me stay in this shithole?" Janaki said, before stuffing some sort of chili dog into her mouth. Dennis's head rotated over to her – whatever she was eating, it smelled like absolute escape, absolute heaven.

Catching himself, Dennis jumped to his feet, wiping his cheeks clean. "I should be getting home myself--"

But before he could make a clean escape, Janaki dumped another paper tray holding another of those gorgeous chili dogs down onto the bricks where Dennis had just been sitting. "You expect me to believe you're gonna walk away from a free Ben's Chili Bowl half-smoke?"

"A free …? But-- isn't that your--?"

"I know," Janaki said – or Dennis thought she said, through the chili filling her mouth, "it's unfathomable how big an oinker I am. I shouldn't have ordered two. So you take that one and, bingo, no more guilt."

"You're sure?"

"Yes, I'm frigging sure, my eyes are bigger than my stomach, please rescue me before it's too late."

Dennis smiled, picked up the tray, found openings in the chili where he could cleanly get his fingers around the bun, and brought the half-smoke to his mouth for a giant bite. His nose hadn't lied to him – it *was* heaven.

"Really?" Janaki glared up at him. "A girl brings you dinner and you're not even gonna sit down and at least act like you enjoy her company while you eat it?"

Dennis slammed his ass down on those bricks as fast as he could. "Thorree," he said through a mouth full of chili and spiced pork.

"Just eat. I know what it tastes like, you don't have to pretend like I'm as interesting as it tastes."

Dennis took another bite, and Janaki followed with a bite of her own. They sat there and ate, Dennis realizing he was chewing with a gigantic grin on his face. Eventually, Janaki finished hers two bites before he did.

"You know, I just started with Judge Goldman two months ago," she said as she wiped her fingers clean with a napkin. "My first day was the day of the attack, actually. He made me cry twice that first month."

Dennis's eyes went wide. He wanted to say something, try to defend himself, assure her she hadn't seen what she thought she had seen, he hadn't been crying – but she had happened to pick the moment his mouth was most full to broach this topic.

"I would tell myself I was emotionally fragile," she continued. "We all were, all on edge from the attack. But no, it wasn't me. It's him. These are insane fucking crazy people we all work for. That's part of the job. We work our asses off, then go home and cry. They don't get to see that, they don't get to see what they do to us, because we do that at home." She looked into his eyes, made sure he was getting it. "As long as we're doing it at home – we're doing our jobs."

Dennis swallowed, but didn't need to say anything. His look of thanks said enough. Then he took the last bite of what he would always remember as the best meal of his life.

The pudgy man estimated he had followed Jason seven miles into the Huron at least. Eleven more to go, he thought, and Lancaster would be close enough to Polis to attract the attention of the Minutemen. The man would help him attract this attention, of course – that was his mission, to confirm Jason made it to the coordinates he had given him, make sure the Minutemen noticed him there, and then get himself the hell out. Get caught himself, and his story would be blown; Lancaster would know he had been set up.

He was careful to keep his distance as Jason broke for the night, just as he had kept his distance throughout their seven-mile trek so far. From several football fields away, he watched the popping glow of Jason's fire light up the trees above it, and wished he had something to warm his own freezing limbs and extremities.

Jason's fire eventually faded out, and he disappeared into his sleeping bag. Watching him through high-powered binocs, Jason's pursuer imagined he would be dreaming about that crazy bitch he was searching for, and chuckled. "Don't worry, pal, you'll see her soon. Probably day after tomorrow."

Before he buried both hands in his own sleeping roll, he pulled out the photo of his wife and daughter, the one he had shown to Jason yesterday, and smiled as he held it up above his eyes. He couldn't even make out their shapes in the darkness, but knew every pixel of the image by heart, every wisp of his wife's hair and tooth in his daughter's smile, and just the comfort of having them that close to his eyes made him smile. "And we're gonna have a great weekend at home." He brought the photo to his lips, then tucked it into his pocket, not pulling his arms back out of his sleeping bag as he followed Jason into slumber.

THIRTEEN MONTHS EARLIER

One of the advantages of understanding that everything eventually turns to shit is that it gives you the balls to have a lot more fun in the meantime. Jason Lancaster didn't go to the batting cages, he didn't go for hikes or read books. Jason bungee-jumped, he sky dove, he rappelled down cliff faces. And why the hell not? All of this would end in dirt and worms sooner or later; he was going to enjoy the fuck out of his time while he had it.

With Thanksgiving approaching on Thursday, the Supreme Court wasn't hearing any arguments this week, and half of the Justices had left Washington altogether. But clerks were still droning away and tours still shuffling through, so the in-house police force was still on duty. Miranda had scrambled their schedules so they each worked fewer hours, and Jason found himself able to sneak away for a couple hours on Monday afternoon to hang with Mooner. Mooner was in country for the first time in a year, and when he emailed to invite Jason to drive a wealthy friend's race cars around the track of the Maryland International Raceway, Jason wrote back with an emphatic, "Fuck. Yes."

Afterward, it was back into Washington for burgers with Mooner, who was also staying in DC proper. Bullfeathers – a Capitol Hill classic named for the word that, according to legend, Teddy Roosevelt had used in place of profanity – was his suggestion. Jason had heard other Court employees mention it over his three weeks there, and had been anxious to give it a try.

These two could talk shop for hours. Jason's Third Special Forces Group had been on multiple joint ops with Mooner's CIA Special Activities Division – the Company's own in-house special forces teams deployed on missions to collect intel or carry out paramilitary operations – and he loved hearing the small little hints Mooner could give him of what they had been up to over in the 'Stan. As happy as he was to be out of the Suck and retired from the military, Jason could feel one small nostalgic bone somewhere deep in his breast, missing his adventures over there.

When Jason came to him three months ago for advice on how to handle the Captain Tyrol incident and his impending discharge, Mooner had tried to recruit him over to SAD. But Jason's father was in hospice at the time, and as little as Jason cared about 'Sarge,' he did feel the tug of familial obligation. His sister sure as hell wasn't going to carry her half of the load, not with two kids of her own and a trunk-full of resentment for the man. Mooner didn't hold that decision against his young protégé; indeed, he was the one who forwarded Jason an email about the Supreme Court opening and recommended how he bolster his resume to land it. Mooner was the first person Jason emailed with shock and elation when he got the call that he had won the job; he was also the sounding board for all the complaints Jason had about the job already.

"Gimme a fucking break, Jase," Mooner gave Jason an elbow as he polished off his second beer and signaled the bartender for another (he had declared his intentions to try all thirty-one of the draught brews before the night was over). "You're working in the most beautiful building in the country, protecting a bunch of Harvard brains who just sit around and read books all day. You were in Afghanistan for almost, what?"

"Nine years."

"Nine years. What could you possibly have to complain about now?"

"It's really … it's my boss. The Marshal, I don't know, she's just--"

"*--an unconscionable ball breaker!*" they finished in unison, breaking out a paraphrase from *GoodFellas* they loved to use when describing horrific COs. Jason told Mooner about how Miranda had required him to wear the traditional morning suit with tails everyday, eliciting jeers and laughter from his colleagues in regular cop dress or even business attire; how she had downgraded him from the usual Threat Assessment office on the second floor down to a small, windowless closet in the underground garage level; how she had ordered him to write detailed summaries of every threat report his predecessor had ever filed. "She even knew about Tyrol."

"What? I thought that was struck from your record."

"It was. I don't know how the hell she found out about it, but she did. She ambushed me in my interview with it. She even had a picture of the asshole--"

"Shut the fuck up."

"I'm serious. And I mean a picture from that night, with all the damage I'd done to his grill."

"That's crazy."

Suddenly, Mooner's gaze whipped up and over Jason's shoulder, in the direction of the entrance to the bar. "Whoa, don't look, don't look. But there's one fine little piece of tail walking in here right now."

Jason smiled. "All right. The bet is twenty dollars."

"Twenty dollars!" Mooner hollered, falling into their familiar routine from another of their favorite films, *Top Gun.*

"You have to have carnal knowledge," Jason pointed at Mooner and looked at him sideways just like Anthony Edwards had Tom Cruise three decades prior, "of a lady this time. On the premises."

"On the premises," Mooner smiled back, loving this.

By now, the object of desire had crossed around into Jason's view, taking a stool at the bar behind Mooner, a couple perches down.

"Oh fuck," Jason swallowed.

"Hey, that isn't the next line. 'C'mon, Mav, a bet's a bet.'"

"My boss."

"Huh?"

"The Marshal. That's her, that's my boss."

"What, no shit?" Mooner whipped around to check her out. Well aware long before this that they were talking about her, Miranda raised her glass and gave the CIA officer a wink. "Holy shit," Mooner said to Jason as he spun back. "You didn't tell me she was hot as shit."

"She's very good at making me forget it." Jason knew he had no choice in what he had to do next. He had been made. He sucked down the rest of his drink, melted off his stool, crossed around behind Mooner and leaned up against the bar next to Miranda just as the ice was settling in the bottom of her own glass, drained of liquid.

"Looks like my timing's impeccable. Can I get you another one of those, Boss?"

"Sure," she nodded. "Ginger ale."

Jason smirked, then raised a finger in the direction of the crusty old Irishman who seemed to live back there. "Uh, excuse me--"

"Jimmy," Miranda assisted.

"Jimmy! Two ginger ales."

She looked at him sideways. "Are you mocking me, Lancaster?"

He smiled back. There *was* one thing she didn't know about him. He grinned as he turned back to the bartender, just arriving with their frosty glasses. "Jimmy, can you tell my lovely boss here what I just ordered over there with Mooner?"

Jimmy looked at him like he was insane, but obliged. "Ginger ale." As the barkeep walked off, Miranda looked at him sideways again.

"Three years sober." Jason raised his glass for a toast.

"Eight years," Miranda said as she returned the gesture with a light clink against his glass. She took a sip, then added, "Giving up the drinking was easy. I couldn't give up bars. The people watching, the conversations you overhear, the regulars both behind the bar and on our side of it."

"You come here a lot?"

"Just for lunch. One hour during which no one needs anything from me. It's meditative actually. I know I sound like a crazy person--"

"No, it sounds great. You always come alone?"

"Always alone. I've been coming here my whole life. It's much nicer now, but I miss the old character of the place."

He sat down on that stool next to hers, and kept up the small talk as her pastrami sandwich came, as she ate a few bites of it, shared a couple fries. At one point, Jason looked over to Mooner, but he waved off any notion of joining as a third wheel, and ordered yet another draught he had never heard of.

"Can I ask you something?" Jason finally asked as Miranda was tipping and signing her credit card receipt. "Something I've needed to ask since my interview."

"Shoot."

"How do you know Tyrol?"

"Ah."

"No, you must know him, right? That's how you knew what I did to him, even though those records are sealed. He's your friend. Maybe more. That's why you hired me, just so you could punish me for what I did to him." He finished his ginger ale, his forefinger off the glass, pointing in her face. "And that's why you've been shitting on me ever since I started at the Court."

Miranda finished her drink, then called down the bar, "Thanks Jimmy." She stood up, bringing her face close to Jason's, boring into his eyes with those gorgeous orbs he had found so alluring the first time he met her. "I would never do anything as *stupid* as hiring someone for one of the most important positions on my Police Force just because of some sort of grudge. I hired you because I thought you were the most qualified applicant. But there were six or seven people on my force who wanted that position too, some of whom have been at the Court much longer than me, some for over a decade. I can't just let a newcomer walk into Court and go above their heads without earning his keep, paying his dues. That wouldn't be right." She patted his cheek. "Don't worry, you're passing with flying colors."

Jason didn't move as she marched right by Mooner – "I'm Freddy, by the way," he offered with an outstretched hand – and out the door.

From that day forward, Jason Lancaster spent almost every minute of the rest of his life thinking about Miranda Whitney.

WEDNESDAY

Dr. Goldman was surprised when, for the first time in weeks, no reporters accosted her on her walk to work. And then she realized why they had left her alone: they were all congregated outside the entrance of her medical building, just waiting for her there. She stopped for a moment to appreciate these surprising few steps of peace. She took in several deep breaths, preparing herself to fight through the throng to get to the entrance – there was only one to the building, so she had no choice but to go right through the reporters and cameras – then started her march toward them.

But something very strange happened: none of them did their part of the dance; none of them leaped to their feet or raised their lenses. They just kept standing around or leaning against walls, smoking and chatting, their cameras not moving from their shoulders or their necks. That's when Dr. Goldman realized she had made quite the presumption, assuming the paparazzi had come for her. They weren't there for her, but those two black Escalades on the curb. They were there for whoever had arrived in that caravan of obnoxious luxury.

One cameraman did notice her –the one with the 'MSNBC' logo emblazoned on the side of his camera. "Excuse me," he said, not even raising his lens yet, "aren't you Judge Goldman's ex-wife?" The others picked up on his discovery, raising their own recorders. She was almost already to the door by the time they had realized who they had missed. She kept her head down, didn't say a word this time, pushing in through the glass door into her building's lobby. Big Hung, the sumo-sized security guard who always greeted her with a smile, was out from behind his desk and at the door, making sure no one followed her in. "What'd I tell you?" he barked at the media hounds. "Don't cross this line, don't cross this line!"

"Mr. Hung, you're a godsend," she sighed after he pulled the door shut. She was already aboard the elevator as he moved back behind his desk, smiling to her, "I got to get you in to see your VIP patient today, Dr. G."

She didn't get a chance to ask who he was talking about before the doors slid shut. Was that right? She had assumed the owner of the Escalade fleet was here to visit another office – but was it possible whoever it was had come to see her?

She had her answer as soon as she stepped off the elevator on the 12th floor, rounding into the hallway to see two large men in black suits standing outside the door to her office. She stopped fifty feet away, considering just turning around and going home. This looked like a political protection detail, maybe even Secret Service judging from their earwear. She knew whoever it was had come to see her not about any medical concern, but about Isaac. And she had nothing to say about him. She had already said way too much.

"Dr. Goldman?" the largest of the bodyguards asked. She was caught, no turning back now. She nodded and moved down the long hallway, the guard opening the door for her as she approached, revealing:

"Mr. President!" she jumped back at the sight of former President Reginald Irving rising from one of her waiting room chairs.

"Dr. Goldman," he smiled, cradling her hands in his own. The other patients in the waiting room also came to their feet, snapping away with their iPhones. Alice's breath was almost taken completely away. In person, Irving was much more, well, *everything* than she had ever heard: much taller, much more handsome, much more seductive; his hair, smell, the touch of his hands, all perfect. "It's so great to finally meet you." His voice was much bassier, much smoother and more calming, when it emanated from his larynx than when it came out of television speakers. "I was hoping we could chat about a couple things."

Dr. Goldman let out all the breath in her lungs, snapping back to why he was here. "It's a dream to meet you, Sir. I have to say I never imagined this moment when I was voting for you. Twice. But I don't think there's anything to chat about."

Irving smiled to the peanut gallery of patients, then put his arm around Goldman's shoulders, spinning her back to the door and leading her down the hallway. "Your husband's going to make a phenomenal Supreme Court Justice, Doctor. But you probably know that better than I do."

"You are right. He'd be an excellent Justice."

"Well, unfortunately, there's a rabid right-wing tabloid website that's started a nasty rumor about you, about why you left him. I would never ask this of someone if it wasn't absolutely imperative ..." He stopped at the elevators, rotating around so he was looking straight down into her eyes, like he was a first date positioning himself for a kiss. "But I think we may need you to clear things up in order to get him confirmed. If Isaac didn't win a seat over this, well, that would be a real shame for our entire nation, Doctor."

"I can't say I disagree. But unfortunately, I can't clear up the tabloid story, Mr. President."

"Why not?"

"Because it's true."

Reg smiled. "That story should've remained a secret of your marriage. It's no one else's business. It shouldn't be the thing that makes or breaks the greatest moment of your husband's life."

"Mr. President, you wouldn't be suggesting I … lie under oath?"

Reg took a deep breath, burying his hands in his pockets. He had come to one of those moments he hated in politics, the playing hardball moment, the extortion moment. He knew it was a necessary evil; he had just made sure to surround himself throughout his political career with people who could do it for him: his Chief of Staff when he was a young Oregonian Congressman; his VP when he was in the White House, who burned so many bridges over eight years on Reg's behalf it wasn't even worth him running himself; and in this Supreme Court process, his wife. He was the pretty face, they were his enforcers.

But Rosemarie was otherwise detained this morning, so Reg had to handle this moment himself. "Dr. Goldman. I think you'd agree that bending that truth just a little over, say, one ten minute interview with Robin Roberts or the ladies of *The View* would not be some great moral compromise. And to be frank, it'd take up a lot less of your time, and would be a lot less painful, than what may occur if you were to insist on locking your heels in on this. We have a lot of friends who get a rise out of wasting peoples' time. Friends with the IRS, the AMA …"

"No offense, Mr. President, but you can't do anything to me. I'm retiring. I'm closing my practice at the beginning of March. I'm going to have nothing but time." She leaned in, whispering, "The letter hasn't gone out yet, so please don't tell any of my other patients."

She turned and marched back down the hallway, assuring the patients waiting there she would begin seeing them in just a couple short minutes. As Reg watched her disappear into the further depths of her office, he nodded to Mitch, who let the door to the waiting room swing shut. The former POTUS shook his head; he knew he sucked at these moments.

Cecilia Koh wasn't sure where she felt more overwhelmed: in her new chambers in the basement of the Capitol, or in her new Georgetown apartment. With the Court launching right into its new term the very morning after she took the Constitutional Oath, she hadn't had the chance to conduct a proper real estate search; that would have to wait until next summer's recess. (That's assuming they were even given an actual recess – the bombing had put them so far behind, Acting Chief Egan had hinted on more than one occasion that this term might have to bleed into the next.) Cecilia's husband Lindsey had offered to take a leave of absence from his own work and go on the hunt himself while she got her sea legs under her, but living in a home she had played no part in finding just wouldn't feel right to Justice Koh, who had enjoyed the property-buying process throughout her life. So she convinced Lindsey they should let the Acting Marshal find them a temporary corporate apartment, just for the rest of the term, and they would search for their permanent Washington home later.

Acting Marshal Meyers had recommended she rent a furnished apartment, but the idea of sitting at a desk someone else picked out, of reading under someone else's lamp, was just as anathema to Cecilia as letting her husband find them a house. *Well, that was about the stupidest choice you ever made, Cecilia,* she chastised herself after a week in her beautiful new townhouse with exactly one couch, a mattress without bed springs, a TV sitting on the floor and a Keurig – *Thank God for inventing the Keurig* – and nothing else. And none of the fixtures that came with the apartment, from the alarm system to the toilet, seemed to work; yet whenever she got to the Capitol and was sucked into Court business, she subsequently forgot to call the building maintenance guy about any of these items.

Ah, the glamour of the Highest Court in the Land, she thought to herself one night as she sat on the floor eating a microwave burrito while watching *Real Housewives of Something or Other.* Meyers had been right; she didn't have time to deal with any of this, didn't have time to deal with *life* now that the Court was her life.

At work, on the ground floor of the Capitol's North Wing, everything at least worked properly – she just didn't know if she did. Building a rapport with four clerks who had all been fifth and sixth choices of the other Justices, learning the etiquette of replying to another Justice's first draft of an opinion, figuring out how to organize her time so she would have time to read all the hundreds of briefs and thousands of cert petitions and still be able to eat and get more than, say, four hours of sleep a night – it didn't feel like she was doing any of that right.

And then there was her first opinion. It had been two weeks since Egan had pulled her aside as the six Justices stepped into an empty Capitol office for their first conference as a new Court. "You have to promise me something, Sister Justice," Egan assured her with a squeeze of the upper arm. "If I assign you an opinion in there, you have to promise me you're not going to worry. I'll go easy on you. It's customary to give rookies an underhand slow pitch for their first one. You'll do just fine." Cecilia smiled back, thinking that meant the Chief would assign her a unanimous vote, of which there were a couple that day.

No, she instead gave her a contentious 4-2 decision, one in which Justice Bruce Winks wasn't even firmly committed to the majority; if he later switched sides, it would be primarily blamed on the author of the decision for not crafting a persuasive enough document. Hence, it wasn't surprising when the comments on her first draft came back even from the Justices on her side of the vote laden with vitriol and condescension, filled with complaints that not only did the new Justice not understand the law they had used in reasoning their votes, but was too poor a writer to convey that reasoning even if she had. Traditionally, opinions came couched in a certain minimum of decorum, usually starting with compliments for the 'learned Justice' who had penned the opinion; but behind the scenes, Egan had been poisoning her colleagues with the notion that Cecilia wasn't really worthy to sit on the Court, and would never have been nominated under normal circumstances. By the time her first draft was circulated, several of the Justices were lathered up to really teach her a lesson. After reading their join memos, Cecilia was so convinced that she was the laughing stock of even her own clerks that she had retreated to her car in the Capitol Garage to bawl her eyes out.

Fuck it, she thought that night on the floor of her Georgetown townhouse with yet another green chile burrito, *this is why they give us lifetime appointments, I suppose, because the job is actually impossible to do. I'll just do what I know is my best, and stop beating myself up about it. And if my best isn't good enough for anyone, well, that's their problem.*

The next morning, Wednesday morning, Cecilia was running late, but for the first time since her confirmation, it didn't bother her; she wasn't allowing it to stress her out. There were no arguments being heard this morning, no reason she *had* to be in at a certain exact time. She was the Justice; if she felt that extra half-hour of sleep she had gotten was more valuable than a half-hour of extra reading time in her chambers, then more important it was.

This revelation gave her step a renewed vigor as she rounded the concrete walkway to her reserved parking spot – a vigor that the sight of the Escalade idling next to her rented Lexus drained out of her. The driver popped out to open the backdoor, revealing Rosemarie's silhouette waiting inside. "Madam Justice," the First Lady's voice snaked out from the back of the SUV. "I realize you're running late. I promise this will only take a minute."

Cecilia tossed her briefcase across the backseat of her car, slammed the door, then came around to get in with the First Lady.

"I understand you're off to a great start," Rosemarie encouraged.

"I haven't said a word in the courtroom. Or in conference. I royally botched my first opinion. How could you have possibly heard I was doing great?"

FLOTUS chuckled. "Sounds like every Justice's idea of the perfect colleague. More time for each of them to bloviate." Rosemarie's hand landed on top of Cecilia's and the Justice swore she could feel invisible claws sinking in. "And you're in luck. I've thought of a way for you to make your presence felt for the first time."

"O…kay?" Cecilia shuddered.

"One of the cases you heard on Monday, *Agguire v. Detroit.* It was completely improper of Egan to call that case now, when there's less than nine Justices to rule on it. You're going to let her know how inappropriate it was."

"You want me to go to the Chief Justice and tell her what she's doing wrong?"

"I know, it's disgusting no one else has done it first. They're all spineless cowards, cringing before that woman. It's shameful they're leaving this to you."

"Leaving what to me exactly?"

"Leaving it to you to make a stand. To tell her you can't support deciding that case until the other three seats have been filled."

"Madam First Lady, look, I really appreciate everything you've done for me," Cecilia stammered, sliding her hand out from under Rosemarie's grasp. "But I'm a Justice now. I will always take your opinion under advisement, I owe you that, but ultimately I have to set my own path now."

Rosemarie stared at her for a moment. And then, broke into a smile. "You're right. My apologies if I've overstepped my boundaries. Forget I said anything."

Cecilia breathed out hard, her exhale forming into a smile, so proud that she had stood up to someone. "Thank you," she said as she opened the door.

Rosemarie was now peering out her own window as she casually tossed over her shoulder, "And maybe Mifa won't have any idea it came out because of your cowardice."

Cecilia froze. She was staring at the asphalt below the car, still looking at her foot stepping down, when she replied, "What did you say?"

"If you think that because you're now a Supreme Court Justice, that means I have forgotten what I know about you, about your daughter, forgotten that thing that only, what, eight people on this planet know, well, then, I think it's time you woke up, Madam Justice." Rosemarie leaned over, piercing into Cecilia with a whisper. "I will always remember that. I will always have that on you. So you will not only take my opinions under advisement, you will consider them law."

Rosemarie leaned back against the leather, smiling as she moved her eyes off Cecilia and out her own window again. "You don't just owe me your Supreme Court seat, Madam Justice. You owe me your daughter."

Cecilia threw the door all the way open, jumped down and slammed it right back in Rosemarie's face. The First Lady watched her storm to her own car, then leaned forward, patting the back of the driver's seat. "Okay, Edmund, we can go."

"Um, could I ask just one question?" one of the White House IT guys smacked through his gum, without lifting his face off the monitor of Becks's computer.

"What's that?" she answered from the other side of her desk, not raising her own eyes from her redlined copy of the DHS report on the Iranian group in Portland, Oregon.

"Are you really sure someone would want to steal a memo to the agriculture and rural development subcommittee of Approp-- OUCH!" He recoiled from the sharp elbow his IT partner had driven into his lower ribcage. "No, I'm serious. This memo has already been seen by, what, 13 Senators? And all their staffs? Is that something someone would really need to break into the computer of the White House Chief of Staff to steal?"

Becks slammed the stack of papers down hard on her desk. "You let me worry about why. You just tell me who broke into that computer, and how they did it."

The tech's eyes whipped right back to the screen. "Yes, Ma'am."

Becks went back to the report, but her concentration was ruined. Of course the IT guy was right; no one had stolen an irrelevant memo to an obscure Senate subcommittee. She had put the memo in that passlocked file only that morning – replacing the item she believed *had* been stolen, and forwarded to the President.

"Wait a second." The other IT tech was now leaned over his compatriot and had taken full control of the keyboard. "Did you know another computer has access to your webcam?"

"*What?*"

"Yeah, I thought if we ran a diagnostic, something might show up that would explain how the thief stole the, um, the memo. I can't answer that yet, but I can see that another IP address is connected to the port your webcam is using."

"In Ingles, por favor."

"Someone can see everything your webcam can see," the other one replied, now looking straight up into her eyes. "If he's watching, he can see us right now." He twiddled his fingers in front of the tiny eye above Becks's monitor. "Howdy, mother fucker. I mean-- excuse me, Ma'am."

"Fuck ME!" The computer guys recoiled from the keyboard. Becks paced away from the desk, thinking. "Fuck-fuck-fuck--"

Then suddenly, charged back to them. "*Wait.* You said another IP address – can't we trace this other computer using that address?"

"Theoretically. Although anyone good enough to do this here, to your computer, I'm sure they masked themselves by bouncing across several IPs."

"Ma'am, at this point protocol dictates we should bring in White House Security on this, the Secret Service--"

"*NO!*"

Becks stopped herself, lowering into the guest chair across her desk from them. She closed her eyes, thinking of the running streams and calming sitar of the meditation CD she often played when she couldn't fall asleep. Then she opened her eyes again with a smile. "I mean, I will bring them in on this, of course. I just want to go to them with all the information. I need to know if this is something I did wrong, so I don't lose my job over this. You understand?"

"Yes, Ma'am."

"Just walk me through who could have done this. I lock my computer whenever I leave the room--"

"Oh, it wouldn't need to be someone physically on your computer. It was probably someone who got you to open an attachment on an email. That attachment had some sort of virus embedded in it that gave this guy access to your webcam."

"So – it was someone I knew?"

"That's looking likely. Social engineering has been proven to be the most effective means of infecting computers."

"But we still should've detected this open port on the White House network," the other one chimed in.

"Good point. Whoever did this would have to be someone with some serious game."

"And someone who knows this network fairly well."

"Like one of us. OUCH!" His compatriot had shot another elbow into his ribs, a sharp comment to his bad joke.

"All I want to know is how we catch him."

"It's going to be tough, Ma'am. We're talking about someone with some serious NSA-type resources. Someone who--"

"Goddammit!" Becks shot to her feet, slamming her open palms down on the wood once again. "That's it!" The answer had hit her like a ton of bricks.

"That's what, Ma'am?"

"Get out," Becks spit. "Now."

The techs sat stunned for a moment, then scrambled to their feet and darted out.

Becks knew what had happened, knew who had been watching everything she did. But it would have to wait for tomorrow. Tonight, she had an election to win.

As soon as the command van had paralleled back into a spot on Everett near 4th, George rose from shotgun and moved back into one of the open seats before the monitor bank. He picked up a radio receiver and placed the buds in his ears, first hearing the FBI HRT members confirming their coms were in working order. But George didn't chime in or shout orders or feel the pressurized adrenaline that came with being in command; at this point, he was only a spectator, an observer. The Bureau was running the show now.

It had been a whirlwind 24 hours: first came word late Tuesday from Kingman Summers that the Secretary wanted to move on the halfway house, that George's team had until start of business DC time Wednesday morning to put everything they had gathered over their month of surveillance into a concise report which the Attorney General could use to procure arrest warrants for Mohammed Mullin and several other residents of the Pencil Pals.

"And what if we don't have anything?" George protested into the speaker phone.

"What the hell does that mean, don't have anything? You've been watching these guys for a month, of course you have something."

"I'm sorry, Sir, but I don't think we do."

"Georgie, off speaker, now." After George had picked up the handset, Kingman let him have it. "This plan comes from on high, Georgie. You understand what I'm telling you? I mean, all the way up, *above* the Secretary. So when you go to sleep tonight, you better *convince* yourself that you have something."

George of course understood: it was the President that wanted the halfway house raided. This course of action had been chosen for political considerations.

It didn't surprise George; sure, decades ago now, he had registered as a Democrat because he thought they were above such things, making military moves or risking lives or creating spectacles just for political purposes. But after working in Washington for over two decades he knew that by no means did one political party corner the market on that behavior.

George wasn't the least bit surprised when the meeting was called for 10 AM Wednesday morning. Not even four hours after they had sent in their report, George and his three closest subordinates were to report to the FBI's Portland field office, just blocks from Portland International.

George wasn't introduced in the meeting, wasn't asked to give a report on their month of work. The FBI's elite Hostage Rescue Team had been flown in for the operation, and their commander would be running the show from here. George was familiar with this unit and knew their name didn't do justice to their full range of expertise; HRT was the most elite counter-terrorism unit legally permitted to operate on US soil.

"Thanks to the diligent intelligence gathered by our colleagues at DHS," the HRT Commander nodded towards George and his neutered colleagues, "one of our teams will be executing search and arrest warrants on the property on Flanders Street known as 'Pencil Pals' at approximately 7 PM tonight. Each of you is getting a floor plan texted to your tablets now. DOJ believes some of the individuals on this property may be linked to the Supreme Court attack." He paused, letting his boys coo with excitement. They would be making history tonight; they would become American heroes tonight. "I don't think I need to tell you that this operation will need to be handled with the utmost precision and caution. We believe some of the residents of the halfway house may have been handpicked by the Ayatollah himself, to wage war right here on our soil. We cannot afford anything less than your A games tonight."

And eight and a half hours later, George's ears rang with the chatter of an HRT op. "Aaaand – here we go! Go, go, go!" the HRT Commander barked in a combat whisper. Displayed on the wall of monitors arrayed before George were the green-tinged night vision POVs of several different team members as they charged out of the back of their Lenco BearCat and rushed down the damp, dark streets of Old Town Portland.

President Salas sat forward, hands on his thighs, focusing all his attention on the array of screens displaying the feeds from the helmet cams of several of the FBI HRT members, foot soldiers in black kevlar running down a Portland street. Becks stood, just over his shoulder, even more nervous than he was, convinced that if this whole endeavor went down smoothly, it could be just the tide-turner they so desperately needed. If all went according to plan, this would be over in less than ten minutes and no one would even notice. In a week or two weeks max, they would break one of these guys, and the President would finally have something to announce in the Supreme Court bombing investigation.

There had to be a breakthrough in that halfway house. It was the only lead, the only theory they had – it had to lead somewhere.

Of course POTUS had seen the DHS report, and had played a ruthless Devil's Advocate to his team that morning, raising his voice perhaps the loudest he'd ever raised it with Becks, hammering her that they didn't have enough to bring these guys in.

But the bombing had been an act of war, and sometimes rules had to be bent to find justice in war, procedures warped in the name of making the American people feel safer. His Attorney General made sure the warrant requests went to the perfect judge, and they were off and rolling.

C'mon, Salas argued with himself, *this is nothing compared to extraordinary rendition, to enhanced interrogation, to the shit that went down in the years following 9/11.* Kingman Summers of Homeland Security had assured him that many of the Iranians at the halfway house were suspected of *something*, they had just done such a good job of keeping themselves squeaky clean since the bombing, their specific link to that attack couldn't be ferretted out simply through surveillance. They needed to get inside these guys' skulls, they needed to interrogate them, they needed to *break* them to get to the truth.

"FBI!" The HRT Commander was at the door of the strange oval facility now, pounding on the front door. "Open up, we have warrants to serve on this address!" Salas sat back and gripped the armrests of his chair. Soon, it would be over. Soon, he could make the American people feel safer.

The point agent banged on the metal screen door covering the front entrance to the old preschool with the side of his fist, making it clang like a warped timpani. "Last warning! Open up!"

Still hearing nothing from the other side, the point agent tried the handle of the screen door – and finding it unlocked, pulled it open. He then wiggled the main wooden front door, but that didn't budge. He stepped back, nodding to the agent with the small battering ram. He stepped forward, rearing back and thrusting it into the wood of the door *once*-- *twice*, the wood cracking on all sides-- *three times*, the door slamming backwards off its hinges.

"FBI! NOBODY MOVE, ON THE GROUND, NOW!" the agents shouted in a cacophony, charging in with M4 carbines raised and at the ready.

Women and children screamed, all dropping to the floor as ordered. Some men were arguing, but the agents quickly convinced them to join their families on the ground with the persuasive stares of both their eyes and their rifle barrels.

In the DHS van, George's agent running the monitors looked back at him with supportive eyes. This was Jerome, the only African-American on his team, the one who had been surveilling Ali Kazemi up until yesterday. George had mentored Jerome since he first joined I&A two years ago, and Jerome had a soft spot in his heart for his superior. "Sounds like smooth sailing, bos--"

A SNAP-CRACKLE-POP from the speakers cut Jerome off.

"FREEZE!" "OFFICER DOWN! OFFICER DOWN! OFFICER DOWN!" came the screams, then a snare drum symphony.

"HOLD YOUR FIRE, HOLD YOUR FIRE!"

But the fire continued as George threw open the rear doors, letting them slam behind him as he sprinted to the Pencil Pals.

George rounded the corner onto Flanders, already pulling out his ID as he approached the kevlared G-Man left guarding the door. He held it in his face as he rushed in.

"Sir, we've got a live fire--"

But George didn't hear any more firecracking. He knew it was done. It was just a matter of who was on the ground with the shell casings.

He could count four bodies in the clearing smoke as he ran up behind the yelling HRT grunts. One with 'FBI' on his back, then two Iranians staring glassy-eyed back at him. One of them he recognized as Ali Kazemi, the young man Jerome had tailed, a smoking Glock in his limp fingers.

And finally, George noticed the body of the ten-year-old girl.

The coordinates were spot on. In a clearing in the middle of the Huron National Forest, several treacherous miles from any road or civilization, someone had erected a compound.

Jason had arrived a couple hours before dusk, giving him the opportunity to case the perimeter. His face was covered with green mud, his clothes all black, making him essentially invisible as he circled Polis, utilizing his old Special Forces skills to stay whisper-silent as he took mental notes on this hidden, self-sufficient civilization. The sheer scope of it was impressive – Jason couldn't even fanthom the amount of manhours and manpower that went in to transporting the materials used in the construction of the dozen wood structures. He counted a cooking unit, a school and chapel, and what appeared to be a makeshift firearms factory; it couldn't have been completed over one summer and fall, but most likely took a number of years. And still, the supply wasn't enough to meet their demand, with several large tents also erected between structures. It was a full community, just as the man back in Mio had explained, with as many women and young children running around its open grass flats or taking treks out to the nearest body of water as there were men practicing hand-to-hand combat or taking turns patrolling the perimeter.

Jason took special note of their routine, how many patrolled at a time, how long their shifts were. Could he sneak around them onto the property and just search for Miranda? Or would it be more effective to walk right onto the property with his arms in the air and ask if Miranda Whitney was a resident here? No, he wasn't sure yet of his best plan; he would sleep on it. As darkness fell on Polis, he would slink further back into the Huron, maybe trek a mile or two away just to be sure no early-morning hunters or fishers might stumble onto him, then camp for the night. He would return in the morning with a--

A gunshot blasted through the air – Jason covered his ears – it was fired just a few feet behind his head, nearly deafening him. He spun around, looking back—something was tearing through the leaves, *someone* was sprinting away from him, away from Polis, hard and fast. But it was already too dark to make out what or who.

Voices, shouts from Polis, pierced through the ringing in his ears, making him turn back. "Shots fired, shots fired!" one of the perimeter guards was yelling into his walkie, as another ran to his side. "Possible trespasser, quadrant A, quadrant A!"

Jason hit the deck, hugging the ground. The other guard had a flashlight up, sweeping it over the brush just above Jason's head. "I got something! There's someone back there!" Had they seen him? Or spotted the guy running away, the guy who had fired the gun in his vicinity?

Dogs were barking, as were the voices of more men. More silhouettes darted from the buildings, all charging with AR-15s or 9MMs in hand. "Do not move! Whoever you are out there, you are trespassing on sovereign territory. Do not move or we will fire!"

Jason didn't move. But he knew he would be forced to if he was going to get away – one of them held a doberman taut on a leash, its nose pulsing with his scent, its throat already growling. One of the men made eye contact with each of the sentries, giving silent orders with his hands.

The soldiers of Polis spread out into a flying wedge, advancing into the trees, closing on Jason.

ELEVEN MONTHS EARLIER

Jason was pretty confident he could beat a lie detector if it came to that. He had suffered through several intense sensory deprivation and interrogation exercises as part of his Special Forces training; how hard could it be to keep his vitals level with a blood pressure cuff around an arm, or some little plastic pieces around his chest and fingers? Yeah, Jason was sure that he could convince a polygraph machine that by no means was he planning his visits to Bullfeathers around Miranda Whitney's schedule.

It hadn't been difficult to figure out her lunch pattern: never Mondays because the football fanatics would start to trickle in early and the TV pregame shows were turned up extra loud; never Fridays because she wouldn't leave One First Street in case the Justices summoned her to conference; that left only the three midweek days, and Jason had no problem eating at the tavern three days a week in order to 'run into' her.

He didn't know if it was because of their lunches, but the 'hazing' portion of his job seemed to finally be waning. Just last week, she had shown up in his office in her own morning suit and tails, a uniform he had learned the Marshal was only expected to wear during oral arguments. "I figured it's only fair if I'm going to make you wear this crap all day, I have to wear it too." They had gotten their picture taken together by some admiring clerks, then Miranda had told him she was relaxing his dress requirement and he could come to Court in simple business attire starting the next day.

Their lunchtime conversations, meanwhile, had reached a depth he had never imagined. It had only taken them one or two shared meals to get into why they were sober, sharing their wake up calls, their 'Jesus come to meeting' moments.

"I wasn't drunk when I beat him up," Jason said out of the blue as they waited for their check one Thursday.

"What?" Miranda asked.

"Tyrol. When I-- what you saw in that photo. I was sober when I did that."

"Why are you telling me this?"

"It's just been hanging over me. Not many people know about that. I didn't want you to think--"

"That incident happened almost a year ago. And you've been sober for three. I already did the math."

"Good. Thank you."

"I do believe you when you tell me things," she smiled as she fished into her purse for a pack of gum.

"Good," he smiled back. "New topic."

"Shoot," she said, popping a piece out of its sleeve and into her mouth.

"You ever been in love?"

Miranda made a guttural sound like a game show buzzer. "Try again."

"C'mon. That bad?"

"I was young and stupid. It wasn't real. What about you?"

"No-- but I've been in Afghanistan, it's a little difficult."

"Well, I don't think we're so different. I've only ever had time to be in love with my job."

"And what is it you love about your job?"

Miranda swallowed, then took another deep breath, looking away from him, thinking this through. "'Equal justice under law.'"

"What it says on the building?"

"Our Court is the only place in this country where everyone is represented. You don't need a special invitation, or have to donate thousands of dollars, in order to get a guest pass to our proceedings; you get in line early enough in the morning, or enough days in advance, and you'll get a seat. First come, first served. Any American can write a petition to the Court, and someone will read it and answer it. It's like March Madness; yeah, all the big boys are there, but every once in a while, the little guys' voices are heard too. And the system for picking the Justices – there's no redistricting, there's no electoral college. As time moves forward, the composition will shift according to the times, but at all times, everyone has someone representing them. It's the one place where justice always prevails."

Jason felt a shiver trickle down his spine. To this point, he had only seen it as a job, no different than any other.

"At least, that's what I used to think." Something had just happened. Some-- *darkness* had draped over Miranda. She had gone from passionate patriot to somber depressive.

"Used to? What happened?" Jason asked.

"It's just a job, Lancaster. A job is just a job."

"Hey. At least I'm there now, right?"

Miranda looked over at him with those eyes. She squinted them as she smiled. She tried to hold it in with all her might, but just couldn't stifle a laugh.

Those goddamn eyes. The eyes hadn't gotten easier for Jason to look at. Their power over him had only grown over the last few weeks. They pierced in through his irises, down into his soul, made his heart thromb.

And he was pretty sure her eyes were calling to him to do what he did next. They had gotten used to sitting so close on their stools, closer and closer each lunch, that he didn't have to stretch at all, just reach up with his right hand, cup her cheek and lean forward, bringing her lips into his.

She didn't stop it, didn't pull back or put a hand on his chest …

But she didn't go with it either. Just let it sit there, their lips holding each other as tight as strolling lovers on a winter night. Her mouth was open just a little, just enough for his lips to taste the mint off her tongue.

Finally he pulled back. She didn't say anything, so he stumbled through something. "The thing I used to love most about being drunk was that tingle in the air when you're drinking with someone of the opposite sex, that unspoken electricity that says anything might happen because we've both got booze as our excuse. We can just completely give into pleasure and craziness and recklessness because we're drunks. I used to think that was one of the magic things about being drunk, one of the things I missed most about it. And then I started meeting you for lunch, and I realized you don't have to be drunk to get that feeling."

Miranda looked down at the floor, shaking her head. She started to rise off her stool.

"I'm sorry," Jason pleaded with a hand on her wrist. "If I misread this, or if you think this is totally inappropriate because of work, forget it ever happened."

Miranda didn't yank her wrist away or storm out of the bar. She put her other hand on top of his. She didn't want this to come out too harsh, didn't want to be cold.

But she knew she couldn't ever do what they had just done – ever do one of their lunches – ever again. "I'll see you at work, Jason." She patted that hand and left the bar without him.

It wasn't that awkward. They saw each other three separate times that afternoon, falling right into their usual roles, with no discomfort between them at all.

Jason was relieved. That was the most impulsive thing he had done since Afghanistan, and as much as he believed he did have feelings for Miranda, as much as he believed they would enjoy each other's extended company, as much as he believed in *those eyes,* he didn't want to screw up this job. He was glad the rest of the afternoon had proceeded as normal and tried to think of anything *but* Miranda as he rode the Metro back to Bethesda that night.

He was just about to cross Wisconsin Avenue and start his short trek up Old Georgetown Road when he heard the voice behind him. "Lancaster!" He started to turn--

And her lips were on his. She grabbed his neck and attacked his mouth, sucking his lips and mouth with such intensity his pants were already tightening around his crotch.

After the initial shock had worn off, he took control. He grabbed her by the back of the hair with a primal hunger, spinning her around, pushing her back into a dark alcove in the front of the Solstice Bank branch where no one could see them. He slammed her back against the concrete, gnawing on her neck as he drove his hardness up into her pelvis.

She was panting, her hand reaching down to rub his bulge. Then she took his hand and shoved it up her skirt, onto her panties. He caressed her mound with the tips of his middle and ring fingers, the fabric getting damper and damper, her hard breaths warping into deep moans. "Do it," she begged.

"What?" he whispered back right into her ear.

"Right here. No one's coming. No one can see us."

He pulled back. The moonlight caught on the green of her right eye. "C'mon," she teased. "We're adults. Why shouldn't we? What's stopping us?"

She didn't know what hit her. His left hand was back between her legs, pushing the cotton aside to reveal her opening. His right was unsheathing his staff--one thrust--

And he was all the way up inside her. She clenched up, her throat tightening with surprise. Her tailbone ached as he pounded her back against the concrete wall, but this was such ecstasy, she didn't care. He hammered away at her until she grunted in his ear that she was coming. He yanked himself out, finishing onto the pavement beneath her feet.

Then he collapsed forward, bringing his forehead to rest on the concrete beside her face. They both giggled at the sheer release.

"Okay," she eventually said, sliding out from underneath him. "See you tomorrow."

She stepped out of the alcove, and disappeared back in the direction of the Metro stop. Jason slouched back against the bank wall and didn't move for several minutes, trying to process what the hell had just happened.

Three swipes in the card reader and the light still wouldn't move off red. "This thing broken?" Jason asked the Court Policeman stationed at the garage elevators as he whipped his ID through the reader a fourth time.

"Let me see that," the guard requested. Jason handed the card over, and the guard copied his employee number into his computer. "Oh I see," he grunted after the monitor beeped. He picked up his phone and spoke quietly into it. "It's Dave, on G. He's here. He just arrived." Hearing an answer, he hung up then smiled back at Jason. "Someone will be right down."

"Someone-- to fix my card? You mind if I just go through and whoever's going to fix it can meet me in my office?"

"Actually, I need you to wait just another minute," the guard smiled.

Jason looked over at the elevators, seeing that none of their displays were lit up green. As a security precaution, there were no up or down buttons; only this guard could call an elevator for you.

Seven minutes later, one of the lifts opened and Deputy Marshal Gregor Meyers stepped out with a banker's box filled to the brim. "Gregor, what the hell is going on?" Jason asked, standing from the waiting benches where he hadn't sat since the day of his first interview. Meyers responded by dumping the box into Jason's arms. "What's this?"

"That's yours."

Jason skimmed the top contents – a couple desk tchotchkes, his recent certificate from the Gavin de Becker course – it *was* his shit, all the shit that should've been in his office. "What-- This stuff is from my office."

Meyers seemed blindsided. "Oh. No one told you? I thought she had told you."

"Told me what? Who--"

Gregor grit his teeth into an awkward smile. "You're being replaced."

"*What?* Why--"

"I, I don't know. Miranda made the decision herself."

"You tell her to come down here right now--"

"I'm sorry," Gregor grimaced, backing up toward the elevator. "I have to get back to work …"

"Gregor!"

But he was already gone, the doors already closing over his face, as if some-one was watching them and had assisted in Gregor's perfect escape.

Jason looked down into his box, his whole upper body releasing a huge ex-hale of defeat. He wanted to ask the guard to call up to Miranda and demand she come down here, but he knew the response he would get, knew the answer he would receive if he called her secretary and asked to speak with her.

Jason turned and headed for his car, already trying to calculate how much time off his meagre savings account could handle.

THURSDAY

Jason had been able to evade the Minutemen search party. They were enthusiastic, suffused with energy, but eight weekend warriors were no match for a former Green Beret.

Whe he returned to the outskirts of Polis early Thursday morning, three times the armed sentries now patrolled the perimeter of the camp, all running on much higher adrenaline and much more caffeine than the day before. Women and children were on lockdown, only coming outside for the bare minimum time required to move from one building to another at the beginning of meal or schooltime. And any building with Polis citizens inside had at least two guards posted at each door. Jason knew that whoever had fired the shot that alerted them to interlopers had eliminated any chance of his sneaking onto the premises and finding Miranda. Take that approach, and he would find only the business end of an AR-15.

So he took the other approach. After the sun had been up at least a couple hours, and it appeared most people had eaten their morning meal, Jason just walked right into the clearing. He had washed the camo paint off his cheeks, so he didn't look quite as much like Schwarzenegger in *Predator*. The Minutemen still surrounded him with guns raised, still ordered him to get on his knees with his hands behind his head. They pushed him face down into the muddy grass, yanking his wrists together with plastic flex cuffs, then pulling him back up into a kneel.

"Holy shit," one of them remarked as he examined the .45 pistol he pulled off the back of Jason's belt. "Check out the inscription: 'LAPD SWAT 114.'"

"Jason Lancaster," one of the others, unimpressed by the gun, read his name as he rifled through the wallet from his back pocket, "you are being placed under arrest by the citizens of Polis for trespassing on our sovereign property. You will be entitled to a trial before the citizenry. This trial will be governed by the laws of Polis. We will not recognize the laws of any other federal, state or local entities in your prosecution. Do you have anything you'd like to say for yourself?"

"Yes. I'm here on friendly terms. I'm not here to spy or report on you. I'm looking for a friend. I need to deliver her a message."

"It says here you're an officer of the Supreme Court." The lead guard must have just found the Court ID in his wallet, Jason figured.

"I was. I don't know if you get internet out here, but the Court isn't there anymore."

"It's just the beginning, Mr. Lancaster. The implosion of the structures of government-- that's why it's all the more imperative we don't have people like you jeopardizing our security." He nodded to two of his larger men; they put their hands under Jason's armpits and pulled him to his feet, then led him across the property – past all the eyes looking up from their work, or the lookee-loos peeking out of every window – and to one of the smaller structures on the far opposite end of the clearing.

It was pitch black in this one-room building, save for the slivers of sunlight fighting around the boards covering the one window. "Will you at least deliver my message for me?" Jason asked as they lowered him onto the bench along one wall. "Miranda Whitney, that's her name."

"There's no one here by that name."

"If you reach into my pocket, I have some photos--"

"You reach into your own pocket," one of them mocked, getting the other to chuckle.

"How long will I be in here?" he called after them as they turned back for the door.

"Until your trial."

"And when is that?"

"When it's time," the other one gruffed out, before they sealed him up in darkness.

Becks was impressed how deep into the Pentagon her ID card, her title, and of course, her forceful hurricane of a personality could get her. Turns out the White House Chief of Staff is allowed to make surprise visits on the DOD whenever she sees fit, and Becks used that power to get all the way to the lobby outside the executive suites of the National Security Agency. The crone of a receptionist there tried to shine Becks on, promise her that if she was just patient, the Director would be with her in a few minutes. But this visit was an unplanned addition to Becks's schedule, and she couldn't devote more than five; she had a 9:30 with the President on how to handle the botched raid in Oregon. She couldn't be late for that, especially with Salas on the hunt for someone to blame, someone to throw under the double-decker bus.

Becks stood again and walked back over to the reception desk, placing her hands down on the desk and leaning over the little beldam. "Please tell the General that if I'm not in that office in the next three minutes, Fox News gets an exclusive about the White House computer network being hacked."

"I'm sorry?"

Becks smiled back at her as she returned to her seat. "The General will know exactly what I'm referring to."

Two minutes and thirty-nine seconds later, Becks was being shown back into General Graddon's office. She stormed right up to the desk as the General's aide closed the door behind her. She hadn't been this deep in the NSA nerve center before, hadn't ever been in this office before, but the last person that would intimidate her was a woman she had screwed a dozen times. "My boss, Gail? Sending that video to my goddamn boss?"

"Rebecca," the older woman sighed, trying to act like she was too busy to even look up, "shouldn't you be more worried about the video images coming out of Oregon right now?"

Becks grabbed Graddon's wrists with surprising quickness and strength, stopping her bullshit busy work in its tracks. "I know how you got it." Her saliva spackled the General's papers. "I know you hacked my webcam."

Finally Graddon looked at her, peering at Becks over the tops of her reading glasses. Becks had often requested this 'slutty librarian' look when they were dating, demanding that the two-star general let down her bun and whip her hair out before Becks descended and went to work on her. "I'm sorry," the General needled, "but I thought we were meeting about some *proof* you have of the White House computer network being tapped? Absent that, I have a very important meet--"

"We both know the media doesn't require proof. A new story about the NSA overreaching? Sounds like something they'll absolutely salivate over."

Graddon sat back, taking off the glasses. She was well aware she had been brought in – *a woman* had been brought in, the first woman Director in the history of this agency – to create a picture of a house cleaning, of a brand new NSA that would leave the controversies exposed by Snowden and other leakers far behind it. "You're really going to make me spend my next month in a congressional hearing room?"

"Not if you admit it was you. Apologize. And shut it down."

Graddon sighed, returned the glasses to her nose and went back to reading some lengthy memo. "Have IT check the network when you get back to the White House. The port will be closed."

"That doesn't sound like an apology."

"Have you thought that perhaps you're the one who should be offering one?"

"Me? For what? For fucking--" She leaned in and lowered her voice. "For fucking Irving? You and I broke up in East Hampton, Gail, in case your memory is going now too?"

"You can do whatever and whomever you want. I just thought we had--*something,* I don't know--"

"We each had someone who knew how to make us come our brains out. But it ended."

"It was more than that for me. I thought you understood that. I never would've let myself go like that … if I'd known you …"

"Known what?"

"Known you were straight."

"Why do I have to *be* something?" Becks shook her head, turning for the door.

"You're not like me, that's all I know!" Graddon slammed on her desk and shot to her feet. "I know I don't want men. I've known that since I was a teenager. I know I want to love a woman. I thought you knew that about yourself too."

Becks stormed back, right to the edge of the desk. "You know what I know about myself? I know I like fucking Power. Male or female, I want to fuck Power. I was the first female White House Chief of Staff fucking the first female NSA Director. Then a former President wanted to fuck me-- so I did that. That's what I am. When I was a little girl and my seventh grade class came to DC, I knew I wanted to spend my adult life here. I also knew boys always followed me around drooling. So I used my talent to get my goals. Welcome to America."

As Becks walked back to the door, Graddon called after her. "But you're much more than that. You would have gotten here even if you were completely chaste. You didn't have to get here that way."

Becks opened the door, keeping her hand on the knob as she looked back one final time. "I guess we'll never know if that's true, will we?"

The Secret Service had recommended to Acting Chief Egan that, much like the oral argument schedule, conferences be called on a more randomized schedule than usually prescribed by the Court procedures, making it impossible to predict when the six Justices would be in the same room at the same time. Hence, rather than the customary Friday at 10 AM slot, the previous week's conference had been called immediately following oral arguments on Wednesday. This week, it was Thursday afternoon when the Justices and Clerks heard Gregor Meyers marching down the Capitol hallways ringing the makeshift conference bell, summoning them each to the room which was also doubling for Robing.

Egan tried to imagine herself at the head of the conference table at One First Street, rather than the flimsy catering table unfolded before her. She tried to ignore the smell of overworked heating ducts and coats drying from the morning rain, and instead place the memory of their old home's warm wood and polished marble in her nostrils. She tried to envision herself in one of their high-backed leather swivel chairs, a brass nameplate reading 'CHIEF JUSTICE EGAN' on the back, rather than a standard-issue Senate office chair rolled down from one of the upper floors. And she thought if she squinted just right, it appeared like the ornate chandelier of the old conference room was reflected off the glistening cheeks of each of her fellow Justices, rather than the florescent tubes that no one had even bothered to trade out for energy-efficient bulbs, figuring this office wasn't used enough to warrant the expense.

But no matter the limitations of this room, it wasn't going to dampen her ability to lead a conference, in her humble opinion the most important of the Chief Justice's many extra tasks. She was quite proud of how skillfully she led them through discussion of the six cases they had heard argued over the past three days, the group maintaining decorum through each of their debates. She knew what her critics would contend, that it was easier to lead a conference of six Justices than the full nine – but due to the closed and confidential nature of the conferences, no one outside the Court knew how difficult a task it was to keep even two of these Justices civil with one another. No one knew that perhaps the most stubborn, cantankerous Justices, the ones Chief Lapadula had the most trouble controlling in his own unruly conferences, had survived the bombing and were among the six still on the Court; no one knew that some of the most vicious rivalries had survived the October tragedy. Perhaps everyone was making a concerted effort to limit their aggression in light of the state of things, but Egan liked to think the calmness with which her conferences were conducted was in fact more a result of her skillful leadership than anything else.

Egan couldn't help but sneer to herself about Rosemarie Irving's impertinence as they effortlessly eased their way through the final discussion of the day, *Agguire v. Detroit.* As the Junior Justice and therefore last to speak on each case, Cecilia Koh hadn't added much to any of the discussions of the day; Egan figured the scathing responses to her first opinion draft had demoralized her. (The Chief made a mental note to stop by her makeshift chambers for a Friday pep talk.) Cecilia's fewest words came when *Agguire* reached her, on which she added no reasoning or precedent they should consider, just said, "I'm, um, not sure of my vote yet."

"Well, it's no matter, I count a majority either way. You'll let us know after you read the opinion and dissent drafts." Egan took the majority opinion for herself, with a snide dig at Justice Winks for his failure to distribute even a rough draft during the previous term, which she considered the reason the case had been relisted.

Egan updated her opinion chart as the room cleared out, then tucked it under the nearly 150 cert petitions they had voted on. They charged through them so quickly, she was always nervous she would discover she had neglected to record a vote, or wouldn't be able to remember which way the Justices had decided, so she had made a point over the last three weeks of double-checking her chicken scratches immediately following the conclusion of any session, and turning them around into legible instructions for the Court's administrative staff before she even left this dreary room.

"I need to talk to you about something," a little voice squeaked from the far end of the table. Egan looked up to find Cecilia still in the room.

"Of course. I was going to come by your chambers tomorrow, actually. I told you not to worry about your first opinion, and that goes for--"

"This isn't about that opinion. It's about a dissent I'm going to write."

Egan swallowed a chuckle. "Are you sure you even want to attempt that before you've successfully completed your first--"

"The dissent I'm going to have to write when you refuse to delay the *Agguire* decision."

"Excuse me?"

"That's exactly the tone of voice I thought you'd respond with." Cecilia lifted her chin higher, trying to imagine Lindsey coaching her to stay strong. "So I came prepared to tell you that if you refuse to postpone that case, I will have to withhold my vote."

Egan squinted, trying to peer into the junior Justice's soul. "I see. This is how you pay for your seat."

"I will also publish a dissent," Cecilia continued, ignoring that implication, "explaining to the public that I am withholding my vote because of your poor leadership skills, and saying that I believe the President should name a new Acting Chief as soon as possible."

Egan shot out of her chair, crossing the room in three large steps until she was nose-to-nose with her most junior colleague. "Now you listen to me. All of us here owe our seats to someone. But as soon as we get in, all obligations, all debts, are forever erased. I am your master now, you understand me? Unless you want to spend the rest of this term writing our responses to every habeas corpus appeal we receive, stuff that'll just make you slit your wrists, you will take back every threat that just came out of your beady little mouth, you will give me your vote, and you will walk out of this office and get back to learning how to craft an opinion that won't embarrass the hell out of this Court."

"Madam Chief Justice, with all due respect … without my vote, you don't have a quorum. You can't decide this case without me. I'm sorry. But there's nothing for us to negotiate. My mind is made up."

Cecilia turned and walked out, ignoring her Chief's demands that she return "right this second." Instead, she marched right back down the hall to her chambers, not letting go of the inside of her lower lip with her teeth. She didn't care if it bled; she needed the pain to occupy her mind, and keep it off of the career suicide she might have just committed.

Once the slivers of light around his boarded-up window had gone black, once the sounds of the courtyard guitar performance and the crowd that had gathered for it had gone silent, Jason lay down on his bench. It wasn't built for sleep, his legs hanging over the sides of the narrow plank, his arms still linked with cable into a fist dug into the small of his back, so he soon moved to the dusty wooden floorboards.

He had no idea how long he had been asleep, how many hours it had been dark, when the door of his cell opened and a silhouette entered. He was still blinking the cobwebs out of his brain when the silhouette closed the door, so quickly he couldn't process its shape, its height or weight.

But when the silhouette mounted him, he knew who it was. He recognized that weight on his pelvis, recognized that smell, not the smell she might have at the beginning of a court day or as they departed on a 'date night,' but her natural smell, the smell of the beginning of a morning, or the end of a night spent intertwined with one another on the couch binge watching *Game of Thrones*.

"Rand …"

And her taste – exactly what he had tasted that first time he had kissed her at Bullfeathers, the same taste of almost every kiss since. Her gum, she had somehow gotten her favorite gum, the kind that comes in the black packs, delivered here, or she had brought enough with her.

He just wished he could see those eyes.

She pulled off his lips and brought her mouth to his ear, emitting such a tiny whisper a person lying next to him wouldn't have been able to make out the words. "I'm going to tell you exactly how you get out of here."

He nodded, then listened.

Finally, she pulled her lips back into his, one last kiss.

But that wasn't enough for him. His wrists still bound, all he could use to protest was his head, nestling his nose hard into the pocket of her neck, sucking and nibbling on her flesh.

She grabbed both sides of his jaw in her mitts and kissed him again. That's when he felt the tears hit his cheeks, the tears from her eyes.

She lifted her pelvis into a crouch, reaching her hands down to unzip his fly, to dig him out of his pants and caress him to full firmness. She then undid her own pants, pulling her underwear down to just above the knees.

She lowered herself onto him, each slow, gentle pump letting him in just a little more. Soon he was sliding all the way up and then out of her. She pulled his chest close to hers, breathing so hard in his ear.

"Someone … rufied me. Is this what it feels like to be rufied?"

"I'm saving your life, Jason."

No. No, Jason put those thoughts out of his brain. He wanted this moment to be perfect, he wanted to *be* in this moment, he wanted new memories of Miranda that erased all the rest.

Their tears coagulated into one of those perfect, beautiful moments, the rest of the world frozen all around them.

And then she was gone. He collapsed back against the floor, sinking into his deepest sleep since the bombings. He wanted to review her instructions in his mind, but that would have to wait for morning.

ELEVEN MONTHS EARLIER

Jason didn't rise from the high-top table when she entered. He didn't want to corner her, didn't want to pressure her, or insist she have a conversation she didn't want to have. Bullfeathers had been her place, her domain, her escape, long before Mooner had introduced it to Jason. He wasn't here to confront her, just offer her an opportunity. If Miranda chose to keep on walking when she saw him, proceeding to her usual stool at the bar without a word to him, he would let her go. He would finish his salad in silence, pay his tab and depart for home, where *Pardon the Interruption* and Monster.com awaited him.

But after noticing him from the door, Miranda didn't move to the bar. She marched right over to Jason's table, just as he thought she would – though he had only known her six weeks or so, he somehow believed he had gotten to know her well enough to guess this is exactly what she would do.

"I'm very sorry about how things went down last week," she explained, "how quickly I had to move on things. That happens sometimes at the Court. But if you're here to convince me to give you your job back, I'm afraid that just won't be possible."

"Oh I'm not here to convince you to give me my job back."

Jimmy appeared around Miranda's shoulder, setting a second ginger ale in front of the open seat across from Jason. "No, Jimmy, I'm not--" Miranda protested, but the barkeep had already moved on.

"I didn't ask him to do that," Jason assured her. "Look, it was a great job and I'm grateful you gave it to me in the first place. But there are other jobs out there. I already have some other interviews. I'm here to convince you to have another meal with me."

"What?"

"I liked our lunches. I miss them. I'd like to have another one. Even better: you let me take you out somewhere new, maybe even after the sun goes down."

Miranda smiled and shook her head. "I want you to know I'm an adult. You can come here every day, anytime you want – it won't scare me off from having lunch here. Good to see you."

She started to turn-- but Jason wouldn't let her off the hook. "Look, I get it. Things got a little out of hand last week. And you woke up the next morning and remembered you don't like to shit where you eat."

Miranda turned back. "Actually, that's not it at all."

"You obviously like spending time with me. You also thought I was impressive enough to hire. I totally understand if you think those two things can't coexist. But you just eliminated one of them. I don't understand why you have to rob yourself of both."

Miranda took a step closer, leaning over the table. "Just so we're on the same page, Mr. Lancaster: reading people is maybe the most important skill of our Threat Assessment chief. Last week, not to mention today, you have continually shown yourself to be incredibly poor at reading me. And I take responsibility for misleading you. You misjudged a moment of impulsiveness--"

"A moment of impulsiveness?" Jason repeated with a sly smile. "You're sure now that's all it was?"

Miranda opened her mouth to respond … then, thinking the better of it, just tapped the table lightly and turned. "Good luck on those interviews."

"Wasn't this some sort of sexual harassment?"

Miranda kept walking backwards to her stool as she rejoined, "Hey, if you wanna sue someone who's friends with nine Supreme Court Justices, be my guest."

"He raped two servicewomen," Jason said, stopping her in her tracks one more time. She turned back, but without a word this time. "Our group would move all over the place, depending on our mission. We bunked up in a lot of different bases, cohabitating with a lot of different units over the years. Perfect scenarios for a predator like Tyrol to chew them up, spit them out, and be long gone before he had to pay any price for his transgressions.

"First time I caught wind of one of his attacks, I just came right out and asked him about it – didn't confront him, I wanted to keep an open mind – I just loved him so much, we all did, and didn't want the story to be true. He said she had gotten trashed and thrown herself at him, then cried rape the next morning. I'd never met the girl, so of course I took his word for it.

"And then, about three, four months later, I'm walking through tent city late one night on my way to sack out and I hear a scream from around a corner. He was in the middle of doing it right there, out in the open. He was so shitfaced, he didn't even care. He was laughing about it as I pulled him off her. She just booked it out of there – I called after her, told her I'd take her to help, asked her for her name.

"And he looks up at me, and he says, 'She doesn't have a name, Jase. Her name is Private, and my name is Captain, and she needs to learn to follow orders.'"

Jason moved his eyes off the nebulous zone of memory he had been gazing off into and back into Miranda's. "And maybe you're right. Maybe I'm not good at reading people. But that night, I could *read* in his eyes that he had done this before, too many times to count. I could read he was going to do it again, and again, and he was never going to stop."

He paused, soothing his parched throat with ginger ale. "The main reason I stopped drinking was because when I mixed drinking with anger, time would get away from me." He couldn't look at her for this next part, something he had glossed over in their previous talks about sobriety. "I'd feel myself getting angry at someone, sometimes for the stupidest shit, drunk shit, and then--" he snapped his fingers, "they're on the floor. I had just hit him. It had *just* happened and I couldn't even remember it. Dewar's was my gamma rays.

"Except it wasn't the Dewar's. It was me. I hadn't had a drink in two years, but when Tyrol said those words to me with that shit-devouring grin, time got away from me again. That was his last day on active duty. He went home with a purple heart."

Jason reached down to his belt, unsnapping his holster, pulling out his sidearm and placing it on the table. Miranda tensed up.

"I later found out, the private he was raping, she had been the only female member accepted into the LAPD SWAT Team when she was called back to the 'Stan. The morning after I pulled Tyrol off her, I'm in the brig. She came in and left that for me. Kimber 1911, custom made for SWAT officers.

"I still haven't spoken to her. But I've carried it every day since."

He looked up at her with a sheepish, incongruous smile. "Anyway, I just wanted to make sure, if this is the last time I ever see you or ever talk to you, that you at least knew what really happened."

"I knew it already."

"What?"

"Tyrol is the reason I got out of the Corps, came back to the world. When I was an MP, he came to our attention after assaulting one of our NCOs. She let me depose her on record, and we brought him in. But the next morning, he's walking. Your team was too important to rob of its CO. Not for something as trivial as a rape. I raised a holy shitstorm about the whole thing. Went above my superior about it. Wrote letters to six Senators."

"And then what?"

"And I got a dishonorable discharge, that's then what. But a couple years later, I hear scuttlebutt from one of my old colleagues about what happened to the scumbag. I had to see that face. And then I had to meet the man who did it to him." Miranda picked up the extra ginger ale. "That photo, that's why I hired you." She turned one last time and moved to her usual barstool.

Jason considered chasing after her, but he had promised himself he wouldn't. He holstered his weapon, finished his salad, paid his tab, and departed for home, somehow resisting the most maddening, the most electric, the most confusing, the most *irresistible* woman he had ever met.

FRIDAY

Kingman Summers was watching some Southern Congressman spit fire and brimstone over C-SPAN when his secretary ushered George in. George knew he was walking into a royal ball busting; that was Kingman Summers's specialty. *Especially since I was supposed to be finding him fall guys that would make his cover up of the bomb evidence moot*, George thought to himself.

But when George sat down across from the Under Secretary, his younger superior didn't say a word for what felt like an eternity. After a while, George started to listen to the televised diatribe – piqued by phrases like "racial profiling" and "harassment of perfectly legal immigrants"– and he soon realized why it was so interesting to Kingman. The Congressman wasn't complaining about the other party or his President; he was flaying *them*. He was burning Homeland Security in effigy.

"You think if they put this investigative committee together," Kingman's voice popped up, "they'll subpoena me, or just the Secretary?"

"I wish I could say. But whatever happens, Mr. Under Secretary, I want to personally apologize. The whole thing is an embarrassment for this entire agency, for this division, for you, and I want you to know I take full responsibility--"

"Ha! No you don't, Georgie. You don't *take* anything out of this. I'm *giving* you the full responsibility."

"And you're right to do so. I ran a subpar surveillance, which they were obviously able to detect--"

"What I want to know is, did this actually surprise you? Huh? How this all turned out? What do you think happens when you abandon your team every week?"

"I'm sorry?" George looked up. He had scripted this meeting in his head, but Kingman had just gone off book, just thrown him a knuckleball.

Kingman sat forward, reading off a piece of paper. "November 22nd, Alaska flight 764 to DCA, return to PDX on the 25th. Another trip on the 29th, December 6th, 13th …" Kingman looked up over the top edge of this single piece of paper.

"Turns out the team you were supervising, the twenty-four/seven surveillance team I ordered you to supervise, only had the honor of your presence three and a half, four days out of each of those seven. Because you were flying back here every weekend."

"I can explain--"

Kingman sat back, lacing his fingers on top of his stomach like he had just inhaled a spectacular meal. "You think I don't know why you've been coming back?"

George tread with caution, unsure whether he should try to lie or obfuscate, or if it was too late and his CO already knew too much.

"I know what you do when you're here. I know where you spend all your weekends, Georgie. I know why your wife popped enough Ambien that eventually she never woke up."

George quivered with rage. He wanted to leap across the desk at Kingman, wanted to pull his necktie tight against his Adam's apple, revel in his choking gargle until his neck just popped.

But George wouldn't do that. George never did anything like that. *And I know you're somehow involved with the bombing,* George wanted to say, *and I'm going to figure out how.* But he just sat there and kept his trap shut.

"And I know why we totally fucked the pooch on this mission. You spent half of it back here in Washington at the Waterford!"

Kingman sat forward, leaning his elbows on his desk, picking up another piece of paperwork. This one, George recognized; he remembered the colorful green and white brochure from his first visit to the Waterford Villas. "I gotta say, place looks pretty expensive, Georgie."

At the end of her sophomore year of high school, Brenda Aug was ranked third in her class, was active in three clubs and the school newspaper, and had scored a PSAT result that qualified her for a National Merit Scholarship.

She would never finish high school. It was early in her junior year that George and his wife started waking in the middle of the night to some sort of rhythmic pounding emanating from Brenda's bedroom. On the second night of this disturbance, George got up, crossed the hall, and knocked on his daughter's door; not getting a response beyond more pounding, he stormed in to find her banging her forehead into the wall – bam-bam-bam, in perfect mindless rhythm – just hard enough to have depressed a crater into the drywall.

It was the only method Brenda could think of to make the voices in her head go away.

George's wife had dedicated her entire life to their only child. Sixteen years earlier, they had been trying to get pregnant for over three years, and had finally started the adoption process, when they suddenly became pregnant with their "miracle child." Brenda was everything to George's wife, her whole life.

But as Brenda grew less and less social – her eccentric-to-begin-with personality dulled by either her mental illness or the drugs she took to treat it, no one could say for sure – George's wife disappeared deeper and deeper into her own depression. George had wanted to cut way back on his hours at DHS, maybe even retire in order to help Brenda, but as it became clear that her future was now considerably narrower, that she wouldn't be able to hold down even the most remedial job let alone seek higher education, George realized he would have to work harder and more hours than ever. The public housing options that Brenda could afford herself on her SSI disability payments made George sick to his stomach, and the only way the Augs could afford to put their daughter in a top shelf facility like the Waterford would be for George to work a boatload of overtime.

Just *paying* for Brenda's room and board at the Waterford wasn't enough. The Waterford wasn't a full-service hospital; as Brenda was now a legal adult, the Augs couldn't force her into one of those. The Waterford was a beautiful condominium complex that just happened to also have medical and psychiatric staff on site, free daily housekeeping visits, even an on-site café that opened for breakfast and lunch. But someone still needed to make sure Brenda took her meds, someone still needed to make sure she got out of bed everyday, someone still had to make sure she remembered to eat. Things had gotten that bad.

Within weeks of Brenda's move into the Waterford, it became clear that George's wife had developed too many issues of her own to handle these things for Brenda; and soon enough, she was gone, quitting on her husband and daughter. It was up to George to do everything. He had to get up at 5 AM and get over to Brenda's to start her day, then head into the office for eight hours of work (and another two or three per day once the Court went down), then get back to Brenda's to make sure she'd had another meal and her meds and got into bed.

When the Oregon assignment came his way, George considered explaining all of this to Kingman, asking to be taken off and kept in Washington. But he had been in the Under Secretary's shithouse for weeks at that point, since that first week after the bombing, and he couldn't be sure he would keep his job if he begged off the first real responsibility he had been given in a month. Plus, there was the per diem that came with a road assignment, and the bonus that would be due everyone on the team, especially its CO, if they made headway in the investigation …

No, George *had* to take the assignment. He had to make it work. Brenda had gotten a little better, a little more independent, and could survive without him two or three days a week. And his surveillance team in Oregon could do the same – especially as it became clear they weren't surveilling much of anything anyway.

Kingman suddenly slammed the Waterford brochure down, jarring George back into the present. "Look, I'm not high. I know this mission wasn't perfect to begin with. But that's not for us to say. This mission was *our job.* We can call this agency whatever we want to make ourselves feel good, but it's a political organization. Our primary mission is to keep all the politicians who appoint us, employ us, and fund us, and the voters who elect them so they can do all that, happy. So it's imperative, after this--" he waved his hand at C-SPAN, on which the Congressman was still going "--that I bring them something that permenantly erases Oregon from this country's collective memory banks post fucking haste.

"And you, Georgie, are gonna find it for me." He sat back, cupping the back of his head in his intertwined fingers. "Because, trust me, you're not gonna like moving your retard daughter to a facility you can actually afford on unemployment."

The door to his small prison opened. Two guards entered, helped Jason to his feet, and escorted him to the Polis courthouse for the second time today.

The first time, he had done as Miranda had instructed: after being presented with the trespassing charges against him, he was given the opportunity to say anything he wished on his own behalf. "I want to assure you that I did not come here to spy on you or report back on what I found to any outside entities. I came because I was looking for a refuge from all the shit that's going on out there right now. I witnessed it myself. I was there the morning the Supreme Court came down. I can't just sit out there anymore, waiting for the conflagration to spread. I needed to find a place, a group of people who are ready for what's coming. That understand the time has come for the people to again govern themselves. I imagined this might be that place. But thanks to all of you, what you've accomplished, it's beyond even my wildest dreams."

"It took years," said one of the men in the triumvirate seated behind the card table before him.

"What about this Miranda Whitney you said you're here to find?" one of the others asked.

"Maybe she's not here. Maybe she was never here. She is the one who told me about Polis, and for that, I am grateful to her. But I am here to find Polis, not to find Miranda Whitney.

"And now that I'm here, I think I can add value to your community. I've been a Green Beret for almost a decade. A combat engineer – that means I specialized in explosives. Once the shit goes down, I have skills you guys might want to have on your side."

The trial wrapped up quickly from that point. The trio of judges conferred amongst themselves before announcing they would adjourn for two hours to make their decision on how to proceed. On the march back to his cell, Jason whipped his head this way and that, but didn't see Miranda amongst any of the faces staring at him from every corner of the compound.

He didn't know how much time passed after he was returned to his prison, but it sure felt like less than two hours before that door opened again and he was again led to the 'courtroom' – just another bare nondescript building with some folding tables and chairs set up. The room was much more packed this time, every chair on all sides of him filled, even some onlookers crammed into corner standing room. Jason didn't have time to scan the entire crowd, but he didn't see Miranda in the first quick glances he was able to steal.

Looking down at that central card table, he realized that he wasn't the draw for the large crowd: this time, only one man sat behind it. The man now had a beard and neck-length waves of blonde hair curling from under his ears, but Jason still recognized him:

Benjamin Bratten. The Solstice Bank shooter.

"Our courtroom is not as ornate or elaborate as yours, Mr. Lancaster. But you don't need marble columns or hand-carved busts for a courtroom. Just a group of people who crave justice. This is just such a group of people."

"My courtroom isn't looking so good right now."

"Things have a way of collapsing under the weight of their own pretension." Bratten had a small stack of paper before him, and skimmed the top sheet with his eyes. "Your introduction to our community has worried some of the people here. Some have recommended banishment, or an even more permanent punishment."

"I'm sorry. I didn't mean to scare anyone."

"So why did you discharge a firearm so close to our perimeter?"

Jason paused, considering how to answer. He decided against explaining it was someone else who had fired the shot, someone who had followed him out here – it was in his best interests to get the Minutemen into as calm a state as possible as quickly as possible, and the notion that someone else was still lurking around in the trees beyond their clearing would only keep them on high alert.

"It was a misfire," Jason lied. "I wanted to make sure all my weapons had their safeties on before I introduced myself, but then accidently discharged my .45. When I saw the reaction to the sound of the shot – an understandable, correct reaction – I panicked. I ran and hid. By the next morning, things had calmed down a bit, and I felt better about introducing myself."

Bratten set down the paper, and stood to come around the table, closer to Jason. Every other person in the room remained silent and still, as if each word rolling off Bratten's tongue were part of a holy sermon. "This is not a time for the people of this community, of this country, to bicker and strife amongst themselves. That is what the true criminals, the ones in Washington, want us doing. They like it when we're petty, not looking at the big picture. They like our attention off them; that keeps us subservient.

Our attention *must* remain on them, and the terrible fruit their crimes against the Constitution, their sham elections and their fiscal incompetency, have finally wrought.

"What happened to your Court, Mr. Lancaster, that is just the beginning. More insurrection, more destruction, builds on the horizon. I don't know how it will come – be it revolutionaries, or creditors calling on our massive debt, or the United Nations seizing our land – but the complete collapse of the charade we once called a Republic is nigh.

"They know this is coming. They have already started to panic, and lash out at groups they feel might threaten them, sending the same FBI team that struck at Ruby Ridge, that burned down Waco, sending that very same team to terrorize those peaceful Muslims in Oregon." By this time, many in the gallery were nodding along or even verbally affirming each sentence, lost in the emotional throes of his homily. "When cornered, our Jefe-in-Chief and his illegitimate government will strike back with deadly vengeance. If we let them, they will create a new slave class for this century. That is why some of us here have already struck blows in this early revolution …"

So that's what you call walking into a bank and slaughtering seven people these days, Jason sneered to himself.

"…and when the rest of us are called to fight, we will dutifully leave this nest and bring the battle to the enemy, keeping everyone here safe to nurture and build our community the way we want it built, the way we want it governed. Polis will remain untouched by any retaliation, any enslavement."

"We are ready to fight for you, Benji!" one of the men yelled from the back, and many chimed in with their own verbal agreement to this sentiment.

Bratten was now nose-to-nose with Jason, his eyes no more than six inches from the Court policeman's. "Are you ready for this revolution, Mr. Lancaster?"

"It's why I'm here."

Bratten smiled, raising his open palms as he backed up, arms stretched out wide from his shoulders, like he was speaking for the entire compound. "Then we shall welcome you."

"I'm surprised we're not meeting in one of *my* rooms," Rosemarie quipped as she lowered into one of the couches of the Oval, rehashing her running tease of the President for not redecorating any of the Residence rooms she had designed while her husband was in office.

Salas sat forward on the couch opposite her, hands wrapped around a tumbler she imagined contained a fine variety of tequila. "I thought we both liked to save the East Sitting Room for celebrations. And with this pot revelation--"

"You know I'm handling it," she assured him with a stern stare.

"There's not a doubt in my mind. That's not why you're here. I actually …" He took a soothing, calming drink. "You've been such a great help with the Court. I thought maybe, if you don't mind, I could bounce something totally unrelated off you."

"Mind? I serve at the pleasure of the President."

"The Iranian community center we raided in Oregon--"

"I wish you'd called me before the raid. That's Reg's old district."

"We're getting eaten alive for it. You've seen the protests outside? It's worse in eight other cities. CNN has been doing half hour profiles on all the saintly women who lived inside and scrounged together pennies as housekeepers and dishwashers back in Iran just to get to this country. Chris Matthews asked if Wednesday night was my Kristallnacht."

"You're kidding."

"But on a positive note, you'll be happy to know Sean Hannity is investigating if Sharia law was being practiced in the halfway house." He stood, pacing with one hand on his waist, other on his glass. "My cabinet was almost unanimously for this thing. I don't know who to listen to anymore. They're all just bending over backwards to cover their own asses. I needed to talk to someone on the outside. I thought I'd start with you – especially in case, worse comes to worst, this somehow impacts the rest of our efforts to fill the Court."

"First off, I'm honored. And it won't. You won't let it."

"I'm listening."

"How strongly can you link any Iranians to the bombing?"

He paused, almost ashamed. "Not beyond a reasonable doubt. Not yet. We weren't planning on announcing this thing until we had that link sewed up."

"Release everyone now. Get them out of that building and into homes of other Iranians in the community. It's already starting to look like the Superdome during Katrina, if not Japanese internment camps. Release everyone-- except the two or three men who have records that make them sound the most dangerous. Even if it's just shoplifting. If they're the two or three that look scariest on camera, even better. Announce that you have the suspects you hoped to find in the community center, and you're very sorry about the tragedy that ensued. But it was imperative for national security, and to prevent future attacks.

"Now these guys are going to have Gloria Allred showing up to represent them. That's fine. Give them their due process. Release them after 48 hours if you don't get anything out of them, but have the FBI issue a very carefully worded press release that implies they did glean a lot of valuable information from these guys in their time as prisoners."

"Great, great, this is great."

"And one more thing – this is the most important."

"What's that?"

"Fire someone."

"Believe me, I lectured--"

"It's not enough. Your constituents need to know you were angered enough to *do* something about this."

"Someone has to take the fall."

"You won't even need to say that. You're above that. You're the President. The press will say it for you."

Salas stood at the door of the Oval, watching Rosemarie bid goodbye to his secretary Dolores, then disappear down the hallway. Every time he spoke with her, it was more obvious how much more she had meant to Irving's success over the years than as just a First Lady or mother-to-his-children. Antonio's mother taught him to never believe in regrets, but he still couldn't help wondering if he had made a mistake when he didn't make the pursuit of a wife a greater priority in his younger years. None of the women he had dallied with had the intellect or gravitas he needed now – not even Eunice Yamaguchi, the KCAL anchor back in Los Angeles, the woman with whom he had come the closest to marriage. He never missed having children, or even frequent sexual partners, but ever since he had ascended to the Presidency, he had needed an advisor like Rosemarie, someone he could actually trust, someone with no reason to have an agenda, who truly valued POTUS's best interests above her own. Alas, it was too late for him to date now, at least for five more years; as much as he loved *The American President,* it just wouldn't be possible to date anyone outside of his immediate inner circle, not with the country on high alert in the wake of a terrorist attack. Can you imagine if TMZ caught the President necking at an ice cream parlor, while the Supreme Court bombers were still running loose?

"Mr. President," Delores rose from her desk, "you promised Mr. Crabbe some time before his next press briefing."

"Of course, Delores," Salas replied, despite the fact the last thing on Earth he wanted to do right now was speak with his Press Secretary. "When he gets here, have him wait with you for five minutes, then send him in." As Delores picked up her phone to carry out the command, Salas whipped his eyes over to one of the few people he could trust. "Hifrael."

POTUS's lead Secret Service agent followed him into the Oval, shutting the door behind him. Salas made a point of talking as he walked back to the Resolute Desk. *Chickenshit,* he acknowledged to himself, but he couldn't bear to look Agent Fernandez in the eyes as he made his next command. "What we spoke about a couple days ago – asking MMA something about the Irvings?"

"Sir?"

“I need some deep background on their marriage.” He arranged some stacks on his desk, trying to keep his gaze busy. “Specifically on the fidelity of President Irving – whether or not he’s currently engaged in any extramarital affairs, etcetera. You get the picture.”

“Mr. President … this is a most unusual--”

“Hifrael.” Now the President’s eyes were on his guard’s. “This is a matter of national security. I can’t explain why. But you have to trust I wouldn’t be asking this of you if it wasn’t.”

Hifrael nodded.

“Knock-knock?” the Press Secretary had poked his head in the door.

Salas raised a hand, beckoning him in. “Come on in, Alistair. Gracias, Hifrael.”

But Hifrael didn’t return a word of acknowledgement as he exited.

“And our final announcement concerns Case 18-012,” Craig Barton, acting Public Information Officer of the Supreme Court, told the pool reporters gathered around him in row three of the gallery of the Court’s old chambers. Public Info was one of many Supreme Court departments that didn’t have its own temporary office at the Capitol, and Barton and his staff had been working out of two rooms in the Rayburn House Office Building. But to lessen the travel demands upon the media, he was conducting all his briefings in the actual Court chamber, when it wasn’t otherwise being used. Several of the old desks and benches had been removed during the retrofit to make room for more seating, so there was more than enough for these briefings.

“*Agguire v. The City of Detroit*,” Barton continued, “has been restored to the calendar for re-argument at a time in which the Supreme Court has been restored to a full capacity of Justices. Have a good weekend.”

This final of several announcements caused no murmur among the sedate Court reporters; it inspired no uproar. They simply scribbled this footnote into their notepads or clicked off their iPhone recording apps. None had any inkling that if they were to ask a former First Lady, she would tell them this was the biggest Supreme Court news since the bombing in October.

Rosemarie was in the back of her Escalade when the announcement was made, on her way from the White House to her foundation offices, sitting with Dennis in the backseat, flipping through a stack of judicial bios he had retrieved from their corkboard at the Capitol. It was her husband who alerted her. "Congratulations," was his first word over the speaker phone.

"You know how I feel about sarcasm, honey."

"Nothing sarcastic about it. I guess you didn't hear. No *Agguire* until we have nine Justices."

Rosemarie slammed the bios down hard on her lap, making Dennis flinch. "God-*dammit*, that is fantastic! Egan caved."

Dennis tried to quiet the motor mouth in his head, but it was impossible. *There's that case again. And she's this obsessed with it? Did she really ask me to research it for her in the Vault as a test, or was I just telling myself that to make myself—*

No, Dennis. Stop it. Shut the hell up and keep handing her bios.

"Koh came through for you, after all," the former President was chuckling over speakerphone.

"Earned her keep," Rosemarie agreed.

Cecilia Koh? Justice Koh? She's already played a part in this case? No, no, you're misunderstanding—

But didn't that sound suspiciously like they had gotten her confirmed just for this purpose, to somehow affect the Agguire *outcome?*

Take a deep breath! Do you realize what you're saying, you moron?

"Dennis," Rosemarie snapped in a whisper. "Who's next?"

Dennis caught himself, then frantically flipped through the stack to find the next candidate he thought might be worthy of a nomination.

"I'm headed to the townhouse," Reg said. "Shall we celebrate?"

"Only if you meet me at the office. We need to be ready when Goldman is voted down."

Reg sighed, but he knew she was probably right. Earlier that afternoon, the Senate Judiciary Committee had voted 10-9 to send a negative report on Judge Goldman up to the full Senate.

"Isn't Mac ready to step right in?"

"The timing isn't right. The point was to get the strong liberal in now. Without Goldman, everything falls into disarray." She lowered her forehead into her hand, showing a weakness that Dennis didn't know she possessed. "I'm sorry, this is my fault, I was so focused on dealing with Egan on *Agguire*, I let my eyes off the ball."

"He could still pull out a miracle in the full Senate. You used to be so much more of an optimist."

"That was before you taught me how to count votes. Unless there's a ram hidden in the bushes somewhere, I'm afraid next week will begin with the sacrifice of Isaac."

ELEVEN MONTHS EARLIER

Miranda had been sitting outside Jason's brownstone for two hours and fifty-three minutes when he emerged for his morning run. She had left the Court at 3:21 AM, got in her car and drove to Bethesda. She paralleled into a spot across the street from his front stoop at 3:48. She had remained in her car without nodding off, without turning on the radio, without even checking her phone.

And at 6:46 AM, Jason came out of the front door and descended the steps. He was thumbing through his iPod shuffle for a song he wanted to start with when he heard Miranda's car door shut, looking up to see her crossing the street. "Well, good morning," he spit-taked.

"Mr. Lancaster. The Supreme Court would like to invite you back."

"You … haven't hired anyone else yet?"

"No one was right. You were right." She swallowed. "The Marshal of the Court was in error."

"I'm flattered, but … I started something else. On Monday."

"And it's as good a job as your job with us?"

Jason paused, then let out a shrug, caught. "No."

"Good. Then you'll come back."

"Can I … go running first?"

"Of course. See you at 8:30." She turned to walk back to her car.

"I know why you fired me." He waited for her to turn back, then explained, "And I won't let things go there again. I won't mistake your impulsiveness for anything else."

"I fired you because every man I've ever liked or respected has turned out to be a huge fucking disappointment."

"Jesus."

"Yes, even him. You're not going to turn out to be a huge fucking disappointment, are you?"

He took a step forward, looking into her eyes, really *looking* into them for the first time. He had avoided them for so long, not wanting to drown in them, get lost in them, get hurt by them before he knew if he had any real chance with her. Now, he looked into those eyes, trying to coat his next words with all the assurance and truth and honesty coursing through his bone marrow. "Never. I might be a dried-out drunk with a temper, very little sense of humor and an unhealthy obsession with a football team with a racially insensitive name. But I also know I will never lie to you, I will never break a promise to you, and I will do everything in my power to make sure no harm comes to you." He smiled. "Or those Justices we're supposed to protect."

A grin broke out on her lips. She nodded acceptance of their pact.

"*But,*" he continued ominously. "I do have one condition to add." She looked at him what-now sideways. "My sponsor had a heart attack last week ..."

"You can't have someone you work with as your sponsor."

"It kinda feels like we'll be breaking a lot of those rules about what you can or can't do with people you work with, doesn't it?"

She shook her head. "See you at 8:30." She turned and walked back to her car, swiveling back just once more. "You know, you are pretty good at reading people."

He smiled back at her, returned his buds to his ears, and jogged away.

Miranda grimaced as she sat down in the driver's seat. Making sure Jason had already disappeared into the morning mist at the end of the block, she lifted her shirt to examine the damage along the left side of her torso, a massive continent of purple bruise already breaking through her skin from hip to armpit. She touched her lower ribs-- and breathed in hard, eyes soaking with tears as immense pain shot through her. She had felt her lower ribs ache whenever she turned the steering wheel left on the drive from DC, but that initial pain was dulled by the adrenaline still coursing through her veins from the attack. Now that she had relaxed, this was real pain, pain coming like a freight train with no brakes.

She would grin and bear it, put the car in gear and head for the office, and never see a doctor for these injuries. She would never know she had three broken ribs.

MONDAY

The gentle electronic ditty broke through George's dream. He shot up in bed and pawed for his glasses, then his phone on the bedstand. Was it a call, was it the Waterford? He always remembered to leave his phone on its loudest possible ring when he went to sleep (he had even done extensive testing to determine which ringtone had the loudest maximum sound), in case someone from the Waterford needed to get in touch with him about Brenda.

His fingers moved more frantically than usual – his dream had been a nightmare, a recreation of the scene he had found in the Pencil Pals, but this time it was his girl, his Brenda, ten years old again, when she was a normal little girl, bleeding in the dream, dead in the dream. Was this a premonition? Was the Waterford calling because something had happened to--

No, the number was '**UNKNOWN**,' according to the display. He cleared the sleep from his throat as he dragged the answer bar across the screen with his thumb. "Aug," he coughed into the bottom of the phone.

"Agent Aug," the crisp voice on the other end of the line answered, "my name is Dean Rikeman, I'm with Allied Armament Security Consultants. Are you familiar with our company, Mr. Aug?"

"I am," he nodded. George knew they had assisted in the recovery efforts after a couple different Southern hurricanes, and that Jason had received a lot of assistance from the contractors in November. "You're the ones in Detroit?"

"We are. I'm City Commander of the Detroit division, in fact."

"Okay," George hummed along, a little amused by that title.

"I understand you are one of the Agents of record in the Supreme Court bombing investigation."

"Under Secretary Summers is leading our task force, but I'm on it, yeah."

"We have obtained a video that I think might be of great interest in your investigation."

"I'll give you my email, and I can look at it when I get to the office."

"I think you're going to want to look at it as soon as it arrives in your in-box, Agent Aug."

In total, fifteen of the twenty-six members of the Senate Armed Services Committee were in the conference room: eight members of the Subcommittee for Personnel, five from Readiness & Management Support, and two Senators who served on both subcommittees. It had all been arranged by Rick Israel (R-MI), chairman of Personnel and one of the young hotshot new members of the Committee who the RNC had their eyes on for big future plans. Israel had been working on his fellow Senators for months, singing the praises of the fast work Allied Armament had done in cleaning up the mean streets of Detroit, building up company founder F. Walsh Howard's December visit to DC as a time for everyone to just sit down for a basic, no-pressure, get-to-know-you. A couple of the most Court-watching members had mentioned some trepidation about holding the meeting while *Agguire* was still pending, but with the announcement that it would be reheard several months down the line, the sit-down was a go, and any repercussions of that ultimate decision on what was discussed Monday could be sorted out at a later date.

As was his style, Walsh travelled light, no entourage, very little pretention. The only person he brought with him was 'LT,' (everyone assumed this stood for 'Lieutenant,') Allied Armament Head of Operations, a fellow Afghanistan veteran who had served as Walsh's CO during his one tour over there. LT bore the scars of war – a limp from a bum knee, one glass eye that looked real enough that you didn't realize it was false until it didn't track into eye contact with the other during a conversation – but once you got used to his idiosyncrasies, he was charismatic, knew their business backwards, forwards, sideways and upside down, and lent real military legitimacy to the company.

"Ladies and gentlemen," Walsh curtailed the small talk, "I'm from Texas, so I could talk football or the weather all day long if you want to. But there is one thing Senator Israel wanted LT and I to do while we're here, or he's not gonna feel right about buying us lunch. We're just here to get a dialogue opened up. We brought some nice, pretty brochures so you can take a look at all the expansion we've had going these last coupla years."

LT distributed the glossy booklets, adding some narration. "Howard doesn't like to boast. So I'll tell you that we just broke ground on a new headquarters we're building down in Lubbock that, when complete, will total over a hundred thousand square feet of training, planning, strategic and tactical facilities. We have our own airfield down there, with 38 aircraft, and more on order. And we just topped 50,000 employees, with a waiting list of about double that."

"The point LT is dancing around here," Walsh jumped in with a smile, as if this was a routine the two had choreographed, "well, y'all are used to talking about budgets and revenues and debt ceilings all day long, so let me just boil it down for you: you spent about a hundred thirty-five grand on each soldier you had on the ground in Iraq and Afghanistan at the peak of those two wars. Well, we wanted to plant a little seed. The next time a big deployment like one a' those comes around? We could do it a helluva lot cheaper."

Whoever says pot doesn't leave you with a hangover is a damn liar, Judge Goldman cursed nearly every morning. Perhaps he didn't get them when he was young, when he was first smoking as a law student in the early '80s, but as he got older, his mornings-after got more and more unpleasant. Sure, a night of cannabis didn't implant that queasy compunction to vomit right into the center of your gut like serious alcohol benders, but for an intellect like Goldman, what it did was worse, dropping a dull haze over his brain that seemed to make even the simplest task complex and annoying and even debilitating.

Having never played any sports that didn't involve skates, an ice rink and a bunch of Canadians, Goldman shocked his family and friends when, in his 30s, he out of the blue picked up running. Right out of the gate, he was running four or five mornings a week. Little did they realize that Goldman ran not for health or fitness or vanity or runner's high, but because he found it was the only thing, better than a red eye coffee, that could wake him up, clear the cobwebs, cure him of even his most wicked marijuana malaise.

Over the years, it had become more of a passion in and of itself, beyond just a hangover cure, and at his peak fitness, he even ran the NYC Marathon in under four and a half hours. Goldman especially loved runs in cities he didn't know well, loved getting lost for a couple hours, loved not knowing where the hell he was, then turning a corner and, whattaya know, there's the Washington Monument or the Arc de Triomphe or the Trevi Fountain.

He was definitely going to start this week off with a run. Over the weekend he had smoked the most weed he had smoked since he married his wife a quarter-century ago. And who could blame him? According to the press, he was a dead man walking, the moment of his ultimate humiliation scheduled to occur Monday morning when the Senate took its full confirmation vote.

Goldman's phones – both his cell and the Hay-Adams landline – rang off the hook all weekend, but he didn't answer them, sure that the President and the last First Lady and every member of the Democratic Party were calling to beg him to withdraw before POTUS had to suffer the embarrassment of a rejection vote come Monday. But Isaac Goldman's mother taught him that the worst scum on Earth was The Quitter, and he wouldn't desecrate her name by quitting now. He was going to see it all the goddamn way through to the bitter end.

He didn't even answer the violent pounds on his door on Saturday afternoon, big, brutish, fist-knocks that sure sounded like someone's Secret Service retinue. He only answered Janaki's lighter knock and plea to open the door early Sunday morning; she dropped off a bag full of air fresheners and forced him out on a walk. (Which, no, didn't work nearly as well as a run.)

Judge Goldman made a point of starting his Monday run late in the 9 o'clock hour, 9:37 AM to be precise, so that the vote would be long over by the time he returned. (He wasn't a quitter, but he wasn't a sadist either.) After four miles, he started his sprint; at 10:14, he was zipping by the K Street McCormick & Schmick's at full speed--

He wrenched to a complete stop. He had seen his wife, he had seen Alice, in there. That was impossible.

He backtracked to the front of the restaurant, cupping his hands around his eyes to peer in through the window:

And displayed on the TV above the bar was the face of his wife.

He rushed inside, ignoring the call of "Sorry, sir, we're closed!" from the manager storming out of the kitchen.

"Turn that TV up," Goldman pleaded, finger pointed at the screen. "Please, you've got to turn that TV up." He had gotten close enough to read the CNN chyron: "**SENATE JUDICIARY RECONVENES FOR TESTIMONY OF NOMINEE'S WIFE.**" Alice's eyes were pointed down, as if she was reading from a prepared statement.

"I'm sorry, Sir," the manager explained as she approached, "but we don't open till 11--"

"Please, that's my wife, you've got to let me hear what she's saying."

Below the TV, Goldman saw a busboy whispering to the bartender, who stopped wiping dishwasher stain off his beer steins. *The kid knows who I am,* Goldman guessed, *he's telling the bartender who I am.* Whatever the busboy told him worked, as the bartender grabbed the remote and cranked some volume into Dr. Goldman's voice:

"… oncology practice in Philadelphia. I wanted to speak to all of you today to explain some things about the relationship I have with my husband Isaac, whom you are currently considering as a nominee for the Supreme Court. Although I would not pretend to be as qualified as this Committee, or the Senate body as a whole, to judge any candidate for the highest court in the land, I do have to say that from my perspective, no nominee could be better qualified, prepared, caring or conscientious than Isaac. No matter the criteria, I cannot imagine him falling short.

"If he is voted down, and it is primarily because of the prevalent belief that he is addicted to marijuana, then let me say as clearly and concisely as I can, at no point in our 25 years of marriage did I believe Isaac was addicted to marijuana. Indeed, as a medical professional, I have never seen research that argues marijuana is as addictive as alcohol or tobacco. For all of you I see with Starbucks cups and coffee mugs up there, it is not even believed to be as addictive as caffeine.

"Yes, Isaac believes in the legality of marijuana, believes its decriminalization is an inevitable advance in our society, and would not deny that he does use it himself from time to time, just as he may have a glass of Scotch from time to time. But at no point did marijuana affect our marriage, at no point did it affect his career and at no point did it affect his faculties as a judge."

Dr. Goldman paused to look up from her paper, giving the reporters and Senators and aides scribbling notes a beat to calm down. She spoke the next section directly to the Committee, eyes never returning to her notes, throat fighting the emotional waver creeping into the bottom of her voice. "Now, a lot has been made of theories as to why I left Isaac. My leaving Isaac had nothing to do with his marijuana use. It had to do with Isaac *asking* me to leave, after I committed adultery."

The Committee room exploded with activity. Clyde Dudley tried to speak over it, tried to regain control and begin the questioning.

And the manager of McCormick & Schmick's offered a paper napkin up to Judge Goldman. "Kleenex?" He took it with a nod of thanks, and dabbed at his tear-stained cheeks.

Dr. Goldman was shown back into a small green room where a lunch ordered from Wagshal's Deli had been laid out across a long table. But when she walked in, her eyes didn't go to the sandwich table; they went right to her husband standing in the center of the room. Alice heard the staffers shutting the door behind her, leaving them the room. Isaac looked good, hair perfect, the suit one of his best, his eyes full of light, cheeks flush with color. Maybe he *was* clean.

"I would've brought flowers," he shrugged, "but that would have looked like bribing the witness."

"Please tell President Irving, I didn't do this because of what he said."

"What did he say?"

"It doesn't matter. I did this for you, Isaac. I couldn't bear to see you humiliated."

"I, I always thought you didn't even meet Elia until six months after you moved out. Was what you said--"

"A complete and total lie."

He smiled his thanks. Never had his breath been taken from him like this. "Have you … gotten my messages? I know Elia's a great guy, but … we're still married. I've given up smoking, Al, or pot of any kind."

"I'm proud of you. But it's too late, Isaac. We have a three month trip planned, Europe, Morocco, Israel, for right after I retire."

He looked down at the carpet, swallowing hard. "Right."

"I hope you can forgive me someday."

Goldman looked up, puddles under his eyes be damned. "I always forgave you. I forgave you as you were walking out. That's what I love you means."

She reached out and touched his cheek. Then left him in that room.

"I feel like we should be toking after this one," President Salas joked as he clinked his Yuengling – chosen to celebrate Judge Goldman's Pennsylvanian heritage – against Rosemarie Irving's. Less than nine hours before, Alice Goldman had delivered the most powerful testimony before the Judiciary Committee since Anita Hill. In those nine hours, the Committee had re-voted on their recommendation (now 16-3 in favor of the Judge) and the Senate had held its own post-lunch debate for only three hours before confirming him with a resounding 55-41 tally, the Republicans in their arguments not mentioning any negatives about the Judge himself, just trepidation about following a President who would order the rounding up of innocent immigrants without evidence.

"I wonder if you're the first President to use the word 'toke.'" Rosemarie smiled as she brought her bottle to her lips.

"I don't know, it sounds like a very Nixon word to me." He took a long sip of the beer, sitting down in one of the couches. "Wow. This actually tastes like shit."

"Blasphemy!"

Salas grinned and beared it, taking another big gulp. "Someday you'll tell me how you got Dr. Goldman to do what she did."

Rosemarie sat across from him. "We didn't have to do anything. That's marriage."

Salas shrugged this topic off with a chuckle, wary of exposing that part of himself most plagued by doubt.

"Someday you'll find your own perfect partner," she assured him. "That person who's ready to supplant all her own goals for the goals that the two of you share. That person who wants nothing more than to form a conglomerate with you, a team of two. Don't worry, your instincts are so good, when you meet that person you can trust implicitly, that person you never have to worry about straying or betraying you or your unified dreams, you'll know it."

POTUS didn't respond, locked in a full Greco-Roman wrestle with his conscience, grappling with whether it was worth it, or his place even, to open the eyes of this woman he had come to respect so much. Or should he wait until he heard back from Hifrael, with more intel, more specifics from MMA?

Laughter from the hall pushed them both to their feet. Reg was coming into the West Sitting Room, his arm around Becks, both of them in the throes of mirth. Salas recognized that laughter, not small talk laughter, not the banter of colleagues, but the deep gut-giggle of flirtation. "Well, here you two are," the former President transitioned when he saw the room already occupied, dropping his arm from the Chief of Staff's shoulders. Salas looked over to Becks's eyes, and saw that she was much more rattled by this surprise.

"Just celebrating being halfway home," Rosemarie explained, turning back to the Betty Ford Bar to retrieve two more beers. "You two can join us."

"Actually," Salas interjected, "we just need one. Becks, I need you over at the VA in a half-hour. They're expecting you."

She lifted her iPad, scrolling through her calendar. "The VA? I didn't have anything--"

"You have a meeting with the Secretary and his senior leadership to catch you up on everything, get you up to speed."

"Up to speed … for …?"

"Veteran Affairs has been in shambles, and an embarrassment to this government and this office, for decades. No offense, Reg."

"None taken."

"Nothing is more important to me than honoring and caring for our veterans. So I'm taking a bold step and making the restructuring of the VA a top priority of my administration and our next five years by naming my Chief of Staff as the new Chief of Staff for the VA."

"*Wh-what?*" Becks stammered. "I mean, thank you, sir. But with all due respect, that's going to be seen as a demotion --"

"Your President is grateful for your sacrifice, Rebecca."

Becks grit her teeth, somehow controlling the dragon in her breast that wanted to leap at Salas and rip that condescension right out of his throat. She nodded obedience, spun on a heel and disappeared down the hall.

"Wow," Reg shook his head as he accepted a beer from his wife. "You do realize the press is going to say you fired her?"

Salas looked over at Rosemarie with a wink. "I had no idea."

"Mr. President," Rosemarie smiled back, "while I have you, we do have a little bit of business to discuss as well." She set her own beer down on the bar, retrieving her leather folder, pulling out a headshot and one-page biography she handed across to the President. "After Judge Goldman takes the oath tomorrow morning, you should pivot right into the introduction of your next nominee."

"If you think he's ready," Salas agreed, looking down into the eyes of Vice Admiral Kennesaw MacTavish.

Mac had received the call from Dennis about two hours before: he was green lit. He would be introduced by the President in the East Room of the White House tomorrow morning at 10 AM following the swearing-in of Isaac Goldman. He should be prepared to answer questions from the press for ten or fifteen minutes, but that would be no problem with all the rehearsing they had done, including the session with the President's Deputy Press Secretary last week, which he passed with flying colors. Mac had been interacting with the press for years, after all. The next morning would bring the single greatest moment of Mac's life, a greater moment than most Americans will ever experience.

And yet, he found himself drowning in the depths of depression.

He had gone a week without listening to any of Shareef's messages. It was easy while he was in the midst of Dennis's vet, spending eight hours a day in the White House basement casino, keeping a routine of a quick room service dinner and one glass of Jack Daniel's upon his return to the hotel, before crawling right into bed; then straight to the gym in the morning before the car came for him at 9.

It was this past weekend that had doomed him. He had been given the option of going home if he followed strict guidelines, but had stayed in the Sheraton because he knew the second he returned home, he would fall into all his old patterns and routines and be unable to avoid calling or hunting down or seeing Shareef. He had stayed in the hotel – not realizing how quiet and lonely and dull it would be over the weekend. Long workouts, a biography of Stanley Forman Reed (the last sitting Justice without a law school education) and a walk down to the multiplex for the latest *Star Trek* movie would kill only so much time.

Saturday night, he had two Jacks. He found himself staring at his voicemail screen, counting Shareef's messages (all 19 of them). After sucking the last drops of golden liquid from the ice, then brushing his teeth and changing into his sleepwear, he lay down across his bed and listened to them, all of them, some of them more than once.

He woke up in a panic on Sunday. He didn't leave his room the entire day; he couldn't risk the compulsion to reunite with Shareef, and didn't want to end up anywhere with even more dangerous trade. He masturbated in the shower that morning, and then again in the afternoon to some trashy internet porn, hopeful that with the FBI background check behind him, no one would be examining his laptop history for the next long while.

But the physical release didn't help. Something much, much deeper than simple animalistic hungers plagued him.

Monday morning was like emerging from under a dark cloud, back to the glorious sunshine of his routine: long workout, room service breakfast, car at 9

AM, back under the White House for his vet, much of which was spent watching the Alice Goldman testimony and subsequent votes on the Sports Book screens.

But that phone call at just after 5, less than 30 minutes after he had returned to his room, was the point of no return. The next morning, he would become an official nominee for the Supreme Court.

He should be leaping with joy. But all he could think about was how he would never speak to or interact with Shareef again.

As Mac watched *Monday Night Football,* he listened to the 21 messages (Shareef had called twice more in the last 48 hours, his relentlessness finally starting to waver), deleting each one, then permanently deleting them from the phone's memory, pausing only to wipe the tears from his face as he went.

The resignation letter was already sitting on the Resolute Desk when Salas returned, eradicating the slight buzz he had acquired up in the West Sitting Room. "¿Qué demonios es esto?" he shouted as he looked up at Hifrael standing sentry by one of the doors.

"I'm sorry, Sir," the agent answered sheepishly in Spanish. "But I can't honor your earlier request."

"Okay, but you don't have to go and quit over it."

"If I can't honor any request you make of me, Sir, then I'm not the right person for your detail commander."

"Goddammit, Hifrael," Salas slammed the letter down on the desk, "I'm withdrawing the request. Forget I ever asked. And don't worry, this whole incident isn't going to affect our relationship, either professional or personal, in the slightest."

"Sir, I'm sorry … I wish I could say the same."

Hifrael turned and left. Salas dropped down into his chair, falling back against it like he had taken a punch right to the gut.

9 PM, and Janaki still had over 20 boxes to unpack. And not only did His Honor want them unpacked by his swearing-in (Chief Egan had moved oral arguments to the afternoon tomorrow, so Goldman could jump right in), but the movers had crammed all 20 into her half of their partitioned office; she wouldn't be able to

get to her desk chair without completing an obstacle course until they were all unpacked and out.

"It's not bad luck to unpack before he's even sworn in?" a voice asked from the door. Janaki swiveled to find Dennis leaning across the threshold from the hall.

"Don't get cute with me, Coutts," she snapped. "I'm tired, starving and have enough paper cuts to supply the Red Cross for the next blood shortage."

Dennis came all the way into the room, dropping a paper bag into the madness of her desk. "Well, you can cross off one of your problems. And I could run out and get you coffee and band aids?"

Janaki opened the maw of the bag wide, breathing in the delectable aroma pouring out. "Amsterdam Falafel?"

"I know it's no Ben's Chili Bowl, but--"

Janaki swallowed his words with her kiss. Dennis's eyes expanded – she had moved so fast, showing off that old D-I field hockey speed, shooting up from her chair and grabbing his cheeks and planting one on him before he even know what hit him.

She pulled away with the sexiest grin he had ever seen this up close and personal. He let out a giggle, as giddy as a school boy after his first post-prom hook-up.

"I fucking love Amsterdam Falafel," she assured him, then smacked one more on his lips.

She returned to her seat and started pulling out the food. He sat down on a stack of two banker's boxes. They ate, and laughed, and would kiss twice more that evening in the midst of their unpacking.

George returned to his sedan in the Waterford lot at 11:04 PM on Monday night. He stared at his phone sitting in his cup holder where he had left it when he went inside. He still hadn't dealt with the video from drikeman@aasc.com. He wasn't sure what to think of it – it couldn't be real, could it? If it was real, George would have to doubt all the skills and instincts he had developed over two decades in this business. If it was real, he would have to show it to Kingman Summers, and explain that they'd had one of the Supreme Court bombers in their custody in the first 24 hours after the attack, and had let him walk. If it was real, George would have to get on his phone and his email and start working on convincing Jason to meet him somewhere. He would have to lure Jason into a trap.

He picked up the phone, unlocked it, and navigated through to the video. Maybe with the sun down, and less glare on his little screen, he would be able to see more detail, be able to catch that little imperfection that clinched it as a fake.

'**7 OCT**,' the date stamp read, the day of the bombing. '**03:22:16 HRS**.' Less than six hours before the bombs would start going off. And the hallways in the image – there was no mistaking what hallways they were: the portraits of old white men in judge's robes on the walls, the giant statue of Chief Justice John Marshall which had sat at the end of the Great Hall since another Chief, Warren Burger, petitioned to have it moved from the Capitol in 1981, the sculpture still sporting the head that would be blown off less than six hours later …

And there was Jason Lancaster, making his way through the building, heavy backpack on his shoulders, moving from camera angle to camera angle, head on a constant swivel, making sure no one was watching him or following him.

Jason ordered one last cup of whiskey for the road. He thanked the bartender, then exited the compound canteen, traipsing through the falling snow for his assigned bunkhouse.

After a Saturday of orientations and introductions, he had just completed his second day assisting the nut job they had building small portable explosives (mostly rudimentary TATP-based stuff) in one room of their arms manufacturing building. Jason had some mixed feelings about building bombs for a militia led by a seven-time (at least) murderer, but he quieted these concerns by reminding himself he was here to find Miranda and get her out, and he would do whatever it took to achieve that end.

Unfortunately, he hadn't seen Miranda since her visit to the brig, but he wanted to get a few more days under his belt here, get some rapport built with a few more of the residents, before he started asking around about her again. She had not given the Minutemen her real name, which was only a small obstacle considering the photo cards he still had in his pocket – but he only wanted to give those out to people he absolutely trusted, lest he raise suspicion and end up back in the prison shack.

Jason timed his steps so that he had one large swallow of whiskey left in his plastic cup when he reached the door of his bunkhouse. He brought it to his lips--

And someone ripped it right from his fingers. "What the fuck is this?" Miranda said as she came around from behind his left shoulder, bringing the drink to her nose, then with a grimace, tossing it over the snow. "What the hell are you doing drinking?"

Jason smiled back at her, trying to keep himself from wobbling. "You drank first, remember?"

Miranda grabbed his arm, dragging him away from the door and any prying ears inside. "You were supposed to leave!" she spat at him in a stage whisper. "As soon as they took the cuffs off, you're out of here – remember?"

"Not without you. I've been looking all over for you. Go grab whatever you need to travel light. I'm taking you out of here."

"No, you're not. I'm not going anywhere."

"Okay, no packing," Jason grabbed her right elbow, turning them towards the woods. "We'll leave now."

"No, we won't. Jason!" She ripped her arm back, out of his grasp. "You're shitfaced. What the fuck is wrong with you?"

He grabbed her arms again, pulled her into his chest. "I once promised you I wouldn't let any harm come to you. I'm here to keep that promise. I'm taking you out of here. I have a friend at Homeland Security. You're going to explain everything you know about the bombing to him, and he'll take care of the rest. We'll never have to think about it ever again."

"I can't do that."

"Oh yeah, why not?"

"Because I don't want to spend the rest of my life in prison."

"What? What does that mean?"

"You shouldn't be here!" she ripped away from him again. "I never should have left you that fucking message."

"But you did. You wanted me to come."

"It was a mistake. You're my old life. *This* is my life now. This is the only place I can escape what I did."

"What you did--"

"You know what I did."

"Rand … on your message, you said you had done a bad thing … you couldn't have meant--"

"Wake the fuck up, Jason. What do you think I meant?"

He just stared at her, unable to even comprehend the concept. There was no way he could have been prepared for this moment. In her voicemail, she had implied some involvement, but he had discounted that, for his own sanity – and for the sake of his motivation in this quest.

"Someone ... rufied me. Is this what it feels like to be rufied?"

She had rufied him. Yes, it made perfect sense. She knew the bombing was coming.

"I'm saving your life, Jason."

He had really known it all along. All she was doing now was confirming it, coming right out and saying it.

Sensing the resistance had drained out of him, Miranda shook her head, turned and walked deeper into the compound. Outside her own quarters, she turned and looked to the outskirts of the courtyard one last time.

Jason still hadn't moved.

BENCH MEMO

BOOK FOUR OF THE SIX-PART CONSPIRACY THRILLER
FOUR SEA
AARON
COOLEY

FEBRUARY

On festive mornings like this, those rare mornings of the year when the Supreme Court is foremost on every American's mind, Chief Justice Quint couldn't help but harken back to his first swearing-in as an Associate Justice some thirty-odd years ago, to that frozen image seared into his memory for eternity: Chief Justice Warren Burger holding the Bible under his palm, the face of the 40th President looking on from just over the Chief's right shoulder. Supreme Court swearing-ins weren't yet the spectacle they would become; no cameras were present in the Court's East Conference Room, just the other Justices, the President and Nancy, Quint's children and grandchildren and the love of his life, Darline.

President Reagan had assured his constituents that William Harvey Quint's record cleaning up Atlanta as its aggressive District Attorney portended of a Justice in the fine Conservative tradition, one who would prioritize law and order and the safety of America's streets above all else. Quint was also a faithful churchgoing man, Reagan's vetters had assured him; the most hopeful right-leaning observers were soon panting with elation about a certain ruling from the early '70s he might play a part in overturning.

Soon into his tenure, however, it became clear that Quint actually came from that most powerful genus of Supreme Court Justice: the Moderate. From his very first term, he positioned himself as an unpredictable voter, dedicated to prioritizing precedent above ideology, willing to vote in any direction, for either side, on any particular issue. Whenever the four Supremes on the left and the four on the right would fall into their predictable roles, the final verdict – and in many cases, a great precedent that might very well affect American law for decades to come – would rest in the hands of William Harvey Quint.

Despite this, Quint didn't make enemies, only friends. He didn't hold his power over anyone's head, didn't inspire grudges or demand debts. He was universally respected by his colleagues, who valued how closely he seemed to listen as they each took turns visiting his chambers to lobby for his vote. He was revered by his clerks, whom he treated as true collaborators and teammates, rather than subordinates.

He was admired by both sides, and would eventually be confirmed as Chief Justice by a Democratically-controlled Senate, with the full, boisterous support of the Democratic House. He was beloved by all of his colleagues, and on the day of his retirement, even his most frequent dissenter, Claudine Egan, shed tears.

He was so esteemed by nearly every American that former President Irving and his wife Rosemarie had seven years later recruited him to return to the Chief's chair when his Court faced its darkest and most uncertain hour.

"When I set out to select my nominee for this vital position," President Salas explained to the crowd gathered in the White House East Room to witness the investiture of the new Chief Justice, "I knew that whoever took the center chair would inherit a Court at the most tumultuous moment in its history: a Court under attack, not yet recovered from the destruction of its home or the loss of so many of her personnel from both behind the bench and behind the scenes. Truth be told, we as a nation, and our Court, must never fully recover, or ever fully forget, those wounds." Quint nodded and hummed, pleased with the respectful tone and timbre of the words the President and his communication staff had chosen for this historic moment. Darline's squeeze on his hand tightened, a silent agreement with her husband's assessment.

"There is no doubt in my mind," the President continued, "that the person I selected to replace the late Chief Justice Lapadula is better qualified, prepared and willing to lead our Court into its future than any other human being on this planet. Ladies and gentlemen, I am truly humbled to introduce to you, the next Chief--"

The gunshot would be the last sound William Harvey Quint would ever hear. He saw the commotion the blast inspired in the East Room – the people rising from their seats in terror, the President being shoved to the ground by his gun-toting security detail – but he was already fading into the muddled acoustics on the edge of consciousness. He could feel Darline squeezing even tighter, could peripherally sense her mouth opening in a scream for help. But he didn't hear her actual plea. Everyone seemed to be moving in slow motion, and as the curtain lowered on Chief Quint's life, his final thought was that same burning question haunting everyone witnessing this spectacle:

Had someone just assassinated the Chief Justice?

BOOK FOUR

BENCH MEMO

ONE MONTH EARLIER
A MONDAY IN JANUARY

House Speaker Robert Hatfield (R-OH) let a dramatic pause sit over the dumbstruck reporters after the snarky blogger representing *Salon* or *Daily Kos* or one of those other liberal sites not worth remembering had asked his question. Hatfield had just finished announcing what would surely go down as his signature decision of the session – not the passing of a budget or a defense spending authorization or a bill to help the poor or sick or elderly, but ordering the formation of the House Select Committee on the Oregon Halfway House Controversy. He was going to be damn sure he milked everything out of his day at the top of America's cable news programs. "We as a nation have got to face facts, Markos: the American people no longer trust their President. It's not pleasant to talk about, but it's the reality. They don't have faith this President and his Justice Department are doing everything they possibly can to bring the Supreme Court bombers to justice. It's our duty as a Congress to make sure they are doing just that."

"Speaker Hatfield," another reporter called out, "are you implying that the residents of the Iranian halfway house did have something to do with the bombing?"

"I'm saying I have no idea. The American people have no idea. And a month after the fact now, that's completely unacceptable. That's what this committee is going to get to the bottom of. We still don't know why Homeland Security and the FBI targeted those people. Did they have good reason to raid that building with guns blazing and make those arrests, or was this, heaven forbid, some sort of racial profiling or something?"

"And if they did have good reason to surveil this facility," Hatfield's counterpart in the Senate, Majority Leader Clyde Dudley (R-OH), leaned into the mic, "then why the heck do you release the guys we did arrest after only four days? Is that even time to question them properly?"

"Why weren't they taken to Guantanamo or a secure military facility?" Hatfield drafted off the Senator, like the two were members of a well-rehearsed boy band performing a familiar routine by rote. "Let's not forget, some of these people aren't even American citizens. If they came here as our guests and committed an act of war, doesn't that mean their detention and interrogation should be carried out under a whole different set of rules? These are the types of questions the American people want answered, and we want them answered too."

"Senator Dudley, it's unusual that the Senate Majority Leader would help announce the formation of a *House* committee--"

"Great question, Mike, I'm glad you asked," Dudley licked his chops, stepping in front of the mic, almost blocking Hatfield from the cameras. "I offered to join my friend from the House here today not only because I support wholeheartedly the formation of this committee and will be doing my part over in the Senate to ask these tough questions too, but because I believe this entire controversy does have bearing on the President's final year that we have just begun and all those big plans he announced in his State of the Union last week. The Republicans of the Senate want the President to know that we have our own thoughts on this coming year; this morning he will be receiving a letter from us explaining that we are giving him two more business weeks – I'm talking from today, until the end of next week, the 24th – to make his final nomination for the Supreme Court. After that, we're going to be into February, and I personally, and my fellow Republican Senators, don't feel it would be appropriate for any further decisions of this magnitude to come out of the White House until we know for certain who our next President is going to be."

This bombshell got the pens scribbling, the thumbs hammering out quick bursts to editors who would within seconds blast it out across the tops of their sites on blinking red breaking news banners. "Leader Dudley! Leader Dudley!" Dudley nodded to one of the raised hands and the rest lowered. "Won't some people say you're just blatantly refusing to carry out your Constitutional duties if you refuse to--"

"Let's take a deep breath and think this through, Luke. We have dutifully confirmed the President's first two nominees, and are in the process of considering his third, Admiral MacTavish. But at a certain point, we have to remember we're in an election year, and it would be irresponsible to give carte blanche to a man who may very well not be President in a few months. I would remind you all there is a precedent for this: the Senate filibustered President Johnson's promotion of Abe Fortas to Chief Justice in his last year in the White House, for these very same reasons."

His sentence was barely complete before the cacophony kicked up again. Hatfield didn't feel like spending any more of his day listening to Clyde Dudley answer questions – this was his press conference and he was going to end it his way. He raised a hand, turning to walk away from the mic with a polite, "Thank you."

"You see that shit?" the President chuckled out of the speaker phone. The three TVs embedded across the back of the front seat of the Irvings' armored Escalade were muted now, but they had heard the entire Hatfield-Dudley joint presser before Rosemarie's phone rang with Salas's call.

"You had to know they'd do *something*," Reg assured him. "The halfway house is all any Fox News host has talked about for the last month."

In his private study off the Oval Office, Salas rolled his eyes at Reginald Irving's tone. He had called Rosemarie's cell for *her* counsel, and wasn't thrilled he had gotten the party line instead.

"This committee will bore the hell out of anyone who watches it for even five minutes," Rosemarie jumped in, "and by next month, it will be long forgotten. By October, Benedict will be a fool to even bring it up in a debate – it will just serve to make him look like one of the kooks himself."

"It's not the committee that bothers me," POTUS sighed into the phone. "It's this deadline."

"This is exactly why we came to see you the very next day after the attack," Rosemarie said. "This is why you had to start picking your nominees immediately."

"And I'm glad I did. But now they're giving us only enough time for one shot at the Chief's seat. We don't get this last one right, we have to live with Claudine Egan for the next year."

"Which is why we've gone in precisely the order we have." Rosemarie held up a hand as if Salas could see her, as if she was a crisis counselor talking someone off the roof of a skyscraper. "You're ending with the most iconic, popular Supreme Court Justice alive today. Someone the public universally regards as one of the fairest, down-the-middle, most reasoned jurists in the Court's history. And someone who's already proven he can lead the Court as its Chief Justice quite capably."

"And he's originally from the South," Reg chimed in. "The Right can't touch this guy."

"The game is over, Antonio," Rosemarie continued, ignoring her husband's raised eyebrow at her use of the President's first name. "You've won."

"In fact, I'd leak the final name right now," Reg added. "Get those talking heads off that committee already. They won't be able to help themselves. They'll spin into absolute tizzies about how exciting and historic and perfect this choice is."

The vehicle bounced, the chained tires galloping onto a long gravel driveway. A pearl white Virginia plantation house awaited them at the end of it, almost invisible against the waves of falling snow. But even this camouflaged view filled Rosemarie with that warm feeling of homecoming that most college kids get when they return on their first winter break. "Or maybe wait an hour, until we can make sure he's accepted our offer."

"You think there's a chance he won't?" Salas's throat quaked with panic.

"Don't worry," FLOTUS smiled. "He will."

Even after decades of marriage to a public figure who often in his career drew the ire of violent activists, Darline Quint still wouldn't allow a security guard or housekeeper or any other person who wasn't *her* to answer her front door. Darline had grown up in a small farm house in North Carolina, and even as her husband's fame and stature grew, she refused to forget her roots. Her family was what America was all about, she always reminded her husband; it wasn't about marble columns and armed security guards and debates over moral stances that politicians looking to build rabid bases had whipped up into national controversies decades after the Court had settled them (in the case of the most partisan dispute, rather decisively too, in a 7-2 vote). America was about having dinner with your family, about knowing your neighbors, about saying hello to all your fellow shoppers as you bought food from your local grocer. America was about answering your own door.

So it was Darline Quint herself who answered the door when the former President and his bride rang the bell. "My favorite young couple in the world," she still called them, stepping forward to hug Rosemarie, to lean into Reg's kiss of her cheek. "To what do we owe this honor?" she asked as she led them into the foyer where Margaret took their coats (she had long ago told the housekeeper to let her do that, but Margaret continued to join her employer at the door; Darline was convinced it was probably William who had told her to ignore that order).

"How is the Chief, Mrs. Quint?" Rosemarie asked.

Darline sighed. "He served with all four of the Justices we lost. All he's done these last few months is sit in his law library, reading. He told me he can't put off reading all those books on the shelves any longer, because he never knows when it's all going to end." Rosemarie rolled her eyes; that sounded like her mentor, all right. "Can I get you two anything?"

Rosemarie turned to her husband, brushing his biceps with her fingertips. "Honey, why don't you help Mrs. Quint with some tea, while I say hello to the Chief?"

"It would be my pleasure," the ex-President smiled, cocking his arm to offer it to the elder woman. She slid in through his elbow with a grin and patted his shoulder as they turned for the kitchen.

"Have you come to drag me from my summer recess already?" Chief Quint asked without turning to the door or even looking up from the large tome open across his lap. Rosemarie smiled; even past 80, his hearing remained his finest sense (his late mother had always claimed it was because he had refused to submit to a vision test until well into his 20s, at which point their local optometrist declared he had probably been legally blind since puberty).

Rosemarie crossed her arms and leaned into the doorway. "What did I always say when you returned to chambers after a break?"

"'Mr. Chief Justice, thank God you're here.'"

"'*Your country needs you!*'" they completed in unison.

As Rosemarie laughed, the Chief closed up his book and set it aside, then readied his hands on his armrests for leverage, pushing himself to his feet. Rosemarie rushed in to assist, but he bade her to keep her distance with a predictable, "I've got this!" He was already in a full suit and tie; those who didn't know the Justice might think he was expecting her, not realizing he still wore his Court 'uniform' five days a week, even in retirement. "It's about time you came for me."

"The first two weren't easy." She knocked on the oak bookcase closest to her. "Luckily, the Admiral looks good so far."

"I thought you might save me for last. Smart."

"So you expected to be asked?"

"It makes sense, doesn't it, given the climate, given what the nation has been through?"

"President Salas will be so grateful."

"Now, hold your horses. I didn't say I was going to accept."

Rosemarie caught her smile. It was never easy with the Chief. Fun, but never easy.

"I'm an old man. To go through a confirmation hearing with all those jerks they got in there now--"

"Will be fun as hell and you know it. We both know you can't wait to tie them up in knots."

The Chief let a devilish grin crack through his countenance; Rosemarie still knew him better than anyone outside of his wife. "I'm just not sure I'm up to the job anymore. Not without my favorite clerk."

"You're in luck," Rosemarie grinned. "She happens to be available."

Jason Lancaster had remained at Polis about 28 days longer than planned. Miranda had no intention of leaving, and whenever he had cornered her about getting out of there, she had stuck to her guns that this was the only place she could escape punishment for her role in the bombing of their old workplace.

Jason still didn't know the full extent of her involvement, let alone her motives, and had for the time being compartmentalized those concerns into a little box in the back of his brain to be opened at a later date. He had travelled the length of four states and spent three months finding her; he had decided he would allow nothing to deviate him from his goal of getting her out of the Minutemen compound. Once that was achieved, he could open that little box and figure out what to do with whatever was found inside.

But a week before Christmas, the snows fell, blanketing the miles of Huron National Forest all around them in a sea of white. No one – not Jason, not Miranda – would be going anywhere until it got warmer, until the green started to break through again. Jason agreed to a couple guest appearances as Santa (the theory being that many of the children hadn't met this newest Minuteman yet, and wouldn't recognize his voice behind the ho-ho-hos, or his eyes above the white of the false beard) and settled into his role as assistant bomb maker to Dreyfus, a middle-aged Ohio 'Nam vet who had lost as many fingers as he had wives (three).

Dreyfus did all the talking for the two of them as they toiled away six days a week in their one small, windowless room of the compound's designated weapons manufacturing building. Jason had misgivings about making explosives for this group, of course, and from time to time couldn't help but debate whether he should request another work duty. But he knew trust was a commodity in a community like this, especially with an unstable element like Benjamin Bratten at its head. Jason could feel everyone starting to trust him, think of him as one of their own even, and didn't want to chance upsetting that apple cart. He reminded himself he wasn't here on behalf of the government, or any law enforcement entity; his mission was a personal one. His mission was to get Miranda out of here, and until he had accomplished that, it was in the best interest of that mission to keep being a productive member of the Minutemen and doing whatever Bratten asked of him. He promised himself he would work slowly (Dreyfus was too long in the tooth to work any faster himself, and no one here knew Jason well enough to know how quickly he could actually build this shit), never introduce Dreyfus to more efficient techniques or more explosive materials, never grimace during any of Bratten's incendiary town hall sermons, and continue to work on Miranda during her once or twice-weekly visits to his bunk for hurried, unconnected sex.

She didn't stick around after these trysts for even two minutes of pillow talk, so he had to manufacture times running into her on the grounds or in the mess hall to remind her why he was here, to try to convince her they should leave the compound. Miranda was trying to maintain the ruse that she had never seen Jason before his arrival at Polis, and would cut these conversations short after a sentence or two were exchanged.

Jason had long ago stopped debating the possibility that Miranda was here with the Minutemen for some reason other than the one she had given him – hiding out, escaping justice for her own high crimes – and it had been weeks since he considered that there might be some other person connected to the bombing here in Polis. He had never for a second thought that the odd duck Dreyfus might know something that could restart his stalled quest. The vet had complained many times about the Supreme Court over their three and a half weeks together; he had denounced every branch, agency and division of the federal government. He had more than once expressed that he thought the Justices got what they deserved with the bombing. "Playing God from the bench," he would shake his head, "not what the Founders intended, nosiree." While Jason nodded and listened, Dreyfus would espouse elaborate, outlandish theories about several prominent cases of the last handful of years, gripped with paranoia about the far-reaching effects of each decision. The NSA was now using every cell phone in America as a listening device, so one of his theories went. In another, he explained how the federal government had been secretly granted the power to use Medicare rolls as a euthanasia list in the event of a national food or water shortage.

But it was a complete surprise when, one afternoon in January, Dreyfus came right out and said, "And I know who did it, too."

Jason stopped what he was doing, looking up at his work partner. "Say that again?" The surgical mask covering the bottom half of Dreyfus's face muffled his words; Jason couldn't have heard what he thought he just heard, right?

"The Supreme Court," Dreyfus explained as he reached up to pull his mask down below his chin, as if only to reveal his cocky smile. "I know who blew it up."

"Bullshit."

"And I know why too." He winked at Jason. "C'mon, Lancaster, you don't really think we all believe it's just a coincidence that you, a former employee of the Supreme Court, shows up here right after it comes down, do you?" Dreyfus re-covered his face, returning to his task packing volatile triacetone triperoxide into a plastic housing.

Jason didn't move his gaze off the other bomb maker for several seconds, his mind swirling with possible interpretations of what he just said. Did Dreyfus know Miranda had played a part in the bombing? Did he know more about why than even Jason did?

Or was this not about Miranda at all? Was someone else at Polis also involved?

George Aug had spent the last month obstructing justice. In his four decades of law enforcement, he had been taught to trust his instincts, and those instincts had never once let him down. He found it impossible to believe that his instincts about Jason Lancaster had been so wrong.

He had turned in the Supreme Court surveillance video of Jason Lancaster to the head of his Homeland Security division, Intelligence & Analysis, the very day after Dean Rikeman, City Commander for the military contractor now running police and fire in Detroit, had emailed it to him. But what George hadn't told Kingman Summers was that he had been in loose contact with Jason for over two months, since the day DHS released him from custody. He hadn't told Kingman that the last they had spoken, Jason was trying to find a Michigan-based militia known as the Minutemen, which he believed was led by the Solstice Bank shooter, Benjamin Bratten. George hadn't given Kingman the video still Jason had sent him from the lobby camera of a small motel in Mio, Michigan, a still showing a man who would prove to know the location of this militia.

George kept all of this close to the vest as Kingman sent him up to Detroit to interview Rikeman about his own brief dealings with Jason Lancaster. (Kingman now knew about George's mentally incapacitated daughter and gave George the choice of redeeming himself for Oregon or going on early retirement; George not only needed to keep his job, it was important to him that he be involved with any investigation of Jason, out of self-preservation if nothing else.)

Rikeman described Jason as a nice enough guy, if one obsessed with the Supreme Court bombing and his ex-boss, Miranda Whitney. Most of George's follow-up had less to do with Jason and more to do with the video itself, and how Allied Armament had happened to obtain it. Rikeman explained it was found on a large server confiscated during a video piracy investigation and George was welcome to re-interview all the hackers behind the file sharing program, each of whom had no idea which of their users had uploaded it to their service. In fact, as their service utilized BitTorrents for uploading, different pieces of the video file had come from hundreds of different users.

Launching off a photo of Minutemen (including one Miranda Whitney) making an arms deal in Detroit, George and his team spent the next couple of weeks following the same steps Jason had tread weeks earlier, culminating in Mio, which seemed to be the last place any future Minuteman was seen before disappearing into the 439,000 acres of the Huron National Forest. But offering assistance to Homeland Security about anything, let alone the location of the Minutemen, was the last thing anyone in this paranoid little town wanted to do. DHS's first aerial searches had turned up zilch before the winter storms made helicopter flyovers impossible. George and his team had just begun searching what satellite imagery beyond Google Earth they could get their hands on.

"We are here because we have determined the location of Polis," Dean Rikeman explained to George, Kingman Summers and several other I&A analysts in late January. Rikeman had made the trip to Washington, to DHS's Ops Center, accompanied by Allied Armament's Head of Operations, a vet known as 'LT' by his subordinates, whose own body was a map of the scarring of the early Iraq War.

"Where what is?" Kingman asked for clarification.

"It's the name for the compound the Minutemen are rumored to have built somewhere in the Huron," George explained. "*Polis* was the Greek word for city-state."

"A declaration of their self-governance," Rikeman added.

"Copy that. So where the hell is it?"

Rikeman looked over to his superior with an uncomfortable grin. George and Kingman turned to LT, each hoping they weren't staring too obviously into his glass eye. "Gentlemen," he smiled back, "Allied Armament Security Consultants is prepared to share with Homeland Security the exact whereabouts of the Minutemen militia and the fugitive they are harboring, Supreme Court bombing suspect Jason Ian Lancaster." As he spoke, he opened a leather folder and passed a short document across the table. It was Kingman who picked it up, but George got just enough of a flash of it to identify it as some sort of contract. "We do have some conditions to proceeding with such an arrangement."

"Conditions?" George scoffed. "How about we don't hit you with obstruction?" George felt Kingman's hand land on his wrist, an effort to calm him. *He's not actually going to kowtow to these amateurs,* George fretted.

"Agent Aug," LT responded with a condescending smile, like a parent in a teachable moment, "Allied Armament is a business. We have to do what's in our best business interests. And let's be honest here." He leaned forward on his forearms, pushing his upper body almost halfway across the table. "Their compound is miles from any drivable road, in the middle of a forest currently blanketed in a foot of snow. DHS would have to farm this out to a specialized law enforcement or even military unit – just as you did with the Iranian halfway house in Oregon." No one in the room missed the implication dripping from the last part of LT's sentence: if DHS chose to go after Lancaster themselves, they were liable to cause themselves more embarrassment. "We happen to employ a full team of men that Uncle Sam's best ass kickers personally trained for the most treacherous passes of the Hindu Kush mountain range in the dead of the Afghan winter. We can get to this guy." He shrugged. "And if we get a press release or a couple camera-ready moments out of the arrest, what harm is that to you?"

"There's still a snow plow's worth of questions we need answered first." George shook his head. "Where this video even came from, why it's edited in such a way that we only see Lancaster – we know there's no way he was working alone, so where's video of the other--"

"George," Kingman's voice stopped him in his tracks. George sat back. He knew it was futile to try to spoil his superior's best chance at covering his own malfeasance in this investigation. He pulled the hanky out of his pocket and used it to dab at his perspiring brow. "The arrangement you've proposed makes a lot of sense," his superior continued. "I need to bring it to the Secretary, of course, but we should have you an answer within the next day."

Vice Admiral Kennesaw MacTavish had gone AWOL. He had witnessed so many political figures in Washington become so important, they became literal prisoners of their own success (Bill Clinton had called the White House "the crown jewel in the federal prison system"); Mac had just never expected this to happen to him. Sure, he used to do press conferences a handful of times a year after successful JSOC missions, and occasionally a young enlisted man or woman who had read one of his books and aspired to a career as decorated as his would approach him for an autograph or advice. But now that he was the nominee for the third Supreme Court seat opened by the October bombing, in the thick of his confirmation hearings, there were very few places he was permitted to go: the Russell Senate Office Building where the Kennedy Caucus Room was located, and his hotel, the Hay-Adams. That was it. The Irvings hadn't stooped to putting an actual security detail on him, but they had given him the name of a young aide on his prep team he was to call, twenty-four/seven, if he needed anything or required a trip beyond his approved locations.

Mac wasn't sure what the hell he needed or where he wanted to go. He just wanted to get out of Washington and have one night where he felt like a normal human being again. (He had already decided he wasn't moving from his Virginia neighborhood even in the event he was confirmed.) He exited the hotel just after 7, wandering a couple blocks to the MacPherson Square rail station, where his familiar blue line happened to connect. He climbed aboard and rode it back down into friendly territory, into Virginia. He didn't know or care where he was going, just that it would feel more like home.

Not wanting to risk being recognized, he rode for a few random stops past the Pentagon, disembarking at the King Street/Old Town stop. He wandered again for a few blocks, just enjoying the crunch of the snow under his boots, the frigid winter air stinging his cheeks.

He smiled when he heard Hank Williams emanating from around a corner – and this was the original article, Hank Senior, not the guy most famous for singing about football. He turned down this alley, stepped into the subtle pub he found there, hung his jacket above one of the open booths, and slid onto its leather bench. He ordered a Jack from the fixture of a waitress, and then the burger she recommended most off their single-paged, five-by-eight menu. He sat back and sipped on his old friend as he glanced at the college basketball game above the bar, noticing that he had been so busy he hadn't even realized Monday Night Football was finished for the season. He dug out his phone to check up on the playoffs, but his dinner was delivered before he got that far.

It was as he chewed his first bite that he noticed the boy checking him out. Mac pegged him for his early- or mid-20s (as the leader of many young men, he had developed a decent eye for identifying age), but in comparison to the Admiral, 'boy' was still an apt descriptor. He was handsome and athletic, taller than Mac, with the body of someone who cared about his health and fitness, and a UVA hoodie that Mac told himself was indicative of intelligence and education. The boy was at the table adjacent to Mac's, but had chosen the bench opposite his; with no one sharing either of their booths, they were staring across two tables right into each other's eyes. Mac tried to look off the awkwardness, but the boy embraced it, keeping his gaze locked on the older man as he brought his Michelob Ultra to his lips, sticking his tongue down its maw in a folded origami before tipping it back for some drink.

Eventually, Mac had no choice but to acknowledge the stare, giving a clenched half smile and a nod to the boy before returning to his burger for his third bite. This only encouraged the young man; he next licked his top lip with a slow, wide swipe of his tongue.

And then, he got up. He topped his bottle with a coaster to indicate he wasn't gone for the night, traded eyes with Mac one more time, then moved for the door in the rear of the bar which, in the brief flash it was open, Mac could see led to a long-out-of-order pay phone between restrooms.

Mac finished his burger. He knew what he was supposed to do next. Honestly, what he wanted to do next. But there were so many reasons he shouldn't do it. There were the common sense safety concerns to think about. There was his confirmation to think about.

There was Shareef to think about.

That blip of Shareef, the first waking thought the disciplined Mac had allowed himself to have of him in days, served to remind Mac why he *should* do this. This would be how he would finally get Shareef out of his system. He would officially move on, starting with a more appropriate partner (as much as a young man 30 years his junior could be considered appropriate). A military man all his life, he had never done this sort of thing. *Isn't it about time?* he couldn't stop asking. He swallowed his last bite, rinsed it down with the last of his Jack, got up and walked back to that little alcove of phone and restroom doors. Giving the wall a quick spatial examination, Mac predicted a one-seater behind the narrow little door with the male icon. He tried the handle – locked.

But he didn't leave the alcove. He stood there for several seconds, not stepping any closer, just listening for some sound of rushing water, for movement, for anything from inside. But there was nothing. Mac raised his fist and brought it to the door, just holding it there for a few moments. Then finally, he used it to knock on the door just twice.

He could hear the lock unlatching. He quivered with nerves, adrenaline pumping harder and faster than it ever had before imminent combat.

The door flew open. "Can't wait to get in?" the boy teased him. He reached out and grabbed the Admiral's wrist – Mac had to lock down his instincts, remember not to rip his hand back – pulling him inside, slamming him up against the wall tiles, ravaging his lips with a primal kiss as he booted the door shut with the side of his foot. The kiss was nice, Mac thought, though less controlled, less considerate, than Shareef's.

Shut the fuck up, Old Man! Mac scolded himself, promising he would not spend this encounter comparing it to Shareef. It was time to forget Shareef, to start forming new muscle memories. He couldn't help it; Shareef was one of only three men he had ever been with, and the only one in the last four years.

"Lock," Mac panted into the boy's mouth, "you need to lock it."

The boy pulled his face away, and as he sealed the two locks on the door with his left hand without even a glance over to them – clearly not the first time he had locked himself in this room in a hurry – he gripped the bulge in Mac's jeans with his right. Mac moaned with delight, eyes rolling back, and clocking this reaction, the boy smiled. At this moment, he decided to make this encounter a public service, all about bringing this older man, who had grown up in repressive, stifled times and hadn't gotten enough in his life, ultimate pleasure and release. "That's right," the boy grinned, "I know what I'm doing. You don't need to worry about a thing." He dropped into a catcher's crouch, grabbing Mac's belt strap and pulling it loose in one practiced move. "You're gonna sleep so well tonight and put those fascist Senators in their place tomorrow."

All the heat in Mac's body rushed up to his forehead. The boy knew who he was. Maybe everyone in that bar knew who he was. How often does this bar get a Supreme Court nominee for a customer? Everyone was watching him closely. They would notice that both he and this boy were spending an awful long time back in the alcove at the same time – someone might even come back here and try the door and realize they were sharing what was supposed to be a one-seater. They would know *what* he was. He wasn't supposed to be here. He wasn't supposed to be doing this.

"No, no, I'm sorry," he protested, taking his belt back and looping it closed again. "I'm sorry, I can't--"

He was out the unlocked door before the boy could even get back to his feet or utter a word. Mac couldn't give him that chance. He knew how easy it would be to convince him to stay.

Tonight was Janaki's turn, but she had broken their rules.

Over the past three weeks, she and Dennis had traded off, picking up dinner and delivering it to the other at the office, engaging in a contest of one-upmanship to see who could deliver the other high-profile aide dinner from the hipper, greasier, more carcinogenic DC landmark. The meals had started as deliveries to their respective offices on the ground floor of the Capitol, but last week, Dennis had taken the unprecedented and bold step of announcing he would be ordering his next turn's meal to be delivered to his own apartment, and hoped it wasn't too presumptuous to ask Janaki to join him there. She did, and they had a great, fun evening.

That didn't stop Dennis from flagellating himself in the days since about whether or not the evening should've been *more* – about whether he should've *made* it more, whether she wanted him to make it more, but he had just been too much of a coward. He went over their hello kiss over and over again in his mind, then their goodnight kiss three hours later. There hadn't been anything to report beyond that. But should there have been? Dennis relived each minute of her visit with a fine tooth comb, picking over her every breath for hints that she wanted him to be more aggressive, try for something more, hints he was sure he must have missed.

Or could the unthinkable be true – could he be in the Friend Zone without even realizing it?

Janaki had emailed him on Sunday and said she wanted to return the favor by inviting him over to her place for Monday night dinner and the latest episode of *Pro Bono*, the laughable Netflix legal show they were binge watching. (As much as two people involved with the Supreme Court could do anything with the word binge in it besides binge-vetting, or binge-brief-reading; they had averaged about 0.4 episodes per week since they started the show separately, discussing what they had seen whenever they next saw each other. Realizing during their 'date' in Dennis's apartment that they were on the same episode, they had watched one together for the first time. (Okay, Dennis watched this episode for the second time; he had fibbed when he said they were on the same one, excited by the prospect of sharing the rest of the season together. He admitted to his white lie as the end credits rolled; Janaki was touched.))

Upon his arrival at her door, a brief hello kiss (*Are they getting briefer?* Dennis interrogated himself) was followed by Janaki stepping back to theatrically reveal a table set with candles above a long tray of immaculate sushi. "Is this from Taro?" Dennis guessed. "Kaz? Are we going to have to set a price limit?"

But Janaki didn't answer, just stepped behind the table, slicing off pieces of fish with a butcher knife, rolling them up into sticky rice with seaweed paper, then adding them to the tray. "Wait – you did this? We said no cooking. That was our one rule!"

"You don't cook sushi, Coutts. It's raw. Here, taste this." She brought some roll packed with a rainbow of colors to his mouth; it both crunched and exploded as he bit down into it.

"Holy wap," he sloshed out of his full mouth. "Dat's incredible!"

"It better be, if someone who grew up in her parents' sushi restaurant made it."

"Wait – your parents' restaurant, it's Japanese?"

"Millbourne already had an Indian restaurant. Racist." She tossed a roll at him; he caught it on his chest and gobbled it down.

An hour later, Dennis slouched back against his chair, full of rice and fish and a little drunk on wine. Their conversation had quieted for a moment; it happened from time to time, which always seemed to make Janaki nervous – what did it mean when two lawyers didn't have anything to say? But Dennis argued they shouldn't worry about it, they should cherish it. They should embrace the silences, revel in them together, since they got so little of them in their work days. The night of her sushi meal, he looked at her and soaked in the silence, finally breaking it with, "Do you know how much I admire you?"

"Sushi isn't as hard as it looks."

"I read one of your stories."

"Wait, *what?*"

"Okay, I read all three of them. I passed Justice Goldman in the hall last week, and he pulls me aside and says, 'You realize how talented that girl is?'"

"Oh shit. Does he know we--?"

"I was as shocked as you. I pretended I didn't know what he was talking about. And he says, 'C'mon, Kid. If there's one thing Jews are good at, it's seeing when two young people are a perfect match.' I turned turnip red. He tells me to relax. And then says, 'I bet she hasn't told you I hired her because of her short stories.'"

Janaki brought her hands to her forehead. "This is so mortifying."

"No, it's not. He was right. They're just-- I was blown away. They're friggin' great."

"You have to say that. I just made you dinner."

"No, I'm serious. I had this powerful, emotional experience reading them …"

She swatted him playfully. "Shut the hell up."

"Hear me out, hear me out! I used to be so *stressed* all the time about how my career was going. I had this whole thing mapped out, since I was 8. Here I am 28 now, I'm supposed to have clerked for both a circuit judge and a Justice. I told myself I would be a complete failure if I didn't clerk on the Court someday. Then I'm supposed to go to a big firm. Four, five years as an associate, then I make partner."

"You do realize how miserable that life is?"

"It doesn't matter. It's what I was *supposed* to accomplish, if I was going to be the first member of my family to stop living in the past, in our dead form of government, and *take over* this one. If I was going to someday be the first American Indian Justice. And I've done okay--"

"Right, just okay, Mr. Assistant to the Irvings."

"Well, I usually walk around thinking I'm a complete failure. At least, until I read your stories."

"And then you saw what failure really looked like."

"Shut up for a second. As I was reading them, I suddenly realized, I didn't care about that shit anymore. I realized I didn't care about that plan I had made for myself. I just cared about being happy. And living a simple, happy life with you. And working hard enough that you can write the greatest Great American Novel this country's ever seen."

Janaki sat back, stunned. "Wow."

Dennis pulled his hands back. "Shit, I went too far, didn't I? I'm sorry, I didn't mean to talk about life – you know, beyond next Tuesday – and, and scare the hell out of you. I shouldn't have said that."

She leaned forward, pulling him closer. "You can never go too far." They met in a kiss, the deepest, warmest kiss he had ever experienced.

She pulled back, her eyes almost touching his, then stood up, took him by the hand and led him back to her bedroom.

She sat him down on her bed. He put his arms around her waist, pulling himself closer to her than he had ever been before, laying his face against her stomach. "You've never done this before, have you?" she asked him.

He looked up into her eyes. "I'm sorry."

She assured him it was all right with just her smile, then pulled back, enough to get her arms free to reach up under her skirt. Dennis had noticed the skirt earlier – she never wore a skirt to work -- and loved this first look he had gotten at her perfect, sleek, brown legs. "Oh my God," he whimpered as she pulled her panties – such perfect, colorful, sexy, *but not too sexy*, panties – out from under that skirt and slid them down her legs and off her feet.

"Now you have to promise you won't get the wrong impression of me. Promise?"

"I promise."

She moved to her dresser, digging into her expansive purse. "I knew you wouldn't know when it was time to buy some." She pulled out a condom, bringing it over to Dennis, kneeling between his legs, opening up his pants and pulling him out. "And I've wanted you to fuck me for a long time."

Dennis couldn't move, his mouth agape, his eyes quivering, as she rolled the condom onto him. She spread her legs and straddled him, guiding him in with her right hand. His arms jutted from his sides with lives of their own, wrapping around her, pulling her close as he pushed himself deeper and deeper up into her with each pump. "Easy," she cooed. "It's been a long time."

It felt like he was at most halfway inside her when he cried out in ultimate elation – it was all over. He buried his face in her chest, panting, "I'm sorry."

"It's okay," she assured him, raising his chin up with her fingers until their eyes met again. "I bought a full pack."

With the juke box now vibing out Maceo Parker, Mac couldn't hear the taunts, couldn't hear the cries. It wasn't until he was all the way outside in the frigid alley air that he heard the laughs, that he heard the first "Fag." Three drunk brutes were standing over a body, crumpled on the ground up against the dumpster, globs of blood coughing out onto the asphalt.

"Just a word to the wise, Sally," the smallest but of course most pugnacious of the three spit down on top of the clump of broken flesh, "the next time some drunk assholes like us talk shit to you, you just roll with it, you just laugh it off. Embrace it! Because you talk back like you did, and look what we have to do." The middle-sized of the three reared back and shot a solid goal kick right into the victim's solar plexus for emphasis, a final goodbye. Each chuckling, they turned to walk out of the alley--

And a granite fist cracked the largest one's nose back into his skull. *Neutralize the biggest one first,* Mac's thoughts flew, *then work backwards from there. If one's left standing long enough to get some free shots in, it's gonna be the small one.* He brought his foot up into the big one's groin – he could feel something soft and satifisfying smash on his toes – then, as the brute crumpled over, brought his left elbow down on the back of the guy's skull, putting him down.

The Middle One came at him next, swinging at him from behind, a drunk, unpracticed, unfocused roundhouse. Mac spun to catch the guy's wrist, then twisted the arm into dislocation, turning him to face the ground. Mac wrapped his left elbow around the guy's neck, then brought him forward like a runaway train, smashing the top of his skull into the bricks lining the back wall of the bar, dropping the guy into instant unconsciousness.

The Admiral took a moment to collect his breath. He still had it. He still loved it. It had been way too long since he had engaged in some good old fashioned fisticuffs. He forgot he liked it almost as much as sex. It had all the same allures – the pure unleashing of all his pent up physicality, the thrill of committing acts usually forbidden. Moves like the ones he used to ravage these gay bashers weren't legal of course when he was wrestling at Annapolis in the '80s, but like any man, he had watched many UFC bouts and oft imagined what he would do with open rules like those.

The sound of a round being chambered brought him back into the moment. He turned, to find the Small One had upped the ante, levelling a service pistol right in his face. "Arlington County Sheriff. You picked the wrong alley to play hero in, Chuck Norris."

Mac brought his hands behind his head and the Sheriff came around behind him, pushing him up against the wall. As he ripped down the Admiral's wrists one by one to apply the flex cuffs, Mac heard a stirring from the dumpster, and turned to see the original victim of the bashing pulling himself to his feet. He thought it might be the Boy with whom he'd had his bathroom encounter. His beautiful face was now decorated with one bloody nostril and a swollen eye which would surely go shiner by morning. They locked eyes, the boy's drenched with regret, as if he could say he was sorry with his irises, sorry he had pulled the Admiral into this.

"You bring me up on charges," Mac spit over his shoulder at the arresting officer, "you have to explain him."

"Oh, you mean, the drunk moron three of us will testify attacked my buddy?" The Sheriff pulled Mac in tighter, whispering in his ear. "How's that explanation sound to you?"

Mac looked to the Boy again, realizing he didn't know his story at all, didn't know if he was open with his life or kept it close to the vest, didn't know what he told his own father and brothers, didn't know how a legal entanglement like this might screw up his own future plans. Mac just nodded at him – a clear message that the Boy was free to do whatever he needed to do, and Mac would take care of this on his own.

The Boy turned and sprinted out of the alley, kicking up snowy gravel from the backs of his shoes. And the Deputy called in an arrest and an ambulance request, before pushing Mac to his unmarked Crown Vic.

Dennis and Janaki both agreed it made the most sense for him to return to his own bed for the night. They weren't opposed to sharing one bed some night soon, maybe as soon as this coming weekend, but it didn't make sense for Dennis to have to get up two hours early just to go home and shower and change; they would save the cohabitating for when they had planned ahead and he had brought the proper clothes (or vice versa). So after their second, much longer and more mutually pleasurable round (Janaki claimed to be quite impressed with Dennis's natural, giving instincts, in fact), Dennis walked the twelve blocks home to his own apartment, fighting down the urge to jump into the air and click his heels together, or take a Gene Kelly spin around a lamp post.

Before he extinguished his bedside lamp, the wall across from his bed caught his attention for the first time in weeks; odd as it was, it was one of those fixtures of a home to which the occupant grows so accustomed, he stops noticing it's even there. Seeing it now, he had to chuckle at it, a remnant of his life before this magical night.

The wall was filled with a collage the art director of a serial killer film could very well have crafted. Lines of taut colored string wrapped around thumbtacks, linking notecards to photo copied documents, to transcripts of top secret Court recordings that Dennis had typed up, to photos, to a timeline, to a map. It was a mural of sorts, a monument to the only thing that had rubbed Dennis the wrong way in his three months in Rosemarie Irving's employ. It was his own personal conspiracy theory.

Before his mind became occupied with the fears and then elation of his relationship with Janaki, this conspiracy was how he spent the handful of weekend hours he had been permitted away from the office. Rosemarie had shown an unusual interest in one particular Supreme Court case, *Agguire v. Detroit,* an interest that some might argue put her in a huge conflict of interest as the unofficial head of the President's judicial search committee. After fetching all the materials of the case for her from the ruins of the Court, after overhearing several cryptic conversations between FLOTUS and her husband concerning the case, Dennis had to know why this one case was of such significance. What was displayed on the wall was a manic panorama of his theories on the case, a map no person other than he would be able to interpret.

The bottom line was, Dennis hadn't found anything unusual about the case. He hadn't stumbled upon any theory as to why it would be so important to the Irvings. Perhaps Rosemarie's concerns were exactly what she had said they were: that she thought it was irresponsible for Acting Chief Justice Egan to call this case with *anything* less than a full complement of nine Justices available to hear it. It made sense; the First Lady didn't agree with the President appointing Egan as Acting Chief (a decision based purely on seniority, he had made clear), didn't seem to care for her, period. Rosemarie Irving was nothing if not opinionated; it would make sense that she would find something about Egan's tenure that irritated her enough to take some action, in this case using Justice Koh to ensure the case was delayed. It was pretty damn inappropriate, but not *All the President's Men* Deep Throat shit.

Feeling his eyes droop, Dennis reached over and switched his lamp to sleep. In his last thoughts of the night, he teased himself about getting lost in a conspiracy like some loyal *World Net Daily* reader. He was so glad he had found something much more important to replace this obsession. He would take down the mural over the course of the next week. He had a feeling Janaki would be spending a night or two in this bedroom over the coming weekend, and there was no way in hell he was going to let her see that manic mess.

TUESDAY

Mac often wished he had the time to read more history, as much history as he had devoured while majoring in the subject as an Academy cadet. Now was one of those times. He wondered if the answer to the ephemera plaguing him was perhaps recorded somewhere, one of those facts so obscure it couldn't even be found on the internet, only in some long-out-of-print book shelved deep in the bowels of a collegiate library: *Who was the last person to be bailed out of jail by a President of the United States?*

To be fair, it wasn't President Irving himself who had bailed the Vice Admiral out, but Dennis Coutts, the First Lady's pet vetter and do-everything errand boy. Dennis had arrived at the Arlington County Courthouse & Detention Facility and paid Mac's bond less than an hour after he was booked, and it was Dennis who led the Admiral out through the tunnel of Secret Service o-linemen blocking the press vultures, to a waiting Escalade, fully tinted for an anonymous journey back to the Hay-Adams.

But only a couple blocks after they had crossed the Potomac, Mac realized they had turned northwest. "Hey, isn't the fastest way to the hotel to turn--?" Dennis didn't respond verbally, just raised his eyebrows as if to apologize that he couldn't arrange for the Admiral to get at least a couple hours of sleep before his inquisition. Mac sat back with a deep sigh, well aware of who would be waiting for him at whatever their alternative destination might turn out to be.

The SUV soon pulled up under a gorgeous Spring Valley townhouse. A Service agent was waiting to escort Mac and Dennis inside, then with an open palm guide them up the ornate staircase. As predicted, the Irvings were already waiting in the museum-piece sitting room on the second floor. Reg was in a bathrobe, his hair mussed and unproduct-ed, like he had just been roused from REM. But the First Lady looked as immaculate as she might for any press event, as if she had somehow been informed in advance that last night was going to go down the way it had and had stayed awake to primp for it.

Mac slouched down into the couch, facing each Irving in their easy chair perches angled off to either side of him, perhaps staged there specifically to impede any path of escape. “I warned you I wasn’t cut out for this.”

Reg chuckled and winked. “Oh, I wouldn’t count us out so easily.”

“Just tell us what happened.” Rosemarie was much more stern.

“I had a couple drinks. There were some dumb assholes outside, on my way home, who said a couple things to me. And I just lost it. Turns out these assholes belonged to the Arlington Sherriff’s Department.”

“What sort of things did they say?”

“I can’t really remember.”

Reg buzzed his lips together. “Bullshit.”

“I’m sorry?” Mac looked to the ex-POTUS.

“You expect us to believe a man world famous for his cool under pressure lost his shit over some trash talking?”

Rosemarie put her steaming chamomile aside, leaning forward on her knees. “Admiral. We have less than two weeks to get you confirmed and our final nominee announced. We don’t get you through, and the President will be robbed of his right to complete this Court. We are going to get you through. So we need you to tell us exactly what happened. And we will fix it.”

Mac let out a deep sigh that raised his entire shoulder structure almost up to his ears. But he didn’t answer.

Rosemarie slapped her palms down on her lap, rising back up to her full seated height. “I think you need to understand something. We know much more about you than you even realize. After some bumps in the road, Dennis has gotten very good at vetting. Isn’t that right, Dennis?”

That’s when Mac first noticed that Dennis had a folder resting in his lap. He opened it, clearing his throat to stall for another second or two, looking to Mac with sympathetic eyes, giving him one last chance to speak up. Then finally, Dennis sucked in a deep breath--

“They were beating up a kid,” Mac said before Dennis could begin. “Gay kid. But you can’t say that.”

Reg clapped his hands together and laughed. “You bet your ass we’re gonna say it!”

“He’s right, Admiral,” Rosemarie concurred, trying to hold down her victorious grin. “Who was the last Supreme Court nominee to *actually* come to the defense of the oppressed? Not from a cushy seat behind the bench, but on the actual frontlines? This is tremendous.”

"You can't say that," Mac protested, "because then they'll go looking for him, the victim. And he'll tell them we kissed, he'll tell them he had his hands down my pants in the bathroom--"

"Being gay isn't a crime," Rosemarie replied as her mind raced, computing all the possible scenarios this could inspire. "It isn't against the code of military justice."

"Anymore," Reg added.

"We should get ahead of this." It was thrilling to watch Rosemarie Irving strategize on the fly. "Take ownership of this before any of them can ask any questions and brand it with their spin. Write the narrative ourselves. This wasn't you beating up on three sheriff's deputies, this was you taking down three notorious gay bashers." She nodded to Dennis. "Let's find out who they were, and if they have histories."

"And what about when their side comes out?"

"You won't be hearing from those boys again," Reg winked. "Mario Cortez, he's the Arlington Sheriff, he's in the family. Those boys want to keep their pensions, trust me, they'll be forgetting last night ever happened."

"So you want me to say … everything?"

"You don't have to announce you're gay, Admiral. That isn't relevant to your ability to serve on the Court."

"Do you realize how much the press will crucify any committee members if they bring it up, let alone try to *prosecute* you on it?" Reg added.

Mac shot to his feet, walking around behind the couch to the expansive window.

"Is there … something else?" Rosemarie asked.

Mac didn't answer for a moment. Was it true what she said, did they already know *everything* about him? Was his greatest fear in that little folder on Dennis's lap?

"No," he finally answered, but didn't turn back, just kept looking out the Windex-clear glass. "You're right. This is the right strategy. It's the right thing to do."

Mac couldn't see the gorgeous sunrise breaking through the clouds and casting its light upon the snow-covered city. All he saw was Shareef's face staring back at him. He prayed it was a face he didn't see in the Kennedy Caucus Room before the week was out.

The truth was, Admiral MacTavish wasn't the primary target of Congressional Republicans looking to take President 'Salsa' down a peg or two. They knew as well as the Irvings that a man who had commanded some of the most prominent anti-terror missions of the past decade was unimpeachable in this post-bombing climate. Nominating Mac for the Court, though unorthodox, might have been the smartest thing Salas had done since the bombing, and even Republicans on the Senate Judiciary Committee assumed this week's hearings were a formality on the road to a rubber stamp.

No, the GOP was going to have to take its shots at the President through its new House committee.

"Ms. Whitford," Committee Chairman Rutherford Cunningham (R-GA) looked down his microphone at Salas's former Chief of Staff, "we have been sitting here speaking with you for well over an hour now and I can't help but come to the conclusion that there was absolutely no cause for the President to dispatch the FBI to the Pencil Pals halfway house on the evening of December the 18th."

Actually, Becks's grilling in Room 2141 of the Rayburn House Office Building had already surpassed two hours, about an hour and fifty-one minutes of that time spent running around in circles with her questioners. Becks was the first witness to be called who wasn't actually present, who wasn't in Portland on the night of the raid, who wasn't on the HRT or DHS teams, who didn't pull a trigger. She was the first witness called from the Administration. And yet, no call of support from her ex-boss, no offer of his resources, no pledge to set her up with a prepper who would coach her on the questions to expect and the answers that would best serve the Administration. Even as the Chief of Staff of the VA, she was still a member of this Administration.

"That's not what I'm saying at all, Congressman," she chuckled out, at this point entertained by the ability of these politicians to find a hundred different ways to phrase the same statement they thought their constituents wanted to hear. "In my entire tenure with the President, he always had very good reasons for everything he did. I was not privy to every bit of intelligence or information that came across his desk, nor could I come close to sharing it in this forum if I were, but I can guarantee you he felt we had to raid that halfway house on that night; we had to get to the bottom of what was going on in there; we had to ask some of the residents inside some very important questions while we knew where we could find them."

Cunningham removed his glasses and smiled. A former F-16 pilot, he had 20/20 vision, but had adopted the lenses twenty years ago when a very expensive image consultant assured him that if he wanted Southern Republicans to vote for a Black man in a GOP primary, he better seem as brilliant and educated as Cliff goddamn Huxtable. In the years since, Cunningham never once regretted choosing to go Republican (he was 9-0 in his House races, after all), although he couldn't wait until the day he retired to a lobbying firm and could write a book about the most *un*talked-about racist left in America today: the Democrat who insisted every African-American loyal to his or her race must vote blue.

"So there was evidence linking residents of that halfway house to the bombing of the Supreme Court?"

"You know I can't answer that, Congressman."

"All right. Evidence linking the residents to terrorist activity in general?"

"Even if I were to answer that, I couldn't tell you what that evidence was."

"Of course you couldn't. I cede to the Congresswoman from Minnesota."

Becks sat back, allowing herself a modicum of relaxation. Her next adversary was regarded as one of the kooks of the House, sure to lead her down some conspiratorial path; Becks's challenge would be to avoid laughing through her answers with too much condescension.

"Ms. Whitford," Kathy Bart (R-MN) leaned into her own mic, beaming out her famous down-home smile, a professional smokescreen covering a zealous, vindictive anger. "There's one area I'm surprised no one here has asked you about yet. What do we know about the government of Iran's involvement in the Supreme Court bombing?"

Becks froze. There it was, the question she had been waiting two hours for, the only question on which she had been coached. She had let her guard down when Bart took over; she had stopped silently reminding herself of the right answer to that question at least a half-hour ago. "I'm sorry, Congresswoman?" she murmured, trying to remind herself of what she was supposed to say.

"Let me be more specific. I for one think very highly of the American people. I believe they trust that their President did the right thing in raiding that halfway house and, despite the tragedies of that night, arresting the gentlemen we arrested. They understand that we're not always on the need-to-know list, and that our ignorance is usually for our own safety. What I think they do have a right to know is whether or not, on October 7th of last year, another nation unofficially declared war on us."

Becks got closer to the mic, but didn't answer right away, trying to shut out the clamoring reporters behind her and fit her rehearsed response into the parameters of this specific question. "From what I had seen … and again, I didn't see everything … there was reason to believe …" But she trailed off from there, leaving the committee room in abject silence for several painful seconds. The wording of her statement had to be just perfect.

"Ms. Whitford. Did the government of Iran have something to do with the bombing?"

"Ms. Whitford?" Chairman Cunningham jumped in. "Are you going to answer, or enter a plea of--"

"We had reason to suspect that the nation of Iran was somehow involved, yes," she blurted out. The committee room exploded into wild commotion, drowning out the hammering of Cunningham's gavel.

Tuesday mornings were the rare times at Polis that Miranda Whitney enjoyed. For all the libertarian ideals its leaders spouted, the compound was really just a throwback to a time when women were constrained to domestic duties and family care. Everyone on the compound was assigned a variety of work duties, and Miranda's included time on laundry service, kitchen clean-up, the seamstress department, and daycare. She never would have stood for this under normal circumstances, but nothing about her last year had been normal. Complaining wasn't an option; she wasn't supposed to make waves while she was here, just *be here*, and wait for the shit to go down.

The shit was coming. It couldn't be much longer now.

For two hours each Tuesday morning, Miranda actually got to do something she was good at, something she enjoyed. For two hours each Tuesday morning, every Minutewoman over the age of 15 was to congregate in the gymnasium building for a lesson in self-defense taught by the only woman with military experience on the property: Miranda. Bratten may have run the compound like a 1950s Mormon bishop, but he also realized the value of taking advantage of everyone's different strengths – those of both men and women – their different sets of experience, their different skill sets. Hence, Jason's assignment working under Dreyfus, and Miranda's inclusion on the occasional mission off campus (like the

Detroit arms deal in November during which they had been caught on surveillance cameras). Most of the Minutemen with military records had been out a decade or more; Bratten knew that if he needed someone watching his back, the younger Miranda would be one of the most capable Minutemen for that task.

This Tuesday morning, Miranda was shouting the ladies through their warm-up drills, everyone partnered up, reviewing the series of moves they had learned last week, when she noticed a man standing in the back of the room. Miranda turned to the tough little 19-year-old who had begged for weeks to be her assistant teacher, asked her to take over, then marched to the back, grabbing Jason by the arm and yanking him outside into the snow.

"What the hell do you think you're doing?" she barked in his face, looking around at the other buildings to make sure no one overheard. "You're supposed to be working, not leering at these girls. You looking to get thrown back in the brig?"

"I had to talk to you. You lose track of time here, but I know it's been over a week since I saw you."

"You shouldn't expect to see me. I'm not here to hang out with you, or continue my life with you. I'm sorry if I've given you the wrong expectations--"

"You've been outright avoiding me."

"Because it's what's best for both of our own good," was all she would say. She couldn't tell him that the closer they got to what was going to happen next, the harder she found it to be with him, to look at him, to even see him across the courtyard or the mess hall. Seeing him brought her too much pain.

Jason put his hands on her arms, trying to hold her steady, trying to assure her with his eyes that this meeting was urgent or he wouldn't have broken the rules. "I need to know why you're here. Why you came here."

"What?"

"Is the bomber here? Is that why you're here, because someone involved with the bombing--"

"Yes, *me.*" She pushed his arms off. "I don't know what you're talking about. I told you, I came here because of *my* part in it." She stepped forward, getting right into his face to whisper, "I know you think you fell in love with some apple pie perfect all-American girl, but that's not who I am anymore. I'm a criminal. An enemy of the state."

"And someone's onto you."

"What?"

"This is very important. Do you think it's possible someone here knows who you are?"

"No one."

Jason took a step closer, lowering his voice. "I think Dreyfus might. He says he knows who did it." Miranda shook her head and paced. Jason continued: "He says he knows the bombing is why I'm here."

"Listen to me, Jason. There are things I like about having you here. But I can still come get those things if you're in the brig. If I need to, I'll put you there myself."

Jason looked past her shoulders, at the compound surrounding them. "I don't like this place, Rand. I don't like this whole situation. There was a guy in Mio who asked me to get a message to his wife and daughter – and they're not even here. No one's heard their names."

Miranda looked to the ground, gripping her forehead as if she could knead out the aggravation. "I can't have you jeopardizing both of us by talking about this shit all the time. I'm here to forget that shit. You should be too."

She stormed away from him, wincing as he raised his voice to call after her, "Just watch your back!"

As the door shut behind her, she didn't return to the front of the class, but leaned back against it, sucking in hard to lock down any tears from falling. She had gotten very good at controlling her ducts.

Jason was right. There were people who knew the bomber was here. And soon, very soon, justice would come calling for that person.

He just didn't realize that person would be him.

"Thank you, Mr. Chairman," Mac leaned into his mic, "for recognizing me to begin this morning's session."

Mac lowered his eyes to the paper between his hands, pressed down hard onto the table to keep from shaking or fidgeting; after rehearsing this speech twenty or thirty-odd times, he was pretty sure he had it memorized, but wanted to be sure his nerves didn't trip him up. It was imperative he got every word right. "Committee members and staff, members of the press, and the American people. You have no doubt seen the news this morning that I was arrested in Alexandria late last night for Assault & Battery of a Peace Officer. I'm sure you all have many questions about the events of last night, which I will be happy to answer.

But first, I wanted to make sure I explained exactly what occurred. You should know that on my way here this morning, I received a call from Sheriff Cortez, who offered his apologies for what happened, let me know that no charges would be filed against me, and offered to corroborate my story in any forum.

"I was having dinner last night at the Dirty Duck Public House in Alexandria when I heard a commotion outside. I stepped out to find three gentlemen physically and verbally abusing a much smaller, younger man. The language they used, which I think you will agree is not necessary to repeat here, included the vilest homophobic epithets I could imagine."

The chamber erupted into a murmur; this was the first time any Senator or their staff, any reporter, heard any details about what had occurred last night. The theories had been flying all morning across ten different networks, hundreds of websites and social media platforms, but in an instant, what everyone had assumed to be a salacious story of controversy had transformed into a heroic tale of a modern American Good Samaritan. The picture was instantly iconic: a man in uniform behind the mic, explaining how he had bravely fought off a gang of gay bashers; by that afternoon, street vendors in gayborhoods from West Hollywood to the Village would be hawking T-shirts of his image under the slogan, "Do Ask, Do Tell!"

In one of the nearby conference rooms the prep team had commandeered, Rosemarie smiled and rose to her feet. She knew the rest of the Admiral's text, and had all confidence he would perform it perfectly. She also knew the Senators across from him would have no choice but to fawn all over him for the rest of the morning, if not the rest of the week. What could have been the most difficult confirmation of the four had turned into a cakewalk. "Dennis, walk with me. There's someone I'd like you to meet."

Not wanting to have to deal with the press or with traffic, Rosemarie led Dennis and her Secret Service retinue down to the three-car mini-subway line that connected all the congressional buildings of Capitol Hill, and in five minutes' time, they were emerging onto the ground floor of the Capitol itself. As Dennis followed her down the hall to their main office – sneaking in a quick peek at Janaki typing away on an opinion draft as they passed Justice Goldman's outer office – FLOTUS explained, "You're finally going to be getting some of your life back. Our last nominee will require the least vetting yet."

Dennis dug through his nerd banks, trying to guess what that cryptic clue might mean, who the final nominee could be. But he never came close, his primary mistake being trying to remember the layout of faces covering their office corkboard; Quint's photo had never been posted there.

They found Quint standing under that very corkboard. Now vertical down the left side were photos of Justices Koh and Goldman and Admiral MacTavish; the right side was papered with twenty-plus faces, legal luminaries who would never get that call to serve on the Court, or at least, not in this round of openings. Quint's voice creaked when he heard them entering behind him, "Well, you coulda done a heckuva lot better than me, Rosemarie!"

"Dennis Coutts, meet the once and future Chief Justice of the United States, William Harvey Quint." Quint giggled as he shook Dennis's limp fingers. "I've never seen him so star struck," Rosemarie teased.

"No, I know that look. He's spent his whole life looking at photos of me from twenty years ago, and can't believe I'm this wrinkled now."

For the next five minutes, they continued talking at and around him, without Dennis uttering a word. His mind wasn't lost in how he had always dreamt of this moment; he wasn't counting the hundreds of hours he had spent reading opinions this elderly legend had written nor trying to think of questions about the way certain famous decisions had gone down.

His mind was back in his apartment, sitting on his bed, staring up at that crazed chart opposite his headboard, a manic mural that, with the revelation Rosemarie would be putting William Quint back on the Court, didn't seem so crazed or manic anymore.

As Becks walked out of the Rayburn hearing room to a scrum of reporters, a smirk crept over her lips. She didn't hear any of their questions, didn't feel any of their bumps. *How long will it take for the call to come in?* was the only question occupying her mind. Would Delores's voice already be recorded into her voice mail memory when she took her phone off airplane mode? Would the call come in on the town car ride back, or over lunch, or once she was once again buried in the anonymity of her antiseptic prison at the Department of Veteran Affairs?

What she hadn't expected was the commotion of vehicles out in front of the VA building, stop gapping traffic so much she had to get out and walk the final block. She hadn't expected to find the gaggle of aides and secretaries and even presidential appointees all crowded into the tenth floor hallway as she stepped off the elevator, all staring and pointing down in the direction of Becks's office. She hadn't expected the earpiece patrol, none of whom she recognized, forming a perimeter around her door, not allowing anyone to pass – until they parted for her.

She hadn't expected to find her former boss, the President of the United States, seated atop her desk. But the stern look on his face, the arms locked across his chest in disappointment, didn't surprise her in the least.

"Mr. President. I didn't see Hifrael out there."

"No, he had to transfer. Some family thing going on."

"It's good to see you. Can I offer you anything?"

"Sit, Rebecca."

She did, on the couch Restoration Hardware had delivered less than two weeks before. In fact, she realized, she might have been the first person to sit on it, and cursed herself for not heeding her new assistant's suggestion to go to the store and test the comfort of various models.

"Who?"

"I'm sorry, Sir?"

"I want to know who put you up to what you said about Iran."

"Mr. President … I've never been questioned by a congressional committee before. I wasn't prepared--"

"Cut the shit, Becks," he shot to his feet. "Who convinced you to lie under oath?" Not getting an immediate answer, he shoved his hands in his pockets, marching back behind her desk to see if there was any kind of view out the dingy window. "Do you realize the position you've put me in? You know as well as I do we never found any connection between Mohammed Mullin or anyone in that preschool and the Iranian government."

"Sir--"

He whipped back to her, forefinger levelled at her like he was back in his goalkeeper days, instructing his back line. "Goddammit, I told you that day that we didn't have enough, and *you* pushed me to do it!"

"Oh, give me a fucking break."

"I beg your pardon?"

"Sir, if I may speak candidly?"

He threw up his arms with amusement. "As if you've ever spoken any other way."

"You are the President, Sir. You made this decision. I advised you with the best available information at my disposal at that moment, but you pulled this trigger. And instead of standing by your decision, you hung me out to dry."

Salas chuckled. "I really don't think you want to get into the litany of reasons you're here now."

"I could've helped you today. A phone call, an email, a fucking fax from an intern with some talking points – all I needed was some sort of sign that you were on my side, some sort of encouragement, some sort of instruction on what you needed from me, and you know I would've done it. Just like I always did. But I had nothing. So I had to wing it. And I'm sorry if that didn't turn out exactly the way that would've worked best for you."

Silence ruled the next minute. Which made what the President said next even more jarring.

"Waaaaagh."

"Really?"

"I don't buy one second of your whining. You're one of the most brilliant people I've ever known. Trust me, I've needed you much more than you've needed me. I needed you to do an overnight rewrite of my State of the Union and tell me I had to cut paragraphs 14, 18 and 26--"

Becks winced. Those paragraphs hadn't worked at all. She had always planned to tell him that, but was shown the door before she got the chance.

"I needed you to help me get everything we needed in this year's budget. I needed you to help me pick a goddamn Secret Service agent I actually like. I needed *you* to deal with this shit storm you've dropped in my lap today.

"But I also needed someone who was unwavering in her professionalism."

"What is that supposed to mean?"

"You know exactly what it means." He stepped close, lowering his voice into an intense growl in case the walls were thin enough to pick up his full voice. "We both know you picked someone's bed to lie in today. I just can't figure out whose it was. There's too many to choose from."

Becks sucked in hard, a sort of reverse gasp, like his words were a fist up into her gut.

"I want a name in the next six hours. Or you can add 'Fired twice by the leader of the free world in the span of one month' to your bio." He looked around the modest space as he made his way for the door. "And I'll make sure your next landing won't come with a new office."

The memo was one of the first items Dennis had removed from his conspiracy wall when he had started packing it up:

> 10 May
>
> Brother & Sister Justices,
>
> It is with some embarrassment that I must inform you of my failure to properly memorialize the majority opinion in *Agguire v. Detroit.* As I worked through my initial draft, I was consistently struck by the momentous ramifications of such a decision, and must now acknowledge that even more research and consideration is required if I am to give this matter its due. Considering the late hour in this Term, I would humbly suggest that the case be restored to the calendar for reargument come the fall. I beg your forgiveness and understanding.
>
> B. V. Winks

Upon his release from work, he had bee-lined straight home (texting a *lame* excuse to Janaki for cancelling dinner), right to that first banker's box constructed on his bedroom floor. He dug out the copy of the memo and read it again. He knew that Justice Winks had been assigned the majority opinion, and that his failure to complete it during the term had been the reason for the relisting, but he had to make sure, had to again see the exact wording he had used, the reasons, however ambiguous, he had given for his failure.

But this wasn't enough. If he was going to prove that the nomination of Justice Quint had made his whole horrific theory fit together, he had to know how each Justice was going to vote before the case was rescheduled. He had to know *how four particular Justices were going to vote before they were killed.*

He opened his laptop and checked his 'AvD' folder, but he already knew he had erased the audio file, exactly as Acting Marshal Gregor Meyers had begged him to do. Just on a whim, he double-clicked on his Recycling Bin; there were three items there, but they were all files he had deleted in the last week. He had emptied the bin since moving the MP3 into it, probably immediately after, as it had been so important to him, then an overeager novice, to follow Meyers's instructions to the letter.

He picked up his iPhone and searched through his contacts for his one high school buddy who had always had that extra aptitude for computers, that friend who majored in programming for two years at MIT before dropping out, then still landed an amazing Silicon Valley job that paid triple Dennis's starting salary at White House Counsel's office.

"Foster, it's Coutts … Yeah, I know, it's been crazy out here … Listen, I have a computer question for you. Is it true what I've always heard, that you can never *totally* delete something off your hard drive? … Okay, then do you know how I'd recover an audio file I accidentally deleted, oh, two months or so ago?"

WEDNESDAY

Jason was having the same dream he'd had every night since the bombing, or every night of dreaming he could remember, every night he hadn't dulled his brain into a Dewar's stupor. (He would be happy in hindsight that he hadn't had a drop on this Tuesday night, hadn't impaired himself for what was about to occur.)

"Rand, what's wrong?" he asked when he noticed the glisten on her cheeks, the glass of golden liquor sitting on the Bullfeathers bar.

"Nothing's wrong," she claimed, then looked back up at the TV. Chief Justice Lapadula was on the TV, ringing the opening bell at the NYSE.

What? It was evening, hours after the market opened and closed. It was Sunday. That's not what was on the TV that night.

Then what was that bell ringing through the bar, invading Jason's dream, clanging into the past?

Jason shot up in bed. The bell was coming from outside, near the front of Polis. Other bells were ringing now too, from all around the property.

"Perimeter alert!" His bunkmate was strapping a holstered pistol around his waist, then charging out the door. "All hands on deck, hustle up!"

Jason grabbed his LAPD SWAT Team pistol, shoving it into the back of his belt as he followed the heavier man out the door into the courtyard. He had slept hard, he realized: all the other beds were already empty, no one else was exiting as they were. They were the last ones out.

He stepped out onto the snow, into the blue early morning air. His bunkmate was yanking out his pistol, rushing beside one of his fellow Minutemen, standing on the perimeter, guns aimed out into the Huron. Jason pivoted to assess the situation: in all directions, Minutemen standing at the border of their clearing, many of them strapped up in their amateur Kevlar vests, shotguns and pistols and AR-15s pointed out into the trees. "Got another one, another one, tree at ten o'clock!"

one was yelling. "FUCK! Three more, three more, my twelve!" another screamed.

Jason had to squint to see it, but soon enough, his eyes rack focused onto what they were aiming at: white masses up in the trees, or hidden out behind logs, with little streaks of black aimed in at the men of Polis. Soldiers of some sort, fully decked in arctic gear, with military-grade weapons leveled on the place.

"Whoever you are!" Bratten's voice echoed over the property. Jason turned to the front, noticing the head honcho walking behind his men with his own Browning 12 gauge pump in his hands, screaming out into the trees. Jason stayed close to his building, not yet sure he should commit himself to this standoff. It didn't look promising for his side. "You are encroaching upon the sovereign city-state of Polis!" Bratten continued. "Disperse now and we will allow you to go on your way in peace. Remain, and we will be forced to arrest and prosecute you under our laws."

The voice in reply was much louder, augmented with the punch of a megaphone. "*Michigan Minutemen militia. We have been vested by the state of Michigan and the Department of Homeland Security with the full authority to carry out the investigation into the Supreme Court bombing of October 7th*." Though it had been a month at least since he had last heard this voice, Jason recognized its accent and cadence: Dean Rikeman, Allied Armament's City Commander for Detroit.

"Homeland Security?" One of the Minutemen spit a heavy wad onto the snow in disgust. "You mean the agency that opened this country's borders for illegals to come take my job and my social security?" Others murmured agreement with this sentiment, tightening their grips on their firearms.

"Hey-hey-hey," Bratten cautioned with a hand. "Let's hear them out. We will protect our home, but what we don't want is needless bloodshed!"

"*We have reason to believe that a primary suspect in the bombing has taken refuge on your property.*"

Jason whirled, eyes darting around the compound, finding the frightened women and children huddled in packs around every door and window. *Rand. Where are you, Rand?* he panted in his thoughts. *They're here for Rand. I can't let them have her. Where the fuck is she?*

"*We will be happy to leave the area peacefully and let you continue with your lives, as long as you stand down and allow us to serve our warrant for the arrest of Jason Lancaster.*"

Jason tensed up. A tiny chorus whispered around him, coming from all sides. He looked up – there were even points and whispers coming from a window above him. All the women and children of Polis were pointing at him. He stepped away from the building, eyes spinning for new shelter.

"I never trusted that guy," one of the Minutemen near Bratten – one of the perimeter guards who had arrested Jason on his arrival here – said over a shoulder to his leader. "Doesn't sound like a bad deal."

"No!" Bratten shouted, not at this Minuteman but out into the snow, out at Rikeman and all the soldiers surrounding them. "Every citizen of Polis has come here and joined us for the protection of our laws from your imperialism." A professional in dramatics, Bratten pumped a round into his shotgun for emphasis. "We will never surrender one of our citizens to your regime!"

Several tense minutes passed. None of the Minutemen lowered their weapons. None of the white blobs hidden in the snow came any closer. Bratten moved around his guards, patting their backs for encouragement, keeping his line strong. "Hold the line! All they fight for are their paychecks! We fight for the passion of our convictions!"

"How long we going to wait this out?" one of his men asked him as he passed.

Bratten backed up closer to the center of the property, looking to the skies, a huge grin spreading across his face, the sun breaking through the clouds reflected in his eyes. "We have nowhere else to be."

Just as he had with the previous three nominees, Dennis began his vet of Chief Quint right at 8 AM. He arrived in the Casino under the White House at 7:30 sharp; the Chief walked over from the Hay-Adams 30 minutes later. (Quint was not required to spend his vetting period at the Alexandria Sheraton like the first three candidates; a former Chief Justice staying at the Hay-Adams wouldn't raise the suspicion of any reporter, and besides, with all that was going on, the Irvings thought it might do the President some good were this nomination to leak sooner rather than later.) Chief Quint's vet was different in that he paid only half-attention to Dennis's inquiries, if that. Between them sat an overflowing wheeled cart of thick briefs, all pending petitions for certiorari being considered by the Court that already had the support of three Justices; a fourth vote to grant from Quint would mean these cases could be scheduled for oral arguments later in the term. (Decisions required five votes, but it only took four to grant cert to a case.)

But what did Dennis really need to ask Quint, anyway? His life was an open book, with thousands of pages in print covering his boyhood through his 35 years on the bench. Unless he had committed a crime, taken up an addiction or joined a hate group in the last seven years, America already knew all there was to know about William Harvey Quint.

"Mr. Chief Justice?" Dennis had to repeat a third time as he began one of his questions.

"I'm sorry, I've just been thinking," Quint replied, then held the dueling petitions in each hand out to Dennis. "To which of these do you believe your Supreme Court should grant cert?"

"Oh, I'm not qualified to--"

"Well, of course you are." Quint looked at Dennis sideways, with eyes of teasing disappointment. "Or you wouldn't be the one doing this job."

"Thank you, Sir."

"Rosemarie's told me all about you. She told me to keep an eye on you as a potential clerk."

"That's nice of her to say that," Dennis blushed, though not about FLOTUS's comment. *You wouldn't be so nice if you knew I stayed up until 3 last night trying to determine your connection to the bombing,* was the thought Dennis feared could be read on his face.

"So. What do you think? Pretend you're doing my pool memos on these two petitions."

Dennis skimmed their top pages; for him the choice was easy. He slapped the one down on top of the cart. "*Sacerdoti v. Attorney General of California.*"

"Oh?" Quint replied as he picked it back up. "Tell me why?"

"Since *Citizens United*, twelve states have enacted laws limiting the amount that entities from outside the state can contribute to in-state elections. California's new law outlaws those contributions altogether. A decision on that case could decide the constitutionality of all of them."

Quint looked up from the petition with a mischievous grin. "And with six Democratic nominees on the Court ... maybe even overturn *Citizens United* altogether."

Dennis shrugged, feigning as if he hadn't thought of that. "You never know."

Quint closed the thick packet up with a boisterous laugh, setting it atop the small pile to be delivered to Acting Chief Egan's chambers later in the day. "I like the way you think, boy!"

Quint caught himself, placing a subtle hand on his heart as he continued. "Now then, you had a question for me?"

"Yes." Dennis had to look back down at his questionnaire to remember it. With his eyes down, he didn't notice the Chief grimacing ever so slightly, or squeezing his hand into a fist he pressed into his chest in an attempt to burp. "What is your greatest regret from your years on the Court?"

"If you mean a case, I don't have one. No, not even *Citizens United.*" As if his mind was somewhere else entirely, Quint rose to his feet. "There were plenty of decisions I personally didn't agree with, but that's the nature of a voting body. This will never be a perfect union, Son; our charge is to strive to make it a *more* perfect one." He had already turned his back on Dennis, making as fast a beeline as he could for the corner restrooms. "Now, if you'll excuse me, before we go any further, duty calls."

Shareef was in the process of changing his life. His last bizarre encounter with Mac a month ago – interrupting one of his parties in the middle of the night with an envelope of twenty K in cash and a promise that they would never see each other again – had been an unexpected wake up call.

No, Mac was by no means the first of Shareef's johns to declare *It's over.* But this particular repudiation had for some reason stuck with him for many more hours and days than he had expected. If any other john had walked away cold turkey like that, Shareef wouldn't have given it a second thought, well aware that he could blink, and there would be three new ones wanting to transact with him. If any other john had given him that much lettuce as a goodbye present, it would have been up his nose and his friends' noses by the end of the month.

But Shareef was well aware that Mac wasn't any other john. Mac had encouraged Shareef to reach out to his brother in Syria over email and set up the series of Skypes that had restarted their relationship. Mac had emboldened Shareef's dreams by buying him an acting class at the Little Theatre of Alexandria as a birthday gift, a course Shareef had renewed with his own money after the initial three-month unit was up. Mac had always told Shareef he could be so much more than he was.

Shareef had only had two other appointments since he last saw Mac, and that was because those assignations were already on the books. He wasn't surprised when neither new client contacted him for a second tryst; Shareef's heart hadn't been in those encounters, his mind elsewhere. Shareef hadn't sought out new business in the last month, nor changed the 'UNAVAILABLE' status on his *MeetLocalMen*.com ad.

Most surprising, Shareef hadn't spent Mac's money on drugs or clubs, but had signed up for two classes at Northern Virginia Community. (He thought he would give it the old college try – his friends groaned at this pun, one he sadly remarked to himself that Mac would've appreciated – and make sure he could handle what he was getting into before committing to a full course load.) He was in his second week of those two classes and already buried under the study requirements. But he was determined to not quit, as he had so many other things in his life.

The pounding at the door woke him. He had fallen asleep while reading, his basic econ textbook still open across his chest. He squeezed his eyes open and shut to try to clear the fuzz. That wasn't an ordinary knock that had stirred him, but the pound of serious urgency. "Just a minute," Shareef grogged out as he rolled his legs off the couch.

Shareef knew there was trouble, knew he should have checked the peephole first, when he found three men in the navy blue windbreakers of government agents waiting on the other side of his front door. "Shareef Summarai?" the largest one, the solid African-American standing in the center, asked.

That's when Shareef noticed the reflection in the front window of the unit across the way. The mirror image was faint, but the three yellow letters on the back of each windbreaker were bright enough to read: **ICE**.

Immigration & Customs Enforcement.

Shareef whipped around, sprinting back into his triplex unit. He heard the agent smash right through the screen door behind him, and rushed for the bathroom. If he could get there, if he could get it locked and maybe get out the small window above the toilet before they could—

The ICE linebacker tackled him from behind, caving his back ribs, smashing him down hard into his small Ikea table, shattering it to the floor, obliterating the lamp underneath his sternum. The agent laughed about the damage to both property and prisoner. "Been too long since I got to do that."

Shareef cried out in abject pain as the agent ripped his arms behind his back, then pulled flex cuffs tight enough on his wrists to draw blood. "Hey! Police brutality, bitch," Shareef protested.

The ICE agent wrenched him up to his feet, pulling Shareef's ear close enough to his lips to gloat, "Those protections are for citizens. Bitch."

Dreyfus didn't like the order, but he had grown to respect Bratten's leadership, and from his years in Southeast Asia, knew well the value of a chain of command in crisis moments like this one. As one of the older Minutemen with the poorest eyesight – not to mention the fewest fingers, though Dreyfus assured anyone who asked that he had more than enough to operate any weapon – he would be one of the three men who would round up the women and children and get them into the three bomb shelters that had been built underneath Polis. Once they were all safe, he could return to his perimeter position and help guard the compound from encroachment.

He was showing a group of eight to the stairwell when the ladies all gasped. He spun too late to steel himself against Jason grabbing his shirt in two fists, dragging him around the corner to a spot where they could have some privacy. "Lancaster," Dreyfus smiled almost with admiration when Jason pushed him up against the wall. "You're a better bomber than you let on."

Jason pulled his shirt tighter, hauling him in close. "You know I didn't do it. You said you knew who blew it up."

"What?"

"Who blew up the Supreme Court. You're gonna tell me who did it."

"Hey, chill the fuck out, Man, I was just--"

The barrel of Jason's .45 smashed hard into Dreyfus's front teeth, forcing open his mouth. Jason pushed the pistol down his tongue, almost into his throat. "This is what's next," he instructed. "You're going to tell me who you think did it. Then you're going to promise me that when those assholes out in the woods move in and arrest everyone, you're gonna promptly forget." He pushed the gun in even further, gagging the Vietnam vet. "We clear on the agenda?"

Dreyfus nodded, and Jason pulled the pistol back out. The older man let out a few hard pants, which morphed into a full-fledged hack. "I thought you fucking knew. I thought that was why you came here."

"You tell me first."

"The government did it to themselves. Right? They do this shit, like clockwork, whenever they need to keep us in line. Like they did Oklahoma City, then 9/11. Just like they're doing us today."

Jason back pedaled. Dreyfus was just another batshit crazy old man, a burnt-out, paranoid conspiracy theorist. They had nothing to worry about. There was no threat. No one here knew who Miranda was. Her secret was safe, even once Allied Armament moved in and arrested everyone.

As long as they didn't arrest her.

Without a word, Jason shoved his gun back by his sacrum, then took a step back around the corner in the direction of the shelter door. Maybe she was hiding with the other women and children; he should try all the shelters, and he would start with this one.

"But there's something you should know," Dreyfus called after him. Jason turned back to see the vet grin at him one last time. "You haven't known Benji for too long. He ain't gonna let any of us get arrested."

During the first 15 minutes Chief Quint spent in the restroom, Dennis didn't think anything of it, his thoughts occupied with the cleaning up of his vetting notes and, of course, the pet conspiracy theory now ever-present in his thoughts.

It was over the second 15 minutes that Dennis started to worry. He asked the Secret Service agent watching over them if he had noticed how long it had been since Quint stepped out. He asked himself if he should maybe check on the Chief. Telling himself that older men often have bags and apparatuses and medical conditions that turned visits to the bathroom into adventures, he put off any action for another few minutes.

Once they passed the 30 minute mark, he felt there was no choice. "Would your mission to make sure nothing befalls either of us," he asked their guard with a forced smile, "maybe even cover something as mundane as, say, checking on the Chief in the men's room?"

The agent looked at him sideways with a wry grin of his own. "Why don't you go check on him, and if you yell for me, I'll be there."

Dennis sighed, and nodded. He stepped up the carpeted steps onto the upper level of the Casino and rounded the corner to the restrooms. Cracking open the door, he inquired within, "Chief? Chief Quint, you okay in here?"

The groan emanating from the back of the room pulled his eyes to the floor under the stalls, where a jumble of fabric and pink flesh was scrunched up next to one of the toilets. "Chief!" Dennis shot for the back, past the two urinals, to the last of the three stalls. The door was locked, and didn't budge when Dennis wrapped his hand over the top of it and shook. "Can you unlock the door? Chief? Stand back!" Dennis reared back, taking aim at the door-- charging right for it, shoulder first--

"Oww!" He bounced off hard, landing in a clump on the floor, remembering why he had quit freshman football after three practices.

And the door was still sealed shut.

He raised a foot, to try the sole of his shoe instead. One – two — on the third kick, the door snapped open.

The little ball next to the toilet was Quint, pants down on his thighs. He looked up at Dennis with a weak smile, as if just waking from an afternoon nap. "Darline," he quivered.

"Oh God. No, no, Sir, it's Dennis." Dennis rushed to him, putting his hands under the Chief's arms to try to help him back up onto his perch. "It's not your wife."

The Chief had his hands on his belt as Dennis wrenched him up onto the toilet seat, pulling his pants back up onto his waist in the same move. "I know that, you loon. That's not what I meant."

Dennis kneeled between the Chief's legs, keeping his hands on his ribs to make sure he didn't topple. This close to the toilet and floor, he was glad the facilities in this room had only been used by a dozen or so people, and were serviced by some of the most meticulous cleaners in the nation. "You want me to call your wife? We can do that, we can call her."

"No. She'll just be humiliated someone other than her has seen me like this. I was just answering your question. My greatest regret from my years on the Court."

"I won't tell her you called her that, Sir."

Quint chuckled and continued. "My only regret, proud as I am of my work and our accomplishments as a Court, is that I picked a profession so difficult on a marriage. I could've worked at home more often. I could've told her more often that I loved her." He patted Dennis's hand, still in place over his left ribs. "Someday you'll realize you only have so much time left, and you'll wish you had spent every last minute the Lord had given you with the ones you love. You'll wish you had told them how you felt about them a thousand more times."

"Mr. Chief Justice, I have to ask … what happened in here?"

Quint sat forward, reaching for the metal toilet paper dispenser. "Oh, it's nothing. Sometimes I get light headed when I urinate. The only drawback of having such low blood pressure. I'm supposed to pee sitting down, but it just feels too damn silly."

Dennis accepted this, choosing not to ask the Chief why, if he was indeed urinating, the seat had been down. He just nodded and assisted as Quint used the dispenser as leverage to push himself to his feet. "Sir, you know I'm going to have to report this," Dennis mentioned when they had reached their full heights.

Quint patted his hand again. "I know, Son. I know."

Sometimes, Antonio Salas forgot he even had a Vice President.

Richard Ruby hadn't been his first choice, or even his own idea. He had been foisted upon him by the Democratic National Committee – a stroke of electoral genius, it would turn out. The chairman of the Senate Intelligence Committee, Ruby had assuaged all concerns about the lack of foreign policy experience on Salas's resume (Antonio may have pulled California out of recession, but he had just two stamps on his passport (Mexico's and Spain's) when he filed his name for the Democratic primaries) and helped Salas win swing voters who might have been concerned he wouldn't give enough attention to a Middle East overrun by terrorist groups. Ruby was a moderate who had once voted to authorize the Iraq War while a Republican, then later retained his seat despite (or maybe because of) switching parties. Although Salas had trouble respecting a man he felt had switched parties just to avoid being associated with the architects of Iraq, he also had a national election to win, and in an intense pow wow on an upper floor of LA's Biltmore Hotel, the DNC Chairman had convinced him he should announce Ruby as his running mate on the Staples Center floor before the Convention was over.

Like nearly every VPOTUS before him, Ruby had spent the last three years drowning in frustration over his 'bucket of warm piss' of a job. He had been dispatched all over the world to make personal appearances and meet foreign leaders on behalf of the President, but it was the Secretary of State who was making the real decisions in these arenas. He had been in many of the most important meetings and videoconferences with the President since the Supreme Court bombing, but it was easy to read Salas tuning him out whenever he expressed his strong belief that, should they discover a foreign entity had anything to do with the attack, they should hit them and hit them hard, with more finality and force than they had used since Fat Man and Little Boy.

In the heat of the Convention, when he had officially offered the slot to Ruby, Salas had promised him he would always have his ear, that they would schedule private lunches at least once a fortnight to make sure they were on the same page on everything. This was their first such meal in over six months.

They were just so different: Salas, the son of immigrants who had pulled his own bootstraps from the barrio to the White House; Ruby, the career politician who had referred to Washington, and not his home state, as 'home' for more than a decade now. Secretly, POTUS wished he could hit the do-over button and make a new VP choice for his second term, but he trusted his campaign advisors who had told him jettisoning Ruby would only make the President himself look weak and regretful about a first term they should be celebrating.

Salas felt so disconnected from Ruby, they didn't even talk official business until the dessert course had been wheeled into the Family Dining Room; the first hour of lunch had been spent on the controversial final play of last fall's USC-Notre Dame game and a long update on one of the VP's granddaughters whom Salas couldn't even remember meeting.

"I'm glad we're doing this again," Ruby smiled as he licked down a first spoonful of ice cream. "We should do it more often. If you have the time, Mr. President."

Salas sat back and wiped his mouth, locking eyes with the Secret Service agent in the corner. He had pre-warned this guard that he would ask him to step out at some point during the meal, and on this signal, the agent turned to the closest door and took his leave. Ruby watched him go, suddenly feeling very uncomfortable.

"I asked you here today, Dick," Salas said, "because I wanted to thank you for something."

"Oh yeah?" Ruby wondered, confused.

"Thank you for waiting until she had moved on to start fucking my Chief of Staff." Ruby's spoon clanged onto his china saucer as Salas continued, "I thought that was very professional. Showed a lot of restraint."

"Sir," Ruby coughed into his own napkin. "I have no idea what you're talking about."

"Relax. No one outside of this room needs to know. I just stumbled upon it. I was watching those kangaroo hearings the other day and had to wonder who could've brainwashed that headstrong 34-year-old woman I knew and loved into perjuring herself. The answer was, of course, you."

Ruby squeezed his eyes into tight little orbs and leaned across the table. "What she said was completely true, Sir. You're just not looking in the right places, or asking the right people the right questions."

Salas laid down his spoon. "This is really what you want? War with Iran?"

"With all due respect, Sir, if you had utilized me properly, you'd already know exactly what I want. What I think you, what this nation, should want. Our deal was that you would include me in moments like this. Yet this is the first one-on-one conversation we've had in almost a year. I had to get your attention in other ways."

"It's not just *my* attention you've got. Over forty percent of this country now thinks we should invade a nuclear-capable country as retribution for a crime they had nothing to do with. And that number is going up every day."

"I've been in this game much longer than you, Mr. President. Iran is a sore we've let fester for far too long. We should've hit them over the hostages. We should've hit them when they bought their first batch of uranium. And I suppose you tell yourself they didn't know anything about 9/11 before it happened?"

"There is absolutely no evidence they had anything to do with the Supreme Court."

"It doesn't matter. You're going to do what six of your predecessors should've done before you. It's a decision that will save more lives than any other decision you will make while you're in office. Even if it's not about the 124 lives we lost on October 7th, it's about the lives we will someday lose, the lives the Israelis will lose, the longer we let those Muslims go unchecked."

"This is the argument you expect me to bring to the American people?"

"Six months after we invaded Iraq, seventy percent of the American people thought Saddam had something to do with 9/11. *Seventy*. You don't get seventy percent on anything." He leaned forward, jabbing his spoon, its tip whitened with vanilla, at the President's face. "Vanilla ice cream doesn't have seventy percent approval. I can sell Congress on this. You play this right – *we* play this right, Sir – and you'll wipe a scourge from this Earth and score your highest approval ratings, all in one fell swoop."

"Mr. President?" the voice of Salas's young body man turned him back to the door.

"Didn't I say we weren't to be--?"

"You did, Sir, I'm sorry, but there's something going on in Michigan right now you should probably be aware of."

POTUS rose from his seat. VPOTUS didn't move.

The weather could not have been more perfect for Benjamin Bratten.

With only a scattering of clouds spackled across the icy blue sky, two of the three Detroit news stations he had contacted over satellite phone rushed to get news choppers out to the coordinates he had provided. The distant warble of their rotors on the horizon was the signal for which he had been waiting all day: time to end this stalemate.

Rikeman's last warning – that the Allied Armament cadre had night vision goggles and targeting scopes and would be at an extreme advantage as soon as the sun disappeared – was of course correct, and with no more than an hour of sun left, Bratten thought the time was right to advance this little drama. It wasn't the advantage the dark would give the mercenaries he was worried about, however. He cared only about what it would do to those helicopters, to their cameras trying to catch the action below.

All Bratten cared about was those cameras. And now, they were finally in magic hour, the hour of the day's best, camera-ready lighting.

"In exactly ten minutes' time," Bratten yelled out into the trees, in the direction of Rikeman's hidden megaphone, "sixteen hundred hours by my watch, we will allow the passage of three men through our borders! You will be met by three unarmed negotiators, who will explain to you the terms of our surrender of Jason Lancaster!"

"*You expect me to send three of my men into the middle of your property?*"

"Your men can carry all the arms they want. My negotiating party will carry no weapons. A trade of advantages."

Rikeman thought for a moment, before agreeing. As much as he knew they could tear through this place once night fell, he didn't feel like cutting down dozens of innocents in a first-person shooter exercise just to get Lancaster. He was concerned about the safety of the meeting Bratten had offered, and so decided he would be one of the three Allied Armament representatives involved.

Some of the Minutemen were surprised when Bratten put 'Perfect Paul' in charge of their negotiation team. Twenty-one-year-old Paul Tighlman had been with the Minutemen for less than a year, after returning from a tour in Afghanistan minus half his left arm. But anyone who had ever spoken with Paul knew he was perhaps more dedicated to the cause than anyone else in Polis. He lived, breathed and dreamt pure Benjamin Bratten.

He believed in Bratten so much, he was even willing to do what he asked him to do next.

When the row of armed Minutemen along the front property line split open for Dean Rikeman, he could see Paul and two of his compatriots waiting a hundred yards in the distance, smack in the middle of an open expanse of snowy land between compound structures. Rikeman kept his hand on his hipped Sig Sauer as he marched his two men, both hugging their HK416 assault rifles close, toward the negotiating party.

Soon, they were facing off, three on one side, three on the other. Rikeman nodded to one of his men, the larger African-American one, who stepped forward and frisked the three Minutemen one by one, confirming they were unarmed as promised.

"I didn't realize you were bringing the TSA," Paul quipped when it was his turn for a frisking.

"And I didn't realize I wouldn't be meeting with Bratten," Rikeman said as his frisker returned to his side.

"That monkey doesn't get to meet Mr. Bratten," Paul nodded to the black one.

Rikeman put a hand before his man's chest, just in case that cheap shot actually got under his skin.

"Mr. Bratten has instructed me and fully authorized me to make this negotiation," Tighlman continued in an emotionless, brainwashed monotone.

Rikeman didn't like it, but he just wanted to get this over with and get Lancaster in chains while those cameras above could still see it. "Now that the news copters are on us, we can't just take Lancaster and go," he began. "But you tell Bratten: you let us confiscate ten, fifteen weapons along with him? That I can sell, and we can leave you in peace."

But Paul Tighlman wasn't listening to Rikeman, wasn't even looking at him. His eyes were skyward, watching the two news choppers, confirming that they had figured out this spot was the center of the action, and were now hovering right over them, the camera lenses on their noses peering down on the negotiation omnisciently.

"Son," Rikeman took a step closer, "do you understand what I'm--"

Paul puts his hands behind his head, his two compatriots following his lead. Almost in perfect unison, their six knees dropped to the snow-covered ground.

"Hey," Rikeman protested, stepping forward to grab Paul under the right armpit. "What are you doing? We didn't tell you to do that."

Rikeman glared back at his men, and they rushed to follow, the black one grabbing Paul's left arm – his false arm, which came off in his hand, leaving Paul only a stump.

Paul's head rotated to look up into his eyes, an evil glint to his smile as he said, "What else you gonna steal while you're here… *nigger*?"

The Allied Armament grunt reared back with Paul's disconnected arm – "No!" Rikeman protested in vain – and smashed it across the boy's skull. As Paul caught himself on the snow with one hand, grunts of displeasure passed like a wave through the Minutemen watching the action from all around them.

"Hey!" Rikeman screamed, pointing at his man. "Stow that!" He leaned over Paul, patting his back with his hand. "Hey. You're all right. You'll just have a welt, that's all. You had your big moment--"

Paul pushed back up to his knees, revealing a small hole, a compartment in the snow between his feet, a small trapdoor he had pulled open while he was down.

Paul now gripped a .38 special, retrieved from that compartment.

"N--" Rikeman got out before Paul raised the gun to his forehead and blew a hole out through the back of his skull.

For several slow motion moments, time on Polis, on all of the Huron, time wherever those helicopters were broadcasting their images, froze. No one moved as Rikeman fell backwards, floating down down down, until his lifeless head bounced on the hard, packed snow. No one moved until a full puddle of his blood started matting under his hair. His soldiers didn't move until they looked down into his glassy eyes and recognized that those eyes would never move again.

They were the first to move. They whipped their rifles around to Paul – his eyes closed, the smile of a young man who knew he had pleased his God across his lips – and shredded his torso, then those of his compatriots, in a torrent of fully-auto hollow tip rounds.

Before they could even turn to beat their retreat for the trees, the Allied Armament representatives were in turn themselves sliced to pieces by Minutemen on the perimeter unleashing their own shotguns and pistols and AR-15s.

Some Minutemen convulsed as they fired, feeling the rounds slamming into their own backs from behind. Those soldiers still out in the trees were firing in at them. With the two AASC grunts now collapsed upon the other four bodies in the center of Polis, the Minutemen turned their attention back out into the Huron, letting rip at any moving white mass or incongruous flash of black they could make out in the shrubs. Many darted for cover, finding buildings they could crouch behind and still have some sort of firing angle into the woods.

From the distant safety of the school building, Benjamin Bratten looked out at all the crumpled carcasses lying across the reddened snow, from the pile of six that had started the whole dance, to the men littering the perimeter who had served him so faithfully. He smiled.

Perfect Paul had done exactly as he had asked.

Ensconced in the Hay-Adams after another breezy day of confirmation hearings, Mac was as riveted by the images he saw from Polis as anyone. One of the news helicopters had veered off after that first shot snuffed out Rikeman's life, but the other had stayed as long as their fuel reserves would allow, beaming its bloody images across the nation. Though at this point the same highlights had been repeated over and over again for hours – each time with new commentary about which side instigated the violence (most analysts pointing to the Allied Armament grunt yanking out the Minuteman's arm and bashing him over the head with it as the spark), or whether or not the President should or even could get a troop presence out there – this felt like one of those history-in-the-making moments off which you couldn't wrest your eyes.

At around 2200 hours, Mac choked down his last Jack and forced off his television, mindful that tomorrow he had to again look rested and warm for his own fleet of HD cameras. (Although what was the chance even C-SPAN would cover his hearing with this going on?) After brushing and flossing, he returned to his iPhone on the desk to turn it off and charge it for the night. That was when he noticed he had missed a call he hadn't heard vibrate over his Fox News, a call from an unrecognized source. He pressed the series of buttons to play the voice mail over the speaker--

Mac sucked in hard when he heard the voice. It was Shareef's first message in over two weeks. He had left over 20 voice mails in the first days after Mac had cut things off, but those had dwindled into nothing when he realized Mac *wouldn't* be calling back.

Shareef had been more and more in Mac's thoughts: another man's mouth on his, another man's hands on him, had not helped him forget Shareef as he had hoped, but had only made him long even more for Shareef's mouth, for Shareef's hands. As Mac listened to the message – the tremble in his voice, the tears caught in his throat, the *fear* behind the words – Mac realized *why* Shareef had chosen tonight to re-establish contact.

It took Mac twenty minutes, through several phone calls to Dennis and the Irvings' office, to convince someone to patch him through to Rosemarie. "Admiral, please, calm down," she interrupted his initial babbling, "you've got to calm down and explain to me what's going on."

"I just got a message," he panted, pacing from one corner of his tiny room to another. "There's a young man, his name's Shareef, Shareef Summarai, I've-- I've been mentoring him. I just got a message from him that he's been taken into custody by ICE. They let him make one phone call and he called me. They've got him in some sort of holding facility before they send him back to Syria."

"Admiral--"

"Please. You don't understand. If he goes back … he had several prominent family members who fought with the rebels in the civil war. If he's sent back, through official channels like that, through an airport, they'll snatch him right up. You don't understand what they'll do to him."

"Admiral. I know you're very upset. But you need to understand how important it is that I know every pertinent detail about this young man. Do you believe he was in this country illegally?"

"I, I don't know. Probably. He came here on a student visa but that was a few years ago."

"Is he employed?"

"I … I really don't know."

"Admiral--"

"No. Not in any way that matters."

Rosemarie's deep sigh came through the phone. "I'm sorry, Admiral. I'll discuss this with Reg. But you have to be prepared for the likelihood that we can't do anything--"

"Of course you can do something, you were in the goddamn White House for eight years, you know you can fix this."

"But right now, in the middle of your--"

"It has to be right now. He might already be on a plane. If we wait till I'm confirmed, he'll be dead."

"But you do understand what it would mean if it came out a nominee for the Supreme Court helped someone stay in this country illegally? Helped him circumvent Immigration--"

"I don't think you understand. *This is more important to me than my nomination.*" Mac squeezed his eyes shut. He couldn't believe he was saying this. "You need to do this for me ... or I'm out."

The buzzing in the phone grew louder and louder, filling the silence that dominated the next minute.

Finally, Rosemarie responded, "Let me see what I can do."

Mac hung up, thumbnailed his ringer switch forward again, slumped down onto his bed, and turned his TV back on. He didn't turn it off until it was time to shower up for another day in the hearing room.

You might be able to list on a single piece of paper the number of people who had ever known that the Supreme Court Conference – the private weekly meeting of the Justices in which they discussed arguments recently heard, cert petitions being considered, made their preliminary votes, and split up opinion assignments – was recorded. Every conference of the past 73 terms had been recorded, in fact.

The practice had started in late 1945, the final term of the Harlan Fiske Stone Court. It was a surprise to most Americans when Stone collapsed in the middle of reading a dissent and later died in his home of a cerebral hemorrhage; but his fellow Justices had noticed Chief Justice Stone exhibiting neurological issues months earlier, often complaining of debilitating headaches that kept him from seeing an issue clearly or completing his work in a timely fashion. Most alarming, he was more and more often starting to forget what had been discussed or decided or assigned in a conference.

The most senior Associate Justice, Hugo Black, had brought a letter signed by five of his colleagues to Marshal Thomas Waggaman, requesting that he very discreetly investigate ways they might be able to document what occurred in the conference session without embarrassing the Chief. A week later, Waggaman had alerted Black that he thought it would be possible to wire the Conference Room for sound recording over the course of a weekend. All remaining conferences in Stone's tenure would be recorded (the Associate Justices were relieved that they never ended up having to 'go to the tape'), and the practice continued following his death, the system receiving annual check-ups and updates as technology progressed.

Many people passed through the Court ranks never knowing about the collection of recordings. Only the Chief and the next senior Justice at any one time were required to be notified of its existence. Most clerks were unaware of the practice, save for those whose direct bosses had spilled the beans (Rosemarie Irving never knew about the system, even though she had served in Chief Quint's chambers for a term). The Marshals over the years had shared the system with only a handful of colleagues on a need-to-know basis (Miranda knew about the recording system, but had never even shared it with Jason).

Because Gregor Meyers had never been officially initiated and groomed and trained as Marshal, and had only filled in after the apparent death of Miranda Whitney, he was forced to learn many of the protocols of the job, including just how close to the vest he should keep the conference recordings, on the fly. When Dennis asked for everything related to *Agguire v. Detroit*, when he made it clear that this request was on behalf of a First Lady of the United States, it was only natural for Meyers to believe the recordings of last term's *Agguire* conference should be included. Thus, something Dennis should have never even known existed was copied onto a compact disc and removed from the Court (or the ruins of it, to be precise). But as soon as Meyers had informed Dennis of his mistake, the First Lady's aide had not only sent the CD through a shredder, he had deleted the offending files from his computer.

Dennis, however, was right about what he had always heard: you could never totally wipe something from your hard drive (or, at least, no amateur could do it simply by emptying his or her 'recycle bin'). With his old high school buddy Foster talking him through it over the phone, he was able to recover the MP3 that had once spent a couple of days in his 'AvD' file.

The first time he had accessed the recording, he had given it the most cursory skim; now, he sat riveted to the Justices' words. A chill ran down his spine as he heard legal dignitaries expounding with the confidence that comes only in the prime of one's life, unaware that for nearly half of them, death was a scant eight months away. As each Justice, from Chief Lapadula to the senior Egan to the junior Salovey, proclaimed a vote on *Agguire*, Dennis kept a tally on the legal pad next to his keyboard.

The routine complete, Lapadula moved the discussion to cert petitions. Dennis let it continue playing, but wasn't listening, lost in the grave ramifications of what he had heard. He now knew which direction the 5-4 vote had swung – exactly the direction he had feared. He understood why Lapadula had assigned the opinion to Winks; he was the Justice who had spoken with the most confidence on the surety of his beliefs and, as the most gifted writer on the Court, would no doubt be able to assure any of his colleagues who might be wavering in their positions that they were right in their initial conference vote. He might even be able to sway a vote or two from the other side.

Nothing in Winks's self-assured diatribe matched up with the floundering, indecisive memo in which he had surrendered his opinion and suggested a reargument.

Dennis's phone punched through the silence, shimmying across the table. He jumped – the recording had ended several minutes ago, and he hadn't even realized it. "Shoot," he whispered under his breath when he saw Janaki's name on the display; he wasn't annoyed she was calling, just with himself, for failing to return her last three messages. "Hey," he smiled into the phone after answering.

"Is something wrong? I haven't heard from you all day."

"No, everything's great, I just got caught up-- crazy day. I'll tell you all about it."

"I mean … I don't want you to think I'm getting clingy or attached or anything. Don't go getting all cocky on me, Coutts."

"It was important, or I would've called, I'm sorry."

"I thought nothing was more important than me," she joked, but Dennis was in a serious mood.

"Nothing is. I'm sorry, J. This is exactly what I don't want to be like."

"Hey, I get it. Imagine when we're in full session and I'm writing half of Goldman's opinions for him."

"There's no excuse." Dennis couldn't help but think of Chief Quint on the floor of the bathroom; his answer to the question of regret rang in Dennis's ears.

"I love you," he suddenly blurted out. "That comes first."

It took Janaki a moment to process this bomb-with-a-capital-B he had just dropped.

"I'm sorry, I know that's heavy, but I've been thinking about it a lot and I wanted to say it before I get buried again."

"No, no, I-- I'm glad you did. I think … I want to say it back. But I've never said it to anyone before."

"I don't want you to say it just because I did. I want you to surprise me with it, make your moment all your own."

"I appreciate that. I'm sorry--"

"You have nothing to be sorry about. You're perfect. I'm deep in something very serious right now, and I'm sorry it's taken up all my time, but when it's over, I'm going to call in sick for a week and just cook and clean for you."

"That's when I'll really say it."

They talked for a few more minutes, but Dennis's mind had already started to wander onto his next day, onto how the hell he was going to handle what he had discovered. It wasn't easy, figuring out how to accuse two Supreme Court Justices of conspiring to blow up their own court.

Jason refused to even consider whether Miranda had been party to whatever grand ploy led him here. He had compartmentalized all those thoughts, shoved them into the same little box where his thoughts about her connection to the bombing had been hidden, and kicked that box to the very back of his brain. Unfortunately, as he struggled to find her in any building or bomb shelter, the firefight carrying on into its sixth hour, that box seemed to keep rolling back into the front of his mind. *Did she know Allied Armament was coming? Did she flee long before they arrived?*

What Jason did know beyond a shadow of a doubt was that Benji Bratten was a class-a murdering con artist. He had orchestrated this whole bloodbath with that sham of a negotiation he had controlled like a puppet master. However many bodies Bratten had claimed in the Solstice Bank had been tripled tonight.

Jason hadn't found Miranda, but he did happen to see Bratten sneaking to the back entrance of the Polis weapons factory, the back entrance that led right down a short hall to the bomb workshop he had shared with Dreyfus.

Bratten was already kneeling on the ground over some small device when Jason entered behind him, .45 drawn on his back. "Did we pass inspection?" Jason startled him. He leaped up to his feet, hands raised, but Jason saw he had already accomplished what he was here to do: red digital numbers counting down from **15:00:00** on the device between his legs.

"It's great to see you, Jason. I get a chance to thank you."

"Thank me?"

"You, after all, are the reason this whole thing is happening here today. You're going to make me a folk hero."

"With that?" Jason nodded to the device at his feet, which he now could see was wrapped with potent little bundles of C4. "When that goes up, when this room goes up, it's going to take the whole compound with it. Anyone who didn't get to a shelter is toast."

"Just like Ruby Ridge. Just like Waco. This century finally has its martyrs to the second amendment, to living tax free. To freedom. Every Minuteman will die a legend. Especially their leader." Bratten grinned. "But unlike Koresh, unlike Randy Weaver, I get to live to enjoy it."

Jason thumbed back the hammer of his pistol. "You're sure about that?"

"You can't kill me."

"Actually, the great thing is, I can."

"Not if you want to know where Miranda is."

Jason hesitated, his barrel lowering just slightly. "Who?"

"You're so pathetic. This has been so way over your head all this time, and you didn't even pick up on it. You didn't think I was in on the deal to let you come here and become one of us? You didn't think I knew who she really was?"

"I … don't know what you're talking about," Jason grunted out, not even sure why he was still keeping up the ruse.

"I know where she's been hiding during the attack. Which I'll tell you," he brought his hands down, cupping them together, "once you throw me your gun."

Jason's jaw quivered with rage, all the anger, all the uncertainty, all the paranoia of the last three months rushing to his temples. With a guttural scream, he ran at Bratten, tackling him up against the barrels of fertilizer lining the back wall. "*Tell. Me*," he growled in the killer's face.

Jason screamed and jumped back, pistol flying from his grip, landing on the concrete floor and skittering away to a corner. He cursed himself – his attack had been so brazen, so reckless. He looked down his arm, to the hand that had gripped his gun, now sporting a deep red gash from inside his elbow to the center of his palm. Bratten had surprised him with a knife.

Bratten came at him, swinging his blade one way, then the other, Jason jumping back just enough to keep out of range of its deadly point. Bratten grit his teeth and took a full lunge at him – Jason matadored his thrust, letting him blow right by him – then grabbed his arms from behind. Bratten fought, but the stronger

Jason shoved his left hand back up, and into his own abdomen. He could feel the give as the blade cut into flesh, finding purchase beneath the protection of Bratten's ribs. He gargled as Jason twisted the knife up and back, severing vital connections between the heart and the body it served. As he felt the life leaving Bratten's body, the devious bastard just laughed. "Tomorrow … I will be the most famous man … in America …"

And he was gone. Jason let him go, let him slide off his chest and onto the floor.

He heard the jangle before he heard her voice. "You're going to put these on." He hinged around – Miranda was standing in the corner, his .45 now in her grip, pointed at him. From her left fingers dangled a pair of handcuffs; she tossed them into his chest. "Cuff yourself to something, something that won't move."

"Rand …"

"I have no choice. I did what I was supposed to, I got you here. When they find your remains …" She paused, fighting back emotion. For just a moment, Jason thought this emotion was for him, an outpouring of grief for what she was doing to him.

Then he heard her next words: "They'll find your remains, and I'll get to see my baby again."

THURSDAY

"Reach into my pocket," Jason said after he clamped the second handcuff, its chain threaded through a drawer handle of the lab work island, around his left wrist.

"What?" Miranda glared at him, stopping just before she reached the door.

"Just do me this one thing. Reach into my left pocket."

"What the hell are you--"

"*One thing, before you leave me here to die.*"

Miranda shuffled forward, keeping the gun trained on his head as she moved it from her right hand to her left, her eyes locked on his as she crouched forward and reached her open hand into his pocket and pulled out the tiny box inside. She breathed in hard. "What the fuck is this? Goddammit, Jason."

It was a ring box, the same box of robin's egg blue that George Aug's Homeland Security team had pulled out of the crawl space of Jason's brownstone.

She screamed as her feet flew out from underneath her. Jason had kicked out her legs, knocking her to the ground. She fell forward into him, and he wrapped his right elbow around her throat from behind. She gagged as he exerted pressure. "I was going to give you that. Maybe for Christmas, maybe your birthday, I hadn't figured it out yet. And I never got the chance. I've carried that in my pocket, all the way from Washington, to find you here."

Miranda still had the gun. She raised it, aiming its barrel backwards so it almost touched his skull. "Let-- me go--" she choked out.

"You're gonna have to shoot me."

But she didn't. She just lowered the gun. With her free hand, Miranda held onto his bulky forearm, but didn't pull on it or try to break free. She just closed her eyes. "Kill me."

"And what about the baby you mentioned? Huh?" Tears streamed down Miranda's cheeks, but she didn't answer. Jason looked over to Bratten's ignition device. "We have four minutes. Unlock my cuffs. I'm taking you out of here. You're not abandoning that baby."

"If you get out of here … I'll never see him again. You have to go to jail, or die--"

"Listen to me: I don't know who the hell promised you what. But these aren't the kind of people you can trust. You can trust me. I'll get him back for you. I promise."

Miranda hesitated, then reached into her pocket, raising the key up high enough for him to grab it from her grasp. She dropped to her knees as he unlocked the cuffs. Jason charged to the door-- before he realized she wasn't by his side. She was still on her knees, on the floor.

"Hey. We gotta go. Three minutes!" He moved for her, stooping to take her under the arm and try to pull her to her feet.

But she yanked her arm away. And with her other hand put Jason's .45 to her temple. "Rand!" He kneeled beside her, putting his own hands around the gun. But he couldn't pull it off; she was still the strongest woman he had ever known.

"You're not doing it," he whispered in her ear. "I'm going to keep you safe. Just like I promised. I'm going to reunite you with your baby. I wasn't here just to find you, I was here to make sure you live happily ever after. And I don't care what it takes, I'm not resting until I've done that."

Miranda sucked in hard, shutting her eyes and holding her breath—

Then released it all, lightening her grip on the gun, just enough to allow him to pull it from her hands. He pulled her to her feet like a rag doll and dragged her out of there.

Once outside, he pulled the hood of his parka over his head, hoping that and the dark would be enough to shield his identity from any Allied Armament soldiers they might encounter. He put his hand on Miranda's head and kept her low as they darted for the nearest edge of the woods. They heard the report of dozens of competing weapons, the zip of rounds whipping over their heads, but didn't think about where the bullets were coming from, which side was winning, or whether the slugs might be aimed for them. They just kept their heads down and kept moving.

Only once they had made it a few meters into the brush did Jason hear the muffled explosions from inside the bomb factory. Not sure how wide the conflagration might spread, how far the shrapnel might fly, he ground to a halt. "Down!" He pushed Miranda's head behind a log for cover.

The whole arms building went up, as blazing as the sun, enough to brighten the night sky into a day blue, its rumble as loud as a sonic boom. Any gun men within a few hundred feet (and at this point, they were mostly Allied Armament gun men, cleaning up any surviving Minutemen stragglers) were blown apart or blown off their feet. The buildings closest to the eye of the storm also took the brunt, the impact tearing through foundations or rupturing walls or hurling out flaming debris to take root in any nearby roofs. The tents were next, skin melting under blue flames, in no time leaving only smoldering skeletons.

As the explosions themselves died down, the sounds of news helicopters once again started to build on the horizon, and the few men left alive on the compound began the struggle to their feet. Jason let Miranda up. “Let’s go.”

They walked away, as Polis burned to the ground behind them.

Shareef’s holding cell had no windows, no lights, no openings to the outside world whatsoever – so he had no idea what time it was when the light streaming in from the open door forced open his eyes. He squinted at the sudden shock to his irises, but it was momentary; the silhouette of the large black ICE agent soon blotted it out, then shoved a tight blindfold over his head and down onto eyes. “I need to speak to a lawyer,” Shareef pleaded.

“Again, a guarantee of my Constitution,” the agent quipped back, “not yours. Hands forward.”

Shareef complied, and the agent again yanked flex cuffs tight enough into his flesh to elicit a yelp of pain.

“Up. Time to walk.”

Shareef obeyed, and the agent led him toward the door. “You can’t deport me without some sort of due process,” the young Syrian argued as the agent shoved him out. “Do you understand me? PLEASE, WHOEVER CAN HEAR ME, I HAVE RIGHTS!”

Throughout the 45 minutes of his blind journey, Shareef would beseech whoever was escorting him to provide him with representation or protections like these, but no one ever responded, not even with a laugh or a snide remark. The only sounds Shareef was met with were the chirps of early morning birds as he was led outside, a car radio being switched off as he was sat down on the leather seat of a vehicle (probably an SUV, Shareef surmised from the height of the seat), the thrum of the highway, followed by the claustrophobic drang of a tunnel or garage. The vehicle came to a smooth stop, and Shareef got out into what sounded like a hallway, lights and vents all emanating the hum of a top-of-the-line corporate building. He was led a few steps forward, then turned to the right, and with the whish of doors sliding shut behind him, realized he was in an elevator. His stomach shot up into his ribs as they plummeted down.

The elevator's electronic bell pinged its landing announcement. Shareef was pushed out into--

No, that couldn't be right. All those bells and whistles going off, the electronic ditties dancing from corners all around him, none of it made sense. Why would ICE have brought him to a--?

"Sit," a voice said, then a hand on his shoulder forced him to accede. Shareef's bottom bounced a little as he settled into a leather seat. And then there was light, as hands from behind his head lifted his blindfold up and off. His eyes adjusted; there was only one person, a woman, sitting before him.

What. The fuck? This woman looked a helluva lot like …

No, it couldn't be. Shareef moved his head around to confirm what his ears had told him: ICE had brought him to a casino? And they had brought him here for a meeting with a woman who could've been a wax figurine of the last First Lady, President Irving's wife, what was her name again-?

"Good morning, Shareef. My name is Rosemarie Irving."

"Why …?" was all that came out of his dumbfounded mouth.

She smiled. "I'm afraid that's what Bogdan and Elizabeth Jarzebski named me. My first name, at least."

"Why would you want to meet me? Is this for some sort of charity? Are you going to use me in some kind of speech?"

"You're here because of the phone call you made. To your friend, Vice Admiral MacTavish? He asked me to make sure you weren't sent back to Syria."

Shareef's eyes welled. His spine shook and he curled into a little ball, letting the tears flow out all over his cheeks. "Oh thank you. Thank you thank you thank you …"

"I'm afraid this good deed doesn't come free of charge." Rosemarie turned to her left, and for the first time Shareef noticed a thick stack of papers sitting on the blackjack table nearest her. She picked it up and held it out for him to take. "There are some very simple conditions to your staying here."

Shareef took it, and though his hands were still cuffed, was able to lay it down in his lap and flip through its first few pages.

"As I'm sure you're aware," FLOTUS explained, "Admiral MacTavish is on the verge of the greatest moment of his distinguished service to this country. *Your* country, as you'll see on the last page ..."

Shareef let out a giant wheeze of elation as he skimmed that last page.

"... *if* you follow this contract to the letter. You will be drug free for six months. You will submit to weekly tests for narcotics and methamphetamines, and missing even one of these appointments will be considered the equivalent of a relapse. You will engage in no romantic or sexual activity for the next six months ..."

"None?"

Rosemarie put a hand, that same hand that had touched Mac a few times, on Shareef's knee and leaned in seductively. "I can't claim to know the full extent of your relationship with the Admiral. I just know how important you are to him. You will find there is one exception to the romance clause."

Shareef let out a little of the cocky smile Mac loved so much. "No offense, but how would you even know if I broke that one?"

"Suffice it to say that at every moment, every minute of your every day of the next six months, I will have someone watching you. You will learn very quickly, if you're not already aware, that the government of your new home is far from perfect, but the one thing we do very, very well is watch people."

Shareef's smile was gone, but his excitement wasn't dampened. "If I sign this ... in six months I get citizenship?"

"Candidates for US citizenship are required to take a test. We'll just call this yours. Pass, and you will be sworn in come the fourth of July. Fail, and you get to see Damascus again."

"I'll sign it. Just give me a pen, I'll sign it."

"There is one more thing." Rosemarie returned to the blackjack table – there was one sheet of paper remaining where the contract had once been stacked. As she had before, she picked it up and handed it across to him.

"What's this?"

"Those are the answers you're going to spend the rest of the day memorizing."

Jerome had been Justice Winks's driver and messenger for all but his first year on the bench, 33 years now and counting. Jerome and his kids were welcomed into the Winks home for both Thanksgiving and their annual day-after-Christmas soiree. Jerome was a member of the extended Winks family.

Today would be the first time in 33 years that Justice Winks would have to consider firing Jerome.

On Thursday morning, when Winks climbed into the back of the Jaguar XJ he had bought for Jerome to shuttle him around, someone was already sitting in that backseat, waiting for him. Winks cherished mornings on his way to the Court, the last chance of the day to just watch the great monuments of America roll by while listening to motown emanating from the stereo. Jerome had committed a very serious offense, allowing the young man in the backseat to violate this cherished time, with no warning, no permission.

"Jerome," the Justice whined, locking eyes with him in the rectangle of rear-view mirror.

"Your Honor, I'm sorry," his driver replied. "He said it was official Court business, and couldn't wait. He said Rosemarie Irving sent him."

Winks had already recognized him: the young Native American who had been serving as Rosemarie Irving's assistant as she helped the President nominate replacements to the Court. Winks had never been a fan of the Irvings, and considered it inappropriate and negligent of the President to turn his search over to them (although, unlike Acting Chief Egan, he was quite impressed with the nominees they had recommended). Whatever this young man was ambushing him about, it was on behalf of the Irvings, and he would be as uncooperative as he felt he could get away with.

"Justice Winks, I appreciate this and I'll make it quick," Dennis appealed as Jerome put the car in gear and started pedaling it to the Capitol. "I know we both have busy days ahead." Truthfully, the only reason Dennis had time for this at all was that Chief Quint would be at Walter Reed all morning going through a battery of tests; Dennis noted the irony in the Chief's failing health giving him this opportunity to further his 'other' research. "I just need to ask you a couple quick questions about *Agguire v. Detroit*."

"I'm sorry? Young man, that's completely inappropriate while the case is still--"

"'As I worked through my initial draft,'" Dennis read out of the file in his lap, "'I was consistently struck by the momentous ramifications of such a decision, and must now acknowledge that even more research and consideration is required if I am to give this matter its due.' Do you remember writing that in a memo to your colleagues?"

"How did you get that?"

"Just hear me out. I did an analysis of each date an argument was heard versus its opinion released over the last eight terms; those are all the terms with the same make-up of the Court we had at the time of the bombing--"

"Jerome, stop the car--"

"Justice, you had the shortest turnaround time. You're the fastest writer on the Court. And the way you were talking in the *Agguire* conference--"

"Ex*cuse* me?"

"--you knew this case backwards and forwards. You knew exactly the way you thought it should be decided. *Agguire v. Detroit* was heard in December, you should've had the argument turned around a month or two later, not been filing for an incomplete on the tenth of May!"

"How dare you tell me how I should do my job?" Winks squinted in rage as the car rolled to a stop on the curb.

"We both know you didn't have trouble writing the opinion."

"Young man, there is so much that goes into a Court term that you can't even begin to comprehend--"

"Like someone asking you to delay a case?"

Winks shut his eyes and rubbed his forehead, searching for the easiest words to just get this kid out of his car. "For your information, the Chief Justice came to me and explained that he felt the case should be delayed. I honored that request."

"Do you have any idea why he would want it delayed?"

"How the hell should I know? There could be any number of reasons. It wasn't my place to ask. It could've been as simple as the amount of media the Court could accommodate on the remaining decision announcement days …"

"And just to be clear, you do mean *Chief Justice Lapadula* asked your help in delaying the case?"

Winks's head whipped around, his eyes bulging and bloodshot. Dennis knew he had hit a nerve. "I don't know what kind of authority you think that woman gives you, but she and I will be having a discussion about you. This conversation is over."

Dennis opened his door but didn't exit the vehicle yet. "Okay, I was just surprised to hear you say Chief Lapadula had asked you to delay it. I thought you were going to say it was *Chief Quint*."

Winks's jaw dropped in shock. "Jerome, call the Capitol Police!"

Dennis stepped both feet out of the car, but kept his body leaned in; he could hear Jerome trying to approximate their location to a dispatcher over the phone. "I've seen the meal records in the Court Vault, Justice. You had lunch with Chief Quint in the Marbury v. Madison dining room three times between the *Agguire* argument and the relisting--"

"We've been friends for years!"

"--including *three hours* before you wrote that memo backing off your opinion!"

Winks didn't move, didn't say a word. He didn't need to. Dennis could read his eyes confirming what he was saying.

"Justice Winks, did you know William Quint is on the board of Allied Armament Security Consultants?"

The tires screeched into movement, and Dennis jumped back to save his toes from being run over. Dust and exhaust spit up into his face, caking onto the front of his wide, toothy smile.

Salas was returning from his third Sit Room pow-wow on Iran when he noticed the rock wall of a Mexican-American standing up from the waiting chair before Delores's desk. "Hifrael!" the President exclaimed when he saw that familiar face.

"Mr. President. I've been trying to meet with you for three days."

"That can't be right. Delores?"

"It's the new COS," the decrepit secretary proclaimed. "He's got me locked out of your schedule. Doesn't want me touching it."

Salas winked at her. "I'll have a talk with him." He opened the door to the short hallway down to the Oval Office study, tossing over a shoulder, "Hifrael, sígueme."

POTUS stepped behind his small study desk as Hifrael shut the door behind him. "I wanted to apologize about the way I left last month, Sir," the guard started to explain in Spanish.

"Already forgotten," Salas declared without even looking up at him. "You're back on my detail, effective immediately. I'll let Joe know." He continued to shuffle papers when a sealed manila envelope landed in the middle of everything. "What's this?"

"It's what you asked me to get you before. About President Irving."

Salas slumped down into his chair, letting out the air from the pit of his core. "I regretted that. It was wrong to put you in an uncomfortable--"

"I'm in the United States Secret Service. I serve at the pleasure of the President."

Salas leaned forward, tearing open the top of the envelope.

"I don't think I have to tell you, Sir--"

Before he pulled out any of its contents, Salas nodded, placing the envelope in a locked desk drawer. "No one will know about this except me and you. It will never get back to MMA that you've shared it with me."

"Actually, Agent Aldridge would never reveal those things, Sir. He's worked for the Irvings for far too long. There's someone at HQ who owed me some favors. She was able to get me President Irving's movement logs, visitation records for both their residence and foundation offices ..."

"Well, thank you for using up your favors on me."

Hifrael nodded and opened the door. "De nada."

The deep snow had made Jason's journey out of the Huron much more challenging than his trip in a month before. He was confident they were going the right way – he had made a point during his hours of avoiding the AASC/Minutemen standoff to collect some easy-to-carry survival supplies (some rations, some fire-starting tools), and to reorient himself on the way back to the nearest road (he had a compass and a topographic map with him) – but it was still eighteen miles at least to that road, and the conditions were making each mile take sometimes up to two hours.

His main concern was that, as deep in the trees as they were, the temperature had been falling in the afternoon hours, and would plummet once the sun was all the way down. They would have to make camp for the night, and without sleeping bags or tents, take shifts keeping a fire alive in order to prevent freezing to death. They found a nice, flat spot, cleared snow from the ground and circled some rocks into a makeshift fire pit.

As Jason starting searching for dry (enough) firewood, he realized he wasn't sure it was a good idea to let Miranda out of his sight. She had almost killed herself just last night, and that was after almost leaving Jason behind to be blown to smithereens. Nearly their entire journey had been in silence, and he recognized that he had no idea where her head might be. "If I go get us some firewood, you're still gonna be here when I get back, right?"

"Where do you think I'm gonna go?"

"I don't know anymore." But what choice did he have? He turned and stepped over the fallen log marking the edge of their camp, bending to examine twigs sticking out of the snow as he went.

"You should've left me there, you know. You'd be moving a lot faster without me."

He turned back. "You know I wouldn't do that."

"I set you up. I almost killed you. Whatever you thought you'd be getting back when you found me … it'll never be the same. You'll never get that me, that us, back."

Jason let out a deep sigh, his eyes moving off her and into his memories. "My whole life, the only thing I ever wished was that I knew my mother. Not knowing her was the only regret I've had in my life.

"Whenever other kids would talk about their moms, it wouldn't just make me sad. It would make me *angry*. In high school, I even thought about killing myself just so I could meet her. That is, until Father Oliver explained in his class that suicides go straight to hell. I knew she wasn't in hell. I could barely remember my mother, but I knew she was perfect, and was in a perfect place.

"So, about six months after you and I met, I'm riding the Metro home one night and I realize I hadn't thought about Mom in a long time, a few days, and rarely at all in the last few weeks. I wasn't yearning to meet her anymore. I realized, right at that moment, I had a new regret. My only regret was that she'd never meet you."

His eyes returned to hers. "I refuse to lose belief in you. I can see in your eyes, I *know* this has all been out of your hands. I know you regret it. And I'm gonna help you fix it."

Jason turned and continued his wood hunt. Miranda covered her face and silently sobbed.

"You see Wyley chase me down back there?" Mac grinned to Reg as they approached his prep room. "He wanted me to know he was going to push for a committee vote tomorrow afternoon."

"That's fantastic."

Mac nodded. "Just one more day."

Reg stopped outside the closed door to their conference room to put a hand on the Admiral's decorated shoulder. "Let's make sure of that." He double-patted Mac's biceps, then opened the door. There was no prep team around the large circular table, no Secret Service presence, just three people: Irving's wife, her assistant Dennis and …

"Shareef?" Mac gasped.

Shareef rose and ran to him. Mac didn't move when Shareef planted a kiss on his lips, so the young man awkwardly rotated it into a hug. "It's okay," he whispered in the Admiral's ear. "I'm okay. They saved me. Everything's going to be okay."

Mac looked to Rosemarie as Shareef pulled away. "Thank you."

"It's our pleasure of course," she replied.

"Shareef, can I show you to one of our other rooms?" Reg smiled. "We'll leave Rosemarie to explain what's going to happen next."

Shareef nodded, mouthing to Mac, *So handsome!* as he followed the former President out.

"Happen next?" Mac wondered as the door closed him in with the First Lady.

"We have made an agreement with Shareef to be made an American citizen in six months' time … provided he follows certain behavioral guidelines."

"I'm sorry?"

"Admiral. We know Shareef's profession. We know how much you've paid him over the years. We know who pays the lease on his Mercedes. We know the drugs he's convinced you to experiment with--"

Mac took a step forward, fists balling up at his sides. "I didn't ask you to do this. I just asked you to make sure he didn't go back--"

Rosemarie shot to her feet. "You think I'm the only one who can get this information? You think everyone bought your Captain America story about the Arlington Deputies hook, line and sinker? You do realize who hasn't questioned you yet, I hope – Miriam Ekman, Republican of *Utah*? We happen to know she has her full oppo team working 18 hour days on *you* right now. There are vultures circling you, Admiral, even if you can't see them.

"Now when my husband was in office, when he gave you an assignment, he left you alone in the Pentagon to do your thing your way because he knew that was your job and you'd get results. Well, *this* building is our Pentagon, Admiral. You have to trust us."

"The committee's recommending me tomorrow. The vote will be Monday! And then-- they won't be able to do anything!"

"You're right. That's why we're going to make sure you get to Monday."

Jason heard her grunts before he could even see the cleared ground of their campsite in the dusk light. "Rand!" he yelled, sprinting forward and leaping over logs and rocks as fast as he could with his arms loaded down with wood.

As soon as he saw her, saw the damage, he threw the kindling aside and dropped to his knees at her side. "*What did you do?*" He lifted the large rock off her lower leg and tossed it aside, making her howl. He depressed the mangled ankle underneath; she hissed in agony as he tried to turn it, then whimpered as he examined it with his thumbs. "It's broken. What the hell did you do?"

"Now … you have to leave me." She rested her damp neck back against the log behind her, shutting her eyes to try to shut out the pain. "You can't get out of here with me. You have to leave me."

"You'll die out here."

She held up her cell phone. "I turn this on, and they'll find me tomorrow. You can't get me out of here like this. But they can. And I'll tell them you're dead."

"They won't believe you."

"I don't care. I have to try. I can't risk what might happen if they think you're still out there."

"Who? If *who* thinks I'm still out there?"

"I was supposed to make sure you got arrested. If they think you're out there … I can't risk what might happen to my son."

Jason put his palm on her face. "A son? Why didn't you ever tell me you have a son?"

"Jason. I did."

He looked away. Did she? Yes--

"I have a son. I want you to know I'm only doing this to save my son."

She had told him that night, after she had rufied him. She had explained the whole thing-- he just couldn't remember any of it.

"Does someone have your son? Is that why you helped bomb the Court? Who has your son, Rand?"

The frozen tears glittered as they crystalized on her cheeks. "I don't want you in this anymore, you understand? You're going to run – and disappear. And I'll tell the world you're dead. Maybe we can still fix this."

Jason knew how headstrong she was, and knew he wasn't getting any further with this. As much as he wanted to fight, he just nodded, then rose and returned to his pile of tinder. He moved it to the fire pit, organized it into an efficient arrangement, and started to work on getting it lit.

Since even before the bloodbath in the Huron began, George had been wracking his brain for all the other leads he had amassed in the last quarter of a year, all the leads that pointed to theories other than Jason's guilt: There were the four people DHS had tagged in surveillance videos visiting the Court five times in the year prior to the attack; the moneyed folks, all with Washington ties, behind the real estate development firm that had purchased the hospital in Detroit where the detonators had been tested; and that anonymous emailer who called him or herself 'DC' and claimed (s)he worked closely with the judicial search committee. (S)He had found disturbing links between that committee and possible motives for the bombing, (s)he claimed.

What links? George had never gotten the opportunity to dig deeper. DC's emails had stopped coming, his/her responses dwindling to nothing well over a month ago now, after just little teases at the information.

And then, on a Thursday in January, he received this text:

> *Sorry vanished. Wasn't sure bout my theories but theyve proved scary accurate. If you still want 2 meet, will explain more – DC*

George wrote back immediately: he had to hear these theories; they must meet tonight.

Too soon, DC explained. Immersed in a work project and wasn't sure he could escape. But by tomorrow night, his schedule should be clear. Tomorrow night they could meet.

George agreed, but he wasn't sure he could wait. He called down to a buddy in Science & Tech and asked what he could find out about the phone number from which he had just received a text.

The fire radiated heat for their chilled bones, and Jason just prayed he had built it too low for any Allied Armament hunters to see. He sat close, as did Miranda – he had moved her nearer against her protests, and had even set her ankle with two pieces of wood and some gauze from the first aid kit he had grabbed from the Polis infirmary. She didn't refuse the ibuprofen, but wouldn't eat.

"They had better food in Afghanistan," he chuckled through another bite of field rations, then held it out to her again, but again she declined. Jason set it down, then pulled out one of the three airplane-sized bottles of liquor he had also grabbed in his last hours on the compound. He cracked off the top and brought the plastic opening to his lips--

"Don't." The first thing she had said in an hour. "Just promise me, wherever you go, you won't drink. Please promise me that."

Jason lowered the bottle, but kept it open between his legs. "I'll make you a deal: you tell me who has your boy, who made you bomb the Court, and I won't ever touch another drop ever again."

She didn't answer, just stared into the crackle of the flames. Jason cleared the bottle in one pull, then tossed the empty into the live embers.

It was when he was about to open the third bottle that she spoke again: "All I did was let them in. Make sure the videos were erased, that there were absolutely no records of them coming and going that night, that's all I had to do and I could get my Gordon back."

Jason smiled. "Gordon." It was a smart and serious name, a nice, old school name, one you didn't hear much anymore.

But Jason had heard it just a few weeks ago, in the family room Miranda grew up in. *"Jason, do you know where Gordon is?"* Rand's mother had asked him. Then Ollie had, too. Finally the questions made sense.

Jason wanted to meet this kid. He wouldn't say it out loud, but he even wished he could be the father to this kid. He still loved Miranda that much. "Why didn't you ever tell me …?"

"No one on the Court could know. No one knew. But somehow these … these *assholes* found out. And used him against me. I let them into the Court that night, I erased them. They were supposed to give him back." She moved her gaze off the fire, to his eyes. "But once they know they have you, they never let go. Next, they tell me I have to call you. Just leave a message, it didn't matter what I said, just tease you that I'm still alive. Then I was to embed myself with the Minutemen, until you came and found me. I was supposed to wait there with you, until you got arrested. You'd be accused and convicted of the bombing, they told me. And *then* it would be over. Then I would get him back. That's what they promised."

Her eyes returned to the blaze. "But they're never going to let me have him back. That's what I realized back in Polis, when you should've left me to die. They're never going to let me see him again."

"Who, Rand?" He moved to his knees before her, put his hands on her shoulders. "Who has him? Who made you do all this?"

"What's always the answer to anything in this country? Follow the money."

FRIDAY

The crackle of a walkie-talkie woke Miranda. The first image she saw as she wrenched apart the crusted sleep from her eyes was a still from the set of a polar sci-fi B-movie: three men in white snow suits, eyes behind goggles, mouths behind masks, their alien-killing laser rifles levelled right into camera.

But these weren't laser rifles; these were very real, very ass-kicking Heckler & Koch assault rifles.

"Stay right there. Don't move those hands. Stay right there on the ground."

One of the others nodded to her splinted ankle. "She ain't going anywhere, Sarge."

The Sergeant rotated his head to his walkie and thumbed it to transmit mode. "Zero-one-two, zero-one-two, we have found the female suspect." One of the others was crouching to pick something up from the ground near Miranda; he held it up for his CO to see. "Suspect was located with the phone signal we detected." He turned a full 360, sweeping the surrounding woods. "No sign of Lancaster, repeat, no sign of male suspect Jason Lancaster." He let his thumb up, then motioned to the two foot soldiers behind him. "Sweep it, go, go!"

As they darted off in separate directions, he crouched down to her, close enough that she could see the dried blood spackling different patches of his snow suit. *Minutemen blood,* she thought. He put his goggles up on his helmet and pulled down his mask, revealing a friendly smile. He let his Tulsa drawl come out as he spoke, knowing from years of flirtation the calming effect it could have on the fairer sex. "That's one nasty break," he whistled. He turned the ankle to test it, and Miranda wheezed, shooting up into sitting. "Oh good, you still got some life in there." He rotated his rifle onto the back of his shoulder, pulling some flex cuffs from his belt. "C'mon, let's see those hands."

She lifted them towards him and he pulled the cuffs tight on her wrists. "Now you just stay right there, darlin," he winked, rising back to his full height and turning his mouth close to his walkie again. "Zero-one-two, we have female suspect Whitney comma Miranda in custody, repeat, Miranda Whitney in custody.

But she's hurt pretty bad. Please advise nearest possible LZ to our location for a medevac."

Miranda wilted her shoulders back down onto the dirt, turning her head with a sigh, her eyes catching on the airplane-sized bottle left displayed near her head, its plastic still full of liquor, its seal still unbroken.

"Mr. Chairman," Mac exhaled into his mic, then paused to let his mind adjust to his voice's amplification, echoing off the corners of the committee chamber. "Let me first start by thanking you for allowing me to open another day of hearings with a brief statement." His eyes moved down to the paper between his hands, just as they had at the start of Tuesday's session. "Ladies and gentlemen of the Judiciary Committee … and my fellow Americans … I have enjoyed our time this week getting to know one another as you consider the very weighty question of whether I am fit to serve on our nation's most important judicial body. But as the week has progressed, I have realized that I was feeling less and less comfortable not sharing one very special part of my life with you. I did not share it immediately, because I do not believe it will have any bearing on my performance as a Justice, nor should it be used in the consideration of any candidate for a post in our government. And yet, it is a very big part of my life.

"This especially haunted me on Tuesday as I described for all of you my actions in Alexandria on Monday night, coming to the defense of that young man. Was I really as brave as you all said I was, as the media was portraying me, as I was portraying myself, if I wasn't willing to share my complete story with the American people?

"And so today, I would like to introduce you to the young man sitting on my right. His name is Shareef Summarai and for the past three years, we have been very much in love."

A giant black Sharpie line was drawn under this paragraph on Mac's cheat sheet, a reminder to pause here and allow the commotion this revelation would kick up to die down. From the seat next to him, Shareef wanted to reach over and put a hand on Mac's knee, squeeze it for support, but their strict instructions dictated that they would have no physical contact until they had gotten through this fiasco and returned to the cozy confines of the prep room.

The Irvings were in that prep room already, watching these proceedings on a closed circuit monitor; the small bustle gave Reg an opportunity to lean over to his wife and whisper, "You're sure about this?"

"He just became the first Supreme Court nominee – or Justice – to come out. *Ever.* No Senator can touch him or the kid now."

"Shareef's life is his own," Mac continued his statement in the hearing room. "He loves soccer and the arts and is working on completing his education. He did not ask for all of this" – Mac gestured around the chamber with his eyes – "when he fell in love with me. We ask that you respect his privacy, and judge my judicial fitness on my qualifications, and my qualifications alone, which I trust I have laid out very clearly for you over the course of this week.

"Again, I have enjoyed the week, enjoyed getting to know all of you, and deeply appreciate your consideration. Thank you."

Mac sat back as a deep silence draped over the committee room. Chairman Dudley, at a loss for words, shuffled through his papers, trying to remember who was up next to lead the questioning. Behind him, one of his aides scribbled, 'Ekman,' onto a piece of scratch paper and leaned forward to set it before the Senator--

But before Dudley saw it, another Senator, another *Republican* no less, had pushed to his feet. He projected from his diaphragm as if he was addressing a town hall meeting, knowing his distance from his mic would add echo behind his words: "Admiral MacTavish, I applaud you." And indeed he did.

In no time, all the Democrats on the committee had joined, both with their hands and on their feet. The Republicans, even Miriam Ekman of Utah, were right behind them, as were their staffs. Soon, every member of the press, *everyone* in the committee room save Mac and Shareef were on their feet, fêting them with a full standing ovation.

Down the hall, as their prep staff cheered and hugged all around them, Reg and Rosemarie just looked at each other with those victorious grins that had become so familiar over the past three months. Rosemarie winked at Reg, and he just shrugged, conceding that she was, of course, always right.

At his table in the Judiciary chamber, Mac swiveled to Shareef, who didn't know whether he should be wiping the streaming tears off his cheeks or just letting them go and hoping the cameras wouldn't pick them up. Mac remembered his instructions from the Irvings, but at this moment, couldn't give less of a shit.

He reached over and laid his hand on top of Shareef's, squeezing as tightly as he could.

Mac and Shareef entered the prep room to another rousing standing ovation, barely 11 AM and already their third of the day. They had arrived an hour or two earlier than originally scheduled; Dudley had made a motion that the committee move to vote right after lunchtime, and the two members who had yet to ask questions – one Democrat, and of course, Senator Ekman – waived their turns, the greatest sign of respect they could offer for what the Admiral had just done. But the interrogation wasn't over, of course: Mac and Shareef were bombarded by the press on their way out. Shareef answered all the questions fired his way as naturally and effortlessly as a seasoned talking head.

An hour later, as Mac and Shareef made their way around the conference room table, trading hearty thank yous for each prep team member's congratulations, Rosemarie turned to her right, where Dennis could always be found, and said, "Thank you."

"It's my job, ma'am," he nodded back.

"And I've been trigger happy to criticize when you've struggled in that job. But this time you were perfect. If we hadn't known everything, right from the beginning, we wouldn't have been able to control it." She put her hands on his shoulders and squeezed hard, turning her eyes sideways to him with a coy grin. "You've gotten very good at research, haven't you?"

Dennis smiled back, using the strength in his every tendon, his every sinew, his every limb and every joint to try to keep from shaking while the First Lady's hands were touching him.

Shareef on the other hand was disappointed he didn't get the chance to speak to Rosemarie one last time and thank her for making everything work out. Before he had gotten around to that end of the table, the Irvings were on the move, being shuffled out for the hallway by their large African-American Secret Service guard--

Shareef froze, his brow furrowing with confusion. Either the black ICE agent who had arrested him two days ago had a twin brother, or he had in the last 48 hours switched to Secret Service and joined the Irvings' detail.

Dennis waited four brutal minutes after the Irvings had departed before he felt he could safely make his own escape. He waited until he was in the hallway, out of the eyes of any preppers or aides or interns who knew him, to pull out the small disposable flip phone he had been carrying in his left front pocket (his iPhone always went in his back right), thumbed it open and started tapping out a text. He recognized that Rosemarie's words were probably meant at face value, that she couldn't have had any idea of the extracurriculars in which he had been engaged, but regardless, his nerves had gotten way too frayed for his own good. He had to end this now, pass along what he knew to the authorities and get it out of his mind, or it would drive him insane. He would crack and expose himself to the wrong person.

Still on for 9, the text to George Aug read. *Dupont circle. North 19 st bench if it's open. DC.*

Dennis had gotten Aug's name weeks ago, from a friend who had moved from White House Counsel's office over to Homeland Security's legal department. He recommended this George Aug as the most honest, straight-shooting, no-bullshit, no-politics agent on the bombing investigation team. Dennis hoped he was right.

His conspiracy mural was going to be George Aug's problem now. Dennis had one more vet to get through. He had a girl he had fallen in love with that he should be spending his nights with. He *had* to get this out of his mind.

The report was much worse than Salas could have even imagined.

The President had retired to his study at around 5 to read the fat binder of information his national security team had prepared for him on the new Iran crisis: the list of all, even the most tenuous, links between the residents of the Pencil Pals halfway house and the Iranian government (of which there were embarrassingly few); a summary of the response in Tehran to the ramp up of hostile language in the American news media (daily parades of burning American flags and Salas dolls on nooses, as well as several terror groups releasing videos announcing plans for an attack on US soil); three possible invasion plans waiting for Salas's green light (at least one, if not two of these three plans resulting in decades of US occupation); and the most recent intelligence on what was believed to be the current state of the Iranian nuclear program (still very active, despite all best efforts to sabotage it in recent years).

POTUS had done his duty and given this material a cursory skim, but had then moved on to the real material he had come in here to digest. He unlocked his top desk drawer, pulled out the envelope Hifrael had given him, finished tearing it open and slid out the contents from inside.

His jaw went limp as he read through the Secret Service logs. He didn't expect Becks to have been the only woman for whom Reg had strayed, but the sheer volume of names was stupefying.

He spent 43 minutes sifting through this comprehensive report, going all the way back 12 years to the very first day the Irvings had a protection detail assigned to them, the day Reg clinched the Democratic nomination. The rest of that year alone, the future President had sexual encounters of some variety with at least three different women, all before he was inaugurated the following January. That was just the first five months of the one hundred forty-nine covered in the report; and by no stretch of the imagination did Reg slow down once he moved into 1600 Penn.

Salas was to a certain degree impressed; he thought he could see why Irving hadn't been outed as a louse the way Bill Clinton had numerous times in his early career. Reg had clearly made a point of not fucking interns or aides or girls just off the bus from Nebraska; he fucked powerful career women, ambitious women, many of them married themselves, who all had just as much to lose as he did should their dalliance become public. There were cabinet secretaries in this log, there were ambassadors, there was even one prominent chancellor of a Western European power.

And there was a Deputy Press Secretary, who would later become Salas's very own White House Chief of Staff.

His eyes happened to glance over the clock, and he jerked upright, realizing it was just after 6. He was late. The full Senate vote on MacTavish should've been complete (as he had in the Judiciary, Leader Dudley had pushed for a full confirmation before everyone went away for the long Martin Luther King weekend) and POTUS was due up in the West Sitting Room for a celebration. He locked his secret envelope back in its top drawer and shoved his binder of Iran materials under his left armpit to head upstairs.

He hadn't made any decisions on Iran yet; he had promised himself he would keep his mind open on how to proceed until he had consulted the one person whose advice he had come to trust implicitly. It would be against protocol and the security clearances to share the binder under his arm with Rosemarie. But he was President; who was to say he couldn't share it with, and seek the advice of, whomever he wished?

"Bartender!" he called out as he marched down the second floor's center hall. He was excited to see what beverage she had chosen to celebrate Admiral-- that is, *Justice* MacTavish's confirmation, a tradition began after getting their first two nominees through. He feared that, in a nod to the Navy, she would be waiting with some type of 'grog,' a putrid mixture of beer, wine, rum and fresh water that 18th-century sailors and pirates would drink to combat scurvy. "What's the drink special for tonight's happy hour--?"

The figure at the Betty Ford Bar turned to face the door. It wasn't Rosemarie, but her husband. Salas surveyed the couches, the corners of the room – she wasn't here. Just two Presidents.

"Sorry, Reg, I thought Rosemarie was meeting me--"

"She's at Walter Reed," Reg answered.

"What?"

Reg raised his hands to calm his predecessor. "It's Chief Quint. He has stage five kidney disease. He's been on dialysis for four years."

"Oh my God."

"We wouldn't have even known, but the doctors say it can exacerbate heart disease, and the Chief had a minor heart attack while Dennis was vetting him the other day."

Salas turned away, his eyes going to the carpet, mind spinning with the ramifications of this news. "That's it. The deadline is in a week. We'll never get another nominee vetted in time." He turned back to Irving. "We're going to have to settle for eight Justices for the rest of this year and have one ready to go right after the election."

"Actually," Reg smiled, "we have another idea."

There were still people who picked up hitchhikers, especially in the part of the country where Jason had spent his last two and a half months. The dusk sky was still purple when he broke through the snow and reached the sweet pavement of State Road 33. After a half-hour or so of walking its shoulder, a large FoodTown truck appeared on the horizon. The driver responded to his thumb and chauffeured him out of the park. He had originally entered the Huron from Mio in the

North, but now emerged in its southern opposite, Rose City, an even smaller hamlet with just over a quarter Mio's population.

Jason had the trucker drop him at the Dairy Queen off 33, where he figured he could get dinner and start to make a plan for what the hell to do next, how to follow up with the only clue Miranda had given him: *Follow the money.*

He had just inhaled his first quarter-pound Grillburger when the television above the TV turned to local news:

"*... unit for the military contractors based out of Detroit is being hailed as heroes nationwide for their deadly firefight with a Michigan militia accused of harboring some of the perpetrators of October's bombing of the Supreme Court.*"

On the screen, a handcuffed Miranda was led through a throng of press, trying to keep her face down and out of the various camera lights as Allied Armament soldiers pushed the lenses out of the way and led her to the back of one of their matte-black Hummers.

"*Today they announced the arrest of Miranda Whitney, formerly the Marshal, that's the chief law enforcement and administrative officer, of the Court. Allied Armament, in conjunction with Homeland Security, is now asking for any information that might lead to the whereabouts of this man, Jason Lancaster, Whitney's subordinate at the Court and the primary suspect in the bombing. Allied Armament today released this chilling video of Lancaster inside the Court the night before the bombing.*"

Jason's tray bounced as he shot to his feet. The news anchor had been replaced by surveillance footage. There was the statue of John Marshall, the portraits of the Chiefs – it was the Court all right.

And there he was, walking down the Great Hall. All was dark, and the timestamp in the corner of the screen read, **7 OCT 03:08:12 AM**. The image of Jason was soon right beneath the camera, firing his flashlight up into its lens – and it went dark, as if he had hit it with some sort of jamming pulse.

The footage was HD; that was him, but how had someone done that? They could've just changed the date stamp, of course, but Jason was sure he had never been at the Court in the middle of the night, after it had been closed. And he definitely wasn't at the Court the night before the bombing.

Or was he? He realized he still had only scant memories of what had occurred between finding Miranda at Bullfeathers and waking up at home at 8:11 AM the next morning.

"If you or anyone you know has had any contact with this man," the anchor's voice continued over Jason's official Court photograph, "*please call the number at the bottom of the screen. And proceed with caution. The suspect should be considered armed and extremely dangerous.*"

Jason could feel all activity around him slowing, the father of four putting down his burger, the teenager in her cheer outfit freezing with fries half-chewed in her mouth, the cashier pausing in the middle of typing in an order. Every pair of eyes turned to him, stared at him, quivering with the recognition of a terrorist they had just seen on their local news feed.

Jason was already gone, half his food left uneaten on his plate. He continued his walk south, thumb held high, thankful that no one would be able to see his photo on their car radio.

"Sit Room!" POTUS announced to Delores as he shot out of his study and stormed by her desk. She yanked her phone out of its cradle and shoved it between shoulder and chin, starting a phone tree while also sending out a mass email to the other secretaries whose bosses would be required.

Hifrael was on Salas's heels, buzzing into his wrist, "Aguila on the move, Aguila moving." He stayed three paces behind the President onto the elevator at the end of the corridor, riding down with him to the ground floor, then made sure he exited just a step ahead so he could use his own swipe card, then his own thumb print, to get them past the two reinforced doors into the Situation Room.

The Joint Chiefs, the National Security staff, all were just trickling in through the room's other two doors as Salas marched to the head of the table. With the next move in the Iran conundrum up in the air, they had all taken temporary offices at the White House, available for any Sit Room meeting like this one without having to travel up from the Pentagon. (Still, Vice President Ruby wouldn't get there for ten more minutes and would spend the next two months bitching that it was over before he arrived.)

Salas looked right to Admiral Percy Holmes, head honcho of the Navy, the first Joint Chief to have found his seat. That was perfect, because what Salas was about to do concerned the Navy more than any other branch of his military. He couldn't wait for Rosemarie's counsel any longer, not with her mind now occupied with grief over Chief Quint and the new task he had given her. And there would be plenty of opportunity for her to advise him in the coming weeks.

Salas held the Iran binder over his head. "The third plan in here--"

"Attack Plan Gamma, Sir," Holmes nodded.

"How quickly can we get the strike groups into the Gulf?"

Holmes traded eyes with his fellow Joint Chiefs, then back over his shoulder to his Operations Deputy, who darted out – Salas hadn't even given an order yet, but the wheels were already starting to spin. "Strike Group Twelve, the *Roosevelt*, Sir, she's in the Arabian Sea. We'll get you an exact ETA, but I would imagine they can be there in a matter of hours. The other three CSGs will take some time--"

"Get them there. Four strike groups, just like you proposed in here." He tapped the cardboard cover of the binder three times with a hard finger. He was well aware this was the first serious military action of his Presidency: four aircraft carriers carrying over thirty squadrons of fighter jets, eight guided missile ships, a handful of *Los Angeles*-class attack subs, and over twenty thousand American men and women, all converging on Iran's shores in the coming weeks. "Get them there. I want everyone to know we're serious, that we're thinking about this." He held up a finger, pointing it in the Admiral's face. "But that's it for now. They hold there and wait for my order. No one sneezes on that country until I say so."

He about faced and walked out. "Sir!" the Joint Chiefs announced in unison, leaping to their feet in deference to their leader who, for the first time in the four years of his Presidency, felt like a Commander-in-Chief.

Janaki was ready to say it.

It had made her sick to her stomach whenever she thought about how their conversation had gone down Wednesday night, whenever she reflected on how she had left Dennis out to dry like she had. She had resolved right after they had hung up that night that she would say it the next time she saw him in person, even if it was at work, even if they were both coming out of the bathroom.

But she hadn't seen him. He had been at Russell for the last two days, while she was cramped up in Justice Goldman's office in the Capitol helping write his first opinion.

She would see him tonight, finally. The MacTavish confirmation was signed, sealed and delivered, and Dennis had also promised that he was about to complete that extra project he had been working on, freeing up all his evening and weekend time to devote to her. He would be turning in his final report, and then heading right over to her place to celebrate. They would have the weekend together. He had a feeling the Irvings would want him in the Capitol helping weed out possible replacements for Quint, but he didn't care. He was going to turn his phone off and just spend all weekend wrapped up in her arms.

Janaki had decided she couldn't wait any longer. She had to say it now, even if it was over the phone. She wanted to say it to him over the phone and then again in person and then in bed and over breakfast and all through the weekend and the rest of their lives. She knew his meeting was at 9, and called him at 8:40, thinking he would be in transit. She got his voicemail, so she tried again seven minutes later. Maybe he was in the Metro. And again five minutes after that. Where the hell was this meeting anyway?

It was on that third call that she just said, *Fuck it,* to herself.

"Coutts, it's me. Maybe this is terrible I'm going to say it over your voicemail, but we're lawyers. I thought you might want this as an official record under oath that I did say it. And maybe you'll like having it to listen to whenever one of us is too busy working to talk. *I love you.* I've never been in love before, and yet, I know with every fiber of my soul that that's what I feel for you. I can't wait to see you and say it again and spend the rest of the weekend and the rest of the year and the rest of who-knows-how-long together. Ha! Now look who's gone too far. I don't give a shit. I love you, Dennis Coutts, and together, we're gonna go as far as we want in this world."

Dupont Circle was a great choice for their meet, George had thought on the Metro ride up. It was enough blocks out of the center of Washington that they would be unlikely to run into anyone either of them knew from work (this assuming that 'DC' had been truthful about being a part of the judicial search committee). And anyone they should run into would assume they were there not to trade in state secrets, but in sexual congress; after dark, this green circle where Massachusetts, Connecticut and New Hampshire Avenues NW, and P and 19th Streets NW all converged, ceased being a trendy people-watching point and became a way station for druggies on the hunt for a fix or gay men cruising for a quickie. George figured now that DC must be a male, otherwise why pick this circle? No one would bat an eye at two men getting to know one another on one of the park benches facing in from the circle's outer edge.

But George struck out on the kind of score he was yearning for tonight. His pal in S&T believed his texts had come from a burner that had probably already been discarded. At least, it sure seemed that way: George had sent him three texts since it turned 9 PM forty minutes earlier – *Am I in the wrong spot? / Where are you? / You okay?* All had gone unanswered.

After an hour, George decided to throw in the towel. Part of him wanted to stay all night, but he knew DC must have gotten cold feet. He rose from the bench, and decided to walk the long way around the circle, giving him time to write one last message before submerging in the south 19th Street Metro entrance. But tired of having his texts go unanswered, George muttered, "What the heck?" to himself and pushed the 'Call' tab instead. Why not try to call this kid and see if by some crazy stroke of luck he picks up?

George hadn't even brought the speaker to his ear when an array of flashing lights pulled his eyes up to the eastern mouth of Mass Ave. Two ambulances, a fire truck, yellow tape and several on-lookers surrounded a body on the ground, its face covered in a shroud. Someone had been hit and killed trying to cross the street. George shook his head at the fleeting nature of life.

And then he heard a phone ringing. The cops and paramedics converged on the body, digging under the blanket and reaching into the deceased's pocket to pull out a lit-up flip phone.

George looked down at his own phone, attempting to ring through to DC's burner. He thumbed the red button – and the ringing in the paramedic's gloved hand cut off mid-stream.

ONE WEEK LATER

The doctors had predicted that Chief Quint wouldn't leave his bed again, that he had only weeks to live, that he should expect another heart event soon, and that this next one could be much, much worse. None of this stopped him from asking Darline to help him into a crisp white shirt, or from looping up his favorite tie around his neck in preparation for a visit from his favorite clerk of all time. None of this stopped him from asking Darline to fix bloody marys with celery stalks, pickled green beans and plenty of tabasco, upon Rosemarie's arrival. ("And we never have to suffer through virgin ones ever again," he winked to Rosemarie as he took his first sip.) None of this stopped him from holding court, so to speak, on the history of the judicial branch, as he always did for his favorite pupil. This would be her final lesson; later today, she was finally going to graduate.

"*Brown* could have started another Civil War, if not for Warren. Even before his recess appointment was made official, he was working the Justices, needling them. Hammering them for a *unanimous* decision, until he'd convinced every last one of them. 'We can't leave any opening for those segregationists to say they have a rational, legitimate counterargument. We have to *bury* their argument. We can't leave them one intellectual leg to stand on.' You can almost imagine his words, can't you?" Quint didn't reveal that he had *actually* heard Warren's words, heard all the tapes of all the conferences in which *Brown v. Board of Education* was discussed; Quint believed in the rules of the Court almost above all else, and knew Rosemarie would be informed of the conference recordings when the time was right. He wasn't going to bend that rule prematurely. "And he got them all, even Jackson and Reed. The Court issued one singular decision, in one voice. Not one dissent. And then, five years later, he knew they had to do it again with *Cooper v. Aaron.*" Quint shook his head and chuckled with admiration. "He was a political master, Earl Warren. That unanimous decision in *Brown*, that was one of the most important *political* decisions in our nation's history." He snaked his fingers up through her left hand, giving it as good a squeeze as he could muster now. "You don't ever let anyone tell you it's not a political body.

It's all about politics. And it took me less than a week to identify you as the best politician I'd ever had in my chambers."

"Thank you, I think?"

Quint put his drink down, so he could pat her hand between his, assuring her of his complete belief, his total trust in her. His eyes passed over the television, past the endless CNN coverage of the protests spreading across America's streets: demonstrations against last month's Iranian halfway house tragedy in a dozen blue states, vigils for the militiamen slaughtered by Allied Armament in several red.

"You have all the votes you need?" The muted pictures had put Quint's mind back on business.

Rosemarie raised her eyebrows. "It won't be unanimous, like *Brown.*"

Quint shook his head. "I'm not sure any important one ever will be again. Ideology has become more important than history."

"But I understand it was 4-2 when they conferenced it in December. After our final confirmation, it'll have swung 5-4 our way."

"Be careful. No vote is ever a sure thing."

Rosemarie was about to concur, when she heard the nurse coming in. "It's time for Myra to give you your dialysis, Dear," Darline announced, entering right behind her.

Rosemarie stood. "And I have to get going. Kind of a big day."

She started to turn away, when the Chief's hands pulled her back one last time. She looked down into his eyes. This moment right here, even after all the years they had been through, was the weakest he had ever looked to her. The realization dampened her eyes. "Rosemarie. Thank God you're here."

"*Your country needs you,*" they whispered together in unison.

She was able to hold back the tears until the backdoor of her Escalade was closed, wiping them from her cheeks as MMA whisked her to the White House.

The Old Supreme Court Chamber was closed to all but the Court personnel on Friday morning, its seats about a third full with clerks and Court police. Behind the wood railing under the east arcade, seven of the eight thrones were occupied, including Justice MacTavish's on the far left. The empty chair belonged to Justice Goldman, who stood before it to address the room. "Though Dennis Coutts was never officially vested as a member of this Court, his assistance to a great many of us made him a member of the Court family. To some, he became even more than that." Goldman was well aware when he wrote that line that he would have to avoid Janaki's eyes when he said it; the tears streaming down her face would only make him break too, only prevent him from continuing. He didn't look at anyone in particular as he recited them, just looked across the room to a nebulous spot on the west wall like a yogi trying to keep his balance in a difficult pose.

"We are honored today to be joined by Dennis's first family, his parents Hok'ee and Elizabeth, who have come all the way from Arizona to help us honor him." He moved his eyes down to the front row, to Dennis's family, the only four people in this room who didn't work for the Court. "They have shared with me that Dennis's greatest dream was to become a clerk of this Court, a dream none of us have any trouble imagining was destined to come true in the very near future. So today, they have agreed to help me make sure that Dennis's dream does come true."

He gestured with an open hand to the railing, and Dennis's parents stood and stepped forward, leaving his two young brothers in their seats. Goldman held out a Bible, and Mrs. Coutts placed her hand on it (when they had walked through a rehearsal an hour earlier, his father had refused, which Goldman said was fine, he understood, and one hand on the book was all they would need).

"We, the parents of Dennis Yiska Coutts," Goldman began, reading off the copy of the usual oath onto which he had scribbled some alterations appropriate to the occasion.

"We, the parents of Dennis Yiska Coutts," they followed along.

"... who has been appointed a clerk of this Supreme Court ..."

"... who has been appointed a clerk of this Supreme Court ..."

"... do solemnly swear on his behalf that he will truly and faithfully enter and record all orders, decrees, judgments and proceedings of this court ..."

Janaki didn't hear a word of the oath. She couldn't see anything through her tear-logged contacts. She wouldn't remember meeting Dennis's parents, or the celebration lunch that followed this ceremony, or any part of the rest of this day.

The Coutts family would get the VIP treatment not just at the Capitol, but also the White House. Rosemarie Irving, their son's mentor, had escorted them there in her own Escalade, then led them on an all-access tour of her home of eight years, culminating in the East Room, where she set them up in the front row of chairs in front of all the media members waiting to hear the President announce his nominee for the final open seat on the Supreme Court, the Chief Justice's seat.

Rosemarie knelt before them, her right hand on Mrs. Coutts's knee, her left on Mr. Coutts's. "I hope you know, we wouldn't have gotten here – *this country* wouldn't have gotten here – if not for your son. You should be so proud."

They nodded their thanks; she patted their legs, stood and walked down the red carpet, to the doors of the Green Room. The President was just coming in from the hallway entrance at the same time, his eyes reviewing the remarks one of his communications deputies had just handed to him. "Do you even need those at this point?" Rosemarie joked.

He shrugged, then tucked the paper into an inner coat pocket. "You know what, you're right. I don't think I do. I know this nominee pretty damn well."

"I'd say you do, yes."

"Actually, something I haven't told you … I almost suggested this nominee, before we went with Quint."

"Really? Why didn't you?"

Salas paused, realizing he couldn't answer that truthfully without outing his favorite Secret Service agent. "This last one … I have a feeling they're going to play ugly. It's their last chance."

"Don't you think we know all their dirty tricks by now?"

Salas looked away, keenly aware of the vile direction the next set of hearings could take. That was his only hesitation in making this choice, but with such limited time, he knew there was no other he *could* make.

"There's just one thing I've had trouble getting my head around," he murmured to Rosemarie as they stepped up near the Green Room doors and watched POTUS's Press Secretary present the order of events to the gathered crowd.

"What's that?"

"You've been close friends with Chief Quint, with the Quint family, since you were a clerk. I understand you guys even spend a couple holidays with them each year. And you really didn't know he was sick?"

Rosemarie stared at him coyly, whether because she had been caught or just enjoyed teasing him, he would never be sure. "And what if I did know all along? Would that give you second thoughts?"

He bored back into her with his own eyes. "That would make me want you all the more."

"... and gentlemen, the President of the United States." On cue, Salas bounded down the red carpet.

Christian Sacerdoti and his fiancée Shelly had a standing agreement to never make Friday night plans. The rest of the week was a social whirl for the king and queen of the Conservative Camelot – political events sponsored by Freedom-Lovers, Sacerdoti's very own SuperPAC; dinners with political aspirants hoping to win their blessing and more importantly, some of their ever-flowing 'dark money;' fundraisers at which they could give back to those less fortunate while getting their photos snapped for society pages – but come Friday nights, Sacerdoti was so exhausted he wasn't even pleasant to be around. Shelly would stay in her Upper East Side apartment on Friday nights, while Christian crashed in his Nolita loft. He would pick her up on Saturday morning for whatever the first event of their weekend might be, as refreshed as the morning after a spring rain. Friday nights he must have gotten his best night's sleep of the week, she figured, and she never took it personally.

What she didn't know was that Friday night was Hooker Night.

Though he acknowledged Shelly would never understand, Christian didn't think there was anything wrong with Hooker Night. It kept his legendary sexual appetites sated (his life would never have turned out like this if that girl he had gotten rough with at Stanford had decided to press charges); after a Hooker Night, he was less aggressive with Shelly, less nasty and frustrated with the rarity of her own hungers. And it wasn't like he was being *truly* unfaithful, *emotionally* unfaithful to her with these women. A man knew the difference between sex and love; the two weren't always a package deal. *Why can't women comprehend that?* he would ask himself. He never stopped loving Shelly since that first moment he had seen her in a Rand Paul campaign office in Lexington. But these women, these *professional* women, they just knew how to turn him inside out.

Nic, Leesa and Jessy had a new bouncer with them when they arrived on Friday night, but Christian didn't give it a second thought. He would be waiting out in the living room, after all, while Christian had his fun.

"We got something special planned for you tonight," Jessy purred, dragging her claws along Christian's chin as she led the girls in.

"What would you think about turning the eyes in the sky off tonight?" Leesa asked after they were all into their second drinks.

"You know I can't do that."

Nic slinked up to him, bringing her lips right to his ear to say, "We can only do what we're planning to do if we have some privacy. You're not gonna want any record of what we've got planned." She gave his burgeoning bulge a good grip before she walked away, her teammates joining in on her seductive laughter.

Christian chuckled, then grabbed the nearest wireless, dialing the code into the security office. "Mike, it's me. I need some privacy for the next hour. No, I know, everything will be fine. You mind shutting off all your eyes?"

In immediate response, the red lights in each upper corner of the room, from each surveillance cam, went dark. The girls giggled their approval, then each took a different extremity of Sacerdoti's and led him into the bedroom, leaving the bouncer out in the living room with the TV.

The most fun part for Christian was always seeing who would play what role on a particular night: Which one would turn on the house music and start a seductive strip on his left? Which one would grab his right hand and bring it up and under her skirt, pushing his fingers up inside her? Which one would work on his belt, pulling down his pants until his growing member was unfolded from his boxer briefs, then start working on its tip with her tongue, stroking him with one hand while bringing her other fingers up and under and between his ass cheeks, penetrating his most forbidden hole with one of her sharp talons?

It was Leesa stripping on this Friday night, and Leesa who revealed the big surprise, pulling a vial of white powder out from between her cleavage as she danced. "Oh, I like this surprise," Christian hummed his approval as she poured thin white lines on a wrist, then a shoulder blade, then a breast, letting him snort each one off. He quivered as she bent over in his face, taking down her panties so her womanhood stared right back at him. She dipped her finger in the coke, then dabbed it along the edges of her wet hood. He giggled with delight as she straddled him, lowering her frosted womanhood onto his face and letting him lick the narcotics off.

He heard a jangle as she spun around above his chest, revealing she had also come armed with hand cuffs. "Yes, yes, yes!" he growled, and Leesa lifted his right wrist, locking it to the bed post. Nic was already on his other hand with her own set of manacles, doing the same, completing this portrait of a debauched, coked-out Christ. He didn't notice that Jessy had moved off his cock and back to her phone, from which she was sending a text.

The double doors to the bedroom slammed open off the bottom of the bouncer's boot. The hookers yelped as he charged right to the prone Sacerdoti. "Hey, what the fu--" the young billionaire got out before the hooks of a taser landed in his chest. They screamed as Christian convulsed with 1200 volts of electricity. One of the girls was sneaking up on the bodyguard from behind, vase held high to clock him out--

"Get the fuck out!" The bouncer spun around, .45 pointed in her face, eliciting a chorus of gasps. "Out! Right the fuck now!" He swiveled the gun from one girl to the next. They grabbed their clothes and sprinted out into the living room.

"Mother fucker! You said he'd like what you were going--"

"Out! Your money's on the counter!" he yelled out after them, then waited until he heard the front door slam, the footsteps silenced.

"You're so … fucked …" Sacerdoti dribbled out onto his chin. "Someone is … coming …"

"Actually, by my watch," Jason Lancaster checked his wrist, "we've got another 46 minutes of privacy left."

Jason had spent the last week doing just as Miranda had advised, following the money. And he had called in reinforcements to do this: Miranda's kid brother Ollie.

"Ollie, I need you on this. *Rand* needs you on this. Let's go back to the hospital."

"What's the fucking point, man, you forget it was a dead end?"

"It just came back to life."

Ollie sent Jason everything he had found on Detroit's United Community Hospital two months ago, including everything on the real estate entity that owned it, the April Group Property Development. Nothing had ever been published in the media about who owned this group, just its face men, its figureheads, its CEO and CFO whose names would top any press releases regarding new acquisitions.

Jason and Ollie had to go to the source. Jason got himself to New York on Wednesday and paid a visit to the April Group's midtown offices. Getting access to their network was easy from there – all he had to do was find some unsuspecting secretary who would believe he was from the IT department and needed to run a quick update on her computer. He could plug the thumb drive Ollie had sent him into any of the computer's USB ports and in seconds, a screen sharing program would be downloaded which would give Ollie the ability to access this computer remotely. He then waited until late into the evening hours, when there was no doubt that secretary had gone home for the night (and when Ollie's evening was just getting started anyway) to go hunting for internal memos, documents or files that might offer clues to the owners of the April Group and United Community.

The list of controlling partners was short and offered almost as many dead ends as answers. Several of the owners weren't human beings, but other corporations or trusts that would require just as much work to tear open. But there was one name that fired off firecrackers in Jason's head: Christian Sacerdoti.

You couldn't live in Washington without hearing the name Christian Sacerdoti. He was just as infamous, just as talked-about, as any cabinet secretary, as any member of Congress. He was perhaps the man most despised by the liberal sect, having personally made the Republican takeover of both houses of Congress in the last midterms possible with his SuperPAC money. He had become the living embodiment of the One Percent buying elections, of *Citizens United*, of the Liberal's worst nightmare.

Jason had always remained apolitical (or if anything, leaned Right, having been raised that way), and hated the idea that this billionaire might be even more villainous than the cartoonish conceptions of him on the Left. But everyone who worked at the Supreme Court knew that Sacerdoti had a petition into the Justices. It wasn't that Jason kept on top of every cert petition to pass through the Court's doors, but when you're working with a clerk base that's 75 percent liberal, there are some cases you start hearing about in the corridors, in the cafeteria, on the basketball court on the Court's third floor well over a year or two in advance.

Sacerdoti's case was one of those cases. Hoping to curb the out-of-control *Citizens United*-inspired campaign spending in their state, the bleeding blue California legislature had resoundingly passed a bill outlawing contributions from out-of-state entities. Sacerdoti sued the state, claiming a violation of federal election laws, and a suppression of his free speech. If ever following the money would lead you to a case, this was the one.

That alone of course wouldn't have convinced Jason of Sacerdoti's guilt. But his 52 percent ownership of April Group Property Development, and through it,

United Community Hospital, sealed it. United Community was where the bombs used at the Court had been tested a week prior to the attack.

United Community was where the surveillance video of Jason had *really* been filmed.

Jason knew something about the surveillance video seemed familiar when he first saw it in the Dairy Queen, but he was too shocked, too concerned about the other patrons suddenly staring at him, to process it at the time. It would require a couple more viewings, which every network and cable news show in the country made easy with their incessant replaying of it.

It was his hand holding the flashlight as he brought its beam up into the surveillance lens that provided the answer. *What was that white bulge around his knuckles?*

A sock. A bloody fucking sock.

It was the sock he had wrapped around them after that stupid bar brawl in Detroit, the same exact night – right before, in fact – Dean Rikeman let him into the hospital. That video wasn't from the Court, it wasn't from October; it was from Detroit in November. Someone with the skills of a Hollywood VFX artist had lifted his image from the hospital and transposed it into video of the Court.

Jason explained all of this to George over Sacerdoti's phone as he held the conservative kingpin, still handcuffed to the posts of his bed, at gunpoint. "I've got him, George. I've got the guy this all started with."

"Haven't you been watching the news, Jason? This isn't my investigation anymore. I shouldn't even be talking to you. That video--"

"It's a fake. It's from Detroit. Someone lifted my image from a different video and put it over shots of the Court."

"You're going to have to explain that to a Grand Jury now. Allied Armament took the video to the DOJ, they have a warrant for you--"

"And where did Allied Armament get it?"

"I don't know."

"What do you mean, you don't know?"

"They wouldn't tell us. They brought it to us, they said it was real, and the guys above me went with it."

Jason's mind spun. Allied Armament had control of the hospital. Could they be running that live surveillance camera he had found inside? Could they have been the ones who used his image to make the fake video?

Jason's whole visit to Polis had been a set up. Miranda had explained that. It was Dean Rikeman who had first suggested he find the Minutemen, Dean Rikeman who had showed him that very convenient photo of Miranda embedded with the militia. Two months later, Dean Rikeman had led a battalion to that militia's compound to arrest Jason in front of live TV cameras.

And the guy who had given Jason the coordinates of the compound didn't actually have a wife and daughter stuck there. Jason had asked a dozen different people; there had never been an 'Evelyn' or a 'Hope' at Polis. Could that guy have worked for Allied Armament too? Christian Sacerdoti, after all, wasn't the only one with a case pending at the Court.

Allied Armament also had a case on the Supreme Court's docket.

"Hey," he spit at Sacerdoti, "what do you know about Allied Armament?" He crossed around the side of the bed, digging the barrel of his pistol into Christian's temple.

"What …?"

"Allied Armament, the security contractor. They have anything to do with this?"

"I told you, *I* don't have anything to do with this," he sobbed. "I don't know any of this shit you're talking about, man, I swear. I haven't even heard about that company since I was asked to invest in it …"

"What? Someone wanted you to invest in Allied Armament?"

"A long time ago, right when they were just starting, one of the other partners in my real estate company. But I didn't do it, I have nothing to do with that company, I promise you."

"All the other partners in your real estate company are trusts and corporations. I need a name."

"Fuck. The name doesn't matter. I never even meet with them, I just know their money guy. It's a blind trust, they probably don't even know about it."

"Christian. You do realize I'm wanted for murdering about 124 people?" Jason pushed the gun in harder, moving his finger from atop the trigger guard down onto the firing mechanism. "You think one more's gonna make one bit of difference in my sentence?"

"No, no, man, please, I'm, I'm getting married-- She's a sweet girl, you gotta--"

"*A name, Christian.*"

Christian's eyes suddenly went wide. "Oh my fucking God." He wasn't looking at Jason, or Jason's gun. Jason followed his gaze out into the living room, where he had left the TV running while waiting for the hooker's text that the handcuffs were on. News images from earlier in the day filled the screen: Rosemarie Irving stepping out next to President Salas at his East Room podium.

The red bar at the bottom of the screen read, '***PRESIDENT NOMINATES FIRST LADY TO BE FIRST FEMALE CHIEF JUSTICE***.'

Janaki had decided she was going to break in, but that wouldn't be necessary. When she reached the sidewalk right below Dennis's apartment, she noticed the lights on up in his window. She was tempted to turn back, but wouldn't be deterred from her mission.

"Hello," Mrs. Coutts answered her knock.

"Mrs. Coutts, I'm Janaki. We met briefly at the Court today."

"You were a friend of Dennis's?"

Janaki paused. She realized she didn't know what the hell she was. They had never established titles, never discussed any sort of official exclusivity, things were just happening. "Yeah. I … left something in his room."

Mrs. Coutts smiled, as if she understood what that meant. She opened the door for Janaki to enter. She was introduced to the other family members packing up boxes in the living room, then quickly made her way to the back. She didn't want to linger, lest the reality of what they were doing set in, and the deluge start yet again.

Janaki opened Dennis's closet and knelt before his laundry hamper. She pulled out a T-shirt and brought it to her nose. It was *him.* All that remained of him. That sweet, young, energetic, uniquely Dennis smell was still on the shirt.

She shoved it in her purse. She tried one or two others, but none of them had retained their Dennisness as well as that first one. It would have to get her through this week. She hoped it lasted that long. She stood to make her way out--

But the strange artwork on the wall opposite the bed gave her pause. It was a collage that the art director of a serial killer film could very well have crafted. Lines of taut colored string wrapped around thumbtacks, linking notecards to photo copied documents, to a timeline, to a map, to photos of Chief Quint, and Justice Winks, and Rosemarie Irving.

Janaki reached back into her purse and pulled out her iPhone, opening the camera app and raising it to the wall.

LONE DISSENT

BOOK FIVE OF THE SIX-PART CONSPIRACY THRILLER
FOUR SEATS

THE SECOND MONDAY OF FEBRUARY

"Thank you, ladies and gentlemen, members of the United States Congress, and Supreme Court Justices both senior and new," Jason heard the President's voice echo from speakers lining the East Room as he topped the stairs on the State Floor. He kept his head down as he moved for the door to the Green Room, and only one Secret Service agent gave him even a sideways glance as he passed. Jason held up his old Supreme Court Police badge, his thumb strategically placed to cover most of his name. The agent responded with a half-smile and turned back to the nearest door to eavesdrop on the speech.

Jason laid his left fingers on the handle to the Green Room door, but before opening it, looked both ways down the corridor, then moved his right hand behind the small of his back, up under his jacket, removing the plastic .357 pistol from his jeans and pushing open the door. *Don't just start blasting away*, he reminded himself of his plan. *Force a confession. Clear Miranda's name. Make sure the world knows she was just a pawn, once and for all.*

"… I knew that whoever took the center chair," POTUS's voice rang through the open door on the opposite side of the room, "would inherit a Court at the most tumultuous moment in its history …" *You've got no idea,* Jason thought. Salas's nominee for Chief was the only other person in the Green Room, a silhouette filling that open door leading out onto the red carpet and the President's podium.

Jason raised his gun, aiming its mouth at the perfect spot to penetrate through to his target's spleen. The bullets were only plastic too, but when they hit just the right spot at a close enough range, they had been known to be lethal.

"I know you planned the bombing," he said in a low voice, just loud enough for the other occupant of the room to hear, but not enough to carry out into the East Room or for a microphone recording the press event to pick up.

Rosemarie Irving turned around with slow and calm, as if she had been expecting these words for weeks. Jason swallowed, blinking the sweat out of his eyes. He was face to face with the person who had ruined his life.

"I know who you are," she answered. "I'm very sorry you got caught up in all of this."

"*You* blew up the Court," Jason continued, punctuating his words with the nose of his gun. "And I know why." He reached into his pocket, pulling out the simple little digital dictaphone he had cash purchased at a Best Buy only two days earlier. He thumbed the red button, and aimed the tiny microphone hole in her direction. "You're going to talk. You're going to explain it all for me."

"Jason," Rosemarie opened her palms, trying to calm him with her eyes. "Whatever you think you might know, I can explain what's really going--"

"I know everything! You're a majority shareholder in Allied Armament!" Jason's forefinger tapped up and down on the white trigger guard, as if it had a mind of its own. "Their Supreme Court case will determine the whole future of the company. There are billions on the line. Unimaginable future power."

"I know all that, Jason. And I'm the only one who knows how to stop them. You have to trust me. You have misread my motives. If you kill me, you will make Allied Armament invincible. Justice will never be served."

Jason shook his head with a whimper, then swabbed the streams of sweat off his forehead with the back of the hand holding the glowing-red recorder. He had expected her to be persuasive; he had prepared himself for that. But he didn't expect these doubts burrowing into twelve different places of his brain, clouding his whole plan with confusion. He thought he would be so confident, so sure. Instead, he found himself wishing he had time to hear her out, a chance to judge if she was possibly telling the truth-

But there was so little time. Jason knew there might already be an agent behind him, ready to pounce. Every precious last second had to be spent compelling her, *forcing her* to confess.

He moved his forefinger from the guard, down onto the trigger. He tried to hold it there, but it vibrated against the mold, like he had just chugged a whole thermos of caffeine.

Rosemarie could smell his frantic nerves, and started to herself panic. "Jason, if you just give me a chance, I can prove all this to you!"

"… there is no doubt in my mind," the unaware President was continuing out at his podium, "that the person I selected to replace the late Chief Justice Lapadula is better qualified, prepared and willing to lead our Court into its future than any other human being on this planet. Ladies and gentlemen, I am truly humbled to introduce to you, the next Chief--"

The gunshot cut Salas off mid-sentence.

Everyone exhaled that strange mix of gasp and scream that signaled the start of a horrific crisis, most ducking for cover as Secret Service agents yanked out side arms and rushed in front of POTUS, his personal guard Hifrael Fernandez shoving him to the ground with one hand as he screamed into his opposite wrist for a report.

On the floor behind the podium, Salas felt around his chest, then pulled his white shirt taut to check for red. Nothing. Wherever or from whomever that shot had originated, it hadn't hit him.

"The Green Room, the shot came from the Green Room!" he heard Hifrael yell to his men, several of them rushing down the red carpet back into the room from whence the President had emerged moments ago.

The Green Room.

Salas rose, puffing his chest to follow his men. But Hifrael grabbed him from behind, hard, holding the former Team USA goalkeeper in place. "No, Sir," he whispered in Español. "This is our job." Salas nodded, but grit his teeth in agony. If shots had been fired in the Green Room, he knew who they were intended for. The target had been his new Chief Justice.

The target had been Rosemarie.

BOOK FIVE

LONE DISSENT

FIFTEEN DAYS EARLIER
A FRIDAY IN JANUARY

Jason had never intended to get out of New York alive. He knew going into Christian Sacerdoti's home that even if he coerced a confession out of the GOP money man, none of it would be admissible. Sacerdoti would lawyer up the minute he landed in official custody and it would probably take DHS Officer George Aug weeks to put together the evidence he needed to bring him in properly, weeks that Miranda and Jason would continue to be the lead suspects in the bombing, weeks that the video doctored to show Jason stalking the halls of the Court would remain the most powerful piece of 'evidence' in the case, especially in the court of public opinion.

But Christian Sacerdoti wasn't involved with the bombing, or at least, Jason didn't believe so anymore, not after hearing the genuine fear and confusion behind his gunpoint denials. The visit to his Nolita loft had still been of great value to Jason, as the whole exchange had opened his eyes to another entity with its very future at stake in the next Supreme Court term: Allied Armament Security Consultants.

Jason had scoffed five months earlier when he had heard some clerks just back from their Labor Day weekends theorizing over the lunch table that an Allied Armament victory in *Agguire v. Detroit* could remove any limitations or restrictions on the type of accounts the contractor could legally take on. Win that case, one clerk feared, and the company would have the legal right to do what their founder had boasted in a recent, much-shared *Time* interview: replace the entire United States military. But months later, Jason heard George recount the contractors' extensive involvement in the investigation, and instantly realized how his own interactions with them had all been manipulations designed to lead him to the Minutemen and make him look like a right wing nutjob. *They really believe it's possible. That's their motive. We're not just talking billions of dollars, we're talking an eventual seat at the Joint Chiefs table, maybe a Secretaryship for its founder. Real American power on the line. More than enough motive to sacrifice 124 American lives, chump change collateral damage in order to take out four Justices. With the right influence, those four Justices could turn into four votes in their favor.*

And it just so happened the person influencing the selection of all four new Justices – the person nominated to be the next Chief Justice herself – sat on the Allied Armament board.

Like the snap of a match to fiery life, everything that had occurred in the past three months instantly made sense to him. Only a finely-honed military unit could have been pulled off such an attack so seamlessly. And this same military unit had influenced so many of Jason's own decisions. He had been their pawn. Was Miranda their pawn too? What was her connection to them? What did they have to do with the kidnapping of the son Jason never knew she had?

Jason had intended all along to be on the phone with Aug from Sacerdoti's apartment no longer than five minutes, or maybe seven or eight max if absolutely necessary. This was the first time Jason had called George directly in three months, a precaution against the likelihood that George's phone had been tapped. As soon as Jason realized he was in the wrong place – that Allied Armament and Rosemarie Irving, not Sacerdoti, were his real targets – he put his escape plan in motion. He returned to the kitchen and went out the service door to the undecorated elevator reserved for maids and house staff. He figured however fast it took the FBI or DHS or whoever to get here, they would have a small enough team at first that they would split up among the most prominent lobby-level elevator and stairs, neglecting the service elevator that didn't even have a ground floor stop, but went straight to the garage. Whoever came after him would be flying blind, whereas Jason had scouted this building for four full days.

He didn't even hear any sirens as he bounced his stolen Camry up out of the garage and onto the darkened streets of Manhattan. But by the time he was barreling east on Houston, there were two birds in the air, the spotlights on their noses scanning the roads below for any car that might be him. Jason started weaving around people, flying through red lights; he had a plan on this night, and anonymity was not a part of it.

There were several sirens behind him when he ripped around the terminus of Houston and flew down the on-ramp onto FDR Drive, sirens not just from the black SUV that had to be filled with some variety of G-men, but the wail of a few good ol' NYPD Blue & Whites, having either gotten word over their radios of the VIP in this car, or just drafting onto the pursuit of a reckless high-speed red-runner.

"*JASON LANCASTER,*" a loud voice-of-God boomed down from one of the choppers. "*PULL OVER. JASON LANCASTER. PULL OVER.*"

He knew the forces amassed against him were surely setting up roadblocks ahead. His goal was just to get north of 42nd, to the covered section where the road crossed underneath the UN complex. Jason knew from his scouting drives that the road would go down to one lane there, that the two lanes on his right would be filled with orange cones and helmets and vests, with the machines of construction. He also knew that, in this one stretch of road, the barrier keeping traffic from sailing off into the East River had been removed.

There it was up ahead: the signs telling traffic to slow, the amber display of a reader board arrowing him into the far left lane. Once Jason was zooming past the construction site on his right, he said a quick little prayer that he wouldn't hit any of the workers – then jerked his wheel this way and that, like a man who had lost control of his vehicle. He cranked the wheel right in one final motion, smashing through the flimsy barriers and bouncing through the unfinished gravel, slowing his vehicle just enough, he hoped, to allow any workers to leap out of his path.

But not slowing him enough to keep from tearing through the tarp on the edge of the cliff – and sailing down nose first into the East River.

As the car started to submerge, Jason could already hear the choppers converging above him, could feel their white hot lights piercing through the back window and onto his hind neck. But just 87 seconds later, the surface of the River had blotted out those beams.

Several different helicopters would hover over this small section of river for the next five hours, trading out in shifts. Eventually, NYPD boats would amass here too. Divers would disappear into the murky depths, and plans would be made to pull the vehicle out come morning.

The car would be empty when it rose out of the bog, draining of greens and garbage and an old shoe or two, but no Jason Lancaster.

TEN DAYS LATER
THE FIRST MONDAY OF FEBRUARY

"Mr. President." Salas forced on a smile as he entered the suite of the Warwick Hotel, offering an outstretched hand to his Iranian counterpart.

"Mr. President," Ghaznavi nodded back, giving POTUS one of those vicious squeezes meant to establish the highest status in the room.

They sat, the protests from the street below creeping up into the brief silence. But before Salas could begin his practiced remarks, the other President in the room was beating him to the punch. "I turn on the television here and learn you are about to go to war with us."

Salas stared down into the carpet for his response. "Mr. President," he raised his eyes back up into Ghaznavi's, knowing each moment he spent looking away would be interpreted as weakness, "the American people just want answers for the attack on our Supreme Court. They just want justice. I believe if we can work together to investigate and prove that there is no Iranian connection to the bombing--"

"I can't do that."

"I'm sorry?"

"I can't do that. Because there is a connection. I ordered the bombing."

Everyone in the room tensed up, like this was an old west saloon, and a spit of chaw had just landed on someone's boot. Salas sensed Hifrael changing his stance, opening one side of his jacket to allow even easier access to his hidden sidearm, in unison with Ghaznavi's detail doing the same.

Before Salas could say anything, Ghaznavi was on his feet, crossing from his plush chair to tower above the POTUS in his. "It took me three years to plan it, to slowly trickle our team in through your porous borders. I started on your election day, Mr. President. I knew the Americans had elected the weakest President in their history, and that now was finally the time for us to strike." He leaned down into Salas's face. "You know, now that there was a dirty Mexican in the White House. Or what is it you're often called? A spic?"

Salas's right cross smashed awkwardly across Ghaznavi's cheek, connecting with more wrist than knuckles, but still enough to knock him down. With a guttural scream, he leaped up and out of his chair, right on top of the Iranian, grabbing his skull to bash it down into the carpet--

But all the other men in the room were in the fray now too. Voices were yelling, guns were out, strong hands were pulling Salas back--

His eyes shot open. His bedroom in the Residence was still dark.

He had ordered that the drapes were never to be closed, so at the latest, he would wake at sunrise each day (and most days, his alarm went off long before that). He rolled over onto his other shoulder, eyes going to his clock: 3:25 AM. Still over two and a half hours until he was to rise, until his day was supposed to officially begin.

Still three and a half days until that meeting with the President of Iran about which he had just dreamt. He had met with plenty of heads of state in his first three years as POTUS, but never one whom most Americans believed had ordered a terrorist attack on their soil.

Antonio swung onto his back, staring up at the carved shapes of the ceiling. Now was one of those times he wished someone else was there to share this humungous Emperor-sized bed with him, to snuggle into his side, to demand a head or neck rub, its droning rhythm enough to help the President himself back into slumber. But the bed remained lonely on this night, and Salas's eyes never closed again.

At 4:38, he rolled out, switching off his alarm before it got its chance to pierce the air with its awful whine.

Clyde Dudley needed this meeting months ago. He was now just five weeks from his primary against a young whippersnapper Republican far to the right of him – hell, far to the right of the NRA. And although the polls showed Dudley and his opponent running neck-and-neck, his office's own internal polling indicated the Majority Leader was in danger of losing his seat by more than five percentage points.

Dudley was an old school Republican, a Reagan Republican, a fiscally conservative Republican, a non-whack job Republican. He had prided himself on keeping his party grounded during these tumultuous times: America under terrorist attack once again, and this time with a (gasp) Mexican in the White House.

(What difference did it make that Antonio Salas was born in Ventura, California; Mexican blood was Mexican blood.) The GOP's capturing of both the House and Senate two years earlier could have led to all sorts of madness – to impeachment attempts, to the militarization of the southern border, to weeks wasted drafting abortion restrictions the President would just veto – but Dudley had worked hard to make sure his beloved Republican party didn't squander its chance at leadership, didn't take this opportunity to devolve into the Party of the Quacks. And now he was paying for this philosophy back home, faced with a rabid, bloodthirsty, good ol' Southern constituency that thought he had wasted the last two years.

The woman having tea with him in his Dirksen office on Monday morning was one big reason why. Terri Anne Stoval had been elected the first female president of L.I.F.E. (Legislate and Inspire Fetal Empowerment) just the past August, and had spent those six months touring the country throwing the group's support behind ultra-right primary candidates that she felt would better represent the rights of the unborn in the halls of the Capitol. Clyde Dudley had failed to bring one pro-life bill before the Senate in his two years as Majority Leader, making him her number one target. LIFE had spent more money against Dudley than any other incumbent; Stoval had made more treks to Kentucky than any other state.

"You do have a good eye," Dudley smiled at her through the steam of his English Breakfast. "My opponent is a very sharp young man with a very bright future. But he can't give you the Supreme Court."

"Excuse me?"

Dudley set his China saucer down on his quaint pre-Civil War coffee table; he was nearly shaking with excitement at the genius of his plan and didn't want to risk spilling on the Asian rug his wife had hauled all the way back from Singapore. "Follow my math here for a second, Ms. Stoval, if you would. Based on their voting records, we believe two of the five Justices who survived the bombing to be pro-life enough to at least consider overturning *Roe v. Wade.*"

"I would agree with that."

"Add in Cecilia Koh, the President's first nominee this past November, that brings us to three."

"And the buck stops there."

"Did you know that Admiral MacTavish's father was a Pat Robertson delegate in 1988?"

"Really?" Stoval's saucer tinkled in her lap as she returned her cup of chai to it. "But of course that's no guarantee that the son is pro-life."

"There are no guarantees of anything in this life. But for the sake of this discussion, let's be optimistic, shall we?"

"It doesn't matter. Reginald Irving was the most pro-choice President we've ever had, and his wife was right there by his side every time he authorized more funding for Planned Parenthood. Complete the Court with her confirmation, and we're still down 5-4, even under your best case scenario."

"And what if I were to tell you that I could defeat Mrs. Irving's confirmation?"

Stoval chuckled, knowing it was a pipe dream. "And guarantee this President will nominate someone pro-life next?"

"No, but I know how important your organization is to our *next* President."

"I assume you're talking about Bradley Benedict?"

Dudley rose and came around behind his chair, laying his fingers over its intricate hard-carved back of white wood. He had cancelled on his trainer in order to hold this meeting with the LIFE leader in the 7 AM hour, inviting her to his Dirksen office rather than his more public HQ in the Capitol, hopefully minimizing the number of press members that might notice it was taking place. But his legs felt tighter than usual as a consequence of skipping a work out. "At the end of this week, Congress is taking a four week recess. We skipped several weeks of vacation after the bombing, then in the months since in order to get all these confirmations complete. We're spending that banked time starting next week. In other words, if we don't have a Chief Justice by the end of this week, we disappear until late March – and I can promise you my caucus isn't going to come back and vote on any more judicial candidates for the rest of the year, until we know for sure who wins in November. You and I, and any registered Republican who's voted in Iowa and New Hampshire and South Carolina, all know that will be Brad Benedict. And come January, he'll nominate a proper replacement for Chief Lapadula, someone you can be very happy with."

"With all due respect, Senator, how the heck do you think you're going to avoid a vote on Rosemarie Irving after an 18-0 Judiciary vote to recommend? She's the most qualified of the four nominees so far – the only one to clerk for the Court, the only one to argue a case before the Court. Her First Lady resume was completely unimpeachable, a litany of bake sales and school lunch initiatives. She sleepwalked through her hearings. Even you voted for her in the Judiciary, and now you're going to--?"

"That was before I acquired some new information."

Stoval raised an eyebrow. "Information that will sink her?"

Dudley smiled. "I don't have to sink her. But I do believe the committee must reconvene to investigate this new information. And if that investigation is involved enough," he shrugged, "who knows if we'll get to her vote before everyone clears out on Friday."

"Well, I am intrigued, I'll give you that."

Dudley came around his chair, returning to his seat for the coup de grace. "And all it will cost you is an announcement that you're changing your primary endorsement for the fine state of Kentucky."

"Thanks to Allied Armament," President Salas declared, "this country is one step closer to learning the dark motivations behind the Supreme Court bombing, and a great deal safer today."

F. Walsh Howard III, founder and chairman of the security consultancy, almost had to pinch himself. He had never been a huge Salas fan, but who the hell cared right now. He was sitting *with the President* before the Oval Office fireplace, their chairs angled 45 degrees out to the assembled cameras, in that classic head of state photo op like he was the Prime Minister of frigging Israel.

"With suspect Miranda Whitney now in custody," the President was continuing, "we hope to learn something in the very near future that will help us determine who else might have played a role in this terrible tragedy."

"Mr. President, Mr. President!" the reporters panted like rabid hyenas, before one voice, one question, rose above the rest. "What of reports that Ms. Whitney took an outreach education class at a neighborhood mosque when she was in high school? Has there been any indication that she has a connection to the Iranian cell that Homeland Security uncovered in Oregon at the end of last year?"

"We're not ruling anything out, Kasie, and we're not jumping to any conclusions either. We're going to take our time, and ask her *everything* – and hopefully, she will be cooperative."

"Mr. President, what do you hope to accomplish in your New York trip this week?"

Salas hesitated, not wanting to show his trepidation about the trip. Other reporters gladly filled the void:

"Are you going to the UN to build a coalition to attack Iran?"

"When you meet with Iranian President Ghaznavi, how do you intend to answer his inevitable questions about the four aircraft carrier strike groups you've moved to the Gulf?"

Salas smiled. "You know, I hadn't really thought about it yet."

The reporters laughed along, but the NBC correspondent pushed forward with another question. "Are there any plans for ground units to also start preparing--"

"I think you know me well enough to know I'm not going to reveal plans for our military in this sort of forum. But I will say if you look back at the foreign policy speeches I've made since I was a candidate for this office, I firmly believe the American people are tired of having their sons and daughters on the ground in the Middle East, and nothing in the last three years or three months has changed my feelings on that."

Hearing the President answer foreign policy questions a mere five feet away gave Howard the chills, and put him into such a daze he almost didn't hear the next question, this one meant for him. "Mr. Howard, are you personally involved with the interrogation of Ms. Whitney, and is there any news on finding the body of her accomplice Lancaster, um, Jason Lancaster?"

Howard wiped his sweating palms on his powerful thighs with a smile. "We handed Miranda Whitney over to the FBI and Homeland Security, so I'll have to defer all questions about her to them. All we did was catch her, which it was our great honor to do. We are also assisting in the Lancaster investigation, and although his body was never found, it is believed with some certainty that he perished in his crash into the East River in late January."

"All right, that's all we have time for," Press Secretary Alistair Crabbe interjected, stepping between the staged chairs and the press. The President stood and offered his hand to Howard, the cameras erupting one last time as they shook.

Howard couldn't believe what he did next – but this was his only chance to do what he came here to do, and he acted on pure Howard family instinct. His Daddy, his Daddy's Daddy, they hadn't built the Howard empire by passing up chances-of-a-lifetime. Over the President's left shoulder, he could see his righthand man LT nodding at him, imploring him to do it. Howard gripped Salas hard, pulling him in a little closer to whisper something near his ear. "Mr. President, I know you're a busy man. But there is one brief private conversation my team and I would love to have with you before we leave."

"I think we have five minutes," Salas looked to his new Chief of Staff, who held up his watch wrist with a sideways glance. "Bryce, I think we should give Mr. Howard five more minutes."

Howard didn't want to risk that the answer was no, and seeing that over half of the media had already made its way into the hall, none of the remaining stragglers paying them any mind, he made sure to dangle one tantalizing tease while he had the chance, a morsel the President wouldn't be able to resist. "I sympathize with your refusal to send ground troops into Iran, Mr. President. And I think I have an idea of how to help you stick to that promise."

"Oh?" The eyebrows of the President of the United States raised high on his brow.

"Strange being back here." Justice Isaac Goldman looked around the casino hidden deep in the caverns under the White House. Indeed, it had been more than six weeks since he had last been down there, for a quick rehearsal for his oath and investiture press conference. "You know, without Dennis."

The others – Justices Koh and MacTavish and nominee Rosemarie Irving – hummed their agreement, raising their coffees and Diet Cokes as if toasting their departed friend with Irish whiskeys. Three of them had spent dozens of hours in this very room being vetted by the young man, Rosemarie many more than that, and each of them had developed a rare fondness for Dennis Coutts.

"How is Janaki holding up?" Cecilia Koh asked. "Weren't they--?"

"She's thrown herself into her work," Goldman answered. "She offered to take a leave, worried she would be too distracted, but I convinced her that was exactly what she *shouldn't* do. I've heard her crying a few times from inside my office, but her work hasn't suffered one bit."

The next few minutes passed in silence, save for the symphony of dishes being cleared by the small wait staff. This was the first time the post-bombing class had gathered as their own little group, the first time any of them had been in the casino or alone with their benefactor since their respective confirmations. "Thank you all for coming," Rosemarie finally said, when she felt they had paid Dennis's memory the proper respect.

"We really weren't supposed to, you know," Mac answered.

"Egan's reminded us each time a new nominee is announced," Cecilia chimed in. "Supreme Court Justices stay out of the process. We don't interact with nominees until their confirmations are official."

"A rule which, under normal circumstances, I would totally agree with," Rosemarie replied. "But I know we all agree that nothing about the last four months, or the manner in which each of us came to be here, is normal. I trust that now that you have all been on the Court for at least a couple of weeks or more, you're well aware of the dire backlog this whole scenario has created, well aware of how much those terrorists halted the progress of this nation."

"Egan mentions almost every conference how we probably won't get a summer recess this year," Goldman rolled his eyes.

"If I am lucky enough to become your Chief, my first duty will be making sure the Court gets back on schedule, that the docket is properly prioritized to allow us to decide the maximum number of cases over the next five months." Rosemarie was already reaching down into her large leather satchel on the floor, pulling out a leather-bound folder. "And making sure they're the most important ones." She removed three pieces of white paper from the folder, handing one to each of the new Justices. "This is the docket I would propose for the rest of the term."

"This starts at the beginning of March," Cecilia noticed. "You'd have to announce it now, alert the lawyers they need to be in Washington--"

"I don't want to denigrate anyone else's work," Rosemarie nodded, "but suffice it to say I believe the way the last couple of months have been scheduled has unfortunately set the Court back even further. It is imperative we get back on track immediately if we are to achieve everything we need to achieve this term."

"And when's the soonest you're going to be confirmed?" Goldman raised an eyebrow, noticing how she was already speaking of it as a foregone conclusion.

"Justice Koh is right. This can't wait for my confirmation. This schedule would need to be announced this week."

"You know Egan better than any of us," Mac chuckled. "You think she's going to let you make one single decision before you've officially taken over?"

"I know what Justice Egan really wants. And the reason I wanted to meet for lunch today is to tell you how you can help me give it to her."

The video first hit airwaves in select markets at 5 PM EST. *TMZ* mastermind Harvey Levin decided not to release the video in whole on his website until 24 hours after its initial airing, hoping to garner his syndicated show its best-ever ratings on that Monday night. (It was iPhoned and YouTubed so many thousands of times in the first hour of its broadcast that Levin changed his mind and put an HD version front and center on his homepage just before 7.) It was after 10 when the President saw it for the first time, in his private study just off the Oval Office.

The webcam video was silent, and started just a millisecond after the woman in the center of the frame had stood from her desk, turning her back on the lens. The video was cut and censored to hide her identity – but the man who appeared behind her was unmistakable. The tall, lithe matinee idol who took the beer bottle from her hand and brought it to his own lips was one of the most famous men on the planet, having just three years prior served as the leader of the free world. He spun the woman around and shoved her down onto the desk – her face now pixelated. His pants came down and he thrust into her from behind, leaning down to whisper dirty nothings in her ear, bringing his face only more into the light, even closer to the camera.

Harvey Levin had somehow acquired the first-ever video evidence of a President of the United States committing adultery.

"Yep, that's the Stray Dog, all right," the current POTUS's Chief of Staff Bryce Sando murmured from the rolling chair next to Salas, his feet up on the computer desk.

"What was that?"

"Stray dog, Mr. President," Sando sat up straight. "When I first met Reginald Irving, we always used to call him the Stray Dog. Cute as hell, but he'll go home with anyone who'll feed him."

Salas didn't reply, his face buried in his fingers. He of course knew it was indeed his predecessor in the video, and knew that Miss Pixels was none other than Bryce's own antecedent, Rebecca Whitford. He had seen the video months ago, when someone with a grudge against Becks had found a way to get it into his email in-box without it being firewalled. But this wide release, on TV and computer screens worldwide, this was *his* fault. Becks had to be the source of the leak – why else would her face be blurred out? And he was the one who had given her cause to do this, cause to be vindictive; *he* had given her a thirst for revenge. He had demoted her to the VA, he had confronted her two weeks previously about her lies before the special Congressional committee on their handling of the Iranian halfway house. Delores had told him in passing that Becks had quit the VA a week ago and left Washington; he had just sighed with regret – another young person this city had chewed up and spit out – not pausing to think that this might not be the last he would hear of Rebecca Whitford. Hell hath no fury like a woman fired.

Of course she would go after the Irvings. It was her inviting them to pitch themselves as Supreme Court consultants that had started her downward spiral. That was what brought Salas and Rosemarie so much closer, that was the moment the First Lady became the President's most trusted de facto advisor, replacing Becks as the person he would turn to with his most difficult conundrums and dilemmas. Becks would no doubt correctly ascertain that it had been Rosemarie who had advised the President to make his Chief of Staff the fall gal for the PR debacle in Oregon, who had recommended he make a show of demoting her to take the heat off of himself, who had even recommended her replacement.

Little does that cunt Rosemarie know, Salas imagined Becks stewing from behind the wheel of a U-Haul on I-95 bound for Massachusetts, *I've got something that will make her life – not just her confirmation, but her whole life – a living hell. She never should've fucked with me.*

Salas slammed the laptop shut just as Harvey Levin and his young staff were getting on one of their snarky rolls. "I'll see you in the morning," Salas instructed Sando without standing.

The President's thoughts stayed locked on only one person for the rest of the night. No, not Becks; he didn't blame her, not after the way the Men of DC had treated her.

His thoughts weren't even on Reg, or even on how his now-tarnished legacy would make him much less valuable in this year's election than he had been four years before, going from swing state to swing state, practically commanding his loyalists to become Salas believers. The President hadn't counted on Irving; he had seen his predecessor's history in such sordid detail recently, he had been operating under the assumption that it was only a matter of time before a great unravelling such as this one.

Salas picked up the landline, then set it right back down again. *You can't make her feel better*, he chided himself, then stood, pulling his jacket off the back of his desk chair. *Her whole world fell apart tonight, Antonio. She has her own house to clean up. You just want to call her for <u>you</u>, because you want to talk to her, not because you can actually help her.*

He walked out, heading upstairs for the Residence. It was the first of four times he would pick up a phone and consider making that call.

The Irvings' publicist had gotten wind of the *TMZ* video an hour before it aired. Rosemarie had told Suzie to go home at 4:30, allowing the hundreds of requests for comment as well as the gloating-disguised-as-condolence-calls to go to voicemail. She could count the number of people who had her personal cell number on two or three hands, and all of them knew not to call on this kind of night. But there was one call she was still expecting, regardless of the events of the past six hours.

She was on the fourth floor of their townhouse, just high enough that the mass of press vultures gathered before their front stoop wouldn't be able to make her out. All the lights were off, so she could stand at the window and stare down at them without herself being seen through the slight security tint upon which Secret Service had once insisted. The phone vibrated in her hand, and she brought it to her ear without even having to read the caller's identity. "I thought we were going to speak earlier."

"I didn't … uh …" Walsh Howard sputtered out a response. "I don't know, y'know, with all that's going on …"

Rosemarie rolled her eyes; one of the most important men in politics didn't know a thing about how to be politically smooth. "How did it go?"

"He heard us out. He doesn't know what he's going to do in Iran yet, or even how to do it. But the idea of using us clearly made it more palatable to him. You could just see it in the way his eyes lit up when I proposed it."

"Excellent work."

"I guess my first meeting with the President went okay."

"The first of many. Until you're on the other side of the Resolute Desk someday."

Howard huffed out an orgasmic grunt at the very thought. "From your lips to God's ears. But this is all moot if … you still think you can close him?"

"Don't worry about me for a second."

"I know. I know how good at this you are. It's just-- after today ... I hope you know how to navigate these extra wrinkles. Without you, this whole thing falls apart. We need you to deliver President Salas, Mrs. Irving."

"You need to stop worrying, Walsh. I've been planning for today my entire adult life."

1992

Rosemarie hadn't expected this. The moment she walked into the strip mall's ground floor suite, a charge of energy shot up her spine. She had never been interested in politics; to her, it had always been a game of photo ops and pork deals played by people who, with rare exceptions, were prettier or more charming than they were intelligent. *The Law* was where the real power lay, where the unsung intelligentsia controlled this country's fate. The Law was where she had spent her educational and formative years; the Law was elevating her from her parents' immigrant, blue collar roots; the Law was where she was investing her bright future.

But she couldn't deny that when she entered the retail space engorged with red and white and blue bunting and posters and signs and buttons, with young people frantically working phones or running in to grab more paraphernalia before darting out to pound more pavement, she felt a tingle under her skin. There was an electricity to this place, a hopefulness, a belief in everything this country was built upon. She didn't necessarily feel this when she walked into a law library, any law library, even the Library of Congress Reading Room or upstairs at the Supreme Court. Sure, there was a weightiness to the air in those places, and of course in the Courtroom itself, especially when it was filled for arguments or decisions; on those days, the air was suffused with a buzz of history being made. But this energy she was feeling in this campaign office – the urgency that filled every young volunteer's eyes and feet and dialing fingers even though the election they were attempting to win was still almost nine months away – this was like nothing she had ever felt before.

And she was terrified by how much she liked it.

"Volunteer or press request?"

"I'm sorry?" Rosemarie snapped out of her reverie.

"Are you volunteering, or do you have a press request?" the pretty blonde worker repeated.

"Oh, I'm here to see Congressman Irving. Reginald Irving? I'm Rosemarie Jarzebski, I was told he'd be here at this time."

"Yes, he's just practicing his speech. I'll let him know you've arrived."

The volunteer turned and walked the length of the large retail space, disappearing into one of the offices in back. Rosemarie rested against the nearest desk, continuing to soak up the excitement all around her.

She was patient for at least the first ten minutes, understanding the career importance of this speech the young Congressman was currently busy practicing. In only the second year of his own tenure as an elected official, he had been flown cross-country by the DNC to help warm up the crowd before the introduction of the Southern Governor who had suddenly become the favorite for the party's nomination. This wasn't a speech on just any old stump, but an *unveiling* on the biggest of stages, in perhaps the most important of battleground states. It was the highest profile gig Reginald Irving had landed yet, in a quickly-rising career. Rosemarie chuckled to herself, realizing how silly it was for her to be taking up even five minutes of his precious time. But this meeting had been suggested by one of the partners in her firm, Bryce Sando, a college classmate of Irving's. The most junior partner at A&R, Sando was expected to be a rainmaker, bring in new business, and Irving was the first new account he had brought into the firm. He had personally asked Rosemarie to jump on the Irving team, and had suggested she introduce herself while the new Rep was briefly in Columbus.

It wasn't until the 20 minute mark of her wait that she started to lose her cool. She understood he needed to hone his speech, but would it have been too much trouble for someone to check on her once or twice, to ask if she wanted anything to drink? Where was that aide that had disappeared into one of the back offices? It was at this 20 minute mark that Rosemarie remembered that she had as little time as Irving to waste on this meeting; he may be a Congressman with the biggest speech of his life tomorrow, but she was a week away from arguing her first case before the Supreme Court.

Thirty minutes was her absolute limit. She pushed up from the desk and started to turn to the door – but stopped herself. She wanted to just walk out, but what if it got back to Sando, to any of the partners for that matter, that she had ditched on their new client Irving? They would hear some version of the story that wouldn't include her long wait, or how she had been ignored. She should at least apologize to *someone*, give them a message to pass along to the Congressman.

Rosemarie followed the same path the young aide had taken a half hour before, looking in on the transparent walls of each back office as she took a lap around them. But not seeing her anywhere, she was about to turn back for the front door--

When she realized she *could* see the aide's head through one of the walls, just the back of her head, a man's fingers intertwined in her blonde locks, his palm guiding her up and down on his crotch. The man's eyes were closed, but Rosemarie recognized him from his Congressional website, which she had visited when Bryce Sando had first recruited her to his legal team three months ago. With a deep moan from the pit of his ribs, Reginald Irving pushed the girl's head in one final time, opening his eyes– to stare right through the glass wall into Rosemarie's own.

Mortified, Rosemarie spun on a heel and marched for the front door of the storefront, turning left as she pushed out the door to rush for her car.

"Wait!" She heard not only his voice behind her, but the jangle of his buckle as he attempted to re-latch his belt. "Rosemarie, right?"

She fumbled with her keys, not even looking back as she got one into the lock of her driver's side door.

"Hey, I'm sorry, she didn't tell me you were waiting. I mean, she told me *someone* was waiting, she didn't tell me it was you."

"It's a great honor to know you might have put a blow job on hold if you'd known it was me." She slammed down onto her seat, reaching for her door--

Too late; Irving had positioned himself between it and the car, preventing her from shutting it. "You're funny."

"If you don't mind, I'd like to shut my door."

"Let me buy you dinner tonight. Please. Sando didn't tell me you were so gorgeous."

Rosemarie rolled her eyes with a chuckle, moving them off him and out her windshield. "Oh, please. I think we both know what you look for in a woman, and I've never been known for my lips."

Reg laughed again, but didn't move. Her attitude had only enticed him further. Reginald Irving had never met a woman he didn't think he could conquer; the greater the challenge, the more insatiable the sex seemed to be when it finally happened. And it *always* happened eventually. "Please, Bryce told me about your case. It's something I'm very interested in."

Rosemarie's eyes spun back to him. He had found her Achilles heel.

"Forget dinner, we'll have breakfast or lunch tomorrow. Just business."

"Isn't your rally tomorrow afternoon? You don't think you should be practicing that close to--"

Reg scoffed. "Don't tell anyone in there, but I can give a speech after reading it once. No cards, no prompter."

"Bullshit."

"Everyone's got a gift. I guess that's mine. And Sando says yours is that you're the smartest lawyer he's ever met."

"He has to say that."

"Look, I'm surrounded by dumb kids kissing my ass all day long. I need some, some substance. I'd love to hear your take on everything going on in the world."

Rosemarie stared at her speedometer, already regretting where her mind was going, disgusted with herself for actually considering his offer. She rationalized to herself that she was doing this to appease Bryce Sando, to make a partner, to make all the partners, happy. More importantly, she could be on this man's account for decades, and didn't need to spend the first year of it drowning in awkwardness, avoiding any solo phone calls with him, or any direct glances when they were in the same conference room.

"Fine. Lunch."

Reg smiled, and backed out of her door.

"I thought we were going to talk about my case," Rosemarie said as she took an initial bite of her angel hair. The first 25 minutes of the meal had been filled with the usual openers: where they were from, basic dossiers on their parents and siblings. The thought of this meal being a date nauseated Rosemarie, and she took the first opportunity to pivot to business.

"A confession." Reg didn't even look up from cutting his New York strip into bite-sized pieces. "I don't know what your case is. Bryce sent me a piece about it, but I didn't get a chance, I've been so swamped--"

"Practicing your speech."

"Oh right," he smiled as he shoved one morsel between his teeth. "I already blew my best excuse with you. See how weak you make me?"

Rosemarie put down her fork and dabbed at her mouth with her napkin. As much as she wanted to stand right up and walk out, she saw no need to humiliate a rising politician in Columbus's hippest, busiest restaurant, or at least, not as long as he was also a rising client. "So much for substance."

"Substance is exactly why I'm here. Substance is why Sando wanted us to meet."

"Okay. Then what should we talk about *of substance?*"

Reg leaned in to make sure she was the only one in the restaurant who could hear what followed. "I don't think I'm being clear. I don't have any substance."

"I'm sorry?"

"I need someone like you to provide it for me."

Rosemarie averted her gaze. "I think I should get something straight. I thought we were meeting because you wanted to know all the lawyers on your team."

"My father was Attorney General of Oregon. I went to law school, spent six months as an Assistant US Attorney, and now I'm in Congress. One thing I don't need is to meet another lawyer. I need help."

"Help?"

"I can win a congressional district with this face and an above-average speechwriter. But to not screw it up now that I'm there – to take full advantage of this opportunity while it's mine – I'm going to need a lot more than that."

"You have amazing self-awareness."

"One of my greatest strengths, my biggest advantages over everyone else in this business, is that I know not to take myself too seriously. I know I fell into this by blind luck. Enough experts – the D-triple-C, my lawyers, some of the biggest Senators and Congressmen that have ever lived – they've all told me what it is I'm lacking, what it is I really need. I'm man enough and just smart enough to listen to them." His hand reached across the table, landing on top of hers. "They've told me I need someone by my side. Someone who not only looks stunning on camera but is as smart as anyone in Washington."

She slid her hand out from under his. "Congressman …"

"Reg. Please."

Rosemarie shook her head with a laugh, bouncing her fork a couple times on the soft table linen. "Okay. First, why don't you tell me why you're doing this."

"I told you. You're gorgeous and brilliant, and I need--"

"No. Why you're in politics in the first place. What do you—*feel* when you think about this country? What fills you with energy, what gets your blood boiling?"

"I think I have a problem. I've never been patriotic."

"Huh?"

"I mean, I don't dislike this country, don't get me wrong, I love it and intellectually know it's the greatest place on the earth. I've just never-- You know how some people at a sporting event, when the national anthem comes on, their hand just robotically moves to their heart, and they have to sing along, loud and full voiced? How some people get the chills whenever they're watching the Olympics and we win a gold and our Star Spangled Banner plays?"

"Uh huh," Rosemarie nodded. She was one of those people.

"That's not me. None of that ever happens to me."

"Oh-kay. What do you want to accomplish?"

"Nothing."

"Excuse me?"

"I don't really care about anything. I don't have any real causes -- outside of the fact college football needs a playoff system. And not like a cop-out plus-one or four team system. I mean an honest-to-goodness, eight team, can't-argue-with-it system. Hey, I'm serious!" he smiled in unison with her laugh. "This was never my dream. Someone with the D-triple-C saw me give a speech in law school, and said he'd give me a million bucks for a campaign."

"Wow."

"See? This is why I need you. I need someone to tell me what I want, what I care about, what I'm going to do. I don't even know what your case is, but you say the word, and it becomes the most important cause of my next legislative session. However high this face can take us – you'll be running the show."

Rosemarie changed the subject, ricocheting off his football comment into a comparison of the strength of that year's Big Ten vs. Pac-10. Irving was quite proud of his alma mater, who had three years before won a bowl game for the first time in thirty-three seasons and seemed to be on their way to elite status. Rosemarie chuckled at the notion that a football team called the Ducks could ever be elite, and countered that her Buckeyes were only five years removed from their last conference title, and had come oh-so-close again last season.

It wasn't until the dessert course that Irving came in for his follow up. "So, what do you think? Can I see you when you're in Washington next week? I mean, after you've given your oral argument, of course."

Rosemarie put down her spoon after two bites of ice cream. She had been thinking about how to let him down throughout the entire last hour. "Reg. You are certainly charming and—fun." She couldn't help but let out an unexpected smile. "This has been more fun than I've had in a long time."

"Me too."

"And I'm sure you will find a brilliant and gorgeous woman to become Mrs. Irving soon. But politics has never been my thing--"

"Bryce said you had to navigate some pretty serious office politics to convince your partners not to take this case away from you when it was granted cert by the Supreme Court. You realize how many third year Associates in the history of this nation have gotten the opportunity to appear before the highest court in the land?"

"That's not politics. I'm a lawyer. I have dedicated myself to the law. I think you and I could have a lot of fun together from time to time. But the next morning, I would never have time to discuss your campaign platform, or the wording of the next big bill you're sponsoring, or who to pick to run your press office. I'd always have to go back to my work, to my briefs and arguments and discoveries and depositions. That's my life. You need, you *deserve* much more than that."

After a beat, Reg nodded. He never took rejection well, but could tell she had at least given it some thought over the last hour, and he appreciated that. "Thank you."

They stayed for 25 more minutes, time enough for cappuccinos and comparisons of the legal education one got at a state school vs. the Ivy League. They said goodbye at the valet stand with a professional hand shake, then leaned in to kiss each other's cheeks, new friends, if nothing more.

TUESDAY

Before her eyes even reached the second case number, Acting Chief Justice Egan recognized the fingerprints all over this proposed docket. She shook her head as she set it aside on her desk. “I’ll take it under advisement,” she said without even looking up at the Irving Three (as Sean Hannity had dubbed the three new Justices everyone by now knew the Irvings had handpicked), then returned her eyes to the dull brief she had been battling to get through all morning.

The Irving Three looked at each other. Rosemarie had coached them on what to say if Egan refused to follow this schedule, but none of them had even considered the possibility that Egan wouldn’t give them *any* answer, that she would just *receive* their proposal like it was next week’s lunch menu, without giving any indication whatsoever what she thought of it. What would FLOTUS want them to do now? Do they press her on the urgency of it? Demand an immediate answer?

Mac was the first one to just raise his eyebrows, then turn for the door leading back out into Egan’s chief clerk’s office. A career military man, he was of course the most stringent rule-follower of the three, and had the strongest reservations about breaking protocol and interacting with Rosemarie in the first place; there was no way he was going to stick his neck out any more than the bare minimum for her inappropriate request. In seconds, Koh and even Goldman were right on his heels. They had almost made it out of the room before the Acting Chief added one more thing: “Uh, Cecilia? A word?”

With her back to Egan, Koh squeezed her eyes shut, then put on a forced smile before turning back around to face her. “Of course.”

“Doesn’t it make you wonder?” Egan was holding the proposal aloft in her right hand.

“I’m sorry?”

“When you saw this schedule. It didn’t make you wonder why *Agguire v. Detroit* is so damn important to Rosemarie Irving?”

The former Notre Dame professor stammered. “I, I don’t know--”

Egan pulled the wastebasket out from underneath her desk and tossed the proposal in. "Two months ago she was so desperate to delay that case, she brainwashed you into refusing to vote on it. Now she's got it scheduled for March 2nd – the very first case she'll hear as Chief."

"Chief Egan, that, that schedule is actually just something the three of us put together to help--"

"Oh, spare me the bullshit," Egan spit, and Koh wilted under her laser gaze. She had never been a good liar. "The three of you feel indebted to her for your seats, so you ignored the rules – ignored my instructions – and met with her with her confirmation still in doubt. I don't blame you, Cecilia. I'd probably *kill* for President Bush. The elder, that is.

"But I don't have to pay one damn bit of attention to her meddling until she's officially sworn in," Egan leaned in on her elbows, "whether that's tomorrow or next week or next year. She's just going to have to wait to reshuffle the docket schedule until she's moved into this office. And if that means it takes an extra month or two before we consider *Agguire v. Detroit,* well, that's just tough titty."

"Have you considered the possibility she's doing it for your benefit?" Justice Koh felt the words, the words Rosemarie had suggested using when she gave them the proposal, just flying out of her mouth.

"Excuse me?"

"I don't expect you to believe this, but she doesn't feel it's right to take over your court in the middle of a term. Not after all you've done in this horrific time. She wants to honor your contribution, your leadership. Change the schedule now, while you're Chief, and it will look like your decision. This will always be remembered as *your* term, the term you scheduled, the term you led this court through tragedy all the way to its conclusion.

"But if she has to come in and do the reshuffling herself – to the press, that's only going to look like you didn't know what you were doing, so Rosemarie had to change everything, had to clean up your mess, the second she walked in the door. You would be looked at as someone who really just kept the seat warm, who filled in, and didn't even do it particularly well.

"So, yes, I believe the First Lady thought this was a way she could honor you, and make it look like your term through and through. Like you were so good at this job, she just eased into it, following your schedule and procedures, learning from a true master until she takes over next term."

Her arms crossed, Egan rolled her sharp fingernails up and down her biceps with an impressed grin. The rumors of Cecilia Koh working as a litigator before she entered academia were actually true. She knew Rosemarie Irving herself had probably crafted this argument, but Koh had delivered it passionately and persuasively. "And let's say I were to fall for that. That still doesn't answer the question of why this particular case should be so important to her."

"I can't answer that. And, yes, I agree it's fair to be a little concerned when you look at the way she's manipulated the scheduling of that case. But she's still just one vote of nine. I can promise you she's never once hinted, implied or even come right out and said how she wants me to vote on *Agguire v. Detroit*. It was never mentioned in my vetting, nor has it been mentioned to Isaac or Mac."

"You're sure about that?"

"Yes, I'm sure. You don't think I noticed she was a little obsessed with this case? So I came right out and asked them. I don't know how they're going to vote on that case, but I can promise you, Chief, Isaac Goldman and I are not going to vote the same on much of anything during this or any other term."

Egan looked to the floor, wrestling with her thoughts. "Anyway," Cecilia concluded, "I've said my piece." She turned and left the Acting Chief to her decision. She had done her part, she had delivered every point of Rosemarie's argument.

She wasn't in the room when Egan returned to her chair, pulled the wastebasket out from under her desk, and retrieved Rosemarie's proposal.

"His name is Ramin Bastani," the CIA Director explained as he stepped up next to the handsome Persian photo displayed on one of the Sit Room's screens. "We developed him when he was just a student at Cal Tech. We've had him under the deepest cover since, no contact with him in the 16 years since he returned to Iran. He had probably grown to wonder if he had totally imagined his entire recruitment. Until two weeks ago, Mr. President, when we reminded him it was very real."

Salas was reading Bastani's dossier on his own tablet. "He's a physicist inside their nuclear program."

"Deep inside, Sir. He's such a valuable asset, we didn't want to take any chances contacting him until circumstances made it absolutely imperative. We weren't even sure how'd he react. How could we be sure he hadn't grown loyal to his country? How could we be sure we'd even hear back from him?"

"But we did?" The President set his personal device down on the table and looked up over the heads of his Joint Chiefs to his DCI.

"That's an affirmative, sir," the Director nodded. "Dr. Bastani was able to give us a clearer picture of the Iranian weapons development program than we've had in years. And it's not good." He swiped the scientist's photo away, replaced by a map of Iran, covered with red dots. "These represent covert, underground enrichment laboratories previously unknown to us. Iran has now enriched enough fissile material for not only several atomic warheads, but Dr. Bastani confirms the Revolutionary Guard has successfully developed a delivery device--" He swiped again, filling the screen with a blueprint of some sort of missile. "--the Koussar-4, an intermediate-range ballistic missile, with a range of over 5000 kilometers. 3000 miles, Mr. President."

"Enough to get to Israel," he realized almost in a whisper. "How has this gotten to this point? How have we not done anything--?"

"The last administration, Sir," the DCI threw up his hands. "We had the greenlight to assist in anything the Mossad ran point on--"

"Like Stuxnet," the National Security Advisor chimed in.

"The computer worm?"

"Only set them back a year or two."

"Your predecessor wanted as far away from anything in the Middle East as possible. We could keep our network in Iran, but not initiate any actions of our own."

"We've known about the Koussar program, Sir," his DIA Director spoke up, "we just didn't know they would be able to outfit them with nuclear warheads."

"This means if we hit them," Salas asked, sitting forward, "we can't just give them a little slap on the wrist. We can't just take out the mastermind behind the bombing sitting at home in his condo."

"If we even knew who that was," someone in the room grumbled. Salas couldn't place the voice, so he moved on:

"We have to hit them so hard, in the right places, that they don't turn right around and retaliate on Tel Aviv."

Admiral Percy Holmes rose, stepping to the main screen as it filled with another map of Iran, this one shaded in different colors to illustrate a potential attack plan. "We've been working on this for the past couple of weeks, Sir. You'd want concentrated air strikes on these cities, every location with an underground facility." He created circles on the map with his finger. "Build a perimeter around each lab, and knock out each airport. Then move JSOC teams in to neutralize each facility. And we're gonna wanna keep an eye on no man's lands like these, here and here, with drones at the very least, to prevent them from moving any of the offending material before we can take it out."

POTUS brought his hands together over his mouth, biting into one of his forefingers. "One of those labs is under Tehran. You want to bomb Tehran, then put boots on the ground?"

Percy sighed. "Mr. President. We believe indefinite occupation would be a likely necessity. Their infrastructure is going to be devastated. If we just bomb the hell out of them, then fly away into the night, we'll have not only created a breeding ground--"

"We'll have created a brand new third world country, robbed millions of food, created how many thousands of orphans ..."

Percy just raised his eyebrows. It didn't sound promising to him either.

"No, I'm asking you, Admiral. How many orphans? How many casualties will there be? How many orphans are we going to create?"

"Long term ... surely in the six figures for the duration of our occupation, Mr. President. There's no doubt there would develop some sort of insurgency element that we project would surpass even Iraq."

"We would kill a hundred thousand Iranians?"

"That's in the first decade. Sir."

Salas's chair rocked as he fell back into it. "Let me ask you this – does this even make sense? They've got nukes now, why would the government of Iran sponsor a terrorist attack that kills about a hundred people?"

"Maybe it wasn't the government."

"I'm sorry?"

The CIA Director had returned to his seat, and now sat forward. "Ever since the Ayotollah Khomeini first declared a fatwa saying nuclear weapons violated the Muslim religion, it's been unclear if his predecessors or the other Muslim clerics that really run that country support them. Maybe that's why someone, maybe one of their homegrown terror groups, maybe some disillusioned military elements, wanted to give us this little prick. They wake the sleeping giant and the United States has to invade Iran – an invasion the clerics deem unwarranted, a response to a terrorist bombing they believe they had nothing to do with. Well, surely then, at that point, even the clerics would get behind using any weapon available against their enemies the United States and Israel."

The Chief of Staff of the Army let out a scoff. "That would be suicidal."

"That's exactly what I'm worried about," the President murmured.

"You don't have to torture yourself." Reg Irving heard his wife's voice entering their home theater behind him. He had been cooped up in here for the last two hours plus, not missing a single second of the Senate debate on whether the Judiciary Committee should reconvene after the release of the sex video starring the husband of their latest Supreme Court nominee. Rosemarie came around to join him on the couch, handing him a hot drink to match her own.

"Whoo-hoo!" His neck whiplashed from his first sip. He had expected chamomile, not some sort of variation on the hot toddy.

"How often do we get to call in sick and have a TV day?" she winked back at him. They had no choice but to keep themselves locked up in their townhouse, prisoners in their own palace, at least until they were ready to respond to YouTube's most popular video of the past 24 hours, already with an eight-figure number of hits and climbing towards nine fast. The hope had been that the Senate would still vote on her confirmation in short order; sure, the count would be much tighter now than it should have been, many Republicans finding the excuse they had been yearning for, but she would still get through.

With the debate over the video now entering its third hour, however, Rosemarie realized drastic measures had to be taken.

As always, Reg was much more emotional than his wife. "I just can't believe, after all these years, this had to happen-- *now.* I just can't tell you how sorry I am." He intertwined his fingers in hers, locking in on her eyes. They may have had a relationship any outsider would consider odd, but it was still one of deep caring and affection. "This was supposed to be your time."

"I just can't believe you let her film you. You used to be smarter than that."

"Goddamn machines. The sci-fi writers had it right all along. Our machines are going to kill us. They're just doing it much more creatively than shooting us up with machine guns or launching our own nukes at us. They're destroying our privacy. Our freedom. And we're going right along with it with fucking smiles on our faces."

"You have kept your promise to me, at least?"

Reg broke from her grasp, reaching over to the side table next to him to retrieve a hanging folder so full it had to be held together by two rubber bands. He set it between them on the couch. "Never slept with anyone we didn't have an *Infinite Jest*'s worth of oppo on."

"Reg. It's me. You don't have to pretend you've actually read a book in the last decade."

"Sorry," he smiled back.

Rosemarie stood. "Let's get the word out. I will testify before the committee tomorrow, and put this thing to bed."

"I'll let Wyley know," Reg nodded. Volunteering to re-testify in this climate might normally be an insane strategy, but this was Rosemarie. He held up the file again. "And I'll get the highlights from in here to Xan."

As she headed for the door, he scratched at an old stain that one of their dear departed dogs had left behind on the couch. "Hey. How rough you going to be?"

"Not so bad," she turned back from the threshold. "Just enough to make that girl regret the Lumière brothers ever invented the motion picture."

1992

"Cough drops, aspirin, ibuprofen. Unfortunately, we can't fill prescriptions yet, but believe me I've been working on it." The lawyers filling the Lounge chuckled louder than Chief Clerk H. K. Baskin's cheap jokes merited, desperate for anything to break the tension gripping most of their spines as they prepared to deliver their oral arguments before the Justices. "You're all gonna do great in there. Break a leg. Just don't do it until you're outside the building, please, our insurance just expired."

As the octogenarian stepped away from the podium, the assembled lawyers feted him with applause, not only for his efforts at lightening the atmosphere, but out of respect for his decades of service culminating in this, his final term.

Alone in the back row of chairs, Alterman & Richbourg Junior Associate Rosemarie Jarzebski was the lone lawyer who hadn't laughed, who didn't applaud. This wasn't because of fear, or because she wasn't fond of Baskin (he had made her chuckle, honestly chuckle, during many a loopy, delirious all-nighter of her clerkship), or even because she was intimidated after meeting her opponent in her case, President Bush's Solicitor General. Rosemarie had just been laser-focused since leaving her hotel room, hungry for blood, ignoring everyone she knew, even Rusty the pro-life hobo when he shook his coin cup at her as she passed the Methodist building. Rosemarie wouldn't be, couldn't be diverted from her fixation on one image: the Justices sitting rapt as she wowed them with her argument. The look in her eyes was one her father had noticed when she was a little girl, calling it her 'orzeł oczy' in Polish; her eagle eye. Nothing was going to distract her or take her off the game in her sights – not even the Marshal's aide who entered the room calling out, "Ms. Jarzebski! Package for Ms. Jarzebski!"

Rosemarie turned in his direction and raised her hand with a slight look of confusion. These messengers were only to disturb the sanctity of the Lawyers Lounge with an urgent message pertaining to one of the cases about to be argued, with new information from the lawyer's firm or one of the parties involved with the case. It was an unspoken rule that not even life-and-death emergencies should be relayed in this room; these attorneys were about to appear before the Supreme Court, after all, and that superseded life and death; this was history, this was the future of America. It didn't make sense to Rosemarie that someone from her firm would have an urgent message to relay; she had taken this case on herself, she had convinced her clients to threaten to leave the firm if the partners had taken Rosemarie off of it once it was accepted by the Court. This was her case, and she knew everything about it; there would be no new information to surprise her at this late hour.

She signed the aide's clipboard, then returned to her seat with the small package, tearing it open low in her lap – she didn't want to give any other lawyers an advantage over her in this case or any future ones by seeing whatever it contained at the same moment she did.

'Your reward for winning today,' the handwriting on the plain white, 8 ½ by 11 inch piece of paper, folded in thirds, read on one side. *'I hope you won't make me wait until January to see you again.'*

With her fingers gripping only one edge of the paper, the bottom third dropped open, the thin item folded inside fluttering down to her lap, landing front side up.

79th Rose Bowl Game, the colorful ticket read. **January 1, 1993.**

Rosemarie shoved it inside the inner pocket of her leather binder, infuriated with Reginald Irving for breaking her concentration.

She felt her lips curling into a grin. Okay, maybe not so infuriated.

"We'll start today with argument in Case number 91-4176, *Rostron v. Richard B. Cheney, Secretary of Defense*," Chief Quint announced. "Ms. Jarzebski?" Only when her old mentor said her name did Rosemarie raise her eyes to the nine robed figures behind the bench, her eyes catching on those of the Chief. She had thought it might be a mistake to look at him, to let her mind relax in the comfort of their relationship, an escape from the scared, ruthless place she needed it to be. Indeed, the slight wink she caught in his left eye did jar her for a moment, like a stage actor falling out of character for the briefest of moments after peripherally noticing her parents seated in the darkened front row.

But in an instant, Rosemarie was back in character, stepping to the lectern an unrelenting advocate who would stop at nothing to win her clients justice. "Mr. Chief Justice, and may it please the Court: I am here today on behalf not only of

Miss Katherine Rostron, but nineteen other young men and women who have served this country with bravery, honor and distinction in the Gulf War for Kuwaiti freedom. All of my clients have dedicated their lives to defending this nation, and yet, when they themselves came under the most vicious attacks imaginable, we were not there to defend them.

"Each of my clients was sexually assaulted by fellow military officers, in the majority of these cases by their superiors, but in not one of these cases was the assailant prosecuted or punished in the slightest, not even with the proverbial slap on the wrist. My clients were told their accusations were baseless, unpatriotic and treasonous; that the attacks were largely their own faults; and in each case, were not even permitted to seek a transfer to another officer's command. In nearly half these cases, this led to repeat offenses at the hands of the same perpetrators. The psychological damage wreaked upon my clients could never be quantified, but they hope today you will help them find some small--"

"Let me get this straight," a booming voice rang out from two chairs to the Chief's left. Rosemarie jerked her eyes down to her notes. The one unbreakable rule she had set for herself was that she wouldn't look in this particular Justice's eyes. She knew he was the only thing in this room that could throw her off her game. And now her worst fear was being realized, that he would interrupt her and dominate the Justices' questioning. Not that she wouldn't be able to answer any query – she knew she could do that – just that she wouldn't be able to parry with this awful man without looking in his eyes. She hadn't looked in those eyes in the final nine months of her clerkship, or the three years since. She had pledged never to look in them again.

"These accusations are horrific; no one could deny they are." Justice Warren Lapadula's linebacker's baritone reverberated off the walls all around her. "But you're arguing that the Secretary of Defense is responsible for the actions of sergeants and lieutenants and captains thousands and thousands of miles away from him? Men that he's never met and never will meet?"

"This is about a failure of leadership all the way at the top, inside the Pentagon," Rosemarie answered, locking her eyes on the wispiest hairs floating off the top of his coif, avoiding his eyes or his arrogant mouth or his granite jaw at all costs. "The failure to establish a system of military justice that properly punishes rapists in the military ranks has led to an atmosphere of anarchy, one in which soldiers are tacitly *permitted* in their off hours to prey on--"

"Ms. Jarzebski, are you familiar with *Gilligan v. Morgan*, decided by this Court in 1973?"

Not only did she know it, she had prepared for just this line of counter attack. "The Kent State case, of course I know it. That was a case pertaining to the free speech and safety of civilians, not--"

"But it was in this case that Chief Justice Burger wrote of the military, 'it is difficult to conceive of an area of governmental activity in which the courts have less competence.'"

Rosemarie grit her teeth. She knew Burger was a particular hero of Lapadula; a recent biography contended he had legally changed his own first name in high school after President Nixon had named Burger the 15th Chief.

"'The complex, subtle, and professional decisions as to the composition, training, equipping, and *control* of a military force are essentially professional military judgments,'" he continued, "'subject always to civilian control of the Legislative and Executive Branches … intended by the Constitution to be left to the political branches directly responsible – as the Judicial Branch is not – to the electoral process.'" He grinned as he set aside that prepared reading. "In other words, Ms. Jarzebski, as detestable as these tales are, I'm just not sure there's a thing this Court can legally do about them."

The white light on Rosemarie's lectern lit up, indicating she had but five minutes left in her half of the argument hour.

"Justice Lapadula, if I may," Chief Quint butt in, trying to come to his protégé's rescue.

Lapadula smiled; he figured the Chief would attempt to come to his former clerk's rescue, and consequently had made sure to come armed with enough ammo to run out the clock. "Your clients should petition their elected officials. *Change* those elected officials if they don't like the results they're getting. Start a national campaign to get their President's attention, and the attention of future candidates for President."

"Mr. Justice, if I could just get back on topic, I'd refer to my brief, which outlines the dishonorable discharges many of my clients have been forced to accept, which have damaged their abilities to get jobs for which they are otherwise *over*-qualified--"

"This seems to me to be the way your clients could find justice," Lapadula soldiered on as if he hadn't even heard her. "Not by dragging a cabinet secretary busy keeping America safe into a litigious court battle he doesn't have time for."

The white light extinguished, the red light next to it popping to life in its place. Rosemarie's time was up, and she could feel a line of sweat dive bombing from her right armpit all the way down her ribs. "Your Honor, if I could just--"

"Thank you, Counsel," Chief Quint's voice quivered, his eyes drenched with sadness. But rules were rules, and he could show no favoritism for Rosemarie, not even after the way Lapadula had unfairly brutalized her. It was his job to keep the Supreme Court on schedule, and that superseded everything. "Mr. Starr?"

The Solicitor General stepped up to the lectern, and after she got her pure, unadulterated shock under control, Rosemarie returned to her seat a few feet behind it.

Rosemarie didn't want to go up and see Chief Quint that afternoon, not after the humiliation she had suffered. She wanted nothing more than to go straight back to her hotel and spend all afternoon nursing her wounds with every bottle of brown liquid she could find in the mini-bar her firm was paying for.

But she understood she didn't have a choice. William Quint wasn't the type to be offended or hold a grudge if he felt slighted, but it would undoubtedly hurt his feelings at least a little if she disappeared without paying her respects, and the very thought of her favorite man in the world experiencing any sort of pain discomfited her.

She never even considered the possibility of what would actually happen next. What was the chance there would be no one else in the long, uninhabited hallway outside the Chief's office when Justice Lapadula stepped out of his own office a few paces away? Noticing Rosemarie waiting to be called into her mentor's office, Lapadula chuckled under his breath. She didn't look over at him, just *sensed* his presence, and though she didn't believe in prayer, realized she was at this moment praying, pleading with some force greater than herself that the Justice let her be and turn the other way.

But Warren Lapadula wasn't one to pass up an opportunity to gloat. The click of his alligator shoes echoed up and down the polished marble as he crossed to Rosemarie's chair, stopping to tower over her, right hand in his pants pocket, his left bringing a bright green apple to his horse's teeth. "A noble cause you fought for today, Ms. Jarzebski," he grinned through a mouth full of fruit flesh. "Perhaps in the hands of a more experienced lawyer … Alas, I guess it wasn't meant to be."

Rosemarie decided her best course of action was to not acknowledge him, to keep her eyes locked on the ground, to not say a word and turn her higher power requests towards the hope that one of the Chief's clerks would come out and fetch her, rescuing her from this nightmare.

Warren Lapadula never took kindly to being ignored. He leaned down on his powerful thighs, bringing his face level with hers. "I think you need to understand something. I am going to make sure you never get this close to my Court again. And if by some miracle you do weasel your way in here, you will find the reception you receive next time to be ten times worse. It is only a matter of time before everyone in your firm, their every client, everyone in this *country* knows they can't trust Rosemarie Jarzebski to bring a case before the Supreme Court – because she can't win there."

He spun on a heel, strutting back the way he came. He didn't hear her rising from her chair behind him. "You think you're so fucking invincible?"

The Justice stopped. "Excuse me?" he called over a shoulder.

"You forget I can tell *everyone* what you did to me?"

As he spun back around, another chuckle spawned from deep in Lapadula's chest. He slithered back toward her until he was staring right down into her eyes. For the first time in nearly four years, she wasn't avoiding his eyes, but locking in on them, defying the control he had held over her since the moment they met. "And who do you think people are going to believe?" he growled. "A dykey second-rate lawyer or a Justice of the Supreme Court?" He turned one final time, spitting out some last words as he walked away from her: "Everyone leads with their resumes in this town. Call me when you've got one."

Reg was the Asshole.

For at least the forty-fifth time this year, the residents of the C Street house known as 'Demo Tau Demo' were passing the night away with collegiate drinking games. The living conditions in this house shared by six Congressmen – ranging in age from 36 to 76 – were so putrid that one had to be drunk to even stomach them. And most of the residents agreed that the quickest and most fun way to get drunk was the card game Asshole, at least since Reg had introduced it upon his arrival six months ago. The house hadn't been updated since the late 1970s when

Marcus Carpinello (D-NY) – now its most senior resident – bought it, and the cleaning service's weekly visits weren't frequent enough to sanitize after six grown men who didn't even have the time to pull their clothes out of their suitcases and put them on hangers.

But it wasn't renowned for being the lap of luxury – it was renowned for its five-block proximity to the Capitol. Being one of the chosen few invited to rent a room was a great honor that had by no coincidence also been a springboard for many young congressional careers. It couldn't hurt to spend every night one had to spend in Washington getting drunk and smoking cigars with five of one's most powerful colleagues, now could it? Reg still wasn't sure how he had earned the invite – which came via a phone call from Carpinello the very next day after he won his seat – but figured his benefactors at the Democratic Congressional Campaign Committee were looking out for him once again.

"Yokah!" Reg yelled out as he threw down four sixes, a declaration his high school best friend 'The Seabass' (Sebastian Falcone) had invoked whenever he had earned a 'Social' – a stoppage of play in which all participants were required to stand and take a simultaneous, ceremonious sip of beer. Reg didn't know what the hell 'yokah' meant – chances were The Seabass didn't either – but the phrase had stuck everywhere he had used it since, from U of O to law school to Demo Tau Demo. The three other elected officials at the table (one of the housemates was home in his district; another had his wife in town and she had insisted on a hotel) chugged down beer, before elderly Carpinello pulled over the nearest garbage can and calmly released a quick, quiet stream of vomit with the urgency of casting a fishing line. This sent the other players into hysterical fits of laughter, beer even shooting out of Reg's nose. Carpinello slammed down into his seat, grabbing his sizable stack of remaining cards. "Four of a kind clears back to you, Irv Griffin."

Reg clapped his empty hands together. "I'm out of cards, Carp. President next game, bitches!"

They continued playing, Reg sticking around to watch each card and drink along with his fellow players, until the doorbell interrupted their fun. "Beer bitch should get the door," one of the other players clarified. (House rules called for rankings of President, Vice President, Beer Bitch and Asshole in any four-man game; while Asshole dealt, Beer Bitch was charged with retrieving beers whenever any player had an empty, and these duties often extended into a variety of errands.)

Carpinello rose with a sigh. "He's right. House rules. I got it."

Irving burst out laughing. "You can't get the door, Carp. You smell like puke."

Carpinello looked around at his fellow players like they were insane. "I will have you know my up-chuck doesn't smell. I invite you to confirm this with Knox Overstreet."

"Who the hell's Knox Overstreet?" one of the others forced through a guffaw.

"My roommate at Hotchkiss. Unfortunately, he died in 1976." That elicited another round of uproar, before Carpinello disappeared to answer the doorbell.

Three minutes later, Carpinello's voice reached them from the landing below. "It's a lovely young lady for you, Reginald."

"Big surprise," one of the others quipped.

"Don't start without me," Reg commanded as he rose. "President picks his pile." He shot down the stairs, passing Carpinello huffing it back up the bannister, then opening the door to find a dripping vision standing out on the front stoop in the rain. "He didn't invite you to come in?"

"He did," Rosemarie answered. "I wasn't sure I wanted to."

"We get that a lot."

It took Rosemarie a few seconds to get out her next sentence. In the energetic burst that got her over here, she had neglected to script what exactly she was going to say. "I've thought about you," was what finally came out.

"I've thought about you, too."

"You're going to stand for universal single-payer health care. You're going to champion an immigration policy that includes amnesty. Take us to rehab for our greatest addiction: fossil fuels. Fight for limits on clips and magazines, rather than on guns themselves."

"Restrained but effective. Love it."

"And you're going to make sure that any sexual predators finding safe haven in our military are brought to justice in civilian courts of law."

Reg felt not only a huge smile spreading from ear to ear, but something more, something deep in his core, something right behind his eyes, something under the skin of his arms and down his legs. For the first time in his life, he was getting that tingle he knew so many people got when they were feeling patriotic. *This woman,* this fascinating, power-packed, insanely brilliant woman had this magic ability to make him finally feel the potential of politics, the magic of America.

And on top of that, she looked hot as hell sopping wet.

"You sure you don't want to come in? We've got lots of beer."

"I've been drinking Macallan all afternoon."

Reg stepped aside, opening the door all the way with an underhanded butler's flourish. "Liquor before beer, you're in the clear!"

WEDNESDAY

The President marched down the hallway to the Oval determined to make his first meeting of the day a short one. He had ordered Bryce to cancel Fleisher four days ago, only for Bryce to retort that no one canceled on Jacob Fleisher, not even – *especially* not – a President of the United States. (Salas was already starting to not like Sando, but he also knew he was right.)

Jacob Fleisher was not only the owner and founder of the first social media platform to surpass Facebook in popularity, but had also single-handedly contributed almost a tenth of Salas's entire campaign funds four years ago, over one hundred million dollars in 'dark' (its source undisclosed) money to Democratic SuperPACs. That was without mentioning how vital Fleisher's site was in stirring up and focusing the passion of America's newest eligible voters. So, though Salas thought it inappropriate to be spending precious time meeting with a social media magnate while on the verge of war in the Middle East and in the midst of the humiliation of his final Supreme Court nominee (and close friend), he also knew he shouldn't, he couldn't, say no to Jacob Fleisher, not with his second campaign about to kick off. Besides, there was something he needed to make very clear to the 28-year-old.

"I appreciate you keeping our meeting, Mr. President," Fleisher smiled as he sat down on one of the couches. Salas didn't even flinch at his jeans or hoodie, by now used to the young billionaire's ever-casual attire. Besides, those jeans probably cost more than his suit; the hoodie, more than his shoes.

Salas sat down across from him, as he had in all their Oval Office confabs. Fleisher had first requested a private, one-on-one meeting with the President in the initial one hundred days after his inauguration, a request that was of course honored, if only for a few minutes, and it had since become a tradition for the two of them to hold these pow-wows a couple of times a year. Nothing of substance was ever discussed, but their brief conferences made Fleisher feel like he was listened to, like he was almost a de facto member of the Administration – like his money had been well spent.

"I wanted to see you too, Jake," POTUS said. "There's something I've wanted to tell you, and I've wanted to do it in person: with everything going on, I've put off thinking about the election for at least a couple more—"

"I'm not here about the election. I'm here about Israel."

"Israel?" Salas had to think for a moment – had he even known for sure that Fleisher was Jewish? When he had first heard his name five years ago, when they were courting him to be an early believer, he had assumed him to be of Jewish descent – but that was the last time he had thought about it. He had never known Jake to express any religious priorities, let alone concern for the Jews' ancestral homeland.

"Mr. President, when you're at the UN, you should be building a coalition *against* Iran. You can't validate President Ghaznavi by meeting with him."

The President rubbed his hands together. He wanted to let Fleisher off easy, without making it too obvious he would never take suggestions from him on anything, let alone foreign policy. "I have to give him a chance to explain what he does or doesn't know about the Supreme Court."

"You know what he's going to say. He's gonna act all nice and obsequious, then go on Al Jazeera and rail about how weak you were. As soon as you moved carrier groups into the Persian Gulf, you had already played our hand. We don't do something now, and Iran will know we're never going to do anything. They'll know we didn't retaliate after they hit *us*--"

"Look, Jake, I know what they're saying on cable, but we still don't know they had anything to do with that."

"They'll think they can finally strike at Israel, and we're not going to do a damn thing about it."

"You know that's not true."

"It doesn't matter what I do or don't know. How many Israelis might die because President Ghaznavi, or more importantly his Supreme Leader, thinks it is true?"

"Everyone knows we support Israel."

"You proposed cutting our aid to them by a billion dollars."

"I proposed cutting aid to many nations. My point was that in this economic climate, we need to closely reexamine who really *needs* our money. Does Israel really need three billion a year from us right now, and can we afford to give it?"

Fleisher shut his eyes, well aware of how heated discussions about Israel could get in a hurry. "Mr. President, I'm not here to argue about Israel with you.

Just to let you know that this issue, what we do in the Middle East, is a priority for me, as I consider how involved to be with the next election."

"I'm glad you brought that up, Jake. Your contributions were very valuable four years ago. But I can't govern based on what's important to a few key contributors. You know I can't. If that means I need to go on this journey without you this year – I'd be saddened, I've come to consider you a friend – but I'm prepared to do that." Fleisher sat back, pushing a forced, staged laugh out of his gut. "We've run some numbers," the President continued, "and even if you gave zero dollars this year, we still expect to out-raise the Benedict campaign. And that's assuming Benedict is the nominee. The other GOP candidates don't have nearly the fundraising reach he's got."

"You think this is about money? You think that's the greatest thing I have to offer you?"

"You're one of the ten richest men in this country."

"Money is nothing. You didn't win four years ago because of money. If I want, I can make sure no one on my site ever sees anything but negative articles about you. I can make it so every other post any user on my site sees is a positive article about your opponent. Mr. President, I have 250 million Americans interacting on my site each month, at least 200 of them voting age, and if you don't govern based on what's important to me, I can convince all of them that their mom, dad, sister, best friends and the first boy they kissed back in the 3rd Grade are all tired of you and are voting for Bradley Benedict. Maybe that's no big deal. But last I checked, I only have to swing, oh, about two percent of them, five million of my users, and I can personally pick the winner in a presidential election."

"Jake, are you actually threatening me to wage war on another nation?"

"No one says we have to go to full-out war with them. I just think it's about time we finally carried a big stick again."

There were numerous routes Rosemarie Irving could have taken to the Dirksen Senate Office Building on Wednesday morning without being seen or detected by the press. The underground garage to the Irvings' townhouse was connected by a secret bomb-proof tunnel to what appeared to be a public parking garage half a mile away. And yet, Rosemarie chose to step out of her front door and stroll down her front steps, elected to fight through cameras and shouted questions to reach MMA at the back door of her Escalade. And twelve minutes later, she asked to be dropped off right in front of the iconic steps of the Capitol, which she would mount cinematically through another media throng, before taking the Capitol mini-subway to her date with the Judiciary Committee. In both encounters with reporters, Rosemarie didn't answer any questions – but inside, she savored them all. "Mrs. Irving, has your husband told you if he was seduced by Rebecca Whitford?" "Madame First Lady, what would you say to Ms. Whitford if you ran into her today?" They were the exact questions she had predicted, the very questions she had wanted. Their plan was working to perfection.

Xander Peabody had been a friend since Reginald Irving had first arrived in Washington as a young Congressman – back when Xan was Carl Bernstein's assistant, long before he worked his way up to executive producer of *Morning Joe*. Leaking Rebecca Whitford's identity and sordid history was as easy as one phone call to Xan. Suddenly, the story was less about the former President's infidelity and more about all the powerful men a confused, abused-as-a-child career seductress had fucked on her way to the top. Overnight, Reg had gone from being a filthy adulterer to the victim of a conniving, social-climbing venus flytrap. Conservative outlets like Fox News wouldn't let him off the hook, of course, but even they couldn't help but cast Becks as this generation's Tonya Harding or Heidi Fleiss.

"Mr. Chairman," Rosemarie said into the mic. It was 10:05 AM, on an unexpected sixth day of hearings on Rosemarie Irving's candidacy for Chief Justice Lapadula's vacated seat. "Members of the Judiciary Committee. Thank you for reconvening so I could have the opportunity to make this statement." Rosemarie had written the remarks the night before, but she didn't read them; the words flowed like they were forming spontaneously in the deepest core of her heart.

"First, I want to make sure everyone here understands that I did not volunteer to appear before you today to talk about an amateur video that has surfaced of my husband having sex with another woman." A buzz passed through the press section behind her, and most of the committee members shuffled with discomfort at the first mention of anything salacious in this hallowed chamber since Anita Hill was describing Long Dong Silver and pubic haired Cokes. Chairman Clyde Dudley was the only one who didn't move, a small respectful grin glued across his lips, his eyes locked on the First Lady as she spoke, savoring this little ballet he had personally choreographed. "I was of course gravely disappointed and hurt by his betrayal, as any wife or husband whose partner has strayed would be. But he has promised it was just one slip. He has begged my forgiveness, and I have given it, as Christ teaches us to do.

"I have also forgiven the young woman who was the other half of this equation. I cannot begin to identify with the set of circumstances that would inspire one to initiate a sexual relationship with another woman's husband, but I grant that the Lord has not blessed everyone equally, and that some of the most frustrating people in our lives need our deepest compassion and patience.

"I am also not here because of my nomination. Today has nothing to do with me. I enjoyed our conversation last week about my qualifications and legal philosophies, and I trust you got to know me well enough then to pass judgment.

"I was compelled to appear before you one final time because of the injustice I observed in the Senate chambers over the last two days. Although the debate was ostensibly about me, I feel that it is truly the women of America who were victimized. I am here because I had to come to their defense. This week, the Senate committed a crime that has been perpetrated for millennia, that ancient belief that somehow, when a man strays, the woman is to blame. She didn't give him enough of what he needed, and so he *had* to stray. Somehow, when a man beats his wife, the woman is to blame. She should have left long ago; she must have somehow provoked him; he *had* to hit her. Somehow, when a man rapes a woman, it is because of what she was wearing, how much she had to drink, and how aggressively she came on to him. He just *had* to rape her. *The woman is to blame.*

"My nomination has nothing to do with my husband. My husband will in no way affect my knowledge of the law, my dedication to stare decisis, or my ability to lead your Supreme Court from the ashes of tragedy back into its home opposite the Capitol where it belongs. Am I worthy of the great task our President has set before me? I ask you to judge this from what you know of *me* – whether we have known each other for many years, or had our first opportunity last week – and not from my husband's actions of the distant or recent past.

"Thank you for this time. It will be my pleasure to take any new questions you may have."

There were no additional questions. After a few moments of silence, a female Democrat from California leaned into her mic to suggest, "Mr. Chairman, I'd like to make a motion that we honor last week's vote to recommend and adjourn." This motion was unanimously accepted, and Clyde Dudley's dream of dragging the Rosemarie debate into later in the year was dead. By the end of the day, MSNBC's *Cycle* and Fox's *Five* were themselves collectively unanimous for maybe the first time ever: No Senator would be able to vote against Rosemarie Irving now, not if they hoped to win another female vote in their careers. They all agreed the First Lady would by week's end become the first nominee confirmed unanimously in over three decades, and may even garner the first ever 100-0 vote (many votes before the 1960s were collected by voice, but still, an impressive feat).

Dudley made his way back to his Russell Building office alone, riding the subway in silence, without even an aide by his side. He nodded to a couple people he knew as he made his way to the elevator, then up to the seventh floor where his office had been located for the past thirteen years, since his first ascension to Majority Leader. He made sure to appreciate everything he loved about these facilities, resigned to the fact he was now in his final nine months of using them. He smiled at his sweet secretary as he passed her desk, but again didn't say a word, nor pause when she rose with one forefinger raised, as if to warn him of something.

She was going to warn him that Rebecca Whitford was waiting in his office, along with eleven other women ranging in age from their late 20s to early 50s. Dudley knew who they were without even having to ask. He and his Chief of Staff had secretly christened them, 'The Dirty Dozen,' twelve women who had shared beds with Reginald Irving since he wed Rosemarie Jarzebski. Becks had told him she had an entire group that wanted to speak up (and there were dirty dozens more where these came from), and they were all ready to jump into duty when the need arose.

"I'm afraid it's over, Ms. Whitford," Dudley shook his head, coming around his desk to sit down, nonplussed that she was perched on the front of it. "You didn't see her speech? That woman is invincible now."

Becks stood and turned around to face him, putting her hand on the shoulder of the closest woman to her left, a beauty with the coffee skin of Indian descent. "Before you kick us out, Senator, I think you'll want to at least hear what Nundhini has to say."

When George visited his daughter in her Waterford apartment on Wednesday night, Brenda was very … *Brenda*. She was already in her pajama bottoms, an oversized XXL shirt draped on top of them, some SyFy show on the TV behind her. She claimed to have already eaten dinner, and George hoped that was true, it now being past 8 PM. He had been taken off the Supreme Court case because of his failure to hold Jason Lancaster back in November. (Luckily no one had noticed George had been the last person to speak to Jason before his death in the East River or he would be out of a job, if not his freedom.) But he still had to report to the Ops Center each day, and with the nation on high alert ever since that attack, no one was allowed to leave after banker's hours, not even someone like George, assigned to nothing more than staring at his own email. He had been leaving at 7 for the past week, usually too late to get to the Waterford in time to dine with Brenda. And that was okay with him; as long as she was remembering to eat on her own, his feelings weren't hurt that the meal wasn't consumed sitting across from him.

After some pushing, George railroaded her into letting him at least join her for some television. George was always reminded during these little squabbles how Brenda's mother had never believed in pushing Brenda, and because of that, could go months without getting any quality time with their daughter. It was one of the things that had driven mother and daughter apart, and made George pledge after his wife's suicide that he would from then on never stop insisting, never stop pushing.

George and Brenda shared three sentences during the next two hours of programming (some reality show about cosplay followed by an episode of that terrible *Star Trek* series with the Russian woman from the Netflix prison show at the helm), but George was satisfied. This was all he needed. He was there for his daughter. He was the best father he could be. He was the one who had cursed her with these genes; he was the one who should be there in case she ever needed him. It was rare, but once a year or so she had a breakdown or an incident, once a year she needed someone. And he was never going to miss one of those times again.

He still believed in Jason; there had just been something in his eyes, in his voice over their few phone calls, in the way he talked about the love of his life, that made George believe this was an honest young man just trying to get to the truth of what went down on October 7th. But he had started to acknowledge that maybe his instincts had for the first time, on what might very well be the final marquee assignment of his career, failed him; maybe Jason had poisoned his thoughts about Kingman Summers' handling of the unexploded ordnance recovered from the ruins of the Court; maybe everyone else was right and *Jason* was the bad guy all along.

And what did it even matter now? He hoped he had survived his plunge into the East River and would be forever hiding out, bearded in Nome or Cartagena or Amundsen-Scott South Pole Station. But deep down, George knew he was dead.

The simple fact was, the more days he spent away from the case, the less George cared. This helpless girl sitting on the other side of the couch from him – she was all he cared about now, not some stranger he met four months earlier who most likely was a terrorist.

As the 10 PM program began, George checked his watch. "Getting late isn't it?"

"I'm 25, you know," Brenda responded without breaking her eyes from the HD glow.

George stood, and as he came around the back of the couch, he patted her shoulder. She *was* 25. She could decide how late she stayed up on any given night. And if she was tired the next day, she could find time to take a nap. Everything was going to be fine. He was there to support her. That was all that mattered.

It was after he had started the engine of his Volvo that he felt the press of cold steel against the back of his neck. "*Easy* now." He recognized Jason's voice instantly. "Just drive home. I've got a lot to explain to you."

1996

"So … your ring being cleaned?" Chief Quint finally asked as he stirred his virgin Bloody Mary with the celery stalk. Rosemarie figured he had noticed her bare ring finger right when she walked into the Marbury v. Madison Dining Room – Chief Quint always noticed *everything* – and she had spent a considerable portion of their meal wondering when he was going to come right out and ask about it.

"We separated," she admitted, looking down at her outstretched left hand, at the tan line the two-carat diamond and its yellow band had left behind. Rosemarie was more honest with this man, more connected to him, than any other person on this planet. She didn't sugarcoat anything with him or his wife (the way she would for her parents), and wasn't going to make up a lie here, even as plagued with doubt about her decision as she was. She hadn't even told the elder Jarzebskis yet. When it came to anything in Rosemarie's life, Chief Quint was often the first to know.

"Oh, Rosemarie, I'm so sorry." He reached over for her other hand, patting pure love into it. "But the new baby--"

"Reg cheated on me," she stated flatly.

"The schmuck bastard."

"He threw out the first pitch for the Portland Beavers last week--"

"There's a Don Rickles joke in there somewhere."

"They're our Triple-A team. In the third inning I caught him in the bathroom of our suite with some girl from their marketing department. I moved into the Benson that night."

"*You* moved?"

"He has to stay in Portland." She played with a loose string of the table linen. "I have nothing keeping me there. I could go back to Columbus. I could come here."

"So that's it?"

"He came to the hotel the next night. He was sobbing. He begged my forgiveness. He promised he would never do it again."

Quint set his drink down. "Rosemarie. You believed him."

"Is that wrong?"

Quint shrugged. He had made enough mistakes with his biological children; he wanted to make sure he never pushed her too hard down any one path, but allowed her life to play out the way it was meant to play out. "Not if it feels right."

"At that moment-- He was so honest, so naked. It was the first time I'd ever seen him like that. He said he'd started seeing a shrink, a-- Dr. Siegal, I think?"

"If it's Walt Siegal, he is the best."

"He's helping Reg identify the origin of his sex addiction."

"Sex addiction," Quint scoffed. "What we used to call a schmuck bastard too self-centered to ever turn it down. Sex addiction." He shook his head, finally taking that first taste of spicy tomato.

"He never knew his father. His mother brought around so many different men when he was growing up, and in their tiny two bedroom apartment, he could always-- *hear* them… He thinks, in some weird way, each conquest is just another attempt to make his mother love him more."

There was something behind her eyes Quint had never before seen in this ruthless creature of pure ambition. "You still love him."

"I don't know." After a beat, she collected herself and took the first sip of her own virgin cocktail. "Maybe he was never the right one for me."

"Every person, every love is different, Rosemarie. I can't tell you if he's right for you. No one can. If this man is the one for you, the one and only, then even his faults, his mistakes, will be worth suffering because you love everything he gives you in spite of them."

"I don't know, I just-- I used to have such grand goals. I used to think my destiny was to be so much more than a politician's wife. To be defined on my own terms, not by whom I'm married to."

"You still have that destiny. That destiny cannot be denied or broken, and you know that. What you don't know, what none of us know, is how we are going to get to our destinies. Perhaps this is just one necessary step to put you in position to someday seize that which is rightfully yours."

"But what if Reg has a ceiling? What if by staying with him I would somehow be stagnating myself?"

"Oh come now, Rosemarie," Quint grinned. "His ceiling's as high as *you* build it, and we both know it."

Rosemarie wasn't in Chicago for The Speech.

She had specifically decided to go to the Benson Hotel gym at the exact same time that Reg would be appearing before the Democratic National Convention two thousand miles to her east. She had left Baby Chad with Reg's Mom, explaining that she wasn't sure she could watch Reg give a speech right now, but wanted to make sure her son, as young as he was, didn't miss it.

The President had taken note of Reg when he introduced him in Ohio four years ago, had noticed the reaction he stirred up in a crowd, and had been keeping tabs on him, grooming him, ever since. She wasn't sure how missing this career pinnacle she herself had worked so hard to help Reg achieve was going to make her feel, and being in the gym gave her the option of ignoring it. Or, if she did find herself missing it, if she thought she could handle it, she could turn the TV above her exercise bike to one of the cable news nets and catch the whole thing while at the same time doing something good for herself.

As she often did, Rosemarie got so engrossed in her workout, she lost track of time and forgot that Reg's time to go on had passed. This was Rosemarie's routine, drowning out an entire room behind a cacophony of techno (she didn't even particularly like this genre, but loved how it didn't allow her to pause and think, just keep moving). As she increased the intensity of her workout, as she pounded all her anger into that bike, her mind disappeared, focusing only on the pain.

It was after she finished one of these grueling sixty minute sets on the bike that she noticed the gaggle of women (and even a couple men) gathered in one corner of the gym, packed so tightly – the ones in back trying to peer over the shoulders of those in front – she couldn't even see what they were looking at.

Then she heard Reg's voice. *What is he still doing on?* she asked herself. *He was supposed to go on a half hour ago, and the speech was only twelve minutes when we clocked it.* Another towering, heroic sentence, another one she didn't recognize. *What is he-- he's adlibbing!* She heard the eruption of the United Center on the down beat of every line. She heard some of the girls at the TV tittering and laughing and even cheering, heard them whispering about what a hunk he was, before others shushed them. She heard him in the flow of perfect improvisation, feeding off the energy of the crowd, giving them exactly what they needed and wanted in return.

Rosemarie stepped in front of her bike, reaching up on her toes to tap at the channel button on the hanging television until it found her estranged husband's handsome visage. Then the angle shifted, tracking some of the rapt, elated faces in the crowd all around him. Many of them had never seen this Reginald Irving before, or even heard of him. But this charisma, this delivery, this passion and energy and *perfect fucking hair* – he was like a younger version of the President. This was never more evident than when the President made a surprising appearance at the conclusion of The Speech to hold Reg's arm aloft like a heavyweight champion. Looking at them standing there, the Dems filling the United Center couldn't help but dream of a Democratic dynasty. They had quietly been fretting for weeks about their dull-as-paint VP, and his not-so-slam-dunk prospects to succeed the President in four years.

Tonight, they had found his true heir. Tonight, they had found a star.

After three additional days of DNCing, Reg should have been exhausted. He was anything but. He was so keyed up he could only stay in his seat during take-off and landing of the small Gulfstream the campaign gave him for the trip to and from Chicago; every second above ten thousand was spent pacing or dancing or hitting on the flight attendant or mixing another drink. He knew it would take something a little extra to get to sleep on this night, and knew exactly what that little extra needed to be. He emailed his assistant Adam from the air and had him make sure the limo company would pick Candace up from her Beaverton apartment before coming out to Hillsboro Airport to get him.

Reg had already had one orgasm by the time the town car crossed into Lake Oswego. Candace had tried to start with the small talk, that pretense of mutual interest in which all prostitutes seem to come well schooled. Reg was having none of that: as she peppered him with questions about the Convention, he silently raised the opaque partition up to the driver, then undid his belt and lowered his pants to his ankles, revealing his readiness. "Well now," Candace smiled, swiveling to move onto her knees.

Reg grunted his disapproval and held her on her seat, then reached up into her skirt and yanked down her underwear around her own calves. He lifted her up, then down onto his lap, keeping her face away from his, just staring at her quaking rump as he held her by the waist and lowered her up and down until his business was complete.

He was tempted to take her back to Beaverton, but remembering that Rosemarie and Chad had moved downtown, decided that he might as well bring Candace home and get the complete value of the full evening he had already paid for. They had just stepped into the foyer of the house, the limo's headlights washing away on the ceiling above them, when Candace slammed him up against a wall and started kissing him again. "I want to come this time," she purred in his ear. "You made me so wet before, then didn't finish me."

"You want to be fucked again?" Reg smiled, taking her arms and backing her towards a small display table, covered with generations of Irving family photos, from sepia-toned to color printed.

"Take me to your room."

"No," Reg insisted, pushing his arm past her, sweeping all the photos off the table and onto the floor. He lifted her up and set her ass down on the table, reached up to once again remove her panties, then got her ready with one hand as he lowered his pants with his other and stroked some life back into himself. Finally, he was firm enough to make his entrancc, her head rolling back with a groan as he went all the way in, up to his full depth.

He rutted away for several minutes, Candace's moan finding a steady rhythm – but never building to ecstacy. She could feel he wasn't his full hardness, probably too drained from their first go-around. "Are you going to come?" she finally panted. "I don't think I--"

She suddenly screamed, sitting straight up.

"What, what is it?"

Without words, Candace turned a little, looking back over her right shoulder into the kitchen – where *someone* was seated at the table, in the shadows, staring out at them, watching them.

Reg couldn't see her face, but recognized the silhouette. It was his wife.

But he didn't pull back, didn't pull out of Candance. He could see Rosemarie's right hand around a glass of red wine. He could see her other hand between her thighs; he could imagine where her fingers lay.

Almost on instinct, he started thrusting again. Candacc's grunts grew deeper, as she felt Reg growing larger and larger inside of her, bigger than she'd ever felt him. She leaned her head all the way back, looking upside down at the woman at the kitchen table, her fingers picking up speed on her own pleasure center.

Reg also never moved his eyes off Rosemarie, realizing as he went that it was her he had imagined when he closed his eyes in the town car.

Seconds later, all three of them screamed in unison ecstacy.

Reg pulled out, falling back against the wall behind him, sucking wind. Candace grabbed her underwear up off the floor and stormed out the front door. She didn't know what exactly had just happened, just that it was weird as fuck, and that she would happily walk a few blocks in the summer night air until she reached a major enough road that a cab would pass her by.

Reg stared into the kitchen at his wife, more surprised by her than he had ever been before. She stood up, downing the rest of her pinot noir in one swallow. All he could think to do was smile and make a cheap crack. "Maybe if we'd tried this earlier--"

"You don't have the willpower or maturity I wished you would have. I understand that now. I'm not going to try to change you like some stupider women might."

"Hey, there's no reason to get nasty about--"

"Nothing nasty about it, Reg. I came here tonight to tell you I'm going to let you be the man you are. I'm not going to hold it against you. I'm not going to divorce you over it."

"Okay," he looked at her sideways. "What's the catch?"

"There are two of them. You're going to be a helluva lot smarter than you've been. No college interns, no sports marketing PAs, no hookers who can later extort us. You're only to fuck women you've cleared with me, that we both agree would never betray you without great personal cost to themselves."

Reg nearly laughed at the sheer strangeness of this situation. "And what's the other?"

"You're going to do whatever it takes to become President of the United States."

THURSDAY

George's hand shook as he splashed ginger ale onto the ice cubes stacked on the bottom of one glass, then did the same with the next. This was the first time he had ever hosted a suspected mass-murderer in his home.

"They're trying to get in on whatever we do in Iran, I guarantee it." Jason was pacing, foaming at the mouth like a rabid dog. But when George offered up one of the tumblers, Jason did take a five second break to down his entire glass in one attempt. "They've got the men, they've got the materiel." He slammed down his empty, shaking his head with a cynical laugh. "Sick fucking brilliant plan, huh? A company blowing up the Supreme Court so they get the contract to run all combat operations against the country we blame for blowing up the Supreme Court."

As he nursed his own drink, George got his first real good look at Jason. And he looked like shit, like he hadn't slept or eaten anything more nourishing than a freeway exit burger or lukewarm rest stop coffee in weeks. He had given George only the barest details of his whereabouts since his plunge from FDR Drive: His parents had always owned two acres in Appalachia, in Southern Virginia where it was just a little warmer, where the ground was damp but not covered with bumpers of slush. Left in his sister's married name when the Sarge died, it couldn't be linked to Jason without some serious digging. Still, he wouldn't dare sleep in the actual cabin; any day now, Allied Armament or the FBI or DHS or frigging Navy SEALs could raid the place looking for him. (And besides, it looked like it might cave in on your head at any moment, that's why they had never VRBOed it.) He instead found an old cranny between the overgrown trees where he used to hide as a boy to lay down a tarp and sleeping bag. He made daily treks into Big Stone Gap for a wi-fi signal on which he could check on Allied Armament, on the Supreme Court and Rosemarie Irving, and it was during yesterday's check of the news that he realized he couldn't afford, *this nation* couldn't afford for him to hide out any longer.

"Jason," George pleaded, "all of this, Allied Armament, Rosemarie Irving, you told me all this over the phone, when you were in Sacerdoti's apartment--"

"And you didn't do a thing about it."

"You have no inkling how little political capital I have left."

"I don't blame you. This is *Manchurian Candidate, Parallax View*-level shit going down. These assholes are this close to running this country. They win this case, they'll be handpicking every war we fight from now on based on their profit margins. Going up against them is taking your life into your hands. I know you have a family--"

"A daughter. Yes."

"I know I'm the only one who can do this. They targeted me. They *framed* me. They took everything from me."

"There's no part of you that thinks all that might sound just a little ... outlandish?"

"Outlandish?" He stopped now, eyes searing deep into George's skull. "All that stuff that's been on the news from my past, from Miranda's past, about our interest in Islam, our possible connections to terrorists? *That's* outlandish. It's all been made up out of whole cloth."

"And they chose to pin all this specifically on *you* because ...?"

"Not *they*. I know who chose me. One man chose me. I know why."

"And you want me to help you take him down?"

Jason finally sat. "We don't have time for that. That's exactly what they want, for me to get selfish like that and do something stupid and walk right into their trap. No, there's only one way to stop them now.

"But time is already running out. The Supreme Court changed their schedule. They just announced it yesterday. The first case they're going to hear under Rosemarie Irving is Allied Armament's case. When I saw that change, that's when I knew I was right. When I knew we had to act *now*."

"And do what exactly?"

"Make sure the Court never hears that case. At least, not with the makeup of Justices that Rosemarie Irving's worked so hard to get nominated and confirmed."

George covered his face in his hands, then pushed his elbows down into his knees, rising up to his feet. He took a lap behind the couch, before turning back, planting both hands into pillows and leaning closer to Jason. "A lot has changed since I met you. I've been kicked off this investigation, I've been put on review. My whole career's worth of pension, and every benefit I use to take care of my sick daughter, is on the line now. Everyone else – *everyone* – believes that you were a part of this bombing. So you must see how it would be just a little difficult for me to put everything, to put my *daughter* on the line, and keep trusting you?"

Jason's eyes brightened with an idea. "You're right. You're absolutely right. It's not me you should listen to at all."

Salas could have called the Irvings during the ride in his Tanque out to Andrews, but he wanted them on teleconference. He needed to see their faces, needed to look Rosemarie directly in the eyes, when he delivered this news. They snapped onto the Air Force One conference room's main 65-inch screen in clearer, crisper, HDier resolution than most people got on their Skypes at home. The President recognized the logo on the wall behind their heads and realized they were in the conference room of their foundation offices, a bitter irony considering the extortion Dudley had just moments before wielded against him.

"It's just the three of us, correct?" Salas asked before they had even traded good mornings.

"Correct," Rosemarie confirmed straight into their webcam, as Reg nodded at someone off screen, shooing the last person out.

As soon as he heard a door shut on the Irvings' end, Salas began, "Clyde Dudley pulled me aside after the National Prayer Breakfast. Rosemarie should withdraw, he casually warned me, or he's got at least a dozen more women prepared to come forward and talk about their own affairs with Reg."

"He couldn't possibly be that stupid," Rosemarie responded.

"Let him go right ahead," Reg agreed. "It doesn't matter if there's one hundred girls instead of one. Everything Rosemarie said yesterday is even more apropos. If this moron tries to say she's not qualified to be Chief Justice because of my infidelity, the women of America will have his balls in a sling."

"Reg. This will destroy your legacy--"

"My legacy's been written, Tony. This is Rosemarie's time now."

Salas saw their arms moving closer and realized they were taking each other's hands right below the frame line. "We know our marriage may be hard for many people to understand," Rosemarie concurred, "but it's worked for us. We've been preparing for the day when we have to explain that to the men and women of America for the past--"

"He has a girl who says she was paid to keep her mouth shut." This stopped them cold in their tracks. "With Foundation money." This smashed through their confidence like a bullet through a plate of glass. Rosemarie's shoulder moved away from her husband's, her hand retracting from his.

"It's not true," she murmured.

"It doesn't matter, once that's let out of the box--"

"Get us a name." Salas heard her fingernail pounding down into the conference table with each word. "We can destroy anyone's credibility, we just need a couple of hours to make phone calls--"

"RM," Reg announced solemnly. "It is true."

For several seconds, the three of them just sat there in silence, the three most powerful people in the country rendered powerless.

Then Reg was on his feet, pacing manically, in and out of the webcam frame. "No. No, we're not letting one of these bitches burn us down--"

"Hey. Reg."

"We'll hold a press conference. Yes, we'll beat them to it. Tony, tell that asshole Dudley we need 24 hours to decide. In the meantime, we tell the American people our side of this. We make the narrative ours. We explain that Rosemarie didn't know anything about this. It's all me, this has nothing to do with her or her confirmation. And we've been working through our issues. We've been in counseling. Dr. Siegal, he'll gladly get in front of the mic and say whatever we need him to say, he's offered many times. They're going to believe us. I'm the President. Americans want to believe their Presidents." He returned to camera, leaning down into it. "Don't worry, Tony, we'll fix this. This is what we do." He bounded out of the frame, and Salas could hear the door opening again, then a yell fading down the hall: "AMBER, WE NEED A PRESS CONFERENCE TOMORROW!"

Rosemarie and Antonio stayed connected, but neither was able to look at the other.

Her eyes rose again suddenly. The pain, the confusion was gone, replaced by straight, cold business. "There's something else I've needed to talk to you about. I know about your meeting with Allied Armament."

"It was a photo op, a thank you for their--"

"I know they want a piece of whatever we do in Iran. A big piece. I understand what they can offer must be very appealing to you."

"Rosemarie--"

"I don't want to know what you're planning. I just want you to do yourself a favor, and not plan on using them."

"Excuse me?"

"Don't rely on Allied Armament. I'm not going to let them become our corporate military."

"Look, there's something I need to say too. I think maybe the last few months, I've let you become too involved with some of my--"

"As soon as I'm confirmed, I'm going to lop their fucking balls off."

Salas grimaced, gripping his temples between forefinger and thumb. "I don't want to hear this. You know I can't hear this."

"I just don't want to see you embarrass yourself."

"Like you're letting your husband do?"

"What?"

"If he holds a presser tomorrow-- he's going to be the first President to confess to a crime since Nixon. He could go to jail for this. And … we both know it's not going to save you. This is too deep. This is too ugly. I'm sorry. But it's over."

"I know."

"You can't let him do this. You guys need to end this gracefully."

Her eyes raised into his. "I know."

She killed the connection.

Salas didn't move for several more seconds, just staring at his reflection in the sleek screen until he felt the floor dropping beneath him, and heard the Captain announcing they were descending to New York.

"Ms. Whitney, my name is George Aug, I'm with the Department of Homeland Security," George introduced himself. The burly guard finished locking Miranda down to the metal table and made his exit, sealing George in with America's most notorious criminal.

She didn't look up at him, so George tilted his head down to look up into her eyes. Her cosmetic-free face was as ragged and tired as her gait had been hobbled by her injured ankle. But George could still see a foundation of great beauty and understand how she had once stolen Jason Lancaster's heart.

"It appears you haven't answered any questions posed by any of the investigators that have visited with you here. I thought I would give it a try and see if maybe you feel up to it today." She didn't look up, her lips not even flinching.

George had read the transcripts of every interrogation session since Allied Armament found her in Michigan's Huron National Forest, and expected no less. She had yet to utter a word in her three weeks in West Virginia's United States Penitentiary, Hazelton. (Though technically a men's prison, the nature and notoriety of Miranda's alleged crimes had led to calls that she be detained in no less than supermax-level incarceration; she was being kept in segregation, separate from the men.)

"Maybe we should start with something simple. Your name is Miranda Whitney, is that correct?"

Nothing.

"These stories I've heard, about you being curious about Islam, taking classes at a local mosque when you were younger, is any of that true?"

Still nothing.

George suddenly brought his hand to his mouth with a hard intake of breath. He stuffed his other hand in his front pants pocket, pulling out a hanky, also bringing that to his nose before letting out a loud sneeze. George's sneezes were infamous in the DHS Ops Center, always the loudest of anyone's, and he had never failed to make everyone within earshot start with surprise when they heard him blast one out.

But still, Miranda didn't flinch.

"Darn winter allergies," George smiled, tossing the hanky onto the table between them.

He didn't say anything more, didn't ask another question, for a handful of minutes. He stared at Miranda's eyes, but they didn't move.

Then they raised ever so slightly, passing over the hanky for just a hair of a second, just long enough to light up with realization, exactly as Jason had predicted.

"Y--" she tried to verbalize, then had to clear her throat of everything that had built up on it over weeks of not being used. "Yes," she moused once her vocal pathways had opened.

"Thank you," George said with a wink, a nod and a smile. He crumpled up the hanky and stuffed it back in his pocket, then stepped up to the door behind him to knock to be let out.

He wasn't sure he was free and clear until his car was a few miles off the premises, wasn't sure his old collegiate acting skills were still good enough to pull off that sneeze, wasn't sure that the cameras monitoring the interrogation cell weren't HD enough to pick up the words he had Sharpied onto his hanky:

DOES ALLIED ARMAMENT HAVE YOUR SON?

"Mr. President." Salas smiled as he entered the suite of the Warwick Hotel, offering an outstretched hand to his Iranian counterpart--

But President Ghaznavi's hands were occupied, holding a shirt box, a white soccer jersey with red and green highlights displayed inside. "Mr. President. It is my pleasure to present you with the official kit of our Iranian national football team, which advanced past the group stage for the first time in the last World Cup."

Salas took it in his hands and chuckled with pleasure. He had been dreading this meeting for weeks, and the Iranian President had disarmed any tension in the first five seconds. "I'm touched, Mr. President."

"A love of football was the strongest bond my father and I shared," Ghaznavi said as they sat. "We were very blessed financially, and were able to afford a satellite dish. We used it to watch every football match we could find. Any nation, any league. We saw your ten saves against Boca Juniors in Copa Libertadores Final."

"Just needed one more," Salas blushed.

"Ah, penalty shoot-out says nothing about the goalkeeper. It is such a, a gimmick!"

"As much as we all love soccer," the voice of Salas's VP, Richard Ruby, cut off their laughs from the President's left, "we're here about much more serious business."

"Of course," Ghaznavi nodded.

"Mr. President," Salas took over, "I'm sure you've heard all sorts of ridiculous things in our news media since your arrival here about what we should be doing in your country. I wanted to meet with you to assure you that I'm not going to do anything rash, or leap to any judgments. I just need answers, the American people want answers, about the bombing of our Supreme Court."

"Give us the perpetrators," Ruby frothed at the mouth, "and nothing *unfortunate* has to happen."

"Please believe me," Ghaznavi answered with open, empty palms. "I wish I could. But we know no more about this terrible tragedy than you do."

"It is really disapointing to hear that," Ruby sat back. "We can't promise--"

"I'd like to speak with President Ghaznavi alone," Salas abruptly shut down his aggressive second-in-command.

"I'm sorry?" Ruby scoffed. "Mr. President, you know we can't leave you two--"

"One guard each. Hifrael for me."

Ghaznavi turned to his guards, sputtering something in Persian. And at his command, most of his delegation, all but the one guard over his right shoulder, started walking for the door.

Bright red, Ruby stood and moved for Salas's shoulder, whispering down into his left ear, "What the hell do you think you're--"

"I'll call you in an hour," Salas said full-voice, castrating him full volume. "Thank you. *Dick.*"

Ruby glared down at his President as he raised up to his full height, but followed the Secret Service guards out. The door closed and sealed behind them, leaving only Salas and Hifrael, Ghaznavi and his own favorite attendant.

"I appreciate this," Ghaznavi nodded. "This is no time for brash shows of strength or ultimatums. I have many men like Vice President Ruby in my own administration. But I wanted to meet with you, President Salas, to offer to open our borders to any investigators you'd like to send in. I can offer the full assistance of my Republican Guard in helping you find--"

"It's a wonderful offer. And I wish I had time for that. But I do that, and before they even have the proper time to find answers, I will be replaced by someone who will be much less interested in working with you and building on our relationship. It's imperative, for both our countries, that I give the American people something *now*."

"I wish I had something to provide you."

"Mr. President," Salas stared deep into his eyes, penetrating into his soul, "I need you to tell me: Did you or anyone in the Iranian government have anything to do with, or know anything in advance about, the bombing of the Supreme Court?"

IRVING PRESIDENCY, YEAR SEVEN

The First Lady was not easy to shock. But that was exactly what Chief Quint had pulled off.

Rosemarie had not been summoned to the Court for any stated special reason; he hadn't lured her back into his warm oak-lined office for a secretive hand-off of the traditional Letter-to-the-President; he did it during one of their bi-weekly lunches in the Marbury v. Madison (always with bloody marys, and always virgin ones, unless they happened to be meeting on a Friday), handing it across the table in full view of anyone who happened to be looking over at them at the time. This would at first annoy Rosemarie – how irresponsible, to give her the letter in a location where someone might be able to take their photo, or guess the contents of the envelope he was handing across their lunch table.

But she just as quickly realized how silly she was to be worried: no one would have guessed that William Quint would ever retire from the Supreme Court – least of all her.

Quint held the letter out over the table without any warning or preamble. "I thought you might be the quickest way to get this to him," was all he said after their salad plates had been cleared.

Rosemarie noticed the words '*My President*' hand-scrawled on the cream paper. "No," she said as she took it from him, already guessing its contents. "You can't do this. I refuse to accept this."

"I'm afraid it's not addressed to you, my dear. But I did leave it unsealed so you could read exactly what it said."

Rosemarie hoped this was all some sort of practical joke, that the paper inside would read something along the lines of, 'GOTCHA!' or 'APRIL FOOLS!' despite the July date.

But it said nothing of the sort:

Supreme Court of the United States
Washington, D.C. 20453

Chambers of
Chief Justice William H. Quint

10 July

Dear President Irving,

This is to inform you of my retirement as Chief Justice of the United States, effective upon the nomination and confirmation of a replacement Chief and a new Associate Justice to the Supreme Court. After thirty-one Terms, I leave the Court with a heavy heart, and undying respect for the role it plays in our Constitutional democracy.

Sincerely,

W. Quint

"You can't do this," Rosemarie stammered. "You always said they'd have to wheel you out of here in your coffin."

"The lifetime appointment is necessary for total autonomy of the Court," Quint sighed, looking around the old room, "but when you are someday privy to all the secrets these walls have seen and heard, you will realize it has its drawbacks. Some Justices, even some Chiefs, have severely hurt this Court in their eldest years. This nation can't afford that."

"But you, you're in perfect health--"

Quint didn't have to say a word in response, just reach across and pat one of Rosemarie's hands, as he had been doing for over twenty years.

"No." Her eyes blotted with tears, a sight the Chief never thought he would see in his prized pupil. "What is it? What's wrong?"

"It's all going to be fine."

"I can get to your wife, you know. Darline will tell me."

"We both will. Just not here. Once I'm home."

Rosemarie would acknowledge that how she handled the delivery of the letter was not entirely appropriate. She could have given it to her husband's secretary, his Chief of Staff, or even left it on his nightstand. But she felt the Chief had implied she should hand it off personally (or so she rationalized to herself) and it took her over three days to get some face-to-face time with him. (Both travelling, they hadn't even shared their bed in over a week.) Besides, she knew Quint well enough to know he wouldn't complain, knowing she was waiting to give it to Reg at the most appropriate time possible.

The most appropriate time possible turned out to be late Friday afternoon. Reg had his forehead buried in his palms as Rosemarie marched in one door of the Oval, a FEMA team marching out the other. "Your scheduler's been giving me the run-around all week," she griped.

"I know, I'm sorry about that, I just-- with this hurricane, and the immigration vote, I had to prioritize--" His eyes rose, lined with red veins, drenched with exhaustion. "But, school lunches are important to me. So," he forced some energy into his bones and sat upright in his chair. "What's the latest update?"

Her elegant fingers laid Quint's sealed letter down before the President. "This is a new matter."

His curiosity piqued, Reg picked up the envelope, tore it open and read. "Oh shit. What happened?"

"He says they'll have us over for dinner when the entire process is played out and explain it then."

When he lowered the letter, he realized she had laid something else, a single white sheet of paper, seven names typed in 11-point Times Roman, down on the Resolute Desk in its place. "A list of possible replacements," she explained.

"Isaac Goldman? He's a nutcase. We can't get him through."

"We can – if we promote Claudine Egan to Chief first."

"RM," Reg jeered, starting to collect his things to return to the Residence and prepare for the evening's itinerary. "C'mon. I can't promote a Republican to Chief."

"Actually, you very much can. And you should. Chief Justice is almost a purely administrative position. The Chief holds no more voting power than any of the other Justices. Getting your first and maybe only opportunity to nominate someone new to the Court – that is infinitely more important than promoting someone to Chief.

"But if you nominate Egan to Chief, the media and the Senate will get so lapped up in a fervor over the possibility of the first female Chief Justice, they won't give Judge Goldman nearly the scrutiny he might normally get."

Reg rubbed his lips between forefinger and thumb, telling Rosemarie she wasn't getting through to him. "It's happened before," she argued. "The Senate was so tied up in knots about whether to promote Rehnquist to Chief, they on the very same day confirmed an Associate Justice nominee with very little examination and a 98-0 vote. His name was Antonin Scalia."

Reg set the list down, intertwining his fingers with a sigh. "I don't know."

"Reg. This right here, this moment, this is why I'm still here. Why I stuck it out all this time. Adding to the Court is the most important thing a President does in office. *This* is why you married me."

His eyes rose to hers. "I married you because I love you."

Rosemarie chuckled, then walked out without saying goodnight.

FRIDAY

Rosemarie knew things had turned for the worse right when she walked into Quint's bedroom and noticed he wasn't in a tie or a clean, crisp white shirt, but an old v-neck soiled with spittle; when she saw the oxygen tube looped under his nostrils; when it took him a moment to wake from a napping state and sit up for her; when she took a sip of her bloody mary and realized the alcohol had been left out.

"I think this will be our final meeting," Quint grumbled.

"What? Never."

"You don't need to waste your precious time on a dying old man."

"I'm going to need you next week," she said, drawing his eyes back over to her with a firm hand on the shoulder. "No one else can deliver me the oath."

Quint nodded, but looked away. "Your oath. I always imagined myself doing that for you." His voice was saturated with regret, but Rosemarie wasn't sure if this was because he knew he was no longer capable of getting to the White House to do the honors, or because he no longer believed she would make it across the confirmation finish line and earn that moment. "No matter what happens, Rosemarie," he said, his eyes returning to hers, "nothing is more important to the future of this country than the Allied Armament case. No matter what happens this week or next, you *must* find a way to finish what we've started."

"They will be out of business before the year is out," she assured him. She patted his hand just as he used to do hers and stood; the press availability was scheduled to start in under an hour.

But before she could get out the door, Quint added one thing: "You can't let Reg hold this press conference. Over the years, I've come to understand how much you care about him. And you can't let him do this. You know you can't."

Rosemarie smiled. "Come now, Chief. Don't you think I know how to handle him by now?"

Reginald Irving understood how much he owed his wife. She was the most important thing in the world to him. He believed in his soul of souls that were she to have said at any point in the past 25 years that she didn't want him having any more affairs, that no matter how meaningless or unemotional they were, they were damaging to her, hurtful to her, he could have cut them off. For her, he could have done anything. He realized the sacrifices she had made for him over the years and was quite aware of where she could have been at this point had she dedicated her life to herself rather than her husband.

All this made Reg care more about this press conference than any other in his career. He wanted to give Rosemarie everything she ever desired, and she had always desired the Chief Justice's seat. From the moment he met her, he knew it even if she never said it. She never had to say it. Today, he would finally make it happen for her. He owed her that, and so much more.

He rehearsed his opening remarks eleven times, or nine or ten more times than he had ever practiced any other speech in his life, even the '96 DNC appearance that had made him so famous. He met with their publicist the afternoon before to pick the perfect location in the Irving Foundation offices, to talk out where the reporters should sit, what images he wanted displayed behind him. He had his favorite make-up and hair girls come to the townhouse before he departed; he would look perfect for the cameras, without any of the reporters realizing this was at least partially an artificial achievement. He didn't take any calls or make any chit-chat on the ride over to the office, instead whispering his speech and talking points over and over again on the way.

All of this was before MMA pulled the SUV up in front of the Foundation façade, and Reg saw Rosemarie already there, on the front steps in front of the colonial columns, surrounded by dozens of salivating journalists.

She's giving her own presser?

No reporter, no camera, realized who was behind the tinted glass of Reg's Escalade; no one turned their lenses on him, keeping their focus on the last First Lady. But what was she saying?

He flipped on the backseat TV, thumbing the remote to MSNBC so he could hear her without lowering his window. "--realized earlier this week that funds donated to this foundation I worked so hard to build have in the past been used to pay off and cover up my husband's extramarital affairs. *The second* I learned of this, I alerted my husband that I would be initiating divorce proceedings against him, that I wanted him to resign from the Foundation immediately, and that I would be moving out of our Portland home and Washington townhouse and into my own home here."

The flashbulbs popped, and the gathered reporters shouted out questions with a bloodthirsty intensity; she pointed to the one she would answer first. "Madame First Lady, have you thought about whether these revelations, and your impending divorce, might be distractions that could impact your performance as a Supreme Court Justice?"

"Of course I've thought about that, Dana. It is my duty to the American people to think about that. But let me explain one thing very clearly: the greatest mistake a woman can make is to allow her husband's failings to prevent her from her own destiny. No man would ever miss out on an opportunity, a job offer, or even tickets to a football game just because he was going through a messy divorce. And I will not allow my husband to rob me of the chance to serve on the greatest judicial body this world has ever known."

Everyone could feel Rosemarie was on a roll now. But when she opened her mouth to say more-- she paused. Reg looked out through his window, to where she stood fifty yards away on the top of the entrance steps, and their eyes seemed to lock even through the tinted glass. Was that regret he saw in her eyes? Was it some sort of an apology?

Reg knew what he had to do for her now. He ordered Mitch to drive out of there, to head back to the townhouse, to leave this moment to his wife.

"Today I am getting a divorce," she continued on, unfazed, "and when the Senate calls me, I will be ready to marry the rest of my life to the Supreme Court."

The President was aboard Air Force One, flying back from a night of Broadway and donor dinners, when Bryce advised him to turn the conference room monitor to Rosemarie Irving's press conference. It had been over for about five minutes, commentators on both MSNBC and Fox again speculating that the Senate politically had no choice but to confirm her, when he heard a commotion at the door. He turned and rose to find Hifrael holding his Vice President back from entering the room.

"I don't care how much he loves you," Ruby hissed in the Secret Service agent's face. "You get your hands off me or you won't be able to get a job with the Mexico City Police."

Hifrael of course didn't budge-- until Salas ordered him off in Spanish. He left President and Vice alone in the room as ordered.

"I can't believe that shit you pulled yesterday," Ruby barked as he attempted to flatten out his wrinkled suit. "I want to know exactly what went down after you kicked me out. I *need* to know, Mr. President, if I'm going to be able to do the job you always said you wanted me to do."

"I asked President Ghaznavi if he had anything to do with, or knew of any Iranian involvement in, the Supreme Court attack."

"You *asked* him? Oh, I bet that was insightful."

"He looked me right in the eyes, and he said he knew of no connection."

"He looked you right in the eyes?"

"And I believed him."

"Oh my fucking Lord. It was the soccer jersey, wasn't it?"

"It was my instincts, Dick."

"Well, I hope you realize if you go before a camera and repeat that trough full of horse shit to the American people, *we're going to lose,* Mr. President."

"No, we're not."

"Oh, I assure you we are."

"*We're* not doing anything. In Seattle in August, at the Convention, I'll be announcing a new Vice Presidential candidate."

"What?"

"You've got six months to decide how you want to handle this. You can leave gracefully, or you can make me fire you. And trust me, I will fire you."

"That's only going to make you look like you made the wrong decision in the first place. Like you're second-guessing yourself. Like you're a rank amateur who was never cut out for this job."

"You know what, it might. I might lose. I might lose in November and have to move to Malibu where I work on a book for oh, an hour or two a day. I would just say 'Fuck it' and go straight to the beach, but I'll have already cashed in Random House's ten million dollar advance, so I'll probably feel a little guilty. So, yeah, one to two hours of writing, then the beach. Fish tacos for lunch, Nobu for dinner. Now doesn't that sound like a terrible life?"

Ruby shook his head with a chuckle, then left the room, never to ride on Air Force One again.

That evening, President Antonio Salas gave a live televised address to the nation for the first time since the day of the bombings. He thanked the Senate for confirming Rosemarie Irving to replace Warren Lapadula, congratulated his new Chief Justice, and explained how President Ghaznavi of Iran had assured him that his nation had no connection to the bombing of the Supreme Court. At this time, there wasn't enough evidence to take retaliatory action against any nation, including Iran.

However, he would present the evidence against Iran to the Congressional Intelligence Committees, and if the Congress voted that war should indeed be declared, he would honor that vote, as was his Constitutional duty.

The American people would just have to wait for Congress to return from vacation for that vote.

George was early to the 14th Street NW Starbucks, giving him time to scroll through his newest emails and see the alert from Kingman Summers' assistant that the Under Secretary wanted to see George the second he came into the Ops Center that morning. Normally this might inspire George to skip his morning routine, forego a work out or maybe even a shower and get his ass into work ASAFP. But George knew what bee had flown up Summers' ass, knew he just wanted to grill George about why the fuck he had interrogated the prized suspect in a case in which he no longer had any involvement.

George grinned as he stood. Colin Caviezel looked just like his dad looked at the start of each work day. George and Colin Sr. had trained and entered the Secret Service in the same class: 1993, right after returning from the Gulf. His boy had a firm handshake, and his impressive physique pulled at the seams of his Service-standard black suit.

"Pleasure meeting you, Mr. Aug," Colin said as he sat. "My Dad thought the world of you."

"A great man. Great American. Just like you are, I understand."

"I've always wanted-- to thank you. You gave us ten more years with him. I can't tell you how much I'll always be grateful."

"Just doing my duty, as you know. As you're doing now."

"About that ... shouldn't there be a more official channel DHS should go through--?"

"This operation is of the utmost sensitivity. Any additional person who knows about it increases the risk exponentially. My superior asked all of us on the team if we knew any agents we could go to directly. I immediately thought of you. And how proud this would make your Dad."

"Thank you, Sir," Colin smiled wearily.

George paused. Colin had more caution, not the rah-rah gung ho abandon of his father. George thought that would serve him well … as long as he wasn't blackballed or incarcerated for what George was about to make him do.

He snapped himself out of it. This was more important than Colin Caviezel, than one young man who had his whole career to recover from this. "You'll see it's very simple." George reached into his jacket, pulling out an envelope and sliding it across the table under a finger pad. "All you have to do is get that name on the White House guest list for Monday."

Colin held the mouth of the envelope wide, peering in at the name handwritten on the card inside. His color went pallid, his eyes wide. "Isn't that the name of--"

"Uh huh."

"So he survived that crash in New York, into the river?"

"Colin. The less you know …"

"Understood, Sir. But you know you don't spell it with two As, I don't think …"

George sat forward. "Agent Caviezel. This is but one small part of a sting operation that we believe is the only way to draw this savage criminal out of hiding. This might be our only chance to catch one of the most dangerous, most murderous men in American history."

Colin nodded, slipping the envelope into his own inner pocket, like George's, right above the heart. "I serve at the pleasure, Sir."

He stood and walked out, and George exhaled. He knew it had worked. In the lexicon of the Secret Service, Colin couldn't have offered a stronger affirmation.

IRVING PRESIDENCY, YEAR SEVEN

The walls of the Oval Office had over the years heard plenty of Presidential cursing. LBJ ordered pants that gave him plenty of room 'down where your nuts hang,' with an extra inch 'back up to my bung hole;' Dick Nixon had described Presidential leadership as 'a balls thing;' and who knows what Slick Willie might have moaned while he was in Monica's mouth.

But those walls had never heard a First Lady swear a blue streak like Rosemarie Irving did as she slammed into the Oval one morning in the seventh August her husband had occupied the office. "What the fuck is this?" she exclaimed, tossing the front page of the *Washington Post* down on her husband's desk.

"Rosemarie," Reg blushed, but the cabinet members there for their own meeting were already taking their cue to slink out.

"Lapadula? Fucking Lapadula?" she continued before the door was even pulled shut, before they had full privacy. "I told you *exactly* how you should play this."

"Listen to me. No one knows this, but Egan has liver cancer."

"Jesus."

"It's stage one. The doctors say she looks good for now, but …"

"There are three other Republicans you could promote."

"C'mon. You know I was never going to promote a Republican to the Chief's chair." Rosemarie turned away from him with another expletive, so Reg added, "By the way, this will allow me to nominate the second name you had on your list, Bruce Winks."

"Bruce Winks is a spineless pussy."

"He was on your list!"

"As a backup. You should be nominating Isaac Goldman."

"Look, RM, I love you, you're brilliant, but you don't understand everything that goes on in this office--"

She stormed back to him, pointed right in his chest. "I understand everything here better than you ever will, and you know it. And you promised me. I would be the one telling you what you want, what you care about, and what to do. However high your face took you, remember, *I'd* be running the show."

"I know. And you know I value everything you say. But this is so different now. This is a machine--"

"I can't get more than ten minutes with you a month, and it's always at the end of the week, when you're exhausted, burnt out and want nothing more than to be drinking a craft beer in front of a Duck game."

A weak smile of affirmation skirted across Reg's lips at the very mention.

"If you give me no other time, if you don't listen to a single word I say over the next sixteen months, at least listen to me on this." Her finger poked hard down into the desk. Reg looked down to see her sharp nail stabbing right into the *Post*'s photo of Warren Lapadula's face. "You can't make him Chief Justice."

"What happened to the Chief not mattering? To it being a purely administrative position?"

"Not this man. Anyone else, any other strategy. But not this man. We give *nothing* to this man."

"Rosemarie. You've had *something* against this man ever since I met you. What is your deal with him?"

He looked into her eyes. He rose, bringing his hand to her cheek. "What did he do to you?"

Her pupils dilated with rage, quivering as they fought back the moisture building under them. In two decades, he had never seen her eyes like this.

"I can't help you if you don't tell me. Why can't you be honest with me about this?"

"Oh, because you share everything with me? You're honest about everything with me?"

"I would be, if that's what you wanted!" His voice had gotten louder than she had ever heard it. "This is the way you wanted it. I promised you this, and I have kept my promise. If you ever want me to change anything about our marriage, I will, just say the word!"

"I want you to change who you nominate for Chief Justice."

Reg ran his hand through his hair, mussing it much more than he would usually ever allow. Then he shook his head and picked up the *Post,* waving it before her face. "The cat's out of the bag. That's politics."

Rosemarie had to look to the floor to keep from bursting into tears – or maybe to keep from leaping across the desk and strangling her husband. She briefly debated telling him everything, telling him about her history with Lapadula, how it had ended, and chastised herself for never doing so in the past.

Then she reminded herself how weak the whole story made her appear, like nothing more than a feeble, fragile, inadequate little girl – the worst kind of woman, the kind she grew up despising, and promising herself she would never become. The kind of woman her mother was, always being interrupted by her father, correcting her or humiliating her by telling whomever that she was always wrong. And she always *allowed* him to get away with that. No one would ever know Rosemarie had for a brief moment also been that weak, not even her own husband.

After a few seconds of recovery, she pivoted and made her exit, avoiding even looking back at him. "I love you too," she tossed out as she opened the closest door.

THE SECOND MONDAY OF FEBRUARY

George had the metal case open on his kitchen table when Jason emerged from the never-used den where he had spent three nights on a fold-out. "Good morning, Sunshine," George smiled, inviting Jason to take a steaming mug of coffee. Jason looked down at the seven strange pieces of white molded plastic sitting in foam as he sipped. There was a stock, a round snub-nosed barrel, a coil. He could see how they might all form a pistol, albeit a very strange one. "Who built this again?"

"No one built it. He printed it. A Nigerian, Boko Haram, on his perfectly legal, over-the-counter, internet-ordered 3D printer. Isn't that a comforting thought? Got this little number all the way through Heathrow security, onto a BA flight bound for JFK. Luckily it jammed, and four other brave passengers were able to take him down."

Jason pulled the largest piece up out of the foam. "Did he have to make it look like Han Solo's gun?"

"Don't be fooled. Packs a .357 punch."

"What about bullets?"

"Plastic ones, made by Speer." George set a full, jangling box next to the case. "Meant for riot control, crowd suppression."

"Non-lethal?" Jason asked.

"Oh, you fire close enough at the right vital organ, they'll do the trick." George looked at Jason sideways, not sure he liked the disappointment had had just detected in his voice. "But, no one's going to get hurt, right? You promised me. You're just going to force a confession out of her, that's all, right?"

Jason was already putting the gun together, making it look easy. Turns out it wasn't just explosives he had taken apart and put back together all his life. "Right," he murmured as he worked.

George sipped at his own coffee, well aware of how this most likely would turn out. He had called Brenda's counselor at the Waterford yesterday, and told her he would be checking his daughter out at 9 this morning. He didn't tell her he would be driving far, far away, nor that he would never be bringing her back.

Jason watched the White House gate guard read his name off his Maryland license, then type it into his computer. "Oh, that's what's going on," the guard murmured to himself, just as Jason had planned. "Whoever put you on the guest list misspelled your first name. So I hope you don't mind the spelling on your badge." He smiled as the temporary White House ID for 'JAASON LANCASTER' popped out of the little box next to his hard drive, then handed it across to Jason. "There you go, Ja-ay-son," the guard laughed, and Jason smiled back. The plan had worked. Without an exact match for his real name in the system, no alarms had been set off. The only potential hiccup had been the possibility of the guard himself recognizing Jason's names from the news; judging the sentry to be in his 20s, Jason figured he had filled his brain with so many Facebook posts and tweets and Instagrams and Snapchats in the weeks since Polis that the name of Jason Lancaster had long ago been pushed out of his memory cortices.

As Jason approached the building, he saw the metal detector station awaiting him just inside the doors. "Everything in your pockets into a bowl," one of the rotund uniform guards commanded as Jason stepped inside, but he took care to remove only his cell phone, keys, and the simple little digital dictaphone he had purchased at a Best Buy two days earlier.

"Journalist?" a female guard smiled at him, nodding at the recorder.

"Something like that," he replied.

"You're a little late. They been up there setting up all morning. Hope you can get a seat."

Jason nodded, being sure to keep his hands on the plastic puzzle pieces in the deep pockets of his winter coat as he stepped through the detector arch--

And set it off with a piercing beep. His face clenched up.

"Your hands, Sir," the female guard barked at him. "Take your hands out."

Jason did slowly, debating in his mind what he would do when she asked him to remove everything inside those pockets.

"I ain't taking your belt off for you. You're gonna have to use those hands."

Jason let out a relieved smile, then pulled his belt off and returned to the other side of the detector to lay it on the conveyer. He stepped through the arch – this time, with a silent result.

Once inside, he took a hard left to the first men's room, stowing himself in the last open stall, where he went to work assembling seven pieces of plastic into an odd-looking pistol.

Rosemarie had been out in the East Room for more than twenty minutes, saying hello to her sister's family, making sure her mother was seated properly in the front row, waving to the law school professor who had shepherded her through Yale as well as the Senators who had been most supportive of her throughout not just her, but all four new Justices', confirmation processes. She had paid her respects to Justice Winks, who, as her husband's only appointee to the Court, had been chosen to administer her oath. She had spent five minutes catching up with her son, making sure the life of a first-year Associate in the grindhouse that was Williams & Connolly wasn't discouraging him too much, needling him about whom he was dating. The whole event felt like a wedding, or a 50th Birthday party: everyone in the world she had ever cared about in one room.

Except that the two men she had spent the majority of her life caring about more than any others weren't there. Rosemarie couldn't stop thinking about either of them, and found herself less elated than she had always pictured herself on this day.

Seeing the President waiting for her at the end of the red carpet, at the door into the Green Room, brought a smile back to her face. She joined him, finding there was no one else in this room besides him.

He shut the door, then raised two glasses of glorious golden nectar. She took one of them with a quizzical glance, bringing it to her nose. "Macallan?"

"I was told it's your favorite."

"A promotion for somebody."

"You didn't think I'd let us skip our tradition after our most important confirmation, did you?"

"Hence the empty room?"

"I didn't feel like giving Fox such an easy headline today. 'President and First Lady Do Shots Before Supreme Court Ceremony.'"

Rosemarie laughed, mimed a toast, and brought her glass to her lips.

"Wait!" Salas stopped her. "You can't toast yourself." He held his own glass aloft. "To going four-for-four. The best Presidential batting average in Supreme Court history. And to the woman who made it all happen. My Chief Justice."

"Not quite yet," she teased, taking her first sip.

"Ooh," the President exclaimed after following her lead. "That is smooth."

But Rosemarie's mind had moved onto something else, her eyes tilted with curiosity. "Were you really thinking about nominating me all along?"

"From the moment the bombs went off. You were the first name I thought of."

"You sure?" she teased, and though her feet didn't move, she seemed to be moving closer to Salas, her warmth, her smell, penetrating his personal space. "Because when you said it, it kind of just sounded like a pick up line."

"A pick up line?"

"I'm not saying there'd be anything wrong with that."

"Why, Mrs. Irving--"

"Not for long," she hummed. Her face was so close to his now, her eyes dancing down to his lips, as if she was wondering what they might do next, or even considering doing it herself first. "You know, after all these years, I thought I might never find that-- *connection* with another man again."

"I'm sorry you've lost it with Reg."

"Reg?" she nearly laughed. "No, I never had it with Reg. He's always been my partner, the best partner anyone could ever wish for. But no, this connection ... I only had it once, many, many years ago."

"What happened?"

"It all turned out to be bullshit. I always figured it was probably never real. I was just a child." She locked her eyes into his. "I didn't think I'd ever find it again."

"I didn't think I'd ever find it myself," he whispered.

"Ladies and gentlemen ..." Press Secretary Alistair Crabbe's voice seeped under the door from the East Room.

POTUS sighed and set down his drink. He took his nominee's own drink and set it on the same table behind the door, out of the sightline of anyone in the East Room. "See you out there," he said, then opened the door.

He marched down the East Room's strip of red carpet with a pep he hadn't had in his step since his inauguration. But before he could reach his podium, every member of the press, Congress and the Court rose to their feet to fete him with applause. He stopped a few paces short of his mic, taken aback; he hadn't received this kind of reception before the swearings-in of any of the other judicial nominees. Looking around the gallery, taking in those smiling, appreciative faces – appreciative of *him* – he realized that they were all, every last one of them, just as *relieved* as he was that this was all over, that maybe after lunch, Washington would feel normal again.

He stepped up to his podium where his prepared remarks sat waiting, raising his hands to signal the adoring guests to take their seats. None of them were here for him, after all.

"Thank you, ladies and gentlemen, members of the United States Congress, and Supreme Court Justices both senior and new. We are all here to celebrate and bear witness to the investiture of the nineteenth Chief Justice of the United States."

Jason heard the President's voice echo from speakers lining the East Room as he topped the stairs on the State Floor. He laid his left fingers on the handle to the Green Room door, but before he opened it, looked both ways down the corridor, then moved his right hand behind the small of his back and up under his jacket, removing the plastic pistol from the back of his jeans and pushing open the door.

"… I knew that whoever took the center chair," POTUS's voice rang through the open door on the opposite side of the room, "would inherit a Court at the most tumultuous moment in its history …" *You've got no idea,* Jason thought.

And there she was. Rosemarie Irving was the only other person in the Green Room, a silhouette filling that open door leading out onto the red carpet and the President's podium. Jason raised the gun, aiming its mouth at the perfect spot to penetrate through to her spleen.

"I know you planned the bombings," he said in a low voice.

Rosemarie turned around with slow and calm. "I know who you are," she answered. "I'm very sorry you got caught up in all of this."

"*You* blew up the Court," Jason continued, punctuating his words with the nose of his gun. "And I know why." He reached into his pocket, pulling out the Dictaphone, thumbing it to record. "You're going to talk. You're going to explain it all for me."

Ever a believer in the necessity of impartiality of anyone associated with the Court, CNN was Chief Quint's cable news source of choice, much preferred over hysterical Fox News or holier-than-thou MSNBC. The TV in his bedroom was turned to CNN, Darline at his side, as they waited for Rosemarie to be introduced for her swearing-in.

"When I set out to select my nominee for this vital position," President Salas was saying on their 42 inch screen, "I knew that whoever took the center chair would inherit a Court at the most tumultuous moment in its history: a Court under attack, not yet recovered from the destruction of its home or the loss of so many of her personnel from both behind the bench and behind the scenes. Truth be told, we as a nation, and our Court, must never fully recover, or ever fully forget, those wounds." Quint nodded and hummed, pleased with the respectful tone and timbre of the words the President and his communication staff had chosen for this historic moment. Darline's squeeze on his hand tightened, a silent agreement with her husband's assessment.

"You have to trust me," Rosemarie Irving continued at gunpoint. "You have misread my motives. If you kill me, you will make Allied Armament invincible. Justice will never be served."

Jason shook his head with a whimper, then swabbed the streams of sweat off his forehead with the back of the hand holding the glowing-red recorder. He moved his forefinger from the guard, down onto the trigger.

Rosemarie could smell his frantic nerves, and started to herself panic. "Jason, if you just give me a chance, I can prove all this to you!"

Jason hesitated for just a moment – a moment that cost him his entire plan.

Two-hundred-pounds-plus of pure granite slammed into his back, pushing him down towards the carpet. He could see dark brown fingers wrapped around his wrists, forcing the aim of the gun off the First Lady. Jason tried to move his finger, pull it off the trigger – but as the weapon hit the floor, smashing his finger under the guard, it forced down the trigger--

Out in the East Room, everyone exhaled that strange mix of gasp and scream that signaled the start of a horrific crisis, most ducking for cover as Secret Service agents yanked out sidearms and rushed in front of POTUS, Hifrael shoving him to the ground with one hand as he screamed into his opposite wrist for a report.

On the floor behind the podium, Salas felt around his chest, then pulled his white shirt taut to check for red. Nothing.

"The Green Room, the shot came from the Green Room!" he heard Hifrael yell to his men.

The Green Room.

The target had been his new Chief Justice. The target had been Rosemarie.

The gunshot would be the last sound William Harvey Quint would ever hear. He saw the commotion the blast inspired in the East Room, but he was already fading into the muddled acoustics on the edge of consciousness. He could feel Darline squeezing even tighter, could sense in his periphery her mouth opening in a scream for help. But he didn't hear her actual plea. Everyone seemed to be moving in slow motion, and as the curtain lowered on Chief Quint's life, his final thought was one of terror and sadness:

Had someone just assassinated his Rosemarie?

MMA wrenched Jason's plastic gun from his fingers, shoving it in the back of his belt for safe keeping. Rosemarie's personal Secret Service agent then wrenched the failed shooter's arms behind his back, linking his wrists in flex cuffs.

"FREEZE!" about a half-dozen Agents were screaming in the round, like they were performing some complicated version of 'Row-Row-Row Your Boat,' all brandishing Glocks and Berettas and even an Uzi as they charged into the room.

"Suspect secured!" Mitch Aldridge exclaimed, his knees still holding Jason's spine down. "Room check!"

The other agents darted around the room, checking the doors and closets, behind the furniture, before singing out in a chorus of "Clear!" "Clear!" "Clear!"

Another agent crouched at the wall, passing his fingers over the new, small hole there. "One round in the wall. Only one round fired?"

"Confirmed," MMA barked back. "Only one round fired."

Hifrael was last in the East Room door, barking into his wrist. "We need the palace locked down. One shooter in custody, not sure if there's more. All exits closed *right now*."

MMA pulled the shooter to his feet, and he and Rosemarie locked eyes for a moment – before the President bounded in behind her. "Are you all right?" he panted, grabbing her arms and pulling her towards him in a more comfortable, familiar gesture than one might expect. But no one even flinched, no one had an eye for such detail right at this moment.

"I'm fine," she nodded. "I'm all right."

"What happened?" Salas looked over to Jason.

Rosemarie opened her mouth to answer – when the East Room behind them erupted into a cascade of flash bulbs and screamed questions. Salas turned around – but everyone out beyond the podium was on their feet, hands stretched to the ceiling, holding their cameras or phones aloft, blocking any view of the epicenter of the commotion.

Rosemarie moved her eyes to the small monitor over near the couch on the other side of the room, its screen filled with an image of Warren Lapadula, microphones and recorders and iPhones shoved near his mouth from all directions.

Strange, she thought for a moment. *Why would CNN go to file footage of Chief Lapadula right now, in the middle of* this*?*

And then she heard the booming voice from out in the East Room, that familiar voice, that voice that to this day poured shivers down her spine.

"Yes, I'm in perfect health," Lapadula answered one of the journalists out in the East Room, "and I am here to announce my intention to return to the Supreme Court as its Chief Justice, effective immediately. Correct me if I'm wrong, but I don't believe a replacement has taken the oath?"

CERTIORO

BOOK SIX OF THE SIX-PART CONSPIRACY THRILLER

FOUR SEATS

AARON

1989

Rosemarie Jarzebski sat somewhere in the middle of the five stories of marble stairs and bronze banisters. There were two of these majestic circular vortices, marvels of engineering supported only by the steps themselves and their attachment to the walls, wound up inside the palace of the Supreme Court. She had dreamed of working here most of her life, but could never have nightmared an evening like this. Rosemarie was unsure how close to the ground or the apex of the helix she was – she had stumbled off the second floor, where her boss's office was located (really the third floor; the level of exhibits, cafeteria, and John Marshall statue was known as the ground floor) and in her delirious haste couldn't remember if she had gone up or down. She just needed a moment to collect herself; that's all she required to choke back the pain, to breathe back the chunky blood clotting up her nostrils, to spoon mascara from those wells under her eyes that had formed during these past few grueling weeks of opinion draft output.

Seldom used, more wonders of design than utility, these ornate staircases were two of the only places a clerk could hide in the Court building; hole up in a bathroom stall, and other clerks or Court employees would hear her sniffling whimpers and start a chain of gossip about who had most recently seen whom enter. And her own office was but an antechamber of her superior's, a room through which he would pass in and out on his way to the restroom, another Justice's chambers, or eventually, home for the night.

Rosemarie's Justice was the last person in the world she would allow to see her right now, to hear her tears or see her gripping her left side in agony. She refused to give him that satisfaction. She would be back in his office tomorrow morning, clothes perfect, foundation and concealer and whatever-it-took making her face perfect, as if nothing had happened the night before. Would that be submitting to him, letting him get away with what he had done, perhaps even giving him tacit permission to do it again? Maybe, but she allowed herself to think of it only as a fuck you, a big fat middle finger right in his face, an announcement that no matter what he did to her, he couldn't break her, couldn't divert her from her destiny.

Imagine if her grandparents had let the Nazis break them, or her parents the Soviets. Where would she be now if they had been too frightened to risk their lives to escape Bydgoszcz and bring their lone daughter to America? That unbreakable defiance, that's what Bogdan Jarzebski had beaten into her, that's what had made her tough, made her who she was, gotten her through high school and Harvard and Yale Law and all the way to this clerkship. And she wasn't going to let some asshole take all that away from her – especially when, she had to acknowledge in her heart of hearts, she herself deserved some of the blame for what had occurred. She had let her guard down, she had broken some of her most cherished rules, she had taken her eyes off the ball and placed personal goals above the professional ones that had driven her whole life to this point.

"Ms. Jarzebski?" a smooth, kind voice rang up from the landing three stairs down. Rosemarie pawed for the railing, pulling herself to her feet, grimacing but refusing to utter a single sound of ache. "Is that you?" She of course knew that voice; it was the most famous voice in the highest court in the land. Rosemarie turned, placing a foot on the next step up. She would return to her floor before the Chief could see her face; she wouldn't go back to the office, but straight to the elevator, which would shuttle her down to her Civic in the garage. Sure, someone might share that elevator with her, might see in that harsh light the hematomas forming across her jowls, but that was better than Chief Justice Quint seeing her--

Too late. The older man had caught up to her lumbering, injured pace, and now placed a caring hand on the small of her back, causing her to start. "Criminy!" Quint exclaimed, he himself recoiling when he felt her spine jerk under his fingers. "Are you all right?"

"I'm fine, Mr. Chief Justice," she replied, trying to keep her face turned away from his. "I was just leaving for the night, actually--"

"Have you been crying?"

Her shoulders wilted. "I, I was in such a hurry-- I've been working so much, I tripped, I fell down the stairs a little ..."

"Damn it, I've wanted to close these off since I took over," he shook his head. "I think I've finally got my excuse."

She forgot her appearance for a moment, and turned all the way back to him. "No, please, don't. Not on my account. Everyone loves them so much. I'm over-tired, I was just careless."

Quint stared deep into her eyes, almost as if he could read the events of the past hour behind her irises. He reached forward, thumbing away the line of mascara down one cheek. "You're sure that's what happened, now? You fell down the stairs?"

"Yes, Sir, I'm sure."

"Because if I knew that anything untoward was going on in my Court—"

"Thank you for your concern, Sir, but everything's fine. I promise." She was three steps above him now, ascending back to her own floor, her mind already off the Chief, and onto prayers that her own boss wouldn't catch her between stairs and elevator.

"Mr. Sando is leaving."

"I'm sorry?" She stopped, spinning on a heel to look back down on him, just hoping that condensation she felt dripping from her right nostril was clear, not blood red.

"My clerk, Bryce Sando? He's going to have to leave early, move back to Ohio. His mother needs a bone marrow transplant, and he happens to be a perfect match."

"Oh, thank God she found one so easily."

"Now there's an unwritten rule in this situation not to poach another Justice's clerks. Our penalties for recruiting violations aren't as stringent as the NCAA's, but it's still something we all endeavor not to do." He clasped his hands behind the small of his back, tilting his head to her. "But if a clerk were to come to me of her own volition--"

"The commerce clause!" Rosemarie blurted out, then covered her mouth. She had been accused of legal Tourette's throughout law school and into her clerkship, but it had never reared its ugly head in so inappropriate a situation, in front of so important a personage.

"I beg your pardon?"

"I'm sorry, Sir, I didn't mean to say that out loud--"

"But you did, and now I want to know what it means."

Rosemarie took a deep breath; she knew there was no going back. "Your opinion draft in *Rosenthal v. GE*. You're in danger of losing the votes, Sir. But I think if you were to redraft your opinion to focus much more on the commerce clause, then my boss for sure, and from what I hear from their clerks, maybe even Salovey and Robinson would--"

"How quickly could you have such a new draft on my desk?" Quint craned his neck back, examining her with new eyes. He had heard this Rosemarie Jarzebski was the most impressive young clerk to come through these halls in quite a long while, but in one short stairwell conversation, she had blown even that reputation out of the water.

"How about tomorrow by lunch?"

Quint choked on his tongue. "That would mean working every minute from now until then, all through the night, and I'm still not sure you could do it. How about when I walk in the door Monday morning?"

Rosemarie took a deep breath. "Believe it or not, Mr. Chief Justice, tomorrow would be easier for me. I'm supposed to get into Justice Lapadula's concurrence in *Werner v. Holmberg* starting tomorrow afternoon, and--"

Quint smirked as he turned to descend the stairs again. "You let me handle Justice Lapadula. You won't be writing another word for him."

"With all due respect, Sir, I would be truly honored to transfer to your chambers, but I feel it's only right I give the proper professional notice--"

Quint didn't turn back, just kept winding down the spiral below her. "If Warren doesn't want the events of this evening ever spoken of again, then he'll have absolutely no issue with you starting on my desk first thing tomorrow morning."

He was a full story below her when she spoke again: "Do you think I should speak of them?" This time he stopped, but again didn't turn to look up. "The events of tonight. Should I do something?"

Quint's shoulders rose and fell with a deep sigh. "It's quite difficult to take action against someone with a lifetime appointment decreed by the Constitution. You have to know this will come to define not only his life, but even more so, yours. I have considered such action in the past, only to find it's a fool's errand if you don't come armed with a nuclear payload." He turned half his face to her, a reassuring grin on his profile. "But someday, we will be."

Quint kept shuffling down, until he vanished through the dim doorway onto the garage level, and Rosemarie Jarzebski smiled.

BOOK SIX

CERTIORO

THE SECOND MONDAY OF FEBRUARY

Jason Lancaster was pretty sure he wasn't being held in Homeland Security's Ops Center, or anywhere near the cell in which he had spent a couple of nights four months earlier. Not only did this holding pen look different – walls of sleek white, rather than bricks of dull gray –the smell was different, the hum of the HVAC emanating through the ceiling above him different. The lighting was different: at DHS, he had been kept in complete and total darkness; here it was bright white bulbs set to a level of constant burn on the pupils. Jason couldn't be sure where he was, but he knew he hadn't been put in any vehicles since he was apprehended in the White House Green Room with his plastic 3D-printed pistol pointed at the Chief Justice-elect's back. He figured he must still be on White House property, somewhere deep under the President's residence.

But by far the strangest aspect of his stay here was that four hours, maybe even five had passed, and no one had come to talk to him, to question him or offer him a lawyer or threaten him with Guantanamo or read him his rights or *anything* at all since his plan to force a confession out of Rosemarie Irving had failed.

And then suddenly, it all went black, as black or blacker than that Homeland Security cell. He could hear latches flipping, his door coming open – then footsteps, hands on him, ripping his arms behind his back, flex cuffs being pushed down onto his wrists then zipped welt-tight, his hair pulling as a blindfold was yanked down over his forehead onto his eyes, hands under his armpits pulling him up, then forward, out of this room. More walking, until he was being pushed up and onto a cushy leather seat – the raised backseat of a luxury SUV, he guessed. The road hummed under him, changing its pitch and timbre, once, twice, three times during a ten-minute journey. When they stopped, the door on his right opened again, those hands yanking him out again. Elevator doors whisked shut behind him, then the rush of elevation surprised his gut as this elevator car ascended a few stories. A bing, a whisk, and he was dragged out again, just a few steps – then stopped.

A television droned on about ten feet to his right – and up. *Wall mounted,* Jason thought as he heard a CNN reporter describe the surprise appearance of Chief Justice Lapadula – presumed killed in the October Supreme Court bombings – at Rosemarie Irving's swearing-in ceremony.

"Afraid for his safety, Chief Justice Lapadula told reporters, he had remained in hiding in an undisclosed location for the past seventeen weeks ..."

The harsh clap of high heels on hardwood drowned out the low volume of the commentator – and seconds later, her voice went mute. The timpani of plastic on glass; the remote control being set back down on a table, Jason theorized.

Then a voice, as familiar as it was sultry, speared through the new silence: "You can let him see."

The blindfold was lifted off, and Jason squinted with a grimace. The westward afternoon sun seared in through windows across the room, brighter even than the harsh florescents above his White House cell. He jerked to cover his eyes, but his hands were still cuffed behind the small of his back.

"We didn't get a chance to meet properly earlier," the curvaceous silhouette standing before the windows said. Jason looked around – there were two plush chairs on either side of him, across from a couch, a TV mounted high on the wall to his right, above the hearth, its closed captions continuing to spin a narrative of the heroic Chief. The silhouette stood before the couch, a full tea service laid out on the coffee table between them. *Jesus Christ. Am I actually in ... Rosemarie Irving's living room?*

"You don't mind if I sit, do you?" the First Lady asked, lowering herself closer to the table to fill one china cup with coppery liquid. "It's been a long couple of weeks." She took a sip, then looked over Jason's right shoulder. "It's all right, Mitch." The large African-American Secret Service man behind Jason nodded, then stepped out through the open archway into the hall.

Jason was stunned. Though there was no door, and the guard would see or hear if he tried anything, he had still effectively left the two of them alone in this room. *How batshit is this woman?* He could be on top of her, he could do some serious damage, before he could be pulled off.

"You do remember I tried to kill you about four hours ago?" Jason asked, dumbfounded. "How'd you get me out?"

"I'm friends with the only man in America who can pardon any person of any crime. And after the way our last conversation was interrupted, I wanted an opportunity to correct a misunderstanding." Rosemarie stood again, walking over to the wall, where Jason now noticed a whiteboard perched on the floor, laid back against the wall. She lifted it with one hand and brought it to the couch, setting it in the cushions so he could see the two notecards under magnets, as if they were column headings, one reading, 'AFFIRM,' the other, 'STRIKE DOWN.'

"And I wanted the opportunity to prove we're actually on the same team," Rosemarie continued.

Her explanation was easy enough to follow, especially for someone who had spent the last couple years of his life as a member of the Supreme Court's own police force. "These columns represent the two possible outcomes of *Agguire v. Detroit*, which the Court was supposed to hear this term. If the Court affirms the lower court rulings, the Emergency Manager for Detroit's decision to replace all police and fire services with Allied Armament will be declared perfectly legal." Her finger moved from the left heading card to the right. "But should the Court strike down those rulings, Detroit would immediately have to put their own public-funded forces back on the streets. AASC would lose not only a multi-million dollar contract, the most lucrative in their history, but also lose the legal right to ever make any similar type of deal with any city or state in America ever again. Future profits lost would number in the billions."

"I've figured all this out on my own, thanks," he smirked.

"I know you have," she nodded. "That's why you're here."

The only math that made sense to Jason right now was that he had been brought here to be executed, that he had been bailed out so the Irvings could make sure the knowledge he had gathered over the last four months and twelve hundred miles never came to light. So why keep things close to the vest now? "Allied Armament loses that case," he filled in her blanks, "and all their seed investors never make their money back. The company might even have to fold completely. Now I haven't been able to find out how much of that initial capital you and your husband put in, but I do know it's more than anyone except Walsh Howard himself."

"Actually, we put in as much as him. That's how much we believed in him. Two hundred fifty million dollars."

"Sounds like a pretty strong motive for killing four Supreme Court Justices, and 120 other collateral lives."

"Mr. Lancaster, I know this is hard to swallow, but that isn't an outrageous amount of money for us anymore. It just isn't. There are things we hold much dearer than that money. We have dedicated our lives to public service, to bettering this nation.

"But being on the inside, in private meetings with Mr. Howard and his board, opened our eyes to his ultimate goal: replacing our entire military with independent contractors like Allied Armament. And legal scholars all over the country believe that, should *Agguire v. Detroit* be affirmed, the President will retain the broad authority to do just that. The Justices could even go so far as to specifically authorize that in their ruling.

"Just think about what that means." Rosemarie stepped forward, not even feeling the glass table top pressing into her shins. "A corporate entity, beholden to stockholders and other corporations and its own CEO *above* the Commander-in-Chief. A *business* running the United States military. Carrying out missions not for the good of this nation, but the good of their bottom line."

"Don't worry, I've thought about it plenty."

"When my husband and I realized what Mr. Howard planned to do with his company, what this ruling could mean for our country," she brought a small handkerchief under her eyes, dabbing away any building wetness there, "when we saw the bombs going off, and realized the lengths to which they would go to win this case, our seed money instantly became meaningless to us. We promised ourselves we would do everything we could to make sure Allied Armament lost this case."

Jason chuckled. "Forgive me if my first instinct isn't to take the word of a politician – or a politician's wife – at face value."

"The second the bombs went off," she explained, picking a stack of additional notecards up off the coffee table, "we called Walsh. He wouldn't admit to being behind the bombing, but was more than anxious to jump into how they were going to get new Justices friendly to AASC on the bench. He had no plan, he thought he would just lobby and pressure and flex his political muscle. It had worked for him in the past. He didn't realize what his goals would really require, what he would have to do just to get the President to even *think* about nominations in this climate. Reg and I told him we could handle it. And why wouldn't he believe us? We had just as much to gain as he did. We volunteered to go to President Salas and help him fill the Court with Justices that would vote to Affirm *Agguire v. Detroit* when it was finally reargued."

"And that's just what you did."

"Are you sure about that?" Rosemarie placed a card under STRIKE DOWN – one reading, 'Isaac Goldman.' "A liberal and notorious anti-capitalist."

The next card under STRIKE DOWN: 'Cecilia Koh.' "A law professor who grew up on military bases, her own father and brother still active military."

Then the final card. "And a Vice Admiral of the United States Navy, a veteran of three wars, heroic leader of some of our greatest military missions of the past decade." 'Kennesaw MacTavish.'

"That leaves you," Jason finished her train of thought. "I'm just supposed to trust you were going to vote to strike it down, too?"

Rosemarie put one final name under STRIKE DOWN: her own. "If I really wanted to keep Allied Armament alive, would I have spent the last four months of my life getting three people confirmed who are sure to kill it?"

Jason looked down. Her argument was compelling. It made perfect sense. But one thing didn't. "Okay. Then what the hell do you need me for?"

Rosemarie turned back to the corkboard, adding a 'Winks' card under STRIKE DOWN. She then moved to the other side of the board, placing four cards under AFFIRM, starting with 'Egan,' followed by the names of three other surviving Justices. "We can't know for sure how the remaining Justices were going to rule on this case, but this is my best guess. A four-four tie among the Associate Justices, with the last Justice confirmed, the new Chief, as the tie-breaker." Indeed the STRIKE DOWN column was now one card longer than AFFIRM, with Rosemarie's name on the bottom representing the fifth and deciding vote. "With my confirmation, Allied Armament loses 5-4."

Then suddenly, she ripped down her own name. "But I was never sworn in. The last Chief Justice is still alive. His lifetime appointment still very much alive. He is the deciding vote." She added a new card under AFFIRM: 'Lapadula.' AFFIRM was winning, 5-4. "Chief Justice Warren Lapadula, a member of the board of directors of New World."

"Of what?"

"New World Risk Management & Training, LLC. Chief competitor of AASC in the security contracting industry. Lapadula should recuse himself from this case, but he didn't last year. And why should he? He's in no way affiliated with Allied Armament. Only an entirely separate company, but one that stands to write billions of its own business in cities across America if this ruling is affirmed. They'll even compete with AASC for our military contracts.

"In other words, unless we can get rid of one of these five Justices in the AFFIRM column, we're down to four votes. Four months after the bombing, after all I've tried to do, Allied Armament is still going to win this case."

Jason couldn't help but snicker. "If you brought me here to convince me to murder one of them, I hate to tell you this, but our little encounter in the White House was just a one-time thing for me."

"I thought nothing of the sort. I brought you here because you seem to be the only one who's also figured out this predicament we're in. I brought you here because you've worked in that building, among these people, for over a year." She took a step around the coffee table, coming in for the close. "Surely you know something about one of these people that we can use against them."

"These are some of the most stand-up Americans there are, Mrs. Irving. You don't get to that position without leaving your closet wide open for all to see, with no skeletons hanging inside. You know that better than anyone."

"I was a clerk, almost twenty years ago. I know most of them are exactly as pure as they appear. I also know that no human being is perfect. I know there must be *something*."

"I'm sorry. Maybe we do want the same thing. But working in the Court all that time, I also learned that justice has to play itself out. Every case has a life of its own. It's meant to be decided a certain way, at that particular time in history. That's just the way it is. The Court's made plenty of shitty decisions, but it's also corrected many of them. If I sabotage that process, if I try to change a decision, no matter how well-meaning I may think I am – well then I'm no better than Walsh Howard, am I?" Jason turned to his left, aiming his voice out into the hall where MMA still stood sentry. "So I don't know if you want to take me back to my hole under Pennsylvania Ave, or let me go, or kill me, but I'm afraid this meeting's over. I can't help you."

Rosemarie's shoulders slouched, her gaze moving to the hardwood. "Mitch." MMA stepped into the threshold, and she nodded to him. He complied, snapping open Jason's cuffs with the scissors of his Swiss Army knife.

He turned back to her with surprise as he rubbed his reddened wrists. "What's the catch here?"

"You are free to go. Your name hasn't been cleared, but we're not going to stop you from walking out of here today. All I ask is that you think about what we've discussed, think about these five Justices, and reconsider your decision."

Jason nodded agreement, then turned to walk out, passing Mitch Aldridge's expansive football field of a chest--

"He raped me," Rosemarie's voice drew him back.

"Excuse me?"

"I was hired as a clerk to Justice Lapadula. It was a dream come true. I admired him more than any other Justice. He was the child of European immigrants, just like me, who had risen to nearly absolute power in his adopted nation, just as I dreamed of doing. And I agreed with so many of his opinions, his philosophies – I was a different person then. A deer in headlights. When he intimated he wanted to make our relationship more, that he wanted to see me out of the office, I was elated. I wasn't a virgin, but when I gave myself to him, I truly *made love,* I gave everything of myself over to another person, for the first time in my life. We kept our relationship purely professional inside the walls of the Court, then spent late evenings and weekends together. It was perfect.

"And then it wasn't. One late night when we were going over an opinion draft, and over it and over it again, he told me he needed me, right there in the office, to take his mind off work. But we had promised we wouldn't violate the sanctity of his chambers or the Court like that. And besides, it wasn't the right time of the month for me. I was-- dirty and unkempt, unsexy. So I refused. And he took it anyway. He broke two of my ribs slamming me up against the bricks of his fireplace. He gave me a nosebleed I couldn't staunch for two days, pushing my face away with the palm of his hand. He didn't want to look at me, he didn't want to see my face.

"And as I lie sobbing at his feet, he wiped my discharge off himself, then tossed the soiled hanky down on my head like I was the garbage pile. He didn't love me. He loved my young body. He loved my servitude.

"So no, Mr. Lancaster, not all the Justices of our Supreme Court are the most stand-up Americans there are. They're not all lacking skeletons in their closets. They're not all perfect."

What felt like several minutes of silence passed before Jason could force new words up through his throat. "Why didn't you … ever do anything?"

"He threatened me that night. I was less than a year out of law school, he was an Associate Justice of the Supreme Goddamn Court. He told me I would be ruined if I ever brought it out. Then later, once I was married, when we reached our own great heights-- I just didn't want to make that my whole life. I didn't want my husband to have to answer questions about it every day, I didn't want to just be known as the woman a Supreme Court Justice had raped. I didn't want to give him that satisfaction."

"But now," Jason stepped back into the living room, tasting Allied Armament's doom on his lips, "*this* is how you can bring him down."

"You think so? The woman who was about to be named Chief Justice, before his triumphant return? You don't think that might sound just a tad convenient or vindictive? You think this Republican Congress we've spent the last third of a year manipulating are going to just line up to support *me* over the Justice with the second-most conservative voting record on the Court over the last twenty years?" She nodded at the muted CNN, now covering Lapadula in a press conference. The chyron below his face read: 'MIRACLE JUSTICE.'

"Or you think they might be more inclined to believe *that*?" She turned back to Jason one last time, one last hopeful glimmer sparking her pupils. "Unless you have something …"

Jason shook his head. "I'm sorry. My job … I was focused on anthrax letters and armed protestors and, and bomb threats I eventually couldn't even stop. He won the goddamn Heisman. He's an American hero. If you won't come forward, I got nothing."

"Then we've lost."

Antonio Salas heard only one sentence of the masked man's long diatribe, and he didn't even hear it until his third time through the video.

The images themselves were arresting enough: a man with his full face and head enveloped in a black mask, only his eyes and the small slivers of brown skin around them visible in the gaps between fabric, standing over a Caucasian man on his knees, his hands bound behind his back. After the lengthy and dramatic introduction of his prisoner, an American journalist named Simon Weinbach, the masked man pulled a machete from behind his back, bringing it to the neck of the white man. The masked man didn't chop his victim's head off – they never came off that cleanly, all-in-one-swipe like in the movies; there was much too much sinew and gristle and bone, it required much more grunt and elbow grease. No, the masked man had to *saw* at his prisoner's throat, sending blood gushing down onto his white T-shirt; he had to wrestle with his task like a wino with a faulty corkscrew.

And then, a time cut: later, after the masked man's gruesome task was complete. He held Weinbach's white skull aloft by the top of the hair, its face frozen in a permanent how-the-fuck-did-this-happen-to-me glare.

Thousands of people – no, millions maybe, had seen the video before the President did. It was Al Jazeera that found it first (funny how they always seemed to have a knack for that); a dozen websites from Drudge to Huffington picked it up off their feed. It was at about this point that POTUS was alerted to its existence, but he was busy with his first meeting with the returned Chief Justice, a Secret Service briefing about the intruder to the Green Room, and of course, the bizarre request from the First Lady to secretly give Jason Lancaster over to her. A sanitized, pixelated version made its debut on Fox before Salas had his chance to see it. All three major cable news networks had preempted their Lapadula coverage in favor of the video by the time the President's schedule was interrupted so he could be brought to a private place to review it.

After the first viewing, he asked that the Oval be cleared. Then he watched it twice more.

Seeing it wasn't the important thing. It was the audio that would change the course of American history. The masked jihadist had droned on for ten minutes before he said the key sentence, the only sentence the President would remember in his dreams that night: *"With the support of the glorious Islamic Republic of Iran, we, who call ourselves Qatil Kafii, destroyed your Supreme Court – and we will continue to kill you Americans one-by-one until our next larger strike."*

It was in the middle of his third viewing that Salas's Chief of Staff Bryce Sando came back in to alert him that the Joint Chiefs and his National Security team were waiting for him in the Sit Room. Salas banished him again without an indication of when he would head down there. He didn't need that meeting. He knew what this meant. All the work he had done over the last month to avoid war, the relationship he had forged with Iranian President Ghaznavi, all of that had been for naught.

He didn't want that meeting. He didn't want to start planning for what they would tell him had to come next.

The phone on the Resolute Desk pierced the silence and Salas shook into movement. How long had it been since he moved, ten minutes, twenty?

Bryce rushed in through the door from his office, pointing at the ringing phone, "That's Leader Dudley! You've got to answer that."

Salas already knew that, knew it was only a matter of time before he heard from Congressional leadership. He picked up the handset and pushed the blinking button, but didn't say a word. "Go for President Salas," he heard Delores say through the phone with his left ear, as well as from her vestibule just outside the Oval with his right.

"Mr. President," Dudley's Southern drawl poured out next, "I just got off the phone with Speaker Hatfield. We have recalled all members of Congress from recess, effective immediately. We expect to reconvene tomorrow evening at the latest."

Salas didn't say a word, didn't even hum his understanding. He knew why they were coming back.

America was going to war.

How long had it been since Jason had last been in his brownstone? The floors were still sawdusted with woodchips from the .338 caliber holes in the walls; there was still glass under the kitchen windows and those in the bedroom too; his pantry gun safe sat wide open and empty, all the weapons removed from inside – and from the kitchen table where he had discarded his spent M4 – presumably by the FBI or DHS. The only other sign anyone had been in here were the haphazard cardboard pieces duct taped over the emptied panes, barriers put up by law enforcement to keep anyone out of this crime scene owned by the most wanted man in America.

One hundred thirty-one days since Jason Lancaster last left the building, no one would ever suspect he would return there. No one would be watching it. No one would notice when, just after dark on a biting February afternoon, the man himself snuck under the yellow tape crisscrossing the door and returned home.

The gas and water and electricity had all long been shut down, but Jason didn't mind. All he needed was a bed to collapse upon. His sheets were still strewn where he had kicked them off in a haste to escape the shooter, his pillows still scrunched up against the headboard. All he needed to do was knock off the little yellow markers next to each bullet strike, flatten out a pillow, and lay back his head …

"That mother fucker thought he could get away with it."

Jason's eyes crept open. How many hours had he been asleep? He rotated his head towards the two panes still full with glass, lit up by the full moon.

It had been a full moon night just like this one. The lighting was so similar – all tonight was missing was Miranda's gorgeous naked body reflecting the moon's shafts, casting an even brighter glow onto the floor.

"I went to see him in his office today – and I told him that tomorrow, he's going to die."

She wasn't even looking at him, assuming he was too drugged out to really listen. She was staring out at that full moon, too keyed up to sleep, even after the release of a full orgasm.

"I told him that, when it's time, he shouldn't even bother trying to escape. I'll be right there. And I will make sure he can't escape."

On the first Sunday night of October, that was right where she had stood when she told Jason about her son, when she admitted she had been the one to rufie him. He was sitting on the bed, tearing at the hair nearest his temples, trying to somehow fight off his haze and comprehend everything she was telling him. Miranda was standing right there by the windows, staring out at the moon and streets below, not giving a fuck whether anyone saw her nude body.

On the second Monday night of February, Jason sat up again, this perfect environment taking him back to that night four months before, when nearly everything – the light, the smell, the sound – was all the same, the night before everything went to shit in a handbasket.

I remember.

He remembered her words of that night for the first time since she uttered them.

"Back at the bar, those were tears of joy, Jason. Because tomorrow, Warren Lapadula is going to die."

There usually were only two reasons Mitch Aldridge was authorized to wake Rosemarie Irving from a night's sleep: something had happened to her husband, or something had happened to her son. Starting four months ago, she had instituted a third reason: something had happened to one of her Supreme Court candidates.

Tonight she had decreed a new reason: Jason Lancaster had changed his mind and agreed to help her with her Lapadula problem.

MMA had alerted Rosemarie right before he left the townhouse that he had received a call from Mr. Lancaster on the burner they had given him. This gave her nearly an hour to prepare for Mitch to retrieve Jason and bring him back. She wasn't camera ready by any stretch, but with the lights held low, was presentable enough when Jason was brought into the kitchen where she soothed her throat with chamomile.

"I'm sorry to disturb you and the Pres--"

"Just me. Mr. Irving moved out last week."

"I'm sorry, I haven't been paying attention to--"

"I was told you had an idea for me?"

"We need to get Miranda Whitney out. She can help us."

Rosemarie choked on a swallow of tea. "You know that's impossible."

"You got me out."

"No one knew we had you. Secret Service was still trying to figure out how the hell they were going to spin that they let a wanted terrorist get a hundred feet from the President with a loaded weapon when they got the call that they were to release you. No one outside of five or six people ever knew it was you. The networks were told they had heard an accidental discharge. It was buried under the Lapadula story and that beheading video before an hour had even passed.

"But getting Miranda Whitney out – I'm afraid that's beyond even my talents."

"You're married to one President, and a trusted advisor of another. There's got to be something you can do."

"Did she do it?"

Jason paused, looking down at the stone tiled floor. "She was forced to be involved. She had to do it, her son's life was at stake."

"I'm sorry, Jason. But there's nothing--"

"He raped her. Just like you. Decades later, he was still the same rapist, and he did it to her. I don't know for sure, but I think … he may have even made her pregnant."

Rosemarie stood from the breakfast nook and walked over to the sink. She retrieved a glass from the nearest cupboard, filled it with water, and drank the whole thing down.

She always figured he had done it again, raped other girls after she had left his chambers, after her clerkship had ended and she had left the Court – it had been nearly 20 years, after all. But hearing it brought to her gut a familiar queasiness, that sick feeling she would get every Sunday night those last couple weeks in Lapadula's chambers, when she started dreading going to work, having realized what kind of man he really was, what he was capable of, having realized it was all destined to end in disaster.

How many more had he raped because she hadn't done anything, because she had let him get away with it so many years ago?

"Mrs. Irving?"

"Yes, I heard you. Just a little parched."

"No one's going to listen to her, unless we can clear her name. She's the most notorious criminal since bin Laden. Unless we can explain how she was forced to participate in the bombing, her story's useless to us."

"Maybe." Rosemarie looked out the window above the sink, her eyes finding the full moon through the leaves of the Spring Valley Park across the street.

Jason took a step forward to confirm the strange look spreading across her face. Rosemarie Irving was smiling.

"Or maybe not," she grinned.

TUESDAY

Mitch Aldridge began the three-hour-plus drive out to West Virginia's Hazelton federal penitentiary early in the 6 AM hour to avoid rush hour on any part of the drive. He made good time, and at approximately 8:53 AM pulled his personal Toyota Highlander through the prison's main entrance.

At 9:12, MMA was alerted that the prisoner was being readied for him; ten minutes later, he was led into the visitation room where the inmate, her beauty ravaged by the events of the past four months, sat shackled to one side of the table. Aldridge thanked his chaperone, then after being locked in the room alone with the prisoner, set his small bag on the table and removed his laptop. It took four minutes for him to determine how to connect to the prison's wi-fi, then another three to open Skype and dial up Jason Lancaster's new handle. And finally, a voice emanated from his computer's tinny little speakers. "Rand."

And finally, Miranda Whitney's eyes rose to look into the smudgy, dusty screen.

"Jason?"

"I remember. Everything you told me that night. The night before--" He swallowed hard, knowing their every word was being monitored, recorded and instantaneously analyzed. "Everything you told me the night you rufied me."

Her eyes returned to the table. "I did it to protect you. To make sure you didn't show up for work the next day."

"And you did tell me about your son that night. You had him after Lapadula raped you. Lapadula is Gordon's father."

Her silence, her lowering eyes, confirmed it.

"Did you ever tell him?"

"I never told anyone at the Court," she shook her head. "Not even you. And no one who knew Gordon ever knew what I did. The only other people who knew about Gordon, and my job, was my family." She looked up. From Jason's perspective, it looked like she was looking below him, but he realized that was because she was looking right into the image of his eyes on Aldridge's screen. "I was going to tell you. I had promised myself if we made it to a year, I would tell you. And then … all this …"

"I don't understand how you even got away with it, how you kept him a secret. When you were pregnant--"

"Just as I was getting to the edge of how much of my stomach I could keep covered under my baggiest clothes, Iraq fell under ISIS control. I claimed I had been recalled, that I needed a leave of absence to serve my time in the reserves. The Chief Clerk granted it. He totally forgot about my dishonorable discharge. I had Gordon, then came back four months later. No one ever realized why I had really taken that leave."

"And why? Why didn't you want anyone to know?"

"When I applied with the Court Police, I had applied for thirty other jobs already. Fifty. No one wanted to touch a mouthy girl who'd gotten thrown out of the military. Lapadula knew that. He used that against me. Cry rape, and he would claim it was consensual."

Back in DC, Jason was clenching his fists under the Irvings' kitchen table. Lapadula was a fucking genius at picking just the right victims, young, weak girls who could never speak of what had transpired. "Which I suppose he had emails to prove."

She nodded. "It had started as something real. Before I knew what he was really like, what was really in his heart. He warned me if I ever told anyone what he had done, I'd never hold a government job again. And those were the only jobs I had ever known. The Court-- it was the first place I'd really loved."

"So you had his child."

"I'll admit I didn't want to, for so many weeks. But I could never do anything about it. I realized it wasn't this baby I hated. I was growing to love this baby. I just didn't want *him* anywhere near it. It was him I hated. So I had the baby, and life went on.

"The day I was promoted to Marshal, he came to my office, and congratulated me - then reminded me that he could end it all with one phone call if he wanted to.

"A year later, he called me into his chambers, and he did it again. He did it just to prove he could, just to prove he *owned* me. That's why I hired you."

"Me?"

"When I started falling for you, I was so scared you would be just like him, that you would hurt me, that I let you go. But after he did it again, I realized I wanted you there, *needed* you there – to protect me."

"But he had nothing to do with Gordon's abduction?"

Miranda gritted her teeth. "That was all Allied Armament. I still don't know how they found out about him. They must've been watching me for months. They just-- picked him up from school one day before the nanny got there." Miranda looked around, trying to determine if this conversation was being recorded. She quickly decided she couldn't care; Jason was the only person on the planet who cared about her or could save her and she wanted to make sure he had every bit of information. "That's when they told me what I would do, how I would help them if I wanted my son back." She shrugged. "I found a silver lining. At least Lapadula would be going down with the building." She shook her head. "Except I just had to fucking gloat. I was so stupid. I went into his chambers on Sunday afternoon, he was working on some draft of something, and I told him he was going to die the next day. I scared the living piss out of him. I could see it right there in the quiver of his eyes.

"After I saw on the Court network that he had swiped in on Monday morning, I went looking for him. But I could never find him.

"I felt the booms. The building was coming down around me. I had to get out. He had disappeared to who knows where. I had scared him so bad, he wouldn't come out until I was like this," she held up her wrists, her shackles jangling down onto the table, "under lock and key, unable to do anything to hurt him."

"That's why I'm here," Jason leaned closer to his side of the webcam. "To hurt him. To hurt Allied Armament. Do you have any proof that they were behind this? Did they ever send you an email about Gordon? Anything?"

"No. I can't. As long as they have Gordon …"

"Rand. We have help now. This guy across from you, who brought this computer in, he's with the Secret Service. We finally have the resources to take them down. We've got to do this while we can. This is our one chance. We can get Gordon out."

Miranda took a deep breath before deciding how to proceed.

"I didn't just let them into the building, Jason. It was also my job to erase them from ever being there."

"The security tapes?"

"I didn't erase them. I kept them."

"Rand, DHS has torn the brownstone apart, I'm sure they've done the same with whatever's left of your office, with our cars. If those tapes still exist, they would've--"

"No, they wouldn't be able to find them. But Ollie could. It's everything: them coming in the building, setting the bombs, hiding them."

"That means-- it shows you? It shows you helping them?"

"I helped them, Jason." Now she stared right into the lens above MMA's screen, making sure her eyes locked right in on her old love's. "I have to suffer the consequences for what I did. But so do they."

"I thought it important to hold this first conference today, before we've heard even a single case argued, for two reasons," Chief Justice Lapadula explained to his flock from the head of the temporary conference table, the former linebacker towering over his eight colleagues. "First, to tell you how proud I've been of each and every one of you as I kept tabs on you from afar. I know how hard you have worked to keep this Court on its feet in the past four months – especially Justice Egan, who acted as your Chief in my absence."

The Associate Justices applauded and Egan nodded thanks, then Lapadula continued in his deep, commanding baritone: "I'm serious. I look at this flimsy table, at these chairs you've been sitting upon for the past three months, and it's proof that this Court is so much bigger than a building, so much bigger than a Courtroom, or a conference room, or a fancy dining room. It's about nine people dedicated to serve, and the Constitution to which we have pledged our lives.

"Now, unfortunately, the circumstances of this term have usurped so much of our most precious commodity: time – already stretched to its limit in our *least* unusual terms. This brings me to the second reason I wanted to gather this morning. Put simply, we just don't have the time to hear and decide every case we had originally intended to consider this term. Some will have to be sacrificed, pushed to next term or perhaps, their petitions sent back down, their fates trusted to the very capable lower courts." The Chief sat, bringing a pair of reading glasses to his nose as he consulted a prepared list. "My staff and I have taken the liberty of prioritizing what we have left on our docket and identifying a few cases that might not be the most important we were going to hear."

The procedure was simple: Chief Lapadula would present the basics of a case, and the Justices would re-vote on whether or not to consider the matter.

Court rules dictated that four votes – not a majority of five – were all that was required just for a case to be heard, so their task today was nothing more than confirming that at least four Justices still believed these cases worthy of time and consideration. They wouldn't follow the usual conference protocol of speaking in order of seniority; each Justice would be free to speak up when he or she felt the need, just to give the Chief a general sense of who still supported the hearing of a particular case.

What the others didn't realize was that Lapadula was burying his lede. He started with five cases he knew wouldn't retain their four votes, cases in which three of the Justices who had supported it were no longer with them, or cases he knew would lose votes just because of their new irrelevance when considered under this time crunch. Then came four more he knew would be right on the four vote threshold, but on which it would be relatively easy to convince at least one Justice to change his or her mind.

After less than 90 minutes and the elimination of all nine cases he had proposed, he reached the final title on his list, the one around which he had planned this whole charade. "Okay, *Agguire v. Detroit.*" He tried to not be too obvious when he raised his eyes, gauging the reaction in each of his colleagues.

Justice Winks's audible scoff was the first reply. "We absolutely must decide that case this term," he insisted, almost offended that this case – one of the most important of the term, in his not-so-humble opinion – had even been included on this list. "We should've decided it months ago." His words dripped with his guilt over the reason it hadn't been completed last term: his personal failure to finish the majority opinion on time.

"I voted to grant cert in this case originally," Justice Egan piped up, as Lapadula knew she would. "But having now heard it twice, I am more convinced than ever that this Court, as many Justices have argued in our history, should not be concerning itself with *political* questions, with the everyday workings and tough decisions of the other branches of the government. And this case is the very definition of such a political question."

"The question of standing is where I struggle with it," another of the senior Justices rode her wake. "Were Ryan Agguire's constitutional rights really violated when he was given a *speeding ticket* from an Allied Armament patrol? Sufficiently violated for this Court to jump into the fray? He *was* convicted of going over 75 in a 35. Now perhaps if a police officer or fire fighter were to bring a wrongful termination--"

"I'm sorry, are we really discussing this?" a voice unfamiliar to the Chief spoke up from the opposite end of the flimsy table. "We don't deal with this, and we're tacitly permitting a private outfit to take over the running of one of America's great cities." The Chief locked eyes with his only physical equal at the table, that JSOC Admiral with scarce legal experience, whom Chief Lapadula considered grossly unqualified for this bench. "That's martial law, that's the very definition of *Posse Comitatus*. We have to nip this in the bud right now, or who knows where this precedent could lead."

"I have to agree with Justice MacTavish," Justice Cecilia Koh added. "Military contractors are private companies formed purely for warmongering, for war profiteering. They present a dangerous trend in our society. We have a responsibility to set some guidelines as to when they may or may not be used."

"So that's three votes to hear the case," Lapadula kept track on his sheet, leaving an opening for another vote to speak up. But for several seconds, only silence followed. "Without at least one more, I can't rationalize leaving it on the docket."

Isaac Goldman bit his lower lip. He was one of two current Justices who hadn't heard the case argued in one of its first two appearances before the Court (Mac was the other, but he clearly knew it like the back of his hand). Goldman hadn't studied it enough to vote on its merits, on the petitioner's standing, on *anything* when put on the spot like this. He had been so disorganized over the last week, unraveling since Janaki took her sudden and unexpected leave to deal with her grief over Dennis's death. Goldman had come to rely on her so much, and not just as a ghost writer of his memoirs. She would never have let him waltz into a situation like this; she would have known the Chief might pose this question, she would have gotten the case in front of him and made sure he was prepared.

But despite his lack of readiness to discuss this case, there was one important thing Justice Goldman did know about *Agguire v. Detroit*. He knew it was important to Rosemarie Irving. He had witnessed her going to great lengths to make sure the six-Justice Egan Court didn't vote on it after hearing it reargued in December. He had helped her make sure it was scheduled as the first case the Court would hear after she took over as Chief Justice.

Justice Goldman didn't know this case from his ass, but he knew that the woman who had gotten him on the Supreme Court wanted it heard.

"I'll be the fourth vote," he said with a raised finger.

Lapadula hesitated just a beat, before adding another tally to his sheet. "All right, we shall keep it on then."

Goldman nodded to his fellow members of the Irving Three, each of whom had also had their benefactor in mind during this brief but heated discussion.

None of them were paying attention to the other side of the table as Lapadula traded his own brief eye contact with Claudine Egan. If they were, they would have seen the smiles behind their eyes. Though they had failed to get *Agguire v. Detroit* off the docket, it had been quite clear from the reactions of everyone around the table which way the critical votes would swing, and that the lower court ruling would be affirmed.

Walsh Howard looked around in confusion as Bryce Sando led them down the ground floor hallway. This wasn't the way up to the Oval Office; in their visit to the White House last week, they had gone up an elevator – that elevator they were now walking right past. Walsh leaned into the ear of LT, his old CO from his tour in Iraq and now his trusted Operations Director. "You think they're giving us the runaround this time?" he whispered. "Handing us off to some flunky?"

LT held out his hands and mimed pushing down the ground, his constant reminder to his employer to take a deep breath and keep calm.

Bryce stopped at an unmarked door, extending the keycard from his belt to swipe it through the reader in one quick motion. The door clicked unlocked and Bryce opened it to step inside, Walsh and LT close on his heels, following him not into a room, but a very small-- *chamber* is the only word to describe it, a five-by-five little box, smaller than an elevator, serving only as a passageway from one door to the next. This time, Bryce didn't use his keycard, but pressed his thumb down into a clear electronic reader pad. The second door clicked unlocked, and Bryce opened it wide, ushering Walsh and LT in with an après vous underhand.

Walsh Howard stepped into his wet dream, a room about which the young boy growing up back in Texas playing with little green soldiers, parachutes of Kleenex and dental floss taped to their backs, had always fantasized. Every wall was covered with computer displays, rotating interactive maps of every inch of the globe – illustrating everything from troop deployment levels to nuclear capabilities – with closed circuit feeds from every aircraft, ship, from every frigging helmet cam of every American serviceman and woman around the world.

"Good to see you again, Mr. Howard." As the President rose from the round table in the center of the room, Walsh clocked the famous faces around it. This collection of big wigs was even more impressive than the state-of-the-art technology on display.

"Walsh, Mr. President," he mumbled in response. "Call me Walsh."

"Have a seat, Walsh." Bryce was pulling out the two vacant chairs, beckoning Walsh and LT to sit.

Walsh felt his skin quivering as they came around to their seats. They were about to sit at the Big Table, with the President and his National Security advisors, with his CIA and DIA and DHS, with all his Joint Chiefs.

They were about to sit in on a meeting in the fucking Situation Room.

"I'm sure you've seen the Qatil Kafii video," Salas was saying as Walsh lowered himself into his chair.

"'Silent Killer' in Arabic," the Director of Central Intelligence explained. "A terrorist organization we believe founded and funded by the Iranian government. They've been behind dozens of deadly attacks in the Middle East over the past six years, but before today, had never been connected to the deaths of any Americans."

"And today, that count went from zero to one twenty-four," LT grumbled.

"One twenty-five," the DCI corrected, "counting Simon Weinbach."

"Congress is scrambling to get back to Washington," POTUS said. "We expect a vote by end of business tomorrow declaring war on Iran."

Walsh couldn't move, but LT nodded. "The right move, Sir."

"Our goal is to begin bombing runs on Tehran and other targeted sites within three weeks' time," the one wearing the blue tunic of the Navy said.

Salas leaned forward on his forearms. "Gentlemen. Many Presidents have become notorious for reneging on promises. It's almost an expected pitfall of the job. Not this time. I will not be one of those Presidents. I will not send ground troops into Iran." He pushed himself back, his chair bouncing as his weight fell back into it. "But well-compensated civilian contractors? That's a whole other story."

Truth be told, Chief Lapadula was planning to attend even before the phone call sealed it. He had missed it more than anything else in his time away from Washington.

A season ticket holder for over thirty years, Lapadula hadn't missed more than a handful of the Washington National Opera's shows over the last few decades – until last October. Seven shows had opened and closed during his hiding out period; he didn't always make the holiday program, but he wouldn't have missed the other six under normal circumstances. One of his security guards had shown him how to download all the opera his heart could desire to the computer in the Montana cabin where he had spent the winter, but the internet connection was so slow, the process required several hours per album.

Warren had been a rabid opera fan all his life, since his mother raised him on records of the stuff. He had clung to it when his peers were discovering things like Rock n' Roll and grass. His distaste for both probably made him a better football player, and definitely helped ensure he was able to complete law school.

Hence, when he received the invitation in his Tuesday morning mail to attend the WNO's Wednesday night performance of *Il trittico* (Puccini's rarely performed *Triptych*!), he had decided instantly to attend. The phone call from the company's Artistic Director that evening confirming he received the ticket wasn't necessary, but it did help to make him feel appreciated, and even happier to be home.

"We of course would love to honor you in your box, Mr. Chief Justice," the Artistic Director said during the call. "But we can skip that if you don't feel up to the attention." The gentle sarcasm in her voice was a clue that she already knew how he would respond.

"The problem is, anyone who sees me there is going to wonder why you didn't do it. I don't want to make you guys look bad."

"Thank you, Sir. It would be our great honor."

The Chief heard the quiet knock on the door of his chambers after he had hung up and was gathering his things for the evening. He didn't look up, but when he heard the door shut before a word was spoken, guessed who it might be.

"I told you her disciples would save it," Egan hissed from the door. "I doubt they even know why it's important to her, they just know it is. I'm convinced it's part of their deal with her – she gets them on the Court, they get that case heard, no matter what."

"Stop worrying, Claudy," Lapadula smiled, putting a comforting hand on her upper back as he came around his desk. "I've got it handled."

"You haven't seen her these past months. She's far more cunning and resourceful than you could ever imagine."

"If Rosemarie Irving really did manipulate the entire replacement process so she could control *Agguire v. Detroit*, I'm afraid her quest is going to come up short." He winked at her, then opened the door. "She failed, remember? This is our Court. It will never be hers. Now if you'll excuse me, I must get home. My wife's still cross I didn't think to let her know I was alive. I've explained it's not her I had to keep it from, it's those damn sisters of hers. Goodnight, Justice Egan."

Ollie hadn't answered his phone in over 12 hours, since Jason first tried him seconds after the Skype with Miranda had ended. Perhaps not usually a reason for concern when it came to a twentysomething, but there also hadn't been any answer at the door of his apartment, and none of his neighbors could remember when they had last seen him. His coworkers at FirmWall reported he didn't work there anymore – he hadn't worked there in over a month. He had lost his job after failing to show up for over two weeks, without any warning or reason or notification.

Jason was starting to get very nervous. He had spoken to Ollie in that last month. He had enlisted his help in tracking the ownership of that Detroit hospital all the way up to Christian Sacerdoti. The kid sounded fine in those conversations; he didn't mention anything about losing his job or his life falling apart.

But of course, Jason hadn't asked, had he? He had just given orders and expected them to be carried out with no frills or personal attachment. He knew that, no matter what happened in his own life, Ollie cared about his sister, and Jason had taken advantage of that without one thought for the young man himself. And now he was nowhere to be found.

There were, however, two things working in Jason's favor: one, Ollie was a twentysomething in twenty-first century America, and no matter what happened to him, there's no way he would let it happen without his Samsung Galaxy somewhere on his person. And two, Jason was now working with the Secret Service (or the Irvings' personal agent, at the very least) and as long as it was powered on, the Secret Service could track that Galaxy.

As Jason drove down Atlantic Street SE, staring out at all the brick projects of the Washington Highlands passing by, he found himself almost wishing he didn't find Ollie on this night. Sure, he needed the kid's help – and wanted to make sure he was all right. But if he was to be found in this neighborhood, maybe Southeast DC's worst, it wasn't because he was doing some community outreach or giving back to those less privileged.

"Looks like he's right across the street from you," MMA squawked through Jason's earpiece when he pulled his borrowed SUV to the curb. Jason got out and crossed to the concrete courtyard in the middle of the cluster of two-story tenements, a late night hub of activity, trash talking and bonfire light. Jason had come armed with a photo loaded up on the phone he was carrying, but he wouldn't need it: there was only one white man to be found on this patio, leaned up against a far wall with four other homeless-looking dudes, passing around a pipe that most assuredly wasn't packed with tobacco or even marijuana.

Jason stood over him, realizing the photo wouldn't have helped him anyway. This Ollie was skin and bones, his face dominated by a bird nest beard that hadn't been trimmed in months.

"Ollie, it's me. Time to go."

"Man, I don't know who you talking about." His head spun this way and that like a dreidel, like he had forgotten how to hold it upright and kept having to correct it from collapsing. "There ain't no Ollie here."

Jason didn't say another word, just reached down and shoved a paw up under the boy's filthy armpit, pulling him to his feet and dragging him out of the courtyard and back to his SUV, ignoring the catcalls and hollow law enforcement threats from the rabble they had left behind.

Jason had just thumbed the engine to life when Ollie's bony fist connected with his chin. "Did you just punch me?" He had tried, but had done no more real damage than batting Jason's head two inches to the left.

Jason reached over and grabbed Ollie's wrists before he could do it again, trying to shake some sobriety into him. "Hey. Hey. Stop it. I need your help. Miranda needs your help." Ollie froze, and Jason let go, turning back to the wheel.

But before he could put it in gear, he heard sucking and wheezing emanating from within the younger man's beard. "It's all such a fucking waste, man." He was crying. "She was always perfect. And look what happened to her. If that's how her life turns out-- what the fuck can I possibly do? What can any of us do?"

"You can save her, Ollie. You can help me tell her story. That's what we're going to do."

The car started moving. In less than a mile, Ollie's tears had come to a full stop.

WEDNESDAY

One advantage of finding Ollie tweaked out of his gourd was that he didn't need sleep; once Jason had assigned him his task, he jumped into it with a tireless ferocity. His manic explanation zipped out of his mouth almost too fast for Jason to follow: he had set his sister up with a top-secret, impossible-to-find cloud account, its servers based in Sri Lanka, accessible only by patching to it through four ghost IP addresses. "In fact, anyone watching right now thinks someone in Budapest is accessing the account," Ollie motor mouthed as he opened the account on his laptop. "Budapest, Budapest. Not sure if this IP is in Buda or Pest. Or Pesht. Ishouldfindout."

"I really have no idea what you're talking about."

"She asked me to open this for her, oh, week, weekandahalf 'fore the bombing. Atthetime, no idea why she needed it. Duh! Makesperfectsense *now*. OhGod-Miranda. Never changed her password. Toldherto, but guess she neverdid. Ah-well, makes this much easier. Anywayatthetime she just said she had security concerns at work, needed someplace to stuff some files that no one at work, that no one *on Earth* could see."

"And you at no point over the last four months thought this might be of interest to me?"

Ollie leered at Jason over his shoulder. "No offense, bro, but you're not officially in the family *yet*, kay? She had told me she was nervous about someone at work – you may have seduced her but that still defines you."

"Right."

"And, lookeewhatwehavehere!" A dozen video thumbnails were popping up all over Ollie's screen. Even in this miniaturized form, Jason could see what they were: excerpts from Supreme Court surveillance cameras, angles on every hallway, darkened and dim in their night time lighting settings. Even as tiny as the thumbnails were, he could read all the date stamps in their lower right corners: '**7 OCT**.' The day of the bombing.

Ollie clicked the first one open, and they sat in silence, staring at a rarely-used ground floor side door, until--

Oliie gasped. "It's her," he whispered. Miranda had entered the frame. She opened the side door wide – and five men clad all in black rushed into the building. "Lookatthat. So cocky, don't even think they need masks," Ollie observed.

"Can you open up Google next to this? I'm wondering how many of these guys we can find in photos working for Allied Armament."

"That'd take forever. I can do you one better," Ollie smiled, already opening up another application. "Facial recognition."

"You have that?"

"C'mon. Google and Facebook have that."

"Yeah, but theirs can't be nearly as good as the NSA's or CIA's. If I could get someone's help from inside an agency--"

Ollie snorted. "Google and Facebook pay a lot better than the NSA or CIA. And so does my company." He was already zooming in on one frozen frame of a surveillance feed, his facial recog program going right to work separating an intruder's face into sections, breaking it down and analyzing its color and shape patterns. "Gimme a few hours, I bet we can get most of these assholes. Except this one, of course." He had minimized the recog program and was pointing to another one of the tiny thumbnails: the last of the five men into the building, the one always bringing up the rear as they planted their bombs, he was the only one who had actually chosen to wear a mask.

Fueled by his fix from earlier in the night (and maybe sneaking one or two more since they got here, though Jason hoped not), Ollie was still working away on his laptop when Jason crashed out on his couch, and still working when he awoke just under four hours later to the dawn sun burning down on his face.

"Already found most of them," Ollie summoned him over. Jason crouched behind his shoulder as Ollie showed how he had already identified three of the five bombers through their affiliations with Allied Armament. "This guy here was photographed by the *Detroit Free Press* at their press conference last summer announcing they were taking over the police; this one is in a recruitment video on the company's website; and it turns out this Mensa member here has to Instagram every time he takes a shit or eats a bowl of oatmeal. That leaves just one more, this guy here, who I should have in the next hour or--"

"I already know that one," Jason said. "That's Lance Tyrol."

Despite all evidence to the contrary, the 116th United States Congress could work rather quickly when its members felt like they had no choice. House Joint Resolution 120, "Declaring a state of War between the Government & People of the United States and the Islamic Republic of Iran," had already garnered over 200 votes by 1300 hours on Wednesday, while debate on Senate Joint Resolution 22 (the resolutions' authors had worked together to ensure their texts were identical) had just wrapped up and voting was about to get underway.

President Salas was paralyzed by the votes, unable to move from his private study off the Oval, incapable of peeling his eyes from his five TVs. This time had been cleared off his schedule for him to work on the speech his communications director had prepared for him, to refine and rehearse the address he would give to the nation as soon as the vote totals were official, voicing his support for the decisiveness of Congress and pledging to follow their edict to take immediate action against Iran. (Not that he had much choice, as the final vote totals were expected to well surpass veto-proof numbers.) But he hadn't looked at the speech in over two hours; he just continued to bounce his miniature rubber soccer ball (the same one that used to drive his former Chief of Staff Rebecca Whitford nuts) off the walls between each screen.

Bounce. Bounce. Bounce.

"You're going to want to speak tonight." Salas heard Rosemarie Irving's voice in the doorway behind him, but didn't turn to look at her, didn't rise from his chair.

Bounce. Bounce. BOUNCE.

"Everyone's going to tell you that you have to speak tonight, that the American people need to hear from their President tonight. And I would implore you to use every iota of strength and willpower you have to ignore that advice."

"Oh, you'll implore me?" Salas threw the ball one last time, harder than ever before, smashing a vase to pieces and toppling the framed photo next to it. He leapt to his feet, getting right in Rosemarie's face. "You'll fucking implore me?!"

"Tony--"

"No," he hurried away from her before he did something he regretted, pacing around the room as he ranted. "I need to say something that I should have said a long time ago. *Months* ago. You are not a part of this administration. It is grossly inappropriate for you to advise the President, for you to solicit information on sensitive matters, for you to fucking waltz into my private study without anyone telling me like you still live here!"

Rosemarie held down her initial reaction. She took a step further into the room to shut the door behind her, to add at least some small layer of privacy to the rest of this conversation that the whole of the west wing must have enjoyed so far. "If I've done something to upset you, I'm sorry. Everything I've done in the past four months, *everything*, was in your best interest--"

"No, it really wasn't, was it? It was in *yours*. You drove my Chief of Staff away so I would have to rely on you more. You convinced me to hire a new COS you'd known for twenty years, ensuring your agenda was properly prioritized. You volunteered to lead my Supreme Court search so you could control that search. You put yourself in position to be named Chief Justice so you could control which cases went before *your* Court."

Rosemarie sucked in a tiny bit of surprised air. "I don't know where this is coming--"

"I know you own part of Allied Armament, Rosemarie. A big part." Salas now had his strong goalkeeper's paws on his waist, and with his sleeves rolled up, the muscular sinew of his forearms pulsed with anger. "Jason Lancaster. That's when you went too far. That's when I really woke up to what I've let go on here. This guy comes into the White House and tries to kill you, and two hours later, you're telling me to spring him. You can't be surprised that sent up some red flags."

"Then why did you do it? Why did you spring him?"

Salas opened his mouth to answer, but had to stop himself. After a deep pause, he answered. "You know why."

"Yes. I thought I did. I thought I knew you."

"And I you. But now that I know … know that you had arranged for the Allied Armament case to be the first your Court would hear--"

She took a step forward. "Antonio, you've got to trust me right now, it's more important now than ever. If you can just remain calm and be patient for a little while longer, everything is going to become more clear—"

"I shouldn't have to be patient for things to be clear! I'm the President of the fucking United States, *everything* should be clear! I should've known from the beginning what you were doing, and why. And you know what, I could've helped you."

"I know you're angry with me right now. But just-- *listen* to me. Don't go before the American people tonight. Don't say anything yet. So much more is about to happen.

"Or, if you feel that you must go before them, if you feel that you have no choice but to say something, don't tell them what you've decided."

"What I've decided?"

"To use Allied Armament as our ground force." She opened the door to leave, looking back at him once more. "In 24 hours you'll understand. Everything I've ever done, I've done to protect you."

Just after she had gone, the tiny soccer ball rolled to its owner's feet. He picked it up and hurled it as hard as he could against the closed door.

George sat back from his computer with a prolonged sigh. He had that feeling he hadn't gotten in a long time, and never on this Supreme Court case, not through all the seeming breaks of the past four months. It was that feeling that all the answers had become clear, that light was finally appearing at the end of the tunnel, that all that remained was to bring the schmucks to justice.

George swiveled his desk chair around, hands behind his head, to look at the young man he had for some reason believed throughout this whole prolonged mess. "Bet you can't wait for me to call you when we've got everyone in chains."

Jason Lancaster smiled. "That will be nice."

"*But.*" George turned back to his screen. "We still don't have the proof Walsh Howard ordered them to do it."

Jason was already on his feet, coming around to take control of the mouse. "We've got the next best thing." He opened one of the videos, pausing it on the clearest shot of LT's face. "Lance Tyrol. Allied Armament Head of Operations."

"You'd think he'd be enough to justify one helluva search warrant."

Jason nodded. "He's the General, the commander-in-chief of all their military ops. And a class-A scumbag."

"You sound very familiar with his work."

"He was my CO. Damn good soldier. And an even better rapist." George's head whipped back in Jason's direction, as Jason let the video play. "I gave him that limp."

"You don't say?"

"*He's* when I want you to call me, George. He's when it's over. When that asshole is in cuffs."

George closed the program and pulled the zip drive out of its USB port. "I gotta get back to the office. One thing I don't want to miss is Kingman Summers's reaction when I explain to him--"

"Can you go higher than him?"

"What?"

"Kingman Summers also put some early money into Allied Armament." George nodded; suddenly, some of Summers's behavior immediately following the bombings, his suppressing the agency's analysis of the recovered explosive, made perfect sense. He knew how his next weeks would be spent: gathering hard evidence that Summers was connected to the plot all along. "Might be a good idea to go over Summers's head this time."

George's biggest smile of the past quarter-year expanded across his face. "There's nothing I'd enjoy more in this world."

Warren Lapadula nearly shook with anticipation during the second intermission. It was established fact that the first two one-act operas of Puccini's *Triptych* were far inferior to the third; a century after its debut, *Gianni Schicci* was now most often performed alone, in fact. Throughout the first two acts, Lapadula had gotten more and more excited to hear the company's lead soprano perform "O mio babbino caro," the aria he considered Puccini's masterpiece; she was a sublime Giorgetta in *Il tabarro*, a superb titular nun in *Suor Angelica*, and he had no doubt she would be a transcendent Lauretta.

It was near the end of the intermission that the Artistic Director made her promised visit to the Chief's box, a white gloved usher bearing a tray of champagne flutes right behind her. "Mr. Chief Justice, Mrs. Lapadula," the AD smiled as she held out a glass for Lapadula and his wife, "all of us at the WNO would be honored to toast you on the occasion of your heroic return."

Lapadula chuckled and accepted the drink, but before he could bring it to his lips, the house lights dimmed, and the returning audience quieted to listen to the voice booming over the speakers: "*Ladies and Gentlemen. Tonight, the Washington National Opera is honored to celebrate the return of one of our most dedicated patrons, and closest friends. Please turn your attention to Box 16 and join us in saluting the Chief Justice of the United States – Warren Lapadula!*"

The Chief stood and raised his champagne flute as a spotlight found his box. The audience applauded, everyone rising to their feet; Lapadula nodded and mouthed thank you several times, even sending some kisses flying. As the cheers faded, he turned to clink his glass against the Artistic Director's, then brought it to his lips to drink the whole thing down. The usher took back the Chief's glass, setting it upright atop his tray, then hurried out, the Artistic Director right on his heels.

"He forgot to take my glass," Mrs. Lapadula grumbled.

Out in the corridor, the usher handed the lone glass from his tray to the Artistic Director, just as she had instructed before they had gone in. "Ma'am, I'd be more than happy to run it back to--"

"I've got it, Teddy."

"Uh, yes, ma'am."

With glass in hand, she pushed past her usher and down the hall, the opening stanzas of "Povero Buoso" alternating between loud and muffled as she crossed each portal, finally reaching the box entrance on the far opposite end of the theatre, where a large man in suit and earpiece stood sentry.

"She's expecting this," she said as she handed the glass off to the security guard. He nodded and disappeared inside the box.

Warren Lapadula was a very giving patron and great friend of the opera, indeed. The Irvings were just better friends.

On the night of February 12th, the biggest party in America was in Lubbock, Texas. Walsh and LT had flown back right after their meeting in the White House, and had decided at about 25,000 feet that their 70,000 employees (and soon to cross 100k, with the hiring binge they would have to embark upon) should have the opportunity to celebrate before the serious business, before heavy training for the Iranian invasion, began in the morning. Every mess hall and the three bars on their hundred-thousand-square-foot compound offered free drinks and food throughout the night, and no serious work was to be expected of anyone any earlier than 0900 the next morning. No other AASC employee knew what they were celebrating, although the rumor was already flying that they were going to be a big part of the action against Iran. If only they knew how big.

Despite four scotches, three Tequila shots, and a good portion of a couple bottles of champagne (but how much ended up in your mouth when one was dumped over your head?), Walsh Howard was determined to drive himself home in his Tesla. There was nothing but flat dirt with which to collide between the compound and his mansion, and if he happened to be pulled over, well, Allied Armament owned this town, and every moving violation he had been given in the past two years (including two other 'deweys') had disappeared as fast as he could make one phone call to the mayor's office.

"Sure you're okay to drive?" a voice from the passenger seat asked as Walsh got in.

"HOLY SHIT!" Walsh leaped back so hard, he fell right out of the car, his ass slamming down onto the dusty pavement.

He pulled himself back in, confronting the large black man who had somehow broken into his baby. "Who the hell are you? You scared the piss out of me!"

"A friend sent me," Mitch Aldridge smiled.

Every news anchor and talking head, network and cable, was ripping into him. Sean Hannity was ripping into him and so was Rachel Maddow, as were both O'Reilly and O'Donnell. For one night, everyone agreed: the nation needed to hear from its President. Antonio Salas's decision to cancel his evening address was not only shocking and cowardly, but sapped the American people of any confidence they may have had in the aggressive military campaign upon which they were about to embark. Perhaps worst of all, his November opponent, Bradley Benedict, swooped up his open time slot and delivered the sort of fire-and-brimstone damnation of Iran and radical Islam that the country was really clamoring for.

POTUS didn't know why he was still up, flipping between these channels as he lay in bed, torturing himself with remote control in one hand, Gran Patrón Platinum in the other. But at about 11:45, he felt his eyes begin to droop, his chin to fall. He deposited his empty glass on the table, pushing his body all the way recumbent under the covers, laying his head back against his pillows-- when his phone rang.

The President groaned as he sat up, but brightened slightly when he read 'CHIEF OF STAFF OFC' on the phone's digital display. *Exactly the man I need to speak to.* Salas brought the receiver to his ear. "Bryce," he pushed out, "I made a terrible mistake. I have to talk to the American people, first thing in the morning."

"I agree," Bryce Sando answered firmly. This surprised Salas; since coming on board a month ago, his COS had always pushed for following Rosemarie Irving's guidance. Earlier today, in fact, he had supported POTUS's instincts to listen to the former First Lady's advice, and hold off on any public statements about future war plans.

Bryce quickly explained the change of heart. "A couple bits of new information have just come in, Mr. President. Everything has just changed."

THURSDAY

The early spring sun made its second straight appearance on Thursday, warming the White House lawn enough to convince President Salas he should give his address, sure to be the most gratifying of his Presidency, from the Rose Garden. *Guess Phil was wrong again*, the President chuckled to himself as he stepped out before the gathered press; the famous Pennsylvania groundhog had returned to its burrow two weeks ago, a prediction of six more weeks of winter. Instead, as Salas stepped behind his podium, he could see many of the mounds of snow built up over the harsh winter already starting to recede.

"My fellow Americans," he began when the hubbub had quieted, "since the morning of October 7th, we have understandably been a nation on edge, desperate to find the evil perpetrators who brought us tragedy on that day. And I promise you, no one has been more dedicated to this cause than me. I would like to thank our Congress, for being ready to act when it appeared answers had finally been found.

"However, I come before you this morning to announce that our Central Intelligence Agency has now confirmed that the video that so shocked and angered all of us earlier this week is in fact a forgery. Through the use of advanced facial recognition software and some human intelligence, the CIA has confirmed that the facial features of the head displayed at the end of the video does not match that of Simon Weinbach, the prisoner seen in the beginning of the video. It is true that Mr. Weinbach disappeared while on assignment in Iran two months ago; however, we now believe he has actually *joined* the Qatil Kafii terrorist organization, not as a prisoner, but as a member. War upon and with the United States is a stated goal on the charter of Qatil Kafii, and we believe this video, and their claim of the Supreme Court bombing, was an effort to goad us into just such a war.

"I can also this morning announce that investigators at the Department of Homeland Security have now obtained evidence that links the bombing of the Supreme Court not to Qatil Kafii, or any international terrorist organizations, but to certain high-ranking members of an American company doing business right here on our soil.

"Earlier this morning, DHS and FBI agents executed a raid upon the Texas headquarters of Allied Armament Security Consultants, armed with search warrants from the Attorney General, as well as arrest warrants for four men we have identified as among the bombers. These teams also hope to collect evidence that will answer the question of whether or not the bombers were ordered to cause such destruction by their employers at Allied Armament.

"Before I spoke with all of you, I had a private sit-down with Leader Dudley and Speaker Hatfield, followed by a meeting with the joint intelligence committees from both houses of Congress. Later today, a Joint Resolution will be presented in both chambers that will revoke yesterday's Declaration of War against the Islamic Republic of Iran. I also telephoned President Ghaznavi early this morning to express our apologies for this misunderstanding, and he was very understanding of the confusion and difficulties we have been faced with over the past several months.

"I pray, as I know all Americans do, that today provides the final answers we need to put this horrible chapter in American history behind us, and sleep well with the knowledge that justice has finally been served. May God bless those law enforcement officers representing all of us on this bright morning, may God bless each and every one of you, and may God bless the United States of America."

They came ready for war, and were met with a whimper.

The FBI raid of Allied Armament's Lubbock compound was complete before the President even went before the cameras. Though the HRT Teams stormed the property in their heaviest-duty BearCats, packing their most serious firepower, they found little to no fight in the dorms; there was not one exchange of fire, not one tense stand-off or call for back up. Most of the employees of the security contractor had no reason to run, and they all were much too hungover to care.

It took less than thirty minutes for three of the four bombing suspects to be apprehended, and only one of them provided even a modicum of challenge, darting out of a female co-worker's bunk and charging across the property in just his Jockey boxer briefs, where four FBI G-men tackled him to the turf. Meanwhile, other teams were meeting no resistance in confiscating every computer, every hard drive, every laptop and server on the property.

If he was guilty, Walsh Howard III would never be brought to justice, or at least, not justice in this world. An hour after their arrival on campus, a female FBI agent noticed the Tesla in the executive parking lot with a strange red tint to its windows. She approached with sidearm raised, and only once she confirmed there was no movement from the silhouette inside did she yell into her shoulder-mounted walkie, "I may have a casualty in the East parking lot, that's the executive parking lot. Looks DOA, possible 10-56. Repeat, possible suicide!"

Indeed, after she pried open the driver's side door, she could confirm the Glock in Howard's right hand, the exit wound out the back of his brain stem, the perfect splash pattern all over the otherwise pristine leather. Though she assumed he had taken his life when he realized his property was being raided by the feds, the ME later confirmed that Walsh had been dead for eight or nine hours when found, adding a morbid mystery to the whole saga: *Walsh Howard had just landed the biggest contract in the history of mercenaries; why would he take his own life?* Figuring that he had many friends in government and law enforcement, investigators guessed he had been tipped off to the impending arrests hours before the fact.

Agents would not have to go far to inform Howard's family of his death; his mother was set up with her own apartment on the compound. It was when they were clearing it of all its own data-storing devices that one of the HRT agents realized she didn't live there alone, but shared it with a precocious little four-year-old. As Mrs. Howard was much too old to have given birth to this child herself, it was at first assumed this was a grandson or other relative, or perhaps even an adopted son of her own. They couldn't have imagined *how* he was adopted.

"My mom's like you," the child said as he watched one of the HRT officers box up Mrs. Howard's desktop computer into an evidence box.

"Is that so?" The officer was half paying attention, answering with a grin.

"She's a police occifer like you. Actually, she's the boss of all the occifers."

"No kidding."

"Yeah. She was the boss of all the Supreme police occifers, until bad guys blew up her work."

Jason chose not to watch the festivities on the news, knowing that its wide angle lenses and press briefing versions of events would be nowhere near the satisfying conclusion he craved to his four-month odyssey. Instead, he went back to where it all began, back to Bullfeathers, back to where he had joined Miranda for an ill-fated drink the night before the bombing.

This not being a football Sunday, Jason was able to get his own seat at the bar this time. He chose to sit in the same stool where Miranda had been seated that Sunday night in October, staring up at the TV that had on that night just happened to be showing an old lecture her Baby Daddy had given. Tonight, the screen was instead filled with a Georgetown game. It was another so-so season for the Hoyas, sure to end in the upper-teens or even lower-twenties in wins, but still far short of the postseason glories of Thompson, Ewing, et al.

Jason's pocket buzzed. He knew who it was. Just two or three people had the number corresponding to this burner, and he was expecting a call from only one of them.

"It's done," George's voice crackled through.

"Good."

"And they found the boy. He's all right."

Jason closed his eyes with relief. "Good."

"Jason. They didn't get Tyrol. Did you hear me? Jason? Tyrol wasn't there."

Jason lowered the phone and set it down on the bar without thumbing it dead. He took another sip of his ginger ale. Somehow, this news didn't surprise him. He didn't think LT would go down easy, not after all these years of tormenting him. He had been preparing for this call for the past 36 hours. One memory, or amalgamation of many memories, dominated his thoughts.

"My own piece of heaven. Wouldn't look like much to a fancy city boy like you, Lancaster, but it's all the heaven I need. That's where I'm going, they ever let us come home from this stank hole."

He wasn't sure how many times Tyrol had told him about home. He and Tyrol had been friends; he had looked up to Tyrol before he found him assaulting that girl. They were often sharing cigars on weekends, or going off on stupid-as-hell snipe hunts together when granted short leaves. And Tyrol never stopped talking about going home, back to his little piece of Arizona land, back to his own little piece of heaven.

Jerome, he called it.

He had even given Jason the address before a long leave. They were going to be back in the world for a month or something, and Tyrol knew Jason didn't have much to go back to, just Sarge locked away in a 'home,' sure to do nothing but criticize and complain, cry that he needed help wiping his ass. If Jason needed some vacation in that leave, some *real* vacation, he should fly out to Arizona, drive up to Jerome.

"Look me up anytime, Lancaster."

Jason picked the phone back up off the bar. The Georgetown game was now long over, and George Aug had long ago hung up. Jason had wasted so much time – three years. Time to finish something he should've finished a long time ago. He thumbed one of the two speed dials, and brought the speaker to his ear.

"It's Lancaster. I am gonna need that plane."

FRIDAY

LT hated Jerome.

Sure, when he was a grunt spending most of the year in the Suck, it was the perfect escape, a little mountain cabin acres and acres away from any other humanity. His own Martin Sheen-at-the-beginning-of-*Apocalypse-Now* refuge to drink and drug and punch through mirrors. Ghost town Jerome was just close enough to drive into when he needed whiskey and cigars and meth and titty mags. Two or three people might say hello – the convenience store clerk, the postman – but no one would linger or ask him if he was married yet or generally give a shit. No one would come by and visit him as he sat in the little cottage his grandfather had built and contemplated blowing his brain matter all over the wallpaper his grandmother had hung.

Only one person had ever found LT in Jerome. Two years ago, a caravan of big SUVs had rolled up in the red dust. Out popped Walsh Howard, maybe the worst goddamn soldier Tyrol had ever had under his command. He used to imagine how rich he would be if he had a hundred bucks for each of the times he had wondered how much easier life would be if he just 'accidentally' shot Howard.

How about a million bucks for each of those times?

Howard was there to ask him to run military operations for his new company in return for not only a nice salary, but a five percent ownership stake. Didn't seem like much at that time, but it was sure as hell better than soldiering. And as the company grew and grew, as they built a compound and took over Detroit and started having meetings in the fucking White House, LT was becoming a very rich man.

So why would he ever go back to Jerome? Too many dark fucking moments in that cabin; too many drug-hungry trips in that ghost town. And as he was coming out of his haze, so was Jerome coming out of its own haze, with coffee shops sprouting up and art galleries and its own winery, a fucking winery. The world, not that little shit stain of a town, was now LT's oyster. Why would he ever want to go back to a rat-infested three room cabin with plumbing that barely worked and well water that smelled like rotten eggs and tasted like cancer? When he cashed out of Allied Armament, he would build a vulgar fucking McMansion right on the canals of Venice, he wouldn't go back to *Jerome*.

And just like that, it was over. Just like that, he was back in Jerome. He wasn't complaining; if not for a buddy in the Bureau giving him the heads up, he would be in chains right now, bound for Guantanamo or ADX Supermax.

They would be coming here soon enough. They would connect the dots and realize he owned a piece of land just ninety minutes north of Phoenix, where an Allied Armament Gulfstream had dropped him just 24 hours ago. They might already be here – that's why LT was keeping his distance, camped out about twelve hundred meters away from the cabin. That's why he had a high-powered night-vision scope pointed in that direction, to determine if his property was infested with G-Men or just geckos. He was giving it at least six hours to make sure it was clear, then he would return to the cabin, retrieve the things he couldn't live without: his mother's engagement ring, his birth certificate and other personal files, a few framed photos – and most importantly, the fake passport, bundles of cash and other accoutrements of the false identity he had created a few years ago when it appeared his sexual appetites might catch up with him. He would need these to get across the border in Naco, to escape down to Central or South America or wherever he decided to go, as long as he never decided to come back here.

Tyrol's sleeping bag wrapped tighter as he tried to wrestle himself up. The sound of an engine was floating off the horizon. Between these mountains, you didn't hear that unless they were coming for his cabin, coming for *him.* He had fallen asleep. He wasn't supposed to fall asleep. Sparks of headlights out in the distance, beams slicing through the dust plumes kicked up by wheels – there was a car on his property, approaching the cottage. He shoved his eyes into the scope.

Someone had parked about a hundred yards from the front porch, hiding behind his driver's side door, trying to see in with his own binoculars. As he lowered them, LT zoomed in – and smiled.

"Well, I'll be goddamned. Lancaster, you stupid son of a bitch, finally figured out it was me all along."

Tyrol's finger found the trigger of the Accuracy International AX338 rifle beneath his scope. He'd gotten enough amusement out of Jason Lancaster over the past few months; fun time was over now. LT centered his crosshairs on Jason's back. It was an imprecise science, especially as he was no expert marksman. Then there was the epileptic shake of the scope's image, at almost the rifle's max range from its target. But when you're firing .338 Lapua horse pills, you don't have to be that accurate. Hit Lancaster anywhere and he would be fucked up damn good.

LT applied just a tiny bit of pressure. The rifle quaked under his shoulder. Blood fissured off Jason, and he went down hard, face planting, eating red dirt.

Tyrol rose from the gun with a smile, then started breaking everything down. Now was as good a time as any to return home. He hadn't given it the full six hours, but Lancaster might be just the prelude to a larger invasion, and this might be the last opening he would get.

And there was nothing LT wanted more than to roll Jason Lancaster over with his boot and let a spit loogie descend down onto his dead face. It would be his last moment of pure pleasure in Jerome, and on American soil.

With its replica wooden lockers shoved into its ill-fitting corners, its library-stacks must, its paucity of light, the makeshift Supreme Court Robing Room might be stifling to most. But for Chief Lapadula, entering the room on Friday morning to find his eight comrades was invigorating. Rolling his finger across that brass 'CHIEF JUSTICE' nameplate, slipping his arms down into the fabric of his gown, going down the line of thirty-six handshakes; for the first time since Miranda Whitney threatened him on that fateful night four months ago, it felt like all was right in the world. In moments, the Marshal would summon them to the Court. They would make their first official public appearance as a group since his return, and Warren Lapadula would be Chief Justice again.

But when he reached the end of the handshake line, he noticed a tenth person standing in the door, hands perched defiantly on her hips, here to throw a big rusty wrench into his perfect, beautiful day.

"Madam First Lady," Lapadula smiled as gently as he could manage, "you know you're not supposed to be in here."

"Oh, she has a habit of forgetting that rule," Justice Egan sneered.

"You and I need to have a private little chat, Mr. Lapadula," Rosemarie Irving replied. Cecilia Koh gasped, noticing the First Lady's impertinent failure to refer to the Chief by title.

"Now is not the time and you know it."

"Oh, you'll make now the time. Or I can tell all of your Justices what I came here to tell just you – the story Miranda Whitney woke up and started telling from her cell at USP-Hazelton this morning."

Lapadula looked at her sideways, trying to gauge what she had planned, and how much it should concern him. Miranda Whitney didn't scare him – that's why he had chosen her, because she couldn't scare him, because she would never have the power or legitimacy to scare him. That's why he had chosen Rosemarie so many years ago, that's how he had chosen all his girls.

Still, even the vilest of lies could undermine the greatest of leaders. Even if he refuted the Whitney woman's story, just hearing it might drive several of his Justices away from him. He had probably already lost the newer ones, who of course would believe their patron Mrs. Irving.

"Why don't you all excuse us for just a moment?" he hummed. "Justice Egan, please tell Mr. Meyers I will be out momentarily."

The other Justices shuffled out, Claudine Egan going last so she could bore into Rosemarie with her most penetrating stare. But soon enough, FLOTUS heard the door shut behind her.

Lapadula took control before she could utter a word: "I don't know what the hell you think you're doing. Are you so bitter you didn't get my seat, so jealous that you would come in here and--"

"No, you've got this all wrong," Rosemarie put on her most saccharine smarm. "I come bearing *good* news, Warren. So far, she's only told her tale to me, and me alone. You still have time to keep her quiet, to save yourself."

Lapadula laughed out loud at the very notion of being at the mercy of these pathetic women. "I don't know what you think she told you, but you know as well as I do, no one's going to believe her. No Supreme Court Justice has been more well-known or well-liked since Earl Warren or Thurgood Marshall. No one's going to believe the most famous terrorist in America when she cries rape."

"Oh, we're not going to cry rape. We're going to cry true love."

"I beg your pardon?"

Rosemarie was already pulling a sheet of paper out of the leather binder she carried at her side; Lapadula could see it was some type of medical form or chart. "This is a DNA test proving you're the father of Ms. Whitney's four-year-old son Gordon."

"Son? I, I have no idea what you're talking about. She never told me she had a son, she doesn't have a son--"

"Actually, Your Honor, this proves she does. And so do you. Congratulations."

"Fine, you want to smear my name with this, both of you, go right ahead. I'm protected by a much more powerful piece of paper. It's called the Constitution."

"Ms. Whitney has asked her public defender to visit her today. She's finally ready to make a deal. She's going to explain that the two of you were in love, and that you helped her plan and carry out the bombings."

"*What?*" Spittle buckshot from Lapadula's lips. "Who the hell do you think is going to believe that?"

"When you combine her son's DNA with the fact you're the only two Court employees who had arrived at work that morning and then were able to escape? Mmm, I think quite a few people.

"No, maybe this isn't nearly enough to convict you in a court of law, but one thing I've learned since my clerkship here is that the court of public opinion is actually a helluva lot more powerful than your Court. And if there's one thing the American public loves more than their hero Chief Justice, it's their salacious conspiracy theories."

"I know what you're trying to do here. But it doesn't matter. My appointment is for a lifetime. You can't pull me from my chair without killing me. She failed to do that four months ago and you're both going to fail now."

"You're going to resign, or your legacy will be forever tainted, your Court will become a national joke and eventually, Congress will find a way to remove you." Rosemarie took a step closer. "*Or,* you can walk into that Courtroom right now and announce your retirement. Miranda has promised to cancel her meeting with her lawyer and keep her mouth shut, but only if you retire today. Retire today, on top, and your image will be frozen. You'll be as well-known and well-liked as Earl Warren and Thurgood Marshall *forever*.

"Or," Rosemarie threw up her hands with a taunting grin, "you can throw this moment away and shit all over the Court you hold so dear."

Lapadula stared at the warped hardwood of the floor. His back rose and fell, his lungs hyperventilating as he considered her extortive choice.

"Well," the First Lady smiled, turning for the door, "I'll be in the Courtroom waiting for your decision."

She laid her hand on the doorknob--

And suddenly he was upon her. He still had that breakneck speed that had brought him up and under many a quarterback's chin. He slammed her up against the wall, hand on her neck, thumb pushing into her throat, hard, hot, panting breath in her ear. "When I had you, that night you said you didn't want it, you actually loved it and you know it." Rosemarie could feel his crotch pressed into her leg, hardening at the putrid memory of that night. Her eyes wanted to close, her face wanted to grimace, but she wouldn't give him that satisfaction. His lips came closer, almost colliding with her ear as he spoke. "You know you did. Getting rough turned you on. When I raped you, you were wet."

"Not as wet as I am right now watching you squirm."

Her knee jerked up, slamming his balls back into his pelvis. She left him on the floor of the Robing Room, a groaning heap.

LT could feel the back of his neck burning to a crisp as he crept his way closer and closer to the fallen Jason Lancaster, but he didn't care. This was the moment he had been dreaming about for two years now, since he woke up in that CASH tent too percoceted up to feel his leg or his face throbbing from Jason's beating.

He knew he had tagged Jason good, but still couldn't be sure *how* good, and stopped every few paces to crouch and bring the scope he had removed from his rifle to his eye. Each time, he confirmed the mass of clothes and blood splatter just within his property line, as if he had turned Jason into the Wicked Witch and melted her with water. After each confirmation, he would return his scope to his rifle bag, raise his Sig Sauer P226 pistol with his right hand again, and keep moving cautiously toward his prey, his gun never dropping to his waist. He would never make the mistake of taking Jason Lancaster for granted again.

He hoped Jason wasn't dead yet, hoped he had lived to see who had taken him down. And after LT dive-bombed a spit wad right between his eyes, he would plant a .357 SIG slug there too.

Now just twenty yards away, Tyrol crouched once more and verified the same thing he had seen the other four times he had stopped: Jason wasn't moving at all. *Praise Jesus. I finally got the little shit.* He pushed back up to his feet, and this time left his heavy bag behind so he could secure his gun with two hands as he approached. He could feel a big, wide smile growing on his face as he came around the final large succulent between them …

Oh fuck. Tyrol stood over a pile of clothes, given form and shape by a line of rocks. It was a fucking rock scarecrow. But that meant Jason could be anywhere.

Tyrol shot back up, spinning his gun around in a full 360. *Where is he where is he where--*

It was already too late. When he heard the crunch of rocks under boot just behind him, it was already too late.

He turned right into the blurry Jason, now dressed only in a red-soaked wife beater, coming at him full speed. Jason's left palm went up into Tyrol's chin. He tried to raise his gun, but Jason's same left hand was chopping down on his arm, knocking it off-course as he depressed the trigger. Jason smashed LT's wrist between his hand and knee, disarming him, then spun, bringing the full force of the ball of his hard right foot into Tyrol's chest.

LT went down, wind knocked out of him. He tried to rise again, and Jason backhanded him with that left fist, knocking some teeth loose, filling his nose with warmth, flattening him out on his back.

Everything's with his left hand. He's only using his left hand. LT took a beat to breathe again, and see why: he had tagged Jason's right arm. His right arm was now locked immobile against his side with gauze and medical tape, too flat red rocks holding his humerus in place.

"Got your other shoulder this time," Tyrol laughed through his gums drunk with blood. "Made you symmetrical."

LT planted his hands to push up one last time-- but before he rose, Jason whipped his own pistol from the back of his belt, shoving its barrel right between Tyrol's eyes, right where he himself had been dreaming of shooting Jason.

"You were my shooter in Bethesda?"

"Just trying to do you a solid, put you out of your misery," Tyrol smiled through bloody teeth. "I couldn't believe my luck when I realized blowing up the Court could take you with it. But that cunt had to save you. So I tried to fix her mistake, that first week after the bombing. You were too good. You just had to run. You just had to keep running. You just had to come after us." By now, LT was full on laughing. "I didn't mind. It gave me the chance to fuck with you more. Send you up to Michigan and back. Get this whole fucking mess blamed on you. I beat off every night of the last four months thinking of how much anguish you must have been going through."

Jason pressed the gun harder into LT's brow, so hard it was leaving a cookie cutter impression. "Shauna Diamond gave me this gun. She wore this on her hip everyday with LAPD SWAT."

"Sorry, pal, never heard of the bitch."

"She was the private you were raping when I crippled you. I came here to kill you with her gun."

"*Do it.* Fucking kill me, Lancaster. You know you want to. I ruined your military career. Then I ruined your whole civilian life. Just do it, soldier. Do what you were trained to do."

But still Jason didn't move, his trigger finger didn't move.

"You think you're so much better than me 'cause I got a little rough with a few drunk sluts? You think that gave you the right to fuck up my face? To make me a cripple? Hey, hey, your girlfriend know how many people you've killed? You were good at it, too. 'Combat Engineer,'" he spit out the words. "That's what you called yourself so you felt better about killing as many sand niggers as the rest of us."

"You're wrong. I'm not a soldier anymore." Jason stuffed his gun back in his belt, then reached down to his cargo pants, to the pocket next to his left knee. "I'm a cop." He came around behind Tyrol, planting his foot smack in the center of his back and pushing his chest down into the dirt.

Tyrol grunted as he sucked in the devil dust kicked up by the impact of his chest. "You're not a cop!" LT screamed as Jason wrenched one of his arms behind his back, trapping it under his knee, then did the same with the other. "The cops still want to kill you!" Jason then slipped a pair of flex cuffs down around LT's floundering wrists. "You're nothing! I made you nothing! I destroyed you and everything about you! You can't even get on a plane anymore without getting arrested!"

"Actually, I can be whatever I want." Jason smiled as he zipped the cuffs tight, as tight as they would go, almost tight enough to draw blood. He yanked LT back into a painful cobra contortion, bringing his lips close to his former CO's ear. "I work for the Chief Justice of the United States now." He pulled Tyrol to his feet, and dragged him to his rented SUV.

MARCH

As Jason flipped mindlessly through *Highlights* magazine, he realized his skin was quivering with something very unfamiliar. He never felt this, not in Afghanistan, not stalking the Michigan Minutemen in the depths of the Huron, not even before his first interview for the open Threat Assessment position on the Supreme Court Police.

He was nervous.

He chuckled it aside. He shouldn't be nervous, he should be ecstatic. A week ago, he wouldn't have been able to sit in the lobby of a government agency – or any lobby – without the cops being summoned. But after the four Supreme Court bombers in custody all testified that he hadn't been involved in the attack at all (in fact, three of the four had never even met Jason), and after three Hollywood visual effects experts had been deposed pointing out how the video of Jason in the Supreme Court on the night of October 6th was most likely faked, the Attorney General dropped all charges against him.

Still, feeling the eyes of the room on him, hearing the Child Protective Services employees whispering his name while trying to avoid looking his direction, made him realize that he may be free, but his life had forever changed. The last four months had made him famous – *in*famous, more like – and who knew how long that would last.

The door across the antiseptic CPS lobby opened and the counselor who had given him the rundown earlier – Gordon's likes and dislikes, his habits, the medications he was taking – led the boy out by the hand. Jason stood for the introduction. "Gordon, this is Jason. He's the friend of your Mom's I was telling you about."

Once the bombers had confirmed that Miranda had only let them in the building, that she didn't assist in the planning or the planting, a judge had granted her the right to choose who would take custody of her son while she was incarcerated. After four months at Allied Armament and three weeks in foster homes, the boy's mother was finally in control of where he was going. Jason had zero experience with children. He never had enough of a relationship with his sister's kids to start learning the basics with them. But he didn't want to let Rand down. This would have to be his trial by fire.

He sparked it up by kneeling to the kid's level, trying to give him his warmest smile. "Nice to meet you, Gordon." The boy was as adorable as a stuffed animal; he could see Miranda in his nose, in his mouth, in his eyes as he stared back into Jason's, trying to read if he could trust this man. He saw other features he recognized in that face too, but had promised himself to keep those thoughts out of his mind.

Jason stood back up, opening his hand and offering it to the boy. "Should we get out of here and go see your Mom?"

Gordon didn't take his hand, still staring up, hard into Jason's eyes, like if he just squinted hard enough, he might be able to read his soul. "You *the* Jason?"

"I'm sorry?"

"My Mom always said I would meet Jason someday."

"Aw," the CPS lady cooed.

"'Soon, soon,' she'd been saying, 'you're gonna meet Jason soon.' But then I went on my trip." Gordon rotated his head sideways at Jason as he said this, his eyes warning, *I'll know if you're a liar, Bucko.* "You're him, right?"

Jason coughed a little, fighting to make sure he didn't let any moisture out of his eyes. "I guess I am."

Gordon reached up and took Jason's hand. And Jason led him to the elevator.

"Oyez, oyez, oyez!" Gregor Meyers stood just behind the banister under the east arcade of the Old Courtroom, a silhouette before the windows bright with artificial light. (An expansion of the Capitol in the mid-20th century had blocked out any natural lighting.) The Marshal (or in this case, Acting Marshal) began every session of the highest court in the land with these words, Anglo-Norman for 'Hear ye,' a nod to the English court traditions of centuries past. "All persons having business before the Honorable, the Supreme Court of the United States," he continued, "are admonished to draw near and give their attention, for the Court is now sitting."

From the doorway to Gregor's left, Rosemarie held her politically perfect smile. Meyers was a nice enough Marshal for now, but she looked forward to the day in the coming months when her own pick for Marshal would take over, someone with a voice that would truly command the room, be it this Courtroom or their proper home back at One First Street.

The perfect Marshal, the Marshal she had in mind, he would be someone who owed her. Someone whom she would *control*.

"God save the United States and this honorable Court!" Gregor completed his introduction, and everyone rose from their seats; the Courtroom was packed with press and visitors on this day, not because of any particular case they would hear, but in recognition of the great historic significance of this particular group of nine gathering for the first time.

The Justices processed in along the banister, taking their thrones, Rosemarie fifth in line, lowering into the center chair. The Chief Justice found herself wishing they were in their proper building, entering from behind their red velvet drapes, appearing in place behind each of their chairs. Alas, that ceremony would have to wait a few more weeks.

"Thank you, Mr. Meyers," Rosemarie said as she sat. She didn't look down, jumping into the most important business of the day, of the year, without even having to refer to her notes for a docket number. "We will hear argument first this morning in Case number 18-012, *Ryan Agguire, et. al. v. The City of Detroit, Michigan*."

Just hearing the title flow off her lips eased some of the tension in her shoulders. Finally, after all these months, *Agguire* would be heard in the proper forum, in front of a Court she had constructed. Finally, it would meet its proper fate. And though Allied Armament was in shambles, this was more important than ever: the Emergency Manager of Detroit had already hired New World to send in 5000 emergency mercenaries to take AASC's place, and several other contractors had made big, publicized hiring pushes in an effort to put themselves in position to sweep up whatever business Walsh Howard might have sacrificed. Rosemarie and Jason may have driven a stake through Allied Armament, but the hired gun business wasn't going anywhere unless her Court took decisive action.

The Chief took a deep breath, panning her gaze to the green-topped counsel table to her immediate left. "Mr. Pastor?"

"Thank you, Madam Chief Justice," the petitioner's lawyer nodded as he stood, an acknowledgement of welcome and congratulations to the Chief that he wouldn't waste any of his allotted thirty minutes expressing verbally. "And may it please the Court: one of the tenants of American freedom, going back to the

Posse Comitatus Act of 1878, is the right to streets policed by, and laws enforced by, local entities …"

"Uh, Mommy?"

Jason smiled. Miranda had been holding the hug for what felt like three or four minutes, before finally releasing her hold on little Gordon. "You're gonna stay with Jason for a while, okay?" The boy was wary, but nodded.

"As long as he needs," Jason smiled back, then put a hand on Gordon's shoulder. He wasn't sure he was comfortable doing this just yet, but wanted to put on a good show for Rand so she could rest easy knowing he was up to the job. "But it's only two hours to visit Mommy, so we're gonna drive up here a couple times a week, okay?" The same judge that allowed Miranda to name Jason as Gordon's guardian had also moved her to the far-less-intense federal detention center in Philly, where she would be housed with other female inmates until at least her trial and sentencing. And Jason had pulled some strings to ensure they could use a private visitation room whenever he and Gordon came by. It was the size of a closet, but it was all Miranda needed, as long as her two favorite guys in the world were in here with her.

"Okay," Miranda ran her fingers through her pride and joy's hair, "Mommy's gotta go back to her room now." Gordon understood, and moved to the other end of the table as she mouthed, 'Thank you,' to Jason.

"Oh, there's one other person here to see you," Jason added as he rose.

"What?"

"Yeah, he didn't want to intrude on our time so he waited outside." He opened the door and ushered in Miranda's only sibling, clean shaven, in laundered clothes, as good as new.

"Ollie!"

"Hey sis." He bent down to hug her, and she held him almost as long as she had Gordon. Then she pulled back, keeping her hands on the back of his neck as she looked him over.

"You keeping your nose clean?"

"Heh," Ollie hesitated.

"He's doing great," Jason assisted. "He's been a big part of making sure this all worked out."

"Good," Miranda beamed.

"No," Ollie ground everything to a halt. "It hasn't been good. I haven't been good. I thought I'd be lost without you."

"Oh, Ollie."

He grabbed her head in his hands, making sure her eyes stayed locked on his. "I'm gonna do better. For you, Randi. I want you to know that. I'm gonna do my best to get clean for you."

"Do better than your best."

"I don't know if I can," he broke. "But I'm gonna try. I promise."

She pulled him in to kiss his cheek. He wiped them dry of tears as he stood back up to his full height.

"Okay," Jason put his hand on Gordon's back. "I think we better let your Mom get back to her day."

As Ollie opened the door, he turned to the boy, screaming, "FIRST ONE DOWN THE HALL!" Gordon squealed with delight as he chased his uncle out.

"Hey," Miranda said as Jason turned to exit himself, "thank you."

"Of course. It's great to see you, no matter where we are."

"No, I mean-- I know what rages in that head, remember?"

And suddenly Jason did remember-- more of that night, of his rufied haze, of the night before the bombing.

"No no no," he's sitting on the bed, head in his hands, raving, "don't tell me this, I don't want to hear this." He's on his feet, pacing. "I don't know what I expected. Everything always turns to shit. That's my fate, that's what I deserve." Miranda's trying to get in front of him, hands on his shoulders, but he's too wasted. "Everything's <u>shit</u>. I don't know why I thought it was going to turn out any differently this time. As soon as I'm happy-- BOOM, it all turns to shit, like my life's always supposed to."

"You are a wonderful man, Jason Lancaster," she said in the present, in March. "I don't want to hear you ever thinking otherwise. And this time, everything's going to turn out exactly the way you want it to."

He smiled. "Not 'til you're out of here."

On the evening of her first day leading oral arguments, Rosemarie Irving was the last Justice to leave the Capitol, the last Justice to release her clerks for the night, the last Justice to fill her bag with reading and call for her car.

She was stuffing in one last green brief when a familiar voice hummed from the door of her chambers. “Madam Chief Justice.” She smiled. She thought she would be hearing from him much earlier.

“Mr. President,” she smiled as she turned to face him.

“I believe I owe you an apology. And some thanks. After declaring War, then taking it back, Congress’s approval rating plummeted into the single digits. And the presidential candidate who piled on Iran has fallen five points behind the incumbent who showed restraint.” Salas held up a single piece of paper. “And that’s the Fox poll. You should see how I’m doing in the NBC News one. All of this thanks to you.”

“You’ve done so much more for me, and you know it.”

“There’s only one problem.” Salas stepped further in, shutting her office door behind him. “I’m terrified of being reelected.”

“You shouldn’t be. You’ve been commendable, especially considering the circumstances dumped in your lap.”

He stalked closer to her. “If I win again, I don’t know how I’ll survive without you.” He was right on top of her now, his perfect smell filling her nostrils.

“Good thing you don’t have to,” she purred back.

He grabbed the back of her hair, pulling her lips into his. He drove her back against her desk, pushed her down to sitting on its surface.

She moaned in shock – his hand was up her skirt, wrapping around the crotch of her panties. He slammed a backhand down over her mouth, stifling her gasp as he tore the underwear off of her. “Shh,” he whispered into her ear. “One of your clerks is still out there.”

Rosemarie closed her eyes, gnawing on the inside of his sweaty palm. She grabbed that wrist with both hands, pulling it down off her mouth. “I need you,” she panted when he brought his ear to her mouth. “I need you inside me.”

“We’re saving that for next time,” POTUS smiled back. “I don’t think any President has ever done *this* to his Chief Justice.” He found a wooden gavel on the desk, a cheap, cheesy gift from Congressional leadership, and shoved it between her teeth – then disappeared between her legs, his head up and under her skirt, toying with her with the tip of his tongue.

Salas could hear her screams, her grinding on the gavel ramping up in intensity, and grabbed her backside with both hands. Her knees slammed down around his temples, holding him in place. Her insides tightened around his tongue as her guttural wail announced her climax.

Rosemarie was still shaking when MMA helped her out of the back of the Escalade, her legs still quaking as she walked to the elevator, then rode it up into the townhouse. Her mind swam with fantasies of exotic vacations with the President as she stripped down in her closet, then erotic trysts in various rooms of the White House as she rinsed herself off in the shower. As she dressed in her nightwear and crawled under the sheets of her bed, she even permitted herself to imagine moving into the Residence again. And why not? All her decorations still hung from its walls, her furniture still filled its halls.

Nah, she smiled to herself. *Been there, done that. This is home.*

"You've got to change that rule about no cameras in the Courtroom," Reginald Irving smiled as he lowered the day's *Wall Street Journal.* "Otherwise I might never get to see the Chief Justice in action." He leaned over to kiss his wife's cheek. "How was day one?"

"Perfect. I finally heard from the President, in fact."

"I knew he couldn't stay away forever. How'd that go?"

"Exactly the way we thought it would."

Reg leaned into her again, this time giving her a much more passionate lip kiss. "I need to remind you how it's really done?"

"Well. I do have a little left in me, now that you mention it."

Reg giggled with hunger, slinking down her body, taking the drawstring of her pajama bottoms in his teeth.

JULY

The Supreme Courtroom was packed for the final day of this most tumultuous term in its history. The crowd had started gathering the night before, many sleeping in tents at the bottom of the majestic stairs at One First Street, all hoping to secure one of the few seats in the Court gallery reserved for the general public. Expected announcements in gay and abortion rights cases had stoked this fervor; despite the case's importance in the lives of Rosemarie Irving and Jason Lancaster – and really, every Court appointee and employee – this session wasn't the term's most popular because of the decision that would be handed down in *Aguirre,* a case of interest only to legal scholars and SCOTUSBlog aficionados, especially with the company it would most effect now in shambles.

The reconstruction of the home of the highest court in the land was far from complete, but both its Chief Justice and the President felt it important that the Justices return to their Courtroom as soon as possible, ordering that room to be completed first. It had been two weeks since their first session back in the Courtroom, and though one or two of the most senior Justices groused about having to shuffle through an active construction zone between the car park and their chambers, Rosemarie shut them up with subtle reminders that they were lucky to be alive.

"Before we begin today," Chief Justice Rosemarie Irving smiled as she looked around the standing-room-only crowd gathered for the final day of her first term, "now that we have returned to our old home, I think it's important that we recognize an individual who just re-joined our Court last week. Until the true history of the last year is someday written, most Americans will never know the extent of the tireless and thankless work Jason Lancaster did over the last nine months to ensure that this Court lived on, that it returned here to First Street, and that the perpetrators of the violence against it were brought to justice. Mr. Lancaster put not only his freedom on the line, but his life. As you know if you noticed him calling out that ancient term that begins our every session moments ago, we are all lucky to have him as our new Marshal, the highest-ranking officer of our Supreme Court Police." The gallery broke into light applause, and Jason raised his hand from his box to the far right of the Justices with slight embarrassment.

Chief Irving raised her hands to indicate she wasn't finished. "Now what makes Jason a true hero is that he didn't do any of this for the attention or the spotlight, which he truly despises. He's already cursing me under his breath, I'm sure." She paused for the smattering of laughter. "But I'm afraid I'm going to have to call even more attention to him today by announcing that the American Bar Association, on my recommendation, has also chosen to award him with one of their highest honors, an award given to the person who has made the most positive impact on the American justice system. Jason Lancaster, please step forward and accept your medal as the winner of this year's John Marshall Award."

Jason didn't move at first, even as the entire room filled with applause. It took the Justices to come to their feet, then everyone else in the room, even the members of the press stuffing away their iPhones or notepads so they could bring their hands together, before he stepped out of his box, revealing the traditional full morning suit with tails. He came around in front of the Justices, between their perches and the counsel tables, stepping right in front of Rosemarie so she could lay a gold medal around his neck, adjusting the strap behind his white shirt collar, laying the gold shape in the center of his necktie. Jason turned back with a sheepish grin and a wave of thanks to the crowd, then returned to his box. As he sat, so too did the rest of the assembled guests.

"Now then," Rosemarie smiled as she returned to her own seat and removed the first opinion from her trademark leather binder, "we will draw this term to a close first with the opinion of the Court in case number 18-012, *Ryan Agguire, et. al. v. The City of Detroit, Michigan*. This case concerns the right of the Emergency Manager of the city of Detroit to contract all city police and fire services out to a company by the name of Allied Armament Security Consultants ..."

Miranda had always told Jason that she tuned out when the real work of the Court began, during oral arguments or the reading of opinions. The job of the Marshal was not to understand the legal ramifications of the cases the Court may be hearing, just to protect the Justices so the hearing and deciding of those cases was never deterred. And in these last two weeks of opinion readings (he had started officially about six weeks ago, handling all security preparations of the building before the Justices moved back in), he had done just that, keeping all his senses acute to the Courtroom around him, his eyes always moving, while letting the voice of whatever lawyer or Justice may be speaking to fade into the background.

That's what allowed him to see the girl first.

There were several Supreme Court Policemen stationed around the Courtroom – their number almost doubled from what it used to be – and yet, Jason was the first to react as she stood from the gallery. It may have been because no one else recognized the strange shape in her right hand, rising from her waist to the level of Rosemarie Irving above her as she yelled out, "MADAM CHIEF JUSTICE!"

Jason didn't recognize the shape itself either, he just recognized the distinctive cloudy white plastic of something made on a 3D printer, the same type of plastic as the gun he himself had almost used on Rosemarie Irving five months before.

For Jason, the room seemed to snap into slow motion: everyone screaming, heads ducking, his guys reaching for their side arms – but Rosemarie Irving didn't move, just stared defiantly back at the girl, as her trigger finger started to depress--

Jason was in her chest, shoulder digging hard into her solar plexus, like he was making his first open field tackle in two decades. The girl's head whiplashed sideways, her makeshift gun firing, its projectile going way high, embedding into the month-old ceiling. Jason and the girl crashed into the chair behind her, snapping it in three pieces as they collapsed into the carpet, her skull bouncing on the hard marble underneath.

"Let go of the gun," Jason screamed in her ear, his hand gripping her right wrist as tight as he could, holding her aim at a wall where it could do no damage. "Let go of the gun or I will break your wrist."

She hesitated for just a moment, tears streaming down her cheeks, hyperventilation pumping from her chest.

Finally she opened her fingers, and the gun slid out of her sweaty palm and down onto the floor.

Two other Court cops were upon her, rolling her over, cuffing her, while the others were securing the room, shutting the doors so no other attackers could get in, waving their pistols this way and that, ready to react on a hair trigger if someone else pulled a surprise from their sleeve.

No one noticed the Justice on the far right of their traditional semi-oval standing from his chair, a hand over his open mouth. "Janaki?" Justice Goldman whispered, much too quiet for the girl to hear as she was hauled away.

Tucked next to the Permanent Records Vault on the second underground level of the Court were two secret detention cells where the Supreme Court Police could store any disruptors of Court business or any protestors who got a little too energetic. It was in one of these cells that Janaki Singh was locked while the Court proceedings continued – Rosemarie wasn't going to let a twentysomething with a plastic gun keep the Court from finishing this most important of terms. Justice Koh struck down a Nebraska law forcing the closure of dozens of abortion clinics, Justice MacTavish read the Court's opinion granting full spousal rights to any gay couples covered under the Salas health plan, and the Chief Justice herself announced that *Agguire v. Detroit* had met its end in a surprisingly convincing 7-2 decision.

Janaki's cell had no windows or bars, so all Jason could see of the former clerk was the high angle, black-and-white view displayed on the laptop on the guard's desk just next to the sealed steel door.

"Did you know she was a clerk, Sir?" Jason's deputy Gregor Meyers asked. "From what I understood, a damn good one too."

"Yeah, I just came from Justice Goldman's chambers. He said she never recovered from the death of her boyfriend. Took a leave of absence and never returned. Until today. Hey," Jason raised a finger at the monitor, on which Janaki paced back and forth, ranting and raving through the Dell's tinny speakers, "she been like this since we put her in there?"

"Flash drive, flash drive," she seemed to chant, *"all on the flash drive ..."*

"Yes, sir. She seems to be obsessed with a flash drive. And she did have one in her pocket." He held out the plastic tray of personal effects – a smattering of change, a pack of gum, and a set of keys, which included a small USB flash drive dangling from one of its rings. "You want me to pop it in?"

"No, we don't want whatever virus or worm might be on that thing getting loose in our network. George Aug from DHS should be here to pick her up in the next hour," Jason reported of his friend who had just been named Under Secretary of Intelligence & Analysis. "He'll have someone who can tear that open safely."

"Of course, Sir."

"Make sure you call me when he's here." Jason turned for the door out to the elevator, his ears picking up just a few more of her words as he pulled it open:

"Agguire, *she killed him because of* Agguire, *this whole thing was all about* Agguire ... "

Jason stopped, letting the door shut as he continued to listen to her bloviations. Then, finally, he reached for that tray.

Rosemarie did find it odd for the briefest of moments when her secretary told her that her Marshal had asked to see her in the Justices' conference room. But reminding herself that most of the more mundane and non-essential offices and conference rooms in the building had been saved for the last of the rebuilding and refurbishing, didn't give it much more than that passing thought.

"I was going to apologize for embarrassing you," she chuckled as she entered, finding Jason already standing on the far end of the conference table. "But I'm glad to see you're so proud of that thing."

Jason's hand went to the medal around his neck – in all the craziness of this day, he had forgotten he had it on.

"You look exhausted, Jason," Rosemarie continued as she strolled around the room, taking in its beauty, its smell, for really the first time since they'd moved home; her every other visit to this room so far had been filled with piles of Court business and politics. "I hope you're going somewhere sunny and relaxing."

"Justice Winks was writing to Affirm."

"I'm sorry?" She turned back to him, realizing he had a stapled document rolled up in his hands.

"*Agguire,*" he continued. "He was writing the majority opinion. To Affirm." He unfurled the paper, set it down on the table, then slid it halfway across to her. "You can read his rough draft if you want. Original's down in the Vault."

"Why would I need to?" she smiled back. "My opinion's already written. As you know."

"Madam Chief Justice." Jason shook with nerves, with bubbling rage. "The Lapadula Court was going to affirm *Agguire v. Detroit.*"

Rosemarie spun on a heel, trying to get out of that room before things went too far. "Thank God things turned out the way they did, then."

Jason took a step around the table, veins popping out of his temples. "Allied Armament was going to win. They had no reason to bomb the Court, or kill any Justices. They were going to win their case 5-4."

"Thank God they're morons."

"*You* convinced them to do it. You convinced them they were going to lose and had to force a major restructuring of the Court."

"And what exactly gave you that insane idea?"

"William Quint convinced Justice Winks to delay the case by holding out on his opinion until it was too late in the term. He met Winks for lunch three times last term, including three hours before he sent around a memo saying he couldn't finish the draft."

Rosemarie shook her head and chuckled. "Jason--"

"You had something on him. You blackmailed him somehow to delay it."

"Jason, I know you've only been in law enforcement for a couple of years, but even you should know this is as circumstantial as it gets."

"You and Quint were both on the Allied Armament board. You knew the prospects they had to take over our military. You didn't go to them after the bombing. You went to them before."

Rosemarie crossed her arms and stared him down, a guttural little chuckle emanating from the pit of her breast. Did she really need to keep up this charade? He had nothing on her. Did she really need to waste the energy and brain power lying to this peon, this subordinate?

But there *was* one worry on her mind. "The last time we had a conversation like this, you came armed with a handy little recorder, didn't you?"

Jason reached into his pockets and pulled them inside out, revealing they were empty.

"Then I want you to listen to me very carefully, Jason, because this is the only time we will speak of this. I. Saved. America. Chief Quint and I knew how *Agguire* would be decided. We know this Court better than anyone; we know how every case will be decided before it is. And we knew what Walsh Howard and Lance Tyrol had planned had they won."

"So you killed 124 people--"

"Those people are martyrs. Everyone who died that day is a patriot, an American hero, and I will never let anyone forget them. They saved this country, more than even you or I."

"There's a hole in your ship somewhere and I promise you I'll find it. The masked man, the bomber we never found – he was yours, wasn't he?"

"Has Mitch Aldridge never told you about his wife Loretta? Stage four brain tumor. Luckily, by the grace of God, we were able to help her get accepted for an experimental cancer treatment at the Mayo Clinic, and it's the only thing that's kept her alive. So no, I don't think he'll be your whistleblower. Unfortunately for you, the only other two people I ever discussed this with are dead. Oh yes, and I'm fucking the President.

"So I'm afraid all you've got is a conspiracy theory that would light up the internet. And there's already a dozen different ones about what a psychotic bitch I am. I'm not sure this one even has the juice to go viral."

Jason turned his gaze to the ground, his fists squeezing so hard with rage he thought his fingernails might puncture his skin and draw blood.

Rosemarie just smiled, hands moving to her hips. "I know you feel powerless right now. That's just the nature of this Court, Jason. This Court is beyond the average American's ability to understand. We are the intellectual Gods of this nation, and you, right now, are just visiting my Mount Olympus. We determine the fate of this country because the citizenry is too stupid, and the people they elect much, *much* too stupid to do it.

"So yes, when you think back on what you discovered here today, you'll often feel angry and powerless. *That's how you're supposed to feel.* That's how every average American who's cared to take the time to even think about this Court has felt since it decreed its first decisions. No, it's not fair. As every parent tells his little child, 'Life isn't fair.' You're the little child, and we're your loving parents. Everything we do, *everything I have ever done*, is because of how much I love my children. And you will never understand that, because you will never be a parent, you will never be a God, you will never be me."

A long silence passed between them. Jason's mind swam with visions of his fingers digging into her jugular, but he never moved.

"Now then," she finally continued, "I would understand if this little discussion has made it-- *awkward* for you to continue to serve here. I will leave that decision up to you. I still consider you one of the finest, most impressive men I have ever known. Perhaps more so now than ever. I hope to see you in September."

Jason yanked the zip drive out of the hard disc tower and placed it in his pocket. He hadn't yet decided with whom he would share the contents of Janaki's drive, especially with one brand new audio file added to its wares. He had played it back once to confirm it worked, impressed with the sound quality of the conference room's hidden directional microphones. As he stepped out of the hidden antechamber that looked like no more than a closet door just adjacent to the Robing Room, he crossed one item off his mental to-do list; he would never debrief the new Chief Justice about the recording of every conference of the past 73 terms, at least not unless he was using the room's latest recording to put her in chains.

And he wasn't sure that's what he wanted to do just yet. Check that; he wanted to do it, he just wasn't convinced the time was right yet. The country was not ready for more tumult emanating from the Supreme Court, from *his* Supreme Court, not ready for the political fallout of yet another vacancy, sure to spark an even fiercer battle with the results of a looming election still very much in doubt.

And the truth about Rosemarie wouldn't change Miranda's fate, wouldn't lessen the number of years she had ahead of her in jail. What else did he really care about?

If there was one thing Jason had learned from Rosemarie Irving, it was that every bit of information was a weapon that was to be stored and protected and cultivated until the perfect moment to use it finally arrived. He knew that moment would come for this new recording of his Chief Justice, he just didn't think that moment was now.

Now was vacation. Jason didn't want to spend the next month in interrogation rooms and hearing chambers anymore than Rosemarie Irving did. He wound his way down one of the spiral staircases, past the statue once again sporting the head of John Marshall, out of the building, and down the marble steps to First Street NE.

"Hey, man, save the children."

As Jason headed towards Massachusetts Ave, he stopped before Rusty, the pro-life hobo that had camped out in this same spot in front of the Methodist Building every day of the last who-knows-how-many years, even when the Court had relocated to the Capitol. Rusty shook his cup at Jason, its singular coin bouncing around inside, smiling at him through toothless gums. Jason removed the John Marshall medal from around his neck and dropped it with a clang into Rusty's cup.

Jason continued his walk to Union Station, and rode home in silence to his brownstone in Maryland.

ACKNOWLEDGEMENTS

Just like my last book, this novel was sparked by a gift from my wife, in this case a 2013 birthday present of a book on Supreme Court history that stoked a fascination with the Highest Court in the Land that I didn't even realize I harbored. Twenty months later, I finished the first draft of this novel. Stephen King says you really only write for one person, your first reader, and for me that's Whitney; thank you for not letting me give this up until it was finished.

My manager Brad Kaplan and agents Roy Ashton, Jeff Greenberg and Noah Jones gave invaluable feedback on the earliest germs of this idea, but perhaps no one was more helpful than Rachel Israel and Meghan Mathes when they were still in the Evolution fold. Thanks also to my boss Joel for his initial encouragement when I pitched the concept to him, and for constantly inspiring me with his unwavering hunger to work.

Every early reader of this book contributed something, especially in their areas of experience and expertise, and they each deserve massive thanks: Greg Meyer and John Easton (the workings of government), Danny Haas (military, law enforcement and firearms), Patrick Jacobi (pretty much every geographical and gastronomical DC reference) and Patrick Egan (the legal stuff). If something has been botched in one of these realms, it's not because these guys didn't catch it, but because I was stupid enough to ignore some of their notes in the name of storytelling.

Speaking of Egan, I've realized that *way* too many characters in this book are named after friends or family. I've got family at Homeland Security, friends running Allied Armament in Detroit or working for the CIA in Afghanistan, friends getting abortions, and other friends extorting their mothers. I apologize to anyone who's lent their name to a villain; I promise it is no commentary on what I think of you, just that I love your name!

Although the writing of this book is my proudest creative achievement, the planning of its marketing and release has been even more fun. Thanks to Mike

Reichman for nine judges' robes (or perhaps six judges' robes and three graduation gowns that looked close enough) in which to clad my Justices, Richard Aug, Joanne Austin, James Baskin, Rob Ferriman, Jesse Ivarra, Paula Mittner, Dan Neri, Helene Robinson, and my 96-year-old grandmother Sally Baskin. Thanks to Patrick Wilson-- heck, the entire Wilson family for their contributions to my trailer, as well as Robert Schajer, Patrice Cormier and the team at BUF, Kathleen Chee, and especially Andrew Johnson for music that was perfect in one pass. The biggest thanks of course goes to Joe Otting, a true genius who has now made two little iPhone productions of mine into full-blown cinematic affairs. And John Easton and Brendan Kownacki for working their butts off to lend this book that DC legitimacy (and enabling me to play star struck one evening).

But the most fun I've had on *Four Seats* has been the time spent with my mother June Cooley, designer of the covers for all six installments of the serial e-book release. I miss talking to you everyday, Mom; we must do this again soon.

If I could dork out for a moment, the most exciting part of the writing of *Four Seats* was learning about the branch of our government that a much greater part of our population should be reading up on! The Court's history is not only as salacious as it is fascinating, but in this age of gridlock and partisanship, they're kind of running things. If this book has made you thirst for the real thing, I can recommend several books, but most especially *The Nine* and *The Oath* by Jeffrey Toobin, *The Brethren* by Bob Woodward & Scott Armstrong, *Gunfight* by Adam Winkler, *Five Chiefs* by John Paul Stevens, and *The Rehnquist Choice* by John W. Dean.

See you on the next one.

ALSO AVAILABLE ON AMAZON.COM
BY AARON COOLEY

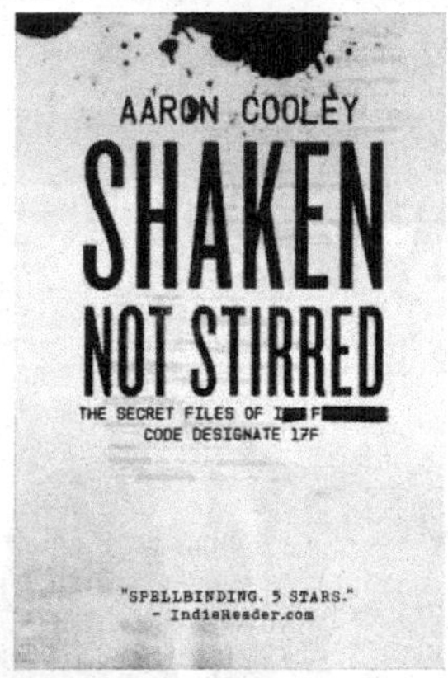

"ONE OF THE BEST BOOKS OF 2013. Spellbinding ... highly entertaining ... 5 stars. "

- IndieReader.com

"Aaron Cooley writes with such galloping deftness and verve that you'll find yourself swearing you were present at the creation of James Bond. "

- James Kaplan, Author of *Frank: The Voice*

"Great details and storytelling."

- Duane Byrge, *The Hollywood Reporter*

"A frenetic thriller ... keeps the story moving without ever losing its sense of fun."

- Kirkus Reviews

"Combines the best ingredients of an edge-of-your-seat action movie and a page-turning thriller into one riveting punch. I wish I could nominate it for an Oscar! "

- **Joel Schumacher, Director of *The Lost Boys, A Time to Kill* and *The Phantom of the Opera***

"CHECK THIS OUT!!! Page turner like a mutha$&@!!!! Congrats to Aaron Cooley."

- Tory Kittles, Star of HBO's *True Detective*

Aaron Cooley is a producer and development executive for famed film director Joel Schumacher. His first novel *Shaken, Not Stirred* was named one of the Best Indie Books of 2013 by IndieReader.com. In 2015, Aaron was hired by MTV to create *The Campaigners,* a politically-themed one-hour dramedy intended to air during the 2016 election cycle, to be produced and directed by Jeremy Garelick (*The Wedding Ringer*). As a screenwriter, he has also developed projects for the companies behind *Pulp Fiction, Transformers, The Wolf of Wall Street, Dallas Buyers Club, Margin Call* and *Let's Kill Ward's Wife.* A native of Portland, Oregon and graduate of Yale, Aaron now lives in Los Angeles with Whitney, Beatrix and Mitten.

https://www.facebook.com/fleming17f

@fleming17f

8/17

CPSIA information can be obtained
at www.ICGtesting.com
Printed in the USA
LVOW13s0840150717
541461LV00010BA/907/P